GOD of WAR

Also by Christian Cameron

GOD *of* WAR

CHRISTIAN CAMERON

First published in Great Britain in 2012 by Orion Books,
an imprint of The Orion Publishing Group Ltd
Orion House, 5 Upper Saint Martin's Lane
London WC2H 9EA

An Hachette UK Company

1 3 5 7 9 10 8 6 4 2

A CIP catalogue record for this book is
available from the British Library.

ISBN (Hardback) 978 1 4091 3267 7
ISBN (Export Trade Paperback) 978 1 4091 3268 4

Typeset by Deltatype Ltd, Birkenhead, Merseyside

Printed in Great Britain by CPI Group (UK) Ltd
Croydon CR0 4YY

The Orion Publishing Group's policy is to use papers that are natural,
renewable and recyclable products and made from wood grown in
sustainable forests. The logging and manufacturing processes are expected
to conform to the environmental regulations of the country of origin.

www.orionbooks.co.uk

For all the members of the SGA

1980–1987

Have you any idea
What we're like to fight against?
Our sort make their dinner
Off sharp swords
We swallow blazing torches
For a savoury snack!
Then, by way of dessert,
They bring us, not nuts, but broken arrows, and splintered spear shafts.
For pillows we have our shields and breastplates,
Arrows and slings lie under our feet, and for wreaths we wear catapults

Mnesimachus, *Philip*

GLOSSARY

Airyanām (Avestan) – Noble, heroic.

Aspis (Classical Greek) – A large round shield, deeply dished, commonly carried by Greek (but not Macedonian) *hoplites*.

Baqca (Siberian) – Shaman, mage, dream-shaper.

Chiton (Classical Greek) – A garment like a tunic, made from a single piece of fabric folded in half and pinned down the side, then pinned again at the neck and shoulders and belted above the hips. A men's *chiton* might be worn long or short. Worn very short, or made of a small piece of cloth, it was sometimes called a *chitoniskos*. Our guess is that most *chitons* were made from a piece of cloth roughly 60 x 90 inches, and then belted or roped to fit, long or short. Pins, pleating, and belting could be simple or elaborate. Most of these garments would, in Greece, have been made of wool. In the East, linen might have been preferred.

Chlamys (Classical Greek) – A garment like a cloak, made from a single piece of fabric woven tightly and perhaps even boiled. The *chlamys* was usually pinned at the neck and worn as a cloak, but could also be thrown over the shoulder and pinned under the right or left arm and worn as a garment. Free men are sometimes shown naked with a *chlamys*, but rarely shown in a *chiton* without a *chlamys* – the *chlamys*, not the *chiton*, was the essential garment, or so it appears. Men and women both wear the *chlamys*, although differently. Again, a 60 x 90 inch piece of cloth seems to drape correctly and have the right lines and length.

Daimon (Classical Greek) – Spirit.

Ephebe (Classical Greek) – A new *hoplite*; a young man just training to join the forces of his city.

Epilektoi (Classical Greek) – The chosen men of the city or of the *phalanx*; elite soldiers.

Eudaimia (Classical Greek) – Well-being. Literally, 'well-spirited'. See *daimon*, above.

Gamelia (Classical Greek) – A Greek holiday.

Gorytos (Classical Greek and possibly Scythian) – The open-topped quiver carried by the Scythians, often highly decorated.

Hetaera (Classical Greek) – A female companion. Usually a courtesan.

Hetaeroi (Classical Greek) – Literally, male companions. In Alexander's army, the Royal Companions, or Guard Cavalry.

Himation (Classical Greek) – A heavy garment consisting of a single piece of cloth at least 120 x 60 inches, draped over the body and one shoulder, worn by both men and women.

Hipparch (Classical Greek) – The commander of the cavalry.

Hippeis (Classical Greek) – Militarily, the cavalry of a Greek army. Generally, the cavalry class, synonymous with 'knights'. Usually the richest men in a city.

Hoplite (Classical Greek) – A Greek soldier, the heavy infantry who carry an *aspis* and fight in the *phalanx*. They represent the middle class of free men in most cities, and while sometimes they seem like medieval knights in their outlook, they are also like town militia, and made up of craftsmen and small farmers. In the early Classical period, a man with as little as twelve acres under cultivation could be expected to own the *aspis* and serve as a *hoplite*.

Hoplomachos (Classical Greek) – A man who taught fighting in armour.

Hypaspitoi (Classical Greek) – In the archaic, a squire, or possibly a servant, who fought 'under the shield'. A shield bearer. In the army of Alexander, an elite corps of infantry – Alexander's bodyguard.

Hyperetes (Classical Greek) – The *Hipparch*'s trumpeter, servant, or supporter. Perhaps a sort of non-commissioned officer.

Kithara (Classical Greek) – A musical instrument like a lyre.

Kline (Classical Greek) – A couch or bed on which Hellenic men and women took meals and perhaps slept as well.

Kopis (Classical Greek) – A bent, bladed knife or sword, rather like a modern Ghurka knife. They appear commonly in Greek art, and even some small eating knives were apparently made to this pattern.

Machaira (Classical Greek) – any knife or sword. Sometimes used for the heavy Greek cavalry sword, longer and stronger than the short infantry sword. It was meant to give a longer reach on horseback, and not useful in the *phalanx*.

Pezhetaeroi (Classical Greek) – The 'Foot Companions' of Philip and Alexander – the *phalangites* of the infantry *taxeis*.

Parasang (Classical Greek from Persian) – About thirty *stades*. See below.

Phalanx (Classical Greek) – The infantry formation used by Greek *hoplites* in warfare, eight to ten deep and as wide as circumstance allowed. Greek commanders experimented with deeper and shallower formations, but the *phalanx* was solid and very difficult to break, presenting the enemy with a veritable wall of spear points and shields, whether the Macedonian style with pikes or the Greek style with spears. Also, *phalanx* can refer to the body of fighting men. A Macedonian *phalanx* was deeper, with longer spears called *sarissas* that we assume to be like the pikes used in more recent times. Members of a *phalanx*, especially a Macedonian *phalanx*, are sometimes called *Phalangites*.

Phylarch (Classical Greek) – The commander of one file of *hoplites*. It could be as many as sixteen men.

Porne (Classical Greek) – A prostitute.

Pous (Classical Greek) – Measurement; About one foot.

Prodromoi (Classical Greek) – Scouts; those who run before or run first.

Psiloi (Classical Greek) – Light infantry skirmishers, usually men with bows and slings, or perhaps javelins, or even thrown rocks. In Greek city-state warfare, the *psiloi* were supplied by the poorest free men, those who could not afford the financial burden of *hoplite* armour and daily training in the gymnasium.

Sastar (Avestan) – Tyrannical. A tyrant.

Stade (Classical Greek) – About 1/8 of a mile. The distance run in a 'stadium'. 178 meters. Sometimes written as *Stadia* or *Stades* by me. Thirty *Stadia* make a *Parasang*.

Taxeis (Classical Greek) – The sections of a Macedonian *phalanx*. Can refer to any group, but often used as a 'company' or a 'battalion'. My *taxeis* has between 500 and 2,000 men, depending on losses and detachments. Roughly synonymous with *phalanx* above, although a *phalanx* may be composed of a dozen *taxeis* in a great battle.

Xiphos (Classical Greek) – A straight-bladed infantry sword, usually carried by *hoplites* or *psiloi*. Classical Greek art, especially red-figure ware, shows many *hoplites* wearing them, but only a handful have been recovered and there's much debate about the shape and use. They seem very like a Roman gladius.

AUTHOR'S NOTE

I am an author, not a linguist – a novelist, and not fully an historian. Despite this caveat, I do the best I can to research everything from clothing to phalanx formations as I go, and sometimes I disagree with the accepted wisdom of either academe or the armchair generals who write colourful coffee table books on these subjects.

And ultimately, errors are my fault. If you find a historical error, please let me know!

One thing I have tried to avoid is altering history as we know it to suit a timetable or plotline. The history of the Wars of Alexander is difficult enough without my altering it. In addition, as you write about a period you love (and I have fallen pretty hard for this one) you learn more. Once I learn more, words may change or change their usage. As an example, in *Tyrant*, I used Xenophon's *Cavalry Commander* as my guide to almost everything. Xenophon calls the ideal weapon a *machaira*. Subsequent study has revealed that Greeks were pretty lax about their sword nomenclature (actually, everyone is, except martial arts enthusiasts) and so Kineas's Aegyptian *machaira* was probably called a *kopis*. So in the second book, I call it a *kopis* without apology. Other words may change – certainly my notion of the internal mechanics of the *hoplite phalanx* have changed. The more you learn...

A note about history. I'm always amused when a fan (or a non-fan) writes to tell me that I got a campaign or battle 'wrong.' Friends – and I hope we're still friends when I say this – we know less about the wars of Alexander than we do about the surface of Mars or the historical life of Jesus. I read Greek, I look at the evidence, and then I make the call. I've been to most of these places, and I can read a map. While I'm deeply fallible, I am also a pretty good soldier and I'm prepared to make my own decisions in light of the evidence about everything from numbers to the course of a battle. I may well be "wrong," but unless someone produces a time-machine, there's no proving it. Our only real source on Alexander lived five hundred years later. That's like calling me an eye-witness of Agincourt. Be wary of reading a campaign history or an Osprey book and assuming from the confident prose that we *know*. We don't know. We stumble around in the dark and make guesses.

And that said, military historians are, by and large, the poorest historians out there, by virtue of studying the violent reactions of cultures without studying the cultures themselves. War and military matters are cultural artefacts, just like religion and philosophy and fashion, and to try to take them out of context is impossible. Hoplites didn't carry the aspis because it was the ideal technology for the phalanx. I'll bet they carried it because it was the ideal technology for the culture, from the breeding of oxen to the making of the bowl, to the way they stacked in wagons. Men only fight a few days a year if that, but they live and breathe and run and forage and gamble and get dysentery 365 days a year, and their kit has to be good on all those days too. The history of war is a dull litany of man's inhumanity to man and woman, but history itself is the tale of the human race from birth until now. It's a darn good story, and worth repeating. History matters.

Why does history matter? I should spare you this rant, after all if you're reading this part of the book, chances are you're a history buff at least, possibly a serious amateur historian, maybe a professional slumming in my novels. But just for the record, a week after I finished the final page proofs of this book, I happened to read a Facebook post by a Holocaust denier. I'm still mad. It's not just the tom-fool anti-Semitism, it's the anti-history. A person who denies the Holocaust happened is denying that history exists; that research and careful documentation, eye-witness accounts and government archives have any meaning. In this kind of relativism, there is no truth. Pontius Pilate wins. And historical fiction is just fantasy without magic.

Well, I happen to believe that the past *really happened.* And that the more we know about it, the more we are empowered to deal with the present.

Finally, yes, I kill a lot of characters. War kills. Violence and lives of violence have consequences, then as now. And despite the drama of war, childbirth probably killed women of warrior age about twice as fast as it killed active warriors, so when we get right down to who's tough ...

Enjoy!

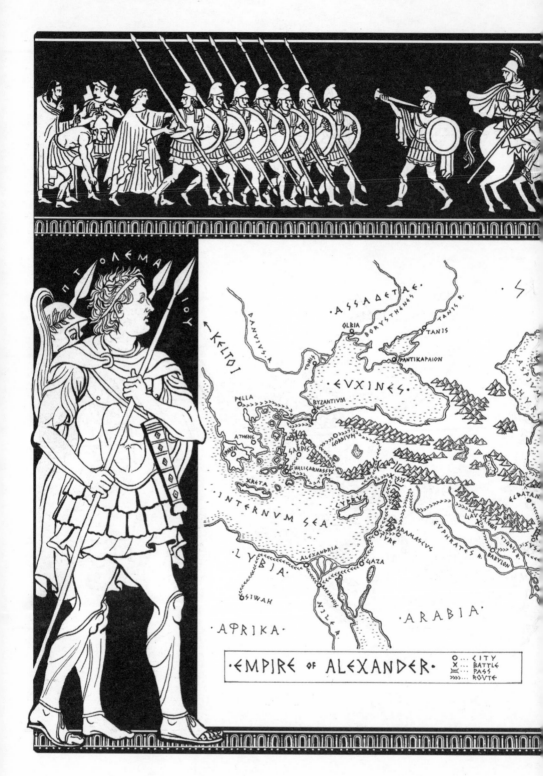

ΠΤΟΛΕΜΑΙΟΥ

KELTOI

DANUVIVS

ASSADETAE

OLBIA   BORYSTHENES

TANIS R.

TANIS

PANTIKAPAION

EVXINES

CASPIVM

HYR

PELLA

BYZANTIVM

ATHENE

GORDIVM

SPARTA   SARDIS

HALICARNASSVS

KRETA   CYPRVS

ISSVS

ECBATANA

INTERNVM SEA

DAMASCVS   EVPHRATES R.   SVSA

TIGRIS R.   BABYLON

TYRE

ALEXANDRIA   GAZA

LYBIA

MEMPHIS

NILE R.

OSIWAH

ARABIA

AFRIKA

·EMPIRE of ALEXANDER·

O...CITY
X...BATTLE
)(...PASS
>>>...ROUTE

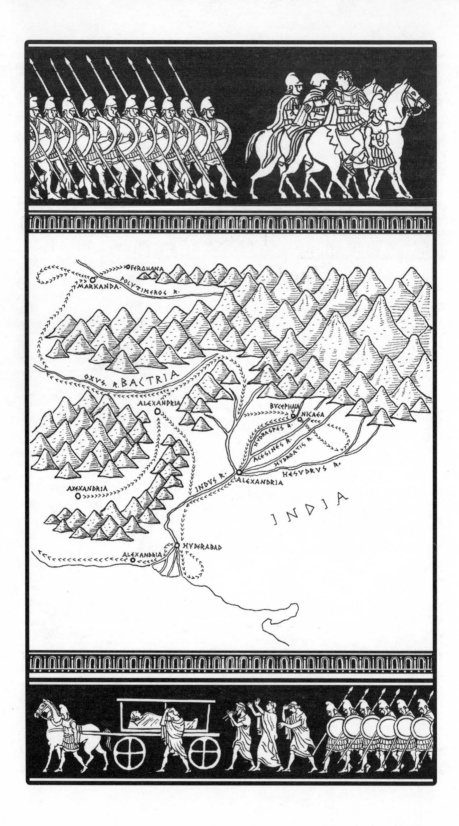

PART I
The Garden of Midas

PROLOGUE

S atyrus had been in Alexandria only a few days when Leon took him to the Royal Palace to meet the King of Aegypt. After Antigonus and Eumenes and four months with a mercenary army, Satyrus should not have been nervous, but he was – Ptolemy was the greatest king in the circle of the earth, and his court kept great state, as befitted the ruler of a land that had recorded history going back five thousand years into the past, whose ancient gods still held sway over most of the Nile valley.

Ptolemy wore the crown of Lower Aegypt on his head, and a strange, un-Greek cowl that went with it, over a chiton of pure Tyrian purple. His sandals were white and gold. In his hand was the ankh – the sceptre of Aegypt. Leon's hundreds of parental admonishments fled – Satyrus could scarcely remember how to bow.

The great king of all Aegypt leaned forward on his ivory throne. 'Kineas's son?' he asked Leon.

'Yes, great king,' Leon answered.

'Has the look. The nose. The chin. The arrogance.' Ptolemy smiled at the boy. 'I'm sorry for your loss, lad.'

Satyrus found his voice. 'She's not dead!' he insisted. The loss of his mother had affected him more than even his sister. Rumour had her murdered on the banks of the Tanais river, but it was still possible that rumour was wrong.

Ptolemy smiled a sad smile. 'Will you stay at my court, lad? Until you grow a little? And I'll put a good sword in your hand and send you out to reclaim your own.'

Satyrus bowed. 'I will serve you, lord, even as my uncles Diodorus and Leon serve you.'

Gabius, the king's intelligencer, brought a stool and sent most of the courtiers out. And he and the king asked Satyrus questions – hundreds of questions – about Antigonus and about how Eumenes died, about the mountains south of Heraklea and about the coast of the Euxine

3

– on and on, battles and deserts and everything Satyrus had seen in his busy young life.

But he was served rich cheese and pomegranate juice and crisp bread with honey. And neither the king nor the intelligencer was rude, or forceful. Merely thorough.

Sometimes Leon had to answer, or had to coax the answer from his ward, but Satyrus had lived with soldiers for two campaigns, and he knew what was expected of him. He explained as best he could the source of Antigonus's elephants, the horse breeds of the steppe and a hundred other details, while a dozen Aegyptian priests and a pair of Greek scholars wrote his words down on papyrus.

When they were done, the king leaned forward again, and put a gold ring into the boy's hand – a snake with his tail in his own mouth.

'This is the sign of my people – my secret household,' Ptolemy said. 'Wear it in good health. And whenever you need me – well, your uncle knows how to find me. You are a remarkable young man – your father's son. Is there anything I can do for you?'

Leon shook his head.

But Satyrus couldn't restrain himself. 'You knew ... Alexander?' he asked.

Ptolemy sat up as if a spark from the fire had struck bare skin. But he grinned. 'Aye, lad. I knew Alexander.'

'Would you ... tell me what he was like?' The boy stepped forward, and the guards by the throne rustled, but Ptolemy put out a hand.

The King of Aegypt rose, and every officer left in the great hall froze. 'Come with me, boy,' he said.

Together, the King of Aegypt and the adolescent boy walked out of the great hall of the palace. A dozen bodyguards fell in behind them. Leon and Gabias came with them, bringing up the rear of a fast-moving column that crossed the palace in deserted corridors or past scurrying slaves.

They entered a tunnel behind the royal residence. Ptolemy was silent, so Satyrus did his best not to ask questions. The one look he'd caught from Leon told him that his guardian was angry.

They climbed steps from the tunnel into a sombre hall, almost as big as the throne room. The walls were of red stone, lit by the last light of the sun through a round hole in the middle of the low dome above them.

The hole of the dome was covered in crystal or glass. Satyrus stared like a peasant.

In the midst of the hall was a dais as tall as a grown man's knees, and on it was a bier – a closed sarcophagus in solid gold, with chiselled features and ram's horns in ivory.

4

Satyrus fell on his knees. 'Alexander,' he said.

The King of Aegypt went to the bier and opened a cabinet set in the side of the dais. There were twenty-four holes – neat boxes made of cedar with silver nails. They held scrolls.

'I kept a military journal, from our first campaign together to our last,' Ptolemy said. He took one of the scrolls – the first – from its box, and handed it to Satyrus. Satyrus opened it, still on his knees. In the first hand's-breadth of parchment, he saw water marks, mud, a grass stain, and a bloody handprint.

Satyrus wanted to raise the parchment to his lips – his awe was religious.

'Of course,' Ptolemy said with the impish grin of a much younger man, 'it's a tissue of lies.'

Gabias laughed. Leon smiled. Satyrus felt his stomach fall.

'He was like a god, but he was the vainest man who ever walked the bowl of the earth and he couldn't abide a word of criticism after the first few years.' Ptolemy shrugged. 'I loved him. I know what love is, youngster, and I don't toss that word around. He was like a god. But he'd have had me killed if I had written everything just as it happened. The way he killed most of his friends.'

Satyrus swallowed with difficulty.

'Would you really like me to tell you about Alexander?' Ptolemy asked. 'I will. I've always meant to put down a private memoir for the library, when it is finished. So that some day someone will have the real story.' He looked at Satyrus. 'Or would you rather I kept it between me and the scribes, lad? It's not always a pretty story. On the other hand, if you plan to be a king, there's a lesson in it you must learn.'

Satyrus looked at Leon, but the Nubian's face was carefully blank.

'Yes,' Satyrus said. 'Yes, I would like you to tell me about Alexander.'

Ptolemy nodded. He smiled with half his mouth, and then he took the crown of Lower Aegypt from his head and handed it to a guard, handed another the sceptre, slipped the cowl over his head. Satyrus noticed that the King of Aegypt's left hand was badly scarred, two of the fingers almost fused, but he seemed to use it well enough. He also noticed that the great King of Aegypt had a dagger on a thong around his neck. Satyrus had one, too.

When he was done taking off the regalia, Ptolemy sat down in the red light of sunset on the steps of the dais. Alexander's sarcophagus lay above him, the figure of the god-man himself reclining over his head, lit too brilliantly for mortal eyes to see by the last rays of the sun on his chryselephantine face.

Gabias leaned forward. 'My lord, Cassander's envoy has waited all day.'

Ptolemy put an elbow comfortably into the relief of the dais, where a young Alexander was putting a spear into a lion. 'Let 'em wait. I need this.' He looked at Satyrus. 'I doubt I can do this in a day, lad. So you'll have to come back, now and then.'

'I will,' said Satyrus. The sunset on Alexander's head was blinding him – he had to look away.

'Well, then,' Ptolemy began ...

ONE

Macedon, 344–342 BC

It's not my earliest memory of him – we grew up together – but it's the beginning of this story, I think.

There were three of us – we must have been nine or ten years old. We'd been playing soldiers – pretty much all we ever did, I think. Black Cleitus – my favourite among the pages, with curly black Thracian hair and a wicked smile – had a bruise where Alexander had hit him too hard, which was par for the course, because Cleitus would never hit back, or never hit back as hard as the prince deserved. Mind you, he often took it out on me.

No idea where Hephaestion was. He and Alexander were usually inseparable, but he may have been home for his name day, or going to temple – who knows?

We were in the palace, in Pella. Lying on the prince's bed, with our wooden swords still in our hands.

There was a commotion in the courtyard, and we ran to the exedra and looked down to see the king and his companions ride in – just his closest bodyguard, his somatophylakes. They were wearing a fortune in armour – brilliant horsehair plumes, Aegyptian ostrich feathers, solid gold eagle's wings, panther skins, leopard skins, bronze armour polished like the disc of the sun and decorated in silver and gold, tin-plated bronze buckles and solid silver buckles in their horse tack, crimson leather strapping on every mount, tall Persian bloodstock horses with pale coats and dark legs and faces. Philip was not the richest or the best armoured – but no one could doubt that he was in command.

It only took them a moment to dismount, and a horde of slaves descended on them and took their armour and their horses and brought them hot clothes and towels.

That was dull for us, so we went back to Alexander's room. But we had seen a dream of power and glory. We were quiet for a long time.

7

Cleitus scratched – he was always dirty. 'Let's play knucklebones,' he said. 'Or Polis.'

But Alexander was still looking towards the courtyard. 'Some day they'll be dead,' he said. 'And we'll do what they do.'

I grinned at him. 'But better,' I said.

He lit up like a parchment lamp at a festival. He hugged me to him. 'That's right,' he said. 'But better.'

It's odd, because that same day – at least in my memory – is the day that we heard Philip ordain the invasion of Asia and the war with Persia.

We must have been invited to the great hall. We weren't old enough to be pages, yet, and we never went near the hall once the drinking started. So I'm going to guess that it was Alexander's birthday, or just possibly the Feast of Herakles, the great one we celebrate in Macedon. I had lain on a couch to eat, with my pater at home, and I had been served by slaves, because my family was quite rich. But I had never seen the reckless rout for Philip's soldiers, courtiers and minions. I lay on a couch with Prince Alexander, pretending to be as adult as I could, trying to be bigger and fiercer and taller and stronger.

After dinner, Philip, who was lying with his general, Parmenio, and a dozen other officers in a circle just to my right, began to carp at Parmenio about how long it was taking him to defeat Phokion and the Athenians, and Parmenio, who was a friend of my father's and my hero, shot back that if Athens didn't have free entry into the Persian ports . . .

Antipater – quite a young man at the time, and already the schemer of the staff – sat up suddenly on his couch. 'To the war in Persia, and the end of Athens!' he said, and poured wine on the floor. 'I send these winged words to the gods.'

We had a dozen Athenians among us – mercenary officers, gentlemen rankers, courtiers, philosophers and a pair of 'representatives' from the 'democracy'. Philip laughed aloud. 'If I took Persia,' he said, 'I would *be* a god.'

At my side, Alexander, who sought, even at age ten, to be in all things the first and best, stiffened and raised himself on his elbows. I caught his eye.

'We'll miss it!' he hissed.

'No we won't,' I said with the total bravado of the very young. 'No we won't.'

And later that year, or perhaps the next – just before I became a royal page – Alexander came to one of our farms. We were among the first families in Macedon, and our wealth was old wealth – we had horses and land. Our stud farms were the best in Macedon, and perhaps the best in Hellas – my father imported stock from Thrace and Asia and even, once, a mare from Italia, and our horses were bred for war – big, tall, perhaps a trifle bony and heavy-faced for the purist, but tough, capable of carrying a man in armour and capable of surviving the Tartarus of horses, a summer on campaign. For that, a horse needs hard hooves – hard enough to stay hard in four days of rain, and hard enough to stay strong over roads that men have worn down to shards of sharp rock. A war horse has to be able to stay alive on the leavings of grass where a thousand horses have already grazed; has to survive a day in the sun without water, if its rider's life depends on it. And it is a rare horse that can do all these things.

But we bred them, and it was my pater's life. He was the old kind of aristocrat, the kind of man who hated the court and never left his own farms if he could help it. I won't say everyone loved him, because he was a very difficult man when crossed, but he was fair, and fairness is all peasants and slaves ask of a master. They don't love us, anyway – but they ought to be able to expect the same treatment and the same justice every day.

At any rate, Pater promoted and freed his slaves and made sure his freemen ended up on farms of their own if they did well for him, and that did as much for our horses as all our priceless bloodstock. Listen – let me tell you a story. It's about Alexander, in a way.

Years after this, I was in Athens – you'll get to that part later – and I went shopping for vases. I wanted to send something to my father and to other friends, and the ceramics of Athens are the finest in the world.

In the Keramaki – the ceramics quarter – were two shops next to each other. Both had big names, and both provided the sort of high-end wares I wanted – one specialised in scenes of gods and war, while the other specialised in scenes from plays.

Outside the latter, a man in a dun wool cloak was beating a slave with a stick. He was thorough and brutal. I passed that shop – interrupting a man beating his slave is like interrupting a man having sex with his wife. I went into the other shop, where two slaves behind the counter were burnishing the surfaces of finished pots with bone tools. Both were older men, clearly experienced, and they were chatting, laughing. At my entry, the nearer jumped up with a smile while the other continued burnishing. I watched him for a while, his quick, even strokes, and when I looked at a wine krater, I couldn't find a spot that had been left unburnished. The surfaces were perfect – almost glossy.

I didn't want scenes from plays, but I loved the sheer quality of the finishes.

Later, after a cup of wine with the master, I went back to the first shop, where the beaten slave, who proved to be the master painter, sat slumped in a corner. The master waited on me himself. His vases were fine, but the finishes were all sloppy.

He saw me looking at the surface. He grimaced. 'You can't get good slaves any more,' he said, and shrugged.

I bought six vases, and all of them had scenes from Athenian drama. One is buried with my father. He loved it that much. In part, I gave it to him because he would have agreed. You can't *buy* a good slave, but you can make him good with fair treatment, and in return, he'll burnish the pot evenly. Understand me, boy?

But I digress.

Alexander came to our farm at Tyrissa, and stayed a week, riding our best horses and watching the running of a great estate with interest. He was not a farm boy by any means – I had been in the fields as soon as I could walk, because in Macedon, lords pick flax with peasants, and at haying, everyone gathers hay. Everyone but Prince Alexander, of course.

But he loved it. We sacrificed to Poseidon every day (every horse farm has a shrine to the Horse God) and we rode, fed horses, mucked out stalls, and watched grooms and pages schooling the next year's cavalry mounts. On this one farm, with eighty slaves and six hundred head of horses, we provided almost a tenth of all the cavalry remounts that Philip demanded every year, because war eats horses far faster than it eats men. In one season chasing Phokion around the Dardanelles, King Philip lost two thousand horses to bad food, disease and exhaustion – and we had to find new ones. In a bad year, the three-year-olds intended to be the next year's cavalry horses are sent out early, green and nervous and flighty. An epidemic or a military disaster could force a farm to use up its stock – the superb horses used for breeding – sent as cavalry horses, and lost for ever. Two straight bad seasons could wreck a farm. Three straight bad seasons could wreck a nation, leaving it without cavalry. Waves of disease – the arrows of Apollo – or bad water, or a long heatwave – and messengers arrived at our farms with letters from the king demanding horses.

I mention this not because Alexander's visit had any long-term effect on his life, but because we are horse soldiers, and we loved horses. And used them and used them up. I have had three great horses, and Alexander had one – and my Poseidon was the best horse I've ever had between my legs. But great horses are as rare as great men, and as fragile, and need the care and attention that other men lavish on a lover or a best friend.

The last day Alexander was on our farm, we built a fort of grape stakes, and with a few of my friends, we challenged the Thracian boys – the children of our slaves – to come and take it from us.

There were twenty of them, and they hooted at us, unafraid as slave children are until they are beaten. They came at us without fear, with rocks and sticks, and we stood our ground with the same weapons, except that Alexander and I had small round shields made of wicker which we'd woven ourselves from old vines.

They attacked twice and we drove them off with some blood flowing, and then we looked out over the fields, with herds of beautiful horses in every field, and fences of woven hurdle between the herds.

'Why are they separated?' Alexander asked me.

I shrugged. 'We have a mare from Arabia in that field, and we're putting her with one of our best stallions – Big Ares, over there. He doesn't think much of her yet,' I said ruefully, because the stallion was at the far end of the field, ignoring the mare.

'And over there?' Alexander asked.

'Pericles's herd. The grey is Pericles – an old stallion, but still one of the best, with a healthy dose of Nisean in him from Persia.'

'And nearer?' he asked. He was clearly impressed with my knowledge. 'They're all different – large and small. Bay and black and white and piebald.'

'Socrates, my father's favourite. That field has a special purpose.' I smiled. 'It is a secret. Pater is breeding horses that are smart. Only smart horses go into that field.'

Alexander nodded. 'I'm to have a tutor,' he said. 'To help me learn to rule men. And yet your horse farm seems to teach all the lessons I need.'

Later that afternoon, the Thracian children came for us again. But we were ready, and we beat them again, and then we chased them – a dozen of us.

I kissed my pater the next day, because I was going to court to be a page, and Alexander was taking me as a companion. We both knew I was in for a long, tough time. But I thought I wanted it, and he was a fine enough father to let me go. He gave me a fine ring, and a bag of money. I guess he'd been a young man, once.

I rode off, excited to be with my prince, excited to be going full-time to court, excited to be a royal page.

I only went back to the farms to live just once, and that was much later, in virtual exile, as you'll hear. I never thought, that bright sunny morning, that I was giving up horses and love and friendship and beautiful mornings to spend the rest of my youth avoiding rape and murder while working like a slave.

A royal page.

Alexander's new tutor was, of course, Aristotle. And almost as soon as I became a royal page, Philip moved Alexander's household to the Gardens of Midas. We were told it was time for him to leave his mother behind. I'll speak more of Olympias later, but she was more like a force of nature than a woman. And she tried to rule Alexander rather than guide him.

As a companion – almost a peer – I was educated *with* the prince. There were a dozen of us at any time, and I think only Amyntas, Cassander, Hephaestion, Black Cleitus and I went through the whole course with Alexander, although I may be missing somebody. At any rate, we sat through lessons together with Aristotle in the Gardens of Midas, and sometimes, when I was the favoured one, I sat beside Alexander on the stone bench – colder than you can imagine on an autumn morning – while the old oligarch explained *exactly* what Plato meant in the *Gorgias*, or the proper conduct of a gentleman in a symposium.

Aristotle was one of us, or close enough – he knew what we were – but he'd been away a long time, with foreigners on Lesbos, and he could be quite naive. He loved the symposium and all of its trappings – the proper wine bowls, the krater, the sieve and the silver ladle, the bowls of good companionship, the small talk and the wit. I experienced them all later, and came to know that the philosopher was talking about something real – delightful, in fact. But you must imagine that we heard him through a veil of our own experience as pages at court, and for us, wine meant trouble. When we were at Pella, all of us – except the prince – were royal pages, and we waited on the guests at the feasts in the great hall. And that was horrible.

Philip's court had three groups. The first, and most dangerous, were the highlanders, the near-barbarians of the ancient upland kingdoms; Elimiotis in the south, Orestis in the west and Lychnitis by the lake, near Illyria. They didn't like Hellenes, didn't like Philip's insistence on the trappings of Athenian culture and didn't very much like Philip. They liked to steal cattle and kill each other and fuck.

The second group was just as dangerous and just as violent. Philip attracted mercenaries the way rotting corpses attract carrion crows. He had the best – and most expensive – captains in the world, and the two I remember best were Erigyus and Laomedon, descendants of Sappho's daughter, from Mytilene on distant Lesbos. Despite their air of culture and their distinguished poetic pedigree, they were hard men, killers with no shame in them, and no page ever came close to them once the drink was flowing.

And the last group was the lowlanders, the courtiers, the great nobles and barons of the rich inner provinces of Macedon, men who had estates the size of small countries. They wore Greek clothing and most of them spoke excellent Greek, and *they* could speak intelligently about Plato. They were also as tough or tougher than their highland cousins, and their national sports were hunting wolves and regicide. My father was one of them, Lagus, son of Ptolemy. Our estates ran for parasanges – we owned people as Attic farmers own sheep, although, as I said, my pater was a fine leader and manager.

The leader of our faction at court was Parmenio, the general – Philip liked to joke that the Athenians managed to come up with ten generals every spring, while he'd only found one in his whole life – that was how much he valued Parmenio. Well he might.

At any rate, when men gathered to drink wine in the royal court at Pella, we pages served as quickly as we could and huddled together for safety under the eaves. Men *died* when the wine was flowing. And if anyone talked about Socrates or Heraklitus, I never heard it. Casual fornication was tolerated – slave girls and sometimes boys were used as freely as wine cups. One of my clearest memories of youth remains serving wine to Erigyus while he rode a girl on his couch. Beyond them, a highlander was kneeling on the floor, watching, incredulous, as his life ebbed away, blood all around him like spilled wine. He'd mocked Erigyus's penis. The Lesbian cut his throat and carried on. *That* was the closest thing we knew to a symposium, and *that* was why it was sometimes difficult to understand what Aristotle was talking about.

I don't mean to dwell on my own youth. I mean this to explain – to myself, if not to you – why we killed the king, in the end. But to understand Alexander, you have to understand everything, and as with Aristotle's lessons, it can be hard to see Alexander through the haze of later events. And to understand the man, you have to see some of the boy.

I observed Alexander on dozens of hunts, but one sticks in my head. We'd been hard at it – lesson after lesson, swordsmanship and ethics, wrestling and spear-fighting and running and ethics, the lyre and ethics. The physical world – the bodies of men and women, with dissection; medicine, in detail – how to make drugs from herbs, how to grind powders, how to administer even the most complex concoctions. And political philosophy, too – we were, after all, the men who would rule Macedon, not a group of merchants' sons, and we were being trained carefully.

Like any group of boys, we had an established pecking order and it was ruthless and yet curiously malleable, and boys went up and down the ladder swiftly. Alexander headed it – he was to be king, and that was that. Indeed, he was not the strongest, the fastest or the best swordsman – but he was *almost* the best in every category, and he was, without a doubt, the most intelligent of us. Sometimes it seemed to us that he alone understood what Aristotle was talking about, and certainly, when it came to swordsmanship, or spear-fighting, what he lacked in reach and leg length he often made up for in subtlety and practice.

Practice. I was busy sneaking over the wall of the boys' compound every night to meet a girl – I loved her. I was fifteen, and her body was smooth and beautiful, and mine, as long as I was willing to risk heavy physical punishment and go for days without sleep, which most fifteen-year-old boys see as a small price to pay for the feel of two breasts under their hands. But I remember coming back from one of these expeditions, feeling like a king, and finding Alexander with a wooden sword in his hand, standing at the stake behind the barracks, practising the steps of a particular blow – hip rotation, right foot rotating around the left, then pushing forward, passing the left, and then another hip rotation that left you facing your opponent from a new angle. Our sword master – one of half a dozen men named Cleitus – had taught us the footwork the morning before, and here was the heir of Macedon in the first pale grey light of day, executing the move over and over. He'd placed white pebbles where he wanted his feet to go.

'Join me,' he said, without turning around.

No one refused a direct order from the prince. Once or twice, Hephaestion, his best friend, had smacked him for us, but none of us, even Hephaestion, ever refused him. So I squared off, tried the steps, stumbled.

'Use the white rocks,' he said quietly. 'They help.' He stepped around the pell and left me to his rocks. They did help, but what helped me more was watching him. He was executing the steps faster and faster, and then he began to throw cuts with his wooden sword as he moved his feet – one, two, *three*. The master hadn't taught us cuts yet – at least, not the cuts that went with the steps.

It was always difficult to learn anything from Alexander – he learned things by observation, usually in one or two repetitions, and he never really understood that the rest of us needed to be shown things slowly and precisely.

I had the steps in ten repetitions. Alexander grinned at me, and we started to do them together, like peasants dancing for the gods, and I picked up his sword cuts just for the joy of doing them in perfect unison. The sun rose, a red ball cutting through the high morning fog.

I got it. What he had reasoned out in the darkness – well, I'm no fool. I got it.

We dressed quickly and we were the first into the dining hall. Leonidas, the athlete, was already there, naked under a chlamys of coarse wool. He had a heavy staff in his hand. He rose and bowed his head to Alexander. He looked at me the way teachers look at boys – boys they know are guilty but haven't caught yet.

'Your pallet was empty, son of Lagus,' he said formally.

'He was with me, practising,' Alexander said.

Leonidas narrowed his eyes, stuck a hand down the front of my chiton and felt the slick sweat on my chest. He nodded. 'Very well,' he said. What he meant was, *Another time, boy.*

That was the prince's way, though. He didn't say, 'Ptolemy, Leonidas is on the hunt for you.' He merely required me to attend him at practice and then dealt with the matter himself. So that if I made an excuse and avoided practising with him in the grey dawn, I would only punish myself.

At any rate, that morning, after we did drills in pairs, the sword master handed out the padded wooden swords and we stripped off our chlamyses and sparred. We were tough boys – indeed, other than in Sparta, I doubt you'd have found tougher – and most fights ended with the loser knocked unconscious, because it was reckoned faint-hearted to raise a hand and accept defeat without showing blood or falling into the deep.

By chance, I drew Amyntas – we were never friends. I hit him and he hit me, and welts were raised. He was cutting at my sword arm – perfectly legitimate, but my timing was off and he kept hitting the same place, and the lambskin wrapped on the oak sword was not enough to keep those blows from causing real pain.

'Keep your sword down and behind your shield,' Cleitus muttered. We weren't using shields yet, but the chlamys was a stand-in for the shield. A good swordsman doesn't show his opponent the sword until the cut is coming in. I was waving my sword about, sending Amyntas signals as clear as if I was shouting out when I meant to attack.

I got back into my stance, got my sword hand down so that my weapon was hidden by my chlamys, and swore to myself that I'd let him strike first.

I waited a long time. The little shit had learned his fancy arm cut and now he was determined to use it over and over.

We circled and circled. The other boys hooted – Hephaestion began to deride us both. Alexander wasn't even paying attention. He was somewhere else in his head – I knew that look.

There were elements of swordsmanship that were exactly the same as elements of things at which I was very good – pankration, for instance, the all-in wrestling that the Greeks love. I'm big and my arms are longer than they ought to be, and I know my distances when I go for a throw. Amyntas was at a loss as to what to do, now that I wasn't throwing attacks, and he was less willing to accept the taunts of the others than I was. I slid forward, closing the distance subtly while circling to the right.

I didn't plan it. It was gods-sent. I *did* stamp my foot to draw him, and he did fall for it. The movement of my front foot drew his counter-cut at my arm. But my arm wasn't there, and I did the steps – one-two-*three*. My sword cut down from his open side, I was at an odd angle to him, and I hit him so hard in the head that I might have killed him – I swear I never meant to cut so hard. He fell like an avalanche falls – every part of him together.

Cleitus narrowed his eyes. Shrugged. Gave me a curt nod. Like a tutor who thinks you've cheated on a test but can't see how.

'Next,' he said. He looked back at me.

Alexander came forward, with my friend Cleitus, the one we called 'the black'. He was the son of Alexander's nurse, and not exactly a nobleman, but he was as loyal as a good dog to Alexander and, as I say, he was my friend. Nearly always, or at least that's how I remember it.

I was covered in sweat, and while slaves dragged Amyntas off the palaestra and revived him, I put my cloak on – it was cold – and real-ized just how badly my arm was hurt.

I stood there, rubbing it and trying to look unhurt and victorious. Manly and aristocratic.

Alexander took Cleitus apart. It was quite an exhibition; Alexander had mastered the step and the associated cuts, and he proceeded to hit Cleitus over and over again. Cleitus scored occasionally – he wasn't bad – but Alexander hit him again and again, smoothly moving through his cutting strokes as if on parade – right to left, bottom to top, as if this was a drill and having his opponent know which blow was coming was expected. But because Cleitus didn't get the new rhythm or the fancy offset offered by the new footwork, the blows came in – one after another.

And then Cleitus's dark face filled with blood. Maybe he thought he was being mocked – maybe one of the blows hurt more than the others. He grunted – it caught my attention, because, to be honest, watching one man carve the crap out of another is dull, and I'd stopped watching, but that grunt had hate in it. He stepped in, took Alexander's blow on his shoulder and caught the prince's elbow – and threw him to the ground. Classic pankration.

Alexander got to his feet, came on guard, measured the distance and knocked Cleitus unconscious. One-two-*three*. Black Cleitus crashed to the ground as if dead.

The sword master looked at him, and then flicked his glance over to me.

'Well done, my prince,' he said. 'A *little* harder than it needed to be.'

Black Cleitus was not dead. He let out a great snort, and blood flowed from his nostrils, and then he snorted like a boar and got up on his knees and vomited.

Alexander held his hair – we all wore ours long. Then he came over and stood by me – according to our traditions, the winning boys stood together.

'Did you see me?' he said. 'I used the new step.'

'Me, too,' I said.

He turned to me so fast I thought he had tripped. 'You what?'

'I put Amyntas down with the same blow you used on Black Cleitus,' I said. I wasn't paying attention to the signals – we were victors together, and I thought ...

His smile came off his face like water draining from a dropped pot. He stood quivering with anger. 'It was mine,' he said. 'Not yours. I should have been *first*.'

He had the same look in his eyes that Erigyus had when he punched his eating knife through the highlander's throat-bole. I admit I stepped back.

When the sun was high, Aristotle came out to find us and take us to the cold stone benches. As always, he asked Cleitus and Leonidas to tell him what we'd done.

'Alexander downed his opponent with the Harmodius Blow,' Cleitus the sword master said. He wasn't a clever man, and his flattery rarely went well with the prince. He was a good swordsman, though.

'Every idiot knows how to do it,' Alexander spat. He stood by himself, arms across his chest, the very image of adolescent anger.

Aristotle looked around. I fancied he caught my eye – perhaps it was just my imagination. 'Victors should be gracious,' Aristotle said.

'I am gracious,' Alexander retorted.

'No,' said Aristotle. 'You are not.'

Their eyes locked, and all the other boys shuffled away.

'You desire to be Achilles? You strive always to be first and best?' His old tutor, Lysimachus of Acarnia, who had complete control of the younger Alexander before Aristotle came, called himself Phoenix, called Hephaestion Patroclus and called Alexander Achilles. Aristotle was human enough to resent the old tutor and his lickspittle ways.

Alexander looked away in angry silence.

Aristotle stepped closer. 'Which boy did you put down with this Harmodius Blow, Prince?'

Alexander shrugged. 'It does not matter.'

'Ptolemy?' Aristotle asked.

'No,' Alexander spat. 'He ...' Then he lapsed into silence.

'It was me, lord,' Black Cleitus said. He was rueful. 'Had it coming.'

Aristotle looked at Cleitus. Then at me.

Leonidas's straight back and flared nostrils suggested that he was none too pleased by this intrusion of the academic into the athletic. 'Held the boy's hair. He was decent enough.'

Aristotle looked around again, like a good hunting dog catching the scent of a distant and elusive prey.

He looked at Amyntas, with a heavy bandage around his temples. The same bandage that Cleitus wore. 'Who fought Amyntas?' he asked.

'I did,' I allowed.

'The same way?' Aristotle asked, splaying two fingers on Amyntas's head and measuring the blow.

I shrugged.

Alexander flushed.

Aristotle laughed. 'Alexander, excellence lies in being better than other men – not in other men being worse than you. I can read you like a book, boy.'

Alexander looked as if he might cry.

What is hard to explain in this schoolboy reminiscence is that I could understand. Alexander felt I had betrayed him. He'd rescued me from Leonidas only to have me go first and throw his blow – a blow he'd risen in the dawn to practise.

So I stepped right up next to the prince and bowed my head. 'I'm sorry,' I said.

Alexander didn't look at me. 'No. I was not behaving well.' His voice was choked, as if he'd just heard that a favourite was dead.

'I'm sorry anyway,' I said.

My pater used to say that if you truly want to know a man, spend a week with him in the wilderness. No one can hide his true self from the companions of the hunt. Freezing rain, stinging nettles, a bad cut from a spear-point, an unwanted offer of sex from one of the oldsters – all the tests of young manhood are waiting in the hills and deep woods, and that's before you meet the boar or the wolf with nothing between you but an ash staff and a few inches of cold iron.

A few days after the sword incident, Erygius and Laodon came from

Pella with some of the king's companions – his Hetaeroi, friends and bodyguards and inner council of state all in one – to take us hunting. It was a test and a vacation all in one.

Macedonian nobles do not hunt like Greek aristocrats, and despite the many ways we copy them, in hunting we have our own ways.

We use dogs to locate the quarry, and other dogs to run it down, and we follow our dogs on horseback. Depending on terrain and the animal we're after, we stay mounted with spears or dismount with spears. The height of courage is to take a boar on foot. Greeks do it the same way, but they don't use horses, and that's slower. And they don't use a double-bladed axe to finish the boar, and that's just foolishness. Trying to finish a boar with a spear is ... well, it is a good way to reduce your supply of available noblemen.

It was autumn, and we went north and west, into Lychnitis. Lychnitis is beautiful – low hills that rise gently into mountains, and old forests that men have never cut, not even in the age of heroes. There're trees lying on the forest floor that are as thick as a horse, and others as wide as a man is tall, so that to clamber over them is like climbing a low hill – and they're just the downed trees. Giants rise on every side, green temples to the immortal gods, and every animal thrives there – the great deer, the elk and the boar. And the wolves.

And desperate men, of course.

We made our hunting camp in a long clearing that kings of Macedon had used for their hunting camps since the gods walked the earth. It was a defensible hilltop, high enough to give warning of approaches, low enough that the boys and the slaves didn't have to go too far for the water that flowed across the northern base of the hill from the spring. The land about was scrubby, but rose to the west and north – to the north the camp was dominated by the first low mountain of Paeonia, and to the west the trees grew and grew, so that the Illyrians said a squirrel could jump from tree to tree from the hunting camp all the way to Hyperborea, where Apollo went to sleep.

The air was as clean and cold as a mother's reproach. The animals were not afraid of men, and came right into camp to steal food. Our horses were skittish unless one of the boys was with them all the time. This was just a year after Alexander gained Bucephalus – a fine horse, though legend has improved him like it has polished his master. In fact, the prince had three big mounts for hunting and a palfrey for riding about. We all did – no one horse could keep going all day over that country, and we knocked them up badly. And that week, the rain fell as if Artemis disapproved of our slaughter – on and on, a light rain that never seemed to end, and in that kind of weather, horses get sick, go lame – die – as fast as children die in the same weather.

I had a horse I loved – a dark yellow golden coat, with blond mane and tail, tall and handsome and fast, which one of Pater's grooms had rather impiously called 'Poseidon'. But Poseidon he remained, and he had the god's own strength, and in my eyes he was a better horse than Bucephalus or any other horse who'd ever lived. He was certainly faster than the mighty bay, but like the other boys, I was not foolish enough to show it.

We spent the first few days deer-hunting – for the meat. Boar-hunting and wolf-hunting are very noble, but they don't feed the troops or the slaves, so a boar hunt usually starts with the massed slaughter of a deer herd. It wasn't like sport at all, or even like war – more like a harvest, as the trained slaves and a handful of the king's cavalry troopers wove screens of brush and set up a long alley of these hurdles, shaped like a giant funnel, between two hills. All the mounted men made a great line before dawn, and we picked our way across the hills, eyes watering with the effort of finding the next huntsman to the right and left in the rain and the dim light – I was off my horse twice on the first morning, flat on my face once and off Poseidon's rump the other, caught looking the wrong way when he trotted under a low branch.

But we covered a lot of ground, driving the deer – and every other living thing – into the open end of the funnel. By full daylight, we closed the net tight. The first day was sloppy, and we pages were blamed for indiscipline. But on the second morning it was well done, and we drove fifty deer down the funnel into the older men, who killed them with swords and spears. Laodon was thrilling to watch, standing coolly with a short spear – a longche, just the height of a man, and heavy in the shaft. He killed a stag that charged him – stood his ground, shifted his weight and the animal was down, and then all the older men finished it. A few deer got past, of course, and soldiers with bows shot them down – shooting carefully, because hitting one of the king's companions was a death sentence. Perhaps they were shooting too carefully, because one enormous stag, a monster as big as my horse, beloved of Artemis, burst through the archers and raced free up the hills and vanished into the deep trees.

Alexander cantered up. I've said he wasn't the best at everything, and he wasn't, but he was the finest horseman I've ever seen – years later, when we rode against the Sakje of the Sea of Grass, I remarked that he was as natural a rider as they. What always amused me is that he took this utterly for granted and would accept no praise for it – never told self-important stories about his riding prowess, never bragged about the horses he'd broken. Horses loved him, and I suspect that's because he always knew *exactly* what he wanted.

Laodon was standing there, naked, wiggling his spear back and forth in the stag's chest, trying to draw it free where it had lodged against bone. He looked up when he heard Alexander's hoof beats, and waved a salute.

Alexander merely pointed at the rump and tines of the great stag galloping for the treeline. A few heartbeats later and the animal would have been gone. But Laodon saw what he had missed, and rage filled his face. He let go his spear haft and walked over to the archers. Words were exchanged, and a man struck to the ground.

Alexander pursed his lips.

Laodon came back and shook his head. 'My apologies, Prince. That beast should never have slipped us.'

'The will of Artemis,' Alexander said. But the way he said it indicated that he meant the opposite. And Laodon knew it.

Next day we went out as scouts, all the pages, looking for the boars. I was with Laodon, and we rode from sun-up until high noon through the woods. The day was beautiful, with a golden autumn sun on red leaves and the most amazing, heady scent in the air of fresh-fallen leaves – the perfume of Artemis, Laodon called it.

I remember that I spent a good deal of time worrying whether he meant to rape me. Just to give you an idea of what Laodon was known for.

He was an excellent hunter, though, and his eye for the field sign was without error, and while I don't remember why I was allowed to accompany him, it certainly wasn't my looks. I was fit – we all were – but you can look at my profile on coins, can't you? I am not a handsome man, and my friends called me 'Georgoi' or 'Farm Boy'.

If it was a privilege, it was a scary one. I was on my guard, never within reach of his arms. That's pretty much how we lived our lives – just so you know.

Noon came, and I was ravenous. What boy isn't? We'd been mounted since dawn, and up and down from our mounts, looking at fewmets and tracks and traces and rubs, and then up again – riding down steep hills, up rocky defiles, or over the downed trunks of ancient trees that had stood like towers when Hector fought Achilles.

We came to a muddy ditch where the trail crossed a stream – the passage of men and animals had worn the end of the trail into the ditch. Laodon dismounted, handed me his reins, and looked into the ditch for a long time.

'A great many men passed this way,' he said, and scratched his beard. His eyes were alive, of a sudden, and he moved his head slowly around like a hawk does when searching for prey.

Then he shrugged. 'I'm getting old, boy, and I see bandits behind every tree. What have you packed us to eat?'

I had a leather bag full of cheese and bread, and a pottery flask of good Nisean wine. I laid it out for him and stood back – pages don't eat with knights.

He nodded curtly, ate some bread, drank some wine and grinned at me.

'That's good wine, young Ptolemy.' He drank another sip from his horn cup and nodded.

I probably flushed with the praise.

'Sit, boy. Eat.' He indicated the food.

I guess my fears were obvious. I sat too carefully.

Laodon laughed. Like lightning, his hand was on the back of my neck, locking me to the ground. 'If I wanted you,' he said with a snort, 'you'd be mine.' He snickered. 'Not my type, boy.' He slapped my rump and picked up his horn cup, which he'd somehow set aside without spilling its contents while he put me on the ground with one hand.

I was shaken, but I managed to eat anyway. Oh, for a moment of that youth now! Beans make me fart, milk curdles in my stomach and too much wine goes to my head. At fifteen, I could go straight from fear and terror to eating without passing through any intervening stages. I remember how good the cheese was.

'Have some wine, virgin,' Laodon said, handing me his cup. He got to his feet. 'I'm going to look around.'

I sat on a big rock by the stream and drank wine from his horn cup. He was an important man and a famous warrior, and to be allowed to drink from his cup was a compliment. My father loathed him – which, at fifteen, can make a man more appealing.

I was wondering whether his permission went as far as a second cup of wine when a hand came over my mouth and I was dragged off the rock.

'Don't make a noise, virgin,' Laodon said. 'There's an Illyrian raiding party on the other side of the ridge. Can you find your way back to camp without me?' His hand came off my mouth.

'Yes, lord,' I said.

'You are absolutely positive? No horse shit?' He turned my head. 'Swear by Zeus?'

'By Zeus, god of kings, and my ancestor Herakles,' I said.

'Good boy. Go! Warn the prince!' he said. He helped me mount to save time. 'Never take lunch by a stream,' he said, shaking his head. 'You can't hear anything.'

'Are they after us?' I asked him.

He shrugged and slapped my horse on the rump, and Poseidon sprang forward.

Almost immediately I faced a quandary. I was not lying – I knew how to get back to camp. But we'd come a great half-circle north and west around the high hill, and the only way back to camp that I knew for certain was to cast all the way back. Or I could cut the circle and ride north and east. Camp had to lie that way – across the shoulder of the high hill, maybe eight stades or a little more. But if I missed the ridge and the clearing – by Artemis, I'd go for ever and never find another man or horse.

I didn't have a weapon, either. I had an eating knife – not really a useful instrument for killing, although you'd never know it from the number of men I've seen put down with eating utensils – but neither spear nor lance nor sword.

I headed across the circle, east by north.

The nerves didn't start until I was over the shoulder of the hill. I'd convinced myself that when I rode over the shoulder, I'd see the meadow, at least from the top. But I couldn't, and all I could see were trees – red, orange, evergreen, stretching in an endless parade to the north and west.

I reined in. Poseidon was edgy, and he fidgeted under me on the knife-edge ridge. I thought about it for as long as a man takes to run the stade – a good man – and then I turned Poseidon north and climbed higher on the ridge.

By the time I'd ridden for a hundred heartbeats, the awful truth was clear – I wasn't on the right ridge. We'd come farther around the mountain than I thought. I wasn't quite lost – but I didn't know what angle to cast on to make it to camp.

I considered going back to Laodon. He might mock me, he might club me to the ground, but at least he'd set me on the right trail.

I kept Poseidon going up the ridge, dodging trees and cursing under my breath every so often. Fearing that I was going to be the death of my prince, because I was lost in the woods. That's a worse fear than battle sickness or fear of a girl's parents – fear of failing others. The worst. Better to die alone than to fail others.

Up and up. The ridge was quite steep now. The trees were thinning, and for the first time I could see for a few stades. I had to dismount and lead Poseidon across a rocky slope at the base of a high rock cliff – old volcanic rock like rotten cheese. Poseidon picked his way across the scree like a veteran, and I looked until my eyes burned for something I might recognise.

Of course, we put out our fires as soon as the day dawned. So there was no smoke.

But midway across the cliff face, I realised what I was seeing. Out of sight over the next ridge was something that drew a lot of carrion birds.

Dead deer, that's what was drawing the crows.

I felt my heart start to pound. My hands grew cold. I made my feet go faster. Poseidon stumbled and I tried to haul him along the scree by force – never a good move with a horse. The horse always wins a contest of strength – my first riding master taught me that. But I was *afraid*. I made mistakes.

I think that the difference between great warriors and dead warriors is that the great ones survive their first mistakes.

I got across the scree and started down the second ridge. I could no longer see the carrion birds, but they were loud and raucous and I could hear them and I rode for them. I cantered where on any other day I'd have walked. I pictured in my mind all the pages butchered or sold as slaves, Alexander as a hostage. Because I'd failed.

Down the ridge – now I was committed because it's easier to ride down a steep slope than to come back up, and once Poseidon got into the vale below, I wasn't sure we'd get back up this high. I cursed under my breath, prayed, and got a lot of branches in the face. Then we came out of the trees.

There was the wall of hurdles – the deer trap. Slaves around the carcasses. I put my head down, clenched my knees and put my heels into Poseidon's flanks, and we were off, canter and gallop and a desperate sliding stumble down another slope of loose rock above the camp, and men were looking at me.

'The prince!' I demanded as I reined in.

Philip the Red, one of the oldster pages, shook his head. 'Alexander is off with Erigyus,' Philip said. 'What the fuck?'

'Illyrians!' I said. 'A raiding party. Laodon sent me to warn the camp.'

Philip was a year older than me, a right bastard to the younger pages, an obsequious lickspittle to the older men. He looked around desperately.

There wasn't a free adult male in camp. There were ten or twelve pages and fifty slaves and some flute girls.

Some men have it. Some men don't.

'Right,' Philip said. I swear his face changed. He looked at me. 'The prince went north. Go and warn him.' He looked around again and saw Black Cleitus. 'Arm the pages, Cleitus! Right now! And get every slave a bow!'

Simple orders. Obvious stuff, you say. But Philip the Red made the grade, right there. Even if he had beaten me to a pulp once.

I had a body slave – a sort of dog-of-all-work, a gift from my pater to go with my new horse – that I called Polystratus. He was older, a Thracian, and I tolerated him and he wasn't all that fond of me. But as I turned Poseidon to head north, he was at my side with a spear and a bow. He put the spear in my hand.

Philip the Red wasn't the only one making the grade.

Polystratus ran with my horse. It's something city people don't know – a horse isn't that much faster than a man, especially over broken ground. The longer the two go on, the more even the race becomes. Over the course of a day, a man and a horse will about break even, except that over ten days, that man on the horse wins, because the man on foot is too tired.

Polystratus and I went north, over a low ridge. It was all very well for bloody Philip to tell me to find the prince, but I really had no idea how to go about it.

Polystratus did. He picked two more Thracian slaves as we went – men hauling deer carcasses into the clearing, big tattooed men with knives.

He looked up at me. 'We follow water,' he said. Shrugged. That was his plan – to follow the stream that fed the next meadow. It made sense – animals need water, and it was probably what Alexander had done. But he'd done it seven hours ago.

'Listen, boys,' I said, leaning down. 'I'll free all three of you if we live and find the prince. Got that?'

Grins all around. One Greek word every slave knows – *Eleuthera*. Freedom.

'I'm going north of the stream. Polystratus stays on the stream. You two – spread out a stade – south of the stream and another stade farther south. And *run*. When you have to stop to breathe – shout!' I looked under my hand into the sun to the west – saw riders on the crest of the distant ridge. 'Tell the prince that there are Illyrian raiders to the north and the west. Philip the Red is organising a defence in the camp. Got it? Now go, by Hermes!'

They grunted – Thracians make Macedonians look very civilised indeed – and ran off, all together at first, and then separating by degrees as they crossed the marshy meadow.

I went due north, avoiding the meadow altogether. The first time Polystratus stopped to draw breath and shout, I heard him, and that put heart into me. Then I was back on the low mountain, riding through enormous tumbled rocks and that startling perfume of mighty Artemis, up and up again. I called and called.

25

After an hour I crossed a stream and realised that I was lost. The ridge had plateaued – in another marsh, and how marshes grow at the top of steep ridges is a bafflement to me still. I had to dismount to get Poseidon around the marsh, and then there was another hill to my left, and I was completely lost. Was this Polystratus's stream? Or another stream?

I stopped at the edge of the meadow, remounted and turned Poseidon to look at the sun, and only that turn saved me.

I heard the buzz of the sling-stone. I knew it for what it was, but the information took far too long to percolate through my head. Then I put my head down and galloped for the treeline.

I crashed into the trees and looked back, and there were three men in skins – they looked like animals. Fur caps, fur leggings, furs worn as cloaks. Behind them were two men on horses – little ponies, really.

I remember saying *fuck* quite a few times.

One of the mounted men gave a whoop, and then both of them were flying across the meadow.

I kept going through the trees. I could easily outdistance their little ponies on flat ground, but in these woods they'd have the edge.

I remember thinking, quite reasonably, just as Aristotle taught us, that I had to kill them. I couldn't chance losing a race. And I couldn't chance leading them to the prince.

I was over the crest of the ridge with the marsh at the top, now, and going down a shallow slope. Off to the right, I saw one of the downed giant trees.

I rode for it, staking everything on gaining its cover before they saw me.

This giant had fallen recently – in the last hundred years – and the great ball of its roots was open to the sky like a natural cage, all the dirt washed away. I rode in among the roots.

Poseidon stopped, and his breath came in great loud snorts. I could just see my back trail. I gripped my short spear at mid-haft and waited. And waited.

When they came, they were loud and fast. But they had cast far to the west of my line – possibly because they were not fools, but Illyrians – and they passed a quarter of a stade from my ambush, robbing me of any surprise. So I let them pass. There was nothing else I could do, really, except charge them and die.

But I did follow them, moving from cover to cover on horseback the way we were taught, both hunting and scouting. Since the penalty for failure was almost always a heavy beating, doing it with the risk of losing one's life wasn't so bad.

The big downed trees were my salvation – that and my excellent horse, which never snorted and never lost his edge. We ranged along with them, half a stade distant, and went north and west. After half an hour, we crossed the track Laodon and I had used in the morning, and I knew where I was. I wasn't sure quite what I was doing – but I had passed from prey to predator, and I was scouting, or so I thought.

The sun was well down in the sky when they came to a cross-track, and one of them dismounted to look at the ground. He frowned, and then he grew a spear in his back and flopped full length on the ground.

His partner whirled his pony.

Laodon was empty-handed, but he came straight at the man on his smaller horse. He took the man's sword cut on his forearm – I winced, even as I pressed my knees into Poseidon's sides – and his right hand grabbed the headstall and ripped the Illyrian's bridle right off his horse's head.

The Illyrian's horse bolted. He threw his arms around the horse's neck.

I put my spear into him as he went by. He probably never knew I was there until he fell from his horse. He hit the ground heavily and screamed – oh, such a scream as I hope never to hear again. And then he screamed again.

I'd never killed a man, and I'd lost my spear in the shock of the successful stroke, and Poseidon did not want to go near the writhing thing on the ground, covered in leaf mould and blood, bellowing and shrieking.

'Finish him!' Laodon shouted. 'Or we'll have all his friends on us!'

I had an eating knife.

I slid from my horse and my knees were so weak I slumped to the ground, and I had to stab him three or four times. Maybe more. I really don't remember. What I remember is the silence and the blood all around me. And Poseidon, glaring at me from one wild eye, *very* unhappy.

My victim's bowels relaxed into the sloppy, smelly embrace of death. His mouth fell open and his eyes were open too. I thought he was dead, but I threw up all over him to make sure.

Laodon came and retrieved my spear. He wiped it clean, then took my knife out of the dead man's neck, wiped it clean and finally pulled the man's sword belt over his head. He had a long Keltoi sword.

Laodon tossed it to me. 'Wipe your face, lad,' he said.

I wiped it with my chlamys. I didn't have anything else. I got some of the blood off my hands and arms, but it stuck in my arm hair.

'I have to know, boy – did you make camp?' he asked.

'Yes. I'm ... I'm looking for the prince. Those two found me – I slipped them.' It sounded foolish. 'I was following them.'

Laodon nodded. 'Well done. If the prince is alive.'

We collected the dead men's ponies and headed south.

I had a sword.

Polystratus hadn't found the prince. He found us, instead, coming down yet another ridge. Laodon sent him off on a new angle, and sent me back to camp, headed almost due south.

I found Hephaestion, less than two stades from camp and blissfully unaware that the world had gone to shit. Let me take a moment to say that Hephaestion and I were never close friends. He was Alexander's favourite – his best friend, almost from birth. Alexander's partiality blinded him to Hephaestion's many failings. That's the nicest way I can put it.

Hephaestion was a bitch queen, and Alexander loved him because he reminded him of his evil mother – that's what I really think. And yet, to be fair, Hephaestion and I stood up for each other a number of times. He was loyal, and that alone was worth a lot.

Hephaestion panicked. Granted, his form of panic was to gallop off downhill to the south and west, looking for Alexander, abandoning the two younger pages he was supposed to be riding herd on – Cleomenes and Pyrrhus, a pair of useless sprites. He galloped off, and there I was with two eleven-year-olds.

Grinning like imps.

'It's an adventure, isn't it, sir?' said Cleomenes.

'Shut up, you two.' They had ponies. 'Can you two find your way back to camp?'

'Oh, yes, sir!' Pyrrhus said in the child's tone that conveys the very opposite of what's said.

'Oh, no, sir!' said Cleomenes, who'd felt my wrath before. 'It's ... that way, I think.' He pointed off towards Macedon, wrong by a quarter of the earth.

'Stay with me, then,' I barked.

Want to rid yourself of fear? Taking care of others is the key. With Laodon I was the weaker – with Cleomenes and Pyrrhus I was the strongest. It might have been comic if it hadn't been so forceful. I led them back over the first ridge and down to the treeline – and then I made them dismount while I looked at the camp.

All I saw was armed pages looking nervous. So I gathered my charges and rode hard into camp.

Philip was unable to keep still. 'That's all you found? Two brats?'

Then he saw the blood on my arms.

'I found Laodon. He's looking for the prince.' I was handed a cup and I took it, drank from it and spluttered – it was neat wine.

'Thank the gods.' Philip paused, met my eye. 'Will you ... go back out?'

Command is hard. You have to make people do things that you could do better yourself – that might get them killed. Philip the Red, one of my many foes among the pages, was asking my permission to send me back out.

I finished the wine. 'I need to change horses,' I said.

Philip nodded. A slave ran for the horse lines.

'Nice sword,' Philip said.

'Laodon did all the work,' I managed. Suddenly we were men, talking about men's things, and I was damned if I would boast like a boy.

Philip nodded. 'I've got archers in the woods,' he said.

'I got in the north way without being challenged,' I said as my second-string horse, a big mare that I called Medea, was brought in.

Philip gave me a hand up on to Medea's broad back – as if I were his peer. 'I'll look at it,' he said.

I took a different angle this time, and the shadows were long. In half an hour or less the red orb would be lost behind the flank of the mountain. Already it was cold – and time for the prince and his hunting mentor to be back.

I missed Poseidon immediately. I'd named the mare Medea for a reason – she was all love one minute and death on hooves the next, and she was in a mood. She made heavier work of climbing the ridges than Poseidon had done, and I had to spend more time dismounted, leading her. But before the sun was down a finger's breadth, I was across the stream and marsh where I'd first left Polystratus, into new territory.

Medea was a noisier horse, too, and she gave a sharp whinny as I crested the second ridge. I put a hand on her neck, but she raised her head and let go a trumpet call, and I heard a horse answer.

I drew my new sword. There were several horses, all coming up the ridge at me. Running for camp was out of the question – we were drilled relentlessly about becoming the means by which an enemy might discover the camp, when we were scouting. In fact, we might have been training for this moment all our lives.

I tucked Medea in behind a stunted, bushy spruce and threw my chlamys over her head to shut her up. I could hear my own panicked breathing, and I assumed that every Illyrian in the woods could hear me, too.

I'd picked a poor hiding place, though. Always pick a place of ambush from which you can *see*. If you can't see the enemy, chances are he can't see you – but you can panic too, while you don't know whether he's outflanking you or wandering into your trap. I crouched there on Medea's back, a hand well out over her head, keeping my cloak in place so she'd be quiet, and I had no idea where in Tartarus the Illyrians were.

But to move now – they had to be a few horse-lengths away.

The next few heartbeats were the longest of the day. And then the gods took a hand, and nothing was as I expected.

I waited. I could hear them moving, and I could hear them talking. They were quiet and careful and they knew that they were being watched. And I became aware that they'd sent men around the other side of my spruce thicket – so I was a dead man.

Best to charge, I decided. For the record, this is a form of fear that probably kills more men than running from an enemy. The need to *get it over with* is absurd.

I pulled my cloak off Medea's head and got her under me, and we were at them.

Fighting on horseback is very different to fighting on foot, mostly because you are not on your own feet, but on someone else's. It's hard to wrong-foot a man in a fight – at least, in the open. But it's not so hard to wrong-foot another man on horseback – if he's got his spear on the wrong side of the horse, say. The first Illyrian had his spear in his right hand, held at mid-haft, slanted slightly down, and I burst from cover and he caught the spearhead in his pony's neck strap.

I missed my overhand stab, but my spearhead slammed sideways into his head and he toppled.

Then Medea took a spear in the chest, and while I tried to slow her, another in the rump, and down we went. It was so fast I didn't have time to hurt, but rolled free and got to my feet.

Got my back against a big tree.

The rest of the Illyrians were already relaxing – they'd thought it was a great ambush sprung on them, and now they were realising that they had one boy, not a Macedonian army.

A pair of them kneed their horses around the spruce thicket, but the rest turned into me.

I got my spear.

A boy my own age laughed, pulled a bow from a long scabbard under his knee and strung it.

So I threw the spear.

It was something we practised every day – if I hadn't been able to hit him at that distance, I'd have had marks on my back like a bad slave.

That took the smiles off their faces. The boy with the bow died with a gurgle.

I drew my sword.

Let's make this quick – they shot my horse, and then they beat me to the ground with spear staves. I don't think I marked any of them. They were good. And thorough. They broke both my arms.

They bound me to a sapling like a deer carcass, and I screamed. It hurt a great deal.

Several of them spoke Greek, and the chieftain – at least, I assumed he was the chief, although he looked like a brigand with some gold pins – came and squatted by me.

'So,' he said. 'You killed Tarxes' boy. He wants to skin you.' The brigand chief grinned. He was missing a great many teeth, and others were broken, blackened stumps. I was somewhere in a haze of pain between consciousness and unconsciousness. 'You look like a noble brat to me, boy. And you have one of my swords on you. Tell me. Who are you?'

I'd like to say I was brave, but all I could do was mewl, spit and scream. The rawhide straps cut off all circulation to my legs but left plenty of feeling in my unset broken arms.

Broken Teeth watched me for a while. Then he took my eating knife out of his belt and rammed it through my bicep. 'Talk, boy,' he said.

I fainted. Thank the gods.

They unstrapped me and threw me into the icy stream at the foot of the ridge. So much for fainting. I couldn't swim. I couldn't even float. It occurred to me that the best thing I could do was fill my lungs with water and go down, but they hauled me clear, and anyway, I'm not sure I had the nerve.

It is a funny thing, but when you are tortured, you are a different person. Weaker, with no pride and no *self*. And yet you want to live. That's the hold they have over you. The desire to live.

They knew quite a bit. They made the mistake of talking about it. They knew it was Alexander with the hunting party.

As soon as I heard that, I knew that one of the lowland lords was playing at regicide. Alexander was the king's only heir.

That thought gave me power. Gave me back my self. Instead of being human garbage ready for sacrifice, I went back to being a royal page who had a master to protect.

See this, lad? That's where they cut my right nipple off my breast. Oh, yes. That's all scar tissue.

They enjoyed themselves. But they weren't as good as, say, a Persian torturer.

I screamed out my name. Several hundred times. It was the only thing I'd say, but I must have said it quite a bit, because I can actually remember when no sound came out at all – just the shrill sound of vocal cords wrecked by overuse.

It would have been nice if I'd passed out again, but I didn't and they tied me to a tree. Blood is sticky and *cold*. I was in shock, of course, and I shook so badly it hurt my arms. Shall I go on? Men came and beat me – quite casually. A fist in the face, a couple of kicks – they must have cracked every rib.

I'm trying to shock you, boy, and that's unkind. On the other hand, you have the satisfaction of knowing that since I'm here wearing the crown of Aegypt, I must have survived, eh?

As darkness fell, half of them rode away west under Broken Teeth. The other half bedded down, with two alert and well-concealed sentries. Tarxes came and put his eating spike into my left hand and pulled it out a couple of times. See the scars?

Then he went off to check the sentries. I was far too aware of everything around me. I wanted to faint or die, but instead I was hyper-aware.

So I watched Laodon slit a sentry's throat. I wasn't sure it was real, because by then the night seemed to be full of ghosts and shadows. The moon was full. The Illyrian ponies began to fuss, and ghosts walked. When Laodon slit the man's throat, taking him from behind with his hand as he'd grabbed me at the stream, I saw the ghosts lap at the fountain of black blood that flashed like a sword in the moonlight.

From my position in the middle of the camp, I saw Erigyus take the big axe that was meant for boars and cut the other sentry in half, or close enough. The axe made a noise like a man splitting a melon for water on a summer's day.

Then the pages flooded the camp and began killing. There was no resistance – the Illyrians were taken by surprise and paid with their lives, and they died on their squalid pallets.

Laodon cut my bonds. I managed a shriek when he reached for my arms, and he lowered me to the ground.

'By Aphrodite,' he swore. 'What have they done to you?'

And next I saw Alexander, his blond head outlined in fire. I can still see him – his profile sharply outlined. The pages must have thrown all the camp's hastily gathered wood on to the fire, and the raging flames backlit him.

'I will never forget this,' he said, and kissed me on the forehead.

It is a hard way to become a royal favourite – to win the absolute trust of the king. My left hand was never good for much afterwards, and I've known women lose the desire to fornicate when faced with the ruin of my left breast.

But without those wounds, and those awful hours, I would not be King of Aegypt.

I was a year recovering. To be honest, it was more than a year – it took me a year to recover my body enough to begin training, and another year to train hard enough to recover my place among the pages. And more than that to recover ... something that Tarxes cut out. Ambition. Aggression. Will.

I recovered for a while on my father's estates, but as soon as I could walk and hold a stylus I was back with Aristotle, and it was then that I came to understand how much my station had changed. I was not Ptolemy, son of an aristocrat, royal page. Somehow I had become the Man Who Saved the Prince, and even my father treated me with respect.

I had to go back to the Gardens of Midas to know why.

Aristotle told me that Alexander saw me captured. That Polystratus – who lived to be free – found the prince and Erigyus, and was leading them to camp when they saw the whole fight – me against twenty Illyrians. Alexander ordered them to be silent. Later, Polystratus said he watched the whole incident like a craftsman watches his work – forging everything into his memory. Alexander and Polystratus didn't depart until Broken Teeth took his men out of camp at nightfall, and they left Erigyus to watch – and came back with the pages and Laodon. As Aristotle explained it, the prince felt I'd sacrificed myself for him. Over the years many men would do the same, but he *watched* me do it. Sometimes the gods are kind.

Aristotle liked to use it as an example of how proper behaviour could result in immediate reward.

I was suspicious of that. It was my left hand that hurt as if it was newly injured every time it rained, not Aristotle's. My smooth-skinned girl screamed when her hand found my scars and she woke her father.

I had nightmares. Still have them. *Nothing* I ever found on the great wheel of the earth ever terrified me like that night in the woods when the ghosts walked, Death prowled and I was in the doorway between this world and the next, my soul stretched thin on the ground, when men wandered out of the dark to hurt me.

But Alexander and the rest treated me like a hero. And that was, in fact, worth the cost.

TWO

Macedon and Greece, 341–338 BC

My best memory of Aristotle is one of my most unhappy memories of myself.

We were wrestling. Before my injury, I had been the best pankrationist – and the best boxer. The effective loss of my left hand, which was just strong enough to grasp the reins and not much more, left me a much worse wrestler and a bad pankrationist. I didn't do much to change that.

It must have been spring in the year that Alexander became regent. Greece was in ferment, Demosthenes was ranting against us every day in the Athenian Assembly, the Thebans were threatening war and nothing was as it had been in the outside world, or in the Gardens of Midas.

The pecking order among the pages was no longer malleable. Hephaestion was at the top, with Alexander – he had no authority of his own, but Alexander would always back him, and the rest of us had learned to avoid open conflict. On the other hand, while I had been on my father's estates, my ribs knitting back together, my arms healing, Hephaestion had changed for the worse – he no longer stood up for the other pages against Alexander. I suspect they'd been lovers since they knew how to do it, but they were thicker than thieves after the hunting camp. Inseparable.

I was a distant third. I was not handsome, and that counted against me with Alexander. But like Black Cleitus, whose loyalty was beyond question, I had special rank, and no other page could touch me.

After us came the best of the other boys – Perdiccus, Amyntas, Philip the Red – by now all leaders in their own right, with their own troops of cavalry. Cassander, Antipater's son, was there – a useless twit then and now – and Marsysas, who even as a young man played the lyre and wrote better poetry than we did; nor was his sword hand light. Indeed, even Cassander – the best of the worst, if you like – was a fair fighter, the sort of man that troopers could follow in a pinch, with a rough sense of humour and a good way with hunting dogs.

Then there was a pack of younger men and boys – the youngest was ten or eleven, and we treated them like slaves, for the most part, while trying to win their devotion at the same time, as older boys do to younger the world over. It was good practice for leadership – for war. Everything we did was practice for war.

At any rate, we were fighting unarmed in the palaestra – a cool spring morning, all of us oiled, naked and trying to pretend we weren't cold.

I went up against Amyntas. I never tried – oh, Zeus, it hurts more to tell this than to tell of being tortured. I never even tried. I basically lay down and let him pin me.

No one said a thing. Because by then, I'd done it fifty times. In fact, I remember Alexander smiling at me.

But after we'd had a bite of bread moistened in wine, while Alexander and Hephaestion were fighting like desperate men – and by then we had seventeen-year-old bodies and a lot of muscle – Aristotle came and put a hand on my shoulder.

'What I hate most about the Illyrians,' he said, 'was that they tortured your arete out of your body, and now you have no daimon at all.'

Sometimes you know a thing is true. I burst into tears.

Every man there turned and looked at me, and the pity in their eyes was like Tarxes' eating spike driven into me again and again.

Aristotle took me by the hand and led me out into the garden.

'Ptolemy,' he said, and he put a hand on the back of my neck as if I might bolt, 'you were the best of the pages. And now you are not even a man. You have the honour of the prince's esteem – you saved him. You alone saved him – with your head and with your sword. Is that to be the sum of your acts? Will you lie on that bed of laurels until it is withered, or will you rise from it?' He turned me to face him. He was not a particularly handsome man, but I've always maintained that his looks made men think of him as *the* philosopher – bushy eyebrows, deep-set, wide, clear eyes, a thin mouth, a high forehead – the very image of manly wisdom.

I'm ashamed to say that all I could manage was some sobs. It was all true. I'd lain down for every contest since I came back, and no one said me nay. I was an object of *pity*.

'Let me tell you what I know of men,' Aristotle said. 'Most men are capable of greatness once. They rise above themselves, or they follow a greater man, or the gods lend a hand, or the fates – once, a man may make a fortune, may tell the truth despite pressure to lie, may have a worthy love who leads him to do good things. This taste of arete is all

35

most men ever have – and they are better for it.' He looked at me. 'Stop blubbering, son of Lagus. I tell you – and I know – you are better than that. I expect better of you. Go and fight and lose. Lose fifty times to lesser men and you will be better for it. You have reached a point where there is no penalty for failure, and that is the worst thing that can happen to a young man. So here is your penalty – my contempt. And here is your reward – my admiration. Which will you have, son of Lagus?'

I'd like to say that I stood straighter, looked him in the eye and thanked him. What I did was to run off into the garden and bawl my eyes out.

And the next day, when we were to box, I faced off against a much younger page – and folded.

Aristotle just shook his head.

And over the next few days, I began to notice a certain want of regard among the younger pages. They had worshipped me when I returned, and that worship was falling off.

That hurt.

Cleomenes, the young sprig I'd rescued in the hunting camp, was my most loyal follower, and he sat on my tightly rolled war cloak in the barracks and glared at me. He had a black eye.

He wasn't eleven any more, either.

'Amyntas says you are a coward,' he said with all the hot accusation that a thirteen-year-old can throw at a seventeen-year-old. 'He says that the Illyrians cut your courage out, and we should treat you like a woman.'

'If Amyntas thinks women are cowards, he should try birthing a baby,' I said. One of my mother's sayings. I sighed. 'I'm not a coward,' I said.

'Prove it,' Cleomenes said. 'Beat the shit out of Amyntas.'

'Why?' I asked.

'Because that's what he did to me,' Cleomenes said with a half-sob.

Life among the pages. Very nice.

It occurred to me to go to Alexander.

But after further thought, I realised that they were all right.

It is odd – I don't think I was ever a coward. I just didn't need to excel, and since the need was taken away, I coasted. Or maybe there's more to it than that. I certainly had a great many nightmares, and my camp girl – I'll explain that later – would wake me in the night with a hand on my cheek because I was screaming and waking the barracks.

I thought about it, and I came to a set of decisions – every one of them nested into the next. I needed to learn to be the man I had been. And I wasn't going to learn with the pages.

Polystratus had become a foot companion – one of the elite infantry-men of the old king – and he had a farm not far from the gardens. So I asked for an hour's leave and rode out to find him, and dragged him from his plough and made of him my sparring partner. His whole idea of fighting with a sword was to hit faster and harder – worthy objectives in themselves, but not a way to win a fight, unless your only goal is to smash your way through the other man's shield. So, in order to arrange to practise myself, I spent two weeks training him.

Two weeks in which I must have interfered with his ploughing and his sowing, too. I all but lived in his hovel, and his wife – another freed slave – feared me. But teaching Polystratus to be a swordsman did more for my own fighting skills than anything I'd learned in the last year. In fact, I think it was those two weeks that put me on the path I'm still on. Somewhere in the teaching of Polystratus I realised – that there was a theory, a philosophy, to combat. That each motion of an attack, a defence, could be analysed like a problem of philosophy.

I was not the first Hellene to understand this. I may not have been the first seventeen-year-old to understand this. But it was like a key to unlock a trunk full of knowledge. Many, many things that I had learned by rote – steps, hip movements, overhand cuts, thrusts – came together in two weeks to form a sort of Thalian singularity, and if you don't know who Thales was, young man, you will have to ask your tutor and report to me tomorrow.

I admit, it was easier with my former slave – easier to risk a contest against him, and unimportant to lose. Why? Because he was a man of no consequence, that's why. What did I care if a former slave could best me?

Except that in those two weeks, Polystratus became a *man* to me. Since that time, I have seen this happen again and again – worthy men develop a kinship with their opponents, just as unworthy men come to loathe them. The worthiness resides in the competitor – if he brings with him an ability to emulate and admire his enemy, then he is a better man for it. Or so I think.

At any rate, after a fortnight of daily struggle in the mud of spring, Polystratus was a passable pankrationist, and probably the best swords-man in the foot companions – not that they ever fought with swords. But still.

All this time, every morning that I was paired with another man in a contest, I lay down – if not literally, then in effect.

Aristotle shook his head, and then, after another week, didn't even bother with that.

But Alexander began to look at me curiously.

37

Cleomenes ceased to come and sit with me, or to flirt with my bed-warmer. I should put in here that Philip had become deeply concerned by Alexander's little ways – with sex. It was known to every one of us that Philip thought that his son was soft – possibly effeminate. A gynnis. There had been loud words exchanged on the subject, and Olympias – never a subtle woman – sent Alexander a hetaera, a courtesan, named Calixeinna.

She was outrageously beautiful, with the sort of body – high, perfectly round breasts, a tiny waist, a long, sculpted face with small, thick lips for kissing and enormous eyes – the sort of body that drives men mad.

All of us – even the prince – lived in the Macedonian version of a Spartan barracks, in messes of ten boys – five oldsters and five young-sters. Some oldsters slept alone, some with each other, some with the younger boys. Some were just sharing cloaks for warmth. Eh? And some weren't. Until Calixeinna came.

The poor thing was appalled to be the only woman in what must have seemed like an armed camp with academics. She was quite intel-ligent – she could recite great swathes of the *Iliad* – but the idea that she had no room of her own, that she had to dress and undress with forty boys, made her angry. She threatened to leave.

Alexander refused to live outside the barracks.

Aristotle bit his lips, cursed and found women for us all, or, if not all, at least a few per mess. Country girls – not prostitutes, no one's father would have allowed that. The king offered them all dowries and regular pay, and I suspect there was no shortage of volunteers – we were good-looking, clean and noble.

Of course, this was also the occasion for his famous lecture on the life of hedonism versus the life of restraint and self-control, too.

The truth is that our barracks life improved immeasurably when the women moved in. The clothes were cleaner, the conversation was bet-ter, and the youngsters began to laugh and play – the women wouldn't allow them to be abused. Women exert a subtle influence – not so subtle, sometimes. They will say things without fear that even a warrior might fear to say.

At any rate, I had a regular bed-warmer from the first. She was named Iphegenia – some parents need a better classical education – and she was pretty enough, with large hips and smooth muscles and breasts. She was scared the first time we were naked together, and after that, not – and she was never put off by my scars. I can't say I loved her – she was the most selfish woman I've ever known well – but she took good care of me, bore my first bastard and my pater put her on a farm for me. I hope she lives yet.

Oh, I'm an old man. I love to think of Genny stripping for bed – the only sign I ever had that she was as eager as I was the way she'd incline towards my sleeping roll like a hunting dog pointing to the prey. Hah!

But Alexander appeared to want nothing to do with his courtesan. She was in his sleeping roll most nights, and a few times I saw her under his cloak, once even wrapped in his arms. He was gracious to her. But that was the limit, and Aristotle openly admonished him against her.

Olympias sent notes explaining how men and women had sex, and how much better sex with a woman was than sex with a man. Just picture getting this lecture from your mother, herself a famous beauty, a veritable avatar of Aphrodite. Zeus, god of kings, what a horror that woman could be, and how much of Alexander can be laid at her door. Sober, she was brilliant and scary, and drunk, she was a lascivious predator with no scruples and a poisonous memory. And her power to manipulate – she was quite brilliant ...

She was very beautiful, with sparkling eyes and curly brown hair, tall, elegantly limbed – please don't imagine her as somebody's mother. She bore Alexander at the age of fourteen, and when I first met her – not first saw her at court at a distance, but actually stood in her presence – she was twenty-five years old, in the prime of her beauty. Her skin glowed, and she herself had a sort of radiant vitality that she passed unmarred to her son. I've known men who hated her, and I've heard magnificent tales of her debauchery, and I know some of them to be true, but let it be said – Macedonian men disliked powerful women, and she was a powerful woman who added to beauty and charm an indomitable will and an almost unbreakable bond with the king that allowed her to call the tune at court. She had many enemies.

She was fiercely protective of Alexander and her protection extended to his friends and companions, and despite having several skirmishes with her myself, as you will hear, I have to admit that she was often our ally against Philip and his companions – the older men who saw us first as children and later as dangerous rivals.

But I digress. That winter, she had got it into her head that Alexander needed a woman, and she decided that the woman of his dreams would also be a useful tool to manipulate him – this is a fine example of how her mind worked.

Anyway, she and Aristotle were adversaries. These days, it has become popular to suggest that Olympias and Philip were the enemies, but I never saw that. It seemed to me that Olympias and Philip were united in wanting their boy to grow up to be a good, solid, dependable Macedonian nobleman – something, I'd like to note, that Philip never was – and Aristotle wanted something more – a great king, an

Athenian-style philosopher who had the mettle of Achilles and the mind of Socrates.

Calixeinna became their battleground. She could flirt, a talent wasted on young men, and she could play the lyre and the flute and recite poetry. She could also do geometry, and this fascinated Alexander and even Aristotle. She was not without weapons. Nor was Alexander indifferent to her. He loved beauty, and she was beautiful.

One day, Alexander was paired with me in a war game. We were to live without supplies for three days, stealing food from the kitchens or outlying farms. This was in emulation of the Spartan training, and deeply unfair – if we were caught, I would be beaten. Alexander was never beaten.

We were taken some miles from the Gardens of Midas, and our horses were taken by slaves. We were to live three days off the country, never being caught or even seen, and then we were to steal food from the manor itself, and finally, we were to surrender ourselves to Aristotle at a set time.

Alexander wanted to be paired with Hephaestion, but for whatever reason, he was paired with me. We were taken into the chora, the farmland west of the manor, and left at the edge of the forest without food, water or weapons of any kind.

Perhaps this sort of thing challenges Spartan boys. Alexander and I had a very pleasant three days. We lay up until dark, stole into the first farm and took the dog leashes off the wall of an outbuilding we'd observed at last light. We slept together for warmth and in the morning we unwove the hemp leashes and made slings. Instead of going into the chora, we went up into the hills and killed every rabbit we wanted. There were ripe berries on the bushes, and Alexander got us not one but two magnificent trout out of a stream by standing stock still in the freezing water until the trout trusted him – and then he abused that trust. He was very proud of his feat and I praised him extravagantly, both while I cooked the fish in clay and later, when my belly was full.

Trout, rabbit – by the gods, we ate more than we ate in the pages' mess, and we slept as long as we wanted. It makes me laugh to think of it.

The second night, we were watching the stars come out. We'd been talking about war – as a generality.

'I want to conquer Persia,' he said, as if the stars had just told him.

My belly was full and I was sleepy. 'I want a cup of good wine,' I said.

He shook his head. 'Don't be an ass,' he said. 'Pater is not going to get the invasion together until Athens is subdued. Athens can't be subdued until the Chersonese is cleared. The Chersonese can't be cleared until the Athenian fleet is neutralised. The Athens fleet can't be neutralised until Persia is conquered. Persia can't be conquered until Athens is subdued.'

He grinned, proud of his deliberately circular logic.

'But this season he's campaigning in Thrace, against the Scyths and the Thracians,' I pointed out.

Alexander laughed. 'You know as well as I that fighting the Thracians and the Scyths is merely an extension of fighting for the Chersonese.'

I did know that, so I laughed. 'But we don't have to beat Athens,' I said suddenly.

'Why not?' the prince asked.

'Athens is a democracy,' I said.

Alexander nodded. 'Good point.'

This was, I have to add, one of the chief features of discussing anything with Alexander. He was so intelligent that when you *did* make a good point, he always – or almost always – understood immediately, which had the boring effect of keeping the rest of us from ever getting to explain ourselves. What I had meant was, *Athens is a democracy, and sooner or later one of their factions will screw up their alliance with Persia, or lose interest in the war, and then we'll have them.* And the moment I said it, Alexander understood.

It saved time in argument, anyway. But our conversations may have seemed stilted to outsiders. The insiders – Hephaestion, Cleitus the Black, me, Craterus – we could often have whole conversations in single words.

At any rate, he lay there and finally he said, 'Until he defeats Athens, he can't send all his force against Persia.'

'True,' I said.

'I will need you, when I go to conquer Persia,' he said. What he meant was, *Philip will never finish with Athens, and I will have a turn.*

I laughed. But he sat up and put a hand on my arm.

'I am serious. There's only a hand of you I really trust. I need you. And to be the man I need, you must stop surrendering in contests,' he said. 'Here, in the woods, you kill game, you cook, you find trails, you cut bedding – you are the perfect companion, afraid of nothing, quick with good advice – but among the pages, you lie down and let lesser boys triumph over you.'

I remember a hot flush of anger – which of us likes to have our innermost failings exposed? And the temptation to tell him that I was practising, that I meant to strike back, was like the pressure of a swollen river on a dam. But I resisted.

'Aristotle has spoken to you about it,' Alexander said.

'Yes,' I said, my voice thick. I wanted to say *fuck off*, or words to that effect.

'Get it done. Our time is coming.' Alexander sounded very sure of himself, but then, he always did.

I struggled for words. But none came, and suddenly he turned to me.

'I know where Calixeinna bathes,' he said. Again, it was as if the stars had spoken to him.

'You can see her naked any time you want,' I shot out, still full of emotions.

'Isn't there something terribly … ignoble, in giving orders to a woman purchased for you by your mother?' he said. He shrugged. 'I love to look at her. She has the most beautiful body I have ever seen.' He shrugged again. 'But I will not order her to disrobe for me.'

I shook my head. 'Give her to me, then,' I said. I meant to be playful, but he rolled over suddenly on our bed of grass and his face was inches from mine. 'No,' he said coldly. 'She is mine.'

Never a dull moment with Alexander.

'I want to go and watch her bathe,' he said.

'Let's not forget what happened to Adonis,' I mused, with the false levity that always follows a serious moment.

'I am not Adonis,' Alexander said. 'She is not Artemis, and anyway, no one will catch me.'

He woke me while the stars were still a cold and distant presence, and we stretched, did some exercises and started down out of the hills. Far from sneaking across the plains, we ran – about thirty stades, I think. Ah, to be young! Alexander had thought it all through, and decided that Aristotle's slaves, pretending to be guards, would not guard anything or patrol at all in the dark. So instead of creeping from tree to tree across central Macedon, we ran down the roads in the moonlight.

As the sky bgan to pale in the east, we ran past the manor house, bold as brass, and went down the orchard lane, past the olive groves and up the big hill to the west of the manor. There was a spring there, and we ran to the spring, drank water and prayed to the gods.

'You must not look,' Alexander told me. 'Go and take a nap.'

So I snuck away, and he concealed himself in a tree. We were enacting his fantasy – I knew him well enough to understand that. He played the game according to his own rules, and this was his way.

But I was a boy on the edge of manhood myself, and I had no intention of letting him have her all to himself. So I found a little knoll of soft grass under an olive tree and lay down, knowing my man. He came soon enough. He was checking to see that I was asleep.

I pretended to sleep, and then, when he was gone and I had counted to a thousand, I went all the way around the hill and climbed up behind the spring.

Waiting in ambush is dull. I waited a long time. After perhaps a full hour, I guessed where Alexander was hidden from the behaviour of the birds and squirrels. And when the sun was well up and I was regretting my temerity and wondering why I *hadn't* just gone for a nap, Calixeinna came.

She had three slaves with her, and they dropped their chitons by the pool and splashed each other, shrieking and calling names. I had a girl of my own – and some experience of women – but I remember being struck almost dumb by the four of them, all beautiful, all splendidly muscled and all very, very different. A dark-haired Thracian girl had short but beautifully muscled legs with heavy thighs, large breasts and a waist and hips that were all swooping curves. A Greek slave was taller and slimmer, with subtler curves, small breasts and a long, graceful back and a magnificent neck. The third woman, a Persian, had the most beautiful eyebrows I had ever seen, graceful hands, and breasts of a different shape from the other two, almost like wine cups. They were all women, all beautiful and all utterly different.

And then there was Calixeinna, who was tall and willowy, with a waist so small that I could have put my hands around it, lips that were the colour of dawn, hair that was a particular blushing shade of red-blond, and heavy, full breasts as yet untouched by age. Her hips were wide and her legs long, and she was *perfect*.

While her women shrieked and played, she swam in the small pool, really only about three times the length of her body, the water ice cold and black in the early sun under the great holm oak that shadowed the spring. When she emerged, it was like the rising of the sun, and when she reached her arms back to wring out her hair ...

Oh, youth.

She played for a while with a turtle by the edge of the pool, and it occurred to me that she knew Alexander was there. I didn't know much about women, but I knew they didn't play naked by pools nearly as much as adolescent boys thought they did.

When she was done with the turtle, she lay on a rock, naked. The other nymphs continued to laugh and scream, and the longer I watched, the more like a performance it seemed.

Eventually, I had to wonder how often it had been repeated, and by

43

what mechanism Alexander had been informed of it, and whether he'd been to the performance before.

Eventually, she put on her chiton – so prettily that one breast was free while a lost pin was found in the grass – and she and the Persian girl skipped away down the hill, arm in arm, and the other two stayed for a few minutes, filling jars.

I snuck back to my resting place, and went straight to sleep.

A little later, Alexander wakened me, looking as if he'd had a religious revelation. Then, in broad daylight, we climbed into the walled compound and went to the slaves' quarters, where we sat to breakfast with the slaves – bad wine and stale bread and a little cheese and some dry figs. They all looked at us, of course. Alexander just smiled.

And we were in our usual places when Aristotle opened his class. The philosopher actually got several sentences into his lecture before he realised that we were supposed to be in hiding.

He was pleased with us.

We were pleased with ourselves.

And I never told Alexander that I had watched Calixeinna bathe. I think he'd have killed me.

My point is, he was very smitten, in his deeply self-controlled and selfish way.

I missed most of the by-play, because the next weeks were the weeks I was off drilling in the late afternoons with Polystratus. But Genny told me everything – sometimes too much of everything. Genny could chatter gossip at me even when her breathing was coming in gasps and her hands were locked behind my back and her nails were cutting into my muscles – 'and then – ah! – she said – ah! – that he …'

It's good to know that, even as king, I can raise a laugh.

I don't remember what occasioned it. We hardly ever boxed – it was considered too Greek and effeminate – but when we did we wrapped our hands. That helped me – my left hand was ugly, and I was young, and having it wrapped helped steady me.

Old Leonidas stood wearing his chlamys and holding a heavy staff of cornel wood. I happened to be the first page out the barracks door with my hands wrapped. And Amyntas came out second.

'Ptolemy, son of Lagus,' Leonidas snapped. 'Against Amyntas …' His eyes wandered, and he shook his head. 'No. A younger boy. Philip the Black.'

'Oh, I'll be gentle with him,' Amyntas said. 'He's ugly, but maybe if I roll him over …' He guffawed, and many of the other oldsters laughed.

Alexander looked hurt. And he gave me a look – the whole burden of his eyes. In effect, he said *do it.*

I must give the prince this – he was horrified when the other pages began to turn against me.

Hephaestion relished my discomfiture. 'He's the only oldster who competes against little boys,' he said to Leonidas. 'Make him fight Amyntas.'

'Hephaestion!' snapped Alexander.

'I'd love to face Amyntas,' I said. 'But I'm no match for him.'

Amyntas laughed. 'Put a bag over your head, Ptolemy!' he said, and his little set laughed, but the other pages – especially Philip the Red, long ago turned from my tormentor to my friend – looked embarrassed.

Leonidas didn't like it, but he put me in the ring of wands against Amyntas.

Losing can become a habit.

Amyntas put a fist in my gut and instead of twisting away – I had stomach muscles like bands of steel and it wasn't that bad – I folded around his punch and lay down.

But when I rolled over, he was pushing his hips, pretending to fuck me for his little audience.

I did my very best to hide my rage. I'd had some practice, since the night with the Illyrians, at hiding my thoughts. I hung my head, rubbed my hip and squared off.

Leonidas struck Amyntas with his staff. 'Don't be a gadfly, boy,' he said.

Amyntas turned on me, eager to have me on the ground again. But he stumbled as he took up his guard – the will of the gods and sheer hubris – and I had all the time in the world to strike him.

I needed it. Losing is a habit. Covering up is a habit, too – fighting defensively, waiting for the blow that will allow you to lose with honour, or at least some excuse and a minimum of pain. That's how low I'd fallen – even after weeks of practice with Polystratus, faced with a real competitor, I was ready to lie down, I think, until that stumble. Ares was good to me.

He stumbled, and his chin came to my fist.

Instead of defending himself, he lashed out with his left and caught me on the nose, and it *hurt.* He didn't break it – but he hurt me, and I saw red. Those two things saved me from myself – his stumble and that haze of pain.

Let's make this brief. I beat him to a pulp. I broke his nose and blackened both of his eyes and made him beg me for mercy.

None of the other boys said a thing. Leonidas stood back and let it happen, and Aristotle ...

... caught my eye and gave me the smallest nod of approbation.

When he was begging, I let him go. I had him under my left arm, his head locked against my body, and I was beating him with my elbow and fist. My hand hurt.

Leonidas waved for two boys to carry Amyntas off.

'Since you are feeling better,' he said, 'you may face Prince Alexander.'

If losing is a habit, so is winning. Alexander always won – both because none of us wanted to beat him, and because he was awfully fast. And practised like a mad thing.

But that morning, in that place, I was bound to try. I was drinking water and I almost choked at the announcement. Cleitus the Black grinned – not an adversarial grin, but the grin of a man who has been there. So I grinned back, and just at that moment, the gods sent Calixeinna. She was not entering the palaestra – that would have been an appalling breach of etiquette – but she paused, going down the steps from the exedra, about thirty paces away. Owing to the way the columns and the buildings aligned, I'm pretty sure I was the only boy she could see.

She smiled at me. It was a beautiful, radiant, confident smile, and it wasn't a brief flash.

Then she turned and went down the steps.

I shrugged off my chlamys and went to meet the prince.

My shoulders hurt and my left hand was a dead thing, and I was back to being embarrassed by the scar tissue on my left breast – competitors are supposed to be beautiful. But when the stick came up between us, I didn't give ground but jabbed with my left – over and over, my left fist like an annoying horsefly.

My fourth or fifth jab connected. Alexander's head snapped back and his lip was split, blood already welling. He was stunned, and I stepped in and gave him my right to the gut, jabbed a few more times, making some contacts, and then my right to the exposed side of his head and down he went.

The other pages were silent.

Alexander got up slowly, putting the cloth wrapping of his fists against his split lip to slow the flow of blood. His eyes met mine – glanced away – came back.

He winked.

And then his lightning-fast right jab slammed into my head, while I was still trying to understand the wink.

*

When I came to, Alexander was sitting by my bedside in the infirmary. He loved everything about medicine, and always told us that if he wasn't king, he'd want to be a doctor. He meant it, too – he was always trying medicines on himself and others, and for years he kept a little journal detailing what he'd tried and with what effect, under what conditions.

He grinned at me when I was obviously aware of him.

'Have I told you, Ptolemy, how much you are a man after my own heart?' he asked.

I smiled. Who wouldn't? He was the most charming man who ever lived, and that smile was all for me. 'Why so, lord?' I asked.

'How long since you decided to come back to us?' Alexander asked me. 'Two weeks? Perhaps three?' He nodded. 'And you hid your intentions carefully, like a wily Odysseus with the suitors all around him.' He leaned forward. 'You'd already started training when we were up the mountain, and you never said a word.'

'My lord does me too much credit,' I said. But I was grinning, too.

'Welcome back, son of Lagus,' Alexander said. 'There is nothing I love better than a man in control of himself.'

He gave me a hug, forced me to drink some foul tea that really did make me feel better – a tisane of willow bark, I think.

Calixeinna came and read to me. I'd never really met her, and she had a beautiful voice and her reading was as good as an actor's – at least, the kind of actors who came to Pella. She read to me from a play of Aeschylus and then she read me some of Simonides' poem on Plataea. And then she recited a long section of the *Iliad* – the time from when Patroclus dies and Achilles is disconsolate.

'You are one of his friends,' she said, interrupting herself in the midst of the hero's rage. 'I just heard today – how you saved him.' She looked at me – at my hand. 'I'm sorry.'

'You are too kind,' I said.

She shook her head. 'No. I'm not. I've been used – I know what torture is.' She squeezed my hand.

My heart fluttered.

'I need help with him,' she said. 'Would you help me?'

I sat up. I really didn't need to be in bed. And she gave off a perfume, and a feeling – some women exude sex, the way some men exude power. Perhaps it is the same. I wanted her, she knew it, it didn't matter a damn to her, and she was prepared to use it against me.

I wasn't a fool, you know. Just young.

She ran her hand casually up my left arm and on to the missing nipple, her nails unerringly just between pain and pleasure. 'I could teach you things that would mean that no woman would ever care about your scars,' she said. 'I need to sleep with the prince. I need to see into his head. No one told me when I took this job that he was a Spartan.'

My loyalty to my prince was absolute – nor had I ever had enough trouble with women, despite my looks, to worry overmuch in that regard.

But to look at Calixeinna was to want her. 'I'll think on it,' I said, and I meant it. I seized one of her hands and kissed it.

Her free hand slapped my left ear, boxed it hard enough to drive my wits from my head for a moment. She was off the bed and across the corridor.

Alexander was in the doorway.

'He has a great deal of life left in him, I suspect,' the prince said. He was smiling.

Calixeinna sank gracefully to one knee and rose again, her back straight. Then she moved away.

Alexander's eyes never left her. I watched him watch her, when he thought that I was lust-raddled myself.

In the same kind of flash that had come to me over the fighting skills, I understood him in that moment. Calixeinna didn't have a chance.

He wanted her.

But to take her at his mother's insistence would involve a loss of a battle.

'I would not poach your deer,' I said.

'You may have her,' he said. His eyes said otherwise.

I shook my head. 'Lord, if I were ... in a moment of hubris, and even if she would part her legs for me – to take that woman, everyone would punish me for it.' I shrugged. 'Your father, your lady mother, Aristotle, the other pages – Aphrodite herself, no doubt.'

Alexander sat on my bed. 'How's your head?'

'The tisane helped,' I said, which made him happy. I took out a stylus and scratched a note on his wax tablet.

'You want her,' I said. Boldest thing I'd ever said to him.

He read the note. 'Yes,' he admitted. He sighed. 'But I cannot. I think ... *do* you understand, son of Lagus?'

'I think so,' I said.

'A king must never surrender to his lusts. A man must never surrender to the views other men have of him. This would be both.' Alexander nodded, having learned his lesson by heart.

He was very serious. Only an eighteen-year-old can be that serious. You should know.

'Have her in secret – win her to your side and have her deny that you were ever together,' I suggested.

'When did you become so wily?' he asked.

It occurred to me that in one blow I could become his confidant, undermine Hephaestion and help him with his mother and father. But that wasn't my intention.

On the other hand, once I'd thought these things, I realised that I had become wily – at some point between the bandit's knife and pulping Amantys. Odysseus, not Achilles, was always my favourite.

Alexander's nails were pressed into his palms. He used pain quite a bit, to control himself – I'd seen it, and he was hardly alone in that regard.

'Prince – you will be king. If you want the woman – let's arrange it.' I smiled.

He didn't smile. 'It is a wrong action,' he said.

Aphrodite, the things Aristotle drilled into him. 'No,' I said. 'Aristotle doesn't want you to have any fun. And your father wants to make you behave like a beast. Surely there's a middle road. Your own road.'

Alexander's self-control was such that he almost never touched his face. Try it – try to go fifteen minutes without touching your face. I mention this because I remember that at that moment he put his chin in his left hand and gave me a long look. 'How?' he asked me.

It took me ten days. I felt a little like a pimp, to be sure.

And of the two, the less willing conspirator was the prince. He did not like to conspire. He wanted to be Achilles. I was listening when Aristotle talked, by this time, and I'd finally figured out why we all love Achilles – who is, let us admit it, venal, selfish and somewhat given to boasting and drama.

What we love is the freedom that comes with absolute mastery. Achilles can do whatever he wants – sulk for days in his tent, as we all wish to, or rage among his enemies, or mourn his dead friend, or take Briseis back from a great king. The limitations on his absolute freedom drive him almost to madness. And because the rest of us don't live that way at all – because we submit to the will of others every day – we admire Achilles' freedom.

Alexander wanted to be Achilles, and sneaking about in the dark was not his way.

As it turned out, my plan was over-complex and almost unnecessary.

My plan involved Cleitus the Black taking a beating from Philip the Red – they could both be trusted. That evening, Hephaestion was to take wine to Aristotle – it was his turn. Every evening, one of the oldsters took him wine and sat and practised 'good conversation' for a few hours.

49

Alexander would go to visit Cleitus – no unusual thing.

But instead of Cleitus, he'd find Calixeinna, waiting on the bed in the infirmary. Not bad, eh?

But on the day, Hephaestion had a virulent head cold and stayed in the barracks. And I was sent for by Aristotle.

Alexander was nursing his best friend – a little too much nursing, and Hephaestion drove him away with his blanket snapping at his friend's head and threw a vial of medicine after him for good measure. Sometimes Aphrodite takes a hand.

I went to see Aristotle. I took a flask of good Chian – my father was rich, after all. This was the sweet Chian made from raisinated grapes. Sweet and strong. And instead of cutting it with water, I cut it with a mixture of wine and water I'd made in advance, and my tutor was as drunk as Dionysus by the time he'd finished his second bowl.

He had a wife – a nice enough woman – whom he largely ignored. His tastes didn't go that way, and she managed his household and not much more. I can imagine him telling others that a wife was cheaper than a slave butler – that's what he's supposed to have said to Alexander. On this evening, she came in, and she was on to me in a moment – saw me pouring my watered wine mixture into the Chian.

She said nothing. Either Aphrodite was with us, or Aristotle's wife was as happy to see him too drunk to move his legs as I was. Before he was done with me, though, he'd told me that I was the best of the pages again, and he tried to kiss me. He really was a moral man, but no man, no matter how controlled, can restrain himself with a jar of Chian under his belt. His wife took him to bed, singing a hymn to Ares of all things, and I cleaned up the wine-serving things – part of the training was learning what to mix and how to judge taste against quality of conversation.

I was never good at the subtleties, but I had just figured out how to knock a middle-aged philosopher out cold.

But I'm a worrier, and I cut across the compound, my slave laden with wine things, wondering if the prince had managed to make love to Helen of Troy, or whether some iron-clad principle had stood in the way.

I thought that I'd just have a look. I had as much right to take a peek at Cleitus as anyone.

I was sorry I looked. Not sorry, exactly. More … intrusive. Sensitive men do not last as household companions to princes – but at the same time, if you have no ability to read and feel other people, you'll never be much of a battlefield commander, will you?

My prince was lying with his head on her chest in the light of the vigil lamp. He was asleep. Her eyes were open. They met mine, and the very smallest smile – the sort that Pheidias put on Aphrodite – flickered around the edge of her mouth.

I slipped away, mortified at his weakness – he looked like a boy sleeping on his mother.

What had I expected?

'Lord, there's a rider at the gate.' That was my forgotten slave, Hermonius, a big barbarian from the north. He was laden with the wine service, and despite that he was alert enough.

'Go and drop the wine things in a chest and wake ...' Herakles – the prince was in the wrong bed. 'I'll deal with it,' I said.

I went to the gate, already wondering what could bring a messenger at this hour. Another way that the fight at the hunting camp had changed me – violence was real. Alone of the pages, or perhaps with Philip the Red, I realised that the Illyrians had intended to take or kill the prince and that meant he'd been betrayed. I'd only told two men – my father, and Aristotle. My father told Parmenio, or so he told me.

The man at the gate was Laodon.

'My lord?' I said, swinging the gate open. And wondering, all of a sudden, if Laodon could have been the traitor.

'Hello, Ptolemy. I need the prince – we're fucked, and that's no mistake.' He was covered in mud, wearing beautiful scale armour and a fine red cloak both fouled from the road. He slid from his horse and embraced me – that surprised me, and pretty much let him off the hook of treason in my mind. 'Glad you are here. Get me the prince.'

'Life or death?' I asked.

Laodon paused just as Hermonius came out of the dark and started to untack his horse. 'Yes,' he said.

I grabbed his rolled cloak and led him to the infirmary. It was still dark – all I needed was some luck. 'Swear on the furies you won't say a word, lord,' I said. 'I stood my ground with you.'

Laodon shrugged. 'He's got that fool boy with him? Not my problem. This is the kingdom, boy – take me to the prince.'

I took his hand. 'Swear,' I said.

'By the furies, damn you!' Laodon said.

I took him into the infirmary. I got ahead of him, leaned over the bed – the oil lamp was still burning, and now they were both asleep.

I woke Alexander with a brush of fingers across his mouth – works on most folks – and he came up with a knife in his hand. But I'd been the duty page before and I knew his little ways.

'News from Pella,' I said. 'Life and death. Gather your wits, lord.'

He looked past me and saw Laodon. Nodded to me. Rolled out of bed, naked but for a knife sheath on a string.

She was awake already. I lifted her, bedclothes and all, off the bed, and carried her out the back of the infirmary. I put her down on the porch – on her feet – and threw the end of the blanket over her head, and she smiled at me and ran. Problem solved.

As if we were in one of Menander's comedies, Hephaestion came through the front door a heartbeat later. He was ready to be hysterical – he thought that he'd caught Alexander with Laodon.

I'd have laughed if it hadn't been so sad, and if the news hadn't been so bad.

Philip had lost a battle – and he was badly wounded. A combined force of Scythians and Thracians – not that the two are all that different – had caught him in the passes where he was carving out new territory, north and east of Illyria. He'd lost a lot of men – veterans – and part of his horse herd, and he'd taken a wound in the thigh.

Laodon shrugged when he was done with the barest relation. 'He's your da,' he said. 'So please accept my regrets. But I think he's done – and the Thracians aren't going to sit on the other side of the mountains and let us rebuild.'

'My father's going to die?' Alexander asked. His voice had a curious timbre to it – hard to guess what he thought.

'Almost dead,' Laodon said.

Alexander didn't raise his eyes from the rumpled bed – 'Where's Parmenio?'

'Chasing Phokion in the south. Or being chased by him.' Laodon shrugged.

'Antipater?' Alexander asked.

'With your father, bringing the phalanx back as well as he can.' Laodon was exhausted – I knew the signs. I poured him a cup of wine and water and he drank it off.

Alexander stood up, and he wasn't just awake, he was quivering with energy.

'I was afraid he would leave me no worlds to conquer,' he said softly. 'Ptolemy – all the pages over fifteen, with armour and remounts, in the courtyard at dawn.'

I thought that one through for fifty heartbeats. 'Yes, my lord.'

'Very good. See to it that the young person is suitably rewarded and silent, if you please.' His eyes flicked back to the bed, but I knew who he meant. His voice was impersonal, military, like the better sort of Athenian orator. Like a king.

I like to think that if Alexander had lain with the courtesan and then had a good night's sleep, it might all have been different.

*

By the time we cantered into Pella, our girths tight and our cloak rolls tighter, we looked like professional soldiers, the bodyguard of a king. We'd trained for it – and three days on the road moving at top speed tightened everything about us. Alexander had reached a new level of remoteness from us – he barely spoke, but when he did, his voice was light and he laughed with everyone.

He was working on a new version, a new mask. From 'serious boy' he was now on to 'golden boy'.

When we reached Pella, the vanguard of the army was already coming in.

Macedon in those days was an armed camp, a state girded for war night or day, winter or summer – indeed, it was one of Demosthenes' chief complaints about us that we made war all year long. Even the Spartans took the winter off, seemed to be the burden of his message.

But while Philip had certainly been beaten, and beaten badly – the Field of Crocuses comes to mind – Macedon was not used to defeat. Pella liked her victory celebrations, with rich, drunken pezhetaeroi swaggering through the streets and wild-eyed auxiliaries glutting themselves on wine and good bread and all the delights of civilisation.

But when we rode into Pella, War was showing his other face.

Philip's companions brought him in. Every mouth was pinched, and every neck and shoulder bore the marks of ten days in armour and no rest. Men were missing helmets – helmets that had cost a year's wages for a skilled man. Men were missing cloaks. Hardly a single knight had a spear, and some were missing their swords as well, and where there ought to have been four hundred noble cavalrymen, there were not many past two hundred.

The horses looked worse, first because so many knights were riding nags and scrubs and hill ponies instead of our best Persian-given bloodstock, and second because where you did see a charger, he was as knackered as his master, and many of them had more wounds than the men on their backs. So many men and horses were wounded that the whole column buzzed with carrion flies and the companions were too tired to brush them away, so that a wounded man, just keeping his saddle, might have forty or fifty flies on the open wound of his face, in the corners of his eyes.

Behind the companions came the pezhetaeroi, the 'foot companions'. They had walked where the nobler companions had ridden, and they had lines like Keltoi work engraved on their faces, and their legs were mud to the thigh. Most of them wore quilted linen corselets, some leather, all splashed with mud and blood. Most of the infantry column had dysentery – not as uncommon as you might think, my lad – and some of them shat while they walked. Oh yes.

And behind the pezhetaeroi, the wounded. In baggage carts that had held officers' tents and nobles' spare horse tack – all abandoned to the foe. On blankets between two sarissas – our long spear, taller than two men. There's a cruel Macedonian joke that every recruit wears the stretcher that will carry his corpse home – his infantryman's cloak. There were quite a few wounded – later I learned that the pezhetaeroi had turned on the Thracians and stopped their last charge cold and then made sure of their wounded. Thracians torture any wounded they find – it is religious, for them, to test a man's courage as he dies, but to us that is blasphemy.

I was sitting in the front rank, a few horses from the prince. Hephaestion was next to him – calm and professional. He was only a drama queen when his own interests were affected. Black Cleitus gave me a grim smile and walked his horse to my side. But I watched Alexander, and he watched Antipater.

'Ready?' Cleitus asked. He had the face of a loyal dog, a big hound that you send in after the bear, but he was as smart as any of us. He hid it from most men, but not from me.

I raised an eyebrow.

Alexander heard him. He couldn't stop the smile from reaching his face.

But he was wrong. We all were.

THREE

Pella and Greece, 340–339 BC

The problem was that Philip did not die.

He was a great man. And there's a saying in Greece that I heard when I was in Athens before the Great War – that great men have useless sons. Phokion, Isocrates, Alcebiades, Leonidas – none of them had great sons.

But maybe the problem is that great men are too fucking hard on their sons, and most sons can't stand the pain, and they fold – I'm just guessing, but sometimes it is easier to just knuckle under than to strive, endlessly, with the man of gold. I speak from some experience, youngster.

But Alexander – no man ever born of woman – or of goddess – was ever so competitive. He had to compete – so deep, the inner need to prove himself to himself every day, all the time, over and over. When you are young, this appears as a great strength. As you grow older, it appears weaker and weaker. Trust me on this. The best men – the ones untouched by gods and happy in their own skins, the prosperous farmers and the good poets and the master craftsmen, the mothers of good children, the priestesses of well-run temples – have *nothing* to prove to gods or men. They merely *are* like the immortal gods.

Then there's the rest of us, of course. Hah!

And Alexander had that need to prove prowess, like a disease. So that he ran, wrestled or studied Plato with the same look on his face that he wore in mortal combat. To him, it was *all* mortal combat. To the death. To prove himself as good as his father. Or better.

Oh, it all sounds like crap – the sort of mumbo-jumbo that priests mutter. And he loved his father and his harpy of a mother, and they loved him. I've known many boys with worse parents. He did well enough. And he really loved them – he didn't murder his mother, and that alone speaks volumes.

Don't look shocked, boy. We're talking *Macedon*.

But he was determined to be like a god – to *be* a god if ever he could be. To be a better man than his father, and his father was a colossus who bestrode the earth and made the mighty – Persia, Athens – tremble like small boys in a thunderstorm.

Your father was a great man in a different mould – but you have to measure up to him, don't you? Aye. And all around you are relatives, tutors, officers – men and women who knew him. You must see the judgement in their eyes.

Good. Point made.

Philip had a bad wound, but he was far from dead. In fact, he never gave up the reins of power. He was lying in a litter, dictating the re-structuring of the magazines from Pella to the Thracian borderlands so that his counter-strike would land faster and better supplied.

He looked up and caught my eye first. He was as white as a new-washed linen chiton, and his lips were pale, and his eyes had sunk into his head like those of a corpse – but he grinned.

'Son of Lagus,' he said. 'You look ready for war.'

'We heard you were dead, lord!' I dismounted. The other pages dismounted behind me.

'Not yet. Where is my son?' Philip looked past me, and I saw him as he caught sight of Alexander, the only young man still mounted. He had his Boeotian helmet off, and the golden hair on either side of his forehead had made itself into ram's horns, as it always did if he didn't wash it for a few days. He looked like a god.

Philip's face lit up – blood came to his cheeks. His smile – I hoped that my father smiled like that, some day, when he saw me. 'Ahh,' Philip said.

Alexander turned and saw his father's litter and slid off his horse with his usual elegance. He bowed. 'Pater,' he said. Voice clipped, too controlled.

'I'm not dead yet, boy,' Philip said. Meant as humour. But delivered too deadpan.

'My apologies, then,' Alexander shot back. 'I shall return to my studies.'

'No – stay.' The wounded man shifted. 'They nearly cut my balls off, lad.' Another try at humour.

Alexander managed a half-smile. 'That would hurt you worse than many another blow, Pater,' he said.

Philip laughed, slapped his leg and roared in pain.

I left them to it, gathered the pages and joined them to the column.

*

In fact, we never went back to the schoolroom. But it will take a long digression to explain how we ended up where we did, and you will have to be patient, because when you are young, life is an endless succession of elders forcing you to learn things, eh?

Throughout my youth, Macedon was at war with Athens. This takes some explaining, because we sent them money and trees for their fleet and they sent us actors and rhetoricians and politicians and goldsmiths. But they had an empire and we wanted it. They were perfidious and evasive and dishonest – and Philip was their match.

There was no principle involved at all. Just self-interest.

Athens held most of the Chersonese and all of the best parts of the Bosporus. Athens' prosperity depended on a free flow of grain from the Euxine – but of course you know all this, you scamp! And that was fine with Philip and Macedon, until Athens started to use all her naval bases in the Chersonese to brew trouble for Macedon. That's a game that, once started, can't be stopped. It's like playing with a girl – you can hold her hand and be in paradise, but once that hand has been on her breast or between her thighs, you can't go back to holding hands, can you? So it is with nation-states. First they slight each other, and then they foment war through third parties, and then they accidentally sink each other's ships – brewing more hatred at every action – and they can never go *back* without a lot of treaties and some *reason*.

Athens and Macedon were well matched. Athens was past her prime, but I didn't need old Aristotle to tell me that Athens always bounces back – her prime is whenever she has a fleet. And Macedon was one generation from being a collection of mud huts in the wilderness, or like enough. In that one generation, Philip had pushed out borders in every direction, built an army as good as Sparta's, built roads and supply centres, fortresses and alliances. But he didn't have a fleet, and Athens could strip Macedon of her overseas possessions a few heartbeats after she acquired them. Macedon's army was the better – but not really very much better, as the Athenians taught us in the Lamian War.

Everything that happened while Alexander and I were growing to manhood was the petting and kissing part, on the way to real war between Athens and Macedon. I can't even remember all the convolu-tions. The truth is, I didn't pay that close a heed – I wasn't a statesman, I was a boy.

But even a very young man in Pella knew who Demosthenes was – knew that he rose every day in the assembly in Athens to denounce our king and our state and our way of life. Now – you're an Athenian citizen, aren't you, boy? I thought as much. So you probably know that we all admired Athens in every way – despite their prating against us, we all wanted to grow up to be Athenian gentlemen. We read their plays and their poetry and spoke their dialect and aped their manners and practised serving wine their way. But when it came to war, we were determined to beat them.

And we knew who Phokion was – their best general, the one even Philip feared, and we knew that *he* admired *us*. Your father's tutor, if I remember rightly. Yes.

All by way of saying, in the spring when Philip came back from fighting Thracians, wounded – we were locked in a state of near war with Athens, and we were having the worst of it. Philip had seized a bunch of Athenian merchants – oh, he had provocation, but I remember old Aristotle saying it was the stupidest thing he'd ever done, and Aristotle was an admirer of wily Philip. At any rate, Athens declared war – a formal declaration, like going from kissing to intercourse. And Philip responded by marching an army into the Chersonese, laying siege to the major Athenian base at Perinthus – and failing.

Then he descended on Byzantium, their most important base – a surprise attack after a fast march, his favourite ploy.

And failed. Phokion outmarched him.

So the defeat by the Thracians, even though it was against only a tithe of our armies, was a bad blow. The Illyrians, always willing to raid us, began to agitate on the borders, and the Athenian privateers preyed on our shipping, and Athens put a vicious bastard into the Chersonese, a pirate called Diopeithes. His son, Manes, is there yet. And he's a vicious bastard, too.

But the worst of it was that Athens had joined hands with Persia. That's what Alexander and I were talking about, in the woods, over a trout dinner.

It's a funny thing – Persia was always the enemy of my youth. We didn't play 'Macedonians and Athenians' in the corridors of Pella or the Gardens of Midas. We didn't play Macedonians and Thracians, or Macedonians and Illyrians. We played Athenians and Persians, and it was always the day of Marathon, with us. Or we played Achaeans and Trojans. And the Trojans were just Persians.

Macedon had been a Persian ally. It shamed us all, that during the wars of Salamis and Plataea, our forefathers had given earth and water to the Great King. Mind you, Alexander – the old one, from those days – did his bit for the Hellenes, and our boys turned on the retreating Persians and routed them at Hennia Hodoi.

And Sparta had a turn as a Persian ally, too. Mighty Sparta, but when the chips were down and Sparta was losing the Thirty Years' War on the peninsula, she turned to Persia, took gold and ships in exchange for promises to remain aloof from Persia's rebuilding of her empire.

Not that the Spartans kept their word. Agisalaos struck – and failed.

My point is that one of the constants of the diplomacy of the day was that Athens did not make deals with Persia. We did – there were almost always Persian envoys at Pella, even though we spoke openly of invading them after we'd subjugated Thessaly. And Philip took a stipend from them for a while, and threatened them at other times. He wanted to own both sides of the Bosporus. And the rest of the world, too.

I'm like a drunken carter roiling farther and farther from the track. My point is that the last thing we ever expected – even in the event of war with Athens – was for Athens to make common cause with Persia. Athenians did not love Persia, and even a rumour of 'Persian gold' was usually enough to send a politician into exile.

Philip's speciality was to divide his opponents – split their alliances – and move on them one by one. He did it as automatically as a good swordsman makes a counter-cut. Wherever he saw a stable alliance, he sought to undermine it. He wasn't above faked correspondence and he had a widespread intelligence net, assassins, bandits in his pay – we knew all this, because all the pages at one time or another were present for his diplomatic correspondence, which he read aloud when the foreigners were forbidden the court, such was his contempt for all the other nations of the earth.

Except Athens.

It had never occurred to him that he might be outplayed at his own game, but on the morning after Philip returned to Pella wounded and defeated, he discovered that Athens and Persia, his two mightiest opponents, had united; that they had added Thebes to the mix, with the best-trained infantry in Greece; and that his own allies were deserting in droves.

Later, Parmenio said that if the Athenians had put their fleet to sea and started plucking our colonies with Persian troops while the Thebans covered the passes into Greece, we'd have been wrecked by summer's end.

But all too often – here's the moral of my tale, lad, and no mistake – men carry the seeds of their own ruin in their own greatness. Demosthenes' hatred of Macedon was rooted in a conservative, backward-looking idealism. He thought he was a democrat, but the men he idolised were the Athenians of Marathon. And although he was personally a very poor soldier, he – like many men – idolised what he was not – the hoplite. Demosthenes did not want to war Macedon down in an inglorious and efficient campaign of commerce-raiding and colony-snatching. That's what Phokion or Philip or Parmenion, the great generals, would have done.

Demosthenes wanted us humbled the old way, man to man on the battlefield, our hoplites and theirs spear to spear, and may the better men teach the lesser what democracy really was.

Demosthenes was more than a hundred years out of date. But his foolish idealism saved Macedon.

At any rate, that early summer we knew that Athens had made a deal with Artaxerxes, and we were, in effect, surrounded. We waited – rebuilding forces as quickly as we could – for Athens and Thebes to invade. Sparta sat it out – but Sparta was a nonentity by then, more a fearsome name than a real power.

And around midsummer, after Olympias danced naked for Dionysus, after Philip discovered that his new bride Meda was pregnant, he gathered the main army – including all the royal companions, all the pezhetaeroi, all the mercenaries on whom he could lay hands and cash – and marched away like lightning, bound for the Chersonese.

He left Alexander, just seventeen years old, as regent. Antipater stood by him, with a regiment of cavalry and a regiment of Macedonian foot, a full taxeis – enough force to use on any rival baron or upstart noble who made trouble.

To our immense delight, as soon as the sound of Philip's hobnailed sandals faded away into the south, the Thracians struck again – this time the Maedi, from up by Paeonia. Antipater concurred that a counter-attack was required, and the pages packed their war cloaks and gathered their horses.

We were going to war, and our prince would have his first command. Summer, in the mountains.

FOUR

The Maedi weren't the wildest of the Thracians. They wore chitons, some of them, with their fox-skin hats – or badger or squirrel. The Maedi weren't squeamish about what they killed – or wore.

But they did like Macedonian girls, and they'd come over the mountains in groups of fifty or five hundred – or five. Grab a girl – or pillage a twenty-mile swathe. They were seldom organised, and sometimes we'd find dead men where they had squabbled among themselves. Herodotus said that the Thracians would have conquered the world, if only they'd stopped fighting among themselves. Old Herodotus knew a thing or two.

Ever since the incident with the hetaera, Alexander had kept his distance from me – but promoted me, too, making me the right file leader of the pages.

By this time we had almost two hundred pages – perhaps we had more, but the pages weren't the huge outfit they became later, under Alexander. A few of us were the scions of the great noble houses, but it's important to note here that quite a few of my fellow pages were the sons of Philip's 'new men'. Philip trusted the new men – after all, they had no power and no place at court except what he gave them, and that meant that, as they would fall if he fell, they could be trusted. The rich men and great magnates of central Macedon were all potential rivals for the king, and their riches and power wouldn't be changed if the king fell. It's an old story – Persian kings and Athenian oligarchs often practise the same policy.

But that led to a double standard within the pages, too. We were all supposed to be equals under the prince, and we received stipends and much of our equipment was provided from the armouries so that we would all match and there would be no jealousy. But in truth, Alexander treated the noblemen's sons very differently from the sons of new men. Alexander believed in breeding. That was the fault of all that Homer, I suspect, and Aristotle didn't help, the aristocratic old fart.

At any rate, as we packed our war gear and looked to our weapons –
for the first time, as a unit that would serve together – Alexander made
his preferences plain. I got one troop, and Parmenio's son Philotas got
the other. Better young men, or those who'd already had some commands, like Philip the Red, were passed over.

I took Philip as one of my file leaders and Black Cleitus as the other.
They were both older than I, and might have been jealous or sticky, but
I had money and a fair amount of goodwill from the hunting camp and
I used both. Philip's father was a senior officer in the foot companions
and I bought him a fancy Attic helmet from an Athenian vendor in the
agora – first-rate work, it made him look like a hero. In fact, it was a
better helmet than his father had.

Cleitus needed everything. One of Alexander's failings was that the
closer you were to him, the *less* he seemed to think about helping you
– as if the very power of his proximity would cure financial woes. New
friends, favourites and foreigners often got presents, while Cleitus had
to look to me or Philotas (who also liked him) to get a new sword and
a pair of riding spears better than the royal armouries provided.

And this was really all boyish nonsense. Our armoury provided excellent equipment. But if you know boys, you know that to carry a spear
marked with the starburst of the armoury was an admission of poverty.
It might be a superb spear – but boys are boys.

Worth noting, too, that boys also left the pages. It was a hard life –
the younger pages did the work that slaves did – up all night in front of
the prince's door or the king's – washing pots, feeding horses, carrying
water. We were beaten when we failed – I was only beaten three times
in my whole service, but it hurt my pride every time. And we never had
enough sleep or enough food. Some boys couldn't take it, and they left.

Some found other ways to leave. The handsomest of all the boys
in my age group was Pausanias of Epirus, and he was as pretty as a
girl. When he was sixteen, Philip took him as a lover, and when Philip
marched away into the Chersonese, he took Pausanias as a royal companion – the youngest. To be fair, Pausanias was an excellent spearman
– but it was his fair looks and his flute-playing ways that got him into
the royal companions. He was the first to be promoted out of the pages
and into Philip's service, but hardly the last – after all, the purpose of
the Basilikoi Paides was to train future soldiers and administrators.

Alexander was going to command the expedition, but Antipater was
doing a great deal of the work, and I was lucky enough to be invited to
attend him. I remember it as terrifying – he wasn't the old monster he
later became, but a handsome middle-aged man who'd seen a lot of war

and who was Parmenio's chief rival at court. I received orders to report to his quarters in the palace, and I went, newly shaved, scrubbed like a helmet, with more pimples than scars, as the Macedonians say, except that in my case, I actually had a few scars.

'Well,' Antipater said, looking down his long nose at me. His son Cassander was no friend of mine, and he had to know it. And had been passed over for command, serving as a mere file-closer. I was worried about this interview, and my hands shook.

I was in armour – I saluted.

Antipater returned the salute. 'Well,' he said again.

He looked at me for a long time. 'Cage your eyes, damn you,' he said. 'If I want to be stared at by a child, I'll tell you.'

I looked at the floor.

'How much grain does a donkey eat in a day?' he asked.

'Eight pounds a day. More in the mountains.' These were things I knew.

'How much grain can you count on getting in the Thracian hills?' he asked.

'None, lord,' I answered.

He scratched his beard. 'How much for a warhorse?'

'Twice as much, and as much again on a day he fights,' I said.

He made a motion with his mouth – when I got to know him better, I knew it was disapproval. 'Kill chargers with overfeeding,' he said. 'Don't they teach you babies better than that?'

I looked at the floor.

'How much grain does a man eat a day?' he asked.

I'd run the pages' mess for two years. I gave him amounts for boys, men, women ...

'You'll do. You have a head on your shoulders and no mistake. What's the most important thing about a campsite? Look at me, boy.'

I looked at him again. His face was grim.

'Water,' I said. 'Water, high ground that drains in rain, defensibility, access to firewood, access to forage for horses, in that order.'

Antipater nodded. 'You remember your lessons,' he said. 'I'm not coming on this expedition. So I'm sending Laodon with you, but you – you, young Ptolemy – are going to run the supplies. I'll send you two of my own slaves, who've done this sort of thing before. They're Greeks – they can do mathematics and they understand how to feed an army. Let me offer you this piece of advice, boy – war runs on scouting and food, not heroism and not fancy armour. Philotas is going to run the scouting and you are going to run the food.'

I nodded, but my annoyance crossed my face. Of course it did – I was seventeen.

'You think you are a better scout and it's the more dashing occupation?' Antipater asked.

'Yes,' I answered.

'Then you're more of a fool than I took you for, and perhaps fit for neither. Yes, it is dashing, but a well-fed army will win a fight even when surprised, whereas brilliant scouting can't get an unwilling army to cross a stream. Listen, boy. There's trouble at court – you know it?' He leaned towards me, and I leaned back. Antipater was scary.

And I never, never talked about court matters with adults – not even my father. I looked at him with my carefully calculated look of bovine placidity. 'Huh?' I said.

'My son says you are dull.'

I shrugged. Looked at the ground.

'Very well,' he dismissed me.

I was still shaking when Philotas and Cleitus found me. They put a cup of wine into me, and thus emboldened, I collected my two new slaves – Antipater actually gave them to me. Myndas was the older and handsomer, and Nichomachus was younger and thin, too tall, with a dreadful wispy beard and pimples worse than mine.

'Zeus, they look like shit,' Philotas said. 'Hey – who are you two and why is Antipater giving you away?'

They both looked at the ground, shrugged and shuffled, like slaves. Nonetheless, it was obvious to me that Myndas had been a free man once. And that Nichomachus never had.

'I gather both of you can do mathematics?' I said.

More shuffling.

But Myndas produced an abacus, and proceeded to rattle off some remarkable maths problems, muttering under his breath. Philotas, who liked cruel games, shot problems at him faster and faster – absurd problems, obscene problems.

'If every soldier fucks his shield-bearer twice a day,' Philotas said in his nasty, sing-song voice, 'and if he needs a spoonful of olive oil to get it done each time, and if there's two thousand footsloggers in the army, how much olive oil does the army need every day?'

Myndas didn't raise his eyes. 'How big a spoon, master?' he asked.

'Whatever you use yourself,' Philotas answered, and Cleitus guffawed.

Adolescent humour. With boys, it is the humour of the stronger vented on the weaker, and nothing is weaker than a slave.

But they were my slaves, and I'd never owned a man besides my shield-bearer, so I shook my head.

'Very funny. Myndas, don't mind him – he can't help himself. Some day he'll get laid and stop talking about it.' I grinned at Philotas to take out the sting, and got punched – hard – in the shoulder.

But he laid off Myndas. It's important that your slaves see you as someone who can protect them, and since I was to command a troop, I needed Philotas to see that I had limits and would protect my own.

All fun and games, in the pages.

I needed horses, and so did Cleitus. My pater's factor was in town with orders to give me anything I wanted – my pater was a distant man, but he did his best to equip me. So I spent his money on two more chargers to support Poseidon, and I gave my two old chargers to Cleitus. I put my two slaves on mules. I went out to Polystratus's farm and offered him silver to march with me. He was a Thracian himself.

He looked at his wife, his new daughter and his farm – a few acres of weeds and some oats. A hard existence.

'Double that,' he said. 'I need some money.'

'That's the pay of a royal companion!' I said.

Polystratus shrugged. 'I don't have to go,' he said. 'My wife needs me, and my daughter. I could be starting on a son.' He looked at her and she smiled, blushed, looked at the ground.

Of course I paid him. I gave him a mina of silver down, and then followed him around while he packed his kit, gave his wife a third of the money and then marched up the hill to the headman. I stood as witness while he used his advance of pay to triple his landownership and to pay the headman's own sons to till the new land for him while he was absent.

Polystratus was not a typical Thracian.

We rode back together, and I bought him a pair of horses. It was all Pater's money – what did I care? I got him a good leather spola and a nice helmet with heavy cheekpieces. He had his own spears and sword, and he spent his own money on a donkey. And by evening, he had a pais – a slave boy to carry his gear and do his work.

I had to laugh. But I did so where Polystratus couldn't see me.

That evening, I found that Myndas was sitting in the courtyard of the barracks, and Nichomachus was writing his sums on wax and saying them back. Since I was the mess-master of the pages, I knew the numbers they were doing like I knew my name, so I stopped and stood with them. They didn't make mistakes, but in a few moments I surprised them by knowing how to multiply one hundred and ninety-eight pages by six mythemnoi of grain.

This was the first of many generational differences between Philip's men and Alexander's men. They hadn't had Aristotle. They'd learned enough maths to buy a slave to do the work, but I could work Pythagoras's solutions to geometry in my head. And so could Cassander and so could Philotas and so could Cleitus, on and on.

Myndas kept his eyes down. 'You ... can you use this, lord?' he asked, rattling his abacus.

'Yes, if I had a mind to,' I admitted. 'But I can do most of the numbers in my head – especially any maths to do with the pages and feeding them.' I slapped him on the back. 'Has the prince set the army yet? I've been gone all day.'

The two slaves shook their heads.

'You two been fed?' I asked.

Both shook their heads.

I waggled a finger at Polystratus. 'Myndas, this is Polystratus. He was once a slave and now he's free – serving me. He is the head of my household, which you are now in. Polystratus, these two are scribes, so don't break them cutting firewood. They haven't eaten since before noon. See to them, will you?'

Polystratus nodded. 'Scribes?' he asked. Shrugged. 'Buy 'em food, or get the cook to shell out?' he asked me.

'Buy it in the market today, and get them on the barracks list tomorrow,' I said. This was the sort of detail you had to remember with an army or with your own slaves – I'd walked off to find Polystratus and left them with no way to get food. So much to learn. Zeus, I was young!

Three days of these preparations, and I spent the last two looking at carts and donkeys and mules, watching wicker baskets filled with grain, shouting myself hoarse at merchants, bellowing with rage when I found I'd been swindled on some donkeys ...

The fourth morning, the sun still hidden in the east. Two hundred pages, a thousand foot soldiers, a hundred of Parmenio's Thessalian cavalry leading the way and fifty tame Thracians in our rearguard – and we were off. My baggage carts and donkeys occupied about two-thirds of the column and moved slower than beeswax in winter, and everyone found occasion to mention as much to me as we crawled out of the capital and up into the hills.

The second day out of Pella, Alexander suddenly took all the older companions – except me – and headed off north and west. Cleitus cantered up to me where I was helping get a cart repaired – a broken wheel, the hub was rotten, and I'd bought the damned thing ...

'The prince says it will be winter before your carts get to the Thracians!' he said.

What could I say? I'd been swindled in every direction. I had the worst donkeys in the market and I had apparently bought every old cart in Pella.

But Alexander rode off with Laodon and all the older pages to win glory, and left me with a thousand foot soldiers and the carts. In command.

I chose a campsite on the river – with water, firewood, forage and an easy defence. And when daybreak came, it was pouring with rain and I stayed in camp. I surveyed every cart, declared half a dozen unfit and sent Polystratus to get more from the local farms. Our estates were within half a day's ride.

Then I took Myndas aside. 'You let me buy those carts,' I said.

He stared at the ground.

So I punched him in the head. 'How much did they pay you, you fuck?' I said.

He curled into a ball and waited to be hit again. But it was obvious to me that the military contractors had paid off my slave to give me crap.

I found a dozen footsloggers who knew which end of a spokeshave was which, and put them to fixing carts. I had the rest – a thousand of them – cut wood for fires. The rain was as heavy and cold as Tartarus, and we needed those fires. Then I had them cut spruce boughs for bedding. The officers backed me. I had the feeling I was in command exactly as long as I continued to give orders that they liked, but I didn't get hubris from a few successes because I was still so angry about the carts.

Just at nightfall, Polystratus came in with eight light carts drawn by mules. He had another twenty mules – all the stock from one of my pater's breeding operations. So the next morning, still wet, by the light of roaring fires, I put donkeys in the shafts of every cart. I gave the useless donkeys to the farmer whose fields we'd wrecked by camping there and we were away, moving almost twice as fast as we'd moved the day before.

One of the officers who was supposed to be 'under' me was Gordias, a mercenary from Ephesus. I'd never met him until we marched – now he rode with me. We were crossing flat ground, just short of the foothills of Paeonia, and he rode along, making jokes and observations, and I felt pretty competent.

'You read Xenophon, lord?' he asked me, out of nowhere.

'*The March to the Sea*? Of course. And *On Hunting*, and *The Cavalry Commander*.' I ran through all the titles I'd read.

'Ever formed a box with infantry?' he asked.

I had to laugh. 'Gordias, when I ordered your phalangites to cut firewood yesterday, it was the first order I've ever given to grown men.'

He nodded. 'You're doing all right. Do more. Let's drill a little – can't hurt, and in bad weather, it's best to keep the lads too busy and tired to think. Let's form the box around your baggage and see how we do.'

So we did. And we didn't do very well.

Not my fault. Nothing to do with me. But I felt their failure in my bones. They were not a regular taxeis, but a bundle of recruits with some veteran mercenaries with recent land-grants mixed in. The veterans hadn't taken charge yet, but were still living their own way and ignoring the useless yokels they had as file partners, and the useless yokels were still too scared of the fire-eaters to ask them for help.

They'd never formed a hollow square as a group – the recruits had done it some time or other, and the veterans a hundred times, but never together. The first time, the left files folded in too fast and the front files formed the front face and walked off, leaving the rest of the box to form without them.

Halt, reform.

The second time, the rear face of the hollow square was left behind by the rest of us. And the baggage contrived to plug the road, so that reforming took an hour.

Halt, reform, lunch. Rain.

After lunch, we got the hollow square formed – pretty much by having every officer mount up, ride around and push groups of men, and sometimes individuals, into the spot where they had to go. For almost an hour, we marched across northern Macedon in a hollow square, with our baggage protected, and then the whole thing started to shred like a reed roof in a high wind – the left face of the square ran into a marsh and the right face just kept going.

I couldn't believe how fast we fell apart.

And then I realised that the sun was dipping and I hadn't chosen a camp.

Zeus! So much to remember. Luckily, Polystratus had taken a dozen Thracians and gone off on his own and found a campsite.

We got our tents up before last light, and fires lit, with four hundred men up on the hillsides gathering wood and another two hundred standing to, ready to cover them. The men were wet and tired and angry, and I heard a lot about myself I didn't want to hear. Two days of cold rain would make the Myrmidons mutinous.

But when the fires were lit and roaring, when I had wine served out from the carts, when the woodpiles were as tall as houses – well, my popularity increased. The wine wasn't very good, but in a cold rain on a windswept night, it was delicious. I'd been suckered on the wine, too.

68

Our tents weren't much – just a wedge of linen, no front or back. They kept the water off your face, and we put four men in each – and no tents for slaves or shield-bearers. They were just wet. The footsloggers weren't much better, and the younger pages – I'd been left with all the babies – were soaked to the skin and didn't have the experience to stay warm or dry.

I was up all night.

The next day was the third day of hard rain, and we marched anyway – lighter and faster yet. More wheels had been built during the night – Gordias kept his wheelwrights at it, I guess. Anyway, now we had spare wheels in one cart, and the wheelwrights, instead of marching with their units, stayed with the carts, so that as soon as a tyre came loose or an axle cracked, we pulled that cart out of the line, surrounded it with Thracian auxiliaries and repaired it from spares while the rest of the column marched on.

We made excellent time that day – gravel roads, better carts, and we were already better at marching. Polystratus found a camp, and we were almost in the highlands. The rain let up for a few hours, and the tents went up on dryish ground – I put half the army out to cut pine boughs and gather last year's ferns and any other bedding they could find, and I strung the pages across the hillsides as guards.

I had halted well before dark, having learned my lesson the night before. Besides, I was tired myself.

Gordias was so useful I began to suspect that my pater had sent him to watch me. Polystratus, too – he reminded me of things every minute, like a wife. But I was getting it done – I could see beef being butchered in the army's central area, and the cooks collecting the beef in their kettles, and already I could see local farmers coming into the camp with produce to sell, which we'd missed the night before by making camp too late. It was all running well, and as I watched, the first fire leaped into being in the cooking area of camp, and there were lines of men carrying wood and bedding down the hillsides …

Down the valley ahead of us, more fires leaped into being, and they weren't ours.

I had to assume that was Alexander and the pages and Thessalians. But at the same time, I'd be a fool not to act as if those fires were enemies'.

The headman of the Thracians was called Alcus. That means something like 'Butthead' in Thracian. But Alcus and Polystratus got along well enough. I sent Polystratus for him, and after a delay that seemed eternal, he rode up and I showed him the fires to the north and west.

He nodded, tugged his beard, looked at Polystratus.

'You want us to go and look,' he said finally.

'Yes,' I said. 'I think you are the best suited for it, you know this country. Besides . . .'

Gordias put his hand on my shoulder. 'Don't explain,' he whispered. 'Just tell them what to do.'

Sigh. So much to learn!

'Go any way you think best, but tell me who set those fires,' I ordered.

Alcus pursed his lips, blew out a little puff and pulled his elaborately patterned cloak tighter around his shoulders. 'Boys won't be happy,' he said.

I was freezing cold, I hadn't slept in two days and I was scared spitless that I'd run into a Thracian army.

'Fuck that,' I snapped. 'Get your arse down the valley and get me a report.'

The Thracian officer looked at me for a few heartbeats, spat carefully – not a gesture of contempt, more like contemplation – and said, 'Yes, lord,' in a way that might have been taken for an insult.

When he was gone, Gordias laughed. 'Not bad, lord,' he said. 'A little temper goes a long way, as long as you control it and it doesn't control you.'

The more I thought about it, the more it seemed to me that Pater had hired this man as a military tutor. I never again ran across a mercenary so interested in teaching a kid.

An hour passed in a few heartbeats. In that time, I had to decide whether or not to keep the firewood and bedding collection going, or to call all the work parties in. If it turned out to be the prince up the valley, I'd look like a fool, and as the rain had started again, my men would have a miserable night. On the other hand, if five thousand Thracians were sneaking along the hillsides towards me, I'd lose my whole command when they swept us away in one attack – I had fewer than fifty men on guard in camp, and nothing else except the pages, and most of them were unblooded teenagers.

Command is glorious. I thought some hard thoughts about my prince, I can tell you.

I decided to keep my work parties at it. I sent Gordias to keep them going as fast as he could. In fact, he withdrew a third of the men and put them under arms.

I took the pages, spread them across the hillsides in a skirmish line facing north, and started probing.

It was a standard hunting formation, and I told every boy that I didn't want them to fight, just to report if they saw Thracians, and then we were moving. It was last light, the sun was far off in the heavy clouds, and if we'd been in the bottom of the valley it would already have been night. It was horrible weather, too – sheets of rain. Our cloaks were soaked and sat on our shoulders like blankets of ice.

But the pages were trained hard, and now it paid off. We crossed a ravine in pretty good order – I remember being proud of them – and then the lightning started, and by the light of it – the Thunderer was throwing his bolts about pretty freely – we moved across the swollen watercourse at the bottom of the ravine and up the other side.

I found a trail running right along the top of the ridge. Not unexpected – if you spend enough time in the wild you get a sense for where animals and men like to walk. Trails are hard to find in the rain, but this one had some old stones along the north side, as if there had once been a wall.

Half a dozen pages huddled in behind me. The trail was so much easier than the hillside – it was natural enough.

There was a long peal of thunder, a brilliant double strike of Zeus's heavy spear, and I was in the midst of fifty Thracians. They were all in a muddle, gathered around something on the trail.

A bearded man in a zigzag-decorated cloak had his helmet off. He looked at me in another lightning flash.

Athena inspired me.

I know a few words of Thracian.

'What the fuck are you doing here?' I bellowed over the rain. It's something you say to slaves quite a bit.

That puzzled them.

'What the fuck are you doing here!' I bellowed again. And then I turned my horse and rode away, waiting for the feel of a javelin between my shoulder blades. I got my horse around, got back to the lip of the ravine, and my half-dozen pages were right on my heels – I prayed to Hermes that the Thracians hadn't seen what a beardless lot they were. We slid down the ravine and our horses got us up the other side – it was full dark now, and in dark and rain your horse is pretty much your only hope to get anywhere.

Below me on the hillside, I heard the unmistakable sound of iron ringing on iron.

The closest page was Cleomenes, no longer quite a child. I grabbed him by the hair, got his ear close to my head – the thunder was deafening, or so I remember it – and ordered him to get back to camp and tell Gordias to stand to.

'You know where camp is?' I yelled.

He pointed the right way.

I let him go.

I rode off down the hillside, trusting to Poseidon to get me to the fighting. He picked his way, and I had to take deep breaths and wait. Patience has never been my strongest virtue. It seemed to take an hour to go half a stade, despite the fact that we were going *down* the hillside and that it was almost clear.

After some minutes, I was suddenly flat on my back – cold water running down my breastplate and under my back. I had thought I was wet – now I was in a stream or a rivulet and I was colder and wetter and everything hurt.

We'd gone over a log and Poseidon had missed the fact that there was a ravine on the other side of the log. By the will of Ares, he didn't break a leg, but it took me another cold, wet, dark eternity to find him and get him on his feet – eyes rolling in the lightning flashes, utterly panicked.

Down again, now with me walking in front of him, holding the reins. There hadn't been fighting in ... well, I'd lost track of time, and was worried I'd been unconscious when I was thrown.

So much to worry about!

Down and down. And then ...

The first Thracian I found was a horn-blower – he had the horn at his lips, the lightning flashed and I put my spear through him. The next flash showed scarlet leaking past his lips – he coughed. And died.

I crouched. I couldn't hear a thing, and I couldn't see anything, either. But that man I'd killed – I was queasy with it, but too busy to throw up – he'd been ready to blow a horn call. An attack?

They must be close around me.

So I froze, moved carefully to a big tree, stood with my hand over Poseidon's mouth.

A long time passed. As the lightning played around us, I began to see them. I counted five men around me. But there had to be more – there may have been a thousand in the lightning-lit forest, with huge old trees that could hide an elephant.

Time in a crisis passes in its own way. You think of the most in-congruous things. I remember thinking of kissing my farm girl at the Gardens of Midas. Her lips had a certain firmness that defined good kissing to me then – and now, for that matter. And I remember think-ing that Philotas owed me a fair amount of money from knucklebones and would be delighted if I died here.

I also thought how many things I'd done wrong, including ... well, everything. I was alone on the hillside with a bunch of Thracians and not in my camp with my army, for example.

I can't even guess how long we were all there, and then the lightning storm began to pass over the ridge and the sound and intensity seemed to go with it. I think – it seems to me, without hubris – that we were in the very presence of the gods, because the air around me seemed charged with portent, and the noise and light were mind-numbing. When they went away, it was merely dark and cold – and I hadn't really been cold for all the time the lightning played.

And suddenly it was *dark*.

I curled up against Poseidon. He was warm. Actually, he was cold, but he kept me warm.

I remained as still as I could.

Time passed.

Then I heard them. Two men were talking. They were very close indeed – maybe two or three big trees away, except that in the darkness, such things can be deceptive.

I could hear them talking, but I couldn't understand even a single word.

Mutter mutter mutter.

Mutter.

Mutter mutter.

Growl. Mutter.

And then that stopped, too.

My hand was clamped so hard over Poseidon's head that my wrist hurt.

I was ashamed of myself, afraid and I needed to piss.

Time marched on, one heavy heartbeat at a time.

I convinced myself that I had to move.

Of all the concerns on my shoulders, it was having to piss that made me move. Let that be a lesson to you. I looked and looked at where I'd heard the voices, and then I had the discipline to turn a circle.

And then the rain came. I'd thought it was raining before, but this was like a wall of water.

A wall of noise, too.

I took Poseidon by the halter and I moved. We stepped on branches and we slipped in mud, but I kept going. And by luck, or the will of the gods, in a few moments I caught a glimpse of my own fires – two stades away across open ground. I was right at the edge of the trees on the hillside.

I mounted before I thought it out, and Poseidon was away – stumbling, because although I didn't know it until morning, he had a strain from the cold and rain and the fall. He wasn't fast. And no sooner were we moving than a javelin struck me square in the back.

That's why rich kids like me wore bronze. But it scared me and knocked the wind out of me. And when I reined in for the sentry line, I was shaking like a leaf.

One of the footsloggers materialised under Poseidon's chest, his spear at my throat. But before he could challenge me, he knew me.

'Lord!' he said. 'We thought you were lost!'

I rode into camp. Half the men were standing to in wet clumps with their sarissas in their hands. The rest were huddled around fires – enormous fires. The tents had mostly blown down.

War is so glorious.

My tent was one of those down. Polystratus took Poseidon, made sounds indicating that I was a fool and he was a mother hen, and he took me to *his* tent, which had a front and back wall of woven branches and a stool. He got my cuirass off, towelled me dry and told me that there were Thracians down the valley.

Nichomachus handed me a cup of wine. I drank it.

'I *know*!' I said, trying not to sound whiney. Gordias pushed into the tent.

'Well,' he said. 'Get lost?'

I drank more wine. 'I got caught on the hillside with the Thracians,' I said. 'Did Cleomenes get to you?'

Gordias shook his head. 'Which one is he? One of the pages? No – I had no word. And not all the troopers here are mine – I had some trouble giving orders.'

That's the moment I remember best of the whole evening. I'd sort of collapsed on arriving in camp – acted like a cold, wet kid rescued by his servant. Polystratus was towelling my hair when I discovered that my message hadn't got to camp.

'Gordias, there's Thracians within a stade of camp. An ambush on the road north, more coming across the ridge. Where are the pages?'

Gordias shook his head. 'There's twenty of the youngest here in camp. I thought the rest were with you?'

'Ares' prick,' I swore. It was my father's favourite oath. 'Put my cuirass back on. Polystratus, get us both horses.'

Polystratus didn't squawk. I put my sodden wool chiton back on – noticing that the dye had run and stained my hips. Gordias got my cuirass closed on me again – say what you will, the bronze is a good windbreak. Mounted on Medea, with Polystratus by me, I went back out into the remnants of the storm. Dawn wasn't far away, and there was a bit of light, and if you've done this sort of thing, you know that the difference between a bit of light and no light is all the difference in the world. I got us up the ridge, found my game trail and there were a dozen of my pages, shivering like young beeches in a high wind – but all clutching a spear close to them, behind trees.

'Good lads,' I said – an old man of seventeen to young men of fourteen. 'Back to camp now.'

'They are *right there*,' Philip Long-nose said. 'Right across the ravine!' He pointed, and an arrow flew.

'Been there all night,' said another boy.

Polystratus whistled.

'I know,' I said. 'Get back now – hot wine in camp.'

The pages started to slip backwards. This was the sort of thing we practised in hunting – observe the quarry and then slip away.

But one of the youngsters made a mistake, or maybe the Thracians were coming anyway. And suddenly they were scrambling across the ravine – fifty or a hundred, how could we know?

I had no idea how many pages I had under my hand.

'Run!' I ordered. 'Camp!'

They ran.

Like a fool, I waited, shepherding them down the trail, and Medea got a spear in the side as a result. She tossed me and ran a few steps and died.

I'd been thrown twice in a night and I wasn't too happy. But I rolled to my feet in time to have Polystratus grab my arms, and we were off down the trail with a tumble of arrows and javelins behind us.

They chased us right up to camp. We had no walls or ditches, and there was a dark tide of Thracians flowing across the barley fields. Their lead elements were a spear-cast behind Polystratus's horse's rump.

And as soon as the Thracians in the valley saw the Thracians on the ridge moving, they came, too.

First light – a general rush.

The pages routed, running past the raw infantry.

It should have been a bloody shambles, but for men like Gordias. The infantry let the pages through and then started to form the hollow square. It was patchy, but the Thracians were in dribs and drabs, not a solid rush – I know that now. At the time it looked like a wall of them, but in fact, there were never more than fifteen men coming at us at a time.

Polystratus got through the phalanx and dropped me in the army's central square. Myndas, of all people – my least favourite slave – appeared with my third-string charger and a cup of wine and a towel. I dried my face, drank the wine and used his back to get mounted – I had hurt my hips falling.

The pages had no trumpeter and no hyperetes – both were with

Alexander. Since the infantry seemed well in hand, I rode around gathering pages – three or four at a time – and leading them into the centre of the square. They were exhausted and most were terrified. But they were royal pages, and that meant they knew their duty. I got about a hundred of them together, formed them in a deep rhomboid and led them to the unthreatened corner of the square. Halted while the file leaders opened the corner for us.

'We're about to ride down the barbarians who kept us up all night!' I called. 'Stay together and stay on me, or I'll beat you bloody!'

My first battlefield speech.

Met by silence.

We walked our horses out of the square and wheeled north. Gordias was on to me in a heartbeat – he began to wheel the 'back' faces of the square – the faces with no opponents – out on to the plain, unfolding the square like a 'W'.

The Thracians hadn't come for a field fight, and as soon as they saw us approaching them it was over, and they started to fade into the trees – first a few, and then the whole of their front.

Over on the west side of the valley was a squadron of horse – or, rather, some tribal lords on ponies. I aimed at them. They'd have a hard time riding into the trees, and I was going to get a fight. I was mad.

The Thracians didn't want that kind of fight, and they turned their horses and rode for it, a few of them shooting over their horses' rumps with bows, and one of my boys took an arrow and died right there – young Eumedes, a pretty good kid.

We were half a stade away. Too damned far. They turned like a flock of birds and ran.

I put my heels into my charger's side. I had a fresh horse, a bigger, faster horse, and I was mad. I hadn't even named my new chargers – that's how much of my time oats and cartwheels took.

The Thracians were mostly gone into the trees. Nearer to hand, the chief and his retinue were beginning to scatter along the valley.

I got up on my charger's neck and let him run. I ignored the followers and stayed on the chief. He turned, made a rude gesture at me and turned his horse into the sopping woods.

I didn't give a shit, and followed him, closing the distance between us at every stride. I'd picked a good remount – this horse could *move* and had some brains, as well, and we were hurtling though the trees, never more than a heartbeat from being thrown or scraped off on a tree – just try galloping through open woods.

But my mount was eating the distance. The chief looked back at me – he was a bigger man, much older. He looked back, measured the distance, looked back again, and we both knew it was too late for him to turn his horse and fight. So he drew his sword and prepared to fight as I came up on him – jigging like a hare, trying to get me off his bridle-hand side.

I wasn't having it. And my mount was smart – as I said. He turned on his front feet, right across the pony's rump, and in a flash we were up with them and I got an arm round his neck and ripped him off the horse – just as the instructor taught. I never even let go of my spear.

He went down hard, rolled. Before he was on his feet, my spear was at his throat. His leg was broken, anyway.

He wasn't the warlord. But he was the warlord's sister's son. And I got him back to camp, having collected my pages from their pursuit. We had a dozen prisoners, and Eumedes was our only loss.

I didn't try and move. Our infantry had seen the Thracians off, and they were a lot better for it. I got a cheer as I rode in with the Thracian, covered in gold – he had a lot of gold on. I ordered all the prisoners stripped of their jewellery and all of it – and everything off the men killed by the infantry – put in a pile in the middle of camp. I had my herald announce that all the loot would be divided among the whole army, share and share alike.

And the sun rose. The low clouds burned off, and it was early summer at the edge of the hills instead of late autumn, and the men were warm. No one grumbled when I sent forage parties into the hills for more fuel.

Gordias slapped my back. 'Well done,' he said.

'You mean I fucked almost everything away, but it came out well enough?' I asked. I *was* feeling pretty cocky. But I knew I'd done almost everything wrong.

Gordias nodded. 'That's *just* what I mean, son.' He shaded his eyes, watching the distant Thracians. 'We have a word for it. We call it *war.*'

That night, I decided to press my luck. Gordian and Perdias, my other mercenary officer, were completely against it.

Even Polystratus was hesitant.

I decided to attack the Thracians in the dark. There was some moon. And we'd had forage parties out all day – there'd been steady low-level fighting, our woodcutters against theirs, all day. We'd had the best of it – mostly because our farm boys had chased their farm boys off in the early morning, and that sort of thing makes all the difference. And while they had a few tattooed killers, it seemed to me an awful lot of my opponents were as raw as my own troops.

No, I'm lying. That's what Perdias said, and later in the day Gordias agreed. I didn't have a clue – but once they'd said it, I took it as true.

At last light I put a minimum of men on watch and sent the rest to bed. Myndas had my tent back up and all my kit dry – there's a hard campaign all in itself – and he'd built a big fire, built a drying frame – quite a job of work for a Greek mathematician. But he was still trying to overcome my anger, and he had a long way to go.

We stood at the fire – the two infantry officers and the commander of the Thessalians, a wild bastard named Drako, who wore his hair long like a Thracian, with twisted gold wire in it, and the Thracian auxiliary commander, Alcus. He and Drako were like opposites – Drako was slim, long and pretended to a false effeminacy, as some very tough men do; Alcus was short, squat, covered in thick ropes of muscle and heavy blue tattoos.

'We're going at them, across the ridge-top trail at moonrise,' I said.

Gordias shook his head. 'Son, you did well enough today—'

'I'm not your son. We have them on the ropes—'

Alcus spat. 'Thracians attack at night, not Greeks.'

I wasn't sure which side he was supporting, but I chose to interpret it my way. 'Exactly. They won't even have sentries.'

Gordias sighed. 'Listen – my lord. We've done well. But we don't know where the prince is. This is *his* expedition. If we fail, we'll be crushed. And – listen to me, *my lord* – if we succeed, Alexander may not be too thrilled. You know what I'm speaking of.'

I considered that for a few heartbeats. 'Point made. We attack at moonrise.'

I heard an enormous amount of bitching when we woke the troops – the camp was too small for me to be isolated from their discontent. The only trooper more unwilling than a beaten man is a victorious man – he's proved his mettle and got some loot, and he'd like to go home and get laid.

They went on and on – they were still bitching about my sexual habits, my incompetence and my errors of judgement when I roared for silence and marched the lead of the column off into the trees.

My plan was fairly simple. I sent the Thracians and the Thessalians down the valley – they were to start an hour after us, and make noise and trouble only after we struck. All the infantry were with me. The pages were staying in camp as a rallying point, and because they were so tired that most of them didn't even wake up for the rallying call. Thirteen-year-olds – when they collapse, they're like puppies, and it takes a day or two to get their strength back.

We crossed the ridge more slowly than I could believe – we seemed to be held up by every downed tree, and we lost the trail over and over, despite the moonlight. Finally I pushed up to the front of the column and led it myself – and immediately lost the trail. People say 'as slow as honey in winter', but really they should say 'as slow as an army moving at night'.

After a couple of hours, the moon began to go down, the light changed and I discovered that I had perhaps two hundred men with me and the rest were gone – far behind, on another trail, or hopelessly lost.

But we were *there*. I could see the Thracian fires.

And I didn't really understand how few of my men were with me because, of course, it was *night*. Really, until you've tried to fight at night, it seems quite reasonable.

I had Polystratus right at my heels – Gordias at my right shoulder.

I remembered my *Iliad*, so I whispered that every man was to pin back the right shoulder of his chiton. I waited for what seemed like half the night for this order to be passed and obeyed, and then we were moving forward again, bare arms gleaming faintly in the last moonlight.

We found that the Thracians weren't fools – they had camped in a web of dykes, where in better times hundreds of cattle and sheep could be penned. Some of the ground between the dykes was flooded.

Really, I had a dozen opportunities to realise that I was being an idiot and call the whole thing off.

I led them along the face of the first dyke wall – over the berm, and down into the evil surprise of smelly waste water on the far side. Disgusting. And up, now smelling like a latrine – over the next dyke, and again I saw their fires. I was off by a stade, already turned around in the berms.

But now the system of dykes worked in my favour – we were inside the outer walls, and we moved west along the north side of a long earth wall, and there was no way a sentry could see us, unless he was right atop us.

I was right at the front, moving as fast as I could.

So, of course, I began to outpace all my troops, until Polystratus and Gordias and I were alone.

We stopped at the end of a long wall – almost a stade long. We didn't need scouts to know that we were there – we could hear drunken Thracians calling one to another.

I poked my head over the berm.

There was the sentry, an arm's length away. He roared, I stabbed at him, missed, his counter-thrust tangled in my cloak and I got my left arm around his spear, shoved it into his armpit, lifted it and slammed my fist into his face six or seven times, and he was down. Gordias killed him.

But every Thracian awake in that corner saw me, and there was a growl from the camp.

Gordias roared for the men to cross the dyke and charge.

I watched my beautiful plan fall to rubble. But since there wasn't any alternative, I drew my sword and ran headlong into the Thracians at the foot of the dyke.

It was dark. I think I wounded or killed two or even three men before they began to realise what was happening.

There were Macedonians coming over the dykes. Just not all that many.

I still don't know how many were still with me at that point. A hundred? Two hundred?

They made quite a bit of noise, though.

Gordias crashed into the knot of men where I was fighting, and Polystratus – who had had the sense to bring a shield – stood at my shoulder, and most of the men we were facing were awake enough, but they had eating knives and dirks – all their gear was somewhere else. (Try to find your gear in the dark when you are drunk.)

And of course they were drunk. They were Thracians.

This is a story about Alexander, not about me – but I love to tell this story, and it touches on Alexander in the end. That fight in the dark was perfectly balanced – a hundred fully armed Macedonian infantrymen against two thousand sleepy, drunk, unarmed Thracians.

Just when they should have swamped us, Drako swept over the wall behind us with fifty horsemen, looking like fiends from the Thracian hell, and they broke and ran off. Alcus bit into another group and then both my cavalry leaders – neither one of whom made any attempt to find or communicate with me – swept off into the dark. They got the pony herd and some stolen beef and headed back to camp.

By now, the sun was coming up, somewhere far to the east, and there was a line of grey on the far ridge and eye-baffling half-light. And more and more of my missing infantrymen were coming in – most of them from the wrong direction. By sunrise I had half a thousand men and full possession of their camp.

They formed in the middle of the valley – a dejected band of beaten men, most of them without spears. They knew they had to take the camp back, and their leaders were haranguing them.

My cavalry had begun to harass them with javelins.

I lined the dyke closest to them – every minute brought me more light and two or three more men, as they scrambled up the earth walls behind me. Most of my lost infantrymen had gone too far north in the dark.

The Thracians were game. They put their best-armed men in front, formed as tight as they could and swept forward to the base of the dyke, where they stood, roaring, getting their courage up. They still outnumbered my men four to one, and we didn't have our sarissas – they were in camp. We had javelins – a good weapon, but not as useful in stopping an angry Thracian as a pike as long as three men are tall.

I walked up and down in front of my men – manic with energy, elated by my success, terrified of the next few minutes. I was at the right end of my line when a helmetless man leaped off his horse and ran lightly up the berm.

'Well done,' he said, and threw his arms around me. 'Hold their charge and we have them.'

He gleamed like a god come to earth. It was, of course, Alexander.

'We will, my prince!' I said – torn between relief and annoyance. But relief won. It's like being angry at your lover – and then seeing her after an absence. Suddenly, at the sight of her, you care nothing for her infidelities – you're too young to know whereof I speak.

The Thracians came up to the base of the berm.

We stood at the top.

A chief roared something – I think he called, 'Who are we!'

And they roared.

Three times, and then they came in silence, rushing up the dyke faster than I could imagine.

Gordias, on the other hand, kept his head.

'Ready?' he called. 'Throw!' he roared, and five hundred javelins swept like birds of prey on the huddled mass of unshielded, unarmed men.

And that's as far as they got. So many men fell in the shower of spears that they turned to run, and Alexander was on them with the older pages and the professional cavalry – Alcus was there, and Drako, and all the younger pages from camp.

We were all around them, then, and with numbers, too. And weapons and armour.

Maybe a hundred of them lived. I doubt it, though. We offered no quarter, and Alexander meant to make an example in his first battle. The cavalry went in again and again, and they had nowhere to run – even our shield-bearers and camp slaves were out, with slings and rocks, lining the forest edge, so that if an armed man burst free of the melee, they shot him down.

Hephaestion said that Alexander killed the chieftain, and that's possible, but when he went down, the rest as good as fell on their swords. All the fight went out of them, and we took fifty prisoners.

And then there was nothing but the vultures and the corpses and the stink of men's excrement, and we went back to camp. We didn't form and march back – nothing so organised. That level of efficiency came later. Instead, men simply couldn't stand looking at the dead any longer – or men snatched up a gold ring or a torc and left, or wandered blank-eyed for a while and found themselves by a fire.

Gordias got some slaves organised and started collecting the rest of the loot. I found Philip the Red and got him to help me organise collection of the wounded – we had a few. We killed their wounded. I found that I was turning my head away.

It was horrible. But you know about that – I can see it in your eyes. And the animals – the dogs, the carrion birds.

Luckily it was daylight.

By noon, we had most of the army in camp. It was a young army, and most of the men simply sat, slack-jawed. Older men guzzled wine.

Alexander paced, like a caged lion.

'We need to be at them,' he said.

Laodon put an arm around his shoulders. 'Sire, there is no "them" to be at. You have destroyed them.'

Alexander shrugged off his arm. 'Do not be familiar, sir. And their villages are open – right now. Not for long – other tribes will protect them.'

Laodon shook his head. 'Your army is exhausted.'

Gordias backed him up. 'My men have been up all night, and fought two days in a row.'

Alexander flinched – a visible shudder. I knew him well, and knew that he was fighting off a temper tantrum.

Instead, he managed a smile. 'Well, then,' he said. He caught my eye. 'Not bad for the baggage guard, eh?' he said.

I grinned.

He grinned back.

'I expected to find you besieged,' Alexander said.

Laodon shrugged. 'We were sent to fail,' he said.

I stood in shock. 'Antipater betrayed us?'

Alexander looked out at his battlefield and then back at me. 'It makes no snese – but they were waiting for us. Laodon said they were, and they were. So we left you to fort up and went off to try and ambush their ambush.'

'You might have said,' I shot back. In Macedon, we're not slaves.

Alexander rubbed the stubble on his chin. 'I might have. But it was a hunch, and I might have been wrong. Or Laodon might have been the traitor.' He shrugged, even as Laodon flinched. Smiled at me. 'I knew it

82

wasn't you,' he said to me. 'That's why you got the baggage.'

I didn't really know what he was talking about. Thank the gods.

He slapped his knees. 'Well, if the men need a rest, they need a rest. We march at dawn.'

And that was that.

The next day, Alexander took the oldsters and the Thracian auxiliaries and rode north-west, into Thracian territory, and proceeded to burn every village he came to. I moved along the valley floors, building small fortified camps or using the stock dykes the way the Thracians had, but with better sentries and sanitation. We covered fifty stades a day and Alexander covered three times that, and after three weeks he'd burned a swathe across Maetian Thrace as wide as the Chersonese and twice as long. Four weeks to a day after we'd broken their army, we stormed their log-walled city. Alexander put in a garrison of veterans from the infantry corps – two hundred men who got five times the land grants they might have expected. He called it Alexandropolis.

My last camp in Thracian territory had a stockade with three thousand slaves – mostly very saleable young women. The soldiers took their pick, and the rest went up for sale.

Horrible. But they did the same to us.

And then we marched home to Pella, with a fortune in gold and slaves, and Alexander gave an excellent speech, and handed out the whole of the loot to the infantry and the professional cavalry. The pages received nothing.

Antipater greeted us at the main gate, reviewed the army and embraced Alexander. The town cheered us.

It was very difficult to go back to being a page, after that. Three nights later, I was punished for being late to guard duty outside the prince's door – publicly admonished by one of Philip's somatophylakes, who didn't seem to know or care that I had just won a night battle, killed my prince's enemies, stormed a city and handed in my accounts for the logistics of the army and had them passed. Like an adult.

He hit me across the face with his hand, and ordered me to spend the night standing on my feet.

Which, of course, I did.

A month later Philip was back. Another failed siege in the Chersonese – another Athenian proxy victory, and now the Persian fleet was gathering, or so men said. It had been a summer of manoeuvre and near defeat for Macedon, and the rumour was that Thebes was ready to join Persia and Athens against us. And the western Thracians, unimpressed by Alexander's near extermination of the Maeti, were threatening to close the passes of the north-east against us. Or perhaps hold them open for Thebes.

Amid all this, Philip came home. He embraced Alexander publicly and praised him to the skies – after all, as Philip was the first to admit, Alexander had won the year's only victory, and turned a raw phalanx into a veteran one.

Then Philip took the new phalanx and marched it away, and changed Alexandropolis to Philipopolis, and we were left to wonder. And to raise fresh troops.

All winter, Philip marched and counter-marched – he lacked a fleet, and he had to keep the Athenians and their surrogates at arm's length with his army. He sent letters – brilliant letters, full of advice for his son the regent. Some provoked a smile from the regent – and many a frown.

I read them to the prince, because I was one of the inner circle – my courage undoubted, my place secure, or so I thought. I would read him Philip's letters while he wrote out his own correspondence – he had secretaries but preferred to write for himself. Philip's advice, like that of most parents, could be internally contradictory – I recall one letter that admonished the regent for attempting to bribe the magnates of inner Macedon, and then in the next line recommended bribery as the tool to use with Thracians. And every time we managed to raise and equip a new corps of infantry, he'd summon them to his field army, leaving Alexander without the means to march against the renewed threat from the Thracians.

The second time this happened, when we'd stripped the countryside of farm boys to form a fourth taxeis of foot companions only to lose it, Alexander threw his ivory stylus at the wall, and it stuck in the plaster.

'He wants everything for himself. He will leave nothing for me!' he shouted.

Certainly Antipater was no longer allowed an army. Even Drako's Thessalians were called away to the field army.

In the spring, Philip turned without warning and marched on the Thracians – a deeper raid than we had undertaken, and with no traitor to lure them out to easy victory, this time the Thracians stayed in their hill forts and fought for time. Philip captured a few towns and lost some others, and began to move out of the hills in three columns – but the centre column made a mistake, or moved too fast, and was ambushed. Philip got another spear in the thigh – the same thigh – and the line infantry got badly chewed up.

Philip came straight back from defeat to Pella. He hadn't won a major victory in two years, and the vultures were gathering. Defeat at the hands of the Thracians was unthinkable – it gave his enemies ideas.

But Philip had gone after the Thracians while leaving Parmenio and Attalus, the king's left-hand man, with his best troops – now he concentrated his armies, and in effect abandoned the campaign in the Chersonese. In later years we never admitted to this, but Athens had beaten us, or rather, Athens backed by the threat of Persia.

On the other hand, although Philip didn't admit it to us at court, he'd decided to risk his empire on one blow. To go for the jugular, like a hunting dog facing a boar.

The Greeks like to maintain that Macedon was an oppressor, a barbarian force from outside marching through sacred Greece with blood and tyranny, but in truth, they hounded Philip unmercifully and left him little choice. Demosthenes and his renewed Athenian empire insisted on facing Macedon, where in fact we might have been allies. We might have unified against Persia. And we did, in the end. Our way.

In the autumn, when we heard daily rumours of a Persian fleet in the Dardanelles and an Athenian fleet ready for sea, Philip marched – not south and east to the Chersonese, although that's what he told all the ambassadors gathered like vultures in the capital. He left Alexander to deal with them – and Alexander did. For days, Alexander sat beside his father's throne and insisted that the army was on manoeuvres in the flat country by Amphilopolis – that his father would hold winter court at Pella, that they intended to dedicate a new set of statues at Delphi together. The statues were shown, the ambassadors sent their dispatches.

It was about this time that the affair of Pausanias came to a head for the first time. Let me say that we were all dissatisfied, as are all young men are who are made to behave as children when they are blooded warriors. We continued to be pages, and the old men at court treated us like pages. In fact, Attalus wanted us all sent back to the Gardens of Midas, even though Aristotle was gone. He said that we were vain, bad for the prince's morals – he said a great many things. We said that fat old Attalus hated us because his own useless cousin Diomedes had been refused entry – another complex story in the web of intrigue that dominated court. Diomedes was a pretty boy, and events proved him a good enough fighter, but somehow he had a reputation as … well, as an effeminate. And the pages refused to have him. Attalus vented his outrage on us every way he could – I took a great deal of it, because Antipater employed me as a staff officer even while I still had to do all my duties as a page.

Young Pausanias had been one of us, and then he joined the royal companions and went off to serve with the men. And he was Philip's bed-warmer on campaign – this was not held to be dishonourable, although it led to some malicious humour. At any rate, Pausanias was wounded in the fight against the Thracians.

In the same fight, Diomedes supposedly stood his ground over the king after he took a spear and went down – held his ground, saved the king's life. Mind you, I never heard any man but Attalus tell that story. But however it happened, after the Thracian campaign Diomedes was invited to join the companions, and he replaced Pausanias completely in the king's affections.

Yes – yes, this really is how Macedon was run. Hard as this may be to believe. Philip had a new favourite every week, sometimes. Men, women – jokes were made about his horses. But he was king, he was in his prime and he had no intention of living anything less than the fullest possible life.

But Pausanias was sent back to the pages. It shouldn't have been possible. One was promoted to a regular regiment from the schoolroom, but no one could remember a man being sent back to the boys.

And we had Attalus at court, and he was poisonous to me, and meaner to Pausanias – insisted he get all the worst duties, made him cut meat for the cooks. A rumour went round that he had been paid money to service grown men among the companions. Not hard to guess where that rumour started.

I didn't like Pausanias much. He was, in most ways, the instrument of his own destruction. He was vain, horribly fragile, weak and easily used. But I was one of the captains of the pages by then, and I did my best when drawing up the duty to soften the blows from Attalus, who, despite being the king's left-hand man, was still nowhere near as big a magnate as my father. I went home for the Festival of Demeter and laid it all before my father, and he must have done something because for the moment, Attalus backed off me and mine.

But the pages hated being treated like boys when we knew we were men, and as we thought, so Alexander thought. Every letter full of advice from his father reminded him that he was regent under Philip's will – and being stripped of troops seemed to be an insult, although from the distance of years, I wonder if Philip simply needed the troops. Hard to know, now.

Pella seethed. They were plotting – I could feel it when I spoke to my father by the hearth. It was the last time I saw him. I could tell from the way he held his tongue that he knew something. Even now, I'm not sure what he knew – not sure what the plots were. It is essential to understand this, to understand Alexander. The old families and the generals were plotting every minute – when Philip appeared weak. When he was strong, they fawned. That was Macedon. Our foes were gathering, Philip had vanished and Alexander wouldn't say where he was, and the men of power were looking for a plot to save themselves, their rich farms and their hoards of gold. Attalus was part of it. Parmenio was not, I'd swear to it.

I was learning about court. Certainly I had grown up there, and I knew most of the dirt – but I was suddenly old enough to see other things, listen to mutterings under the eaves, watch whose slave appeared at whose door. There was political intrigue, there were love affairs …

I remember an evening in autumn. I was standing on the Royal Terrace, because I was about to go on duty, and the prince came out, alone. I had not been alone with Alexander in a month. He hardly spoke to me.

But that day, he grinned his famous grin and came across to me. 'You know where my pater is, Ptolemy?' he asked.

I shook my head.

'Guess,' he said. 'It will be public knowledge in an hour.'

I shrugged. 'Thebes,' I said.

Alexander threw his arms around me. 'You are intelligent,' he said.

Indeed, while I was smarter than the Athenian ambassadors, I'm not sure everyone was fooled. But they were fooled enough to keep their troops waiting for us in the Chersonese and in the autumn, Philip caught them flat-footed, and occupied the passes west of the Gates of Fire.

Demosthenes rose in the Athenian Assembly and demanded an army to meet Philip in the field. It was the best speech of his career. Athens answered with ten thousand hoplites and another ten thousand mercenaries, and by a matter of days' marching, beat Philip into the southern passes and kept him out of Boeotia. My guess about Thebes had been premature.

But Philip sat at his end of the passes and watched the Persian–Athenian détente crumble. The Persians wanted nothing more than to see Athens and Macedon and Thebes rip into one another, and the Persian gold was cut off, the Persian fleet went home and Macedon was saved. Demosthenes spent the winter egging Athens on to greatness, or so he claimed. But as I had predicted at the trout dinner, the democracy did much of the work to destroy the Persian alliance themselves.

Philip sent orders home that we should raise two more taxeis of infantry and train the pages harder. But he also ordered that the pages be promoted to royal companions. We were going to be adults. And when we'd trained the new recruits, we were to bring them to Philip in the field. Father and son were going to war together.

That winter, my father died, and I fell in love. I believe in love – many men don't – and it had been my friend all my life. And my first love was linked to the death of my father.

Many men said then that I was Philip's bastard son. That Philip put me on my mother – by rape, in an affair. And the gods know my pater was always fairly distant. On the other hand, he was closer than Philip ever was to me or to Alexander, for that matter. He didn't have much time for me until I was eleven or twelve, but after that, when I was home from being a page, Pater listened to my tales of the hunt and the court, took me with him on business visits around our farms and we went hunting together ourselves. Some of my best memories are of sitting in the hall, on a stool by the hearth, surrounded by Pater's great boar hounds. We talked about everything, solved many of the world's problems, and Pater became quite a fan of Aristotle – actually bought two of his books and read them, which was quite a turn-up for a boar-hunting lord in the wilds of central Macedon.

Pater never discussed my birth directly. But once, when he was at court – a rare event in itself – Attalus made direct reference to it. And Pater smiled at him and rubbed his nose – his long hawk's beak of a nose.

My nose, too.

My guess is that Mater and Philip were lovers – by his will, I suspect. But the child she bore her husband was theirs. He honoured her all her life, and there was a well-tended shrine to her after her death. Not that Philip ever visited it, either way. If he'd visited the graves of all his lovers, he'd have done nothing else.

Some time in late autumn, when there was snow in the passes and the snowline was creeping over the higher fields, when small farmers stayed in, weaving baskets and carving new handles for axes, and the great families had dangerous feasts where everyone drank too much, slept with the wrong people and killed each other with knives – word came to court that my pater was ill, and Alexander brought me the news himself. I was in Antipater's rooms, copying documents like a scribal slave – lists of equipment issued to our new recruits. Dull stuff, but the very sinews of Ares, and Alexander insisted that it be done right.

He came in, a scroll rolled in his fist. 'Ptolemy,' he said, in that way of his that made you feel like you were his only friend, the centre of his world. He embraced me.

By Zeus, I loved him.

At any rate, he unrolled the scroll – even in a crisis, he couldn't ever stop explaining his latest enthusiasm, and this was no crisis. 'Have you read Isocrates?' he asked.

'No,' I said cautiously. It wasn't always good to admit ignorance with Alexander.

'Another Athenian – but oh, he has some beautiful ideas. He says it is time for a crusade of all the Hellenes against Persia.' Alexander held up the scroll and read. He read well – he had a good voice.

Isocrates.

I had a soft spot for Isocrates, because he was a Plataean, and the Plataeans were, to me, the real heroes of Marathon and of all the subsequent campaigns against Persia. Aristotle used some of Isocrates's speeches in training us. So I was, like any good friend, prepared to be pleased and to support Alexander's latest passion.

And I have to say that, at that time, every side and every voice in the Hellenic world was advocating a crusade against Persia. First, the Persian court and Persian army and every satrapy in Asia were now full of Hellenes, growing rich, writing letters home to describe in detail the riches of Asia and the relative ease with which it could all be conquered. Every boy in the world – the Greek-speaking world – read Xenophon's *Anabasis* at school, and every one of us saw Persia as the empire we would conquer. If our thoughts had carried physical manifestation (something Pythagoras apparently advocated at one time) then Persepolis would have had a bull's-eye painted across its walls like a Cretan archery target a hundred feet tall.

In addition, every faction in Greece saw a universal crusade against the Mede as the salvation of the endless infighting – Athens against Sparta, Sparta against Thebes, Thebes against Thessaly against Macedon against Athens. Even Philip advocated such a war – as long as he could command it. And there, my friend, was the rub. Everyone imagined that we would all cooperate – even Athens and Macedon – if we could get to grips with the King of Kings, but no one wanted to play second flute, so to speak.

Alexander raced back to his quarters and reappeared with a whole bag of Isocrates. 'Read these while you go to your father!' he said.

Now by this point I'd been one of his inner circle for more than a year, and we hunted together – sometimes just the two of us – played Polis, threw knucklebones and sparred daily. I knew him pretty well – but the brilliance and brittleness of his moods still caught me by surprise. He could change topics faster than anyone I've ever met. Other men made allusions to femininity – women are supposed to have fickle minds, or so I'm told – but Alexander's intellectual whims came with spear-points of iron and a will of adamantine, and there was nothing effeminate about them. Only lesser men ever thought so. What happened was that Alexander would finish a subject – often inside his head, with no reference to friends or other company – and *move on*. If you were up to his speed, you could reason out where he'd gone. If you weren't, he left you behind all the time, and eventually stopped trying to talk to you.

In this case, all he'd done was share his passion for Isocrates first, and then remember that he hadn't told me the reason for his visit to Antipater's rooms. My pater was dying or already dead. I was requested.

'Take all the time you want,' Alexander said. 'I know you love him – I've seen the two of you together.' He smiled ruefully. 'I am envious.'

What do you say to that? He was envious. He and his pater were locked in a competition when they ought to have been pulling in harness like matched chariot horses.

'I am lucky, lord,' I said. 'Pater has treated me as a man – since before I was one.'

'Men say Philip is your father,' Alexander said. He didn't mean it to hurt. 'Yet despite the slur, your father sees you as a … a *person*.' He shrugged.

'Lagus is my father.' I was on dangerous ground here.

'I agree. If Philip was your father, you'd be better-looking.' Alexander smiled. 'You are the only one of my close friends with his own estates and his own power – and yet you are completely loyal. Why?'

Chasms were opening at my feet, and legions of Titans preparing to rend me limb from limb. He had that look in his eye.

'Habit?' I answered, with a wink.

Alexander stopped, and his face became still for a moment, and then he barked a laugh. 'By Herakles my ancestor, Ptolemy. Get you gone. Send your pater my respects, if he is alive to hear them, and tell him his son is somatophylax to the prince.'

'I am?' I said. I was delighted – for all his moodiness, he was my prince, and I wanted to serve.

He put a gold ring in my hand. 'You are.'

I still wear the ring. I earned it a thousand times, and I never betrayed his trust. Until I killed him.

Pater was still alive when I arrived – on the mend, it appeared. So we dined by the hearth, all the old servants happy to have me home – Pater was an excellent master, had freed all the good slaves already and paid them wages, and men competed to go to our estates. It always baffled me that men had other ways of dealing with their slaves and serfs than Pater's – he was hard but fair, quick to reward. Who thinks that there's another way? I think it is like raising children. Good estate management takes a few more minutes than bad estate management, just as a little time and a few words are the difference between a good child and a bad one.

We had a good dinner, and I showed off my ring, and Pater beamed at me with approval. I saw him to bed, kissed him and gave him Alexander's respects, and he frowned.

'Your prince is mad,' he said. 'Steer a careful course, my son. He is no Philip.'

I didn't lash out – I only said, 'My prince is worth ten of Philip.'

Pater shook his head. 'Perhaps,' he said. 'But Philip is already looking to be rid of him.'

That was like icy water down my back. 'What?'

Pater shrugged, coughed and drank off a huge dollop of poppy juice. 'I've said too much,' he whispered. 'But people tell me things – and I have some of Attalus's slaves – they've run from him. He's a dangerous man – more like a felon than a general.' He nodded.

'Where are these slaves?' I asked.

Pater smiled. 'Safe. Ask Heron.' Heron was his steward. 'You are an excellent son. Get a wife and make some more! That's my only advice, lad. You have the rest in your hand. Oh – and don't forget to breed Narcissa in the spring.' Narcissa was a big mare – beautiful and wilful and not very interested in boys, but the largest, heaviest, fastest mare we'd ever had.

I held his hand, found myself choked with tears, reminded myself that he was going to be there for a few more nights at least, and let the nurse have him.

He was dead in the morning. He stayed alive for a few days on poppy and willpower to speak to me one last time.

I'm going to cry now.

The gods know I cried then. I wept for a couple of hours, and then I got up and went riding. I rode over our home farms – three farms that had been in the family for ever, since we were smaller men, I suspect – it was winter, and the leaves were off the trees and it was pissing rain, and I didn't care.

I rode up the hill – we had a big hill in the middle of our property, with an ancient ruined stone tower from the old people at the top. I looked out over all of it – my land as far as my eyes could see, or close enough.

Then I rode back down and buried my pater. He was never a king, or a general. He spurned the court, and mostly he was interested in breeding horses and dogs and cattle and pigs. But he was an excellent father and husband and lord to his people.

*

Heron understood that there had to be changes. So I spent two weeks – right through the winter festival of lights – sitting in my pater's chair. I dispensed some justice, walked some boundaries and talked to Heron about the future of the estates. The problem was that most men like me had some brothers or sisters – even bastards – to hold the home fort, so to speak. I was a close friend of the prince, and in twenty years I had every expectation of being a general, or a King's Councillor, or something better. Satrap? Really, when I was seventeen, I saw no limit to my ambition.

Pretty accurate, as it turned out.

So I wasn't going to run my estates myself.

Menander and all the 'New Comedy' is filled with bad stewards and rapacious managers stealing from lord and peasant alike. Those stereotypes exist for a reason. Heron didn't want my unlimited trust. He wanted a system of checks and balances to keep him honest. He was a fair man, and he knew that if I rode away and ignored him – well, he'd be under strain.

So for two weeks we hammered out a new administration of my estates, with what was, in effect, a regency council. Heron ran the council, and I got his oldest son, Laodekes, a vacancy as a page. In effect, I ennobled Heron, and his son became my hostage.

That's Macedon, friend.

At some point in my time at home, I met Nike. She was a house servant – by no means a slave, but rather the daughter of one of Heron's closest friends, brought in to learn the management of a house before she had her own. She was fifteen, with Aphrodite's figure and a nose that aimed at the outright conquest of her face. She was pretty sharp – she knew exactly the border between humour and disrespect to her lord, and she walked it carefully, teasing me a little, trying to get me to smile.

I was not doing very well, those weeks after Pater died.

But I liked her for trying, and all of a sudden, in less than a week, I was following her around the house while she did her work. She was the only person I really wanted to see. I'd never been in love before, so the whole thing rather took me by surprise.

I don't remember how long into the week it was, but I remember standing on the terrace behind the kitchen. She had on a good chiton – good linen – with a zone of braided silk. She always looked like a lady – but the lines were not as clear, then, and her people were not peasants.

She had an apron on, and a scarf in her hair, and a heavy bronze knife in her fist. And what I remember is the moment she turned on me, knife in hand. 'Shouldn't you be working?' she asked. 'Your father worked all day on these estates.'

I didn't know what to say, and so, in the best tradition of seventeen-year-old boys, I stammered a great deal.

She laughed – I remember watching her laugh, and there and then, I understood. I *wanted* her. Up to that moment, somehow I had thought I wanted us to be friends. Or just sought her good opinion.

'I'll go and work,' I muttered – or something like it.

'Good.' She nodded. Then, almost sly, out of the corner of her mouth, with the slightest glance out of the corner of her eye – 'I like to ride – when the work is done.'

A woman who liked to ride? Clearly the gods had made her for me.

We rode out every evening until I left for Pella. I was no blushing virgin, and she burned hot enough that I assume she was not, either. But we had more than lust. The son of Lagus was not going to marry a servant girl, but I went to her father, paid her bride price and when I left for Pella, she and a slave-maid rode with me. And Nike she surely was.

Somehow, I also found time to read Isocrates end to end. It was, after all, a royal command. I read it, and I caught fire. We could do this thing. It was the Thracian campaign writ large – the biggest challenge of men and logistics since the dawn of the world. I read and reread the philosopher's words, and began to dream of a new world, where we younger men conquered Persia. I could see it.

The first night back in Pella, Alexander came to my rooms un-announced. This required explanation, too. In the last year, as we were promoted – first by experience, and then by decree – to the ranks of manhood and made royal companions rather than just pages, some of us received apartments in the palace. Other men stayed in the pages' barracks, and others still bought houses in Pella or rented rooms – re-member, some of our number were as poor as peasants.

I had two rooms in the palace. I kept them – they were close to the king and very useful when I was on duty, or when we were awake all night.

But after Pater died and I had Nike, I bought a house in town. I bought a big house – in fact, I bought the house that Aristotle vacated. I moved Nike in as my mistress – in effect, as my wife – and I enlarged the stables to hold twenty horses and invited Cleitus, Philip and my two other best friends among the pages – Nearchus and young Cleomenes – to come and live with me. None of them had any money, and all of them were, in effect, my men. Oh, that's not fair – Cleitus had his own relationship with Alexander, and Philip the Red was never really *mine*, but we were all close, we shared loyalties, tastes and friends.

I set up housekeeping in a few hours, or, rather, my new chief of staff, Nike, did – she bought furniture, won over my useless slaves, bought food, bought a cook, found all my friends and moved all their kit into our house, assigned them rooms – all while I was on duty with Antipater.

We were deeply in love, but that love was aided by events and by the fact that we were good allies, too – she wanted to run a household, and I needed a household manager. And by the will of the gods, I got one. A brilliant one. She could find chicken stock in a desert – enough for as many guests as she wanted to have. She was delighted by my body every hour I wanted her – scars and all. She was happy enough to occupy herself when I was busy. She never fawned, and she could read.

I still don't know what she saw in me.

I get ahead of myself. I was in my rooms at the palace, unbuckling my breastplate and contemplating the short walk 'home'. In fact, I'd been there once and expected a shambles.

Alexander walked in without warning and started helping me with the buckles under my arms.

'Did you read Isocrates?' he asked. As if he'd been waiting for three weeks just to hear my opinion. Which, in a way, was probably true.

'Every word,' I said. 'Let's do it.'

He stopped fumbling with my buckles. 'You mean it?'

I remember that moment. It was a week of changes for me, and any astrologer would have been able to tell me, I suspect. 'We can conquer Asia,' I said. 'Your friends. Your team, if you like.'

He kissed me – he never kissed anyone, our golden-haired boy, but he kissed my cheek and pressed me to his chest. 'Yes!' he breathed in my ear. 'I knew you would understand.'

I got out of my armour, stripped, wiped myself down and put on an old chiton and a warm chlamys for the walk home, while he babbled plans. Good plans – it wasn't that he was babbling nonsense, but that human speech was too slow for the efficient transfer of everything he had to say.

But I *had* read Isocrates, so I could keep up with him, and nod or cut him short. I won't bore you with this, but conversation often sounded like this, to an outsider:

Alexander: We need a navy.

Me (or Hephaestion or Philotas or anyone in the inner circle who could keep up): Ports. We have the wood.

Alexander: Oarsmen.

Me: Amphilopolis. But Athens!

Alexander (sometimes with a chorus of all of us together): It all comes down to Athens.

Me: Isocrates might help.

Alexander: A gift. But we can't be seen—

Me: We need to find a way to bribe from strength.

Alexander: Good phrase. (So in the next conversation, we'd say 'Bribe from strength' without explanation – just as we didn't need an explanation for the words 'oarsmen' because everyone in the inner circle knew that was a code for our complete lack of trained sailors, oarsmen, shipwrights – you get the picture.)

On that day, though, we weren't with the others. Hephaestion – who knew where he was? He was always Alexander's right hand, but he had begun to branch out himself – serving maids, boys with nice hair – basically anyone who was alive and wanted to fuck. Alexander was tolerant – amused. And not very interested.

And for whatever reason, Hephaestion never bothered to read Isocrates.

I'm taking my time telling this, because while it was the culmination of my career as a courtier, and in some ways the logical development of my career, it was also the moment at which the knucklebones were cast. For good or ill.

So – I had changed into plain clothes, arranged my armour on its stand, buffed a few flecks of dust off the bronze – I was waiting for Alexander to lose interest so I could go home. That doesn't mean I wanted him to lose interest – I was a courtier as well as a friend – merely that in the normal run of things, my time would expire and he'd go back to Hephaestion or go to sit with Antipater or go and read letters from his father – listen to court cases, dine with ambassadors, what have you. I'd been back for three days and on duty the whole time, and while I loved having his attention – his entirely favourable attention – I was really looking forward to putting my mouth over Nike's and feeling her breath in my chest.

Alexander was arguing both sides of the notion of starting the Hellenic conquest of Asia in Aegypt when he looked up. He was a little shorter than I, with tousled, leonine blond hair and darting eyes. My blond hair was darker, with some brown in it, but curly enough – I was taller, and had the big nose. Hah! Still do.

He grinned. 'I'm hungry. Let's go and steal some food in the kitchen.'

I didn't even think. 'Come to my house,' I said. 'I'm sure there's food. Better than stealing from the companions' cook!' I shrugged. 'It's not one of Aristotle's foolish exercises.'

Alexander's eyes flicked away and then back. 'You have a house?' he asked.

'Aristotle's house,' I said. 'I bought it. My pater – well, I'm a rich man now.'

Alexander laughed. 'Wait for me,' he said.

A minute later, he appeared in a companion's dun-coloured cloak. 'Let's go. I hope you didn't buy Aristotle's cook?'

'I didn't. But to be honest, I haven't been home since I bought the place. It'll be chaos. I invited Cleitus to come and live with me – but he's on watch tonight. And Philip and Nearchus, I think …' I remember yawning. Alexander walked along next to me – for a few minutes, we were two young men at large in Pella. And woe betide the bodyguard who was supposed to be on duty.

We walked the three streets in no time. We didn't talk about anything that I remember, until he said, 'Well, it's lit up. That's something. Your slaves knew you were coming.'

In fact, there were two slaves in the door yard – Nichomachus and another I didn't know. Nichomachus saw me, saw Alexander and darted inside. The new boy just kept cutting apples.

'I think we're in luck,' I said. The smell coming into the courtyard was excellent – lamb, fresh bread, something with herbs in it.

Alexander paused. 'You are married,' he said.

'I have a housekeeper,' I admitted. 'I like her a lot.'

He gave a wry smile. 'This I need to see.'

And he followed me into what proved to be my own house.

Philip and Nearchus and Cleomenes were standing by their couches – Nike was nowhere to be seen. There was furniture I'd never seen before, two Athenian vases of flowers at either end of the andron, and the empty niche in the entryway had statues of Aphrodite and Poseidon, flowers, a small spilled offering of wine. A brazier was burning to take the edge off the air, and it had something wonderful in it – myrrh.

'My lord.' Philip, as the eldest, bowed to welcome us. 'We have had the fish course.'

'Never eaten so well in my life!' said Cleomenes, who was too young to be restrained, and always hungry.

Philip gave him a wry smile – the equivalent of tousling his hair and telling him to shut up.

Alexander sank on to the couch nearest the door and Myndas appeared and started taking his sandals. Myndas had never, in a year of serving me, helped me with my sandals.

But he did, when he was done with the prince.

Dinner sailed in and out like a well-ordered fleet – servants I'd never hired or paid for carrying dishes I'd eaten only at court or at home. In fact, it was plain enough – four removes, meat and bread and some eggs, but plenty of it, and everything with some little touch of culinary genius – saffron on the eggs, pepper on the lamb with sweet raisins.

Alexander ate sparingly like the ascetic he was, but he relished the bread, and when the sweets came in – nuts in honey – he ate himself to sticky excess. And he drank, too. It was all local wines – Macedon has no need to import wine, really, and our heavy reds are as good as any in the world. Off in the next room, someone was keeping the wine watered three or four to one, but Nearchus was bright red and the prince was loud.

He put his feet on the floor suddenly, and barked his laugh. 'I want to see her!' he said.

We all fell silent.

Alexander had a wine bowl. 'To the mistress of this house, whosoever she might be. I haven't eaten like this in my life.'

I said something about being at his service.

'Then let's see her!' Alexander said.

I rose to my feet.

'In my court we have many factions,' Alexander said, his eyes a little wild. 'Attalus believes all men are pigs. Parmenio wants us to make war for ever so he can keep his place – Antipater craves peace so he can keep his. Hephaestion would make love to the world.' He grinned. 'But you, my friend, are the only advocate of women. You *like* women. And now you've brought one home, and you are ashamed to show her to me?' He beamed around. 'Do you gentlemen know that he put a girl in my bed? Eh?' he asked.

'I'll fetch her, by your leave, my prince.' I headed for the door.

'Don't you find … Ptolemy, I'm asking you. Don't you find that she makes you weaker? After you put that lady in my bed – I thought of nothing else for ten days. I could accomplish nothing. I was worth nothing. Are you a better man than I?'

Knock me over with a feather – he'd never shown a sign of being besotted. Of course, we'd ridden to rescue his father – for nothing, as it turned out.

I shrugged and went to the kitchen.

Nike wasn't there. There was a cook, a big African I'd never seen before, with a gold earring and a faintly military air. Clearly a freeman – the earring was worth ten days' wages. 'Lady Nike?'

'Changing clothes,' he said, with one hand on a bronze pan and the other on some eggs. 'Don't bother me right now, lord.'

By the time I went back into the hallway, she was there, wearing a fine blue wool chiton in the old Ionian manner, pinned with some very plain bronze pins which I determined on the spot to replace with gold.

I snatched a kiss, with spectacular success. Isn't there something almost miraculous to kissing someone who wants to kiss you? Then she pulled free.

'Don't muss my hair,' she said, and ignoring my attempts to stop her and give her advice, she walked into the andron.

Alexander was drinking again. Nearchus looked ... frightened. Cleomenes was laughing and Philip was laughing with him. But they all straightened up when Nike came in. She was that kind of girl.

She made a low curtsy to Alexander – just the sort of curtsy she'd have made at one of the shrines.

He looked her over with an air that made me angry – as if she were unfit for human consumption.

'The food is excellent,' he said.

'Thank you, lord,' she answered.

'You are a freewoman, I think,' he said.

She nodded.

'You can cook and weave, then? How about ...' He drawled the question – he meant to offend. 'How about reading?'

'I've read Isocrates,' she said.

I've seen Alexander surprised a half-dozen times, I think. Maybe more. Not often, though. But when Nike said 'Isocrates' his eyes opened wider and his brows shot up. Even his mane of hair seemed to move.

'Really?' he asked. 'And what did you gather from his works?'

She didn't meet his eye. 'That he'd like a place at your father's court,' she said. 'And that it is time Macedon stopped playing with Greece and took Persia, instead.' She had a matter-of-fact delivery that was like Aristotle's – it was difficult to contradict her, as I learned early in our relationship, and love never stopped her from being 'right'.

Alexander clapped his hands together, much in the way he might have done for a talking dog, I fear. You have to remember that Aristotle had no time for women at all, and Philip liked them only at the end of his cock, and even then he found them interchangeable with men. Alexander's mother was too feminine, too much the avatar of Dionysian excess. He didn't have any charming, witty, argumentative women in his life.

More's the pity. Aristotle told him that pleasure came with cost, and distracted great men from great deeds, and he took that bait and swallowed it. Domestic happiness puzzled him utterly.

He interrogated her for as long as it took the brazier to burn down, and never asked her to sit. He asked her about her father, about her education, about her views of women as priestesses, as mothers – asked her whether she planned to be a mother.

At first I found it offensive, and then I found the explanation. She was suddenly the ambassador of the tribe of women to the court of Alexander. He'd never really had one to talk to before. And he always kept ambassadors standing because he forgot to ask them to sit – because questioning them about their alien lands excited him so much.

When I understood that, I drank a little to catch up, caught her eye and winked, and she stood calmly and answered him as best she could – some sharp answers, some witty answers, and some plain answers.

When she said that, yes, she wanted to have children, he smiled at her.

'Ptolemy's sons? Or will you wed some lesser man?' he asked.

'I'm not sure that I can answer that,' she said. 'Nor would I, even if I knew.' She met his eye, and for a moment the Prince of Macedon was eye to eye with a tiger. Neither shrank.

'Fascinating,' he said. 'I drink to you, my lady.'

And then he was finished with her. I took her by the hand and led her out, and she walked into our bedroom and threw up in a basin, and then tidied herself and went to the kitchen to see what had happened to the barley rolls. That was Nike.

I walked him home, with Nearchus and Cleomenes and Philip as guards – because people *did* want to kill him, and the streets of Pella after dark were an unbeatable opportunity.

He seemed sober. But just short of the palace, he turned to me. 'I'm not sure that wasn't the best dinner I've ever had,' he said. 'And I'm not sure what to think of that.'

'You are welcome any time,' I said.

'Good. I'll come the second day of every week. I may invite one or two others. See to it that the duty officer knows the way.' He paused. 'I'm sorry, please ask the lady Nike if I might come every Tuesday.'

I grinned. 'I will,' I said.

Those dinners saved his life. And more. But that's another story.

FIVE

—◊◊◊—

I n spring, we marched.

In fact, it was still late winter, and there was snow everywhere, and our farm-boy recruits got to march through it in Iphactrian sandals that made the snow pack in under the soles of the feet – I was wearing them myself.

Camping an army in snow is dreadful. First, because *everything* is wet. Snow is water held close to the ground, ready to turn back to water the moment you are comfortable. In higher areas, it stays snow for a while and you are merely cold, but in spring – water, waiting to happen.

Second, because everything wet is *cold*. Even wood has to be warmed and dried before it will ignite.

There's no casual forage for animals. The grass – old, tough and useless – is *under* the snow. Animals use energy getting at it.

And the process of freezing and thawing turns roads to mush. In late summer and early autumn, a good dirt road has a surface like builder's concrete or better, and can shed water from a long rain. But in early spring, there *is* no surface, and every wheel rut is a potential spiked pit of death for carts or hooves. I was ready, this time – in fact, I was merely Antipater's aide, and didn't bear the full weight of the responsibility, although I'd done a great deal of the work. I had spare wheels in every other cart, my carts were the pick of the litter and not the runts and my draught animals would have been chosen as cavalry horses in most armies.

We had two thousand infantry, almost all recruits. We had all the former pages over sixteen years old, three full troops of fifty, each with three chargers and a fully armed groom. Most of us had three or four grooms, although only one was armed and armoured. Polystratus was mine.

We stopped in Thessaly and picked up two hundred young noblemen. We looked at them with some amusement as they flailed around being miserable, camping in the snow – they were as tough as nails, but this was outside their experience. A man can camp in the snow with his pater and a pair of retainers while hunting and still not have a clue how to keep clean and neat and warm in the midst of four thousand men.

At any rate, we crossed the high passes in temperatures that made all of us bond. I was widely envied for my foresight in bringing my own bed-warmer – Nike came. I was an officer – I could get away with it. And her talent for organisation – and her willingness to win Polystratus as an ally – made her perfect for the life. She had food ready when my duty was over – not just for me but for my mess. Don't imagine she cooked it herself. She simply organised all the servants in our mess like a little military unit and had them rotate all the duties. She got them tents, too. Our little corner of the companions' camp went up in no time, and had a central street, with our tents on one side and the servants' tents on the other and the fires in between. Before we were out of the mountain passes, this had become the pattern for all the younger companions, and we all lived better for it, with our fires and our weapons closer to hand. Not all these ideas were Nike's – some were mine, some Philip's, some Alexander's, some Polystratus's. But we implemented them all on that march, and we had a better, tighter, more defensible camp with happier camp servants and warmer men as a result.

We marched down on to the coast road where Leonidas made his stand at the Gates of Fire, and Alexander stopped and made sacrifice there. Hephaestion made a great show of pouring an enormous and costly libation. The rest of us shared an ox, slaughtered it and feasted over the Spartan dead. Nearchus read the poem by Simonides.

We knew we were the invaders and not the defenders. But our hearts were with those Spartans standing at the wall.

Spring came after we passed the Gates of Fire – or rather, what was late winter in Thessaly was early spring in Greece, with jasmine blooming like yellow fire on the hills. The Thebans were holding some of the passes, and the Athenians the others – over by Delphi – and their mercenary army, ten thousand professional soldiers, held the coast road.

Two nights before we marched into Philip's camp, he stormed the mercenaries' positions. It was his first great victory in years – and one of his best. I wasn't there, but I heard about it in detail from men who were. It was, in some ways, the pinnacle of his achievements – the storming of an impregnable position against superb soldiers, done in bad weather, through a mixture of bribery and audacity. He hit the mercenaries so hard that he drove them off their dry-stone walls in the first charge, and he'd moved a dismounted force of his own companions and a pack of Agrianian javelin men – the fruits of his latest barbarian marriage – across impossible terrain to close the pass *behind* the mercenaries, so that they could not rally against him, or seize another pass to hold. In fact, he virtually exterminated them.

We arrived within an hour of his return to his base camp from the bloody pursuit. He embraced his son – as the victor in a recent battle, he was all love – and he reviewed us the next morning, pronounced us fit to be royal companions and confirmed all of Antipater and Alexander's promotions, including mine.

And then we were off like hounds from a leash – all the cavalry under Alexander, racing down the newly captured passes and into the plains of Boeotia, turning the flanks of the whole alliance and leaving them with nowhere to go but back, abandoning Delphi to us and all the mountain states. With no further fighting, we were in behind them.

Chares, the Athenian strategos, had received a great deal of wine-inspired criticism for his campaign, but in fact he did a brilliant job with the tools he had. The Athenians needed only to endure – their fleet was out on the seas, busy wrecking our commerce. And we could endure only so long, while Athens gathered momentum and threatened to do things like take Amphilopolis behind us.

So Chares held his line of mountains, and when he was turned out of them, he had a plan for that, too, and both armies – Thebans and Athenians – retired in good order. My first taste of combat with professional opponents was in late spring – all Boeotia was a garden and a farm, already tawny with grain, and we came cantering down the passes. Our greatest advantage besides sheer training was that every one of us had three remounts, and we could move for days, changing horses as we went. So we did.

The Thebans had little cavalry to speak of, but the Athenian Hippeis were good – not as good as we, but too good to trifle with. They bloodied our noses in our first skirmish – Philotas charged them as if they were Thracians, and they scattered down a Boeotian road, and Philotas pelted after them, and it was a trap – we lost six men.

But after that, we had their measure, and we'd unfold from our road column into a fighting line at the gallop, racing for the flanks the moment the Athenians were spotted, and after that we flushed their roadside ambushes the way a hunter flushes birds from hedgerows.

And so started the most glorious of summers. The sun was warm, Greece was beautiful and kind, the peasants and free farmers mostly welcomed us as liberators because Thebes is hard to love. We marched to the gates of Thebes and drove in their pickets, then turned and went for the passes to Athens – but Chares, as I say, was no fool, and he took ground at Chaeronea like a dozen strategoi before him.

And there our lightning offensive stopped. Chaeronea has been the scene of a dozen battles for a reason. And it is not for nothing we call that area 'The dance floor of Ares'. It is flat, good going, for stades in every direction. The ground rose towards the Athenian position. They had an excellent view of our camp night and day, without even sending their horse out as scouts. Their backs were to the passes over Parnassus to Athens, and yet they had three roads into the countryside around Thebes, so that we were hard put to watch them all, and in fact, contingent after contingent joined their army without our being able to stop them.

We were in the saddle for days at a time.

I loved it. I had a great deal to learn, and I learned it – I fought skirmishes where I might have gathered information, I ignored heaven-sent opportunities to grab enemy supplies, or I grabbed supplies that didn't matter ...

I got to visit Plataea, and was received as a hero. They hate Thebes, even the shepherds. Probably even the sheep. Philip was already declaring his policy of dismembering the Theban League, and towns that had known independence, such as Plataea, were already ours.

The main army camped opposite the allies at Chaeronea, and Philip made peace offers. He meant them, too. He had the plain of Boeotia and that's all he needed to negotiate – time was now on no one's side, and as long as he could absorb the farm produce of the great plain, Thebes was the city that was in the most trouble.

But Thebes had delusions of grandeur, and so did Athens. They were perfect reflections of each other – living in past glories, even past glories where they'd been enemies. Philip told us one night at dinner that they were like two people who are each spurned by a third and use that as a basis for marriage.

I remember it as a golden summer. Alexander was happy – he led us on raids and long tours in person, and he was brilliant at such stuff – always a step ahead of the Thebans and the Athenians – and then back to camp, tired but happy after three days on the road, to the unstinting praise of his father.

We were shutting the enemy cavalry in a box and dominating the countryside. The Athenian Hippeis had done well against Macedonians in the past – we'd got our fingers nipped by Phokion a few times. It was heady to be better than they in every skirmish. And the Theban cavalry were a sorry lot, and we bullied them. The Athenians never got bullied.

After one encounter, where we chased the Thebans twenty stades and captured a Boeotarch, Philip allowed that, in his son, he might have discovered a second Macedonian general after Parmenio.

Now that's flattery. And Alexander loved him for it, gave him a leg-up when he went for a ride, held his horse when he dismounted, waited on him with a cup in his hand, and was the dutiful son that he secretly longed to be.

Both of them were better men when they were successful, together.

And all the plots fell to pieces. No one at court was going to plot against rampant success. Philip, the best general in Greek history, had a son who bid fair to be his equal. We were headed for glory. Attalus took a fraction of the army and marched off to reduce Naupactus, just to keep Athens at the bargaining table, and after he left, the camp was like paradise.

Sophists and priests like to tell people that war is a terrible thing, and indeed, it can be – dead babes, children starving, horses screaming for a man to come and put them down. Horrible. But war in the summer in Boeotia, between Greeks, men of education, courage and principle, was merely the greatest sport man could invent, or the gods. Those who died, died in the flower of youth and vigour, and we feasted every shade. And those that lived were better for having eaten at danger's table and survived. And that is the other face of war – the contest of the worthy.

It went on for months, and while we faced the allies across the dance floor of Ares, we skirmished with their cavalry every day, we rode in races, we wrestled, we ate well and every night Nike took me in her arms. And Alexander ate with our mess once a week, when he wasn't in the field. And Nike began to organise the camp girls – not that she was one of them, but neither did she put on airs.

Good times. I never tired of her. I captured a beauty one day – captured is too strong, but my patrol snapped up a dozen boys and a girl headed into the enemy camp, and the girl was my share. Hair like honey, big tits and a tiny waist – I sent her home. I had what I wanted. And I did it as a sacrifice to Aphrodite.

The wheat was ripening in the fields and the barley was golden when it became plain that no matter what we offered, Athens intended to fight. The last straw was Naupactus, a vital Athenian naval base. Attalus took it – he was a good soldier, despite being a total shit of a man – and at that point, Athens *should* have wanted peace. Instead, they marched their ephebes over the mountains, brought up four hundred more Hippeis, and the cavalry war heated up.

The new Athenian cavalry were better – the best we'd faced, with excellent horses and better discipline. Of course, they were the real aristocrats, most of whom were politically in favour of Philip – members of Phokion's party to a man. Whatever their ethics, they had superb horses and they were crafty devils.

That's the first time I saw your pater, sprig. He was a troop leader, like me, and we tangled twice in a row, honours even. His troop was excellent – not as rock hard as my boys, but better mounted. He caught me flat-footed at the edge of the hills over towards the Kerata Pass, and I caught him the next day, his troop tired and too strung out on the road – but while the men were tired, the mounts were fine, and I got one prisoner, a scruffy peasant boy named Niceas – he was allowed as he was a hyperetes, which with us is a servant, and I slapped his arse and told him to stay out of the fighting. More fool I. Among Athenians, that made him an under-officer, the troop leaders' right hand.

Laugh at me, will you?

It was that night, though, that Philip called all the officers together and told us he was going to attack. He didn't make a speech – we'd lived it. We knew that we'd done our bit, and that if Athens and Thebes held us here until winter, we'd have to go home and start the whole thing again next summer, storm the Gates of Fire or some other damned pass – on and on.

So he outlined his battle plan, which was simple – that his foot would defeat the Athenian foot, and force the Thebans to open their ranks, and then the Macedonian cavalry would ride them down. And Alexander would command the cavalry.

All the younger men were silent after he announced his plan. Philip was the best general of the day – but we were going uphill into a larger army, an army with the Sacred Band, the most feared taxeis of soldiers in the world; a regiment of pairs of lovers, each bound to the other by ties stronger than steel. You know the Plato—Phaedrus speaks in the *Symposium* and says:

And if there were only some way of contriving that a state or an army should be made up of lovers and their beloved, they would be the very best governors of their own city, abstaining from all dishonour, and emulating one another in honour; and when fighting at each other's side, although a mere handful, they would overcome the world. For what lover would not choose rather to be seen by all mankind than by his beloved, either when abandoning his post or throwing away his arms? He would be ready to die a thousand deaths rather than endure this. Or who would desert his beloved or fail him in the hour of danger?

The Thebans built their regiment just that way. And they were unbeatable.

And behind or alongside them were the deeply ranked professional

Theban hoplites who had beaten the Spartans, and the Athenian hoplites who, whatever their failings, were reputed as the most tenacious in the Greek world. It has become fashionable to view the Athenians as second-class soldiers. Don't ever confuse your own propaganda with the truth. And the younger men had grown to manhood on tales of Athens' greatness.

It didn't sound like a great plan to us.

And the older men didn't like it any better, because Alexander, not Parmenio, had the cavalry. Parmenio wasn't there – he was busy holding the Chersonese and keeping the Thracians at bay – but even Antipater got a subordinate command. Alexander had all the cavalry – all the Thessalians, all the Thracians, all the scouts and skirmishers and, of course, all the companions.

Philip left his horse and went to serve on foot, leading his precious hypaspists. Demosthenes said that Philip had fucked every man in the hypaspists, and Philip retorted that Demosthenes had an extra arse instead of a face.

We moved our camp forward, and Alexander pitched his tent under an ancient oak, and we camped around him, street by street. It was a clear declaration that we were coming to fight – we knew it, they knew it and a hundred thousand men, more or less, had bad dreams, sharpened things, polished things and were afraid.

The allies tried to outflank us to the south, by the citadel, where the rising ground gave them a natural advantage. That's where the fight started, in the first light of dawn, and I was still drinking hot wine and trying not to throw up my porridge. Luckily, I had other people to worry about – an excellent way of remaining brave.

Besides, Nike was watching me. She was right there – not a distant rumour of womanhood back in Macedon, but the living embodiment of feminine opinion, and she did a great deal to make us what we were. Young men will compete for a woman's good opinion, if she is worthy.

Besides, as far as we knew, there was nothing of which she was afraid.

When Polystratus brought my charger, Nike held the bridle, gave me a stirrup cup, said the prayer of Aphrodite over me and poured wine on my sword – and on Nearchus's and Philip's, too.

She kissed me – not a long, lust-filled kiss, but a plain kiss on the lips. 'I'm pregnant,' she said. And grinned. 'So either way, you're covered.'

She meant that if I lived, I had a child to raise, and if I died, an heir.

Not sure if that's what every man wants to hear as he rides to battle, but for me, it was perfect. Something dropped away, and I rode to the prince with a light heart.

To our right, in the first true light of day, the phalanx was forming. In the best tradition of all Greek warfare, our best troops were on the right – the hypaspists and then the foot companions and then the phalanx, but all formed shield to shield in one long line sixteen deep and six stades long, covering the whole of the open ground from the rocks and scrubby ground at the base of the citadel hill, to the banks of the Cephissus river. Across the fields, just a few stades that a fit man could run before breakfast, the Thebans and Athenians formed, too. They had the Sacred Band on their right, so it was facing our rawest levies – not really all that raw.

I need to speak about phalanx warfare. Foreigners think that there's something to be gained by experience – by spending more time in the storm of bronze and iron. If you are a cavalryman, there's a great deal of truth to that assertion. Man and horse grow better every encounter – and when wounded, can ride away. It is a different form of war, on a horse's back.

But down in the dust on a summer's day in Boeotia, the advantage is often with the most fit, with the highest hearts. Older men who have seen battle may stay alive longer – but they also know the fear of the spear that slips past your guard unseen. Of the chance arrow. The fears of all the details that they survived the other times, when friends died beside them.

Sometimes, the bravest men are those who do *not* know what lies in store for them.

The Athenians were an army of veterans – most of their hoplites had made campaigns in the Chersonese, or as marines – against us, or policing their empire. The Thebans – they hadn't seen much action since they carved up the Spartans. No one really wanted to take them on. And opposite me, up that hill, they'd formed twenty-five deep. That did not look good.

But our farm boys looked surprisingly tough, when facing two of the most famous armies in the world. They had a touch of swagger to them that made me nod in respect. Some of our men had been to Asia – most had fought in mountains and plains, in the dark, in storms ...

They trusted Philip.

I sat my Poseidon by Alexander, and we watched them form.

'He's insane,' Alexander said quietly.

That snapped me back to reality. 'Who is, lord?' I asked.

'My father – Philip. He thinks that his hypaspists can go uphill into those Athenians and break them?' He shook his head.

I was caught between loyalties. I was absolutely loyal to Alexander – but Philip was Philip. A force of nature. He could not be wrong.

'If he throws it all away, here, we'll never get to storm Asia, Ptolemy. We'll be lucky to hold Macedon. We'll be some kind of historical side-note, like Alexander I and the battle of the Nine Roads.' His eyes were darting around – here, there, everywhere.

Hephaestion was mounted by now. He rode over to Alexander and they embraced.

A rider came from the king and ordered Alexander to send two troops around the army to watch the Athenian skirmishers on our right. Laodon got the nod, and I went with him. Troops cheered us as we passed behind them. They looked calm, as if on parade. I felt like I had a belly full of bees.

Laodon didn't seem too concerned.

'I don't want to miss the main action because I'm chasing slaves,' was all he'd say about being sent to the right.

When we arrived, we saw why we were needed – there was a stade-wide gap between the hypaspists and the edge of the bad ground, the product of a slight widening of the valley and just possibly a mistake on Philip's part.

We slotted into our place in time to watch some of our Psiloi get driven off the ground by allied skirmishers. It wasn't a hot fight, but the enemy had cavalry mixed in with their Psiloi, and they were killing our lads in short rushes.

Laodon shook his head, pointing at the ground. 'I'm not taking my knights into that,' he said. 'We'll kill more horses then men.'

I had to agree – he was older, and I thought he was right.

But the Athenian cavalry was in there, and they were having a field day against our javelin men. Finally the whole pack of our light armed gave it up and fled. They ran right through us, and rallied behind us.

Then we got to endure arrows and javelins. We pulled back, found a better piece of ground and the Athenian cavalry formed to face us and just sat there. We hooted at them, they hooted at us – our numbers were even, and neither of us had anything to gain from a charge.

Our light armed were ready to go forward again, and their leader was talking to Laodon, when a man came galloping towards us from the Athenian ranks. He halted a few horse lengths from our line.

'I am Kineas, son of Eumenes,' he called out. He declared his whole lineage – how he was descended from Herakles via the heroes of Plataea. He had beautiful armour, and a pair of white plumes in his helmet.

He was challenging us to fight man to man.

Laodon spat. Looked away. Young enough to be embarrassed – too professional to accept.

Not me. I took my good spear from Polystratus. I gave Kineas of

Athens a proper salute, and we went at it. We charged each other from about half a stade – a long ride, when you've nothing to do but contemplate mortality.

He got me. I won't spin it out, you must have heard the story from your uncles – turned my spear, got his spear up and swept me off Poseidon's back. The Athenian infantry at the top of the hill roared, and I was unconscious.

I knew he was the same man I'd faced twice in two days. So I got my sorry carcass mounted again as soon as I was able to think and see straight – he'd creased the top of my helmet so badly that I couldn't get it on my head properly and had to discard it, and I had a lump like an egg.

I got back on Poseidon with Cleomenes holding his head, and that was just in time to see Laodon's troop of companions crash into the nearest troop of Athenians – head to head, no manoeuvre. And their second troop was lining up, and there was no time to worry. My head hurt, but not enough to stop me doing my job.

The boys were quite kind, all things considered. I got some back slaps and some 'get the bastard next time' comments, and then I was in my spot at the head of the wedge. The Athenians were formed in a rhomboid, and they had some slope behind them.

And then we were off.

Troop to troop, same weight of horseflesh, same ground, not much to tell in skill – it might have been a bloodbath. It wasn't. We smashed into them, and I never got sword to sword with Kineas – we struck a few horse lengths from each other, and I was into the Athenian ranks before I had time to think about it, cutting to either side, taking blows on my armour and a heavy cut to my bridle arm – see the scar? But I kept my seat and burst out the other side of their formation and found that old Philip had started his infantry forward.

There was a third troop of horse – Thessalians under Erygius – and they smashed into the flank of the melee, bowling Athenian Hippeis right over with their long lances, and suddenly the whole pack of them was in flight, and the hypaspists cheered us.

I could see Philip, just a few horse lengths away. I saluted with my sword, and he waved. A handsome boy came running from his side.

Up close, I could see it was Attalus's pretty cousin, Diomedes. To me, he looked more like Ganymede.

'The king thanks you and orders you back to the left,' he said.

I saluted, and my trumpeter started blowing the recall.

It was all going according to plan, until the hypaspists slammed into the Athenians and the Athenians rolled them right back down the hill.

My lads were just behind them, crossing back from our right to our left by the shortest route, and we felt it when the hypaspists went into the Athenians. Not for them the sarissa – they had the hoplite spear, the dory and the bigger, heavier hoplite aspis. But they were not all individual athletes like the Athenians, and nor did they have a front rank in leg armour, sometimes arm, face and hand armour – a rich Athenian can look like a bronze automaton.

I heard all the excuses that night – there was a line of animal holes, men fell, the Athenians had dug pits in front – for whatever reason, our front rank stumbled and the Athenians gave a great shout and pushed, and our best were stumbling back.

We companions had to hotfoot along to get clear before they slammed into us and all order was lost. Laodon turned back at this point – against orders, I'll add – and manoeuvred to cover the flank of the hypaspists, in case the enemy light troops got brave. It was a smart move.

Whether Philip had intended it or not, his extreme right – his hypaspists – had engaged first, so that the entire army was echeloned from right to left, with the best troops leading the way and the worst following well behind. I've done this on purpose, but on that morning, I still think it was the result of the king being on the far right when he gave the signal to advance, so that the rightmost files stepped off first and started a sort of marching cascade.

It scarcely matters why – except that the whole army *saw* the king and the hypaspists recoil. And the Athenians raised a great cheer, sang the paean, and their whole line moved forward.

I couldn't rein in and watch – bad for discipline. But it didn't look good.

I kept turning my head and looking back as we rode – and the hypaspists were driven down and down the ridge, even as our rawest troops were marching forward into the Thebans.

When I reached Alexander, he was alone except for Hephaestion, well in front of all the cavalry.

'What in Tartarus is happening?' he demanded.

What exactly do you say? 'The hypaspists seem hard pressed, lord,' I said.

Alexander nodded sharply, eyes everywhere.

With a pots-and-pans sound audible even from a stade away, the centres met. The allies had the smaller town contingents and some dubious mercenaries in the centre. We had foot companions. Ours were better, and almost instantly they started to push the allies back.

Why?

The smaller a town is, the smaller its phalanx. Some towns have as few as three or four *hundred* hoplites. That means they've never served in a bigger phalanx – they usually don't form deep enough, and they aren't used to the terror of a dozen spear-butts with long bronze points licking around their heads. Oh – the rear ranks can be difficult.

But the worst is that the danger spots in a phalanx are always the joins – the places where two contingents line up – say Athens and Thebes. Those two files don't know each other – don't trust each other, don't lap their shields or anything like it. In fact, believe it or not, men from different towns or nations will often leave a gap, even though they know – *they know* – that the gap is a death warrant. Their distrust for other men is so physical they cannot close that gap. I've watched contingents of Medes and Persians do it, watched Aegyptians do it – and at Chaeronea, the centre of the allied army had a dozen little contingents and they had more joins than an old pot that's been thrice repaired.

In our army, of course, we had contingents of about two thousand – every one the same. All Macedonian, or like enough. We drilled them together. We had *no* joins. Our pots never needed repair.

Their centre fractured, as an old pot will when it takes a blow.

That transformed the battle, but it didn't give us a victory. The hypaspists and our right were still reeling back – the Athenians scented victory, and who could blame them? Traditionally, when an army's strong right was broken, the game was won, and the hypaspists were barely hanging together. They were still plodding backwards. The noblest thing I can say about them is that they didn't break, and I think anyone else would have.

But the crushing of the centre halted the Theban advance. Or perhaps the Thebans had never intended to fully support Athens. That, too, was part of Greek warfare. Leaving an ally to die was an old tradition – especially with two allies who hated each other.

Alexander was chewing his lip. His eyes went back and forth, back and forth, back and forth – like a caged lynx I had seen once at Pella. A desperate animal.

On our right, the foot companions to the left of Philip's elite began to bleed men from their rear rank.

'How can this be happening!' asked Alexander.

Hephaestion looked at me. I didn't have an answer.

It looked to me like a race between two men ripping sheets of linen. Would our centre blow through theirs? Or would our right collapse? I feared with every heartbeat that the call would go up that Philip was down, or dead.

Alexander's eyes stopped darting about and fixed on the centre.

'Here we go,' he said.

Remember, he was eighteen, and this was his first battle.

He saw it, he made the call and he led it. And by the gods, he never flinched once he made the call.

'Wedge on me!' he shouted. I pulled in at his back – not my normal position, but I was right there and we were doing this thing right then, I could see.

He grabbed Hephaestion's bridle.

'Go to Erygius – tell him to take four troops from the left and *fix the Sacred Band in place*.' He looked at his best friend. 'Do you understand?'

Hephaestion never really understood. 'I can take the message,' he said.

Alexander had an eye to the men forming behind us and another on the battle in front of us.

'Do you understand, Ptolemy?' he asked.

I knew exactly what he needed. But I wanted to charge with him. To glory. I saw what he had seen – minutes too late, but I knew, now, that Alexander was about to win the battle.

But being a loyal servant of a great prince is not all wine and gold. 'Yes, lord,' I said. In that moment, I hated Hephaestion, as the bitch had a look of triumph – I was sent away, and he was to stay with his lord.

'Take command of the left of the cavalry and do it,' Alexander said. Never one to do things by halves.

I saluted, gathered my reins and rode for it.

Erygius was busy packing his men into the prince's giant wedge when I rode up.

'Erygius – Alexander says I'm to take all four flank troops and go for the Sacred Band.'

If the old Lesbian was angered to be supplanted, he didn't make a fuss. His trumpeter called and the men behind him began to move – cursing to have to change and change again, something all soldiers hate – and Erygius turned his horse.

'We're going to charge the Sacred Band? Is he insane?'

'All we have to do is pin them in place,' I said.

Then Erygius nodded. 'I see.' He knelt on his horse's back and peered under his hand through the thick dust.

'I'm going to go ahead with . . .' I looked around, found that Polystratus had followed me. My men, of course, were part of Alexander's great wedge. 'Polystratus here. Bring the whole body in a column of troops around the left – see the big fir tree by the river? Make that your left marker. I'll meet you there – or just keep coming up the stream. See?'

Erygius peered and nodded. 'Ten minutes,' he said.

I leaned forward on to Poseidon's neck, and we were off like a bolt from a stone-thrower.

We went across the back of the army – by coincidence, across the backs of the two taxeis that I had helped to raise and equip. The indecisiveness of the Thebans had probably saved their lives, and they were clamouring to fight. In front of the Thebans, three or four men in brilliant armour were arguing.

The Sacred Band – the finest soldiers in the world – were standing in confident ranks, at the far left of our line. Just three hundred men. Three hundred Olympic athletes, more like. Even a stade away, they looked noble.

More important, they were about to move to my right – opening a gap.

This is war. What is as plain as the nose on your face becomes complex and fraught with peril. Men make decisions in haste, with limited information, surrounded by death. The Thebans decided to move the Sacred Band to the place that was threatened – an absurd decision. Philip decided to take his best troops uphill into the enemy without support – then was too proud to ask for help ...

Alexander identified the one weakness in the enemy line, worked through a way to exploit it and acted.

Erygius reached the foot of the hill by the tree, two hundred companions in a tight column behind him.

Alexander's wedge was formed. He raised his sword. I waved to Erygius. He led the cavalry up the hill in a column. And he was smart enough to start echeloning them forward into line even as he came.

I rode over to the left file of the newest taxeis. 'I'm about to take my cavalry through here,' I said. 'Can I have another half a stade?'

The file leaders started to call out.

The taxeis commander ran towards me.

The Sacred Band commander noticed me. He looked right at me. We were three hundred strides apart, but I swear I saw his eyes widen.

Alexander's charge struck the gap in the centre. I saw it happen – in some ways, I saw more of it than I would have seen if I'd been at his shoulder.

Erygius had the line formed.

The taxiarch came to my right boot. 'No orders in an hour! What's happening?'

'Alexander has just won the battle,' I said. 'All we have to do is keep the Thebans from winning it back. When my horse goes forward, you come with me. You hit them in front.'

'They'll *kill* my boys.' He looked at me – curiously; he was speaking as one veteran to another.

'Only for a minute,' I said.

Erygius was almost up to me. 'Stay with the horse!' I roared to the infantrymen. They all knew me – I'd handed most of them their first helmets. 'Hold the Sacred Band for a minute, and your names will live for ever!'

One of my best speeches. They roared, and to our front, the Sacred Band commander realised that he'd just given up the safe ground on the flank and now his army had no place to make a stand.

I got my horse into my place on the right of the centre troop. 'Rhomboid left!' I roared, and my trumpeters called it.

The infantry started forward – just fast enough that the Sacred Band no longer had time to march back on to their ground.

When you are sparring, there comes a moment when you miss a parry – it can be dreadful, because there can be several heartbeats during which you know how much pain is coming. When two boys who hate each other are fighting with wooden swords, there can actually be time to cringe. I've done it.

That's how the Sacred Band must have felt.

Our phalanx was well ordered; morale was good, the troopers down behind their small shields, their long spears licking away at the enemy, and they marched forward briskly, with flutes playing to mark the time.

My cavalry were slow off the mark – the product of too many formation changes and wheels, so that the slower men were behind the manoeuvre and the best men were annoyed by the apparent indecision. Erygius had swung them from a column of troops into line, eight deep – now we needed to pass the gap to the left of the phalanx, and that meant forming column on the leftmost troop, and it looked to me as if the order was given before some of the flank men had got into place from the last manoeuvre.

There's not enough papyrus growing on the Nile to give me space to write everything I want to say about the drill of cavalry, but all the priests in the world couldn't describe the depths of my ignorance at seventeen. I didn't know then that there's a moment in a real fight where all manoeuvre goes out of the window, and the good men fight and the poor men cower behind them.

So instead of ignoring the debacle, I rode over, halted the column and gave them time to form.

It was the sort of decision young people make, when they are deter- mined to do a thing well – correctly. The way they've been trained, and know it should be done.

It was a decision that cost a hundred men their lives. Because when our eager, well-formed, well-drilled farm boys hit the Sacred Band, those killers cut them down as a slave cuts weeds in the garden. I have never, before or since, seen anything like it. Our front ranks rippled and moved – rippled and moved – and it took me a moment to realise that the file leaders were being cut down, replaced by the men behind them, cut down in their turn …

I'm sure it didn't happen this way – but in memory, there's a fine mist of blood over the whole thing. A man was dying every time my heart beat, and my heart was beating pretty fast.

I can make an argument that my delay with the cavalry gave us the battle – the Sacred Band focused on the Macedonian pikemen in front of them, and ignored the much greater threat of my four troops of companions.

But that's what Aristotle called a 'false rationalisation'. After the fact, one can excuse anything – and weak men do. But here, beneath his tomb, in the comfort of the gods, I say that I got a generation of Pellan farm boys killed because I wanted my ranks dressed more neatly, and I knew it. No one ever mentioned it to me. I never even saw an accus- ation from them, the poor sods. They saw me as a hero.

Well, well. I'm an old man, and look! I'm maudlin. Cheer up. We're coming to some good parts, and your pater's in most of 'em.

We went forward at a trot, in a column of half-squadrons. The earlier shift of ground by the Sacred Band left a broad alley on their left, between their end file leader and the marsh that had been covering their flank. We trotted into the open ground, even as the farm boys to our right died like butchered animals. We could hear them die.

But they didn't give much more ground than the space left when men fell. That's what I meant before, when I said that sometimes inexperience is everything. They knew the cavalry was coming, they'd been told to hold for a minute, and as far as they knew, this is what happened when hoplites fought.

In fact, they were up against the worst nightmare in all the world of war, and they were standing their ground. Too stupid to run, really. But stupid or brave or what have you, *they* beat the Sacred Band. What we did was to kill them.

It was like the sort of thing you dream about, when you are thirteen, curling in a tight ball under your blanket trying to keep warm, back smarting from a whipping, and you want to go somewhere else in your head, be someone else, someone brave and noble and incredibly tough, who can never be whipped, never be beaten, never dirty or late for class or threatened with rape. Or at least, I dreamed of such stuff – of riding at the head of my troops, being in the right place at the right time, wheeling my squadrons, charging into the shieldless flank of my enemies and chewing them to red ruin before my invincible spear ...

Come on, son – don't you dream of such stuff?

Well, I did. Incessantly.

And here I was.

I raised my spear – someone's spear ...

'Column will form line by wheeling by half-squadrons to the right!' I roared. Just like that. Made you jump. Hah! I still have the voice.

And they did.

The Sacred Band must have known – right then – that they were dead men.

They got their end files faced my way.

You are too young to have been in a fight – let me tell this my way. Depth is everything, even when the men in the back aren't fighting. They are your insurance against disaster, their weight at your back steadies you, and their spear-points guarantee that if the man next to you falls, there's someone to step up into his place.

When we appeared on their flanks, the Sacred Band was fighting thirty-six files wide and eight deep. Chewing their way through three times their number in Macedonian recruits.

Then they faced their flank files. That meant that the whole left end of their formation had no support behind them – all those men turned to face me. Not to mention the miracle of discipline it is to face your flank files while fighting to the front. I had to do it later – several times – and only the best men can.

So immediately, some of the pressure slackened against our infantry. And you must remember – this is a big battle, the line six stades long, with each army almost two *thousand* files of eight to sixteen men wide – and I'm telling you about what was happening in the end forty files. Forty of two thousand – what's that? One fiftieth, that's how much of the battlefield I owned. And remember while I tell you this – the other forty-nine fiftieths of the line were also fighting. Somewhere, Philip was stumbling back, cursing, and somewhere else to his left, the foot companions were getting their butts handed to them by a bunch of pompous Athenians – in the middle, Alexander had burst through the back of the wreckage of the allied centre, and somewhere else again, the Theban line infantry was starting to give a little ground to the

Macedonians and *none of us* knew that any of these things were happening.

Walk. As soon as my whole line was in motion, Erygius had his trumpeter blow *trot*. I angled my path across the front of the cavalry and raised my spear. I was damned if the Mytileneian veteran was going to lead this charge. This was my charge.

In the cavalry school, when you are a page, the instructors – all men with a lot of fighting behind them – say that the crucial moment in a cavalry charge is when you are five horse lengths from the enemy spear-points. They knew what they were talking about. There is some complex mechanism – the sort of thing Aristotle would have loved to analyse – whereby man and horse make a nested set of decisions. I suspect it is the distance at which the horse can really *see* the spears. The horse has to decide for itself – over, around, through, back. And the rider – at once master and passenger – can convey determination or indecision with the slightest shift of his arse. Horses *know*.

I knew the moment I got out in front that the Sacred Band had their spear-points down and we were *not* going over them.

So I turned my horse and raced for the rear corner of their formation, as my charge dissolved behind me.

The companions baulked.

In storybooks, cavalrymen ride infantrymen down – crashing in through their spear-points, hewing to the right and left.

Not in real life. In real life, no horse will go through a formed, unshaken body of men – even if they are armed only with pitchforks or their fists. Daimon is *everything* in a fight between infantry and cavalry. The daimon that motivates men to fight, to stand, to flinch, to run – that daimon.

The Sacred Band were only eight ranks deep, so they had only eight files facing me.

The end two troops were actually well past the end of their line. I raced for them, caught the attention of their phylarchs and started them in a wheel – a broad sweeping wheel into the flank and rear of the Sacred Band.

Some of the men in the rear ranks turned, and some didn't.

I'm a quick learner. Having halted once to dress my ranks and missed an opportunity, this time I didn't wait for perfection. As soon as I saw that at least one troop leader had the idea, I led like a Macedonian should.

I set Poseidon's head at a gap in the enemy ranks where the fourth and fifth men in the rear rank were arguing. The corner of the enemy body was a mess.

This is where horseflesh means a great deal, because Poseidon was smart, strong and well trained. So I let him go. I didn't aim him – he aimed me.

And then – then, it was just me and the Sacred Band. About eight of them, at the right rear corner of their original formation – meaning that I was facing file closers and right file men, the very best of the best, except for the front rank.

I didn't think of all that. I don't think I thought of anything, except that it was good to be me.

Spears came up, but Poseidon had made his call and I made mine. I didn't have a lance – they were never as popular then as they are now. I had a heavy hunting spear, a longche, which Polystratus had put in my hand, and I threw it. It went somewhere – who can tell in a fight?

I got my sword out *after* I hit their line. Poseidon got a spear in his hindquarters, and I got one right in the gut – a perfect shot, except that my cuirass turned the point and my knees were strong – I rocked, but I didn't come off, and the point slid over my shoulder and the shaft rang my bell – remember, I had no helmet.

And then my sword was in my hand – a long, heavy kopis. I cut down and back – a school shot, the one you practise endlessly for mounted combat, and for a reason – and caught something. I remember thinking that this wasn't so bad – that I was doing my duty.

And after that, it was all fighting. Poseidon slowed to a stop, and he reared every time I jerked the reins, but after the first ten heartbeats I couldn't even back him. I'd made a hole in the corner of their phalanx and now other troopers were pushing into it.

I do remember the first man I know I put down, because he was right under my right foot, trying to throw me from the saddle. There's a lot of wrestling in phalanx fighting, and his approach was correct – get me on the ground and kill me there. He got his shield shoulder under my right foot and started to lift, and I cut down – once, twice, a desperate third as my balance was going – cut chunks out of his aspis, and the sheer terror of being dismounted enabled me to get him, as the third cut went through shield rim, the visor of his Thracian helmet and in between his eyes, and he died right there. You don't often see it, but I saw it – saw his shade pass his lips.

Old Heraklitus said it was the best way to go, your soul all fire, in the heat of battle. Compared to rape or torture or cursed sickness or coughing your lungs out – sure. But it was better to be *alive*. Achilles says it – better the slave of a bad master here than king of the dead.

No shit.

He's the only one I remember. I yelled myself hoarse, probably

118

shouting 'Herakles!' over and over, like half the men on that field. The next thing I remember is that the pressure on my knees eased – suddenly there were horsemen all around me, and just a few Thebans between us – and then, before my heart could beat three more times, there were none.

Just like that – a cloud of dust, the stink of death, and they were gone.

In fact, a whole pack of Sacred Banders were still alive and fighting – over by the Macedonian phalanx, where they were safe from the cavalry and we couldn't tell one man on foot from another. But the *unit* was gone, and the whole flank of the Theban phalanx was open.

We never reformed, and we didn't really charge again – we went into their flank files in dribs and drabs, a few at a time – in fact, I suspect most men don't even remember a pause between fighting the Band and fighting the line infantry – but I was isolated at one end of the fight for a long time. Say, fifty heartbeats.

I got twenty men behind me in a small wedge and we rode to the right – our right – and we found another combat in ten horse lengths.

By then, the Theban line must have been coming apart. They were panicked to find us in their rear, and our Macedonian infantry was doing well enough at this end of the line.

I didn't know anything about it. Where I was, there was the reach of my sword and the impacts of their spears on my chest, my back, my greaves – I must have taken fifty blows, and only two wounds. Even with my head bare. I was lucky – and of course, after the Sacred Band, I was mostly facing men who'd already lost the will to fight.

Polystratus stuck at my bridle hand and like most Thracians, he never relinquished his spear, but stabbed two-handed, holding on to his mount with his knees. He used a heavy spear with an odd chisel point – he could punch it right through a helmet or a breastplate. But mostly, he blocked blows coming up from my bridle side – in fact, he was a constant pressure on my left knee, his horse always there like a companion's aspis in a phalanx fight.

After some time had passed, we could hear the cheers, and the men under our hooves weren't making the least pretence of fighting back. But the duty of royal companions doesn't end with victory – far from it.

The thing for which we train, the reason we're brutalised as pages and ride all day, every day and hunt animals on horseback . . .

. . . is the pursuit.

Beaten men don't defend themselves. They are easy to kill. But to-morrow, if you let them rally, they return to being grim-faced hoplites who will gut you if they can. There are a great many myths these days about the superiority of the Macedonian war machine. Perhaps. We had some advantages, some tactics, some technical knowledge and lots of good leadership.

But one thing Philip taught Macedon was to *pursue* ruthlessly. When Philip lost, his beaten troops usually slipped away covered by his cavalry, and when he won – well, men who faced him lost and usually died. They didn't come back to fight again.

Pursuit is an art within the art of war – a cruel, inhumane, brutal art. It requires high conditioning and discipline, because all a warrior wants when he's won a victory is to *stop*. And that's true of every man on the field. The daimon can handle only so much danger, so many brushes with death, so many parries and so many killings. The fatigue of combat is such that most men are exhausted after just a hundred heartbeats of close fighting. Or standing under a shower of sling stone, unable to reply – men are exhausted. Fear, fatigue and pain are all somehow the same thing after the first seconds of a fight. The better-conditioned man lasts longer and is braver. And so on.

Philip trained us to be ready to go on after the fight was over. It was our main duty, in many ways. Alexander had been positioned behind the centre – with all the companions – not to win the battle with a lightning strike into the enemy centre, but to exploit the victory that Philip thought he'd win on foot. That was his plan.

Now that the Thebans were breaking, it was my duty to harry them to death.

I could scarcely lift my arms, and keeping my back straight to ride was beyond me – but I found one of the troop trumpeters and started sounding the rally, and before I could drain my canteen I had twenty files of cavalry at my back.

Erygius was there. He gave me a big smile, smacked my back. 'You're not bad!' he said.

That made me blush.

'We need to get into the rout and crush them,' I said.

The veteran nodded. He shaded his eyes – did his trick of climbing a little higher on his horse and kneeling on his back. 'Hard to tell – the Kerata Pass must be west.' He waved towards what had been the centre of their army. 'Where Alexander charged. No point in carving these fools up – they're already trapped against the hills.'

Mostly, we had Boeotian dust and sunlight, and if it hadn't been for dead trees at the edge of the marsh, I'd have been lost.

'Let's head west,' I said.

He nodded.

Our horses were tired, but we keep our animals in top shape – by riding far and fast every day – and we swept across the back of the allied position, killing or scattering any opposition. Twice we turned to the south, on to rising ground – our objective was to block the Kerata Pass, not to fight every Theban soldier.

But far short of the foot of the pass, we found the rout, and then we became killers. The Thebans were utterly broken, and the Athenian hoplites weren't much better, although some of their best men were staying together. We slaughtered the Thebans – there's no better word for it – and I did so in a haze of fatigue. I was so tired that I didn't fully recognise that I'd passed from killing helpless Thebans to killing helpless Athenians until Polystratus took my bridle and pulled me up so hard I almost toppled off my mount.

We'd come pretty far – almost three stades – I've visited the spot since. The rout filled the pass, and men were forced up the sides like flotsam in a spring rain. My cavalrymen and Alexander's were all through the rout, hopelessly mixed in with the enemy, killing, or in many cases merely riding along, taking prisoners, or sitting on the high ground, watching. There is, as I have said, a limit to what even the trained killer can make himself do. Until Chaeronea I had killed six men – after, I never counted again.

But Polystratus hadn't reined me as a merciful gesture. He was pointing.

Virtually under my spear was a crouching man. His shield was gone, he had a light wound and somehow his chiton had got bunched into his zone so that his butt cheeks were showing – a pitiful sight. And he was weeping, begging me to spare him.

I fully intended to kill him in sheer disgust. But again Polystratus stopped me, pushing my spear away with his own.

'You have ears, or what?' he asked.

I swear that until he said that, the gods had quite literally closed my ears. I hadn't heard anything for hours.

I must have shrugged, or something like. He grinned. 'It's their great man,' Polystratus said. 'He claims ... well, listen to him!'

The crouching, bare-arsed man at my feet was Demosthenes the orator.

After that, I started taking prisoners. I was done killing – my whole body hurt, my right side was sticky and wet and cold with blood, and that reek – the reek of sweat and copper and excrement – was in my nose for a day – in the hair of my horse, in my own hair.

And I couldn't kill any more men.

I just couldn't.

I threatened, and some of them just pushed past me, as if they didn't care either, or as if they knew I was past my limit. It's almost like a failure of courage – your arm rises and falls, you kill and wound and maim, and then – and then, you can't do it any more.

I gathered a dozen prisoners, and as far as I could tell, I was the southernmost Macedonian in the whole host – the rest of the pursuit had halted below me. I didn't see Alexander anywhere.

And then the Athenian Hippeis showed what they were made of. Someone – not your pater, he was already down – kept a bunch of them together, and they came after me. I had to fall back along the rout, and as I went I picked up men – whole files, at times.

It was a curious form of war – I don't think a single blow was struck. We were exhausted, and so were they, but they were willing to fight to protect their infantry, and we were *not* willing to fight them just to kill a few more of the fools.

And no sooner had the Athenians got formed than the best of the infantry started to form on them.

Not enough to prevent the aftermath, but enough to save their precious sense of honour, their arete. Myself, I wasn't so impressed. Only later did I realise – when I was more of a veteran myself – what it took those tired, beaten men to stop running, find a little more courage, turn and stand their ground. I salute them. I didn't know it then, but they were probably the bravest men on the field.

I found Alexander with his father, well back down the field. By then, there were thousands of dead Thebans and as many Athenians – heaps for the carrion birds. Greece died there – old Greece, the Greece of Aeschylus and Simonides and Marathon and Plataea. They spent three hundred years building a golden world. We killed it in a long afternoon.

I've never been happy about it. When I played Marathon as a boy, I never imagined that I would be there when the dream of Athens died in the dust of Chaeronea – nor that my hand would hold the sword.

More wine, here.

Mid-afternoon. Alexander was so elated that he was a danger to himself – when I rode up to him, he threw his arms around me and said, 'Did you see me? Antipater says I won the battle. I did, too – Pater was getting beaten, and I saved us, and we won!' He still had his sword in his hand, and his blue eyes had very faint white rims around them – he looked like a dog in the agora run mad in the heat. Hephaestion looked worried – deeply worried.

His sword beat against my breastplate when he embraced me, and he almost pulled me off Poseidon's back.

'Get him out of here,' Antipater said to me.

I could see Philip, just a few horse lengths away. He had his back to us. His shoulders were slumped, and he looked old. He'd had a bad couple of hours.

'He's not making Philip happy.' Antipater played the court game better than anyone, and I had just enough intelligence left to understand.

'Come,' I said into Alexander's too-long embrace. 'Bucephalus is trembling with fatigue, lord. We need to get these mounts rubbed down and fed – see to our men, too.'

He let go of my neck and his sword pommel slammed into my temple.

'Oh!' he said – almost a giggle.

'Put that thing away!' I snapped. 'Better yet – give it to me!'

I took the blade closest to the hilt, tugged – and he kept hold of it.

'It is stuck to my hand,' he said, his voice a little wild.

It was, too. With blood.

'Zeus Lord of Kings, and Ares of the Bronze Spear,' I cursed. 'Polystratus – water here.'

'I just kept killing them,' Alexander said. He was going to cry. I'd seen it with younger troopers. I'm a callous bastard myself – killing itself didn't unman me like this.

Hephaestion got to us with a helmet full of water.

I poured it over his sword hand, and the sword came free, a little at a time. While Polystratus and Hephaestion got the sword out of his hand, I talked to him the way I would talk to a young trooper – to Nike when she cringed at thunder, the only thing that scared her – to Poseidon when he saw a snake.

'There's a good lad. Nothing to it – see the blood wash away? All gone. Let go, my prince. Well done – we won the day. *You* won the day.' Voice pitched just so.

'We did. I did.' Alexander sighed. 'They are so full of blood,' he said.

'May I invite you to dinner this evening, lord'?' I asked.

He managed a wobbly smile – his mouth folded so that he seemed to smile and frown at once. But he was mastering himself – he had a will stronger than any man I've ever met.

'I would be delighted, if it would not be too much trouble,' he said, his face smoothing even as he spoke.

Hephaestion gave me a small nod. We seldom liked each other much – but when it came to Alexander, we could pull together. But when the sword came free from the prince's fist, Hephaestion whispered in my ear –

'Philip will have a victory dinner.'

I nodded. Alexander was sitting straight, eyes darting – the white rims gone.

'One battle at a time,' I muttered, and Hephaestion gave me a quick smile.

'Let's get cleaned up and see to our horses,' he said to the prince.

I saluted, kneed Poseidon and cleared their path. Then I rode over to Philip. He was surrounded by sycophants – and officers. Older men, mostly.

They were telling him how brilliant his plan of luring the Athenians off the hill had been.

'It was our counterstroke that broke them,' Philip said to Laodon. 'When we turned on them, they couldn't stand.'

I remember thinking, *Oho, so that's how it's to be, eh?*

'Your boy thinks he won the battle himself,' Nearchus the elder said.

'Let him,' said Philip with a hollow laugh. 'Boys always think they are important. And the troops love him.' He shook his head. 'Cavalry against hoplites – what was he thinking?'

Saving your sorry arse, I thought.

Attalus's cousin Diomedes laughed a little too long. 'He's as mad as a dog in the heat, lord. We all know it.'

Philip turned and glowered at Diomedes. But he said no word, struck no blow. Something in this little scene told me that the words had been said before – that the catamite was playing a long game.

But Philip's somewhat careless glare silenced Diomedes, although I noticed that he had a 'cat's got the cream' smile on his over-thick lips. Then Philip noticed me.

'Well fought, son of Lagus,' he said, offering me his hand – a major favour, at court. He grinned – a genuine Philip grin. 'Although you got off to a bit of a rocky start.'

I rubbed the goose egg on my head and smiled back.

'Next time you represent Macedon in single combat, see that you win,' he went on, and most of the older men laughed.

'He was pretty good,' commented Antipater. 'Kineas son of Eumedes. I know him. His father's my guest friend.'

Philip nodded. 'One of Phokion's boys – what do you expect?' He clapped me on the back. 'You look like a man with something to say.'

I couldn't help but grin, despite my fatigue. 'I have a gift for you, lord.'

Philip raised his eyebrows.

I motioned to Polystratus, and he led the wretched Demosthenes forward.

Philip smiled as a wolf smiles at a lamb.

I slipped away, duty done, and suddenly all I wanted was to sleep.

But the path to camp crossed the brow of the hill, and there I found Philip the Red and most of my own troop, still mounted.

They were picking up their wounded and dead, like good soldiers, and I joined them, like a good officer.

That took us an hour – killing the worst wounded and picking up the least wounded of both sides. Something turns over in you – you kill, you can't kill any more, you help save one, and all you want to do is save them all. Men are complex beasts.

And I didn't want to stop. If I stopped collecting the wounded, if I paused in getting water – well, I'd have to start thinking about it all. Besides, as long as Cleomenes and Philip were working, I was working.

Our grooms came out to help.

We got all of our own – there were only eight – and then we started collecting our own infantrymen, and enemy infantrymen. They lay in neat rows, or all muddled together – some men awoke as if from sleep when touched, to stumble to their feet, barely injured – others had screamed themselves to wheezing silence and lay as a deer lies when he has your arrow in his guts and he's run as far as he can and the dogs have ripped his flesh and for some reason he's not dead yet.

Every time I got another wounded man on to the litter made by my horse and Philip's, I swore it would be the last.

But I kept going back. The younger companions were proving something, or saying something, or too young to know when to quit. I didn't know which. But most of us were out there.

Philip's victory dinner was starting – I could see the torches and the slaves – when I found your pater. He was lying almost alone in some high grass – I found out later that his friends had taken him out of the melee and laid him there, and then been caught up in the battle. He had three wounds – rather as I did, myself. Polystratus and I got him on the litter and took him back to the surgeons. He was deeply unconscious. And he'd lost his gorgeous lion's-head helmet, which I rather fancied, I must confess.

I was done. Your pater was the last man I moved off the field. A young healer found me, ordered me to sit, and I went down like a sack of grain. He wrapped the wounds on my arms and my thigh, looked at my scalp and pronounced me fit enough.

'Don't drink wine tonight, lord,' he said. He pointed at my scalp. 'A blow to the head does not go with wine.'

So I stumbled back to my tent. To where Nike had stood waiting, as I heard it, for seven hours.

She embraced me, blood and guilt and all. I never loved her better – except when she washed me clean of the blood, wrapped me in a blanket and laid me on some straw she'd foraged like the miracle worker she was. I was out in a second. Show me a man interested in a tumble in the hay after a fight, and I'll show you a madman. Men talk about it. Show me one who got laid after Chaeronea.

I slept.

For about an hour.

Nike woke me. 'The king has asked for you. At his dinner. He means to honour you. So they say.'

I wasn't stiff yet, and I was young enough that I was able to function, but I felt as if I'd been wrapped in felt and kicked a hundred times by giants. Everything seemed to come to me from afar – words, thoughts, gestures.

Nike was worried. Polystratus had a look – I didn't like his look.

'What's happening?' I asked him.

Just beyond the lamplight of my tent, someone was standing. The messenger from the banquet, I assumed.

'Clean chiton,' Nike said, laying a soft wool cloth over my arm. 'Best gold pins. Myndas, get the sandals on him.'

Polystratus pitched his voice very low. 'The king and prince are not doing well together,' he said.

Nike fussed over my shoulder and the cuts on my arms. 'It's not fair. They can live without you.'

It was Cleitus. As soon as he moved at the edge of the lamplight, I knew it was Black Cleitus.

'Alexander listens to you. He needs to go to bed and stop bragging.' Cleitus shrugged. 'It's bad.'

I sighed. 'He did win the battle.'

Cleitus looked as if I'd slapped him. His loyalties were deeply divided – he loved the king, and he owed everything to Alexander.

'He's not insane, Cleitus. Just vain and tired. He won the battle, and Philip can't face it. I shouldn't have passed out. Who let him go to dinner?'

Cleitus appeared ready to cry – an odd face on a man who always looked like the worst thug in a darkened street. 'Philip ordered him. Hephaestion tried to stop him.'

I nodded, and Nike put my best cloak over my head, the pin already closed – tugged it, and planted a kiss on my lips. 'He's a grown man,' she said.

'He's not,' I answered, smiling, as I always ended up doing, even when we had a spat.

And then I headed off down the hill to find Hephaestion. Cleitus followed, begging me to come straight to the king.

'Relax,' I said. This is where being born a great noble with my own estates had its advantages. I could be late for the king – I could, if I had to, live comfortably *despite his displeasure.* So sod him.

I found Hephaestion standing in the door of the command tent under the old oak.

'Come,' I said.

'I wasn't summoned,' he said. Shrugged.

'I order you,' I said. 'On my head be it. Alexander needs us.'

Hephaestion nodded, pulled on his best cloak. 'Thanks.'

What we found at Philip's great tent was an orgy – an orgy of middle-aged self-congratulation and bragging, the sort of thing that writers of comedies think is only done by boys.

I'm past the age now that Philip was that night. I understand now how much worse the experience of battle is when you are older, when other men are faster, when the joy of the thing is utterly gone, when there's nothing to war but a vague feeling of shame because your *kingdom* is killing all these nice young men. Oh, yes. That, and the endless pain of the body – even the hardest body. The failure of reflexes, the slowing, the dimming of vision ...

... and so, when you win that victory, when you put your man down, when you bed a beautiful girl, it is a greater victory, and you brag as you did when you first did these things – from relief that you still can.

Trust me on this, boy. The only thing worse than experiencing the ageing of the body would be to *not* experience it – to have your body rotting somewhere in the mud.

They were loud, and they were behaving badly. When I arrived in the royal precinct, Philip had just stumbled out of the tent. He had Demosthenes dressed in a purple robe, being prodded along with a spear – a dozen other Athenian leaders were there, too, and Philip was leading them on a tour of the battlefield. He was drunk – drunk even by Macedonian standards. He had most of his cronies by him, too – Attalus was there, and Diomedes, and Philotas, Parmenio's son, and Alcimachus, one of his somatophylakes. And over against the tent wall was Alexander. The prince was *alone.* I'd never seen anything like it – there were no courtiers with him. His face was the face of a statue – pale in the moonlight, and set like good mortar.

'I'll show you poncey Greeks how a battle is fought,' Philip declaimed. He took a spear from the guards to help him walk, and with it, as they went out on to the field, he prodded Demosthenes.

'Demosthenes, Demosthenes' son, Paeonian, proposes!' he roared, and all his cronies laughed. In fact, it was funny. Philip had one gift his son never had – a strong sense of peasant humour. He was parodying the great Athenian orator's delivery – the way he'd rise to his feet and start in against Macedon.

Philip prodded him with the spear. 'Philip son of Amyntas, Macedonian, imposes!' he shouted, and the Macedonian officers roared their approval. I saw Alexander, then – caught his eye.

Just for a moment, I could see what he was thinking before the mask snapped back. He was looking at the king, and his mouth and eyes roared their contempt.

I had never seen him like this.

I got Hephaestion to his side with the same ruthlessness I'd massacred routing Athenians – I stepped on feet, used my elbows – I was richer and better born than they, and they were drunk. I elbowed a swathe through the staff and got to Alexander before he exploded, and Hephaestion actually grabbed his arms.

We started on a battlefield tour.

Battlefields are incredibly grim at night – but you know that. Dead things and things that eat dead things. And a bunch of drunken Macedonians and their prisoners.

I walked with Alexander, Hephaestion, Cleitus and Polystratus for a stade, and then, when I thought it safe, started to slip away. But Philip was wily-old, wily, and somewhere down inside, desperately angry.

'Going to bed so soon, son of Lagus?' He came back through his staff, locked an arm around my neck and his breath stank. 'Drink!'

'The surgeons told me ...' I began, and then Attalus pinned my arms and Diomedes poured wine down my throat. I bathed in more of it than I drank.

I was sober.

Attalus had arm-locked my left arm. He did it casually, and to cause me pain.

I got an arm up, reversed Attalus's hold and slammed his head into the ground. If I didn't dislocate his shoulder – well, I must have hurt it a great deal.

There comes a moment in your life when you must make an enemy. Up until that moment, I was a good boy who served my prince and did what I was told. I never played the factions. I did what my pater had done – stayed clear.

Until fucking Attalus put his arm around my throat and poured wine into me. That was it. I knew what he stood for. Knew who he was for and who he was against, and as soon as I had the leverage, I threw him over my hip and put him head down in the dirt.

'If I want a Ganymede, I'll choose my own. A pretty one,' I said to Diomedes.

He tried to slam the wine bowl into my head.

Alexander got him in a head lock. The prince was completely sober and completely in control of himself. In fact, in his horrid way, he was enjoying the bad behaviour of the others. He locked Diomedes up and began to force his head down against his chest.

'Let him go,' Hephaestion said. 'He's just a little arse-cunt. Lord – let him go. Don't do this . . .' Hephaestion recognised, as I did not, that Alexander meant to break his neck.

All at once, Alexander released his hold and the handsome man collapsed.

Philip had walked on. The entire drama had played out in twenty heartbeats, I had made a bitter enemy and Alexander had acted to support me. Heady stuff.

Philip was already standing near the centre, where our pikemen had shattered the allies.

He was pointing dramatically to the west.

'We'd already turned,' he said, 'and started to drive Athens back, when—'

'Like fuck you had!' said a young man with the prisoners. Your uncle Diodorus – one of the richest men there, and hence, on the guest list.

Philip whirled on him. 'We folded the Athenian hoplites—'

Diodorus laughed. 'Save it for an audience who weren't actually there, King of Macedon.'

Alexander, who until then had been so completely in control of himself, laughed.

Every head turned.

A brittle silence fell, and while it stretched on and on, every one of us waited for it to be broken.

Into that moment came a mounted man, wearing a green cloak and bearing a heavy bronze staff. He came out of the dark, and Hephaestion spoke to him – at the edge of my peripheral vision.

He was a good-looking man, and he dismounted in respect, but stood as straight as an ash tree.

'I am the Herald of Athens,' he announced. 'I request words with the King of Macedon.'

'Fuck off,' Philip said.

The herald started violently.

I thought that the king had misspoken, but he went on. 'Fuck off – Athens is done. I'm the victor here, and if I want to send all these worthy men to my silver mines – it's my whim. Athens is done.'

Demades – another one of the prisoners, and another famous orator – stepped up behind Diodorus, who stood with his arms crossed. 'Philip, stop being a drunken tyrant!'

Odd that no Macedonian uttered those words. Or not so odd, given what happened. Athens had some great men.

'Shut up,' Philip said.

'Fortune has cast you as Agamemnon, and you seem determined to be a drunken satyr,' Demades said. 'Be worthy of your victory, or be forgotten.'

Philip stood up straighter – as if he'd been slapped.

I waited for him to take his spear and gut the orator. I must say, even Demades flinched.

But Philip furrowed his brow and then, with a grand gesture, tossed his wine bowl.

'You, sir, have the right of it,' he said to the stunned Athenian. 'I'm drunk, and playing the fool.' He nodded, five or six times. Turned to the herald.

'Forgive my impiety, friend. Yes, of course great Athens may bury their dead. A three-day truce from now. And I have prisoners – Demades here will know their names. And more of your wounded with my surgeons. I seek no more war with Athens.'

Well.

I like to think that one of the signs of greatness is the ability to know when you've been an arse and apologise. But I've never seen it done so publicly, by such a great man. That was the measure of Philip, right there.

He tapped Diodorus on the shoulder as he passed him, walked over to Alexander and embraced him.

'I might have lost without you today,' he said. 'Whatever spirit closed my mind to it – I see it now. Thanks, my son, for a field well fought.'

They were the right words, and I swear by all the gods he meant them.

About two hours too late.

Perhaps if I hadn't had a nap. Perhaps if I'd stayed by Alexander, or Philip.

Or perhaps it was the will of the gods that two men, both so far above the common man, should demand each other's esteem in a way that could only lead them to war.

The next day dawned bright and clean, despite the stacks of naked corpses. Philip forbade any further pursuit – suddenly he changed roles, and we were to act the saviours of Greece and not the tyrants.

He was always a merciful man—once he'd won his victory, the sort of man who instantly forgives any man he has beaten, in contest or in battle. And he was as changeable as his son, and usually unable to keep to the harsh lines he often set himself. In truth, a few more dead Thebans might have done everyone a world of good, including Thebes, which might yet stand.

I awoke as randy as a satyr, despite stiffness elsewhere and serious pain in my shoulder, and Nike satisfied me with a sort of impatient 'I need to get on with my day' response that moved me to work her pleasure until I made her squeak.

I was, you see, alive.

Alive is better than dead by a long, long way.

I went and saw to my troops and my horses, walked the lines, visited my wounded.

Kineas the Athenian was awake.

I took his hand. He knew me from the fight, and I remember laughing at his confusion, and we shook hands.

'I imagine you'll be with us for a while,' I said. 'Are you worth a ransom?'

He nodded. 'A good ransom,' he said.

I never saw a penny, of course, because Philip declared the Athenians free – even Demosthenes. The Thebans he kept – even sold a few as slaves – but the Athenians walked away.

But Kineas stayed with me while he healed. He and the mouthy Diodorus were fast friends, I discovered, and I included them in my mess, so that every night we ate together – Nike and Kineas and Cleitus and Diodorus and Nearchus and Philip the Red and Kineas's hyperetes, Niceas, who was the boldest lower-class man I ever met. He and Polystratus got along like brothers, and Niceas's open mockery of aristocrats everywhere got into Polystratus's speech as well.

It was a good month. We ate and drank and threw javelins when we were healed – went for rides, sometimes all together, while the envoys went back and forth.

Philip sent Demades with his demands, and Athens sent him back with Phokion to stiffen his spine – Athens' best general, their noblest soldier and my new friend Kineas's mentor. The man was eighty. He was a stick figure of sinew and muscle who exercised constantly. Diodorus called him the 'Living Skull', but Kineas obviously worshipped him. He was guest friend to Philip, and one of the few men in the world who could lay claim to having beaten him in battle.

I didn't see him the way Kineas did, but found him dour, rude and incredibly stubborn. Alexander, on the other hand, all but fell in love with him – sat at his feet, listened to his harsh remedies for men's ills, agreed with his utter condemnation of all bodily pleasure ...

Aphrodite! He was a dry stick. I left them to it and went riding. We had no duties except to move our camp when the men and horses had fouled the ground too much for it to be pleasant to live on – fifty thousand men do a lot of pissing in the dark. So do horses.

Kineas took us across the plains to Plataea. We already knew that Philip was going to restore Plataea's independence – one of his little ploys to pose as the preserver of Greek freedom. Plataea welcomed us again, and ten of us spent days there – we stayed in a fine farm with a stone tower at the top of a low hill overlooked by Mount Kithaeron. Kineas's family owned the farm, and he said that it was the ancestral home. That was a happy time – we ate too much, slept late in the mornings, went to the assembly of the Plataeans and were treated as great men. Nike's belly started to swell.

Kineas ceased to be my prisoner early in the arrangement. We were well matched – he was as wealthy as I, well educated and well read, and he could ride. We raced horses, and talked and talked.

When you are a nobleman, there aren't that many peers to talk to – most want something and the rest are potential rivals. I was never going into Athenian politics, and Kineas was never going to be in the royal court of Macedon. We could agree or disagree – we could enjoy the pleasure of saying 'me too!' in the security of knowing that, as equals, if we said 'me too' we meant it.

Kineas's friend Diodorus had a wicked turn of phrase that I couldn't get used to – like Niceas, he said things that were better left unsaid. And after the peace talks were under way, Kineas's other friends appeared from Athens – Grachus, Lykeles and a few more. We went hunting behind Parnassus, and we spent a week holding an amateur set of military games, all of which was started by Diodorus's claim that Athenians were better cavalrymen than Macedonians. We won. But not by much – and Kineas won most of the contests that he entered. To see him throw a javelin from horseback was to see how it was meant to be done.

And then – one night Nike had a sore stomach, the next she was apologetic about being in bed, and the third – she was dead, and our baby with her.

That's when Kineas and I became friends, young man. I sat with her corpse for a long time – holding one of her hands. I didn't really believe she wouldn't come back to me. I was numb and angry at the same time. And the mound of her pregnancy seemed the harshest mockery – pregnant women are supposed to be immune to disease. And I considered self-murder. She was that much to me that I didn't really see what I had to live for.

I sat there for two days, in her folding chair by her corpse. Alexander came and clutched my shoulder and kissed her. That meant a great deal to me. But he left, and then Kineas came, and left. Cleitus and Philip and Nearchus and Cleomenes came, sat with me, and left.

After a couple of days, Kineas came again. This time he was dressed for riding.

'Come,' he ordered me, and I simply rose and followed him. Don't know why.

We rode through a long afternoon, and camped under the eaves of Kithaeron. He killed a deer and we ate it. I swear that in the whole evening he said only 'Salt?' and 'Have another helping'.

In the cold mist of dawn, we rode on, up the mountain. Up and up. Until we were on the flat of the crest, with the sea a golden blue in one direction and all Boeotia spread beneath us in the other.

'Bury her here,' he said. 'With my people.'

Then I wept, and then I nodded, and then I discovered that her corpse was in a wagon at the base of the mountain.

We burned her in the high place, and her ashes went into a pot with a maiden and a child painted on it, and then we put her at the top of the mountain with all those Plataean heroes.

And the next few days are lost to me. There's nothing there.

But your father and I were ever friends from that day forward.

SIX

—◈—

When I returned to the camp, it was to find that Alexander had been appointed ambassador to the Athenians, with Antipater and Alcimachus to support him. I was to go with him to Athens – in fact, I was the escort commander for the ashes of the dead Athenians. Kineas was appointed the commander of the Athenian escort – fifty troopers in armour as good as that of Philip's inner circle.

One of the worst penalties of loving a commoner is that no one expects you to *love* her. When I returned from burying Nike, Alexander acted as if I should be done with her. She was dead, I had work to do as his escort commander – time to move on. Nearchus and Cleomenes avoided my eye when I showed signs of emotion. As when I discovered that no one had moved any of her things out of my tent – men can be the most thoughtless beasts. I packed her belongings – every chiton, every pin, every present I had given her.

Oh, the pain. Some men and women move in and out of love – it comes and goes. Yes? Not me, lad. I love for ever. I can still feel it – walking into the tent, thinking I was healed, and seeing her things strewn about. Zeus, I was nearly sick.

But royal pages are bred tough, for war. I survived it. I was enraged every time a man threw me a look that indicated that I should 'get over it', and I determined – in fact, I swore to Aphrodite – that the next time I knew love, I'd marry her, even if she was a common prostitute. If only so that I could have a year of mourning.

And the Cyprian was listening.

So as I relate the next few months, keep in mind that Nike was never far from my thoughts.

I'll also note that two men never asked me to *get over it*. They were Kineas the Athenian and Cleitus the Black. Both of them seemed to understand at some unspoken level. One afternoon, I was helping

Myndas make up a fire, and I found that he was using her firebox – a firebox I'd given her. Myndas got the fire started and I just crouched there on my haunches, holding the box in my hand.

Cleitus came to find me for Alexander – crouched by me. Took my hand, and held it for a second or two – pressed it, took the box away and said, 'Alexander wants you,' as calmly as if all had been well.

But perhaps it is the greatest tragedy of being a mere mortal – and greater men than I have written poems on the subject, I know – that all things pass. The pangs of love, the roaring fire of hate – even the pain of loss. Even a week after I burned her corpse, I was in Antipater's tent, proposing to him that we buy a dozen Athenian armourers to have a better product in Pella, and he was agreeing that that was an excellent project. We were both impressed – and a little envious – of Kineas's troop, in their ornate repoussé helmets like lion's heads, men's heads, with silver hair and gold cheeks, or with scenes from the *Iliad* on the cheek-pieces – and still superb work that would turn a heavy blow. Not to say we didn't have good armourers in Pella – but we didn't have fifty cavalry troopers like that fifty.

Later, in the fullness of adulthood, I realised that they sent their very richest, best men – probably with the picked best armour of the whole city.

Worth noting here that soldiers are popinjays. Beautiful armour *is* good for morale. When you are shitting your guts out in a three-day freezing rain, waiting to be sabered by some Asiatic auxiliary, it raises your heart to know that you look like a hero, that your gold-figured spear is the best spear for parasanges. Men who look good are tougher and better. Only armchair generals think that you can coat a man in mud and get him to fight well.

At any rate, I started to use Polystratus as my hyperetes, just as Kineas had Niceas, and he was merciless on details of harness and dress. Men had got slack as royal companions – as veteran campaigners, with servants and grooms and leisure time. I wasn't in a particularly good mood – in fact, I was unrelentingly savage, so much so that Nearchus and Cleomenes found somewhere else to eat for weeks.

But when we marched for Athens, my troop shone like the sun, and if their equipment wasn't as spectacular as the Athenians', the way they filed off from the right looked like a trick rider's performance in the hippodrome, and every spear was held *just so*.

Polystratus got himself a trumpet. It wasn't like any other trumpet in the Macedonian army – it must have been Keltoi or Thracian, with a hideous animal's head and a long mouthpiece. Niceas, the Athenian, made a scabbard for it.

We went up over the passes, and came down the other side into Attika, the richest province in the Greek world. I couldn't *believe* how thickly settled it was. There was a farm at every turn of the road, and it was a struggle every night after we came down the passes to find a campsite large enough for two hundred horse and their mounts and servants. We camped in farm fields, we camped on somebody's recently cut oat stubble – gods, Attika is rich.

It was our third day. On the second, priests came out and blessed us, blessed the road, and welcomed the ashes of their dead home. But on the third, we met the families of the dead men.

Some of them were men I'd killed myself – panicked men who did me no harm, killed in the rout like cattle or sheep in a pen. It is one thing to kill them, and another to be blessed by their priests, and then to have to meet their wives, their sons and daughters – their parents.

They bore us no love, either. It was the mothers, I think, who got to me most. Their eyes would caress me with a kind of ecstatic hate – in my fine armour and on my mighty Poseidon, I was *the Macedonian*. Alexander looked young and innocent – and beautiful (unless you looked deep into his eyes). I looked young and hard and had a big, ugly nose.

Most of the time, it is human to react to hate with hate. Or love with love. But there was something in the hate of those Athenian women that made me feel only pity, anger, shame. Pity for them. Anger at the fools who had led them to fight us. Shame at what I had done in the pursuit.

Perhaps I was insufficiently brutalised as a page. Maybe if I'd been raped by one of the older pages – it happened all the time, as a punishment – I'd have been the sort of murderous bastard who likes a good rout.

But I looked at all those mothers, and I saw my own mother, I saw Nike ...

Well. I went on killing men, so it didn't change me for ever.

Alexander saw none of this. I know, because our first night in Athens, at Kineas's father's house, Cleitus the Black and I had a halting conversation about the mothers, and Alexander looked at both of us as if we were giggling girls.

'War kills,' he said. He shrugged. 'Women weep. Men fight.' He turned back to our host, Kineas's father, Eumenes, and his admiration of Phokion.

The Athenians dedicated a statue to Philip. Demosthenes was exiled

– not for ever, but for a while. We got to meet Isocrates, who somewhat sycophantically suggested that the whole Panhellenic crusade had been Philip's notion and not his own – and his speeches in praise of Philip were deeply flattering. Alexander was made a citizen of Athens.

I spent evening after evening sitting with Eumenes. I missed my own father, and Eumenes was a good man – deeply conservative, well read, equally interested in Plato and in the breeding of dogs. He bore us no rancour – he was sure that fighting Macedon had been a mistake from the first.

Altogether, our reception in Athens was a masterpiece of diplomacy. There were people who hated and feared us – and no one tried to hide that from us. There were people who had always wanted our alliance. There were men like Kineas who wanted our alliance but had fought hard at Chaeronea to stop us.

Every day I learned more about democracy. Democracy isn't a theory of government – it is a code of behaviour that allows a lower-class man to call me a murderer in the street, if he wants to. His neighbour may call me the saviour of Greece. They may share a cup of wine in a wine shop, still arguing.

Not like home. Interesting. It didn't seem to work very well – but the dignity of the commons was amazing, vital and not like anything you'd see at home, where a twenty-year veteran of the king's army would stand in the mud to let a thirteen-year-old aristocrat go by with his feet dry. That just didn't happen in Athens.

Kineas and his friends were very much like us – we shared so many things that it was difficult, sometimes, to comprehend how deeply they were *not* like us. They had a respect for their commons – an acceptance of their power, their needs – that seemed at once weak and noble.

Athens had a great deal to offer, and I drank it in as I recovered from my loss. I had no duties, so I arranged to go to the theatre and to the assembly – sometimes with Eumenes, sometimes with Kineas, sometimes with Diodorus, who turned out to be the political member of Kineas's band. He was an aristocrat – but politically he was a radical democrat and an enemy of Macedon.

'You watch,' he said one day over a cup of bad wine. 'Your Philip is going to demand that Athens send soldiers to support his crusade in Persia. And they'll send the Hippeis – we're all oligarchs, to the mob. And I'll spend my youth fighting *for* Philip.' He laughed.

I laughed back. 'And you'll do it – because you respect the institution of voting.'

He shrugged. 'I'd be a piss-poor democrat if I didn't obey the will of the people. Even when it is wrong.'

Athens had other pleasures. I think I mentioned earlier that Aristotle tried to teach us to hold a symposium. Well, suddenly I was living in aristocratic Athens, and I was invited to a symposium virtually every night. For the first few weeks I passed. My heart was ashes, and somehow I couldn't face the Athenians – as friends. So I sat at home with Eumenes.

But after my third visit to the theatre – the festival of Dionysus, the real thing, in Athens – Diodorus was going down to Piraeus to be with friends. It was like something from Socrates come to life. Too good to miss.

We walked down inside the long walls, and Diodorus pointed out how the walls were built in layers.

'Athenians only spend money on defence when they are in a state of panic,' he said with a nasty laugh. 'Look at the base layer – see the column bases turned on their sides? Pure Parian marble – try to crack one of those with your catapults. That was from the year Plataea was fought, when Themistokles came back from Sparta and led us in building as fast as could be done. And atop it – mud brick, unbaked. That's how it was finished.' We walked along for a while. 'Look here. Another course of marble laid down – and heavy stone atop it – the Thirty Years' War. Niceas, or even Alcibiades. Look at the towers!' He shrugged. 'We do good work when we're at our best. We're at our best when we're threatened, scared, angry.'

'Like men,' I said.

Diodorus glanced at me.

'You aren't what you seem at all, you know that?' he said. 'Kineas said you were ... a thinker.'

'Doesn't exactly show on my face,' I said. 'It's OK – I thought you were just an angry young man, all talk and no depth.'

And stuff like that. Making friends is the best way to pass time that there is – I had months in Athens, and I made friends that lasted me the rest of my life. Kineas, Diodorus, Demetrios of Phaleron ...

But I get ahead of myself. We walked down the hill, talking about ethics and whether it was possible to have trust in a ruling class (my point) or acceptance of the stupid crap that the mob sometimes votes (his point) on faith. We agreed that either way, a lot of people were forced into acting on faith in other people's choices.

We arrived at a beautiful house in Piraeus – Graccus's house. He wasn't as wealthy as Kineas's father, and not as aristocratic – his father had built a fleet of merchantmen to trade with the Black Sea, and despite losses, they remained prosperous. But the house was a delight – pale stone and red tiles, a little above the street, and with a high central courtyard that had steps to a platform in the corner – so that on the platform, you could see the sea. We lay on couches watching the sun set. I had dined outside – what soldier has not? But I had seldom enjoyed it so much, a dinner of fresh-caught tuna and red snapper in parchment; deer meat in strips cooked on a brazier; bowls of spiced almonds in honey and little barley rolls. My mouth waters to recall it. And the wines – Nemeans and Chians, raisinated and clear and red, mixed with sparkling, bubbly water from some local shrine.

Graccus was a masterful host, with a good staff who loved him and worked to make us love him too.

I noted that Niceas, who was friends with my Polystratus and whom I treated as a sort of upper servant, shared Graccus's couch. Later – after four or five bowls of wine – Niceas came and sat by me. He was a courteous man – he sat, but didn't recline, until I indicated that he was welcome.

'I'm not a servant, here,' he said. He met my eye – we were only about a hand's breadth apart. 'I think you handle us well, Macedonian.'

'Are you and Graccus lovers?' I asked.

Niceas narrowed his eyes. 'Not really your business, is it?'

I offer this by way of the thousands of things that showed me how free Athenians were – that this lower-class man could tell me to sod off, and then grin, slap my shoulder and go off to dance.

Dancing, it turned out, was the order of the evening. Graccus had musicians – famous ones, not that I knew who they were, but they were incredible, to me. I was used to a kithara and a couple of flutes. This was a group of seven players, and they played songs I knew – and songs of their own – with a sort of mad, elegant violence, fast, harsh and yet precise. As if I'd never heard the notes before. Later, Kineas explained to me that this was the fashion, created by this very group, and that a lyre player had to be extremely skilled just to get the staccato notes out so precisely.

They had a couple of dancers, who proved to be more like instructors – the whole thing was hopelessly complex, because it turned out that these musicians weren't slaves, but freemen – famous freemen, who could demand high prices for their music and were playing for Graccus for free – because he had helped 'discover' them.

And the political discussion – that all government depends on the trust of one group in another, even in a tyranny – continued all around me. Men I'd never met – one of the kithara players, named Stephanos – sat on my couch, handed me the wine bowl and said, 'Good topic.'

Another man – with curly blond hair like Alexander's – sat down opposite me, on Kineas's couch. 'Are you really an oligarch?' he asked.

'I mean – you really believe in that horseshit, or are Macedonians so pig ignorant you've never thought about the rights of men?'

'Well,' I said, trying to not be offended while getting my point across. He was angry – so I smiled. That always helps throw oil on a fire, I find. 'I studied with Aristotle.'

'Pompous fuck!' my debater said. 'He thinks he's better than other men.'

'As do I,' I said. 'I think I'm better than other men. Debate me.'

There was a little hush – some men were still talking, but Kineas fell silent, as did Diodorus.

'In what way?' Blondy asked. 'I mean, how exactly are you better?'

'In every way. I am well born. Athletic. Intelligent. Rich. Educated.' I shrugged. 'I'm not handsome – which you are. So you are the better man in that respect, eh?'

'You are certainly no prize for looks,' he said, but he said it with a smile.

'So you concede that some men may be better at one thing, and some at another,' I said.

'Look, I've been to the lyceum, I know where this goes.' He shrugged. 'But do my superior looks entitle me to superior political rights?'

I nodded. 'If you combine them with superior oratory skills and a war record based on superior bravery and war skills, then they do – don't they? Athenian?' I asked.

Diodorus laughed. 'Good shot, Macedonian. He's got you there, Charmides.'

'You democrats want to make everyone equal,' I said. 'And in time, you will, if we allow you. You will make war on excellence to raise up mediocrity. Cut the tall trees down and call the trees that remain tall.' I looked around. Even the dancers had stopped. 'What if all this equality costs us heroism? Ambition?'

'Why?' Diodorus asked. 'I see a false assertion.'

'Where?' I asked. I was doing well, I thought.

'Why can't we all be equally great? Why not let every man be Achilles?' Diodorus glowed when he spoke. He was a true believer.

I shook my head. 'I've watched the circle around the king. The great men push other great men – but the petty men push only other petty men. Mediocrity breeds only mediocrity.'

I shut up then, realised I had spoken ill of my own among foreigners. Bad behaviour by any standard.

Diodorus snorted, dismissing my comment with a wave of his hand. 'Just because a passel of Macedonians—'

But Kineas shook his head. 'It is the same in the assembly,' he said. 'And you have said as much yourself, Diodorus.'

Blondy hopped off Kineas's kline and slapped my shoulder. 'All I care is that you believe in *something*,' he said. 'I'm Demetrios.'

Demetrios of Phaleron. The eventual Tyrant of Athens, and another of my lifelong friends. He was a rabid democrat in his youth.

So I count that argument as one for me and nought for the democrats, eh, lad?

The sixth bowl, and the seventh, and the eighth. I was dancing. Need I say more? The notes all made sense, and dancing a complex pattern with twenty near strangers was the most important thing in the world.

We danced the wine out of us – danced through moonrise. Lay back and drank water.

Graccus rose to his feet. 'Now, friends,' he said, and he mixed a fresh wine bowl – one to one, wine to water. Exciting. 'Some of my friends have decried the absence of women at my parties.'

Much laughter. Some finger-pointing, some rude gestures.

'And I thought perhaps to remedy this shortcoming' – he made the words *short* and *come* sound obscene – 'by inviting the most celebrated young woman in Athens to share our evening. Instead of a host of flute girls, I thought to bring one courtesan.'

'Does that mean we take turns?' Demetrios called out.

'Shush – one does not hire a hetaera for such rude stuff.' Graccus smiled.

'How would you know?' called Diodorus. 'You'd hire her as a cleaning lady. You don't even know what a porne is for!'

They were best friends, I gathered, because in Macedon, blood would have been shed.

Graccus made a face. 'I've heard – from friends.'

Everyone laughed.

'I think you are all too drunk to enjoy her wit,' he said. 'I promised her we weren't a bunch of drunken barbarians.' He looked around. 'I am serious, gentlemen. She's here as a guest, and not for wages. Treat her as such, or I send her home.'

Kineas glanced around the room. He was their leader – I don't think I really needed to say that, but in that moment I saw how powerfully he was their leader. He caught almost every eye – looking around. His message was as obvious as if he'd spoken aloud. 'Do not be bad guests, you louts!' he shouted with those eyes.

Kineas had a measure of what Alexander had in bushels. In fact, they had a great deal in common, I think. Kineas was Alexander muted;

he was not as brilliant, but I think more to the point, he had a loving mother and father, sisters, a home. He had never been betrayed, never brutalised, never taught that such things were normal. I saw it all in that glance of his eyes – when he commanded his friends to behave themselves, where Alexander would have enjoyed watching *his* friends make arses of themselves.

On the other hand – Kineas drew lines, and he never crossed them. Alexander never knew what a line was. I don't think Kineas would have conquered the world. Or wanted to.

As an Indian philosopher once told me, there is not just one truth.

As usual, I digress. Graccus brought a woman in, modestly dressed and heavily veiled – wool veils that showed us nothing. She sat, picked up the kithara that one of the players had put by – the players were all guests now – and began to play.

She didn't play the fast, harsh style of the men. Nor was her style particularly feminine. In fact, it had many of the same precise displays of notes – but it was slower, and she had phrases of music that seemed to have a rhythm of their own, like lines of song repeated.

But men are men, and most of the guests, fascinated at first to hear a woman play so well, drifted back to their conversations. I did. I wondered idly what kind of childhood a woman had to be so good at playing. I was thinking about Kineas and Alexander – at another level, I was thinking that in Athens, Nike and I might have married.

Demetrios was back, hectoring me to talk about oligarchy.

'Let him be,' Kineas said. 'He is a guest, not a performer.'

I had to smile at the notion of me, the Macedonian monster, as a performer.

We were swiftly drunk again. Graccus and Niceas kissed – something that would never, ever happen in Macedon. Men may move each other, but never in public! And Demetrios picked a fight with Diodorus, and they rolled on the floor – and they were fighting – fighting hard, grappling with intent to do real injury. Diodorus had the better of it, and they rose, embraced, and Diodorus rubbed the back of his head where, apparently, he'd struck it against the base of a kline early in the struggle. Demetrios fell backwards theatrically on to my couch. 'He's just better than I am,' he said, and giggled.

I had to laugh.

'We're going to go and get laid,' Demetrios said. 'Me and Diodorus. When he's done chatting up the hetaera. He loves them all – swears that if he's ever rich, he's going to buy one.'

Diodorus came and sat with us. 'Why not? Why have a twelve-year-old virgin just starting her courses when I could have a woman who can discuss Socrates and suck my dick with skill?' He shook his head. 'I'll buy her contract for life and have sex whenever I want!'

We were all eighteen, remember.

Diodorus leaned over. 'That's Thaïs. She's new – but a free woman, not a slave. People say she has a scar – never seems to take the veil off.' He shook his shoulders. 'Ooh, I want her.'

'Excellent figure,' I admitted. It is hard to hide a woman's figure under a chiton. This one had strong shoulders, a long back and long legs. And beautiful feet, the only part of her that showed, but a most excellent part.

Diodorus laughed. 'A man of taste, hidden under the barbarian! Come, let's get our spears wet.'

I must have looked at Kineas. He shrugged. 'I'm a prig. I'm for home. Some people need to remember that tomorrow is a feast day – the cavalry must be on parade. Yes?'

So they left – Diodorus and Demetrios together, later inveterate enemies. Lykeles, who had not been there for dinner, came in, played a song, embraced me and left. People were coming and going now, and I was pretty drunk. I remember having a pleasant conversation with a very aristocratic man with beautiful manners who proved to be a former slave and professional musician. Athens.

There were other women circulating, now – four dancers who were, somehow, obviously *not* available (at a Macedonian dinner, any woman you could catch was available) and a trio of flute girls who played very well indeed. They were comediennes, and very funny – they'd play a song, and then play a sort of slur on the same song – the largest girl would start to run her flute in and out of her mouth in a lewd way, and another would ... well, you are too young. Let's just say they *were* available after the eleventh or twelfth bowl.

I went out to piss, came back and found the veiled woman on my couch.

Before I could flinch, she laughed. 'I had nowhere else,' she said with a chuckle.

I liked the chuckle. She was referring to the fact that the larger of the flute girls was entertaining two guests at the same time, and she, the hetaera, was as far across the room as she could manage. But the chuckle let me know that while she was no prude, she was neither afraid nor really interested. Quite a lot to convey in a chuckle.

'Are you from Macedon?' she asked.

'Yes,' I said. I suddenly felt drunk. 'Are you really a hetaera?'

It is hard speaking to the blankness of a wool veil. I noticed that it was very fine, and moved slightly with her breath.

143

She nodded. 'I am.'

I lay back – a sign of intimacy, Aristotle told us. 'How do you choose such a road?' I asked.

'Women can have ambitions, just as men do,' she said.

'To open your legs for strangers? That's an ambition?' I said. Nasty words – I remember thinking as soon as they left the fence of my teeth that I should be ashamed.

She turned her head – a hand's breath away, just as Demetrios had been. But covered by a veil. 'Any way a woman turns, *man*, she is forced to open her legs for a stranger.' She said it without the least heat. But with the utmost conviction. 'I choose who they are, and see that they reward me.'

'A husband—'

'Is a tyrant chosen by others; an owner who pays no price, a client without a fee.' She turned her head.

'But marriage?' I asked. I'd never heard *marriage* indicted before.

'Sex from duty is like killing from duty, don't you think?' she asked. 'I mean, I wouldn't know myself, but I assume that when your prince orders you to kill, you kill, whatever you may feel about it. And when a girl's husband says "lie down", why then, she puts on perfume and lies down, or he beats her and does her anyway. Yes? So you would understand better than most.'

I sat up.

'When I want a man, I can have him, or not. And when I don't like him, I never have to have him.' She also sat up.

'I'm not sure the two are the same,' I said.

She let down a corner of her veil so that I could see one side of her face. She smiled. 'You are not the barbarian they made you out to be. I'm not sure the two are the same, either. But philosophy is the land of assertion, is it not? And I will insist that while most men proclaim that killing is bad, few seem to think that sex is bad. A man should be more careful who he kills, and for whom, than a girl who she beds, and for what.'

I had to think that through – her Greek was so pure, so *Attic*, and she'd just said ...

I got it, and I rocked the couch laughing. 'You are a philosopher,' I said.

'I like a good time, too. Red wine. A fart joke.' She laughed. 'But a girl who can't talk to philosophers won't get far in this town.'

People were looking at us. Graccus raised his wine cup in my direction.

'You are with Prince Alexander?' she asked.

144

'Do you always ask things to which you already know the answer?'
I asked.

'It's a good idea for a woman,' she said. 'Since men seldom listen to
us, and often lie.'

She didn't sound like a whore. At all. Or a stuck-up Athenian philosopher. Her eyes were beautiful – blue, deep as the sea.

'I listened to you. And I assert that I kill for my prince of my own
will.' I lay back.

'Well – I was married at twelve, and it wasn't bad at all.' She rolled
on an elbow. 'In fact, my husband and I had a physical attraction I've
never felt for anyone else.' She got a tiny furrow between her eyebrows.
'Why am I telling you this?'

'How on earth did you go from wife to ... hetaera?' I asked.

She shrugged. 'Things happen,' she said. 'Not things I wish to discuss,' she added, closing the subject. 'You are easy to talk to – like a
farm boy, not an aristocrat.'

'Perhaps being a foreign barbarian has its advantages,' I said. I saw
a little under half of her face, and if she had a scar, I was the King of
Aegypt. She had sharp cheekbones, a lush mouth and a nose – well,
smaller and prettier than mine. But not by much.

'You're staring at my nose,' she said.

'I love your nose,' I said.

'It's huge,' she said.

'Superb,' I said.

'Large,' she said, but without coquettishness.

'You wear the veil to hide it?' I asked.

'You are suggesting that I need to wear a veil to hide it?' she said, and
I couldn't guess whether she was really being sharp with me, or whether
I was being mocked.

'Tell me about Prince Alexander,' she said, after a pause.

'He's better-looking than me, and not very interested in girls.' I was
drunk.

'I hear he's not very interested in anyone.' She had a wicked twinkle
in her eye. 'The party girls and boys say ... that he doesn't.'

I shrugged. Even drunk, there are things you don't say about your
prince. 'Not something I will discuss,' I said, since she'd been free
enough in shutting me down.

She nodded. 'Fair enough. You are married?'

I shook my head, and there it was – without pause, I burst into tears.
Drink, and Nike.

She didn't throw her arms around me, but she didn't flinch, either.
'Bad question. I'm sorry.'

145

It passed like a sudden rain shower. And drunkenness passed into sobriety. I wiped my face. 'Thanks,' I said, or something equally deep and moving.

She shrugged. 'You love your wife. I'm not surprised. You seem ... complete. More complete than most men your age.'

I shook my head. 'I had a mistress. She died – a month ago.' I sat on the edge of the kline. Wondering why I was babbling to this woman. 'I should have married her, and I didn't.'

The hetaera sat up with me. She was quite tall. 'I don't really know what to say. Men usually confide in me about their wife's failings. Not ... not real things.'

That made me smile. Somehow. 'Well,' I said. 'You have a way with you.'

'I'm a happy person,' she said. 'I try to spread it around. Not all the ground is receptive, but some is.'

A slave brought me my chlamys, and I pinned it. Graccus came up, kissed the hetaera on the cheek (she unveiled for him) and put an arm around me.

'You have been a charming guest. I had you for Diodorus's sake, but I'd have you again for your own. Diodorus or Kineas can tell you when I have another evening. I hope that you enjoyed yourself.'

The woman bowed slightly to me while she pinned her veil, so that I had a flash of her face, and then she went to the next kline, and sat with one of the kithara-playing men, who put his arm around her. They laughed together, and though I looked at her I couldn't make her turn her head.

'I had a wonderful time,' I admitted.

'I think she likes you,' Graccus said, following my eyes. 'But I admit, with Thaïs, it's often hard to tell. She's not like any other hetaera I've ever known.'

'No,' I said. I'd only known one, and she'd been ... complicated. I looked at Thaïs again, and she had her head back, veiled, laughing.

I embraced my host, gathered Myndas from the kitchen, drunker than me, and started the long walk home.

That was the first of a long series of symposia, and while I don't recall every one of them, I loved them as a whole. I found that I loved to talk – I loved to mix the wine, when invited. I went to the agora and purchased spices, and carried them in a small box of tortoiseshell. I still have it. I sent wine to friends – I was a rich man, even by Athenian standards.

With the permission of Eumenes, I used his andron and gave my own symposium. I invited Aristotle – he was far away, in Mytilene, and didn't come, but it amused me to invite him. I invited Alexander and Hephaestion, Cleitus and Nearchus, Kineas and Diodorus, Graccus and Niceas, Demetrios and Lykeles and half a dozen other young men I'd come to know.

I agonised over the arrangements – no help from Eumenes or Kineas, who, for aristocrats, were surprisingly uninterested. Eumenes decried the expense, and Kineas just laughed.

'A flash of good wine, a bowl to mix it, some bread and some friends,' he said. 'There's nothing to it.'

I glowered at him. 'I want it to go as well as Graccus's parties,' I said.

Kineas shrugged. 'That's all Graccus has – wine, bread. A good sunset and the right men.'

'Flute girls, actors, music, a hetaera, perfect fish …' I said.

Kineas laughed. 'Frippery,' he said. 'The guests make the evening.'

'Thanks, Socrates,' I said. 'Go away and leave me to my barbarian worries.'

Diodorus was more help. 'Get that girl,' he said. 'The hetaera. Everyone says she gives the best symposia in Athens. I've never been invited. Offer her money.'

'She went to Graccus's house for nothing,' I said primly.

'Are you Graccus?' Diodorus said. 'She's a hetaera. Offer her money.'

In fact, I had no need to approach her, because a week later, after a state dinner where we discussed – in surprising detail – the logistics of the crusade against Persia with Phokion and a dozen of the leading men of Athens, Alexander took me to her house. *Alexander* took me to her house. He walked through the front door as if he owned the place.

'Never known a woman like her,' he said. 'Brilliant. Earthy.' He shrugged. He was lightly drunk.

Hephaestion wasn't jealous, so it wasn't sex. Or wasn't just sex.

At any rate, I don't know what I expected – a brothel? An andron writ large? But Thaïs's house was a house – the house of a prosperous woman – and she sat at a large loom, weaving. She rose and bowed to Alexander, and he took her hands, kissed them and went straight to a kline with Hephaestion.

There were other men there – and other women.

She had no veil on, and she was beautiful. All eyes and cheekbones. And breasts. And legs.

'The Macedonian,' she said to me, quietly. 'I wondered if I had offended you.'

I must have looked surprised. 'How so?'

'I invited you to come,' she said. 'You didn't.'

I shook my head. 'I never received any such invitation,' I said. 'I would most certainly have come.'

She nodded. 'Eumenes probably destroyed it.' She bit her lip. 'He's very ... old-fashioned.'

I found myself smiling. 'I'm giving a symposium,' I said without preamble.

She looked up at me – she was back at her loom. 'Splendid!' she said, with a little too much emphasis.

'I want your advice. Your help.' I blurted this. She smiled and looked elsewhere.

'Advice?' she said.

'I want it to be perfect,' I said.

She smiled. 'It's all in the guest list,' she said.

'That's what Eumenes says,' I shot back.

'He's right,' she said. She was looking around the room. There were eight couches, all full. 'I am working right now,' she said. 'If you were to come back tomorrow afternoon, we might actually talk.'

Alexander raised a wine cup. 'You are not your sparkling self tonight, Thaïs. Too busy weaving?'

She rose to her feet. 'I was thinking about Persia,' she said.

Alexander looked puzzled – as if a pig had just said a line of Homer. Women did not, as a rule, think about Persia. It was odd—he could see her as a woman—even as an intelligent woman. But as someone who could understand politics? Never! Which, of course, makes her later role all the more delicious.

'What about Persia?' he asked.

'I was wondering how old I will be before you destroy it utterly,' she said.

All talk in the room ceased.

Alexander looked at her with wonder. 'Are you a sibyl? An oracle?'

She shook her head. 'No. I am a woman who wants revenge. I cannot get that revenge myself. But I long to see it.'

'Revenge?' he asked. Odd – he was so good at leading men. His questions showed how little he saw in her.

'A woman may crave revenge as well as a man,' she said. 'Look at Medea.'

'For what does a pretty girl like you crave revenge?' he asked.

'Ask me another evening,' she said. 'Tonight, I think I will dance.'

There was suddenly something angry and dangerous about her. I couldn't watch. So I took my leave. Alexander didn't even see me go.

Antipater was waiting outside on the portico, and we walked towards our homes together.

'He's besotted with her,' Antipater said.

That's not what I'd seen.

'He enjoys her company, and the privacy,' I said.

'He's been making some dangerous statements,' Antipater said. 'I know that you've been enjoying Athens, but I need you to spend more time with him. And keep him from getting into trouble.'

I stopped walking and looked at him. 'Trouble?' I asked.

'He keeps talking about what he'll do when he's king,' Antipater said.

I shrugged.

'Philip does not like to be reminded that there may be a time when he is *not* king,' he said.

'Alexander's the heir,' I said. 'He doesn't even have a rival.'

Antipater thumped his stick on the pavement. 'That may change,' he said. 'Listen, boy. Your pater and I were guest friends. You've been a good soldier for me, a good subordinate. Can I trust you?'

I didn't want this, any more than I had wanted the moment in which I had earned Attalus's enmity. Didn't want to take sides.

'I am a loyal man,' I said. 'To the king and to Alexander.'

Antipater nodded. 'Philip has put up statues at Delphi,' he said, 'as if he was a god.'

I shrugged. The things men do, when they achieve power. Look at me!

'He's said things ... that lead me to wonder.' Antipater looked away. 'Never mind. Let's get Athens on board for the war with Persia and hurry home, and all will be well.'

To be honest, I was so excited to have an afternoon tryst with a famous hetaera that I simply gripped his hand, went home and went to bed.

Next day, Isocrates met with Antipater and together they wrote out the basic tenets of the Pan Hellenic Alliance. Philip and his heirs to be hegemons of the Hellenic League and Strategos Autokrator, or supreme commander of allied forces. In the afternoon, Alexander went to the Academy and asked Xenocrates, the heir of Plato, Aristotle's rival, to write him a treatise on good kingship.

I winced. I was there.

Xenocrates was bowing and scraping. All of Athens was there to see the two of them together, and all of Athens heard the Crown Prince of Macedon say, 'I need a primer to keep me from the sort of acts of tyranny with which my father burdens his people.'

And there was Alcimachus, watching it all.

I had missed weeks of this, off enjoying my own life and my own friends. The Athenians were good hosts, and they gave Alexander something he'd never had before – an audience of his own, a willing, responsive, intelligent audience. He couldn't help but respond. He couldn't help but respond as the kind of prince he sensed they wanted him to be – a liberal, educated promise of a better tomorrow. A hero.

I slipped away before cockshut time and arrived at Thaïs's door. The slave there took my chlamys and sandals, washed my feet and led me to her. She was reading.

'How was Xenocrates?' she asked.

'Better ask, "How was Alexander?"' I said.

'He does like an audience,' she said. 'And he's never learned to control his mouth.'

'He's the very essence of self-control,' I said. 'Just not right now, apparently.'

She nodded. 'Your symposium,' she prompted.

'I have my guest list. I want advice on wines, slaves, entertainment. And I'd like you to come.' I didn't even trip over that last.

She shook her head. 'I couldn't. Not in Eumenes' home. He disapproves of me, and by having me there you would offend him. You are far too well bred for that.'

I felt crushed. She was absolutely correct. And I hadn't seen it at all.

She had a stylus and a wax tablet, and she wrote quickly. 'I'm quite sure that your evening will be splendid anyway – but here are the six wines currently most fashionable. Don't bother trying to buy them – you can't. But my steward will send a jar of each. I'm writing the names so that you know what you're serving. The "Dark Horse" is really a Plataean wine from Boeotia, common as dirt, but I like it and it's become rather a fashion.' She grinned around her stylus. 'Please don't tell – I'm making a fortune reselling it. There's a pair of women – they do not do sex – who play kithara superbly. Many houses won't have them because they have political leanings. Women are supposed to be above – or below – such stuff. They're sisters. You will need Eumenes' permission, but if he gives it – well, singing for Alexander will make them. And I'd like to see them made. Do you mind my using you like this?' She smiled at me.

'No,' I said.

'Good. Because as I'm doing you a favour, I'm remorseless in collecting in return. My steward will ask for money for the wine – I assume you can pay?' She smiled. 'Friends need to be honest about money,' she said.

'I am probably the richest man you know,' I said.

'Excellent, then. All the better. I prefer men to be young, attractive, valiant and rich.' She smiled again. She was smiling a great deal.

'Well, so far I'm rich,' I said.

'You are not unattractive,' she said. 'I am in favour of your nose.'

Best compliment anyone ever paid me – half in delivery, and half in the words – the twinkle in her eye worth another half. My own desire to be handsome, revealed.

I blushed. For a Macedonian royal page to blush – well, you work it out. 'You're just saying that because I liked your nose first,' I said.

She laughed. And laughed. 'I like you, Macedonian. You'll need food – you're not having a dinner, are you?'

'I was thinking—' I began.

'Don't. Graccus gets away with it because of the view and the very intimate company he invites. You have to get these philosopher boys to settle down with your Macedonians – just because you like them all doesn't mean they'll like each other. Keep it shorter. After dinner. Less smelly, less to clean up. They'll arrive sober, because it is Eumenes' house. I think you'll be golden. But serve Lesbian rolls – barley rolls, I'll send you the recipe – and have almonds in honey. Again, I'll – oh, Aphrodite, I'll just have cook send you some.' She smiled. 'When people taste them, they'll know they're mine. And that will please some and raise other eyebrows.' She got the little furrow between her own eyebrows. 'Really, I'm taking over. Don't let me. It's your party, not one of mine.'

'I'm delighted,' I said. 'You know, my lady, sometimes there are advantages to being a foreign barbarian.'

She raised an eyebrow. 'Really?'

'Well, I don't know whether I'm supposed to offer you money for your advice,' I said. 'But since I'm a foreigner, I doubt you'll be insulted.'

She chewed a finger for a moment. 'No – I'll make money from your wine and your almonds. And everything in life is not a moneymaking proposition.'

'Perhaps you might view me, as a rich foreigner, as a long-term investment?' I asked.

She looked up, and I realised that I hadn't really looked into her eyes until that moment.

'When the day comes, kill a Persian for me,' she said. 'That's all you owe me.'

Well, well. I was too well bred to ask, so I found myself out on the street with Myndas, wondering why she hated Persia.

*

My symposium was splendid. The food was excellent, the wine was divine and widely commented on, and Eumenes not only allowed the two female kithara players but paid us all the compliment of attending during their performance and mixing us a very mild bowl. He was courtly to them, treating them like visiting matrons, friends of his wife, perhaps, or sisters of his friends, and they, despite being radicals of the most democratic stripe, responded in kind with the sort of well-bred courtesy he must never have expected from them. It was a war of sorts, conducted with manners, and both parties left with increased respect for the other.

And they were the finest kithara players I've ever heard. I remember their Sappho lyrics, a hymn to Aphrodite, and my favourite, which begins:

Some say a body of hoplites and some a squadron of cavalry, and some a fleet of ships is the most beautiful . . .

That Sappho. She'd grown up with soldiers.

The elder of the sisters gave me a clam shell as she left – a folded note on parchment that said only 'good luck', and a laughing face. I grinned for the rest of the evening.

Alexander was at his best. He lay on his couch with Hephaestion, or with other guests, sang songs, danced, once. He was brilliant – capping every quote, but mocking himself for it. The best I remember was the moment when he pretended to be both himself as a twelve-year-old and Aristotle, mocking the pretensions of both.

With Alexander, when he was dark or moody or absorbed in war or politics or any other passion, it was possible to forget this man – the lightning flash, we used to call it among the pages. Funny, witty, self-mocking, aware of what we thought of his flaws – wicked, too, with a turn of phrase that would have made a whore blush. It didn't happen often – and I suspected it was as much a performance as any of the other Alexanders I knew. But when we lay on our couches roaring with laughter, unable to speak at the spectacle of Alexander/Aristotle attempting to seduce Alexander/Alexander with philosophy, with Lykeles actually rolling off the couch he was on to crash to the floor – with Kineas, always so controlled, spitting barley roll, with tears coming from his eyes, and Hephaestion pounding Antipater's back because he'd swallowed wine the wrong way laughing too hard . . .

I was sober – I was too nervous to be drunk. And as he wound to the climax of his amazing, lewd, witty impersonation of a besotted Aristotle with an erection based entirely on his love of Philosophy, I caught his eye.

His face was wild with the exertion of the drama, and yet, as if it were a mask, I caught a glimpse of the actor within, coolly assessing his audience. The strength of his own performance.

I was standing at the wine bowl when he came to the end – clutching the serving table to keep from pitching to the floor.

Hephaestion embraced him. 'Oh, my brother, why can't you always be like this?' he asked.

Alexander's face of command slipped effortlessly back into place. 'Like what?' he asked. 'I've heard of actors crowned, but never a comic.' Aside, to me, at the wine bowl, he said, 'Whenever I do that, I feel less a man afterwards. As with bedding a woman. Or too much sleep.'

He was drunk. Make what you will of his words.

At some point, Diodorus proposed that we run a race to the top of the Acropolis and back. I must have started drinking by then, because I thought it was an excellent idea. So did everyone else, so I suppose Antipater and Eumenes, the oldest men, were gone.

We stripped naked, of course.

Kineas, Diodorus, Graccus, Niceas, Nearchus, Cleitus the Black, Alexander, Hephaestion and me. Polystratus started us from Eumenes' front gate. Every man had a torch – I forget whose idea that was.

I didn't even know where the Acropolis was, when we started, so I followed Kineas. Kineas had a badly formed right leg – he didn't trouble to hide it – and he wasn't very tall. But he knew Athens, and he was probably soberer than the rest of us. Alexander was quite probably the drunkest of the lot of us, but he was a wonderful runner, and it was all I could do to keep the two of them in sight. I ran as hard as I could, and they vanished; corner after corner, I saw the tails of flame as I arrived. They'd always just turned the *next* corner.

Up and up through the town, which washes like waves of houses right to the base of the fortifications. Up and up, into a strengthening wind that blew our torches into blazing fires.

Out on to the broad stones of the Panathenaeum. Up and up and up. Now I could see them, neck and neck at the gates of the fortifications. I got a second wind, or perhaps I was not as drunk as I thought, but I caught them up on the steps below the temple to Nike.

Maybe she came to my aid, for the good of Greece. Who knows?

They touched the columns of the Parthenon together. I couldn't tell you which had won.

When I came up, they were agreeing to settle it with a race back down.

They were greater than human. It's in the eyes. It is a certain glow in the skin. I have seen it a few times, when a man rises above himself, usually in athletics or war. And they both had it, just then.

But they were courteous enough to wait for me.

And Niceas was right on my heels.

'Don't do it,' Niceas panted. 'Down is dangerous.'

Alexander's eyes gleamed. 'Dangerous is just fine.'

'You could fall,' Niceas said.

'I'll fly, then,' Alexander said. 'Kineas?'

Kineas took his hand. 'You could run in the Olympics,' he said.

Alexander laughed. 'Only if they had a competition for demigods, heroes and kings,' he said. 'Come, before they dissuade us.'

Niceas grabbed my shoulder. 'You stay with yours and I with mine,' he said.

And we were off.

Alexander meant to go down the way he'd come, but as soon as we were clear of the steps by the temple to Nike – I touched the wall and said a prayer – Kineas turned on a side path down the hill.

Alexander knew tactics when he saw them. So he turned and followed.

Niceas and I were hard on them – a man can only run so fast down a cliff, even a demigod. And when the goat trail ended on a hard-packed street below a row of tiled roofs, Kineas shocked me by leaping from the hillside on to the roofs and running along the tiles as if they were a road – which they were if you don't mind a slope to your road.

With torches. Leaping from roof to roof. Downhill, never touching the streets – down past the lower temples, past the watering fountains. Somewhere – I don't know where, and I'd never be able to retrace the path except in a nightmare – we came to a drop of ten feet and a gulf perhaps two horse lengths wide – a side street.

Kineas didn't hesitate, but leaped at full stride, and Alexander was with him, stride for stride.

That was the heir of Macedon, sailing through the air with a torch trailing white fire behind him.

Oh, there were gods, that night in Athens.

Another leap, and we were on Kineas's street – I knew by the stables. We ran along the stable roof, and now Alexander lengthened his stride, and Kineas lengthened his.

At the courtyard of Eumenes' house, they came to the end of the roofs.

Neither slackened stride.

I did.

Off the end of the stables, legs still flashing, Alexander a full body's length ahead, the torches streaming fire . . .

A thirty-foot fall to the cobbled courtyard.

I didn't even have time to call. Niceas did. He screamed.

And they were gone.

There was an enormous pile of straw below. And while I gather that Kineas knew that, I swear that Prince Alexander simply trusted that the gods would not let him die.

I slowed, stopped, heard no screams, looked, saw and jumped down.

Alexander rolled out of the straw, his torch out. 'I win,' he said, touching Eumenes' andron door.

Kineas was laughing so hard he couldn't get to his feet.

I went off and threw up.

Good party.

SEVEN

Pella, 337 BC

And then we were summoned home to Pella, and the party was over.

We had our treaty, and the Athenians had buried their dead with honour. My troopers stood in the pale winter sunshine as the ashes were lowered into a marble tomb, and I could not help but think that if the Athenians had put as much effort into fighting as they did to burying, we might have come off worse. Even as it was – when I looked around Athens, watched the great port of Piraeus, talked to the people – the more I looked at Athens, the more I saw to admire. I liked their pugnacious independence, and their desire to debate everything. And they were rich, and spent their money well.

I loved Kineas, and all he stood for. I was bred to war, the way a boar hound is bred to his life – little love, plenty of hardship and pain, to make sure that the object of your training never hesitates at the kill. Shed no tears – I made my life, and it's been a glory. But Kineas, as good a soldier as any Macedonian, as events proved, was more than just a soldier. Where we had a veneer of education from Aristotle, Kineas could quote anything from Hesiod and the *Iliad* to the latest play of Menander. He could speak with ease of Thales or Pythagoras, and he could work out most of the problems of the new mathematics. His scholarly skills were not a veneer, and yet he could sit astride his horse like a Scythian and his spear skills – and his wrestling – were on a par with mine.

I mention this, because Kineas and his friends did something to me and my friends. I'm not sure – it was like some sort of beneficial spell, but after Athens my friends wanted more than cheap wine and fast sex. Because we knew that there was more to want.

And Pella, when we arrived, looked like a tinselled crown next to the solid gold of Athens. Alexander felt it keenly – perhaps even more keenly than Nearchus or Cleomenes.

We came over the last rise, to the point in the pass where outlying farms give way to the public buildings of the city. Except that Pella was no city, after Athens, but a provincial town. Attica had three or four towns the size of Pella. Amphilopolis, our major seaport (once an Athenian colony), was as large as Pella.

Alexander pulled his palfrey up short. He was riding between me and Hephaestion. He looked back and forth between us, and the look on his face was strained – almost like a mask of rage.

'I feel like I have been a god on Olympus, and now I'm being forced to go back to being a pig in the sty,' he said, and gave an uncharacteristically savage jerk to his reins.

Hephaestion raised an eyebrow. We were never truly close, but Athens deepened our alliance – I didn't threaten him, and he admitted that I was part of the family. Together, we'd learned – through fifty symposia and a dozen dinner parties – to manage Alexander's moods.

'Storms at sea,' he said.

I winked – thinking that it would all pass soon enough – and we rode down into the city.

The pigsty.

Pella was small, dirty and provincial. Want to understand what kind of society you live in? Look at a prostitute. In Athens, most of the prostitutes were self-owning – many were freemen and -women. They had houses and a guild. It's rotten life, but they were clean and free. The first thing I saw in Pella was a very young girl – maybe fourteen – wearing nothing but a man's chiton, begging for clients on the road. Her lip was split and she had two black eyes.

Pella.

Philip had changed. I saw it in his body language as soon as we arrived at the palace. He didn't quite turn his back on Alexander, but he was distant, cold and very, very businesslike.

I didn't even hear the exchange, it was so brief. Alexander asked where his mother was, and Philip replied that he had no idea.

So little information. And yet, all the information we should have needed.

I had a home to go to – a house that did not hold Nike. But that's where my horse would be stabled, now, and my armour stowed. So I waited by the gate for dismissal, observing. Noting that Attalus stood with the king, and commanded the grooms as if he were the king himself. Our eyes met, and he smiled.

I felt a chill.

Alexander came over in person – uncharacteristic. 'You can go home,' he said.

Hephaestion was at his shoulder.

'Take care, my prince,' I said. 'Something is wrong.'

'Agreed,' Alexander said. 'I think my mother is in exile. I will dine at your house tonight, I think.'

'I'll do my best,' I said. 'Without Nike ...'

Alexander smiled – a sad smile he'd learned in Athens. 'I know you miss her,' he said. 'Now go.'

I had the feeling that Alexander was afraid.

That made my fingers cold.

I rode around the corner of my street and found that my house was burned. To the ground. The houses on either side were burned, too.

Gone.

Ten minutes of increasingly angry knocking at doors – Polystratus helped – revealed that no one knew *anything*, to a suspicious degree.

Polystratus grew more agitated.

'I need to go home,' he said.

We had Nearchus and Cleitus with us. Cleomenes was on duty.

'Let's go together,' I said. We all loosened our swords in our scabbards, and we rode fast.

Polystratus's farm was ... gone. The house was erased. His fields were under tillage.

We rode to find the headman.

He hid in his house. His wife burst into tears, but barred the door.

And then, while we sat there, Diomedes appeared with a dozen outriders – Thracians. All well mounted and all armed.

'Looking for something?' the king's catamite asked sweetly. 'Lost something you value?'

Polystratus looked at me. It was up to me – we weren't in Athens, and peasants don't talk to lords in Pella.

'We're looking for Polystratus's wife,' I said pleasantly enough. 'We didn't expect to find her moved.'

Diomedes smiled. 'I thought you might come looking. So I came out to help.' His grin covered his face. 'She's been apprehended by the law, and she's back at work with her rightful owner. I'm sure that you didn't know that she was an escaped slave.'

Polystratus choked.

I looked at him.

'The law seized the farm as penalty for the crime of hiding an escaped slave,' Diomedes continued. 'And now that the felon has returned, I have a royal warrant for his arrest.' He held out a scroll.

I reached to take it, but Diomedes swished it away. Somehow this juvenile act enraged me where everything else had merely made me cold.

Diomedes leaned in close. 'Perhaps this time you'll notice when we cut you, you fuck. Because we will cut you until you cease to exist. No one pisses on Attalus and lives.'

I had no idea what he was talking about. But I knew that my friends could take his Thracians. On the other hand, he was the royal's favourite.

I looked back at Polystratus. 'Is this true?' I asked, but I could see on his face that it was. 'You stupid fuck – why didn't you tell me? I'd have bought her freedom.'

Polystratus bit his lip. I remember that it was odd to have the boot on the other foot. He was the older man, the adviser – Nestor to my Odysseus. Suddenly he was the supplicant.

Polystratus had been at my shoulder for a year, and I owed him ... everything. And I had seen Kineas and Niceas, remember. Polystratus was not a peasant. He was a man. My man. Who had helped save me from myself.

I turned back, seized the scroll with one hand and tipped Diomedes into the winter mud by the simple expedient of reaching down, grabbing his foot and flipping him up. I pulled my spear from the bucket at my shoulder with my free hand, pointed it at his chest and looked at the Thracians.

'Move, and I'll have the lot of you sold as slaves.' I said it in their language, and I meant it.

The street was mucky, full of winter rain and ordure, pigs' guts and cow manure.

The Thracians rustled, and my friends had their swords in their hands.

I flipped the scroll open one-handed and read enough of the royal warrant to know that Diomedes was full of shit. I knew the laws – better than most men. I put the point of my boar spear against Diomedes' chest. Every movement of my horse pushed it a little farther into his skin. 'Just lie there,' I said. I read the document to the end.

'Nothing here about arresting my man,' I said. 'Nor anything naming you as an officer of the court.' I smiled down into the mud. 'So you're a brigand with a band of Thracians.'

'You stupid *fuck*,' he said. 'The king will have you killed.'

'I doubt you're that good in bed,' I said. 'Get up.'

He got to his feet, backed away.

I was beginning to see where his insinuations led, even as he scrambled to remount his horse.

'You burned my city house?' I said. Had I been Achilles, I would have killed him then and there. But I am not Achilles. I'm Odysseus, and things were falling into place, like the pins and cogs of one of the astrological machines I'd seen in Athens.

'Oh, very good,' he hissed. 'At last, you begin to see.' He was mounted, and in the middle of his Thracians. I regretted letting him up. 'We'll kill your people. And you. Attalus is going to rule Macedon. You are going to suck my cock.'

'You are a dumb bastard,' I said, because thanks to that outburst, I could see the whole thing.

He turned and rode away, and the Thracians surrounded him. He was already hectoring them for their cowardice, but hired muscle is never the equal of determined freemen.

Well – actually that's not true. Hired muscle often wins. But in the long run ...

Attalus was planning to be king. What had he put into Philip's head?

'Back to the palace,' I said.

We rode hard. We crossed the fields at a trot, staying on the field dividers to keep out of the mud, and we were back on the streets of Pella well before Diomedes.

Into the foreyard of the palace.

I turned to Polystratus. 'We'll find your girl. For now – get ready to move. Stable the horses, but stay close.'

With Nearchus and Black Cleitus at my shoulder, I entered the palace through the stables and moved along the main corridor. Of course we had the passwords, but I could feel the eyes of the companions on my back.

On the other hand, I was an officer, the head of one of the great families. If I chose to use it, I had a great deal of power. I thought that perhaps Attalus had underestimated me.

I made for Alexander's rooms. He was lying on his couch, reading, with Hephaestion on a chair polishing his helmet.

'Lord, there's a plot,' I said.

Alexander rolled off his bed. 'I know there's something.'

I shrugged. 'I don't know anything for certain. But my city house has been burned, all my slaves sold. My man, Polystratus – they moved against him in law, seized his wife and sold his lands. And he's a free-man and a veteran.'

Alexander frowned. 'Nasty, but not a plot against me.'

'Diomedes came out to crow,' I said.

Alexander raised an eyebrow. 'Attalus.'

'Diomedes said Attalus will be king,' I said, and Alexander snarled like a lion. Hephaestion put a hand on his shoulder.

And a frightened page came into the room. 'The king!' he squeaked.

Philip pushed in on the page's heels. Behind him was Attalus, with Diomedes, still splashed with mud.

'Ptolemy!' Philip said.

I pointed at Diomedes. 'Only my loyalty to you, sire, kept me from killing this dog on the road,' I said, because a good offence is always the best defence.

'He says—'

'Lord, he tried to lay hands on me and admitted to destroying my property and selling my people as slaves – while I did your bidding in Athens,' I said.

King Philip's eyes narrowed when I spoke over him – but he listened. Remember – I represented a great family and a lot of loyal service. And a lot of tax money. And political power.

'I wish to swear a case against him,' I went on. 'I withheld my hand from killing him, but I demand justice.'

Philip's face worked. He looked at Diomedes.

'Lies!' Diomedes said. 'Lord, I—'

Nearchus, at my shoulder, bowed. 'My king, I was there. It was as Lord Ptolemy says.'

Attalus spluttered. 'They are all pages – they're in it together!'

Alexander stood up. 'Attalus – I do not remember inviting you into my rooms. Please leave. Diomedes, you as well.'

Philip looked back and forth. 'Ptolemy – no need to swear a case against Diomedes, is there? What is this, some boys' quarrel?' He smiled at us.

Attalus narrowed his eyes. 'Lord Ptolemy has been telling people that he is your bastard son and has as much right to the throne as Prince Alexander.' Attalus grinned so that the fat hid his eyes. 'Or better,' he drawled, 'since he says that he can prove you are his father.'

Philip made a strangled sound.

I can go either way – rage or cold calculation. But Athena stood at my shoulder. 'My king – Attalus is gravely mistaken. I have never made any such claim. And anyone who looks at me can see my parentage in my nose.' I laughed.

I have learned that a laugh – an unforced laugh, or a damned good imitation – is the most disarming technique in the world. And my nose was an excellent witness.

Alexander stood at my shoulder. 'Out, Attalus. You are not welcome here.'

'I come and go as I please, at the king's leave, and not for some foreign woman's by-blow,' Attalus said.

There it was, on the table.

Alexander's face turned a deep blood red, and his eyes glittered.

He was so fast, when he was angry, that Attalus was lying on the floor when Philip was still reaching to stop his son.

'What have you done, Father?' Alexander asked.

Philip wouldn't meet his eye. Diomedes was helping Attalus to his feet.

Alexander's face was suddenly nearly white, and his rage burned like a new-lit fire with too much birch bark. 'Men will not meet my eye. All my servants have been changed. My friends are under attack, and I don't know the pages on duty. What have you done?'

Another commotion, and Philotas pushed in. 'Alexander!' he shouted. 'They've changed the password!'

There was a scuffle in the hallway.

'Father?' Alexander said. It was the last time I ever heard him address the king as Father.

Philip drew himself up. 'I have proof that you and your mother were plotting to kill me. And that you are not my son. You are a bastard child, and I am replacing you with an heir. Of my own body.'

Alexander froze.

Philip turned and strode from the room. Attalus and Diomedes went with him, and all their retainers.

Alexander sank slowly on to a chair.

'Zeus,' Hephaestion said.

Before an hour passed, Philip sent a messenger to apologise. As if you could apologise for bastardising your son.

In fact, he invited Alexander to his wedding banquet.

By then, we had an idea what we were up against. A quick tour of the guardrooms showed me that half of the royal companions had been replaced with lowlanders from small families. The old highland aristocrats and the mercenaries were ... gone. Erigyus and Laodon were nowhere to be found, nor any of the other old inner-circle drinkers.

But whatever Philip had said, he had not actually done *anything* to bastardise Alexander. On the other hand, a few old servants – all found in the stables; the palace itself was thoroughly *cleansed* – told us that 'everyone knew' that Alexander was illegitimate. It was in the agora and in the palace. Soldiers made jokes about it.

We'd been gone six months.

Someone had been busy.

And Philip was marrying Cleopatra – Attalus's niece, Diomedes' sister.

Now, Philip married a girl every year or so. And Olympias never minded. She was a broad-minded queen with interests of her own, and she befriended most of the wives and saw to it they were well treated. And she made sure they were no threat to her political power.

Cleopatra was different, and Olympias had already been exiled.

The more closely I looked, the more it appeared that Philip – or someone else – had decided to rid himself of the highlanders and all the non-Macedonians, starting with Olympias. And to change the succession.

That meant they'd have to murder Alexander.

Most Macedonian political murders happened at banquets. So it didn't take Aristotle's training to show us that Alexander couldn't go to this wedding feast.

But he *was* Achilles. 'I will *not* show fear,' he said. 'I will go to the wedding feast.'

Hephaestion took me aside. 'He has gone mad,' he said. 'I cannot make him see reason.'

I knew an answer. A very Macedonian answer. But I didn't give it voice. Killing Philip – the best king Macedon had had for generations – was the obvious solution to our troubles. But I was too loyal.

I thought about it, though. I wanted to strike at Attalus before he did me any more damage.

I wanted to go home to my estates and make sure that they were safe. But the prince came first, and he was walking rapidly up and down his room, dressed in his best Tyrian red chiton with a garland of gilded oak leaves in his hair, eyes white at the edges, skin flushed to the neck. Even the tops of his arms were blotchy with colour.

I stopped worrying about my own affairs and took over.

'Right,' I said. 'Cleitus, you're on duty.'

'I am?' he asked. And then nodded. 'Right.'

'Full armour,' I said.

Hephaestion nodded. 'Me, too.'

'And Nearchus and Philotas,' I said. 'Where's Philotas?'

Philip the Red was there, already in armour. 'He's gone. To his farm. Said his pater ordered him away from court.'

That hurt. But Parmenio and Attalus were close, and they were the driving force behind the military build-up in Asia. Another thing you could see everywhere in Pella was signs of military preparations. And the army was already gone – in the Chersonese, and some of it already in Asia. Almost a third of our total fighting force. That's where all the old mercenaries and highlanders were, no doubt – far from court, where they could be used but couldn't exercise any power.

I was shocked that Parmenio had turned against Alexander. It didn't seem possible.

Quite a few of our old pages were missing. But Attalus had miscalculated and shown his hand before most of us went home on leave – all the men who'd gone with Alexander to Athens were still with me, and had Attalus waited a week, Alexander would have been virtually alone.

But even as things were – I say this from the distance of years – they'd plotted carefully, but they hadn't plotted completely. It was as if – despite their intent – they couldn't actually cross some invisible line. I still think that Philip was unable to kill his son.

Let me add – in case you don't understand – that bastardising your relatives was an old Macedonian royal house tradition, a handy way of knocking rivals out of the succession. It happened every generation. Some bastards – or so-called bastards – stayed around and became trusted men, generals, members of the inner circle, while some ran off to Illyria or Asia or Athens to live out their lives, or died in pointless counter-coups. Of course, outright murder of relatives was also an important part of life in the royal house.

I briefed six bodyguards – all men Alexander had appointed somatophylakes before Athens – and then I slipped out to the stables. Polystratus had gathered the loyal grooms, and he had the horses – fifty horses. Another advantage – we had just returned from travelling, and in every case our travelling gear was still packed – in most cases, still in baggage carts.

As soon as Cleomenes came off duty, I sent him with the carts and the spare horses – up the road, to my estates, north of the city, towards the Illyrian frontier.

Polystratus stood by with our war horses.

I had all the former pages armed and armoured, in boots, ready to ride. With spears and swords – in my rooms, near Alexander's.

I could have killed Philip that evening. The palace was not well guarded – the new companions didn't know their business very well, and were often in awe of us, the 'veterans'. I could have killed him, but remember, this wasn't my first intrigue, I was truly a veteran of that court, and he was my king. I saw to my arrangements, told a lot of lies to new guardsmen to explain my movements, arranged for the loyal grooms from the stables to ride with us, sent a trio of my men with

Polystratus to the house of Attalus – to fetch his wife. Her location was named in the royal warrant. In some ways, they made it easy.

But in my head, a voice was telling me over and over that we should kill the king and seize power – that running for it was the end of everything.

I wanted to send Myndas ahead of Polystratus – slaves can go places freemen cannot. I promised him his freedom if he did my bidding – which was to scout the kitchens at Attalus's house, locate Polystratus's wife and open the back gate – the gate that would usually open for deliveries of wine or grain.

Myndas didn't grin. My offer scared him spitless. He could barely speak; he had two burning red spots on his cheeks and his lips were pale in the lamplight.

Nichomachus glared at him. 'I'll do it,' he said. 'Free me. Free us both.'

It was odd – Myndas had been born free, and Nichomachus had always been a slave. In theory Myndas should have had the backbone. 'Do it, and I'll free you both – though I hope you'll stay for wages.'

Nichomachus nodded. 'I'll do it, lord.'

Myndas narrowed his eyes. 'No.' He took a breath. 'I'll do it. You have no idea what they'll do to you if you are caught.'

Polystratus put his hand on the man's shoulder. 'I'll cut you out if I have to.'

Myndas managed a grin. 'Better than nothing. Better hope it don't come to that. Let's do it.' He turned to me. 'If I die – I want a free man's burial and a stele.'

The things a panicked man thinks of! 'Of course,' I promised smoothly.

When all my preparations were made, I went to Alexander's room. I hadn't been invited to the feast, but neither had I been forbidden. I put on a good chiton and wore a sword under it, next to my skin. Men did that, at Macedonian feasts. We called it the twenty-four-inch erection.

When we entered the great hall, with fifty couches ranged around it in a broad circle around the central hearth, the only sound was the roaring of the fire. Every head turned. Alexander looked like a god – hair curly from the road, with the ram's horns at his temples that always appeared unless he brushed them out carefully, and his chiton, his bearing, the wreath of gold oak leaves – he was a god.

I was at his heels, with Hephaestion, and we had white chitons with gold-embroidered hems on red, to frame him.

Around us, six companions in the armour we'd purchased in Athens.

Helmets like the heads of lions, thorakes of alternating steel and bronze scales, red wool chitons and dark blue wool cloaks.

They stood at attention while Alexander walked to the couch of honour, the kline halfway around the circle from the king. Cleopatra's father was on it with Diomedes.

Philip the Red and Nearchus tipped them out on the floor. We hadn't discussed this – in fact, it had never occurred to us that Philip would slight Alexander to this degree in public. But Philip the Red acted, and we played it out.

Old Amyntas gave a scream, and ran to the king's couch.

Uproar.

Alexander lay down, and Hephaestion joined him.

Philip rose to his feet. 'What is the meaning of this?' he called.

Alexander remained reclining. 'When my mother remarries,' he shouted, 'you will still be the guest of honour,' and he grinned. It was a death's-head grin, and no one answered it.

I stood for a while, watching the silent, uncomfortable feast. Then I decided that it was safe enough, and I went and lay down on the only empty couch – with Alcimachus. He was alone, and none too pleased to have me as a companion.

'What are you playing at?' he hissed as I lay down.

'What in Hades is going on?' I asked.

He shook his head. 'I thought you knew. I've seen you moving around all afternoon.' He looked around. 'Everyone says that Alexander was plotting to have Philip murdered!'

I had many suspicions about Alcimachus. He had kept us in Athens for a long time – spun out the negotiations when Athens had agreed to everything. When we were there, that suited me – I wanted every minute of Thaïs and Athens I could get. But in that moment, lying on the couch, I thought about his loyalties.

I rolled a little, so he could feel my sword.

'Don't make trouble, old man,' I said.

Those were our last words.

The food was pretty bad, after Athens – too much show and not enough skill, and cold. I'd never eaten a dinner for a hundred in Athens – the largest dinner there was for about twenty. They knew a thing or two.

And then the wine began to flow.

There were toasts to the happy couple – Philip was wearing a groom's crown, and Cleopatra, pretty as a picture and the only free woman in the room, lay on his couch in her bridal crown. I could see the old king fancied her – hard not to show what you like, when all you are wearing is a single layer of near-transparent wool. And despite the tensions of that feast, he fondled her – a maiden, and a free woman. He was the king, and a randy bastard at that, and he got away with it, but it was in poor taste, even for Macedon. She flushed with pleasure and grimaced with embarrassment by turns. And the toasts didn't help her, poor thing – she was fourteen at most, and had probably not heard the king's member described in such detail.

Diomedes was the worst. As the king's current favourite, he was in the complex position of being the bride's sister – and rival. He didn't occupy it well, and managed to offer a toast suggesting that her womb might be good for making an heir, but little else.

I saw Alexander register this. His face grew red, and his eyes glittered.

And then Attalus rose from his couch. He was drunk – annoyed at his nephew, annoyed to have Alexander there to spoil his day of triumph. And weak men work their way to rage slowly.

'To Cleopatra's cunny!' he shouted. 'At last, Macedon will have a true heir, and not some by-blow from the mountainside!'

Alexander was off his couch. 'Are you calling me a bastard, Attalus?' he roared, and threw his wine cup – solid gold – with all his skill, and it hit the older man squarely on the forehead, knocking him to the floor.

Philip leaped off his couch. 'You bastard!' he spat, and drew a sword from under his chiton and leaped across the hearth at Alexander.

His foot caught on Attalus's outflung arm and he sprawled – his head hit the hearth with a thud, and the sword spun off into the rushes.

Cleopatra screamed, sat up and the chiton fell from her shoulders – the randy king had loosened her pins.

Philip lay there, having knocked himself unconscious – his chiton was torn at the hips and stained with wine, and his erection stood out like a satyr's. He looked ... like the ruin of a man. Like a satyr, or a drunk in an alley.

Alexander stood over him. 'This, gentlemen,' Alexander said carefully, 'is the King of Macedon, who says he will lead you to conquer Asia, and cannot cross from one couch to another.'

The hall was silent. I think most of them expected Alexander to do it, then – plunge his sword into his father and make himself king.

But Alexander had tears in his eyes, and he looked at me. I made a motion with my hand, and our companions surrounded the prince and escorted him from the hall – Nearchus and Cleomenes stayed behind until Hephaestion and I were clear.

Then we ran.

We needn't have run. Philip was out cold, and Attalus under him – and until they gave the order, one or the other, there was not going to be a pursuit. I didn't know that. I assumed they'd take Alexander if they could.

We ran into the stables, and there were horses saddled and ready – war horses, our very best. All the companions from the trip to Athens, ready for the road.

Alexander looked at them, mounted in the stable yard. He vaulted on to Bucephalus and turned his horse to face us.

'I will never forget this night, gentlemen,' he said. He reached out to Black Cleitus. 'My friends.' He used the word *philoi*, not *Hetaeroi*. Close friends and equals.

And then we rode off into the darkness.

'Where are we going?' he asked me. 'Odysseus? You have a plan?'

I nodded. 'First to my farms, north of the city,' I said. 'I need to warn my steward. Collect some money and some men. Then – you go to your mother.'

'Epirus?' Alexander said. He sighed. 'By Zeus,' he swore, 'I will yet be king of Macedon.'

Philip the Red camne trotting down the column to us. 'Your groom, Ptolemy, and some slaves.'

I rode up the column, leaving the prince. Polystratus had his wife – I didn't stop to talk.

'Mount!' I yelled at them. Polystratus was bubbling with words – Myndas was glowing with pride. I had no time. 'Mount, you fools!'

Other men's moments of heroism may fuel their lives, but I didn't have time to hear the tale, just then. We had horses for them, and we got them mounted – even the wife, who rode like a sack of grain, or worse.

Then we cut cross-country, right from the edge of the town – across dykes and north on the edge of the river, where there was a bridle path. Before rosy-fingered dawn strode long-legged across the murky sky, we had gone twenty stades. We were cold, wet and scared. Alexander was silent.

But we were safe. We'd crossed the river four times, with Polystratus guiding – he was elated that night, and doing better than his best. No pursuit was going to find our trail after that – not even with dogs.

Mid-morning, and we ate a cold breakfast at our horses' heads.

'What will I do for money?' Alexander asked me, suddenly.

Hephaestion laughed. Opened his leather bag. 'I don't have onions or sausage,' he said.

Instead, he had almost all of Alexander's personal jewels.

Alexander kissed him. And then he kissed me. 'I think you two have saved my life.'

I don't remember what I answered – it was so unlike him.

Noon, and the yard of my manor house. Our horse barn could hold fifty horses – and now it had twice that. I had nobly born royal companions sleeping in the hayloft and in the smokehouse.

Heron was a prominent man now, and had a great deal to lose.

Such men can be suddenly fickle, or disloyal.

Not Heron. I never even suspected him – who betrays a hundred years of family loyalty?

'That's the prince!' he hissed at me. 'What's happening?'

I led him outside, and then out beyond the barns. To the top of the family hill.

'I'm going into exile,' I said. 'Philip is going to change the succession – bastardise Alexander. Get a new heir on Attalus's niece.'

'Gods!' Heron said. 'He's insane!'

I had to admit that that's about all I could think. 'Attalus has worked for a year to poison his mind against Alexander,' I said after a moment's silence.

Heron shrugged. 'Your father hated Philip,' he said.

I nodded. I suspected as much and really, really didn't want to know. And having the old family retainer tell me the secret of my birth was just a little too much like a Menander play. So I raised my hand. 'Speak me no treason,' I said. 'I'm going with my prince. Attalus hates me – it's a long, stupid story – and he will attack you here.'

Heron looked down at the farms. We held more than twenty great farms right here – the core of our wealth – but we had sixty more farms spread all the way across Macedon, and up into the hill country of the west. We were highlanders *and* lowlanders.

I could read his mind. 'You can't defend it,' I said.

He nodded.

'I'll need money,' I said. 'Other than that – feel free to betray me.'

'Betray you?' he asked.

'Seize the lands in your own name,' I said. 'Tell Attalus to sod off, you are the boss here, now. I'll wager you gold against iron he'll make an accommodation rather than sending raids.'

Heron made a face. 'Men will spit on my shadow,' he said.

I shrugged. 'Not for long,' I said. 'I have no heir, and if Alexander fails – well, it's all yours anyway. But I'll need money and horses. I'm going to take every horse you have, and all the coin, and all the men who can fight.'

Heron shook his head. 'I need ten fighters and horses and armour for them.'

169

That was good sense. I couldn't strip him bare – even for the week until he could get reinforcements from the outlying farms.

He scratched his jaw. 'Going to take the prince to Epirus?' he asked.

'Zeus! Is it that obvious?' I said.

Heron nodded. 'Best place for him. His mother will protect him. Get him an army, if required.' He scratched again. 'Take twenty men and forty horses. Make up the difference at the northern farms – strip them, not me. And use them as stopping points. And while you're at it, take the slaves and send all the farmers here for protection. Then I don't have any hostages up there.'

'And all the farmers know that you are secretly loyal to me.' I saw right through him.

He shrugged. 'Yes. No one in the family is going to believe I'm a traitor.'

'Attalus will believe.' I hoped it would at least slow him down. He was going to have other fish to bake over the next few months. I had to hope that, or I was going to return to find my people butchered and my estates burned or worse.

Loyalty is the most valuable thing in the world. You do not spit on it. When a loyal man says he wants something – especially when he wants his reputation protected – you had better listen.

Besides, I liked his idea of closing the northern farms – most of which were pretty marginal, spear-won properties still subsisting on frontier rations. And most of our best fighters were up there. And Heron was right – I could ride right through them.

We were the size of a small army when we rode out the next morning – fifty royal companions, more than a hundred retainers and grooms, ten baggage carts, grain, pork, jars of wine, casks of silver. But we were getting away clean, and any idea of pursuit was a day late. We slept in the open that night, and on one of my northern farms the next.

I think it was three days into our exile that we were all sleeping on the floor of the 'hall' of my poorest farm – a timber hall shorter in length than my great hall at home was wide. Our companions were packed in like salted anchovies from the coast. I sent twenty grooms ahead under Polystratus with all the slaves from the northern farms, to clear the road over the mountains, buy food and prepare the way.

It was pouring rain. Some of the slaves were weeping – their lives were hard already, and being driven out into the winter was pretty cruel. Of course, they didn't know the half of it. If Attalus came here …

But the women wept. The rain fell. And Prince Alexander was sleeping on the floor of a frontier farm. He was between me and Hephaestion. I was lying there in my cloak, listening to the rain, and thinking – I remember this very well – of Thaïs. Not Nike. Such is the power of lust and time. I was imagining … well, never you mind.

Alexander was weeping.

I'd never heard him weep before.

So I tore myself from Thaïs's imagined embraces. 'My lord?'

'Go away,' he whispered.

Hephaestion was sound asleep and no help.

'Lord, we're almost to the mountains and safety,' I said.

'Thanks,' he said. Dismissively.

'Lord—'

'Fuck *off*,' he hissed.

I rolled over, so that we were eye to eye. Once, I'd have let him go. But we had put too much behind us – together. 'Talk to me,' I whispered.

'I'm going to die some fat old fuck at someone else's court!' he said. 'I'll wash up in Asia or Athens, and men will point at me and say – there's the victor of Chaeronea. What happened to him? *Fuck* Philip! Maybe he isn't my father. I should have killed him while he lay there. Then I'd be king. Now I will be *no one*.'

Well – what do you say to that? Eh?

'You know what exiles are like? Hatching useless plots, to feel alive? Fondling slaves, because no free person will be with them? They become like family retainers, or old slaves – drones, feeding off the fat of the house and contributing nothing, with no excellence, no arete – nothing to offer.' Alexander knew what he was talking about, because there were generations of exiles around the fringes of the Macedonian court – Persians, Athenians, even a Spartan. And we'd seen more of them in Athens. Thracians, Persians, even a Scythian prince from the far north.

His voice was thick with unshed tears.

I reached out, squeezed his shoulder hard – and said, 'You don't sound like Achilles, to me.'

Macedonians aren't big on gentle.

He froze as if I'd stuck a dagger into him.

His breath shuddered in and out a few times. Then it steadied down.

I went to sleep.

In the morning, nothing more was said. Except that the man who vaulted into the saddle was the man who led the cavalry charge at Chaeronea.

EIGHT

We passed most of the winter in Epirus, at a court so barbarous that Pella seemed like Athens, and suddenly Olympias seemed a great deal less alien than before. She was a child of this world at the edge of chaos.

I tell this out of order, but I remember once when she came to visit us – she had her own court at Epirus, and as a princess of the blood she had the sort of loyalty there that she probably missed at home – men who would die for her. At any rate, Alexander had his own rooms, and we were having – that is, I was throwing – an Athenian-style symposium. We were lying on couches, and the subject of the debate was love, and I was thinking of Thaïs – not that I loved her, but that she was worthy of love.

Alexander smiled at Hephaestion. 'I love Hephaestion, because he is me, and I am he,' he said.

Truth to tell, we groaned aloud then threw things at him. Which was a good sign, because it meant we were starting to heal. Going into exile is like losing a battle, or taking a beating, or failing, or losing a loved one. It hurts, and the hurt can last a long time.

At any rate, we were lying on our couches philosophising, and she swept in without warning. So perfect was her intelligence net – it always was – that she got past our sentries with all her women – she knew when the guards changed, and when the sentries were lax, and when men went off for a quick fumble – perhaps *with* one of her maids.

The women entered first – a dozen of them, in beautiful wools, and their arrival froze our talk. Her arrival – her beauty, even her perfume – trapped us like bars of adamantine. No one moved.

She stood in the middle of the room – in fact, in my memory, she is *always* at the centre of the room – and she looked around slowly. When her eyes met mine, she smiled.

'Son of Lagus,' she said warmly. 'You do my son good service.'

Lovely words, but they chilled me to the bone. And despite that, as I've said before, I desired her.

She went and sat on Alexander's couch. 'You are safe here,' she said.
He grimaced.

She slapped his side. 'Don't play your foolish boys' Athenian games with me,' she said. 'This is Epirus, not Athens, and I can go where I want. Don't pretend that I cannot.'

Alexander was not happier for that.

She smiled at him, a little motherly superiority etched between her brows. 'You so want to be men. But you are boys. It was well done, getting here, but now you need me. We will raise an army, and Philip will see reason. You will see. And everything will be as it was.'

Alexander looked at his mother, and for once he told her the truth. 'I do not want it as it was.'

She laughed. But her laugh got no echo.

'He will relent. As he gets older, it is harder and harder for him to see—'

'I will kill him, if I must,' Alexander said.

And she met his eye, and something passed between them. And she smiled. 'If it comes to that,' she said.

And he grinned, like a grateful son.

She ruled Epirus. Not exactly ruled, but she did as she liked there, and we saw clearly what she came from, and what had made her so sure of herself, so like a goddess come to earth – I mean one of the less human, more vengeful sorts of goddesses.

Beyond Epirus, men wore skins and tattoos, and no one knew the rule of law. At the 'court' of Epirus, most of the warriors had never heard of Aristotle. Or Plato. Or the *Iliad*. There were men like rhapsodes, and they sang songs – endless tales of the borders, where one man killed another in a litany of violence. I admit that the *Iliad* can sound that way, but it is the *Iliad*. These songs were long and dull and had no story beyond the blood, the infidelity of women, the perfidiousness of the cowardly, the greatness of the men of pure blood – come to think of it, this does sound like the *Iliad*, but the difference is that the *Iliad* is beautiful and powerful and these were dull. And monotonous.

There were Keltoi at Epirus – tribal barbarians from the north and west, with red hair, tattoos and superb swords and metalwork, and tall tales – better tales than the Epirote singers sang, about gods in chariots and beautiful women. One of the Keltoi mercenaries there made up a song that slighted Olympias, and she had him killed.

Remarkably, the other Keltoi took no offence.

It was there, at the 'court' of Epirus, that my lifelong love of writing really started. I had very little to do – for the first time in my life. We organised the companions and the grooms into a rotation of watches on the prince – but with fifty men at arms and a hundred grooms, we each only had a watch every ten days.

I took them out for drills every day. That gave the day structure. I had learned some very fancy riding tricks in Athens – team tricks, the way the Athenian Hippeis did them for the religious festivals – and I taught them to the royal companions. And I put all my fighters on to the grooms and trained them hard, too.

But you can only do so much drill. And I lacked the experience to know that I should have kept them all busy all the time. I had enough trouble keeping myself entertained.

I rode, wrestled – in a town so barbaric that they didn't have a gymnasium or a palaestra, which is funny – when you think of what Pyrrhus has built there now! But at the time, it was hard to train, hard to keep weight off.

At any rate, I started to write. The first thing I wrote was about the Keltoi – what they wore, what they carried, and their marvellous stories. They had beautiful women with them – back-talking, witty, marvellous women with bright hair, slanted eyes and a boldness seldom seen in Macedon. They weren't available – I tried – but they flirted as if they were.

Men who didn't understand found themselves matching swords with the Keltoi men. I understood, because in this way the Keltoi were like Athenians. Subtler, but not weaker.

And I wrote about the mountains, which, despite the lack of culture, were breathtakingly beautiful and full of game.

One of my favourite memories came from that winter.

After a snow, the royal huntsman – who was himself of royal birth and carried the portentous name of the hero himself, Lord Achilles – took us on a bear hunt. I had never been out for bear. I'd seen the fur, seen the animal once or twice, but until then I'd never seen one stand on its back feet and rip dogs to pieces.

It was in a thicket at the edge of a clearing in a high oak forest, well up the mountainside, and that bear had a better eye for terrain than most Greek generals. His flanks were covered by ravines and he had an escape route out the back of the thicket and into the deep trees, and our dogs, loyal and well trained, made hopeless leaps at the monster and died, so that that roar of the baying pack became quieter and quieter. The dogs could reach the bear only two at a time.

Old Achilles leaned on his spear. 'Well, boys?' he said. I was there with Alexander and half of his court in exile, and for a moment it occurred to me that this was some deep Macedonian intrigue to kill the prince.

Alexander raised an eyebrow. And winked at me.

'You and Hephaestion up the ravines,' he said. 'Horn-call when you are within a spear-cast of the bear. Philip and Nearchus and I will go right up the hill into him. All we need is a few seconds – thrown spears will do it if you hit him.'

That was our plan.

I spent half an hour climbing the ravine. You try climbing wet rocks in a scale thorax and smooth-soled boots. With a pair of spears and a sword.

I'd still be there if not for Polystratus, who followed me, or led me, barefoot – handing me up my spears, and pushing my arse when I couldn't find a handhold.

An hour, and the sun was going down and most of the dogs were dead, or beaten. I got up the last big rock, and I could smell the bear, and I could see why the old monster was still there.

One of the first dogs had got through the bear's guard and mangled a paw – a back paw. The bear was bleeding out, and couldn't run.

He was a giant, and he was noble, like some barbaric war chief clad in fur, with a ring of his dead enemies around his feet.

I put my horn to my lips and blew.

The bear turned and looked at me. Out shot a paw – if I hadn't been in armour I'd have died, and even as it was, scales flew as if the bear was a cook in Athens and I was a new-caught fish. I still have the scars – three claws went right through the scales and cut me.

I was taken completely by surprise. I thought that the old bear was at bay – exhausted and done for.

There's a laugh. And a lesson.

Polystratus put his shoulder into my back and held me against the bear. That may sound like a poor decision, but it was a two-hundred-foot fall to the rocks below.

I got my sword into the bear – two-handed. Polystratus was shouting – I mostly remember the bear's teeth snapping at my helmet and the hot, stinking breath. The bear reared back, and then stepped away.

I managed to keep my feet, although there was a lot of blood coming out of me. But the bear grew a spear – Hephaestion, somewhere beyond my tunnelling vision, had made a fine throw. The bear turned towards him, and Polystratus threw – another good throw, and the head buried itself to the shaft, and dust flew from the monster's hide.

I didn't have the strength to throw mine – not hard enough to penetrate its hide – so I knelt and angled my spear at the bear. The

175

bear swiped at the spearhead – I dipped the head and stabbed – and Alexander was there, and Black Cleitus, and Philip, their spears went into the beast, and then Alexander went right in between the claws with his sword – fore cut, back cut to the throat and the beast was dead.

Achilles himself was in at the kill, spear in the beast.

He nodded at us.

'That was well done,' he said. He measured the bear and pronounced us to be mighty.

Alexander watched the bear die. 'He was noble,' the prince said. 'We were many – he stood against us all, like one of the heroes of old.'

Then he turned to me. 'But you went toe to toe with him alone,' he said. Polystratus was stripping my thorax to get at my wounds.

I was on my back. 'And he bested me. Polystratus did all the work.'

Alexander shook his head. 'Isn't this your ivory-hilted sword stuck in him to the hilt?' he said.

My vision was tunnelling tighter and tighter. There was so much blood ...

It was full spring when I regained consciousness, and it was warm in the sun. I had had dreams – dreams of Nike where she called on me to avenge her, and dreams of Thaïs that were rather different, and dreams of Alexander and monsters.

A great deal had happened since the bear hunt.

A bear's claws are filthy, and my wounds – really no worse than what a man might take sparring in armour – became infected. The deadly archer shot me *full* of arrows, and I was sick for a month, raving, out of my head.

I was still weak, but awake and alive in the sun, when we crossed the muddy passes – the highest were still full of snow – to Agriania in Illyria, a place so barbaric that Epirus seemed civilised. But the king here – Longarus – was a guest friend of Alexander's, and despite the defeat we'd inflicted on him, or perhaps because of it, he hosted us.

I get ahead of myself, though.

On the road there – a road I remember as colder than anything I'd ever experienced, I guess because of my illness and wounds – Alexander filled me in on a winter of news.

Cleopatra was pregnant. Very pregnant. Had obviously been pregnant when married. And Philip had won the agreement of the League of Corinth – the new league of Greek allies – to the sacred war with Persia. He'd made them swear to support *Philip and his heirs*.

In Asia, the King of Kings was dead – murdered by his vizier, Bagoaz.

Arses, the new King of Kings, was Bagoaz's puppet, and Persia looked like a ripe fruit ready to fall into Philip's mouth.

Philip had spent the winter training the army, and moving the heavy baggage and much of the artillery train to the Chersonese.

The troops were on the verge of mutiny because they were unpaid. This was hardly news, but took on a different meaning when we were exiles.

My money was almost gone. I'd fed my people for the winter and put armour on all the grooms, and that was the limit of my purse. And there was nothing from Heron. Easy to see evil in that, but the passes were mostly closed with weather and Attalus was absolute master in Macedon when Philip was in Corinth.

Antipater lay low, but he was our source for most of these events. His letters came in with the first caravan. No letters for me, and no money, but news for Alexander. He counselled patience, and reminded Alexander that he was the only adult contender for the throne and that, despite the loud talk at the wedding feast, there was no official word. None of us was outlawed.

But I learned from Hephaestion that we'd left Epirus because Attalus had threatened war if we weren't handed over.

Attalus meant to finish the job himself, it appeared.

The royal fortress in Agriania was built entirely of logs, and everyone wore furs and no one could read. I got a hint of how Athenians must feel at Pella – my first night, I slept in the great hall and listened to men having sex with women – noisily – while two other men gutted each other drunkenly with knives. No worse than Pella, in some ways – but worse, somehow. I didn't sleep – I was still touched with fever, and the two sets of noises combined to give me a hideous nightmare. And Nike came to me again and demanded that I avenge her murder.

But spring came and, with it, some hope, as she always brings. First, a letter from Heron, with several gold bars. And news of Attalus – who at least appeared to have accepted Heron as the lord of my former estates.

Attalus was not having an easy time, as the highland kingdoms were on the edge of rebellion and he was trying to tax them anyway. He sent troops, and there was fighting. And men – highlanders – came and joined us in Illyria, and made us feel less cut off from home. Before the midsummer solstice, a major religious festival even in the barbaric north, Laodon and Erygius came up the passes and laughed at the furs and the meals of meat alone. They'd been sent away from the army. Indeed, all of Alexander's friends were in exile – the actors, the philosophers, even men who'd been paid by Philip to be his war tutors. The two Lesbians brought life and light with them.

And brought me a letter from Athens. Two letters, really – one inside the other. The bigger was from Kineas, who wrote me a passionate letter decrying the perfidy of Philip and asking of news of Alexander. As Kineas was the first Athenian to write – almost the first foreigner – his place in Alexander's estimation climbed like the sun.

And folded inside his letter was a small twist of paper for me. It said, 'Son of Lagus, preserve yourself. Athena, goddess of wisdom, be with you, and Tyche.' It was unsigned, but had a tiny picture of an owl and a smiling face.

Thaïs.

I have it right here, in this amulet around my neck. Don't imagine that I was dreaming quietly of her, that summer, and living like an ascetic. Slave girls were plentiful and cheap, and willing enough, and pretty enough. But the sight of her writing sent a thrill through me, and the happiness stayed with me for days.

The letter from Kineas came just before midsummer, and lifted Alexander's mood. We had quite a little court by then, and we drilled – Laodon knew more cavalry drills than I ever did and he took over, and I let him. We read the *Iliad* together, and Alexander married an Illyrian girl – oh, I know, it's not in the official papers because he repudiated it later, but he needed the alliance just then, and it got us money and food and bought time. Anyway, she came with warriors, and we started teaching them some of our ways. I commanded them later – as you'll hear.

Philip the Red said that teaching Illyrians to be better warriors would prove to be an error. A wise man, Philip.

And we put on plays. Laodon had some scrolls of Menander and one of old Aeschylus – truly, I think it was the first theatre ever performed in Illyria. On the festival of Dionysus, the 'Court in Exile' put on *The Persians*. The Illyrians sat silent through most of it, but applauded wildly for the fight scene we put in – lots of sword-clashing, and Alexander cutting me (dressed as a Persian) down at the height of our 'Battle of Marathon'. Not in Aeschylus's original, of course. But we did some rewriting.

And then, before the Illyrian harvest could come in, word came from Philip inviting Alexander back to Pella.

Cleopatra had given birth.

To a daughter.

Sometimes, the gods must laugh. All Attalus's careful planning, overturned by the chance of the womb. He begged Philip to wait – to spend another winter at Pella.

Philip would have none of it. He'd wasted a year, waiting for his son to be born. Possibly he'd seen the child's birth as the will of the gods. He had the allies in line, the Greeks were quiet or downright willing, the omens for an attack on Persia were favourable. And Philip, like many men whose hair begins to thin, could hear the furies at his back. At any rate, he sent an ambassador to Illyria with his request, and that ambassador was old Antipater, and he would never have taken Alexander to a trap.

I've said before that Philip was a forgiving man. He often forgave enemies that other men would have killed – in this, he was truly great. As I've said before – once men were beaten and acknowledged him master – he was very forgiving.

I think that he assumed his son was cut from the same cloth.

We rode down the same passes we'd climbed in early spring. I was still so skinny that my armour didn't fit, and my boots didn't close correctly and my arms were more like sticks than like the arms of an athlete.

Alexander looked out over the first plains of Macedon. 'I will be king,' he said.

I nodded, or said something reassuring.

He looked at me and raised his eyebrow. 'Listen to me, Odysseus. I need your wily ways and your sharp sword. He will do it again. When I've been home a week, or a month, he will remember that I am the better man and it will gall him again. He cannot abide my excellence.' He looked at Laodon; the Lesbian man was preparing to leave us. He was still an exile, and he was going over the border to Thessaly with his retainers and some of my gold bars. 'And he cannot abide the excellence of my friends,' Alexander continued.

And you cannot stop showing it to him, I thought, but didn't say.

'We'll guard you,' I said.

Alexander shook his head. 'No. The time for defending is over. I mean to have him dead, before he kills me.'

I can't pretend I was even shocked. I'd had the same thought ever since we left him lying there unconscious. Patricide? Regicide? Listen, lad – when you are in the thick of a fight, there's no morality – just kill or be killed. We had two choices – ride away and be exiles for ever, or put the king in the ground as soon as we could.

No other choice, really.

'I'm with you,' I said.

Alexander reached over and shook my hand. 'Knew you would be,' he said. 'When I'm king—'

I laughed. 'When you are king, you'll need to buy off all your

179

enemies,' I said. 'I'm the Lord of Ichnai and Allante. I don't need rewards. I'm your man.'

So we rode down the passes into Macedon, and as we rode, we quietly plotted to murder the king.

PART II
The Path to the Throne

NINE

———

Looking back, I think that it might all have been talk, if not for Pausanias. He hadn't made many friends since he was the royal favourite – he'd been demoted back to page when his accusations against Attalus and Diomedes outraged the king. But he'd served well – even brilliantly – at Chaeronea, and he was well born, if only a highlander. He wasn't a favourite of Alexander's, or mine, or Hephaestion's, but he was one of us, and there were young men in our pages' group who we liked a lot less and still tolerated.

Pausanias had a remarkable way of saying the most dramatic thing instead of telling the truth, which made him untrustworthy as a scout or as a friend – a tendency to exaggerate, not just to make a story better, but because he craved excitement. This is not an uncommon failing in young men, but he had it to a degree I've seldom seen, and the saddest thing was that he had real accomplishments – he was a brilliant runner and a fine javelin-thrower. But he never bragged or exaggerated his real accomplishments.

I only mention this by way of explanation, because what's coming is hard enough to understand.

We returned to Pella and had a public reconciliation with the king. He was entirely focused on the invasion of Asia, and he'd just appointed Attalus and Parmenion joint commanders of the advance guard – picked men, a whole picked army.

It was only then, I think, that Alexander discovered how advanced his father's plans were for Asia. And his anger was spectacular – almost worthy of Ares himself.

I was there – dinner in the palace, with only men from our pages' group at the couches, and Alexander was silent. Hephaestion tried to cheer him, called him Achilles, waited on him hand and foot and recited the *Iliad*.

Alexander was having none of it. I suspected what was wrong, the way all of us do when a favourite or a wife is silent and careful. When we are left to guess for ourselves just *why* the subject of our scrutiny is so silent. I watched Alexander, and I guessed that it was the preparations for the war in Asia. They were all around us, from the horse farms teeming with new geldings ready for war to the piles – literally – of new-cut ash poles outside the foot companions' barracks. We'd done our part, signing Athens to the fight, but Philip had not wasted a moment, and all Macedon – and all Greece – was girding for the war we'd all known from birth would happen some day. The great adventure. The crusade.

And we were going to sit home in Pella and hear our elders tell of how it went.

I remember Hephaestion starting into the recitation of Achilles at the head of the Myrmidons when Alexander let out something very like a screech and stood up. 'Fuck that!' he roared. He flung his wine cup across the room and it was squashed flat with the power of the throw – gold with tin in it.

Alexander scarcely ever swore.

Silence fell over the room.

'He's going to go east and leave me with *nothing*,' Alexander said. '*Nothing.*'

Hephaestion, who often misunderstood his hero, shook his head. 'You'll be regent—'

'Regent?' Alexander was almost crying. 'Regent? I want to conquer the world! I will pull the Great King off his throne! It is *my* destiny. *Mine!* He is stealing my life, the old goat! The rutting monster!'

I haven't mentioned it, but we couldn't miss the fact that Cleopatra, the new wife, was once again heavily pregnant, nor that many nobles acted as if Alexander were already supplanted. Nor that Attalus, who, in Macedonian parlance, had the king's cock by both ends – by which they meant that he was Cleopatra's uncle and Diomedes' as well – was to be commander in Asia for the initial campaigns.

At any rate, I remember Alexander standing there, eyes sparkling and nearly mad, his hair almost on end, his muscles standing out. He was possessed – if not by a god, then by something worse. But he was not human in that moment, and he meant business. Had his father entered the room just then, Alexander might have killed him himself.

It was not Philip who entered, but Alexander's mother, Olympias. Who was supposed to be in exile at Epirus, but was mysteriously back in Pella.

She was hardly the monster that Kleithenes has proclaimed her, but she was capable of *anything*. Beautiful – Aphrodite gave her what men desire with both hands. Long, perfect legs, wide thighs and a waist so small that after birthing a child a big man could still get his hands around her tummy. Breasts not just beautiful to look at but curiously inviting – something about the texture of the skin between her breasts demanded that you touch it. It was smooth and yet never shiny. Her hair was as black as charcoal or a moonless night, and her eyes were seductive – deep, expressive, laughing – Alexander later claimed that she had lain with a god, and if anyone was god-touched, it was she.

Men claimed to have lain with her – or to know someone who had – she had a reputation as utterly wanton. I wonder. I never knew anyone who made the claim and seemed believable. I do know several who made the claim and had accidents afterwards.

But beyond her beauty, which was intimidating, was her brain, which was godlike. She never forgot a name. She never forgot an injury or a service. She knew every slave in royal service and every page who had ever served her son by name and family and value of service. She had a web of informers worthy of Delphi, and she usually knew who slept with whom and what the repercussions were, men and women both.

She couldn't read. But she could recite the *entire Iliad*. She could create lyric poetry extempore, alluding to Sappho or Alcaeus or Simonides, even borrowing a line here and there ...

She was brilliant. Alexander's godlike genius probably came from her, and not from Philip.

Of course, she was almost completely devoid of human emotions, except lust for revenge and a desire to see her son, as an extension of her own will, succeed. They say a child is two years old before he realises that his mother is not actually part of him. Perhaps true – but Olympias never, ever realised that Alexander was not part of her. An extension of her. Those men at court who saw women only as mysterious possessors of alien sex organs – such men are common everywhere, and mythologise women in terms of sex; you know whereof I speak, young man? Good. Those men at court liked to claim that Olympias slept with her son.

Crap. She had no need to sleep with him. She lived through him, and consulted him from childhood on every aspect of her life. She was his priestess – he was her god. It was a deeply disturbing relationship, one that appalled even Alexander, and yet he was always helpless in her presence, unable to be a man or even a boy, usually just a toy to her will.

I did not like her. I avoided her as much as I could, and even now, knowing that she is safely dead at that thug Cassander's hands, I still fear her. Men at court feared her as a witch, a woman, a beauty. They were fools. She was one of them to her finger's ends, and they should have dreaded her as one dreads a boar turned at bay, or a royal Macedonian bent on achieving power.

Again, I tell this because without understanding her, nothing that follows makes much sense.

At any rate, there we were, in virtual exile still, even at the heart of Macedonian power, and we were to all intents under siege. She had been exiled, and if the king had recalled her, we never heard. She hadn't followed us to Illyria, but she had suggested the move, arranged the marriage, given Alexander money . . .

Well, I for one assumed she was still in Epirus, and still in exile.

Apparently not!

She entered the room and Alexander turned pale. We were already silent, but the silence took on a new texture.

'Whining about Philip?' she said. She had a cup in her hand. She stopped near the door, bent with a dancer's grace and plucked the ruins of Alexander's gold cup from the floor. 'Achilles was a petulant arse, too, my dear. That's an element of his heroism I desire that you avoid.'

I remember thinking I would choke. That's how she always struck me.

She sat on Alexander's kline and this time she lay down, as if experimenting with the feel of a couch. She lay back – scandalous in itself. She had golden sandals and her feet were painted. Her feet were as beautiful as the rest of her – and really, she was fifteen years older than me. My lord's *mother*.

She took a sip of wine. 'Well?' she asked the silence.

Alexander was choking. 'This is a man's feast, Mother.'

'No, it is not. If you were a man, Philip would be cold rotting clay in the ground, or bleeding himself out in a pool of his own vomit. He is not, so you, my dear, are not yet a man.' She smiled lazily. 'I predict that soon enough, one of you will come upon a method of killing the king. And then we will take power, and proceed to rule well. Philip must die.' She smiled. 'I shock you. You are still such . . . boys. How dare I – a matron? A mother? Suggest that my husband must die? Listen, boys – he's had a boy or a girl on the end of his cock every day since I first spread my thighs for him, and I laugh, because none of them can give him what I can. But now he wants to be rid of my son – my godlike son, his true heir. And me. And this is not Philip, great-hearted Lion of Macedon. This is little Philip, the lover of Diomedes and the lickspittle of Attalus. Best that he die, before all his greatness is forgotten.'

She got up. Smoothed the linen of her chiton, and handed Alexander her jewelled wine cup. 'There, my dear. A new cup for your old one.

Get it done, my dear. He means to rid himself of you and of me, too. Just this evening, one of my snakes died of something I was to have eaten.' She smiled brilliantly at all of us. 'I was tiring of Epirus. It was time to come back here and make Philip dine on his own vomit. Why are you shocked? I only say what you *think*.' She rose on her toes to kiss her son, and I could see every inch of her body through the linen, silhouetted against the hearth fire, and I thought in that moment – what was Philip thinking? What man would want more than that?

And truly, I think that if she had not been cursed with such a sharp mind, he'd have loved her for ever. But I imagine that she ferreted out the truth once too often. Who likes to feel inferior in a marriage? Especially when one is the king.

On her way out, she paused by my couch and leaned far over. When my traitor eyes left her face to probe inside her linen to the very nipples of her breasts, she flicked her eyes over mine and her lips twitched with a familiar ... contempt? Excitement?

'Where is Pausanias, tonight?' she asked.

Who knows what I choked out.

'You have the best brain in this room, besides his,' she said. 'Find Pausanias. He is now in a position to help us all.' She laughed, a horrible laugh. Later, I knew she was making a pun on the word *position*.

She straightened and cast her goddess-like smile around the room. 'Be good, boys,' she said, and glided out.

I grabbed Cleon and, I think, Perdiccas – and told them to find Pausanias. He hadn't gone into exile with us, and we'd only seen him once since we returned. Rumour was he had allied himself with Attalus – one way you can tell when a man is pre-eminent is that his enemies start to become his friends because they have nowhere else to go.

Poor Pausanias.

Alexander was quiet after his mother's visit – quiet and thoughtful. Since he wasn't up to any mischief, I let him go, and threw knucklebones with Hephaestion and young Neoptolymos, one of the other highlander lords attached to the pages.

There was a disturbance down in the royal stables – loud shouting, someone screaming.

Alexander stepped behind his couch and drew his sword. That's how close to the edge we all were.

Nearchus was on duty and sober. He took two pages in armour and raced off down the corridors towards the stables. We sent all the slaves away.

More shouting, some drunken, some sober. A weapons clash. A scream.

'We're Attalus's men!' clear as day. And another scream. The unmistakable sound of a man with a sword in his groin or guts.

Alexander was in his battlefield mode. His eyes met mine. 'Go and find out,' he said. He even managed a smile. 'Don't die.'

I grinned back, hopped over my kline and ran, barefoot, through the curtains, aware that there were slaves just outside the door, cowering out of my way, and more slaves all down the corridor – it was, after all, the main corridor that connected the king's apartments with the prince's. I could see a pair of his royal companions outside the king's door – not at attention, but straining towards me like hunting hounds waiting to be released.

I waved my sword at them. They knew me. 'If I find anything I'll tell you!' I called as I raced by. Hard to imagine they might actually be trying to kill me.

I got down to the stables without seeing another freeman. The screams were done – so was the shouting.

Perdiccas was just inside the stables, with two dead men-slaves – at his feet. Cleon the Black was holding another man – at first, I thought Cleon was 'questioning' him.

Perdiccas looked as if he was going to cry.

Cleon just looked angry and perhaps disgusted.

'We found Pausanias,' he spat.

The man he was holding in his arms was Pausanias. He was naked. Blood was running out of his anus – thick, dark blood. All over Cleon's wool chiton and his legs. Cleon didn't flinch.

'They raped him,' Cleon said. 'Attalus and Diomedes, and every guest at the party. And then he was given to the slaves, and *they* raped him, too. Fifty men?' Cleon's words were thick with rage.

Pausanias was breathing. It sounded almost like snores – it took me a long time to realise he was sobbing without any voice left. He'd screamed his voice away.

'*He* told you that?' I asked.

Cleon jutted his chin at the two corpses. 'They did. Attalus's stable boys.'

Perdiccas had recovered his wits enough to clean his weapon. 'If we're found – fuck, it's murder. We killed them.'

I nodded. The bodies were a problem. So was Pausanias. He was alive. He would tell his story.

Attalus meant him to live to tell his story.

Olympias, damn her, *knew* already what had happened. She'd as much as told us. So the story wouldn't be secret. I stared around, trying to see through the endless dark labyrinth of Macedonian court politics.

Attalus was making a statement – that Alexander was too powerless to protect his friends.

I thought of Diomedes a year before. Wondered if I had been intended for a similar fate.

It was a fate any Macedonian would dread – now that he'd been used as a woman by fifty men, Pausanias's life was over. No matter that it had been done by force. No matter. He would be marked. As weak.

Even I felt a certain aversion. I didn't want to touch him. I marvelled at Cleon's toughness.

But even while I thought through the emotions, a colder part of my brain went throught the ramifications.

'Right. Cleon – can you carry him?' I asked.

As answer, Cleon rose to his feet and swung the older man on his broad shoulders. A drop of Pausanias's blood hit my cheek and burned me as if it were acid – I felt his pollution. Or so I thought.

'Take him to Alexander. Perdiccas and I will get rid of the bodies.' I looked at Cleon. 'Tell me the king is here, and was not at the party.'

Cleon shrugged.

Perdiccas and I carried the two thugs out of the royal stables. This may surprise you, but despite plots and foreign hatred, the palace itself was almost completely unguarded – two men on the king's chamber, two on the queen's, a couple of pages on Alexander and sometimes a nightwatchman on the main gate. We carried the dead men out one at a time, through the picket door used to clear manure out of the stables.

We carried them through the streets – streets devoid of life or light – and left them behind Attalus's house. I put knives in their hands, as if they'd fought each other. I doubt that a child would have been fooled.

After that, it was open war in the streets – our men against theirs. Pausanias was sometimes a tart and always a difficult friend – but he was one of us, and the outrage committed against him was a rape of every page. We were unmanned together. As we were supposed to have been.

Diomedes led the attacks – sometimes from in front, and sometimes from a safe third rank. Cleon and Perdiccas were caught in the agora by a dozen of Attalus's relatives, challenged and beaten so badly that Cleon's left arm never healed quite right. They were baited with Pausanias's fate. Anything might have happened, but a dozen royal companions intervened.

The next day, I was on the way to my house – my rebuilt house – with Nearchus beside me when Diomedes appeared in front of me.

'Anyone able to hear poor Pausanias fart?' he said. 'Ooh, he wasn't as tight as Philip said he was!'

There were men – Thracians – behind me.

I ran.

There's a trick to the escalation of violence – most men, even Macedonians, take a moment to warm themselves up. Diomedes had to posture – both because he enjoyed it, and to get himself in the mood to murder me.

I turned and ran, grabbing Nearchus's hand as I went.

I went right through the loose ring of Thracians behind me, and took a sword-slash across my shoulders and upper back – most of it caught in the bunches of fabric under my shoulder brooches, but some of the cut went home.

But most of the Thracians were so surprised that they stumbled over each other.

We ran along the street, back towards the palace.

'Get them, you *idiots*!' Diomedes shouted.

But they were foreigners, didn't know the city and had riding boots on. I was a former page wearing light sandals, and I flew. Nearchus was with me, stride for stride – street, right turn, alley, under an awning, along an alley so narrow that the householders had roofed it over, up and over a giant pile of manure – euch – into a wagon yard that I knew well and north, along the high wall of the palace, and we were clear.

Diomedes bragged of our cowardice.

Two days later, despite orders to go in groups of at least ten, a gang of Attalus's retainers caught Orestes and Pyrrhus and Philip the Red. They were stripping Orestes to rape him when Polystratus put an arrow into one of the men, a muleteer, and the would-be rapists ran.

Alexander was exact in describing what he would do to the next man who was caught. 'I care what happens to you,' he said carefully. 'But you must care what happens to us *all*. They are trying to break us. To make us the butt of humour. Humiliated boys, in a world of men. *Do you understand?* he asked, his voice calm and deadly, and we did. I had seldom heard him sound more like his father.

Our wing in the palace became like a small city under siege, and out in the town, our slaves and our houses burned.

One of the slaves who tasted Alexander's food died. In agony.

The next day, Alexander took me aside. 'I want you to strike back,' he said. 'I can't be seen to act in this. I must be seen to be the oppressed party. My father is openly contemptuous of me. So be it. But if we do not strike back, our people will lose heart.'

The next day, I had Philip the Red go to the royal companions' quarters and ask for bread.

They refused. Some suggestions were made as to what Philip could do to get bread.

Philip lost his temper and told them what he thought of grown men behaving in such a way to their cousins and sons. And the whole mess of the royal companions laughed him out of their barracks.

Then I sent Polystratus to scout. On his return, he reported that every entrance to the palace was watched, and he'd been 'allowed' to go out.

Sometimes the best plan is to give your enemies what they expect. That night, while I was on guard, I poured wine for Alexander.

'It will be tomorrow,' I told him.

He nodded. 'Don't tell me any more,' he said.

Later, coming off duty, I went to Olympias's wing and visited Pausanias. The queen was sitting on his couch, singing to him quietly – one of the bear songs of Artemis. I stopped in the doorway. She caught my eye and shook her head, and I retreated.

The queen came out of the room into the corridor and I bowed.

'He is not ready for visitors,' she said. 'Especially not men in armour.'

I wanted to ask her – *Is he broken? Ruined?* But I could not. She shook her head.

'He is better. I will restore his wits. Women know more than men about this.' She smiled, and her smile was terrifying. 'Oh, if only men could be raped by women – the world would be more just.'

I had to reconsider my views on Alexander's mother – because her care for Pausanias was genuine. All her women said she was with him every moment of her day. And this for a boy who had been her husband's lover.

Then she caught my eye. 'Be careful tomorrow,' she said.

That sent ice down my spine.

She laughed. 'Half my maids are missing chitons. I can guess.' She nodded. 'And if I can guess, so can Attalus.'

'Since you know, would my lady condescend to give us some kohl?' I asked.

Eight of us went out of the palace in the first light, dressed as female slaves, with a pair of carts. We left through the slave entrance and we had the same carts that they used every day to fetch bread. I had Orestes and Pyrrhus and Perdiccas, but not Black Cleitus or Philip the Red or any of the blooded men. Polystratus drove one of the carts, but in the first narrow street, he switched with me, pulled himself from the top of the cart on to the tiled rooftops and ran off into the darkness, no doubt cursed by every man and woman sleeping under the tiles.

Our little procession of carts and slaves rolled up the alleys and into the main market, then along the northern edge of the agora to the great ovens where bread was baked. If they were on to us, they gave no sign.

We loaded the bread. And the baker's apprentices behaved so oddly that even if I hadn't already been suspicious, I'd have been suspicious. I didn't let any of my 'girls' get close to the baker's boys, and I kept my distance and spoke low.

The lead apprentice watched the last round loaves loaded into the carts. 'Hurry up,' I said impatiently.

He gave me an insolent stare. 'Fuck off, *maiden*.' He laughed. 'By the time you walk back to the palace, you'll walk more like matrons, I wager!'

The other apprentices tittered.

We moved off with a noisy squeal of wheels. The sun was well up, the temples were opening their bronze gates and there were enough people in the streets that I wondered if Attalus would dare come at us, even if he knew who we were.

We took a different route back to the palace – farther west, through the wealthier neighbourhoods where the nobility had their town houses. They were big houses, two or three storeys, with tile roofs and balconies and exedra – Athens boasted thousands of such houses, and Pella had about two hundred.

We passed within two blocks of Attalus's compound. Our strategy was to hide in plain sight, and baffle ambush by passing too close to Attalus for him to dare attack us.

Actually, that wasn't our strategy at all. That was our *apparent* strategy.

In a street lined with high walls, the squealing wheel gave way, and our convoy had to stop.

Eight slave girls and a broken-down cart full of bread.

We worked on the wheel as slowly as real slave girls. The sun rose, and as far as I was concerned, our enemies had proved themselves too incompetent to live. I was just at the point of moving on – the wheel was fine – when Orestes froze at my side.

'Now what have we here?' Diomedes swaggered. He was on horseback. 'Palace slaves?' He laughed. 'If you aren't girls now, sweetings, you will be soon.'

He had a dozen retainers. Not Thracians, but men sworn to his family. When I looked back, there were at least as many at the other end of the block.

Far more than I had counted on.

Orestes made a pretty girl. He bowed deeply. 'Lord, if you and your men would favour us ...?'

He indicated the wretched wheel.

Diomedes rode in, laughing, and his fist knocked Orestes to the ground.

I wanted him, so I ran forward, bare legs flashing, almost under his horse's hooves.

It is amazing how a woman's dress blinds a man, even when the man suspects that he's dealing with other men. Diomedes should never have let me in so close. On the other hand, he was too stupid to live.

I didn't throw myself on poor Orestes, who had a broken jaw.

I sliced Diomedes' horse from forelegs to penis with a very sharp knife and kept going under, grabbed one dangling foot and pulled him from the dying horse's back.

One of his men was awake, and close at his master's side. He cut at me, and I never saw the blow.

It fell on the shoulder of my scale corselet. We were all in armour, under our dresses.

I screamed something – the blow hurt, the opening of a bloom in spring exploding colour into the world, except faster, because it fell right on my wound of two days before. But the scales held, and my scream had the desired effect.

All my boys had swords, and they turned on anyone near at hand.

Our surprise was far from complete – Diomedes' men must have expected it, because they were trying to keep their distance. Spears were thrown, and we were about to have a vicious street fight. A fight wherein my side was young, inexperienced and had no missile weapons.

Diomedes got his feet under him, and rage overcame any attempt at sense.

He drew, whirled his chlamys over his arm and came at me.

'You seem to like the mud,' I said. I got my woman's chiton over my head in one pull – I'd practised – and around my arm. It was fine Aegyptian linen, and somewhere in the palace the owner was going to be none too happy with me.

They were two to one against us, and yet they hung back. That was human nature – they were freemen and thugs against nobles, and they feared both our superior training *and* the consequences even if they triumphed. I wanted to curse them. I wanted them to come in. But no plan is ever perfect.

As it was, the half-dozen who came at us from the north had no real notion of fighting mounted, and my pages were able to overcome them with simple adolescent ferocity.

I was aware of none of this, except as a distant set of blows and howls, because for all his failings, Diomedes was fast and mean and bigger than me. He was large enough that most of my superior skills were negated.

He hacked overhanded at me, and I had to step quickly to avoid getting my chlamys arm broken. His reach was the same as mine.

I needed to get inside his reach.

I crouched in my guard, flashed a glance behind me to see how the pages were doing – I was worried, by then – and Diomedes took advantage of my distraction to strike.

He went for a grapple. He was big, but he was not trained the way I had been trained. The moment he was in range, I punched my xiphos pommel into his teeth, passed my left foot over my right and threw my left hand into the needle's eye between his sword-arm elbow and armpit. My weight slammed into him as I got my arm up – the gods were with me, and by pure sweet chance my little finger went deep into his nostril and he stumbled – and I had him.

Arm up, elbow locked, turned into the ground.

The simplest control hold in pankration, and I had him kneeling at my feet, my sword at his cheek.

His retainers froze.

And that's when Polystratus and Philip the Red appeared over the walls on either side of the alley with a dozen more men, all armed with bows.

'Lay down your arms,' Philip shouted.

One of Diomedes' thugs turned to run and Polystratus shot him dead.

They dropped their swords and clubs with a series of clatters and a soft *thwop* as the weapons went into the mud.

Diomedes grunted, and I put more pressure on his arm and he gave a little scream. I had his right arm just at the edge of dislocation. As it was, his arm would hurt for a week.

I didn't hesitate to hurt him. In fact, I dragged Diomedes the length of the agora by his right arm, ruthlessly dislocating the shoulder.

To tell the truth, there was nothing *ruthless* about it. I enjoyed it. He screamed quite a bit.

The retainers were stripped naked and tied together by Philip's men. In what we might call 'revealing postures'. If this makes you feel queasy, try to remember that these were the men who had raped our friend.

My sword made a bloody little furrow in Diomedes' cheek. I remember that best of all – the blood running down his cheek as he begged me to let him go.

I didn't. I dragged him into the agora and up to the rostrum where merchants announced their wares and sometimes men accused other men of using false weights or selling bad horses.

In the middle of the agora, surrounded by Athenian merchants and Thessalian horse dealers, I stopped. It was possible that Attalus had grown powerful enough to kill me in broad daylight with fifty witnesses, but I doubted it.

I waited. Diomedes screamed. I thought of Pausanias, lying on a couch in the queen's chambers, his face to the wall, and I twisted the bastard's dislocated shoulder again. And again.

'This man who is screaming like a woman dishonoured my friend,' I shouted from the rostrum. 'His name is Diomedes. He is the nephew of the king's friend Attalus, and he is a faithless coward, a whore and a hermaphrodite. Aren't you, Diomedes?'

And I rotated his shoulder, and he screamed.

Shall I leave the rest out?

But that's how it was, in Macedon.

Eventually, the royal companions came, 'rescued' Diomedes and arrested me. That was the dangerous part – being walked to the palace, I wondered whether they'd let me be killed. But they were serious men, in armour, and Diomedes was a wreck of excrement and fear. He couldn't even speak.

I was dragged before Philip, dirty, disarmed and with my hands tied behind me like a thief. Diomedes was, after all, the royal favourite.

Philip was sitting on an ivory stool, playing with his dogs. As I came in, he scratched his beard and growled, and for a moment he looked like one of his mastiffs.

'Ptolemy,' he grumbled. He looked deeply unhappy. 'What the *fuck* have you been doing?'

I bowed. 'Lord,' I said, 'Attalus is planning to murder us – the older pages. Diomedes tried to trap me in the streets. I fought back.'

Philip spat. 'Attalus – Lord Attalus, the Commander of Asia – is plotting to murder some boys?' He shook his head angrily.

I shrugged. 'Do you know that he ordered Pausanias raped? By fifty men? By slaves?' I asked.

'I am your king, boy. You do not question me. I question you.' Philip picked up a cup of wine, poured a libation on the floor like a farmer and drank the rest off. 'Yes, I have heard that there was some matter involving Pausanias. But the boy always exaggerates everything.'

I shook my head and pointed towards the queen's wing of the palace. 'Go and see him,' I said. 'In this, he need say nothing. Just look at him and see if I exaggerate.'

Philip turned his head away. 'Ptolemy,' he began. Cleared his throat. 'This is more complicated than you can imagine, boy.'

I raised my head and met him eye to eye. 'Lord, your *friend* Attalus is trying to kill my friends – or rape them with slaves.'

'*I* will deal with men who break my laws!' Philip said. 'You cannot take the law into your own hands!'

I shrugged. 'If I had not ambushed Diomedes, his men would have killed me on the spot. Or worse.'

Philip gazed at a tapestry on the wall – the Rape of Europa, of all things.

I was not making any headway, and it occurred to me – for the first time, I think – that Philip could not actually accept what I was saying, because to accept it would have been to give up on a number of his cherished notions of how his court should function. Of his own power. Of his need to dispossess Alexander, although I'm not sure he ever admitted that to himself.

In fact, when you are a royal page, you are so deep in the court intrigue that it is like the blood in your body. And here, suddenly, I had to face the reality that the king himself didn't really know what was going on.

'Does my son plot to kill me?' Philip asked, suddenly.

'No,' I said, although my heart beat so loudly that I was afraid the king would hear it in my chest.

'Attalus says he has a plot – with that bitch his mother. Tell it to me, and I will see that you are protected and favoured.' Philip was showing his old iron – telling me to my face that he knew that something was up.

I remember that, because up until then, I had tried to be loyal to Alexander and loyal to the old king, as well.

But in that moment, I had to choose.

I was smart enough to stay in my role – as an angry youth. I forced a sneer. 'I'm sorry you think I look like the sort of man who informs on his friends,' I said.

Philip grabbed my hands. 'Look, you idiot – if Alexander tries for me and fails I'll have to kill him. If he kills me, he'll never manage to rule – he's too weak, too womanish, too easily swayed. Someone like Attalus will drag him down. Tell him from me – I need the balance. So does he. Let it be as it is now.' He released me.

I shrugged. 'I'll tell him,' he said. 'No idea what he'll say.'

'Does he know his own limitations?' Philip asked the ceiling. 'If I die, the whole thing is gone – Athens wins, and Macedon is a memory. None of the nobles will follow Alexander. He's too ... arrogant. Ignorant. Young.'

Philip saw his son only through a veil of his own failings. Very human, but surprising from the man who was King of Macedon. Philip couldn't let himself imagine that Alexander could do without him.

Alexander couldn't imagine that his father could conquer Asia without him.

I stood silent and judged them. On behalf of Macedon.

'You will make a public apology to Diomedes at the wedding.' He pointed at the door.

I bowed. 'What wedding, lord?'

Philip laughed. 'I am marrying young Cleopatra to my cousin, Alexander of Epiros. Olympias will be removed from the succession and I'll be shot of her for ever.' He smiled and poured more wine. 'I'm inviting all of Greece, boy. Athens will be empty.'

I said nothing. Cleopatra was Attalus's niece, remember. Not the same Cleopatra as Alexander's sister, due to be married to Alexander of Epiros at Aegae. Pay attention, boy – it's not my fault they were all inbred and had the same names.

'And this time next year, I'll cross into Asia. You could be with me, Ptolemy. I saw what you did at Chaeronea. You can lead. Men will follow you, despite that ugly mug you've got.'

Philip poured another libation. Drank more.

'It's like riding an unbroken horse,' he said, after he had allowed himself a sip. 'Sooner or later I'm going to slip and get thrown.' He frowned. I wasn't sure he knew I was there. 'And then it all comes down. Fuck them all.'

I got out of the room as fast as I could.

I was one of the first at court to know of the wedding, but in a few days it was the only topic. The court was to be moved to the ancient, sacred capital at Aegae. The theatre had been rebuilt, there were two new temples and everything shone with marble, polished bronze and new gilt.

Philip was going to sponsor a set of festivities lasting fifteen days, to overawe Greece with his civilised power as much as his armies dominated their thoughts of war and violence. He had hired the best playwrights and the best poets, the best rhapsodes, the best musicians.

I'm telling this out of order, because it's all jumbled up in my mind. I beat the living shit out of Diomedes and then, a week or so later, we rode north for Aegae and in that time, a great many things changed.

Cleopatra – the king's fourth wife – gave birth to a son. A healthy son. Philip was openly delighted.

That night he threw a feast. All were invited – even Alexander and his men.

Pausanias rose from his bed in the queen's wing of the palace and went to Philip to make a formal complaint. He did this before the entire court, two hundred of the most powerful men in Macedon and Thessaly, with fifty more highland noblemen of his own family to listen, most of the royal companions and every one of the pages of his own generation except me.

Alexander ordered me to stay in his rooms. He thought that Attalus would try to kill me if he saw me.

But Pausanias did something incredibly brave. He did what Attalus never imagined he'd dare to – he swore a complaint. He admitted that he'd been raped. In effect, he admitted his weakness, but at high polit-ical cost to Attalus, who thought that the man would suffer in silence.

Attalus pretended that nothing had happened, but they watched – I heard this from Nearchus and from Black Cleitus too – as they watched, Philip turned his back on his senior adviser.

Later – an hour later – when Attalus demanded my head on a platter, the king again turned his back on Attalus. He didn't even respond.

But still later – and very drunk – Philip also dismissed the charges against Attalus, with a weak joke about how everyone knew that Pausanias was prone to exaggerate. The 'joke' carried – intended or not – the suggestion that Pausanias had wanted what happened.

Pausanias turned very pale. Nearchus, who was closest to him, said for the rest of his life that Pausanias stumbled as if he'd been struck.

The next day Philip attended the newborn's naming ceremony. He held the squawking infant high in front of a thousand Macedonians and named him Caranus – the name of the founder of the dynasty, and thus a strong suggestion that he would be King of Macedon. Alexander held his tongue. But he was as pale as Pausanias that night. That part I saw. And the king kept his back resolutely to Attalus, who was forced to accept that the birth of his grand-nephew wasn't going to save him from the king's anger.

And that day – almost convenient, the timing was – we received a dispatch from Parmenio, who was already in the field in Asia, saying that he had taken Ephesus, the mighty city of Artemis, without a fight – that they had opened their gates to him – and that he had set up an image of Philip beside the image of Artemis in the great temple.

All the court applauded. Even the ambassadors applauded. Alexander spilled his wine and then apologised for his clumsiness.

But after two more days of it, Attalus gathered his staff and his picked men – and Diomedes – and rode away to Asia with recruits and reinforcements for Parmenio. He was supposed to have had a major role in the ceremonies at Aegae, but he left. I still think that the king ordered him to go. I think it was something of a working exile.

Alexander knew all about the dispatch from Asia, and he knew all about the preparations for the ornate wedding of his sister. He watched those preparations with the same anger he showed over the preparations for war in Asia. He watched the priests gather, watched Olympias arrange for a new gown with new, heavy gold jewellery, watched the musicians practise.

'The Athenians, at least, will view us with the contempt we deserve.' Alexander shrugged. He indicated a new statue of Philip in marble with bronze eyes, being loaded on a cart.

'My father, the god,' he said.

In fact, Philip seemed to have included himself in the pantheon – a sort of unlucky thirteenth god, but he'd built a small temple at Olympias that could be interpreted as a temple to Philip, and now, in the procession of the gods, he'd included an image of himself. And Parmenio had put his image in the Temple of Artemis. Which seemed to me like hubris.

On the other hand, I was inclined to think that the Athenians would think whatever they were told, at least until they'd rebuilt their fortunes. I had begun to experience that cynicism that comes easily to young people. And to anyone who has anything to do with politics.

We travelled north from Pella to the old capital. Pausanias travelled with us. No one could make a joke near him, but he was alive and apparently unbroken, although pale and subdued. If he had been prone to exaggeration before, now he was merely silent. His hands shook all the time.

We rode up to the old capital in a band, like we were going to war. All the older pages wore armour, and the younger ones too, if they owned any. We didn't dare go to the armoury, which Attalus virtually owned. I, for one, thought his 'exile' was a ruse and suspected he was out in the countryside with a band of his retainers, ready to attack us. There was an agora rumour that he meant to kill the king and seize power.

I was concerned to see that Olympias and her household travelled with us. She was as big a target as we were, and Attalus had apparently stated – in his rage the day after I taught Diomedes a lesson – that Olympias had arranged the whole thing and he'd have her killed.

Apparently Attalus told the king – repeatedly, right up until the moment he left for Asia – that Olympias and Alexander were plotting his death.

The glories of Macedon, eh?

But Attalus didn't come with us to Aegae. And Parmenio, the steadiest of his generation except for Antipater, was in Asia. And Antipater was nowhere to be found – in fact, he, too, was in self-imposed exile, on his farms.

We rode through a summer landscape of prosperity that thinly covered a state in which we were near to civil war – nearer than we had been in fifty years. Rumours were everywhere.

I remember that on the second day out of Pella, we were alerted by Polystratus that there was a column of foreigners coming the other way, and we took up our battle stations – Attalus employed a lot of Thracians, and we were ready for an attack.

These weren't Thracians, but Athenian traders on their way to Pella, where they imagined the court to be. Nearchus turned them around, brusquely enough, but when we discovered that they had a cargo of swords and sword blades, we asked them to open their bales, and we probably put them in profit on the spot – fifty of the richest young men in Macedon. The Athenians had Keltoi swords from north of Illyria, beautiful swords with long, leaf-shaped blades and deep central fullers – much stiffer and heavier than our swords or Greek swords, but easy in the hand, and the longer blades promised a longer reach on horseback.

One of the traders showed me how the Keltoi held their swords, with a thumb pressed into the hollow of the blade. I bought the sword, and rode north playing with it. It was a foot longer than my xiphos.

But that's not what I wanted to tell. What I wanted to tell is that Pausanias came alive at the sight of the blades. He was poor, and I loaned him money, and he purchased a beautiful weapon – the size of a xiphos, but with that heavy leaf blade, sharper than a bronze razor and with an African ivory hilt worked like a chariot and a running team. Superb work.

For as long as he was buying the sword, Pausanias was animated and alive. Even his hair seemed to regain its vibrancy.

And then it was gone. And he sank back into himself, and his face went slack, as if he'd taken a death blow.

We reached Aegae about the same time as the Athenian embassy. I looked for men I knew – I had rather hoped to see Kineas or Diodorus. But the Athenians had not sent any of their great men, except Phokion, and he was a guest friend of the king. He was kind enough to remember me. He clasped my arm – warrior to warrior, a nice compliment.

'Why are you wearing armour, son of Lagus?' he asked.

'Difficult times,' I said, looking elsewhere. Great as was my respect for the Athenian strategos, I was not going to tell him about our internal squabbles.

Indeed, upon arrival at Aegae, we all breathed a great sigh of relief. Aegae was sacred ground – no one would defile it with treason. Alexander and Olympias and Pausanias and I should all be safe, at least for the next fifteen days. Or so we reckoned.

That night, I played knucklebones with Nearchus and Black Cleitus, drank too much, lost at Polis to Alexander. He was withdrawn, even by his own standards.

I offered to go and check on Pausanias, and Alexander shook his head and held out his wine cup to have it refilled. 'Pausanias is with my mother, now,' he said. He said it in much the same voice as a man might have said that another man had died.

The next day, the festivities began. The scale was unprecedented for Macedon, and had I never been to Athens, I think I would have been thrilled. As it was, I could only wince – our most lavish celebration, when placed next to, say, the Panatheneum, was like tinsel placed next to real gold. Philip's crass lack of taste was like a physical blow, and the Theban envoys didn't bother to hide their sneers.

But the Herald of Athens – not a man I knew – announced that all treaties had been ratified, and that any Macedonian criminal to be found in Athens would be handed over – a remarkable concession for Athens to make, and not even something for which we'd asked. It made me suspicious, and what made me more suspicious was that Phokion turned his head away while it was read aloud.

There was a feast that night. Philip let it be known that I was welcome – I put on my best, and my best *was* as good as the best the Athenians had – and lay on a kline with a Thessalian nobleman who was fascinated with everything from Athens.

Philip got very drunk and said a great many things that made all of us wince. He referred to the cities of Greece with the term we use for sex slaves, and he made slighting references to Athens and Sparta and the Great King of Persia. In fact, he sounded like a petty and insecure tyrant, and he scared me.

What hurt me most was that many of the older Macedonians ate this sort of crap up, as if Philip's insults actually made Macedon greater or Athens lesser. And it was in looking around that hall that I realised how many of the older, wiser and better nobles were gone. Parmenio was gone, with Amyntas, in Asia. I hated Attalus, but he was the king's friend, and he was gone. Antipater was present – but not in any place of favour, and none of his own inner circle was there, except me – if I even counted. The king had stripped himself of his closest and best men.

The men he had near him were inferior in every respect, and this crass racism was only the surface of it.

And Alexander watched them the way a hawk watches rabbits. He remained aloof – but it seemed that he might pounce at any moment.

We all drank too much. And Philip ended the evening when he stood up, his chiton open to the crotch, showing his parts, so to speak, and stood by his kline.

'I am the King of Macedon!' he said. 'And this time next year, I'll be the lord of Asia, and if I want to be a god, I'll make myself one!'

He tottered away, narrowly missed falling, and two royal companions escorted him to bed.

Alexander may have said something, but his sneer was so palpable that no one needed to hear him. Thebans and Athenians and Thessalians – and Macedonians – noted it.

There were whispers that Philip needed to go. I heard them.

I walked Alexander back to his quarters that night. He was in a large semi-private house, something of a treasury for his family, and it rankled that he was not housed at the palace. It rankled doubly that we had Olympias. She seemed to be awake all the time, and when she wasn't with Pausanias she seemed inclined to flirt with the pages and Hephaestion.

She was waiting for us, and demanded the story of the evening. Alexander told her, in the pained tones that sons keep for their mothers, and finally forced her to go to bed by refusing to talk any more. He was rude. She was not. She smiled.

'Tomorrow, you will love me as you have never loved me before,' she said.

Alexander turned his back on her. Crossed his arms.

She laughed. Then she stopped in front of me, and all the power of those eyes was on me. 'When you had Diomedes at your feet,' she said, 'did his screams please you?'

I looked at the floor.

'Now, now, my little man,' she said. This from a woman whose eyes were at my chest. 'No lies to the queen. Were you disgusted by his weakness? Elated at your own success? Did you force yourself to hurt him in memory of what he did to your poor friend?' She smiled with real understanding. 'Or was it delightful to inflict terror and pain on him?'

I stood with my tongue stuck to the roof of my mouth.

'Well, we both know, don't we?' she said. 'Don't you forget, or grow superior, eh, Ptolemy?' She laughed at me. 'Why do you lie to yourself?' And walked away, floating on air.

When she was gone, Alexander turned to a slave. 'Wine,' he said, snapping his fingers.

The slave, terrified, spilled wine. Alexander looked at the poor boy and he fled.

I picked up the pitcher. A little liquid still sloshed in the base, and I poured a kraterful and handed it to the prince, who poured a libation.

'To Zeus, god of kings,' he said.

I had never heard him invoke Zeus so directly.

I must have opened my mouth, because Alexander held up a hand. 'Ask me nothing. I do not wish to speak, or play a game. I do not even wish to be alive, just now. Please leave me.'

Startled, I took the empty wine cup from him and went to withdraw.

'Stop,' Alexander said. 'I owe you my thanks, Ptolemy. Your attack on Diomedes was brilliant.'

I bowed. 'It almost went badly. I didn't plan for everything ...'

Alexander managed a grim smile. 'Stop, you sound too much like the cook who always apologises for flaws in the dinner you'd never have found yourself. You humiliated Attalus and put him in the wrong – at just the moment. It all went as Mother said it would,' he said. And shrugged. 'She is ... the very best intriguer I have ever known.'

It hadn't occurred to me that my brilliant and lucky attack on Diomedes had been part of a larger plan. 'The queen planned to have Attalus sent away?' I asked.

Alexander shook his head. 'You have my thanks,' he said. 'Now go away, before I say something I will regret.'

The next day, I had the whole corps of former pages on alert, and Hephaestion said that Alexander hadn't slept all night. It wasn't my duty day, but we were all to march in the parade – the ambassadors and all the nobles, led by Philip in a gleaming white chiton and gold sandals. It sounded like bad theatre to me, but we polished our best armour. Those of us who had been to Athens looked like gods. The rest merely looked like Macedonians.

Olympias appeared in white and gold, her dark hair piled in golden combs and strings of pearls on her head like a temple to Nike, who adorned her head at the pinnacle of her hair – and yet she carried it, weight and drama, as if born to it. Philip, despite his steady distaste for her scheming, came over to compliment her. He looked a little silly in his white and gold – but only until you caught his eye, and then he was Philip of Macedon.

But if anyone there looked like a god come to earth, it was she, not he.

He bent down to speak to her, where she stood surrounded by her women. She laughed at him, and he kissed her – just a peck on the cheek. And she laughed again, caught his head and pulled him down – not in an embrace, as I expected, but to whisper in his ear.

He nodded.

I was standing at the head of the former pages. Technically, we were all royal companions, but everyone sill called us 'pages'.

'Ptolemy,' he said.

I bowed.

'I wish to take Pausanias back into my personal guard,' he said, and held out his hand.

Pausanias was standing close behind me. I hadn't realised that he was there.

Philip smiled at him. In that smile, I read that he – a great king – was being magnanimous, and stating – as he could, because he was king – that whatever had happened, he would take Pausanias as a bodyguard. I'll remind you that he was a forgiving man, when he was sober, and he assumed that the honour would wipe away the stains, and Pausanias – older and wiser – would rise to the occasion.

I could see Pausanias. He paled. And his eyes slipped away to Olympias. And he gave the king an unsteady bow and crossed the long twenty or so paces to where the king's own companions stood.

How he must have feared to cross that gap. We were his friends – they were his tormentors. Or that's how I saw it, because he walked with his head high, but with the gait of a nervous colt.

At the head of the procession, the formal statues on their ceremonial platforms were carried by the strongest slaves – eight slaves to a god. All carved of Parian marble with hair and eyes of pure gold. Aphrodite, decently clothed, and Hera, goddess of wives and mothers; Artemis, effeminate Dionysus, Ares and Apollo and Hephaestos and the rest, and Zeus at their head, a foot taller than the other gods. And next to him, a statue of Philip.

There was a gasp, even from the royal companions.

Philip rode it out and stood like a rooster, inviting compliment.

I admired his brazenness.

The Athenians didn't. Even Phokion, who seemed to love Philip, turned away.

But the sun was rising, and the parade was ready, and we started towards the new theatre.

And then we stopped. It is the way with parades – they start and stop, and get slower and slower.

But what came back to us was an order from the king. He asked Alexander to come and enter the theatre with him.

Something terrible happened on Alexander's face, then. His father had shown him no love at all for more than a year – had all but cut him from the succession. But here – all of a sudden – he was invited to walk with his father in the most important ceremonial of the most important two weeks of the year.

He had a difficult time getting his face under control, and twice he looked at his mother.

Then he walked forward, and he walked with the same nervous gait that Pausanias had used.

I thanked the gods for my own mother and father, that I had not been born to the Royal House of Macedon. And I didn't know the half of it.

As we marched into the theatre, the royal companions entered after the statues and turned to the right, forming their ranks on the sand while the priests put the statues into their niches for the duration of the games. I was bored, and my left shoulder hurt, and I wondered if I would be any good. I had entered the pankration, and I was aware that a win would help restore me to Philip's good graces. And the pain in my shoulder was a worry.

We were behind the king, and my squadron was to form to the left as we entered the theatre, while the king went to the centre and then Olympias and her ladies would enter with Cleopatra (the king's wife, not that other one) and her ladies. Together, because it amused Philip to make them cooperate.

As we started to enter, Philip seemed to hesitate, as if someone had called his name. My front rank appeared to fall apart. I noticed that Black Cleitus, my left file leader, was hesitating. Well, we were cavalrymen being forced to march like hoplites, but I hated to make a bad show. I turned farther and heard the noise, turned back to where Cleitus was looking, and saw Perdiccas spring out of the second rank.

Pausanias went past us, his hand all covered in blood.

Perdiccas didn't follow Pausanias immediately. He looked out on to the sands, turned, and *then* raced after Pausanias, followed by two more of my men – Leonatus and Andromenes, both highlanders. They were all three close friends, a tight group made tighter by shared blood and highland custom. I roared at them to halt, but they were stubborn bastards.

And only then did I realise that there was more wrong than the loss of cohesion in my ranks.

I had thought, I guess, that Pausanias had broken down and done himself an injury and his relatives were running to see to him.

If I thought anything at all.

But somewhere in that horrible moment I realised that Alexander was kneeling in the sand by Philip, who was lying in a growing pool of red, red blood, with a Keltoi sword sticking out of his gut, the ivory chariot team racing towards the heavens.

And only then did I realise what Pausanias had done.

'Seal the exits!' Antipater roared at my elbow.

Antipater – who I hadn't seen to speak to in months – was suddenly at the head of the parade.

It was the right order. I turned and shouted it at my companions, and they snapped to.

But I could see that Philip was dead. Not dying. He was already gone.

And I remember thinking that I did not have the luxury to think. I know that makes little sense – but it all came together for me. Olympias, Pausanias and Alexander. And I knew – in a heartbeat – that it would mean my life to show a wrinkle of suspicion.

So I shouted for my men to close the exits, and Antipater got the royal companions into the northern half of the theatre.

The crowd was terrified.

Phokion was angry. It showed in his posture – the old warrior was stiff, hips set, ready to fight.

I did my duty, kept them in place and watched as Antipater cleared the theatre a bench at a time. Olympias and her ladies were already gone. They had never entered the theatre, and neither had Cleopatra.

Every foreign contingent was sent to their lodgings with a pair of guards – mostly royal companions – with orders to make sure that not so much as a slave got away until Antipater ordered them released.

I wrapped myself in my role and saw to it that the companions did their work. Slaves came and took the king's corpse. No one pretended he was still alive.

That meant that Alexander was king.

We cleared the last of the seats, and for a moment, it was just me and Cleitus, way up at the top, watching the Theban embassy moved forcefully down the ramps.

'Alexander is king!' Cleitus said.

I nodded.

'Pausanias killed the king,' he said.

I nodded.

Cleitus caught my eye. 'We know better, don't we?' he said bitterly.

I remember that moment well. Because I shrugged. 'Philip was going to ruin us,' I said. It was in every man's heart – Philip had turned to hubris and self-indulgence. And in Macedon, when the king slips, you find a new king.

Cleitus thought for a long time. 'Yes,' he said. 'Poor Alexander,' he added.

And that's all we ever said on the subject, except one night in Asia. And that was years and parasanges later, and I'll tell that tale when I come to it.

TEN

You might have thought that having lost his father – whether he actively schemed at Philip's murder or just sat back and let it happen – Alexander might have either suffered remorse, or at least enjoyed the fruits of success.

In fact, the next months are a blur to me, and I can't pretend I remember them well. This is the problem with my secret history, lad – we *never* spoke of these things at the time, and I can't really remember the exact order in which things happened.

On the afternoon of Philip's murder, Antipater ordered the palace locked down, and all the former pages were in armour, as I said – we cleared the theatre, and then we came to a sort of shocked halt.

Antipater was there. And he started issuing orders. For us, the most important order was that we were now the *first* squadron of the royal companions. He ordered me to set the watch bill, and he took Philip the Red and more than half of us to clear the palace, and all of the dead king's royal companions were put under what amounted to house arrest in their barracks and stables.

They went without a murmur, which saved everyone a bloodbath.

Perdiccas rode back covered with blood and told me – and then Alexander – that he had killed Pausanias with his spear – that the man had had a pair of horses waiting, so he had accomplices.

In the morning, I had been certain that Alexander had contrived the murder himself, or Olympias had done it, but by afternoon, my cynical observations were shaken, mostly because both Olympias and Alexander were behaving so ... naturally. They were acting as if they were afraid that the plotters were after them. And the precautions they took were real.

I put a whole troop of the former pages – from now on I'll just call them the Hetaeroi – on guard at the palace. I led them myself. Black Cleitus stood at Alexander's side, and Hephaestion stood behind him, both in full armour.

Aeropus's son, Alexander of Lyncestis, came in just after the sun touched the roof of the Royal Tomb. That part I remember. I was in armour, and he rode right into the palace courtyard, leaving a strong force of men at arms at the gate. I met him. He was the de facto ruler of the highland party, and he had some claim to the throne – distant, but in Macedon perfectly acceptable.

I had a pair of archers watching him with arrows on their bowstrings. 'My lord,' I said formally.

He slid from his horse. 'Ptolemy,' he said, with a nod. We weren't friends, but we had enough in common that, in a crisis, we had some basis for trust. 'I wish to surrender to the king. Will he spare me?'

I remember thinking, *What the fuck's going on?* I shook my head. 'I can't say,' I said. 'I give you my word I won't have you killed out of hand, but ... if you conspired at Philip's murder, I can't save you.' I couldn't understand why he had come in or surrendered himself, and my suspicious nature made me wonder if there wasn't a surprise attack coming at me. I stepped back.

'Eyes on the walls!' I said. 'Watch those men in the alley – watch *everything*.' There's good leadership. Laugh if you like, boy.

Alexander the Highlander was as pale as a woman's new-washed chiton. 'I think my brothers had something to do with it,' he said.

And then Antipater appeared. He was everywhere that day.

'Ah, Ptolemy,' he said, as if we'd made an appointment to talk. 'Is that my useless son-in-law you have there?'

In fact, Alexander the Highlander was married to Antipater's daughter.

It occurred to me that Antipater had just spent two full weeks at Alexander the Highlander's estates.

Alexander met his namesake in the throne room. They talked for a quarter of an hour or so, and then Alexander appeared in the courtyard – my Alexander. He looked around for a long time, his eyes locking on one former page or another, and finally his eyes came to rest on me. He looked at me for far too long. He had a scroll tube in his hand and an old cloak over his white robes from the morning.

He beckoned. As I came up to him, Antipater came out on to the exedra.

'Alexander!' he called. His tone was peremptory.

Alexander ignored him. 'Take twenty men. Your own retainers, or someone else's. Go and take the sons of Aeropus, and see to it they are brought here. Do not use the Hetaeroi – do you understand?'

I understood immediately that I was being asked to do something outside the law – and something for which I was trusted.

'Consider it done,' I said, with a proper salute.

Alexander flashed me that awesome smile. 'Herakles ride with you,' he said. And then he said, 'If I'm still king when the sun rises tomorrow, I reckon I'll be king for a bit.'

He was *scared*. I'd never seen it before.

Antipater was shouting from the exedra. Alexander ignored him.

'Ptolemy!' Antipater shouted.

I looked up.

But before he could speak, Alexander pointed at his best and most loyal councillor. 'Antipater,' he said. Heads turned. 'Which one of us is king?'

Antipater hesitated.

And the Fates wove on.

I took Polystratus and his friends – my own retainers, trusted men, every one – small men who owed everything to me, and had been in exile with me. We rode out into the countryside. The Aeropus clan's local estates were up the valley, two hours' ride. We were there as the sun was setting. I had briefed my troopers carefully.

We were challenged at the outer gate. But they let us in. The outer yard was full of armed men – at least as many as I had with me.

My men rode in under the arch, and Polystratus killed the gatekeeper with a single javelin throw, and we went at them. They had weapons, and they were highlanders – trained men. Violent men.

Mostly what I remember is the suddenness of it. Polystratus threw his spear, and we were fighting. There was no posturing, no yelling, no war cries.

My men had good armour and horses. That was the margin. That, and surprise. I don't know why they let us into the courtyard, but they did. And when we went at them, at least a hand's worth were down before the rest turned into killers. I got one of them with his hand on the release to the dog cages. Then I held the ground when three of them rushed me.

Highlanders are brave, but they are no match for a man who has trained every waking moment from age seven. I don't even remember taking a cut. Polystratus came and helped, and then Philoi, another former slave, and then they were all dead, and we were storming the kitchen – the kitchen doors gave directly on to the courtyard, and there was no reason to wait. The cook died in his doorway, and my people went through that house like a tide of death, killing the slaves, clearing each room. We found the two brothers – Alexander the Highlander's brothers – in the cellar.

I tied their hands behind their backs, put them on horses and then went through the house, looking for documents. I found four scroll tubes and a single scroll chest – highlanders don't read much – and loaded them on a horse.

Then I torched the house and we rode for the palace.

No question it was an evil act. We killed a dozen slaves and twenty freemen and took two princes prisoner. I won't even argue that I was only following orders. I will merely say – and I pray to Zeus you have time to discover this your own way – that if you will be a king, you will kill men. Are they 'innocent'? Is one man worth the life of another?

You decide, boy. But make sure you make your own decision, because, by Zeus, it will come back on your head and in your dreams.

Midnight, and we rode into the palace precinct. Black Cleitus had the Hetaeroi. I saluted and he waved me on. My prisoners were taken to the cellars.

A great deal had happened in my absence. Apparently Antipater counselled caution and Hephaestion cautioned rashness – not for the last time, that particular pairing – and Alexander went to meet the army in person – all the foot companions and the two full taxeis of Macedonian phalangites who had accompanied the king from Pella. He met them at sunset, while I was storming the traitor's estate, and he promised that Philip would be avenged – and that they would conquer Asia. And they cheered him, and declared him king by acclamation.

Wish I'd seen it. There used to be a painting of it in the royal palace in Pella, but I hear Cassander had it painted over. Coward.

I was exhausted, but Alexander embraced me, fed me wine, heard my somewhat laconic report. I didn't feel it was an achievement about which I should brag.

'You killed them all and burned the building?' Alexander asked.

Antipater put his face in his hands. Took a deep breath through his hands. 'We are lost,' he said.

Alexander shook his head. 'Well done, my friend. That's the hydra beheaded.'

But I was wily Odysseus, and I wasn't half done. I stood where I could see Alexander and his mother, who was behind his couch, and Antipater, who looked shaken.

'I have all their correspondence,' I said.

It was far worse than I thought. Olympias flushed and her eyes locked with mine – Alexander froze, and Antipater's eyes flicked between Alexander and me.

'Give it to me,' Olympias said. 'Have you read it?'

I looked her right in the eye – no mean feat, friend – and said, 'No.' But I smiled when I said it, to rob the denial of all meaning. I was playing very hard.

Alexander flicked a look at me – and then at his mother. 'Mother?' he asked quietly.

'I know they are as guilty as if they held the knife themselves,' I said. I carefully avoided mentioning that I now suspected that they weren't alone in being guilty.

You may ask why I was working the situation so hard – eh? No? You understand, don't you, boy? Palace revolution isn't that alien to you, is it? All the rules were changing that night. I was determined to be a main player, and not a small one. Great things grow from small – that is how the interplay of power works. I had missed some important events – I already feared that I had been supplanted as Hetaeroi commander, and I was correct. Six hours' absence – doing the king's secret mission – and I was no longer commanding the Hetaeroi. You get it?

Good. I'll move on.

Olympias came up to me. She was so small that, standing, her head came just above my shoulders. 'Give me the scrolls,' she said.

I sent Polystratus to the stables for them.

'What do *you* think I should do with them, son of Lagus?' she asked.

I smiled at her, an actor on a stage. 'Why, Lady Queen, you should do whatever is best for Macedon,' I said.

She actually smiled. 'I like you, Ptolemy,' she said.

Oh, I feared her. It was all I could do to look into her beautiful eyes and smile back, instead of shitting myself in fear. Because she was considering having me killed, right then and there.

It was almost too late when I realised that I was playing the wrong game. I was still playing the game of pages, whereby I could learn secrets to be the more trusted by the inner circle.

The game had changed. Alexander was king, and now he was playing for the preservation of power, and he observed no rules.

But I had not failed utterly, and Alexander embraced me again. 'Ptolemy is one of my few friends, Mother,' he said. 'You want to hate him because he is as intelligent as we are. Do not. That is my express wish.'

I felt the arrow slicing down my cheek as it passed – death was that close.

Olympias met her son's eyes, and then looked up at me. 'If you read those letters, you are a fool. If you did not, you are a different type of fool. The correct action would have been to burn them with the house. Do you understand, young Ptolemy?'

I shrugged. I was young, foolish, vain and brave. 'Perhaps the correct action was to make copies,' I said.

Alexander turned and handed me a cup of wine. 'Only if you plan to kill me and become king,' he said. 'And I don't think you are in that game.'

'Never,' I said.

Alexander nodded. 'Stop playing with fire, my friend. Mother, he never read the letters. He's baiting you.'

Damn him, he was right.

Olympias sneered. 'Such a dangerous game,' she said quietly. 'I *do* like you, young Ptolemy.'

I went to bed, still alive, and awoke, still alive. I learned a great deal in that exchange, and I never tried to match wits with Olympias head to head again. On the other hand, I was invited to council that morning, as soon as I was dressed.

Alexander presented himself to the ambassadors, and was acclaimed hegemon as his father had been.

And then Alexander ordered Pausanias's corpse to be spiked to a tree. In public.

Philip's corpse was stinking – which many saw as an omen. The ambassadors and the army were already present, so we rushed the burial – his tomb was ready, had been ready since he took the wound fighting the Thracians and began to think of mortality (and immortality).

So the next morning, just two days after the murder, we marched to his tomb, the parade in the same order as the parade into the theatre had been, except that my squadron of Hetaeroi – not Cleitus's squadron – marched first.

We got to the tomb, and the priest of Apollo poured libations and prayed and we sacrificed a bull, four black rams and the two younger sons of Aeropus. My prisoners. They were drugged, and died as quietly as the bull.

This public revenge settled the matter of murder, at least among the commons.

But among the noble factions, men saw it as a clean-up operation, and many men looked at Antipater.

And Olympias.

After that, the factions were quiet. In fact, they were *silent*.

*

We had two immediate problems after settling the local population and killing the two possible immediate rivals. They were that the Greek states would almost certainly revolt, whatever their ambassadors said – and worst of all, Attalus, bloody Attalus, and Parmenio, whichever side he chose to be on, were in Asia with the cream of the army.

And Antipater predicted that every province would revolt except the home provinces.

Well, he was right. We were just starting to move the court back to Pella when the news came trickling in – two big Thracian raids and a string of insults from the Illyrians. The Boeotians expelled their garrison and abrogated the League of Corinth. Demosthenes made a tremendous show in the Athenian Assembly. His daughter had died less than a week before – but he threw off his mourning and went to the Assembly in white, wearing a garland of flowers and saying that Greece was saved.

Bad news travels fast.

There was nothing we could do immediately. Everything depended on timing, luck, the fortune of the gods – and the loyalty of the rump of the army.

Alexander took two steps immediately. We held a council the first night in Pella – Philip was seven days dead by then. Olympias was amusing herself by celebrating his death with more abandon than old Demosthenes. She had a sort of honesty to her, I'll give her that. She decorated Pausanias's body as if he were a hero, not a regicide.

Macedon, eh?

At any rate, we held an inner council the first night in Pella. Antipater was there, and Alexander the Highlander, who dealt pragmatically with the death of both his brothers. Olympias was excluded. Laodon was there – he'd been over the border in Thessaly, where Philip had sent him into exile, and he was already back. Erigyus was on his way and the actor, Thessalus, was recalled. So were some other favourites – mostly small men, but Philip had exiled quite a few of them when Alexander's star began to wane at court.

Laodon had a trusted man – a Macedonian, a veteran, a man whom Philip had trusted as a herald and a messenger, but who had a special relationship with Laodon. Hecataeus was his name, and he'd been Alexander's go-between with both Laodon and with Philip during his exile.

Hecataeus was a complex man – no simple image fits him. He was an excellent soldier, and because of it had made his way from the ranks to effective command of a taxeis under Amyntas. But he was both subtle and utterly honest – a rare and wonderful combination. Men – great men – trusted him. He was, in fact, the ideal herald – respected for his scars and war stories, trusted because he always kept faith, discreet with what he learned. I was not everywhere – I don't know what the roots of his alliance with Alexander were.

But at the council, Alexander ordered him to go to Parmenio. 'Bring him over to me, and order him to kill Attalus,' Alexander said.

Antipater shook his head. 'You may as well order the poor man to kill the Great King and conquer Asia,' he said.

Alexander pursed his lips. 'No, those things are for me to do,' he answered, as if the comment were to be taken seriously.

Hecataeus smiled about one quarter of a smile. 'My lord, what exactly can I offer Parmenio? He has the army.'

Again, there was something so ... well, so reasonable about Hecataeus – it was not as if he was bargaining on behalf of a possible traitor. He was asking fair questions. He was a very able man.

'Short of the kingdom, you may offer him anything,' Alexander said.

Hecataeus shook his head. 'I'm too small a man to make such an offer,' he said. 'I would go with concrete terms, if I must do this job.'

Alexander nodded. 'Well said. Very good, then. Parmenio may have the first satrapy of the spear-won lands of Asia. The highest commands for his sons and himself – my right hand.' He looked at Hecataeus.

The herald nodded. 'That's very helpful, lord. On those lines, I can negotiate.'

Alexander looked around. He was selling the commands of his kingdom to a man who'd either been a rival or held aloof. And we, his loyal inner circle, were clearly *not* going to get those commands.

Black Cleitus made a face. 'I take it I shouldn't get used to commanding the Hetaeroi,' he said.

Alexander slapped his shoulder. 'Parmenio owns the love of more of my subjects than I do,' he said. 'The man has most of the army, and most of the lowland barons. In time, Ptolemy can take over his faction, but for now, I need him. He's sixty-five – he'll be dead soon enough. In the meantime – yes. Make room, friends. The sons of Parmenio will be plucking the choicest fruits.' He shrugged. Parmenio's sons had not been pages. 'I expect he'll want Philotas as the commander of the Hetaeroi.' He nodded to me and Cleitus. 'But you two will command the squadrons.'

Then Alexander turned to me. 'I have a mission for you, as well, son of Lagus, wily Odysseus.'

Well, who dislikes good flattery? 'At your service, my king,' I said.

He nodded. 'I'm sending you to the king of the Agrianians,' he said. 'Get me as many of his warriors as you can arrange. Psiloi and Peltastoi

– light-armed men to replace all the light-armed men my pater has sent to Asia.'

That was our first intimation that the king intended an immediate campaign.

'Are we going to war?' I asked.

Antipater coughed. 'No,' he said firmly. 'We are trying to negotiate from a position of relative strength, and a thousand light-armed men will make us look the readier to march.'

Alexander smiled. He looked around, caught every eye. 'What he means is, yes, unless all my enemies miraculously knuckle under, I'll be fighting all summer.' His grin became wolfish. 'I have cavalry, and enough heavy foot. Go and get Langarus to hand over some prime men. And hurry back.'

So I nodded. Even though I was again going to be absent while the big decisions were made.

In fact, I'd already seen the lay of the land. Alexander trusted us – his young inner circle – with the difficult missions. But it would be Antipater's generation – Antipater and Parmenio and such men – who would lead the crusade into Asia. Not us.

I had a long ride into Illyria to ponder the ways of kings. I took my troop of grooms, and bandits fled at our approach. It was very gratifying. We swept the high passes clear. We practised climbing *above* the passes and closing both ends at once, so we could catch the bandits – and it worked twice (and not the other ten times!). Once, with Polystratus scouting, we took a whole band of them – scarecrows with armour – and executed all of them, leaving their corpses in trees as a warning to future generations.

So by the time we came down into mountainous Agriania, word of our exploits had run ahead of us.

Alexander's young wife was pregnant. Her father quite happily called out a band of picked warriors – useless mouths, he called them. Many of them were his own bodyguard – the shield-bearers, he called them in his own tongue – in Greek, we called them hypaspists. He gave me almost six hundred men – well armoured, but light-footed. And he promised to come with his own army if Alexander summoned him.

That was a well-planned marriage. The girl beamed adoringly and waited to be summoned to Pella. For all I know, she's still waiting.

We returned to Macedon by a different set of passes, and the Agrianians loved our game of climbing high above the passes and then closing both ends at once. In fact, they maintained – as a nation of mountaineers – that they'd invented it.

Their principal warrior was 'Prince' Alectus. He was no more a prince than I, but an old war hound. He was the hairiest man I'd ever seen – naked, he looked more like a dog, despite his heavy muscles. He had red-grey curly hair, even in his ears. To a Greek, he was impossibly ugly, with his wiry hair and his intricate tattoos.

He shocked me, the first night on the road home, by asking me if I was an educated man, and then debating with me about the gods. He was widely read, and yet he drew his own conclusions from what he read.

'Ever think that all this killing might be wrong, lad?' he asked me, that first night. He was drinking my wine in my tent. None of the Agrianians had a tent.

'Of course I've thought it,' I said. 'All you have to do is look at a dead man's widow.'

Alectus nodded. 'Or his children, eh?'

'Some men are evil,' I said, drunkenly cutting across a whole lot of arguments. Aristotle would not have approved.

Alectus sneered. 'And you only kill the evil ones, eh?'

That shut me up.

He was an old barbarian and he'd done a lot of killing, and he was beginning to doubt the whole game. 'What if there's *nothing* but this world?' he asked, on the fourth bowl of wine.

'Oh?' I asked. 'And who made it?'

Alectus shrugged. 'If a god made it, what does he want? I mean, if I make a shield, it's because one of the lads needs a shield. Eh?'

'Where are we going with this?' I asked.

'Talk goes with wine,' Alectus said. 'I like both. I used to like a good fight. But now, I'm beginning to wonder.'

'Are all you hill men philosophers?' I asked.

Alectus spat. 'As far as I can tell, your philosophers ain't interested in what's good for men. They're interested in sounding good and pompous, eh? None of them seems to be willing to tell me what the gods think of killing.'

'Go to Delphi!' I said. I had meant to say it with a sneer, but I'm afraid – then and now – that I have a great respect for oracles.

Alectus drank off his wine. 'You may actually have the makings of a wise man, Macedonian. Will Alexander take me to Delphi?'

I shrugged. 'No idea. But ... if we march on Greece, we'll have to go right past the shrine.'

Alectus lifted the whole bowl and poured a libation. 'To Delphic Apollo and his oracle,' he said, and drank some. 'That was god-given advice, young man. I'll pay more heed to you in the morning.'

217

And then he picked up his sword and walked off into the night.

I liked Alectus.

We were two weeks getting back to Pella and my farms fed the Agrianians. I met up with Heron for the first time in two years and he embraced me – and I freely gave him almost a quarter of my farms. Loyalty is rare, young man. It needs rich reward.

And when we reached Pella, I swore out a warrant at the treasury for the value of the food my farms had provided to the barbarian auxiliaries. That got me a two-year remission of taxes.

Which meant that I made a profit – if a small one – on bringing the Agrianians to Pella.

I won't belabour this point. But I mention it so that you know that managing a great estate is a matter of constant work and constant alertness to opportunity. It is much easier to fritter a great estate away than to protect and expand it.

Pella was an armed camp. There were three taxeis of pikes outside the town – all the men of upper Macedon, townsmen of Amphilopolis and hardy mountain men, all billeted on Attalus's estates. Alexander had ordered every nobleman to call up his grooms, so that we had almost four thousand cavalry. He left his father's royal companions at home, and almost a thousand of the foot companions he retired to new estates – a popular move, and one that left him with a reserve of veterans, if we had a disaster.

Alexander picked the largest and best men from the foot companions (as had his father before him) and added them to the Agrianians, and created his own hypaspitoi. As I say, Philip had had his own – picked men of the phalanx, but they were the very veterans that Alexander had just settled on good estates. Did he distrust them? Or was the new broom sweeping clean?

I wasn't consulted. Later, we had three regiments of hypaspists – the 'Aegema' and two regiments of elite infantry to go with them. They were our only infantry that wore harness all year and never went back to their farms – well, in the early days. Heh. Soon enough, no one was going home at all. But I get ahead of myself.

My grooms went with the cavalry, and my squadron of companions was commanded by Philip the Red, and no man was appointed to overall command of the Hetaeroi. But I found that I was the commander of the hypaspitoi – a job I held many times, and always enjoyed.

Alexander loved to blend. It was an essential part of his success that he thought that men could be alloyed just as metals were – and the early hypaspitoi were his first experiment. It was his theory that big, tough, well-trained Macedonians would serve to reduce the Agrianians to discipline, and that the hardy, athletic and wilderness-trained Agrianians would teach his elite Macedonians a thing or two about moving over woods and rocks.

Well, that's what made him Alexander. I admit I thought he was mad. They'd only been joined an hour before we had our first murder.

Alexander heard of it, sent for me and asked what I planned to do.

'Catch the culprit and hang him,' I said.

Alexander nodded. 'Good. Get it done by sunset.' He looked at me. 'We're marching.'

I was stunned. 'But Antipater ...' I'd just seen Antipater, who had reassured me that the magazines were full and we weren't going anywhere.

Alexander frowned. 'Antipater sometimes has trouble remembering who is king,' he said.

So I rode Poseidon into my lines. It was easy to find the killer. He was one of my men, a pezhetaeroi file leader. He was standing in the courtyard of his billet, bragging to his friends.

Some of my best men. Six foot or taller, every man. Loyal as anything.

I had Polystratus and my grooms. 'Take him,' I said.

He didn't even struggle until it was too late. All the way to the gallows tree he shrieked that he was a Macedonian, not a barbarian. His cries brought many men out of billets, and many Agrianians out of their fields. They watched him dragged to the tree, impassively.

Alectus came and stood in front of them. He nodded to me.

I did not nod back.

I ordered Philip son of Cleon – that was my phylarch's name – to have a noose put around his neck.

I had almost a thousand men around me by then, and the Macedonians, as is our way, were vocal in their disapproval.

A rock hit Poseidon.

I had had other plans, but my hand was forced. The noose was tied to the tree, so I reached out and swatted the horse under my phylarch with my naked sword blade, and the horse reared and bolted, scattering the crowd, and before his fellow Macedonians could get organised, Philip son of Cleon's neck snapped and he was dead.

And *that* got me silence.

'Gentlemen,' I said. It was *silent*. 'One law. For every man in the army. No crime against your fellow soldiers will be tolerated. You are one corps – one regiment. It is the will of the king. In a few hours, we will march to war. If you are angered, save it for the enemy.'

Then I sent for the phylarchs and Prince Alectus.

'When we march tomorrow,' I said, 'we will not march as separate companies. There will be four Macedonians and four Agrianians in every file, and they will alternate – Macedonian, Agrianian, Macedonian. And across the ranks – the same. See to it.'

My senior phylarch, yet another man named Philip – Philip son of Agelaus, known to most of us as Philip Longsword – spat. 'Can't be done. Take me all night just to write it down.'

'Best get to work, then,' I said.

There are some real advantages to being a rich aristocrat. He couldn't stare me down. Social class rescued me, and eventually he knuckled under with a muttered 'Yes, m'lord'.

Alectus merely nodded.

'Don't be fools!' I said. 'You two don't know the king and I do. He'll kill every one of you – me too – rather than give up on this experiment. So find a way to work together, or we'll all hang one by one.'

If I expected that to have an immediate effect, I was disappointed. They both glared at each other and at me, and they left my tent without exchanging a word.

All night, I wanted to go and see what they were doing. At one point, Polystratus had to grab me by the collar and order me into my camp-bed.

The Hetaeroi marched first, in the morning, and we were just forming, and the whole army was waiting on us. And every man in the army knew what had happened.

In retrospect, I gambled heavily on Alectus.

He and Philip Longsword stood at the head of the parade, and called men by name – one by one.

It took an hour. More. We had just slightly fewer than eleven hundred men, and it took so much time to call their names that all the other taxeis were formed and ready to march.

And when we'd formed our phalanx, what a hodge-podge we looked. No order, no uniformity of equipment or even uniformity of chaos – which is what the barbarians had. Instead, we looked like the dregs of the army, not the elite.

But we were formed. I ordered them to march by files from the right, and off they went up the road.

I found the king at my elbow. 'My apologies ...' I began.

Alexander gave me his golden smile. 'Not bad,' he said. He nodded and rode away.

*

220

I remember that day particularly well, because I rode for a while and then dismounted and took an aspis from one of the hypaspists.

You hardly see them any more, the big round shields of the older men. They were better men – better trained, the Greek way, in gymnasiums, and those perfect bodies you see in statues and on funerary urns had a purpose, which was to carry a greater weight of shield and armour than we lesser men today. It was Philip's notion – Philip the king, I mean – to arm his bodyguard in the old way.

You can't just take farmers and tell them to carry the aspis. Well – you can if your farmers consciously train to carry it. But Macedonian farmers aren't the heroes of Marathon, who were somewhere between aristocrats and our small farmers, with the muscles of working men allied to the leisure time of gentlemen. But by making the hypaspitoi full-time soldiers who served all year round and trained every day, Philip made it possible to maintain a body of professional hoplites like the men he'd trained with in Thebes when he was a hostage there.

Alexander wanted the same – but he wanted to add the aggressive spirit and woodcraft of those Agrianians. On the first day, we had a lot of big men of two races who hated each other and were miserably undertrained in carrying the weight of the damned shield. And only the front-rankers had armour.

Two hours into the march, my left shoulder was so badly bruised that I had my fancy red military chlamys tied in a ball to pad it, and I was sheathed in sweat and it was all I could do to put one foot in front of another. Men were falling out – both Agrianians and Macedonians.

I knew what I had to do. This is what the pages train you for. This moment. But it hurts, and all that pain – boy, do you know that pain gets worse as you get older? The fear of pain – the expectation of pain?

At any rate, I stepped out of the file and ran back along the ranks to the very back of the hypaspistoi. I didn't know the men by name or even by sight yet, but I guessed there were at least a dozen men already gone from the ranks. I also noticed that the pezhetaeroi behind us were marching in their chitons, with slaves carrying their helmets, small shields, pikes and armour.

I felt like an idiot. Cavalrymen generally wear their kit, and I was a cavalryman. *Of course* foot soldiers marched with slaves carrying their kit.

On the other hand ...

There was Polystratus, riding and leading my Poseidon. He looked amused. I hated him.

'Get your sorry arse back along the column and find my stragglers,' I barked.

'Yes, O master,' he intoned. 'You could ride and do it yourself.'

I made a rude sign at him, sighed and ran back up the column. 'You tired? Anyone want to run with me?' I bellowed, and men looked up from their misery.

'I'm going to run the next five stades. And then I'm going to rest. You can walk the next five stades and then keep walking, or you can run with me.' I repeated this over and over as I ran from the back of the column to the front.

At the front, I took my place in the lead file – a *much* more comfortable place to march, let me tell you, than the middle files, where the dust clogs your scarf and turns to a kind of mud with your breath.

In my head I started playing with tunes. I could play the lyre, badly, but I could sing well enough to be welcome at an Athenian symposium, and I knew a few songs. Nothing worked for me just then, so I grunted at my file leaders.

'Ready to run?' I asked.

Sullen stares of hate.

Command. So much fun.

'On me,' I said, and off I went at a fast trot.

Let's be brief. We ran five stades. We caught up to the Hetaeroi cavalry in front. By then, we were strung out along three stades of dirt road, because a lot of my hypaspitoi were breaking down under the weight of the shields – ungainly brutes.

But we made it, and I led the files off the road into a broad field – a fallow farm field. I dropped the aspis off my shoulder and, without meaning to, fell to the ground. Then I got to my feet, by which time most of the hypaspitoi who were still with me were lying on their backs, staring at the sun in the sky.

'Hypaspitoi!' I shouted.

Groans. Silence.

'The men of Athens and Plataea ran from Marathon to Athens at night after fighting all day,' I shouted.

Legends often start in small ways. And no one remembers, later, the moments of failure.

My hypaspitoi straggled into camp, and almost a third of my men – mostly, but not all, Agrianians – were among the last men into camp. I had to get my grooms together and use them as military police to collect up the slowest men. Forty men had to be dismissed – home to Agriania or back to the pezhetaeroi.

But none of my friends – or enemies – in the Hetaeroi really noticed that. What Hephaestion knew was that the hypaspitoi had caught up with the cavalry and he claimed we'd hooted at the horsemen and demanded to be allowed to run past. Horseshit. All I wanted to do was lie down and die, at that point. But that's how a good legend starts.

I wanted to go and eat with my Hetaeroi, but I knew that wouldn't work, so instead I put myself in a mess with Alectus and Philip Longsword, and we cooked our own food. Well – to be fair, all the phylarchs had slaves or servants, and we didn't do a lot of cooking. But the work got done, and I do have some vague recollection of helping to collect firewood with two exhausted Macedonian peasants who were scared spitless to find their commander breaking downed branches with them. I had to teach the useless fucks how to break branches in the crotch of a living tree with a natural fork close to the ground. Apparently only lazy men know how to do this.

The next morning, I ordered the armour and aspides packed, and ordered the men to march in their chitons. And I collected the file closers ...

You have never served in a phalanx. So let's digress. A Macedonian phalanx is raised from a territory. In their prime, we had between six and nine taxeis, and each was raised in one of the provinces – three for the lower kingdoms, three for the upper kingdoms and three for the outer provinces, or close enough. Every taxeis had a parchment strength of two thousand, but in fact they usually numbered between eleven hundred and seventeen hundred sarissas. Every man was armed the same way – a long sarissa, a short sword or knife, a helmet. The front ranks were supposed to be well armoured, and sometimes they were – never in new levies, always in old veteran corps.

Veterans were supposed to rotate home after a set number of years or campaigns, and new drafts were supposed to come out to the army every spring when the taxeis reformed. All the phalangites – the men of the phalanx – were supposed to go home every autumn. Only the royal companions – the Hetaeroi – and the hypaspitoi stayed in service all year round.

Each taxeis was composed of files – eight men under Philip, and ten men under Alexander. At times we'd be as deep as sixteen or twenty, but that was generally for a specific purpose. Let's stay with files of ten. A taxeis of two thousand men formed ten deep has two hundred files. Every file, at the normal order, has six feet of space in the battle line – six feet wide and as deep as required. That means that the frontage of a taxeis at normal order is twelve hundred feet. A little more than a stade.

But of course we almost never fight in 'normal' order, but contract to the synaspis, the shield-touching shield formation with ten pikes stacked over the front rank's locked round shields. So that's about three feet per man, two hundred files, six hundred feet width, or about half a stade. Still with me?

Every file has three officers – the file leader, who runs the group and leads it – literally – in combat and on the march. The file closer – the 'last' man; he's the second-in-command, because if the phalanx faces to the rear he's the front-rank man, and because he alone can prevent men from deserting or running away. And the mid-ranker. In many manoeuvres – especially Macedonian manoeuvres – men march by half-files, and suddenly the half-file leader is the leader of a short file. The half-file leader is the third-in-command. Finally, the most promising new man is the half-file closer – the fifth man back, who, if the file is split in two, will be the 'last' man in a file only five deep. See? It was never a real rank, but to be put in the fifth position was to be seen as the next to be promoted in the file.

But the hypaspitoi were more complicated. We were a little over a thousand men and only eight deep. Our eight-man files were clumsy, because no one had worked together. And the file isn't just a tactical unit – a file of infantry builds shelters together, cooks together, eats together, goes to find whores together, kills innocent civilians together, steals cattle together, digs latrines together, uses them together, swims together. You get the picture.

My files had no cohesion. We'd forced a bunch of men together, and they were supposed to be elite, but mostly they were angry and unfed, because dysfunctional files meant no firewood, no shelter and no food.

Their other problem is that Alexander's mixture of magnanimity and paranoia had resulted in his releasing *all* the old hypaspitoi. If it had been me, I'd have released a third each campaign. My beloved king left me with precisely one veteran – Philip Longsword. If I had even a hundred – just one veteran per file – I'd have had someone to teach all the Agrianians how to live as soldiers.

I see your question, young man – how could all these picked men not know how to function as soldiers? Why weren't those woodsy mountaineers clever enough to get firewood and cook?

I'm sure that alone in the mountains, they'd have had their shelters rigged in no time. But when you march with ten thousand soldiers and as many slaves and grooms – twenty thousand men and some prostitutes and hangers-on – foraging is a skill. Getting firewood is a skill. Cooking – quickly and well, with minimal wood use and very few pots or utensils – is a skill. Men going into the mountains take a pot – wealthy men have a copper or bronze pot. Soldiers need time and expertise to collect such things – they need to pool money and resources to get a slave, to buy a pot for that slave to carry, to find, buy or steal food to put into that pot . . .

We hadn't given my boys time to do any of that. There were twenty messes without a cauldron of any kind. I know – I walked around and looked.

But I saw something that suggested that there was hope. I saw one file cook and then hand its cauldron over to another file. They ate late, but they ate.

The army was fed by markets – our own army agora. When we were on home ground, scouts – the Prodromoi – would ride out and warn the farmers for stades around the projected evening camp, and they would bring their wares to the camp before the soldiers even arrived. They'd be set up when the soldiers marched in, and one or two men from every mess would go to the market and buy food – a little meat, some grain for bread, some oil, a little wine.

A lucky or skilful mess had a slave or two. That would ease the process greatly, because the slave didn't have to be with the column. In friendly country, a really good slave – a trusted slave – would go out on his own, buy food in the countryside (where the prices were lower) and maybe even have the fire going when the men marched in. A slave who has reason to believe that expert service will bring freedom – which is a Thracian concept of slavery and something Macedonians practise well – will do all this every day for a year or two. But in the end, the file has to free him, of course, and then they need to pool their cash and buy another.

Or just take one in battle.

And let's just add to this. A victorious Macedonian army accreted slaves – bed-warmers, foragers, cooks, baggage-humpers. And the duty of the footslogger gets easier and easier. He's got a slave to carry his gear, a donkey, two cook pots per mess to make the food more interesting, more cash to buy better food, wine every night and a girl. Or a boy. Or both.

One defeat, and all that is gone. If you lose a fight with the Thracians, they take your camp and all your slaves, all your baggage animals, all your bed-warmers. Gone. And you are back to humping your own gear.

That's the life of an infantryman. I've embarked on this long discourse so that you understand that, despite their status as 'household' troops, my hypaspitoi were pretty much at the bottom of the barrel as we marched out of Pella. We had very few slaves, insufficient cook gear, no tents, no baggage animals at all.

So when my men marched in their chitons, they still had to hump all their gear on their own shoulders, and that was painful. I was not happy to carry my own kit, and my decision to do it allowed Polystratus a long laugh at my expense.

'I dreamed of this, when I was your slave,' he said.

I grunted.

Day two was worse than day one. Luckily, I really don't remember any of it.

But towards afternoon, I took my new palfrey – a nice little Thracian mare with no good blood but lots of heart – and rode up the column, saluted the king and then went north with the Prodromoi. We were in my land, and we'd be camping on my farms. I rode into Ichnai with Polystratus, embraced Heron and sent out my orders.

When the hypaspitoi marched into camp – and they weren't any better off than they had been the day before – they found their fires already lit and their food in bronze cauldrons by their lit fires, ready to cook. Every mess had a fire. A fire, two donkeys and a slave.

It's good to be rich.

After they'd eaten, I collected the whole regiment in a mob outside my tent. I had a tent and I was not going to go without it. There are limits.

'Good evening, hypaspitoi!' I shouted, and that night I got some response besides grunts. 'How was the lamb?'

Shouts of approval. 'More like mutton than lanb!' said somebody. There's always one.

'Tomorrow, you can find your own!' I shouted. 'Those slaves are yours – to keep.'

One hundred and twenty prime male slaves. Even I felt that as an expense. And I'd just stripped four of my farms of workers.

But the grumble from my men had another tone entirely.

'And the donkeys,' I said. 'And the cook pots.'

Cheers.

'On the other hand,' I shouted, and they laughed. 'On the other hand, tomorrow we march in armour, with our shields on our shoulders.' Silence.

I was standing on a big wicker basket stood on end. I raised my arms. 'We're going to be the elite of this army,' I shouted. 'We will march under arms every day, and we will run every day, and we will fight when called upon and still march and run, every day. Use the donkeys to carry your loot, my friends, because they will not be carrying your aspides. Tomorrow we will be the first taxeis on parade. Your slaves will waken you with hot wine when it is time. If you quarrel with them, you are quarrelling with me. Understand?'

We were back to grunts. And scowls.

So be it, I thought.

The fourth day out of Pella. My lads had their shelters built and their food cooked before darkness fell for the first time. I gathered them all under an old oak tree and shouted at them. I asked every mess to send me their best singer.

The phylarchs – a hundred and twenty of them – stayed behind when I dismissed my men to their blankets. Most of them had another man with them – the best singers of their files. Almost all Agrianians.

'How many of you can read Greek?' I asked, and the result was to cut my meeting from three hundred to about thirty in one go. I told the rest of them to go to bed.

I gave the thirty men left a speech from Mnesimachus. 'Put it to music,' I said. 'We'll make a song of it.'

That got a lot of nods.

'Tomorrow, we'll throw javelins after dinner,' I said to the phylarchs. They groaned.

Have you any idea
What we're like to fight against?
Our sort make their dinner
Off sharp swords
We swallow blazing torches
For a savoury snack!
Then, by way of dessert,
They bring us, not nuts, but broken arrows, and splintered spear shafts.
For pillows we have our shields and breastplates,
Arrows and slings lie under our feet, and for wreaths we wear catapults

As it turned out, Marsyas, one of the former pages, turned his hand to writing my song. Marsyas was always bookish – he was the one royal page besides Alexander himself who would happily debate Aristotle, and his lyre-playing was nearly professional in its polish and he played better than the king, who played better than anyone else in Macedon. Nor was he a poor soldier – in fact, his particular skills were raid and subterfuge, and he thought nothing of lying all night in an ambush, because he was a Macedonian, not some lily-handed minstrel. We were two years apart, so we'd never been close, but he was a good friend to my young scapegraces Cleomenes and Pyrrhus. Indeed, the three were inseparable.

And since I didn't go to eat with my former mess, they came to eat with me. The next morning I had all three of them to breakfast when a hesitant Agrianian sang his version. It was rich and dramatic, but hope-less as a marching song, and sounded as if it had been sung through his nose. Still, it was a good effort, and I gave him a silver four-drachma piece.

Marsyas listened, picked up a lyre and began to tune it. Lyres take a lot of tuning, I always find, but Marsyas could tune them as fast as I could kill a deer – I've known him take an instrument down from the wall of some strange hold and tune it while talking and go straight to playing. I suspect that being that fast to tune an instrument is a significant skill – if I'd ever learned to tune a lyre, I'd be a far sight better at playing one, I'll wager.

At any rate, he tuned the lyre – and started to play. He played a song, shook his head, played another, made a face, played a line or a snatch of a line.

He nodded to Philip Longsword, who was watching with rapt admir-ation. Everyone loves music, and it's rare in a marching camp. It was still dark, and the slaves were packing, and here's this Macedonian nobleman playing the lyre on the next stool – of course Philip was attentive.

'Show me your marching pace,' Marsyas said.

So Philip walked up and down a few times.

Marsyas nodded and tried other things. The only one I knew was the beat of the rhapsodes singing the *Iliad*. Who knew you could march to the *Iliad*?

Marsyas did.

Now you do, too.

That day, we were on parade with all the other taxeis, all our gear packed. There was some sarcastic applause from the veterans. And we were in all our kit, with spears and shields.

Twice that day, we ran a stade. Just one stade – it was enough. And then we marched, with those who knew the *Iliad* shouting the verses until our voices were shot. We concentrated on the first fifty lines. For some of the Agrianians, it was the first Greek they had ever learned.

That night, we made camp, lit fires, ate and threw javelins.

It was a pretty sad exhibition. The Agrianians made the Macedonians look really bad. No, that's not fair. The Macedonians were really bad, and the Agrianians were better. The trouble was that in recruiting the *biggest* men, we'd taken more of the city boys who were rich and got meat every day, and fewer of the Pellan farm boys who could bring down a rabbit with a stone.

And the next day, we ran three times, a stade each time, and that night we threw javelins, and this time I offered a big silver four-drachma piece to each of the twenty best javelin men. We threw at marks.

I was the best javelin man. That made me happy. Still does. A thousand men, and I could throw farther, harder and more accurately.

The next day, we sang the first fifty lines of the *Iliad* again, as often as I had the wind to sing it, and we ran three times, a stade each time. And that night, the winners of the javelin throw each took twenty students and ran a javelin class. Alectus and Philip Longsword walked around preventing chaos and bad feeling. I taught a bunch of city boys.

I hit one with my fist when he was slow and stupid. He cried.

I hit him again. That's what you did to pages who cried. You beat them until they didn't cry any more.

That night – I think we'd been on the road a week – Polystratus lay next to me in the tent. I could *feel* that he had something to say, because he was lying on his back, not curling up at arm's length.

'What?' I asked. 'Say it.'

Polystratus shrugged in the darkness. Again, when you know a man – file partner or servant – or lover – you really don't need to see them to feel their postures, do you?

'That boy you smacked,' Polystratus said. 'He's not the swiftest horse in the barn, is he?'

I sighed.

'But lord, he's not a royal page. And if I were you, I wouldn't be using your precious pages as a standard of behaviour.' He chuckled without mirth. 'Beating children is foolish. You wouldn't catch a Thracian beating a child, unless the child was very wicked or very foolish. Beating children breaks their spirits. Make their spirits strong – teach them to rule themselves.'

'My, aren't you the philosopher,' I said.

'You only know one way.' He shrugged again. 'It is a bad way.'

His tone was so final, and so judgemental, that I was angry. 'What do you know?' I asked. 'You were a slave.'

He laughed. 'So?' he asked. 'I know unhappy people when I see them. Your pages are all hate and sorrow. You were yourself, until ...' He chuckled again.

'Until Pater bought you,' he said.

'And Iphegenia,' he added. 'Of course, I found her for you, too.'

'Damn you, Thracian,' I said. 'I'm just toughening him up.'

Polystratus grunted. 'Do all horses respond to the same training? All dogs?'

'Of course not,' I answered. 'Every horse needs to be taught according to temperament – very well, you bastard, I understand what you are saying.' In truth, I remember this so well because I remember lying there, shaking my head.

But you'll note, young Satyrus, that while I have a corps of royal pages, I don't let them beat their young ones or rape them either. Lesson learned. Maybe my pack won't hunt quite as hard. But maybe they won't all turn on each other as adults, either.

I'm leaving a great deal out. Many evenings I worked with my own regiment and then had to go to Alexander's tent to be there for the councils. Alexander was behaving recklessly – he was taking almost all the troops he had and marching on Thessaly, which had refused to pay the tribute they had paid to Philip. Let's put it this way – *everyone* refused to pay their tribute. The Macedonian Empire had ceased to be. Antipater felt that this was to be expected – and in Pella, he'd said as often as he could that all we had to do was work slowly, consolidate the gains at home – the so-called upper provinces – replenish the treasury and we'd be in fine shape in five years. He insisted that the immediate threat was from Attalus and Parmenio.

And Alexander marched away and left him regent, with Philip's old cavalrymen and infantrymen and nothing else to stop the Thracians and the Illyrians. Antipater was a good loser – he accepted his fate well enough. The truth – at least, the truth as I see it – was that Antipater always played both sides. He helped murder Philip – for all I knew, he did all the dirty work himself – and he was right there to help Alexander take control. But we all knew he was personally and professionally close to Parmenio and to Attalus. He had a foot in both camps. If the foolish blond boy marched away and lost the army, why, Antipater would have maintained order, crowned Cleopatra's son and called for Attalus to return from Asia. Or so I guess.

We all knew we were headed for Thessaly, which had the finest cavalry in the Greek world and the plains on which to deploy them.

But the Thessalians, as our scouts discovered, didn't intend to fight a cavalry battle. Instead, they called up their feudal army and rolled it into the Vale of Tempe, twenty thousand men to our ten thousand, and waited for us. By the time my boys were throwing javelins in the evening, I knew we were going to have to fight the Thessalians, who, until a few weeks before, had been so closely wedded to us as to be cousins, if not brothers. And Parmenio, who was, remember, the head of the 'lowland aristocrat' faction, was himself half Thessalian.

You have to wonder what, exactly, was passing between Parmenio, Attalus and Antipater.

On our ninth day, we marched into the Vale of Tempe, with Mount Olympus on one side of us and Mount Ossa on the other side.

Polystratus found me marching with my file, and informed me that the king wanted me.

I ordered Polystratus off his horse and gave him my aspis to carry, and laughed at his glare.

'Just toughening you up,' I said, and rode away on his horse.

Alexander was out front with the Prodromoi. He had Cassander, Philip the Red and a few of the other oldsters with him, and Laodon. I could see a dozen Thessalian nobles in brilliant tack, covered with gold, just riding away with a herald.

Laodon winked at me.

Alexander nodded at the Thessalians. He pulled off his silvered Boeotian helmet and scratched his head. 'They have ordered me to stop marching. They say that if we continue, they will be forced to fight.'

Hephaestion laughed. 'And the king agreed to stop marching!' he said.

I looked at Alexander.

'See that mountain?' he said. He had a short staff in his hand – like a walking staff of vine wood, but shorter. He used it to point. 'See the high pass – see the ridge?'

In fact, I could. 'Yes, lord.'

'I need your Agrianians to run up that ridge and seize the height.' He nodded. 'Can they?'

'The hypaspitoi can do it,' I said.

Alexander caught the nuance. 'Can they? All the better.' He nodded. 'Get it done. Cassander, get all the slaves and all the camp servants together, and get tools – shovels and picks.'

'I get all the best jobs,' Cassander whined.

The Thessalians had ordered Alexander to stop marching. This was my king's notion of high humour.

I had my orders. I rode back, enjoying the clean breeze and the feel of a horse under me, and all too soon I was handing the reins to Polystratus and settling the aspis into the groove it had worn in my shoulder.

I ran back along my column. The pass was quite wide at this point, and the ground level enough, so the army was marching ten files wide, with double the normal order between men, and the baggage and slaves in the intervals. We were in the face of the enemy, yet, for whatever reason, only my hypaspitoi were fully armed.

'Leather bags! Make sure you have water in your canteen! Your chlamys, rolled tight.' I looked at men in every file. By now, they were not so faceless – I knew that Amyntas of Amphilopolis was the useless gowp I'd hit with my fist, and I looked at him and he gave me a weak smile and held out his water bottle and his shoulder-bag straps to show me he was in full gear.

Cleon of Aegae and Arcrax the Unready were two more useless mouths, and both of them had to find their mess slaves and recover their water bottles. No matter how elite a body of men is, somehow they always have a few of these men. Some have hidden talents, but most of them have none.

The column continued to march, and my taxeis marched with them – those men who needed equipment had to run back and forth.

And then we were ready.

I ordered the slaves and baggage out of the ranks.

I ordered the men to exchange their spears for javelins.

Then I wheeled my taxeis out of the column and kept moving, so that my lead files were facing the ridge. It was two thousand feet above us, up a steep slope broken by olive groves, tiny farm plots and copses of ash and oak.

'We are going straight up this ridge,' I said. 'We will reform at the top. First man gets a mina of silver. Last man gets to cook dinner.'

Alectus looked at the slope. 'Any defenders?'

I shook my head. 'No idea. But no one who can stand up to this lot.'

Alectus grunted. 'They're not much good.'

I nodded. 'They're freemen with good arms. Anyone waiting for us on this hillside is a bunch of slaves and lower-class men with bags of rocks.'

Philip Longsword nodded. 'Greeks, eh?'

Greeks were notorious, among Macedonians and their allies, for having poor skirmishers.

'Ready!' I roared.

The royal companions were coming up on our right flank.

'The king is watching us!' I roared.

The high-pitched rattle of our cheer rose to the gods – *Alaialaialai.*

Suddenly, I loved them. And we were off up the ridge.

A two-thousand-foot ridge is a long climb, especially when it has a slope like a barn roof. We went up and up and up and up, and by the end of a tenth of the distance, my thighs were burning like a winter fire and my aspis weighed twice what it had weighed at the base of the ridge.

But I was among the lead fifty men.

So was Alectus, well ahead of me, and Philip Longsword, close by my side, although I suspected that was by choice, not by exertion.

We came to an olive grove with a low stone retaining wall. Some men climbed the wall and I ran around and gained ground, and then I heard fighting off to my right. To be honest, what I heard was the sound of men being butchered, so I just kept running up the bastard hill.

Rocks – big rocks, probably volcanic, were scattered across the hillside at this level, and there were weeds from the farm fields, including the bane of every infantryman's existence, the sharp seed-pods that slip into your sandals and maim your feet.

I hadn't been a page for nothing. I ran on, despite the sharp pains in my feet and the stitch in my side and the trembling of my upper thighs, the feeling that my ankles were going to fail, the weight of my aspis.

I was catching Alectus.

A dozen men appeared behind a low stone wall and threw stones at us. One caught Alectus right on the brow of his Illyrian helmet, and down he went. And I was all alone.

I went over the wall. Once people start throwing rocks and using spears, fatigue falls way – for a while.

They ran. I never caught them – a dozen nearly naked slaves, and they left their little piles of rocks.

Very frustrating. On the other hand, I was a little more than halfway up the hill, and I was in front. I looked back, panting over my pair of javelins, and the hypaspitoi were spread over a stade wide and half a stade deep, and the closest men were just ten paces back.

'Come on!' I called. 'The king is still watching!'

Because he was. I could see him – he had his helmet off, because he always knew how to watch a feat of arms. His blond mane showed over the distance and the faint heat shimmer.

I waved my spear.

He raised his helmet. I swear that I could see those blue eyes across the distance, and I swear some spark leaped from Alexander to me.

I turned before the first men could catch me and I was off again, a different fire in my blood. And close at my heels, afire with emulation, came a mix of Agrianians and Macedonians – about fifty men, all together in a bunch.

Men were laughing.

We ran on.

After another stade, we couldn't really pretend to be running. We were just climbing. It was steeper, the rocks were bigger and the copses of stunted trees came thicker. I was panting every breath, and my mouth was so dry that my tongue stuck to its roof. I was no longer first, either – Philip passed me, and then several Agrianians all together, and then more men.

We were all together when we caught the slaves, though. They were just slaves, and had no wind, and suddenly all our weapons were red.

And as if their blood fed us, we all gained another wind from the gods, and we *ran*. And down in the valley, the pezhetaeroi were cheering – the same *Alaialaialaialai* we'd screamed as we started, and it carried like the very voice of the gods, and rebounded from the slopes of Olympus.

The top of the ridge was only a few horse lengths above us now, and men had to pull themselves from scrubby tree to scrubby tree – and suddenly the ridge above us was full of Thessalians, hundreds of infantrymen. Not true hoplites, more like Peltastoi, with small crescent-shaped shields and leather hats and javelins.

Their problems were twofold. First, it's not that easy to throw a javelin accurately in thick brush, and we were climbing the last of the ridge through dense spruce and old ash – little trees, but probably ancient, starved of water and of food.

Second, by luck or the will of Zeus, the portion of the ridge we'd come up at the last had an odd hump and twist, so that the men above us couldn't actually see us until we reached the very last few feet.

What was best – for us – is that they tried hurling javelins at the sounds we made climbing – because such was the fire in us that we never slackened our assault, even when it became clear that we were climbing into a force larger than our own.

Philip Longsword shot out of the spruce first, and took a dozen javelins in his aspis.

When I came out next to him, I was at the base of a rock taller than a man's head. The enemy was atop the rock and behind it.

Javelins were thudding into my shield like an ill hail.

I looked left and saw a route to the top, and I ran up it, into a swarm of Peltastoi.

It was like the bear hunt all over again, except that this time I had a lot of friends and armour. I took a javelin in my instep and another ripped a finger-deep gouge in my right calf, because I had no greaves. In fact, I'd never have made it to there with greaves. But my good thorax held some blows, and my helmet took its share of abuse, and my javelins were gone – who knows where – and then Philip's long Keltoi sword was flashing in the sun by my side, and then Agrianians were shouting in their own barbarian tongue and one of their phylarchs – I didn't know his name yet – was beside me, with a spear as big as the one Achilles carried.

At first, the Thessalians poured into our position, trying to overwhelm us and push us back off the rock.

We were bigger, stronger and better trained. So we held on, although at least one of my Agrianians fell to his death in that fight.

But as they poured into the centre to repel my thrust, the rest of my hypaspitoi caught up, spread half a stade on either side, and some of them were suddenly atop the ridge with no opponents at all – and with no plan whatsoever, or at least no plan I made, they folded in from either flank like the horns of a great bull.

I could see it from my rock. All I wanted to do was stop fighting – one minute and I was exhausted, and ten minutes and I was wrecked, and spears were coming past my guard routinely. Only my thorax saved me, as many as twenty times. Men – good men – fell there because they had nothing left after the climb, and didn't have armour to keep them alive.

But I could see the wings of my taxeis closing in, and it was glorious.

I took a deep breath, and Athena stood at my shoulder and whispered honeyed words in my ear.

'Hypaspists!' I roared. Or perhaps I croaked it. But they heard. 'The king is watching! And there is Olympus, and the gods themselves are watching!'

And the battle cry came back – from the valley, from the heights above us, from every throat that could still draw breath, so that the very air around us thickened with the sound.

Alaialaialaialaialaialai!

The Peltastoi broke. I *think* they thought from the sound that we'd got behind them. But it doesn't matter. They turned and ran.

They all lived, because none of us followed them. We sank down on our ridge-top and bled.

I drank water, and Polystratus appeared with twenty mounted grooms and bandaged my calves and my instep, and put me in riding boots.

Cassander rode up the shallow end of the ridge, three stades away.

At our feet, two thousand slaves were cutting steps in the hillside. They were fast. They'd been promised cash payment and freedom for the best, and they worked with a will – so fast that we could watch the progress they were making.

Cassander saluted. We were not friends – I've said that. But he grinned. 'That was worthy of the heroes of the *Iliad*!' he said. 'Alexander all but pissed himself with pleasure. Now he wants you to clear the ridge heading south.'

I nodded.

Polystratus handed me a roll of sesame seeds in honey, and I sucked a mouthful out of the sausage skin. The sugar went into my blood like ambrosia. I drank a mouthful of wine, finished the seeds and stood up, a new man.

Youth! How I miss it.

'Hypaspists!' I called. Very little came out.

I looked at Philip, who was busy with two slaves, wrapping the mess he'd made of his sword arm. He shook his head and croaked something.

'My voice is strong,' Alectus rumbled. He had a bandage around his head. 'I missed a good fight.'

'I thought you had your doubts about fighting,' I said.

He laughed. 'You should listen more carefully,' he said.

I had to whisper loudly to get words out. 'We need to sweep the ridge.'

Alectus nodded. He walked out along the ridge and raised his big spear. 'Hypaspitoi!' he called in his barbaric accent. 'Not finished yet, philoi! Take a deep breath, think of happy things and get your helmets back on.'

Not exactly like my speeches, but it did the job.

Alectus led, and we followed. Whatever fire had run through my veins was gone, and I was washed clean – and empty. I couldn't think, and I couldn't form words. Which was fine. Alectus spread us out in a skirmish line across the ridge, as if we were Peltastoi ourselves – perhaps the terrain, or perhaps it was just the Agrianian's way. And we walked slowly, and the remaining Peltastoi and Psiloi simply popped up like hares in a hunt and fled, and we let them go. They wasted some stones on us, and we didn't trouble them with our javelins.

Now, in truth, we lost three men for every one the Athenian mercenaries – that's what they were – lost to us. And in truth, we outnumbered them by at least two to one when all our men reached the hilltop.

But if you ever ride through the Vale of Tempe, look up at Mount Ossa, and tell me it wasn't one of our finest hours. We pushed them off the ridge.

And after that, they weren't going to make a stand anywhere. Maybe they thought we were insane. And perhaps we were.

We camped that night at the southern end of the ridge, overlooking the Thessalian camp. Behind us, the whole Macedonian army was coming up the steps cut by the slaves.

That night, Marsyas came to me. I had no tent – the baggage was still down on the plain. I was eating more sesame and honey, and my heart burned with the sting of it, but Polystratus had found milk, and warm milk and honey is a fine meal on a cold night in the mountains.

Marsyas came to our fire and flopped down next to me.

'Hail, Achilles, Lord of the Myrmidons!' he said. 'Alexander is beside himself with jealousy. Just so you know.'

I laughed, but I knew my king, and I knew I was in trouble.

Marsyas shrugged. 'I have your song. And I think your corps have earned a song, don't you?'

'Slaves and Peltasts?' I said, because that was the Macedonian way. 'On a little hill?'

'If that's a little hill, then Aphrodite has little tits,' Marsyas said. That seemed really funny to me, too.

He had Polystratus fetch my lyre – a little-used instrument, I promise you. He made 'tsk tsk' noises while he tuned it, and then he played.

Well, you know what he played, I'm sure.

By the third time through, Philip and Alectus and even Cassander were singing along.

By the next morning, enough men knew it to make a decent sound as we marched past the king, down the high pass and into the plains of Thessaly, leaving the Thessalian army standing like fools.

Marsyas asked me for a job that morning. As I said, we'd never been close, because of our year groups, but I liked him, and I needed some good officers – and any boy who survives being a royal page is a good officer. So I gave him the first ten files. He dismounted and marched, and later in the day, his slave brought him an aspis.

At any rate, we came down the pass with the Thessalians behind us. Of course, they were between us and home, but we, on the other hand, were between them and *their* homes.

We halted at midday, ate a small and hasty meal and formed for battle. Remember, they outnumbered us two to one.

Alexander rode out, then. He rode across the front of the army, helmet off, Tyrian purple cloak streaming behind him, and he looked like a god. I think – I may be wrong – I think it's the first time I saw him like that.

He galloped across the front and the roar was like a physical thing, right to left across the whole army, a shocking sound.

And then he pulled his horse up in a little display, half a stade in advance of his whole army. And he used his spear to salute the Thessalians, who were pouring out of the pass behind us.

The sound of our cheer rose to the heavens, climbing the pass to Olympus and to Ossa and then bouncing back in a mighty ripple of echo.

The Thessalian army shuddered to a halt.

They started to sort themselves out, and Alexander ordered us forward.

We marched forward about a stade. Our line wasn't perfect, but it was adequate. Later, Macedonian armies did this kind of display all the time, and our drill was magnificent. That summer day, it was enough that we kept our places in line and no gaps opened.

The Thessalians, it was obvious, weren't going to get formed in time. They were just a mob.

A delegation was spat forth from the mounted part of the mob.

Alexander raised his arm, and we halted.

He rode forward by himself.

I know that the Prodromoi started forward, and my squadron of the Hetaeroi. He waved them back, but the Prodromoi shadowed him, moving anxiously ...

They needn't have worried.

The Thessalians surrendered.

In retrospect, you just nod, boy, because what army of barbarians could even look at a Macedonian army without fear, eh? But that was not yet come to pass. We weren't 'Alexander's Macedonians' yet – an army that, by wonderful irony, was always at least a third Thessalian.

I count that day as Alexander's first battle. At Chaeronea, he did what he could with a dull plan. Philip was a brilliant strategist and a fine fighter, but a dull tactician. Alexander ... was Alexander.

Had we rolled forward into the Thessalians, we would have killed a great many of them – and been at war for years. Alexander took a terrible risk. But the circumstances – when every province in the empire was in revolt, and we had no friends – required risk. Or that's how the king saw it, and he was the king.

And Thessaly was ours. The best cavalry in Greece, the finest horses and a nation that immediately offered two years' tribute as recompense for hesitation.

In one day, Alexander had changed the game.

Heh. Alexander, with the help of the hypaspists. And not for the last time, either.

ELEVEN

I imagine that Greece offered many strategoi who could have turned the flanks of the Thessalians and beaten them without a battle. Old Phokion could have done it – it was very much his sort of victory. Philip – well, I suspect Philip would have forced the battle and the massacre, and taken the consequences.

But Alexander wasn't done.

We picked up a thousand noble Thessalians – aristocratic cavalrymen, men who were in almost every way *just like us.* After all, they'd been our allies, almost our subjects, right up until Philip's death – and the only men who'd died on the slopes of Mount Ossa had been Athenian mercenaries. And hypaspists. I lost fifty-five men on Mount Ossa, a number I'll never forget. I didn't even know all of their names. More Agrianians died than Macedonians, because the Agrianians got to the top faster. But, cruel as it sounds, there were enough corpses of both races to bind them together.

We buried them on the plains of Thessaly, in five barrows of eleven men each, and the king came and poured the libations at the edge of night, and fog rolled down from the hills to cover the newly turned earth, and men said that the ghosts of Hades had come to lick the blood of the sacrifices and the wine of the libations.

I was tipsy. I remember that. I'd fought hard, and fighting on foot is exhausting – cavalrymen really have no idea. But I'd also made decisions that killed men, and it was, perhaps, the first time I faced the consequence of glorious victory – the sad, sick feeling afterwards, the same feeling you get when you know you've paid far too much for wheat in the marketplace, except ten times worse. And somehow, the rain of unforced congratulations from my peers only served to make it worse.

Of course, I bore it all with smiles, backslapping, coarse humour – I'm telling the truth here, and the truth is that it never does to show weakness with Macedonians – or any other human animal, eh, lad? But

I was hurt, inside – hurt as if I'd taken a wound – by those fifty-five men who'd died so that my king could *not* have a battle.

So I was tipsy. I drank from the moment the libations were poured, and when the king poured one to Herakles and ordered us all to drink our cups dry, I drank mine and sent it back to be refilled, and smiled at a Thessalian aristocrat-boy so that he shrank away.

Marsyas steadied me.

But Alexander came over and put a hand on my shoulder. 'Yesterday was well done,' he said.

A great many responses came to me, and I bit them down. It wasn't the king's fault so many men had died, and it wasn't his fault – exactly – that it all seemed to be for nothing and the leaders of the 'enemy' army were sharing our funeral feast. So I made a smile come to my face and muttered, 'Thanks.'

'Will your men be ready to march tomorrow?' he asked.

Zeus Soter! I remember that question shooting down my muscles like new pain. My men were exhausted.

But that was not something I chose to say. Good or bad leadership is often a matter of perspective. I was going to make my hypaspists creatures of legend. Creatures of legend do not admit fatigue. Paradox, if you like – I was angry at my losses and eager to keep my men's reputation well shined.

'We could march now, if you want us to,' I said.

Just for a moment, in the flickering torchlight, I saw Alexander's eyes narrow a fraction. And Marsyas stepped forward, took my arm and smiled. 'If they can walk, that is. Come, big brother. I'll steer you to bed.'

I woke in the darkness – fully alert. I got up, kicked Polystratus out of his cloak and crawled into a dry chiton and a heavy chlamys, because the plains of Thessaly had the same fog in early morning as they did at night.

Every muscle in my body protested softly, and a few protested loudly, but the advantage of a life of activity is that even as a very young man you know that none of this is actually pain, and that it will all be gone as soon as you sweat.

I walked out and roused my mess group. Polystratus woke my slaves, and Ochrid, the lead slave, pulled out a quill and blew the coals of the fire into life. 'Morning, master,' he said, cheerfully. Ochrid was a big fellow, a Paeonian. He wasn't too bright, and he wasn't *too* big – he had an open, pleasant face and bright blond hair, and no apparent need to be a freeman. But he was steady, trustworthy – as long as you didn't task him beyond his skills – and careful. He was warm, too.

Let me just say that slaves came and went. A few stayed with me for years, but in general, I tried to keep them moving – to freedom, or to the farms. Being a soldier's slave is brutal work, and it breaks them. And they can never marry, or have children, or have a little hut or a plot of land. Mind you, they can earn their freedom in an hour of looting or a single lucky kill – or die screaming on someone's spear-point, for sport. My point is that Ochrid survived years of this life, and he's got a place in Memphis as my tax farmer there. So he's an exception. Mostly, I won't even mention their names. Sad. But one of those facts of life. Slaves come and go.

Where was I?

Ochrid called, 'Good morning,' and that seemed to allow other men to approach me, and before I had a cup of hot milk in my hand, a dozen men were all around me – could I look at a wound? Did I know that third file was now three men short? Would we be getting new drafts to make up our numbers?

I was starting to know my phylarchs. And I liked most of what I saw. Nicanor was a Macedonian only by adoption – he was a former mercenary, also from Lesbos, a friend of Aristotle – the great man's former lover, in fact. Nicanor was the fourth file commander, thin, small, full of fire. A handsome man, with serious culture.

Astibus, on the other hand, was an Agrianian chieftain's son, tall, blond and outweighing me by half. A giant. Virtually the first man up Ossa, after me. He had an axe – a very old-fashioned weapon indeed – which rested in carefully forged spring-bronze mounts inside his aspis, a vicious surprise when he broke his spear. He put as much thought into fighting as Aristotle did into categorising living things, and the Greek pankration fascinated him utterly – the Agrianians had nothing like it.

Nicanor and Astibus were among the more memorable, but I had one hundred and twenty phylarchs, and they came in a huge variety of sizes and flavours, and one was actually black – an African. He was another former mercenary, and his Macedonian name was Bubores, and he had horrible nightmares and could terrify all of us when he screamed in the night. His Greek was pitiful, but his battlefield power was legendary, and he, like Astibus, had been among the first men up the mountain.

Astibus was stubborn and inclined to argue with orders. Nicanor was arrogant and snide – used big words, and patronised his lessers, which meant nearly everyone. Bubares was often drunk on duty, although his men liked him well enough that they covered for him.

These men exist in every army in the world, I suspect. When the

Hittites rolled their chariots to windy Ilium, I suspect there were old drunks, arrogant poets and brash youngsters.

And new commanders trying to create legends.

But what they all wanted to know, that morning, was who had won the prize at Ossa – who had been first up the hill. The phylarchs crowded around me, arguing the merits of this man and that.

Old Philip laughed. 'Lord Ptolemy was first up the hill,' he said. 'I saw him.'

Alectus laughed. 'Cheap bastard,' he said.

That got a general guffaw.

'I am *not* a cheap bastard,' I said, with mock horror. 'So I'll pay half the prize each to the two men who were *second* up the hill – and without whom I'd be dead!' I sent Polystratus back to my tent for cash, and I gave half a mina of silver – a pretty fair prize – to Philip Longsword and to young Astibus.

That seemed to make everyone happy. Despite funereal hangovers – the night before, my boys had discovered that Agrianians and Macedonians share a belief that the dead are best mourned drunk – despite muscles of cast lead. Despite all of that, we were first on parade, in pitch darkness.

In armour, with our spears and aspides.

I've won battles, and I've killed heroes in single combat. I've slept with outrageously beautiful women I had no business even looking at, and I've climbed mountains and travelled the world. On balance, that moment in Thessaly, standing confidently, arrogantly, despite my pains and my wounded instep and the gouge in my leg – standing bare-legged on parade, with my heroes all lined up behind me, clamouring to start their march – even the slaves all in the ranks, all our baggage packed – we, who had fought a heroic action two days before – and around us, the royal companions and the pezhetaeroi scrambled to be ready – it was one of the most satisfying moments of my life, and I grew taller and handsomer.

The king rode out to me. I didn't see him coming until the last moment – he was riding quietly on a palfrey.

'Splendid,' he said. He grinned – a boyish grin I seldom saw after he was twelve. 'You know, Ptolemy, just now, I think I'd like to trade places with you. Right now, it is you who are a god, and I am merely your commander.'

Sometimes he was impossibly arrogant, and sometimes he was impossible not to love. I took his hand and locked it in a clasp – the way warriors do. He leaned down. 'We are going to conquer the world with these men,' he said. The grin was still there.

The hypaspitoi began to cheer – *Alaialaialaialai.*

Suddenly Alexander laughed. 'Fuck them if they're late to parade!' he shouted, and pumped his hand to indicate that we should prepare to march.

So we marched away from Thessaly to conquer the world. The hypaspitoi led, and all the rest of the army had to catch up.

Beat that story, lad. Those were great days, great men, doing great things.

We made forced marches across the Thessalian plain, one hundred stades a day and sometimes more. We didn't drink wine in the stews of Larissa – we missed nothing, I can tell you – and we didn't bother the shepherd boys on the slopes of Mount Othrys. We crossed Thessaly in five days, and the Thessalian nobles complained we were ruining their horses.

My men laughed. They were marching five parasanges a day, running a third of the distance, keeping up with the cavalry scouts and the king. They were young and strong, and after three weeks in the field, they had bodies as hard as rock. We rested at the height of the pass over the shoulders of Othrys – my men were tucked into rocks and fissures, and there was snow. Men curled up three to a cloak – or rather, three to three cloaks. The man in the middle got a little sleep.

Alexander rode into my 'camp', which means that he asked a few sleepy men and a sentry, and Polystratus woke me.

Alexander had only Hephaestion with him.

'I need another dash from your myrmidons,' the king said. 'I need you to be at the Gates of Fire by tonight. I don't *think* Thebes has the balls to contest my passage, but once I have the Gates, we've got all the time in the world. Tell your boys I promise at least a week's rest at the Gates. But I need this done now – I went to sleep thinking about it, and I woke up just now with Herakles' hand on my shoulder.'

Fuck him. Let's face it, I'm not at my best in freezing cold in the middle of the night after a hundred-stade march and very little sleep.

But there comes a moment – when you are building something special – when you just want to keep testing it, because you cannot really believe how good it is. I've seen a cutler put an edge on a razor and then test it until his thumb is bleeding – grinning like a fool because the edge is so good. That was me.

I got to my feet, smiled at the king and Polystratus bellowed, 'Spears and armour! March in one hour!'

And they got up off their rocks and joked that marching would be warmer than lying in the snow.

We marched along the beach and through the Gates of Fire unopposed. In fact, we had time to stop and make sacrifice to the Spartans who fell there for Greece – though I knew we were better men than they ever were. After all, they were merely Greeks, without even the erudition of Athens.

But they were good, brave men, and all brave men should be brothers, even when they fight against each other. War's bad enough without rules. I hear men say that war should be fought without rules, but I despise such weaklings. Rules in contests are the courtesies of the strong to the strong.

But I digress.

We bought sheep from the shepherds and sacrificed them, and we poured libations to the dead – Persians as well as Greeks. And while we did that, fifty picked men climbed the high pass on our right flank and another fifty prowled ahead twenty stades under Alectus, who neither knew nor cared who Leonidas had been, despite his gleanings of Greek learning.

We were ahead of the Prodromoi, so we laid out the camp – the first time that ever happened – and we got the pick of the sheep. The farmers were thin on the ground, and there wasn't much food. I sent scouts north into Achaea looking for grain and wine and oil.

Towards evening, Alexander came with the army, looked approvingly at the small ash-altar our sacrifices had left, and dismounted immediately to add his own. His devotions were absolutely genuine – he was a very religious man, and the sacrifices of heroes – all heroes, regardless of cause or race – meant a great deal to him. Some he had to equal or exceed – he was locked in agonistic competition even with the very gods – but that didn't mean he didn't worship their achievements. By acknowledging them, he worshipped himself. Or that's how I see it now.

The next morning, we slept in, and held impromptu games in honour of the Spartans. We had only four Spartans in the whole army, but they were made the judges, and we had a wonderful time, running and throwing javelins, riding horses, wrestling, fencing and reading poetry.

It was a first, but like many aspects of that campaign, it was a sign of the future. Alexander the innovator was also Alexander the conservative. He wanted the old ways restored, even at the risk of seeming a little silly to his men. The first games we held had a slightly forced atmosphere – I remember that when the first wreaths of ludicrously over-woven laurel were awarded to the distance runner, men laughed – but the laughter stopped soon enough.

Marsyas found some local girls and asked them to make us proper wreaths, and when I won the run in armour on the second afternoon – running with a spear wound in my left foot, let me add – I received a beautiful wreath, which I was proud to wear all the next day. And those of us who won wreaths ate together that night.

Astibus won the javelin throw for accuracy.

Little Cleomenes wasn't so little now, and had long legs like a woman, and won the two-stade sprint – won it handily.

That one I remember, because Alexander watched that race with something very like lust. He wanted to compete.

I was lounging about, literally resting on my laurels. I was lying on a pallet of new straw watching men run and cheering, and I caught the king's eye. I shrugged. 'Go run!' I said quietly.

He gave me a sad smile. 'Prince Alexander might have run,' he said. 'King Alexander will never run again.'

It wasn't all fun and games. As soon as he made camp, Alexander sent heralds to the members of the Amphictyonic League, demanding – in the most courteous way possible – that they meet him at the Gates of Fire.

In effect, he announced, 'I'm at the gates of mainland Greece, and none of you have the strength of arms to stop me. Want to talk?'

And they all came.

Even before the League assembled, states around us were falling into line. Or rather, back into our allegiance. The cities of southern Epirus begged for forgiveness and insisted they hadn't meant to revolt. Listening to their ambassadors was an education in bad rhetoric.

Alexander stunned them by giving a few of them their independence. It was a complex version of independence, wherein he kept absolute control of their foreign relations, but they had city charters and city magnates. I didn't understand right away, and thought that he was making concessions to the realities – but in a matter of a few weeks his policy became audience. It was his father's policy in Boeotia to liberate the smaller cities and use them as watchdogs on Thebes. Of course they were loyal Macedonian allies – they owed us everything. Plataea comes to mind.

Alexander did the same. And the outer provinces crawled all over themselves to return to the fold. Even the ones we'd left behind when we marched on Greece.

Athens and Thebes did not send representatives to the Gates of Fire.

It is remarkable, when you are a soldier, how quickly after exhaustion that rest gives way to boredom. The change seems to be immediate

– you are exhausted, you have a rest, suddenly you are bored. Bored soldiers are the most dangerous animals in the human bestiary. They fight duels, they get drunk, they rape.

All bad.

By the third day at the Gates of Fire, I'd killed a man who'd fought at Mount Ossa with my own hand – he raped a child, and I gutted him in front of the parade. That gave the rest of them pause. And I learned my lesson – I hope that child's life saved a few others – and I brought in instructors for sword work, for wrestling, for running. We threw javelins relentlessly, and we climbed the cliffs, and we began to master the close-order drill that Philip had insisted the pezhetaeroi learn. We had a lexicon of manoeuvres, and we spent four days marching through them – Spartan counter-march, Macedonian counter-march, files and form to the left, files and form to the right, wheeling motions, half-file manoeuvres and file-doubling manoeuvres. Anything to keep the bastards busy.

The League representatives met, and on the first day they voted Alexander to be head of the League, as his father had been. Alexander smiled and proposed an agenda for the next four days of meetings.

And then we marched away in the dark. All Alexander ever wanted was the League's recognition. As soon as he had it, he was finished with them and their trappings of authority. The Prodromoi marched in pitch darkness, very early on a short summer night, and my hypaspitoi followed them. We had guides we'd recruited from the countryside and paid well, and we moved very fast.

We had to cross the mountains of Phokia, and Alexander, always religious, was determined to march past Delphi. The going was steep, but it was high summer and we'd had a week's rest, and we flew. Three days to Delphi, and a day's rest.

Alectus went to the temple, presented himself to the priests and was refused – as a barbarian.

So I accompanied him, both of us in armour.

Greeks like to claim that we Macedonians are barbarians when it suits them. As Alexander was the head of the Holy League and his soldiers were the guarantors of the temple treasury, I had a feeling they would accept me as a Hellene – nor was I disappointed.

We waited in the antechamber while a trio of Athenians asked detailed questions about business and about Alexander's intentions for their city.

When they emerged, I sent Alectus in alone. And I walked out on to the portico with the Athenians. Two of them were unknown to me, but the third was Kineas's friend Diodorus.

'They say that meetings in the temple precincts are part of the will of the God,' I said, putting my arm around his shoulder. Diodorus turned and we embraced.

'Alexander wants to be recognised as hegemon of the League of Corinth. He'll fight to get it, too.' I held both his hands and looked him in the eye so that he'd see I was being utterly honest.

He nodded. 'Fair enough,' he said. 'And a great deal clearer than what the priestess muttered.'

His companions looked uneasy, and kept their distance.

He jerked a thumb at them, rudely. 'I'm the token aristocrat. They're my fellow democrats – friends of Demosthenes, or followers. More like acolytes – very dull companions. Give me dinner tonight and I'll tell you how happy I am that Alexander is coming to rescue us!' He laughed bitterly.

I sent him on his way and waited for Alectus, who emerged looking troubled.

'She is a real prophetess,' he said, and fingered his beard. 'I could feel her power.'

I shrugged, because only a fool doubts the power of the god at Delphi.

Alectus walked with me back to camp, but I could tell he was not in a mood for talk.

That night, I gave a small dinner for Diodorus, and invited some of the Hetaeroi – Philip the Red, Cleomenes, Nearchus and Marsyas. He was good company, but his tale was a sad one – Athens was in a state of near stasis, civil war, because Demothenes kept the commons united against Alexander – who he caricatured as a fop, a poseur, an effeminate impostor.

Kineas was in the other faction, of course. And Diodorus had finally turned his back on the democrats.

'If that fool has his way, we'll fight you again,' Diodorus said wearily. Then he brightened. 'Say – you know that Thaïs speaks of you often?'

'Does she?' I asked. That gave me a little heart-burst of joy.

'She gave me a party the night before I left – she prophesied that I would have days of dull company and would need to remember her wit.' He smiled. 'Some day, I long to afford a woman like her – to have her all to myself, every day. I'll take her to dinner parties. Shock the matrons. Perhaps marry her!'

I laughed, although I was jealous.

He smiled at me as if reading my thoughts. 'Thaïs said that she had been told by a seer she trusts that she is to leave Athens.' He laughed. 'Hardly news – the old men hate her so much they threaten to exile her constantly. Bad for public morals. Worse than old Socrates. Or so I hear.' He laughed into his wine.

Marsyas leaned over. 'Who is this paragon?'

'Ah,' I said, and took the opportunity every man loves, to discuss his paramour. Or perhaps she wasn't my paramour. I won't have you imagine that every time I lay with a slave girl or a willing free woman, I dreamed of Thaïs. That would have been, if nothing else, rude. The partner of the moment deserves your full attention. If you can't remember the woman with whom you are lying – don't bother!

But I thought of her often, more so as we came closer to Athens, and to discuss her openly with Diodorus was delightful.

At the same time, I sent Nearchus to Alexander when he went on duty with a note explaining the presence of the Athenian envoys and their mission.

Nearchus came back with two grooms and regretfully informed Diodorus that he and his fellow envoys would be guests of the temple for a few days. Diodorus accepted this with good grace. His fellows were obviously terrified.

We marched away in the dark.

We were at Lebedaea before noon, a hundred and ten stades of running and marching, with the Prodromoi just ahead of us and on either side, and the king with them, surrounded by his somatophylakes – the inner companions, the trusted bodyguards. I was one of them, in title.

I knew all morning we weren't going to stop. Alexander was playing for the whole jar of oil, as the Athenians say, and we were going to make the dash. My men were in peak condition, and ready for anything. The Prodromoi changed horses at the meal break – and every one of them had at least two remounts.

The sun had scarcely begun to decline when we started for Thebes, another hundred and twenty stades across the plains of Boeotia, the dance floor of Ares. If the Thebans were going to fight, it was going to be today, tonight or tomorrow. My men had already come five parasanges on foot, in their armour, with their shields on their shoulders. Go and try it. Tell me how you do.

And we were off. The Prodromoi didn't range far ahead. A thousand hypaspitoi, two hundred Prodromoi and twenty somatophylakes in full armour – the cream of the Macedonian army. And the king. Twelve hundred men against the might of Thebes and Athens – against a possible sixty thousand hoplites.

Farmers stood at their ploughs and watched us as if we were an army of ghosts.

Women stood at the edges of fields and watched us pass. Let me tell you what that means. Women are usually locked away when armies come. It's a good idea. If country people get a rumour of an army, their grain is buried, their animals are driven up the hills and their women vanish.

We marched through a Boeotia full of late-summer grain, donkeys and beautiful women watching us march. They had no idea we were coming, and the Prodromoi moved so fast and so professionally that any man among them who thought to saddle his mare and ride for the city was quietly, ruthlessly removed and brought before the king. No one was killed, but by the time the sun was well down in the sky, we had thirty of these honest citizens trailing the king.

And we could see the Cadmea in the distance. Fabled Thebes.

Bastards. Really, an example of bad behaviour to ring through the ages. Only worthy thing Thebes ever did was to beat Sparta, and even there, really the Spartans beat themselves. Otherwise, Thebes was like a weathercock to tell worthy men what not to do, eh?

It is very fashionable these days in Greece to decry the fate of Thebes. Fuck them. They got what they deserved. How's that for insensitive?

Anyway, we kept marching. We were on a superb road by then, rounded at the crest, paved with stones, and we sped up.

We marched right up to the gates. We posted a double line of sentries, paid the farmers of the near Cadmea to provide chicken, lamb and barley, and made a rich dinner. The hordes of Thebes didn't frighten me any, and I slept well.

We were up in the dark, but however early the hypaspitoi rose that day, the men of Thebes were up earlier. By the time I found Alexander, Thebes had already surrendered and agreed to accept a new garrison, and accepted Alexander as the hegemon of the League.

I went back to bed.

I awoke late, to a new world. A world where Alexander, my boyhood friend, was actually going to be the hegemon of the League of Corinth – the master of the Amphictyonic League, the keeper of Delphi. The King of Macedon, Lord of Thessaly and undisputed master of his father's empire.

It was thirty-nine days since we'd marched out of Pella, with Antipater claiming we should sit and negotiate and lay out some bribes.

The first sign of the new world was Amyntas son of Philotas, one of Parmenio's household officers. I knew him well – he'd brought me my first toy sword.

He was waiting with Polystratus when I awoke. We embraced, and he shook his head.

'When I was a young man, I never slept this late,' he said with mock severity.

'When you were a young man, Agamemnon was still king and the siege of Troy was in its second year,' I said. 'And I doubt you ever marched two hundred stades in a day.'

He grinned. 'With Philip? I've made some marches, boy. Watch what you claim.' Then he gave Polystratus a long look. 'Can I trust your man?'

'With anything,' I said.

He nodded. 'Parmenio was always a good friend to your father,' he said quietly.

'Absolutely. Parmenio has my complete respect and admiration. Where's this going?' I asked.

Amyntas shrugged. 'Alexander made my lord an offer.' He looked around again.

I nodded. 'I know all about it.'

He looked startled. 'You do?'

'Command in Asia, under the king. First satrapy, all the high offices for his sons and his favourites. Like you, Uncle Amyntas.' I shrugged. 'You should ask for the hypaspists. Best outfit in the army.'

He twirled his moustache. 'So you know. So – is it genuine?'

'Polystratus, get my Uncle Amyntas a cup of wine.' I gestured, but Polystratus was already gone. A damned good man, Polystratus. Then I turned to Amyntas. He wasn't actually an uncle at all – he was Parmenio's political manager, and he'd been close to my pater.

'You know, Uncle Amyntas – the truth is, it doesn't matter whether the deal is genuine or not.' I grinned. I liked him, but I needed, right then, for him to understand what we'd all just spent thirty-nine days learning. I went on, 'I assume it is genuine – I'm one of the king's friends, and he's never spoken of Parmenio with anything but respect.' I shrugged. 'But truth to tell, Uncle, if Parmenio doesn't ditch Attalus and switch sides, we'll come to Asia and beat the shit out of him. The king is the king. And look around, Uncle. We hold Greece in the palms of our hands. Thebes fell today. This is Philip's son, and the gods love him.' I smiled. 'Don't be mad at me. Just take it on board. He's the king. Parmenio needs to bend the knee. Or ... else.'

'Alexander needs my lord,' Amyntas said. He was in shock. 'You can't honestly believe that the gold-haired boy can defeat Parmenio?'

'In fact, Uncle, you believe it too, or you wouldn't be here. You'd be in Asia, readying your army to come and fight us for Macedon with Attalus. Eh?' I grinned. 'Have some wine. We're not as young as we used to be.'

He rubbed his chin. Ochrid brought a stool and he sat on it, took wine from Polystratus and shook his head. 'I'm to negotiate for Attalus.'

I nodded. 'Spare yourself. Attalus is a dead man.'

Amyntas rubbed his chin as if looking for a louse. Maybe he was. 'Like that, is it?'

'Listen – you weren't there. Neither was Parmenio. But Attalus did things – none of us will ever forgive him. If Alexander let him live?' I shrugged. 'One of us would do him anyway. And Alexander would let it be.' I met his eyes. 'You know how it is, right? When a man has gone outside the laws other men accept? Attalus did that. And he put himself against the king. He's a dead man.'

Amyntas seemed to deflate. 'Is this the stupid business about the boy Pausanias?'

I nodded. 'That's part of it.'

He nodded. 'When Attalus came to Asia, he told us that story. He told it with pleasure. And Lord Parmenio left the dinner in disgust.' He shrugged. 'Attalus carries the seeds of his own death.'

I nodded. 'Let him go, then. Attalus is done.'

Amyntas nodded. 'I hadn't expected to find Alexander in possession of the League,' he said. 'I think I should sail back to Asia and ask my lord to think again.'

'Finish your wine first,' I suggested.

After breakfast I reported the whole conversation to Alexander. If I was to be the new faction leader of the lowland nobles – a job I thought that I wanted – I had to play both ends. I'd given Amyntas sound advice, but the king had to know I gave it from loyalty, not self-interest. All very complicated, as being a courtier – even a martial, active courtier – always is.

Alexander nodded. He made a face – rare for him, because he prized his immobile good looks – and spat. 'I wonder what his terms were,' he said bitterly. 'From the great Parmenio to a poor misguided boy.'

'Better not to know,' I said. 'I told him that Attalus was not negotiable.'

Alexander shrugged. 'Oh, him. He's in his late sixties – hardly a major power—'

I stopped the king with a raised hand – which shocked him – but I was instantly outraged. 'I told him that Attalus was not negotiable,' I said again, quite harshly. 'Now I'll tell you. Or rather, lord, I'll remind you. Your loyal men died or were injured, humiliated, raped – by Attalus. None of the pages will ever accept him. If you forgive him, I'll kill him myself.'

Alexander looked at me, and again, his eyes narrowed.

I was challenging him.

'You are above yourself, Ptolemy,' Alexander said. 'It is not your place to tell the king what he may and may not do.'

Something – something that had been hanging over me since I stormed Mount Ossa – broke.

'You're wrong, Alexander,' I said, and my use of his name was deliberate. 'It is my place. I am your friend and your trusted man, one of your great nobles, the leader of your best troops. If you leave Attalus alive, you tell us, your pages, that our sacrifices meant nothing to you. And that makes you an ungrateful bastard, not a king. Everything is not a trade of this for that, a compromise towards better rulership. Sometimes, you just have to accept that you are a leader not by the will of the gods but by the consent of the men of worth. If you leave Attalus alive, you betray us.'

He turned away. His posture hardened. With a good athlete, you can read anger in every muscle, not just in a few in the arms, shoulders and neck. He had rage in his hips and in his lower back.

'Remove yourself,' he said.

'Fuck you,' I said. Not what Aristotle would have wanted me to say. 'Call your companions and have me dragged out.'

Hephaestion came in in a hurry. I have no doubt he'd been listening. 'You cannot address your king that way,' he said. 'Apologise!'

'Alexander is going to pardon Attalus!' I said.

Hephaestion hadn't been listening as closely as I had thought. He stopped dead. 'What?'

Alexander whirled. 'Not you too! Listen. Attalus is a tool. I need him in Asia. I need all my father's generals.'

Hephaestion made a moue of distaste and glanced at me, clearly caught between annoyance at the king and dislike of me. 'Attalus,' he spat.

I leaned forward. 'My king, you do *not* need Attalus to conquer Asia. You do not need Parmenio and you do not need Amyntas. You just conquered Greece in forty days – with your own men and your own army. And your own head.' I shrugged. 'And I stand on my statement. If you pardon Attalus, I will take my grooms and retire to my estates.'

Alexander paused and just looked at me.

'My father did it,' I reminded him. 'I can live without all this.'

Alexander was as white as a new-woven chiton. 'Leave me.' He waved his hand quickly, like a man dying of suffocation. 'Don't argue. Go.'

I left the tent.

*

That was a bad day. I ordered my kit packed. I called Philip Longsword and told him the whole story – much as I'm telling you now, because my story went back to the hunt with Laodon and the rape of Pausanias. He heard me out, and shook his head.

'Bad,' he said. 'But you shouldn't have defied the king.'

I knew he was right. I knew that in a moment's hot-headedness, I'd lost years of ground with Alexander, and maybe lost him altogether.

So I handed command to Philip, and said some goodbyes, and then sat down on a camp stool – our kit caught up with us that morning when the rest of the army marched in – and waited for the summons.

It didn't come all day.

Men watched me – men who had been my own a few hours before. But they kept their distance. Philip Longsword had told them – on parade – not to come within a spear's length of me, by my own order.

A long day.

As the sun was setting and the evening sacrifices were being made, Nearchus came with a full file of Hetaeroi. Before he could ask, I gave him my sword.

We walked back through a silent camp.

The king was with Hephaestion in his tent. No one else. I took that as a good sign. If he meant to execute me, he'd have to order it done before my peers, and they'd have to agree.

He kept his back to me.

Hephaestion did the talking.

'The king requests that you resign the command of his household guards. And requests – as one man to another – that you withdraw the term *bastard*.' I had expected Hephaestion to be delighted by my fall from grace, but he looked stricken.

'My king, I deeply regret my show of anger, this morning,' I said. 'I withdraw the term bastard, and offer my apologies.'

Alexander turned around. 'And trying to make me alter my policy?'

I shook my head. 'I'm sorry, Alexander. But if you won't give in on this, you will eventually die as your father did.'

Yes, I said that.

It was true. I loved him, and he was about to make a capital mistake at the very start. If he let Attalus live – do you see it, young man? If he let the bastard live, Cleomenes and Nearchus and Pyrrhus and Marsyas would begin to feel the germs of doubt. The kind of doubt that ends with a King of Macedon surrounded in bed by a ring of daggers held by men who were once his friends.

That's the way it is, in Macedon.

Alexander had allowed himself to forget it. Not for the last time.

But he shook his head. 'If I kill Attalus,' he said through clenched teeth, 'I have to give *everything* to Parmenio. I have no counterbalance to him. I *hate* Attalus – but that's not important! I am king! I must do what is best!'

I shrugged. 'I am *not* king,' I said. 'I will be sorry not to command the hypaspitoi. And I will – without any disloyalty – do my best to kill Attalus myself. To spare you.'

'*Do not do this!*' Hephaestion spat. '*Do not seek to bend him to your will.*'

Alexander nodded to himself. 'Very well. I need a man I trust to go to Athens. You will go with the envoys we picked up at Delphi. I do not demand the head of Demosthenes, but I would very much like him to present himself to me as the ambassador of Athens.'

Even through the tension, I had to smile at that image.

'Go and be my ambassador to Athens. They know me there. And you weren't to keep the hypaspitoi, anyway. They love you too well, and they are my spear.' He nodded coolly. 'And I'll no doubt have to give them to one of Parmenio's sons.' He grimaced. 'Go to Athens for me. Get their agreement that I am the hegemon. Tell them that I require five hundred of their best cavalry. Get your friend Kineas.' He was speaking a little wildly, trying to stumble back from the brink I'd brought us to.

That's when I learned how much Alexander loved me. A little too late. And I burned some of that love, buying Attalus's death.

Worth it.

Only a handful of men knew what had happened – the public story was that I was to return to command a squadron of Hetaeroi, and that while I held the ambassadorship to Athens, Philip Longsword would command the hypaspitoi. There was no punishment in public or private, except, in the days before I left for Athens, a certain distance with the king.

I missed the hypaspitoi the way a father misses his daughter, and I wept the first night I was back with the Hetaeroi.

Polystratus told me I was a fool.

I took my grooms and three Hetaeroi. Diodorus rode with me as if he were my hyperetes, and the other two envoys cowered in the rear. Despite their presence, we made excellent time across Parnassus, and on the second morning we were at the gates of Athens. I requested permission to enter, made sacrifice as a foreign ambassador and was allowed entry. Demosthenes was still in shock – Athens had known for less than a week that the Macedonian army was just two hundred stades away. Suddenly, all the tough talk ended.

I sought permission to lodge with your grandfather, Kineas's father, and was accepted. I wish I had not. It was my fault that he was exiled later – my enthusiasm for his company, and his for mine, and Kineas's open pleasure at having me in the city all conspired to seal his fate.

I should have been in the throes of exile and anger myself. I had been ill used by the very king I was striving to serve – had I not?

In truth, I was so sure that I had done the right thing – the good thing – that I was unconcerned by the result. Only young and naive people can act this way, but I was convinced that the king would see it my way in the end.

So I set myself to enjoy Athens. And that began with a visit to Thaïs.

I dressed plainly. It was late afternoon – her public receiving hour. I tipped the slave at her gate, and was escorted to her solar, a big, sunny room with a loom and a set of couches and chairs.

At the sight of her, a thrill ran through me, better than the thrill of a cavalry charge or the racing rush of a galley. How well does Sappho say it? I had not seen her in more than a year, and her immanence was like a breath of incense to a man working in manure.

Her smile was like sunrise. Or noon. Or something nice and poetic. It was beyond artifice, and that was the good part.

She flirted effortlessly with half a dozen of us, and I noticed that most of the men present were quite young – twenty, just free of their ephebe duties – and long-haired boys at that, aristocrats who cared nothing for Athenian virtue.

Diodorus had, indeed, suggested that Thaïs was past her most popular.

I could find no visible flaw – nor, when she sang, could I hear an audible one. But fashions change, and Thaïs represented a freer, more self-confident Athens – not the narrow world Demosthenes wanted – a prude whose sole justification was his hatred of Philip. And now, of Alexander.

But the boys were afraid of me. One made bad jokes at my expense, as if my Greek were so bad that I couldn't be expected to understand. He was doing it from sheer bravado, and he bored me, and angered Thaïs, who asked him to stop.

'Perhaps Demosthenes is right,' the boy said, flipping his hair like a girl. 'Macedon is a land of effeminate poseurs, and this Ptolemy with the barbarian name hides behind Thaïs.'

I sipped some sweet wine. 'Dear Thaïs, if I break the little one, will you forgive me?'

She made a face. 'Yes. But only if I can watch.'

That stung the brat. He sat up. 'Well – if that's all the thanks I get for my wit, I'll go.'

I smiled. 'Don't hurry, laddy. We're going to wrestle first.'

Thaïs clapped her hands.

The boy waved for his cloak. 'I'll decline to wrestle with a barbarian, however well connected.'

'Well,' I said, still smiling, 'then I guess I'll just break your neck.' I caught him by the shoulders, locked an elbow, put him in a hold and threw him out of a window. The window was open, and it was less than the height of a man above the garden.

The garden was a little thorny.

'His father is quite important,' Thaïs said.

'My master is the King of Macedon,' I said. The other boys hurried out. As soon as they were gone, I bent down over her kline and kissed her.

And she let me.

It was quite a long kiss, and without meaning to, I had a hand under her chiton, on one lovely breast and then the other.

I could hear the boy in the garden arguing with his friends. But I didn't care what he decided to do.

My hand drifted over her belly, which was as taut as my own, and stroked her – down and down. My fingers parted her. And then I was inside her.

It all took a deliciously long time. And her slaves must have been remarkably well trained.

And at some point, she was astride me, and she pulled her chiton over her head without unpinning anything, shucking it off as a useless encumbrance. 'Sex should be naked,' she said. 'Like athletics – the participants need to show their bodies.'

I took the hint, although I remember giggling as I tried to wriggle out of my chiton while pinned to the couch.

Am I shocking you?

Let me put it this way. Before that afternoon, I'd never really had sex. She was playful, humorous, lust-filled, languorous, fast, slow, intelligent, as beautiful as Aphrodite, with more cleverness in one hand than all the slave girls I'd ever bedded had in their cunnies. And in between bouts – for sex with Thaïs bore some very real relationship to competitions – she'd talk of things – real things, like love and friendship and war.

I'd like to say we made love six times, but that would be bragging.

'I'm going to be sore tomorrow,' she said.

'I'm sore right now,' I said. I was looking at my penis, which was as red as a Spartan's cloak. She laughed. I laughed.

Put a value on that.

'Come away with me,' I said. 'Live with me. Be my hetaera.'

'On the basis of one afternoon on a couch? You don't have my bill yet.' She smiled and kissed my nose.

Now, I hated my nose. People called me 'Farm Boy' because of that beak. No one had ever kissed it before.

'On the basis of the fact that I think of you constantly.' I licked her lips.

'You've bedded me now – the feeling will pass.' She smiled. 'Men really only fancy what they haven't had.'

I bit her.

She bit me.

We were pretty far down the path when she grabbed my hand – she was strong – as strong as a warrior. 'That hurts. I'm done, sweet.'

I laughed and kissed her. 'I suppose I owe you for the week you'll be out of commission,' I said.

She shook her head. 'I'm not a porne,' she said. 'You'd be surprised how long it is since I had a man between my hips.'

I licked her lips again. 'I'm lucky.'

She laughed. 'Perhaps.'

'I mean it,' I added. 'Come with me.'

'You don't know me,' she said. 'And people will say the most unkind things.'

I shrugged. 'I'll kill them.' That made her laugh.

She wouldn't give me an answer. We drank some wonderful red wine together, and I left to go to a dinner in Alexander's honour.

I didn't see her for two days. She refused my invitations and was not at home to anyone.

On the third day, Demosthenes himself agreed to lead the embassy to Alexander. Athens was racing to throw itself at the conqueror's feet. Demosthenes could never meet my eye. Old Phokion was kind enough to shake my hand and tell me that the exploit of Mount Ossa was as worthy as any feat of arms he'd ever done.

Kineas and I boxed, and he gave me a black eye. Your pater had the fastest hands I've ever failed to see, and that's no lie.

I was done. So I sent Thaïs a note, declaring that I was still sore and that I still wanted her to come with me. I thought a touch of humour might have an effect.

She sent me a bill for ten talents of gold. A year's income from all of my estates.

I sent her all ten talents, and a bill for ridding her of a troublesome guest – one Athenian drachma, payable in kisses.

The next day, I packed my gear. I had no intention of riding with Demosthenes. I detested him. He made my skin crawl.

Mid-morning, while I said my goodbyes to Kineas, his father's steward summoned the old man, who went out for a hundred heart-beats and came back.

'Ptolemy, there is a *person* at my gate. She says she will wait for you. Do you wish me to admit her?'

Kineas looked puzzled. I *was* puzzled.

'Not ... Thaïs?' I asked.

'Yes,' Eumeles said. 'A person of some ... distinction.' He spoke with evident distaste.

'Ah!' I ran down the stairs and out into the courtyard, across the yard and out through the gate.

There were twenty mules in the alley, and a dozen slaves, and Thaïs, robed like a matron and wearing a broad-brimmed straw hat.

'Last chance to change your mind,' she said.

I shrugged. 'At ten talents an ... encounter, I must confess that ours may be a chaste relationship.'

She nodded. 'Platonic, perhaps?'

I laughed. Kineas laughed when I told it to him. He snorted wine over his chiton. She was that funny.

When I left Athens, I had the one thing Athens had that I wanted.

TWELVE

W hen I rode out through the gates of Athens – the magnificent Panathenaic gates – I hadn't given Alexander a thought in three days. And such was my delight in Thaïs that I didn't really think much about him during the idyll over Parnassus to his camp outside Thebes.

But the camp was a buzzing hive, and the first drone to land near me was Hephaestion, who had the inner guards when I rode into camp. I saluted him, and he rode over.

He looked at Thaïs, looked away, and back, and away.

I smiled.

'Who's that?' he asked. Not at his most subtle.

'The hetaera Thaïs, the jewel of Athens.' I smiled. 'She has agreed, of her goodness, to spend a little time with me.'

'She is beautiful!' Hephaestion's admiration was quite genuine, and he bowed deeply in the saddle. 'Despoina, that you condescend to grace our rude camp is like having Aphrodite herself—'

'Hush,' Thaïs said, with a smile, and raised a finger to Hephaestion's lips. 'No hubris, and no calls on the Cyprian that I challenge her beauty – for I do not.'

Hephaestion was smitten on the spot. Who expects a courtesan to be well spoken and witty? Well, Macedonians don't. Athenians do. There's a lot to be said, there.

'The king wants you,' he said to me. 'He's waited for you for three days.' Hephaestion made a face. 'He wondered if you were coming back.'

I sighed. 'I wonder who put that thought in his ear?'

Hephaestion frowned. 'Not me. We need you, even if you are a fool. There's only you, me and Cleitus who will stand up to him, now. But if I were you,' and Hephaestion's eyes flickered over Thaïs, 'I'd take her. He needs to see something beautiful. He's angry. And it's not really about you – but it could become you in a heartbeat.'

259

Well – for Hephaestion, this was almost like friendship.

'Thanks,' I said. I still counted my fingers after I shook his hand. 'I'll change—'

'Go straight away,' Hephaestion said.

Uh-oh.

So I rode to the royal pavilion with Thaïs at my side, and helped her down from her horse. She didn't make a fuss about her appearance or her fatigue – a miracle – but strode in behind me.

Black Cleitus was at the tent door. He clasped my hand and beamed at Thaïs.

'By the *gods*,' he said. 'Alexander! It's Ptolemy, with a goddess.'

Alexander called, 'Come.'

I went in first. Alexander was alone except for two slaves, both armourer's men, who were fitting him for a helmet. Theban smiths make good work, but these men were Athenians – I could see their samples. The best armourers in the world.

Alexander turned to me. 'A goddess, Ptolemy?'

It seemed a promising start. 'Lord, the hetaera Thaïs has agreed to spend some time with me.'

Alexander smiled. 'She is here? The jewel of Athens came to our camp?'

'And will live here, if you give her leave,' I said.

Alexander nodded. 'Well done, Ptolemy. A cunning stroke, worthy of Odysseus. I gather you were crowned with success?'

'A deputation is behind me – ten leading men, headed by Demosthenes himself. Kineas's father, Eumeles, is the actual speaker.' I held out a scroll tube of ivory. 'Athens agrees to have you as hegemon and agrees to provide five hundred cavalry for the crusade in Asia.'

'Well done!' Alexander shook his head. 'You do well at anything to which you turn your hand. The hypaspists – four weeks, and you made them like gods.'

'I had help,' I said, but his praise was like strong wine.

'The last time we spoke, you reminded me that, at the root of it, I am king under the sufferance of my subjects – at least, of my elite subjects.' He was not smiling now.

I rolled my eyes. 'You needed reminding.'

Cleitus coughed.

Alexander shook his head. 'You are just not getting this, Ptolemy. I suspect you don't get it because you are, in fact, so blessedly loyal to me – but a man who warns the king that he can be dethroned by force – is that the man to command the king's inner guard – to win their absolute devotion?'

Sometimes, I am slow. In this case, I had to laugh. 'So,' I said. 'That's what this is about. You were afraid—'

'I am afraid of *nothing*,' Alexander said. He was quite calm. 'But some of my friends are afraid.'

Our eyes met.

'Attalus is dead,' Alexander said. 'Parmenio had him killed. It happened two days ago.' The king shrugged. 'I suspect that you were, and are, right. He had to die. Much as I hate him, I could have used him. As I will use Lord Amyntas and Lord Parmenio.' His eyes never left mine – like a lover's. 'But I saw Cleitus's look when I ordered his death – and Hephaestion's.' He nodded slowly, eyes still locked on mine. 'Listen, Ptolemy. The longer I am king, the less I will understand of what happens outside this tent. The more power I'll have, the less information to help me use it. Think of Pater – Philip – in those last days. He *didn't even know that Attalus had had Pausanias raped.* No one told him until you did.'

I nodded.

'But he didn't love you for telling him, and I'll never love you for it, either. Kings don't say "I'm sorry", and they don't say "You are right". Eh?'

Eyes still locked.

'Find a way to do it,' he said, very quietly. 'Find a way to keep me from … ignorance.'

I smiled.

'But find a way to do it without making it a war between us. I am king.' Alexander's eyes bored into mine, and I realised that I was doing it – challenging him – refusing to break the eye contact.

Quite deliberately, I looked away. Then back, like a flirting girl.

He smiled. 'Now I want you to bring your goddess for dinner. But first, I want you to swear me an oath that you do not now, nor will ever, seek the throne of Macedon.'

It was *right there*, the possibility of my indignation boiling over. *Fuck him.* How dare he? I'd nearly died for him – twice.

But he was the king, and he was not responsible for the shit people poured into his ears. I knelt. 'I swear by Zeus, lord of the gods, lord of slaves and kings, Zeus of the eagle, Zeus of the thunderbolt, may I be burned to invisible ash and no man ever remember my name if I have ever sought the throne of Macedon, or ever do so in future.'

Alexander put his hand on my shoulder and crushed it, his grip was so hard. He left a bruise.

'Thank you,' he said very quietly. 'I cannot give you the hypaspists. What do you want?'

I had Thaïs. 'I'll go back to my squadron of Hetaeroi,' I said.

Alexander nodded. 'Excellent. Perhaps you and Laodon would put in some time improving the grooms, as well. Now – the goddess?'

Cleitus, who could hear every word, held the flap, and Thaïs came in. She was wearing a wool chiton, very plain; a long riding cloak of transparent wool, so light it flowed like silk, and a hat woven of bleached straw, very fine and also white. She was the only woman I knew who owned a pair of Boeotian boots made to her size – open-toed, for riding. She still had her long whip in her hand. Upon entering, she unpinned her hat and made a deep obeisance. 'My lord,' she said. 'You will not remember me. We met at a party.'

'Ah – I would be unlikely ever to forget you, Despoina.' He inclined his head gravely. 'Your presence here is a triumph for Macedon – we have taken the finest thing Athens ever had.'

'But my lord,' she said, 'Athens never had me – I am an Athenian, and I am here of my own free will. I am not an object – I am here to be a subject.'

Alexander looked at me. 'I've seldom been corrected so gently. Perhaps you might teach Ptolemy your arts?'

'Well,' she said, and her eyelashes fluttered, 'I could try, but women of my sort seldom train a potential rival, and Lord Ptolemy is already a very good companion.'

Alexander, who never, ever spoke of sex, blushed. And then laughed, because her joke was so subtle – the Greek word for courtesan was hetaera, but it was merely the feminine form of Hetaeroi – our word for the king's bodyguard – his companions. Damn it – that's funny, lad! She was comparing courtesans and bodyguards ...

Never mind. You're too young. The king laughed his arse off, and that didn't happen often.

'Would we shock the world if we had the Lady Thaïs to dinner tonight?' Alexander asked Hephaestion.

He looked at me as if to say *I told you so*. 'No ambassadors. Possibly the last night it's just the army. So I'd say yes.'

It was quite a dinner. Thebes rose behind us like the backdrop for an Athenian tragedy. Because of Thaïs, the talk was light and witty and educated. Bad as we Macedonian barbarians might be, we had all been educated by Aristotle, and even Perdiccas and Cassander could manage to sound vaguely like men of culture.

Thaïs helped them. She had a way of capping a quote before a man could finish it – as if she understood that he was going to say something erudite, and she loved to help him finish. Cleitus, for example, struggled to participate. Thaïs always liked Cleitus – almost always – and that first night, as he stuttered through a quote from the *Odyssey*, she smiled.

'With you quoting Odysseus's part, I suppose I must respond with Penelope's,' she said.

His relief was obvious – he got the credit for a good quote and she'd done all the work.

It's not the best example, just the best one I remember.

She smiled around the company. 'But I don't want to stay at home like Penelope. If you, my lords, are going to Troy, I want to go!'

Alexander smiled and shook his head. 'The queen of the Amazons fought for Asia,' he said.

'Who needs to be bound by the classics?' she said. 'And what of Atlante? Eh? Or Athena? Not that I compare myself to the grey-eyed, but still.'

Hephaestion smiled. 'What would you do, in a camp of soldiers, lady?'

Thaïs smiled, and Hephaestion blushed. She never said a word. He looked away, and Alexander blushed.

'Laundry,' Thaïs said.

Her timing was beautiful, and the whole tent burst into an approving roar. I'd seen her at work in a symposium in Athens, and so had Alexander, but none of the others had, and they had no idea how powerful was her command of song and speech. She gave them a taste – sang a few popular love songs to her own accompaniment on the kithara – but she intended to remain a guest and not a performer, and she declined to play more.

Alexander came to her couch after she had sung, and sat on the end. 'You spoke of our crusade in Asia,' he said.

'Ptolemy speaks of little else,' she allowed. 'And men in Athens – my friends, like Diodorus and Kineas and their faction. Men say that you will throw down the Great King, and make all Asia subject.'

He breathed in sharply, like a woman at the climax of love. 'Yes,' he said softly. 'But I love to hear it coming from you.'

She smiled. 'When your crusade marches – will you let me accompany you?'

Alexander laughed. 'After one evening, lady, I think we would beg you to accompany *us*. Ask me another boon – anything you like. Your presence will enhance every dull evening on campaign. You make my officers better men just by being here. Perhaps this is what Helen brought.'

'Anything?' Thaïs asked, and her voice was suddenly ... odd.

Alexander caught it – but the need to be Achilles and Agamemnon rolled into one always took over from common sense. 'Anything.'

She nodded. 'May Zeus hear you, Lord King. May we all some day be where I might have my boon. For now, I ask nothing.'

Alexander loved a moment of drama. 'I swear it by Zeus, by Herakles and by the River Styx.'

Cleitus sat up on his couch. 'I heard the shears of Moira – that oath went to Olympus.'

What I noticed was that Alexander did not swear by his father, Philip. A month ago, he had.

That night, I lay with Thaïs in my own tent. She had her own, but she wanted to play, as she called it, and we made love – slowly – under my cloak. She was quiet and careful.

And in the morning, her head was on my shoulder when I awoke. The smile that came to my face stayed all day.

Even when, about midday, when Polystratus brought me sausage and leeks where I was drilling the grooms, he said, 'People need to sleep.'

I tried to pretend I didn't understand.

He just shook his head. 'If I bring a girl and fuck her all night, will you laugh it off?'

I could have told him to go and sleep somewhere else. But that was not the way between master and man, if you wanted loyalty kept. I understood, and he understood.

Alexander didn't really understand, and that worried me, but I had sworn to defend him, and I realised that afternoon that more than anything, I would have to defend him from himself.

In fact, the next day, when Alexander dispatched heralds all over Greece to summon the cities to a meeting of the mighty League of Corinth, Philip's tool for governing Greece, I rode away from camp alone. Thaïs wanted to explore, and she'd begun to collect her own household – a military household. She meant to come with us. She approached it intelligently, and paid Polystratus cash to coach her in her hiring, which won him over in two different ways.

I rode to Plataea. Above Plataea, to the place where Kineas's family had an altar – high on the summit, a day's journey to climb. A day's journey for a man who could run thirty stades.

I climbed alone, except for Ochrid, and I left him with the horses. I went up to the top, where you can see the whole rim of the world. And there I caught a deer and killed it, my own sacrifice to Artemis and to Zeus, and I offered my own oath to protect the king.

Before I was done speaking, thunder rumbled and an eagle, borne on some rapid updraught, shot up from lower on the mountain into the sky on my right, the best of omens and a clear sign of the High God's approval.

I came down the mountain, elated, and like many men who are elated, I suddenly wanted to talk. And I missed my way, somehow, so that instead of coming down by our horses on the northern slopes, I came down the western slopes and found myself above the ancient tomb of the Hero of the Trojan War. They say Leitus went with the Athenians, and came back after many fights and died in his bed, at peace with the gods. And that he never did anything worth recording – he was not an outstanding fighter, or a brilliant runner – except that, on that day we all know in the *Iliad* when Achilles sulked in his tent and Hector drove the Greeks to red ruin by the ships, Leitus rallied a dozen average men – average for the Trojan War, of course – and formed a tight little wall of shields, and their locked shields kept Hector at bay for the crucial time it took to rescue Odysseus, who had taken a wound.

Veterans go to that shrine. Leitus is the hero of every warrior who stands his ground and hopes to go home again – not the ones who seek joy and death in battle, but the sane ones who seek to show courage and then live to plough their fields and their wives. His precinct is always well kept, and there are always ten or fifteen men there at the tomb – an old Tholos beehive, high above the road over the mountain to Athens. I had gone there one afternoon with Kineas, and now I stumbled on it by accident.

An old man was sitting on the steps of the little cabin, and he had a dozen boys and adolescents at his feet, sitting in the dust and the late summer leaves. He was very fit, that old man, with neck muscles like whipcord. He was teaching them, of course.

'What is your duty to the city, boys?' he asked.

They all looked at me, as boys do when they want to avoid work. But I kept my face blank, and the teacher gave me a friendly nod – man to man, so to speak – and the boys guessed that I wasn't going to stop the lesson.

The eldest stood. 'To protect the walls. To stand our ground in battles.'

The teacher frowned, but nodded. 'There is more to life than war, though.'

'To defend our freedoms. To attend every Assembly ready to vote on every issue on the agenda set by our elders,' said another boy in the sing-song voice of one who has learned by rote.

'How is democracy like war?' the teacher asked.

'In war we use spears, and in democracy we fight with words and ideas,' the boys chorused.

'And who is the winner? The loudest?' he asked.

'The last standing!' one boy called out. And they all laughed, even the teacher.

But one boy shook his head. 'Teacher, what if the city is wrong?'

The teacher raised an eyebrow. 'Tell me more, sprout.'

'What if the free man finds himself ... disagreeing – with the city? What if the city orders a wrong action? Say a man goes away to fight for Alexander, and comes back to find that a tyrant has taken his city, or a madness has come over the Assembly, and they give outrageous commands?'

I laughed to hear a fifteen-year-old suggest that a man might go from Plataea to fight for Alexander. Although, of course, it was about to happen, and I knew it.

The teacher nodded. 'It is the duty of every man who votes in the Assembly to accept the will of other men when he is outvoted,' he said. 'To behave in any other way is to be a bad sport, a poor loser. A cheat.' He looked at them. 'But despite that, there can come a time when a city, or a tyrant, or a king leaves the path of good actions. Faction can make this happen, or personal enmity, or a curse, or lust for power.' He looked off into the distance. 'And then a man must ask himself where his duty lies. For war is an ugly mistress, and civil war is the worst hag of the lot. But to allow yourself to be made a slave – is not to be born, is it? So there can come a moment when the freeman must accept the consequence that his state, his city, his king, has failed him.' The old man shrugged.

The boy was amazed that he had participated in something so profound. But he was still curious. 'But ... what should he do?'

The old man smiled a bitter smile. 'He should kiss his wife and child, order his burial shroud and declare himself dead. And then he should gather men of like mind, and march. Not expecting to live, but prepared to die to prove his point. Because such rebellion must never be for personal gain, but for the good of the city.'

The boys were silent. I said, 'You sound like Aristotle, sometimes.'

The old man smiled. 'Never heard of him.'

'A philosopher,' I said.

'Ah!' he said, and shook my hand. 'I'm no philosopher. I was a phylarch under old Phokion, and now I teach war to the boys.' He looked at me. 'You don't look like a philosopher yourself, young sir. Cavalry officer, I'd be guessing.'

'Under Alexander,' I said.

He grinned. 'I fought Philip a few times.' He laughed. 'Outmarched his arse a few times, too!' He looked at the boys, and shooed them away. 'Home to the fields, lads,' he said.

He took my arm and we walked to the edge of the clearing. 'Being Plataean was just a status in Athens, you know. Thebes razed our city to the ground. But Philip saved us from exile, and now we're trying to raise a generation that sees Plataea as their home – not the south slope of the Acropolis!' He shook his head. Picked up an amphora of wine. 'You've killed a man in combat?' he asked. Except it was not really a question.

'One or two,' I said. I mistook his tone.

'It's a serious thing, taking a life,' he said. 'You're just the age where it's going to start to occur to you that every man you put down had a life. That they ain't just meat-bags waiting to help you run up your score. Eh?'

I said nothing. I think that if I'd come on purpose, I'd have been prepared. But I wasn't prepared. And because I was unprepared, I almost burst into tears. It was a sudden thing.

He put an arm around my shoulder.

'Didn't you come here to talk, boy?' he asked.

'Got lost,' I said. 'I went to the top to pray to Zeus.' I shrugged.

'And he sent you here. Come – let's pour a libation together, and I'll set you on your road.' He grinned.

He filled a big Boeotian cup of wine, and we poured it on the rocks at the edge of the tomb.

'I can afford a sacrifice,' I said. I felt wonderful – elated. Hard to describe. I felt the way I felt after making love to Thaïs. Clean.

He shook his head and made an odd face. 'No you can't,' he said. 'Leitus has no sacrifice but men.' He looked away. 'And you, praise to Ares, ain't the one. Sometimes a man comes, and the hero screams for his blood, and the priest puts him down at the door of the tomb.' He shrugged.

I was impressed. And the Greeks called us barbarians?

'Now – you must have come from Thebes, eh?' I notice he spat when he said the name of the city, even though it was just a few stades away.

Plataeans are good haters.

I nodded.

'So your horse can't be far. Take the trail here and head that way. Where the trail forks at the top of the ridge – that's where your horse ought to be, eh?'

I admitted it was.

'Shall I walk with you?' he asked.

I shook my head. I felt ... strange. As if I was in the presence of the hero himself.

'Take wine with me,' I said.

He grinned, and filled the cup again. He took a deep draught, and handed me the cup, and I drank – the rich red wine of Plataea, which men call the Blood of Herakles.

'Drain it,' he ordered, and I did. I was already feeling odd.

He laughed, and patted my back. 'Go conquer the world, lad,' he said, 'with my blessing. But when the day comes, remember what a freeman's duty is, and don't flinch.'

What did he mean?

You'll see.

My horse was right where he said it would be, with Ochrid standing worried by his head. I mounted, took the reins and rode back to camp, feeling a little drunk and a little foolish. In a village so tiny it was really just four houses and a roadside shrine, I bought a raw amphora of the local wine and carried it on my hips all the way down the mountain and across the Asopus and up the road to Thebes.

I saved it for a few days, until we all moved camp to Corinth. The army went north to the Gates of Fire, because Alexander knew that to camp the army around Corinth would be to offend the delegates. But he didn't send the army home, either. And he took my squadron of Hetaeroi.

Parmenio sent 'Uncle' Amyntas to join us. He was officially welcomed as commander of Asia, and any remaining hopes *anyone* had of overthrowing Alexander collapsed. The Athenian delegation reached Alexander – without Demosthenes, who proved just as much of a social coward as he was a battlefield coward. He ran off into voluntary exile rather than face the king.

But to my delight, Kineas came out with his father, and he had Gracchus and Lykeles and Niceas with him. Phokion, of course, was one of the delegates, with Kineas's father.

We had some fine dinners and some ferocious competitions, too – horse-racing and javelin-throwing and a dozen other things. The only one I remember well was fighting Kineas with a wooden sword. We both wrapped our chlamyses about our arms – I don't even remember how this started – and we were showing off for Thaïs – well, I was – fighting too hard, making showy attacks – and we had a flurry – this is the part I remember – that was nearly perfect – cut and counter, back and forth, for maybe as long as it takes me to say this sentence – ended locked up, each grabbing the other's sword-wrist, and we laughed and embraced.

And afterwards, I told Kineas about my visit to the Hero's Tomb. He'd talked of it and we'd meant to visit.

He shook his head.

'What's the matter?' I asked.

He shrugged. 'There hasn't been a priest there in fifty years,' he said. 'Oh,' I said. 'Must be a new man, then.'

I served the Blood of Herakles to Alexander the night that the League proclaimed him hegemon as his father had been. The night that we climbed the high altar of the city and swore an oath – every city, every delegation, and I swore for Macedon because Alexander was hegemon of the whole alliance – to make war on Persia until all the cities of the Ionian were free, and then until our armies held Persepolis and Ectabana and the Great King was toppled and all Asia was ours.

It was a mighty oath. We swore to avenge the insults to Athena and Zeus at Athens, to every Greek temple looted by the barbarian, every violated precinct, every outraged family, every city ground under the Persian heel. We swore to liberate every Greek slave.

We swore.

The delegates were divided, and it was old Phokion who pointed this out to me. We were coming down the steps of the Acrocorinth, and he was taking his time – he was seventy, and he moved like a man in his fifties, but he also took his time – and Kineas and I waited for him.

'Half those men worry that you will fail to war down Persia,' he said. 'And half worry that you won't fail.' He laughed. 'I wish I could come.'

Kineas took his hand. 'Come, master!'

Phokion shook his head. 'Enough to have seen this night. Too long have Greeks frittered away their birthright. Sparta failed, and Athens failed. Let young Macedon lead us to victory. Let Persia tremble. The young king has the fire.'

We walked down the steps, the sun set over the Gulf and the gods listened.

One more thing happened in Corinth – it's a well-known story. We'd spent the morning wrangling with Demosthenes over the Athenian supply of naval stores to the alliance – there's nothing like a petty-minded bureaucrat to bring you down to earth when you've been imagining yourself the conqueror of Asia – and Alexander had had enough.

'I'm going for a walk,' he announced to Hephaestion. He looked at me. 'Come.'

The three of us simply rose and left the negotiations.

A small horde of sycophantic Greeks followed us. Really, that's not fair – your pater was there, and so was Diodorus, and Nearchus, and Alectus, of all people. The army was at the gates, but the hypaspists were outside the city. Just in case.

I assumed from Alectus's presence that we were going to visit the hypaspitoi.

I was wrong.

We walked down the hill towards the Gulf side of the isthmus, and then out of the city proper into the suburbs. You have to imagine – the captain general of the League of all Greece, wandering down alleys the width of a small bed – dusty alleys, alleys with beggars, thieves and some very ordinary people, who were amused, annoyed or outraged. Or delighted.

Oh, it was spectacular. Especially as the captain general didn't know where he was going and didn't want to tell us or ask directions.

We wandered for an hour. I wondered what Demosthenes was doing, and Diodorus began an acerbic commentary on the captain general's sense of direction. Kineas tried to shut him up, but his sharp voice carried, and Alexander heard him.

He turned. 'You have something to say, Athenian?'

Diodorus stood his ground. 'If you are looking for Diogenes the Cynic, you have only to say so. If this is how we're going to conquer Persia – well, it'll be good exercise.' He smiled. 'Unless this is a test of rival philosophies – you wander about like Aristotle, Diogenes sits in his olive garden without moving?'

Most of the Macedonians didn't get it. I got it. I laughed.

Hephaestion glared at me.

Alexander shrugged. 'Take us there,' he said.

Diodorus looked at me. His face was easy to read. It said, *This is not going to end well.* 'Diogenes does not accept visitors,' he said.

'And you know because?' Alexander asked.

'I tried. The first day we were here.' Diodorus shrugged.

Alexander smiled. 'Perhaps you were not Alexander,' he said.

After Alexander walked on, Diodorus made a face. 'Perhaps not,' he said, in a voice calculated to suggest that this pleased him more than the alternative.

But he got us to the philosopher's house, and we knocked, and a slave answered the door and insisted that his master would not receive anyone, no matter how well born, noble or beautiful.

Alexander pushed past him.

I was content to wait outside, but Alectus pushed right in behind the king. Bodyguard. Of course.

But the rest of the followers took that as an excuse to stay with the king.

I shook my head but followed Diodorus. Kineas stopped at the doorway. 'My father says I should never enter a house where I'm not invited,' he said.

I nodded. 'Good advice.'

He smiled. 'I'll wait here, then.'

I went in, against my judgement, to find that we were in a tiny house, far too small to hold twenty well-born men and their slaves and servants. It had a small courtyard, and in the middle of it lay an older man with an average body, a little inclined to paunchiness, naked, sunbathing.

His eyes were closed.

Alexander stood watching him.

Diogenes, if it was he, made no move to speak or welcome us. No rage, no anger, no interest, nothing. He just lay with his eyes closed.

This went on for an incredible length of time. It was excruciating – embarrassing – you have to remember that *no one* had *ever* ignored Alexander. For any reason whatsoever.

Time stretched. Men scratched themselves, spoke in increasingly loud whispers, looked around. If you want to get the measure of men, make them be silent for a long time. See what they do.

On and on.

I just watched. Mostly, I was waiting for Alexander to explode.

On and on.

Alexander stood as immobile as the philosopher.

On and on.

Back up the hill, we were building the alliance that would conquer Persia and change the world, and here in this garden, we weren't worth the shit in our bowels. I knew that the fucking philosopher knew we were here, knew who we were, and honestly, actually, didn't care.

Good for you, friend. Point made. Let's go.

Or let's gut him and leave him to bleed out and see how he feels about that.

I can be a bad man. I had some bad thoughts.

Alexander cleared his throat. I had *never* seen him so ill at ease.

Diogenes opened one eye. Very sporting of him – almost courteous. The pompous twit.

'Yes?' he asked.

'I am Alexander,' the king said.

'Yes,' Diogenes agreed.

'I ... admire you very much. Is there ... anything – at all – I could do for you?' Alexander sounded like a boy with a crush on a great warrior. I'd never heard him sound like that – all his near-mythic certainty veiled.

271

Diogenes closed his eyes. 'You could get out of my sun. You are shading me.'

Hephaestion spluttered.

Diodorus fled. He didn't want to roar out his laughter.

I got out in a hurry, because I was tempted to pummel the philosopher with my fists. Just to teach him respect for his betters. Kineas was sitting on the step, with his stick on his shoulder and one fist against his chin.

Diodorus was moving so fast he was almost running.

Kineas gave me an odd grin. 'I take it that was bad?' he said.

He got to his feet as Alexander emerged.

'I could kill him,' Alectus said, at his shoulder.

I laughed. My eyes met Alectus's and we shared a moment of barbarism.

Hephaestion was shaking. 'Useless, pompous bastard. I'd kick him, but it would soil my feet!'

Alexander stopped in mid-stride, pivoted and put a brotherly hand on Hephaestion's shoulder. 'No,' he said. 'No, you are wrong. He behaved exactly as he should. We intruded in his house. We were not invited. And we deserved nothing better. In fact,' Alexander smiled, 'if I were not King of Macedon, I would want to be Diogenes. And I would expect kings to stay out of my garden.'

'You'd keep yourself in better shape,' Hephaestion said.

Someone laughed.

Alexander looked over at Kineas. 'What did you think, Athenian?'

Kineas shrugged. 'I didn't go in.'

Alexander stopped as if he'd received a blow.

'Diogenes is very careful about his privacy,' Kineas said, as if this statement would make it all better.

'How do *you* know?' Hephaestion asked.

Kineas shrugged. And very wisely, said nothing. It was that night that I found out that he and Diodorus had both been students here for a few months – had sat in that garden and listened to the great man.

Saying so would have been foolish, and Kineas was wise.

But Alexander told the story for the rest of his life. Once, by the Ganges, he told the part about Kineas. He looked across the river and said, 'Perhaps the Athenian was the wisest of all.' The king looked at the ground. He was trying to impress a passel of Indian philosophers. 'He didn't try to enter the man's house.'

And one of the old Indian men shook his head. 'There is no single answer to any question,' he said.

The king liked that.

THIRTEEN

e marched for home. It was late in the year, and there was
snow in the passes again, and the Greeks were happy to see
us go.

Alexander was determined that we would march by way of Delphi so
that he could consult the oracle. We marched two days through snow,
and Poseidon's mane got icy mud in it and it took me a day to comb it
out, with Polystratus bringing pots of warm water. Poseidon was sick,
and I didn't want to lose him. He wasn't getting any younger, though.

Delphi, and the Pythia, was not open for business. She only prophe-
sies a few months a year – the Pythia then, an older woman named
Cynthia, was quite well known and very intelligent. They are not always
like that.

She had her priests send the king a respectful message explaining that
she could not simply sit on the tripod and implore the god, as it was
out of season. Alexander shrugged, dismounted and tossed his reins to
a slave.

'The men and horses need a rest, at any rate. We'll be here two days.'
He looked at me. 'Go and tell her that she *will* prophesy. Negotiate any
way you wish, but get it done.'

I got all the glorious jobs.

So I took Thaïs, and went down to the village to visit the Pythia.

Really, she was a very ordinary woman – for a forty-year-old virgin
who was well born and ferociously intelligent. We found her grinding
barley behind her house. She was using a geared handmill – I'd heard
of them, but never seen such a thing.

She took it to pieces in her enthusiasm to show me how it worked.

She and Thaïs were not immediately friends by any means – in fact,
on balance, I could see I'd miscalculated, and this was a woman who
lived and worked with men, and had little time for women. But Thaïs's
intelligence shone through, and her superlative social skills, and in an
hour the three of us were drinking wine.

'He needs you to prophesy,' I said, finally. 'Blessed Pythia, all Greece needs you.'

She smiled. 'You know that the Great King is one of our patrons?'

I nodded.

She laughed. 'He's doomed. Do you know your Persian politics?'

I shook my head. 'The only politics I know are those of the Macedonian court. Well – Athens. I know a little of Athens.'

Thaïs wrinkled her nose as if she smelled something bad. 'Bagoaz is Grand Vizier,' she said. 'He rules by intrigue and murder. He killed Arses, who was Great King, and he's replaced him with some minor nobleman.'

The Pythia smiled. 'Well! Nicely put. Except that young Codoman just made Bagoaz drink poison and is now master in his own house. But he's only a distant relation of the Great Kings of the past – and many of the eastern nobles do not accept him at all.'

I had never heard so much about Persia. To us, Persia was the great enemy, a magnificent unknown. I suppose that Parmenio knew such stuff, but up until then, I didn't.

'There has never been a better time to invade Persia,' the Pythia said, sipping her wine. 'I speak no prophecy, young man. Codoman has Greek mercenaries, Greek scribes, Greek administrators. He runs his household with Greeks. He is virtually at war with his own Mede nobles. Persia is divided internally, taxes are late coming in, and over a third of the total administration of the country is already in the hands of men sympathetic to your king.'

Thaïs smiled. 'I would like to know more about such things,' she said.

'I will tell the king. But he sets enormous store by matters of religion, and he wants the blessing of the gods.' I shook my head.

The Pythia nodded. 'Then he can return in the spring, and I will prophesy for him.' She finished her wine. 'I have work to do. Tell the king that nothing save force of arms would get me to my tripod.' She smiled, I smiled, and Thaïs finished her wine.

The Pythia forestalled her with a hand on her shoulder. 'Stay with me a while,' she said.

Thaïs smiled to herself and stayed.

I asked no questions. But I summoned Polystratus and sent him to the king with a message.

Alexander walked down to the Pythia's house a few hours later with a dozen Hetaeroi and the duty hypaspitoi. I was reminded uncomfortably of the entourage that followed him to the visit with Diogenes. But it was bitterly cold, and we were all swathed in multiple chlamyses, and many men had fleece hats – all the hypaspitoi. We trooped to her door.

Alexander knocked politely.

Thaïs opened the door. She smiled. 'The Pythia was expecting you.'

Alexander ducked through her doorway, went inside and bowed to the Priestess of Apollo. Then he picked her up in his arms and carried her out of her house.

She didn't raise a squeal. She was not a small woman – she was well enough formed that I wondered at her virginity – but the king was in top shape and carried her easily, without unseemly grunting.

It is four stades from the town to the temple, and all steeply uphill.

He carried her all the way, even though we were all around him. Thaïs followed. She caught my hand.

I looked at her.

She blew me a kiss.

I was jealous – sure in my head that Thaïs had just lain with the Pythia. Angry. Resentful. Puzzled. She'd just gone with that woman. Not a glance, not a look.

So I followed Alexander up the hill, tormenting myself.

Thaïs was *laughing*.

Damn her.

We went up the hill all the way to the temple, and if Alexander was flagging, he never gave a sign. He carried her up the steps of the temple and in through the great bronze screens, which were open. Somebody had accepted a bribe.

He carried her to her tripod, which someone had set over the cleft.

But there were no priests. They were the required intermediary. I knew how it worked – the priestess breathed in the fumes from the cleft, and the god came to her, and she spoke, and the priests translated her words.

Alexander put her on the tripod and set her down. She gave a little squeak – the tripod had been set badly, and it wobbled and she shrieked as it began to topple – back, into the cleft.

Alexander's right arm shot out and caught the tripod – a heavy bronze artifact that weighed as much as a strong man, and the Pythia was no small woman. He caught them both on the brink of the cleft – which was only a man's shoulders wide but as deep as Tartarus – and pulled them back to safety, and the Pythia threw her arms around his neck.

'You are invincible!' she breathed.

But we all heard her.

Alexander beamed with joy like a boy on a feast day.

275

He set her on her feet and offered to carry her down the hill to her house.

She laughed. I don't know how often the Pythia laughed in the temple, but I doubt it happened often. She looked around. 'A most eventful day,' she said. 'If someone would lend me a cloak, I would return to my work.'

Thaïs handed her a long red cloak, which she held for a moment. 'It has your smell,' she said to Thaïs, and I felt a spear-prick.

Thaïs raised her two flawless eyebrows. 'Keep it for my sake, then,' she said.

Alexander turned aside to Thaïs. 'I think you are the first woman to be allowed here, except for the priestess.' He looked worried. I could read his mind – he knew that the 'prophecy' he'd just gained was irregular, and he was afraid that people would point at Thaïs as an aspect of pollution or sacrilege.

'I?' asked Thaïs. 'I am not here,' she said, and walked out of the precinct.

The next day, we rode together. I was still in turmoil. She had slept elsewhere that night, and that happened often enough, but I felt for her in the night. I was angry and hurt.

'You do not own me,' she said. Ares, she was angry.

This is the part I had not understood. I had made *her* angry.

I looked around, made a motion to Polystratus. 'I do not own you. But I love you, and you slept with someone else. For nothing but the pleasure of it, I assume.' Oh, I was being prim and proper and adult.

She shrugged. 'Girls don't make love. They just play. And she's the *Pythia*. I am a priestess of Aphrodite. I cannot refuse the *Pythia*. And she was so *lonely*.' She turned to me, and her eyes, despite some brimming tears, were hot with anger. 'And you made me feel bad about it. Like a jealous boy. I don't want to spend years with a jealous boy. I want to spend years with a noble man.'

'Is that a clever, sophisticated, Athenian way of saying that you can spread your legs for whomever you please?' I asked.

She spat. 'Yes, that's exactly what it is. Listen, Ptolemy. Let me tell you a harsh fact. I spread my legs for whomever I please. All freewomen do. Otherwise, we are slaves. If we can only open and close our cunts when you tell us, we are slaves. Period, end of story, no argument. If you want *me*, you must win me every day. Not just once, and then lock me away for future concubinage. If you cannot accept that,' she sighed, 'I have to face a long, cold journey back to Athens.'

I rode on, tight-lipped. Too hurt to speak.

She dropped back to her women.

Next day, I sent Polystratus to fetch her to my tent. It was colder than the blackest depths of Tartarus and I had a brazier going.

She came, which was a good sign, I felt.

'I want you,' I said.

'Good,' she said, and sat.

'I need to negotiate a treaty with you,' I said. 'I cannot keep you – and win you every day. I cannot. I lack the time, and I have to live in a world of men.'

Thaïs laughed. 'Do I get wine while we bargain?'

'Hot wine, if Ochrid knows what's good for him. First, I have considered your idea of freedom. Even if I accepted it in principle – and I'm not positive I do – I am a senior officer of the king, and a man in a world of warriors, and if you spread your legs for Nearchus I have to kill him.'

'Nearchus?' she asked. She shook her head. 'He's pretty, but he's dumb.'

'Perdiccas?' I asked.

'Spare me.' She sighed. 'You are saying that I cannot truly be free due to the constraints of your culture, in which I am choosing to live.'

I nodded. 'Exactly!'

'Did you consider that I might figure this out all on my own?' she asked. 'The Pythia ... was lonely. And no one needed to know but us.' She shrugged.

'So I was being tested,' I said.

She shrugged again. 'If you like. You are not actually the centre of the universe, my love. Other people exist.'

'Could you stop putting me in my place?' I asked.

She laughed, drank some hot wine and quite suddenly got up, leaned over and kissed me. The scent of her – which I hadn't smelled in two days – threatened to overwhelm me. My penis was instantly hard – I offer this vulgarity not to be salacious, young man, but to give you an idea of her power.

'I will never offend you or yours,' she said. 'You are my friend, my heart. And you will not ever ask me questions. Because if you do, I will tell you the answers. My love, I am a hetaera, not a wife. If you want a kept virgin, go and get one, and leave me be.'

I nodded. 'What if I ask you questions and I can stand the answers?' I asked.

'Then you will be unlike any man I've ever known,' she said.

'Did the Pythia please you?' I asked.

'Beautifully. She is a very skilled lover. Priestesses of Apollo always

277

are.' She shrugged. 'And she is in a position to aid me. Delphi has powerful friends, and makes a powerful friend, too.'

I must have looked spectacularly dense. She made a motion with her hand – dimissal, annoyance. 'Do you know that in every relationship, there comes a moment when I ask myself – Aphrodite, is he as dumb as he seems?' Her eyes bored into mine.

Note that we were not having my conversation – the one where I tasked her with infidelity. I was on the defensive and losing ground more quickly than a badly ordered phalanx in a rout. 'Well?'

'She—'

'I did not make love to her because she can help the crusade in Asia,' Thaïs said. 'But she can do us more service than ten thousand hoplites. Because Delphi is the clearing house of information for all of Hellas – and Asia, too. Do you understand?'

I'm sure I nodded. In truth, I didn't understand. Not until much later.

But I was smart enough to know that I didn't want to lose her, not for anything.

I nodded slowly. The spear-point was there, somewhere down in my belly, grating softly against my ribs, but I was going to learn to deal with it, because this was the woman I wanted.

'She was better than me?' my mouth asked before my brain could stop it.

Thaïs reached out a hand and caught my face in it. 'I never, ever compare. Don't ever ask me to again.'

I wanted to cry.

She shook her head. 'I will teach you the rules, love. It will be worth it. Love, far from being scary, dangerous and horrid, is in fact a marvellous engine of energy and creation – but it needs a harness, and that harness is rules. Please?' she asked, waiting for me to let her on to my lap.

I hesitated.

'Ptolemy,' she said. 'I don't want to play at this many times. If you cannot live with me as I am – let's part now. Right now, this instant. Otherwise, let's move on and make love. The talking is done.' She smiled, and it wasn't a hurt smile or a difficult smile – but it was a deeply knowledgeable one. 'Choose.'

I looked into those remarkable blue eyes. 'You mean, I can choose between sending you away, and having the best sex of my life?' I sighed. 'I don't know. I need time to think,' I said, while reaching my warm hands under her gown.

'Humour,' she said, through my kisses, 'is your outstanding virtue.'

'I thought it was my large penis,' I said.

She laughed into my mouth. We were warm.

We spent the winter training north of Pella. This was new. As I've said, Philip always sent the army home for the winter. Alexander did not. He kept the entire force in the field – funded by the League of Corinth, at a drachma per soldier per day.

We climbed mountains in the snow.

We practised seizing ridges and passes. In the snow.

We charged lines of straw dummies with our lances. On horseback. In the snow.

We practised setting camp and setting fires, digging in, collecting forage – in the snow.

And we drilled.

Ares, it was endless.

Look, I'm good at drill. I love drill. I love the sort of ritual-team-dance aspect to drill – the stamp of a thousand perfectly timed feet sends a thrill down my spine. But that winter was absurd. We drilled and drilled and drilled, and I'm not sure that there's any army in history that spent as much time practising the Spartan Counter-March as we did. Every day, five or six times a day – with wheeling, sprinting, breaking and reforming, marching to the left, right and rear by files, half-files and double files. On and on.

Every damn day.

The troopers cursed him. The aristocrats were good officers at first, but after two months – remember, we'd been at it all summer, too – people just wanted a cup of wine and a fuck.

I had to send Thaïs away, because men were starting to hate me for having her. Which was sad, because she loved it, and she kept people amused – she'd show up in the phalanx in armour and already know the drill, she'd ride a horse shooting a bow, she'd go off with the scouts until they caught her – she could easily pass for a man, but something often gave her away, too.

She had found a hobby. I didn't know what it was and I knew I wasn't allowed to ask, but she suddenly wrote a great many letters – on and on, really. Sometimes a dozen a day. And she bought a pair of Thracian slaves – and sent one home. Into the mountains. I didn't understand that at all.

She smiled at me and dared me to ask.

At any rate, after a month I didn't have to pay attention any more, because I had to send her to my estates. After that, the rest of the winter was a blur of marching and climbing and freezing cold – you climb a mountain in two feet of snow wearing open-toed boots. Go ahead. The pezhetaeroi were in sandals. I had a horse, most of the time – a sort of living leg-warmer.

I knew what we were doing. We were going to blow the Thracians right out of their northern kingdom and carve a road to the Danube – to buy Antipater a defensible border while we were away conquering Asia. It was a good plan, in a general, strategic way. But it was an obvious plan, and every man, woman and child on both sides of the nebulous border between Macedon and the wild Thracians knew we were coming as soon as the passes were free of snow.

Alexander did have one shaved knucklebone, though. He sent our fleet – twenty triremes and some supply ships – from Amphilopolis, around through the Dardanelles and into the Euxine Sea. In part it was exploration – the Macedonian fleet had never attempted to enter the Euxine. In part it was sheer daring – we knew *nothing* of the mouth of the Danube, although we found some Amphilopolans who had traded there. But it was a brilliant outflanking move. If it worked. The ships would leave well before the army marched. If the army marched.

One night, I lay in some straw between Cleitus and the king. We were passing a gourd full of wine. Outside, the wind howled. Alectus had just informed the king that we'd lost a little over a hundred men to exposure and the arrows of the Lord of Contagion that month.

I was keeping the Military Journal, by then – in effect, I coordinated everyone's military reporting, and that had become my major job. Antipater did it for Philip, and he taught me – but I added to the job. I went around to all the regiments and appointed a record-keeping officer – sometimes with the help of the commander, and sometimes in spite of him. Perdiccas called my officers the 'king's spies'. The thing was, the king needed to know the truth. Bluster didn't cut it when you needed a return of effective soldiers, or when we needed to know how many horses and how many riders were available for a particular mission, or which horses needed new tack before the army could march.

And at the same time, the king was paying – with League funds – for a gradual re-armouring of the whole Macedonian army. And that cost money, but it also required endless lists, inventories, record-keeping, tracking inventory . . .

It was all glory and arete, let me tell you.

At any rate, that's why I was lying wrapped in my cloak in a pile of straw in a freezing-cold barn in northern Macedon, snuggled between the commander of the king's bodyguard and the king himself, listening to Alectus tell us his figures on sick and injured, with every word sending plumes of mist rising from his mouth. It was *cold*.

Alexander dismissed him with a cup of hot wine and rolled over. 'As soon as the passes are clear,' he said dreamily.

'Why don't we go now?' I asked. 'I mean, as soon as I can put together a logistics head of food and fodder.'

Alexander laughed. 'Because that trick will only work once, and I want to save it for a tougher opponent.'

Sometimes, he was scary.

But later, when Alectus was obviously still awake, I turned towards him.

'What did you learn at Delphi?' I asked him.

He laughed. 'I learned that I will live a few years yet, and the king is going to be a god.' He laughed again.

The passes cleared. Before they cleared, I had all the grain in north-west Macedon gathered in fifty new-built stone granaries that cost a fortune to build and required men to keep roaring fires going all day and all night to keep the ground soft and let the mortar harden without freezing.

All in a day's work.

We marched from Amphilopolis, headed north, and we moved fast. We had preset camps with supplies waiting at every halt. We flew.

At Neopolis we joined up with our baggage train, and I was reunited with Thaïs, who was fresh and pink-cheeked and looked like a maiden. Most of the army's wives and sweethearts – and prostitutes and sex toys – came to Neopolis and marched with us. We crossed the Nestus and marched all the way to Philipopolis. The Thracians were conspicuous by their absence.

Thaïs shared my tent and my cloak. Her field household was now reduced to three – her steward, Anonius, from Italy, a Thracian, Strako and a Libyan woman, Bella, a big, attractive black woman who drew the stares of half the army wherever she went. However, she seemed capable of taking care of herself.

The Thracian came and went, foraging and visiting. I warned Thaïs that he would desert, and she laughed.

'Give me a little credit,' she said. 'I have a chain on him.'

The worm of jealousy gnawed at me. It must have showed.

She laughed in my face. 'I don't fuck slaves,' she said, and walked out of my tent.

I hope I don't make her sound like a harridan. She was not. But we had a spat every day – that's how we were. She wanted to know every aspect of my business, and I wanted her to respect my privacy, and I didn't see any need for her to know the inner workings of the Military Journal or the Hetaeroi.

Plenty of things to fight about. Making up was good, too.

Strako kept with us. That impressed me. After two weeks in enemy country, I rolled over, pinned her with a leg and said, 'OK, I have to know. Why's he loyal?'

She wasn't angry – I never knew, with her. She laughed. 'Well – since you're keeping me so *very* warm ...' She kissed my nose. 'I have his wife, child and brother at home. At your home. If he runs, they all die.'

Um. So soft. So beautiful. So funny, so warm.

So hard.

She also received as many letters as the king. I know that to be true, because I sometimes functioned as the Military Secretary, in those days. I certainly saw most of the king's correspondence, and I saw all the messengers that came in from Pella – one a day, and sometimes two. She had at least two a day. Some were slaves, some were free, and once, her messenger was a Priest of Apollo.

Two more days, and we were at the Shipka Pass. And the wild Thracians were there – in huge numbers. They had thousands of warriors and more armed slaves, and they had a wagon lager of four wheeled carts lining the top of the pass, where it was about two stades wide.

The Prodromoi brought us word.

We rode forward and looked.

'Impregnable,' Hephaestion said. From his years of military experience.

But he was right. It was impregnable. Several of Philip's campaigns had ended right here.

We made camp.

Just as the light was failing – it was late spring, and the days were getting long – Strako came into my tent. I hadn't seen him in a day. He frowned at me and motioned at Thaïs.

Thaïs was under some cloaks, trying to get warm. She got up, and Strako began to talk while she put on boots.

'He says the wagons aren't for defence,' Thaïs said.

'How do you know about the wagons?' I asked.

'Strako was just up there. In their camp. Listen, love. Tell the king they plan to roll the wagons on you when you attack. And then charge you. They are hoping you'll bring up artillery to shell the wagons. It is a ruse within a ruse.' Thaïs listened to the man.

'You speak Thracian?' I asked.

'It was a long winter,' Thaïs insisted.

I heard the report to the end. And looked at my lover.

'I can't expect to be taken to Asia for my good looks,' she said. 'I have friends in every city, and the Pythia made me more friends. But there are other tricks – that anyone in politics knows. That anyone who has read Thucydides knows.'

I had heard of Thucydides, but I hadn't read him. I made a mental note to rectify this.

'We can trust this report?' I asked.

'Or I'm a complete fool,' she said.

I took it to the king.

Cleitus woke me in the dark. 'Come,' he said. 'We're going to attack. Get up.'

I was up like a shot. I knew Alexander – I knew we were going to attack.

I went for Polystratus and found Bella curled in his cloak. He was mightily embarrassed to be awakened.

'It's not what you think, lord,' he said. 'We were cold.'

I nodded. What do you say?

We armed each other in the light of a single lamp. It was cold.

Alexander was waiting for us by a huge fire near his pavilion.

'We've drilled all winter at opening gaps in the ranks,' he said. 'We'll win this one on simple discipline. It will be a good lesson for the pezhe-taeroi. Tell them to open ranks to let the wagons through – if they are too packed together, tell them to lie flat with their shields over them and let the wagons run over them.' He shrugged. 'Once they drop the wagons on us, it's just an infantry fight.'

He turned to Philip Longsword. 'Straight up the right-side ridge until you are well above the pass – then down into their flank.' He turned to Cleitus. 'Take the mercenary archers and march to the left of the hypaspitoi – get into the rocks – those white rocks there – and start shooting. You'll have them at open shields. Then it'll all be over but the marching.'

It wasn't a complex plan. It was, in fact, an obvious plan.

The thing is, most armies couldn't have done it. It required that the hypaspitoi climb a mountain in full armour, with spears, and then traverse a long ridge and then come down in the enemy rear, while archers climbed the same ridge, took cover and lofted arrows two hundred paces into the Thracians. While the rest of us went right up the path into the carts and didn't just die.

But we knew each other. Alexander dismounted a hundred Hetaeroi, and I led them as the right anchor of the phalanx, which was going straight up the throat of the pass. When we assembled in the first light of dawn, the hypaspitoi were already gone, the last files of archers were just leaving camp and the Thracians were awake, alert and lining their rampart of wagons.

Alexander walked down the line of the front rank. We were only a thousand paces from the top of the pass.

He stopped and shook my hand. Then embraced me.

He went along the front rank and he hugged, embraced, shook hands – a hundred times or more.

While the Thracians jeered, and the hypaspitoi climbed.

And then, when he was satisfied that the army loved him, he waved and ran off to the right. He was going with the hypaspitoi. In person, this time. Not like on Mount Ossa.

I buckled my chinstrap and led my friends up the pass.

The thing about plans is that they are rarely like the eventuality. The idea that we could drop files and half-files to the rear – as a phalanx always did when faced with, say, a small stand of trees in the middle of a plain – was excellent. But the fact was that when the Thracians started rolling the carts on us, they came at us like a ball flung by a child – all angles, no predictable path.

I'd say we were at three hundred paces when they released the carts.

As I said, my Hetaeroi were on the right of the line. We were crammed into the last 'open' ground in the pass, and our end files were virtually crushed against the low cliff that gradually sloped in from our right, narrowing the pass and packing us tighter and tighter.

At five hundred paces, I had six files – almost half my strength – doubled in behind the left files to make space, and there was no place for us to climb above the pass, or I'd have gone.

My point is, we weren't eight deep, we were sixteen deep, and all along the front, phylarchs and taxitoi doubled files to cut their frontage and keep room to manoeuvre.

And then the carts came.

There was no way we could drop files back, because the carts had no predictable path. They bounced, slammed into each other, stopped, exploded against rocks – or hurtled at us like fists from Olympus.

It was a brilliant stratagem.

I'd say we had five carts on our frontage. The fact that the pass was 'v'-shaped – an inverted 'v' like a lambda – with the point at the top of the pass, the narrowest part, and the floor of the pass vaguely rounded out by a small watercourse, meant that all the carts tended to run towards the centre.

Of the five rolled at us, two collided and stopped on the slope above us, and two deviated off towards the pezhetaeroi and vanished.

And one came right at us.

'Lie down!' I roared. It seemed like an insane thing to do, with a ton of cart roaring and bouncing down at us, but Aristotle and Alexander agreed that the wheels should pass over us so fast we'd be uninjured. I got down and put my aspis, sloped slightly, over my head and upper back.

The front right wheel hit my aspis and went over it, then right over my butt and missed my right leg. The rear wheel kicked my aspis hard enough to slam it into my head – my helmeted head – and then ran off down the slope and over the file behind me.

I got to my feet.

Aristotle, damn him, was completely correct. Behind me, Nearchus got to his feet, and then Cleomenes and then Pyrrhus.

The cart that hit us stopped in the seventh file, because the shields slowed it so much. Two files had to roll it off young Calchus. But he sprang to his feet.

In the whole army, men were getting to their feet.

Which was good, because the Thracians were charging.

'Close up!' I roared.

I wanted my men at the closest order – the synapsis, where the shields overlapped. I might as well mention that all the Hetaeroi in the assault had aspides, albeit the smaller, rimless type Iphakrates invented.

The way to achieve that close order was to move the half-files forward into the gaps between files. But what I wanted to do was to get the full files – my right files, my very best men – to move forward through the left files – remember, the right files were all pushed to the rear by the narrowing of the pass. Right?

I could see Cleitus. He could see me. And this is where the trust part – and knowing each other like brothers – came into it.

I caught his eye and yelled, 'Files forward! Synapsis!' Took a breath. 'Not half-files – the rear files! Now!'

Cleitus had it from the first syllable. He was bellowing at his phylarchs, and my front phylarchs were pushing to the right and left to make room, and the Thracians were one hundred and fifty paces away and coming down the slope at a dead run.

Changing formation in the face of the enemy is the very worst thing you can do. It requires rock-solid confidence and enormous quantities of practice. Great officers and file leaders. And no errors, because at this point, two men tripping over each other could spell doom.

But we were Macedonians.

The Thracians were about thirty paces away when the rear files locked their shields to the front-file phylarchs.

I was on the left, by choice – I wanted to be in contact with the centre. So my full-sized aspis – call me old-fashioned – locked up with Laodon, who was commanding his pezhetaeroi from the right file, which was more the norm.

'Spears – DOWN!' I ordered, and Laodon roared the same words, almost at the same moment, and our front ranks put their spears at the ready and the rear ranks pushed forward, locking up so that every man had his shield pushed into the back of the man ahead of him, his spear either point forward, overhand, ready to kill, or, in the rear ranks, erect, the point at the sky, safe until needed. The pezhetaeroi had sarissas, eighteen feet long, but we Hetaeroi had our cavalry spears, just eleven feet long.

No matter.

The Thracians hit us.

Ares, they were brave.

The front men, those who had run the fastest to reach us, were the bravest of the brave, men who sought to make a reputation for ferocity *among Thracians.* They were coming down a steep slope and they were *above* us, and several men leaped into the air and *fell* into our ranks, seeking to break our wall of shields and spears, shatter our formations and make room for their friends to reap us like summer wheat.

A man leaped in front of me.

My spear took him in the air and slammed him to earth, and then it was a blur of bodies and edges and threats and parries. The sun was just rising, and cast a red light over everything, and the noise was every-where, the full-throated roar of the brazen lungs of Areas, and men died, fell wounded, collapsed to earth all around me.

The pressure of the shield at my back was gone, and I stumbled back – downhill – looking for that reassuring pressure, and it wasn't there.

My spear broke. I remember that, because it was disorienting sud-denly to have no pressure behind me and no spear. I raised my shield to cover my head and took a full step back, reaching with my back foot.

Nearchus was down. I found his shield with my foot.

Got my hand on my sword.

Drew.

The Keltoi long sword doesn't come free like the xiphos. A xiphos glides into your hand like a friendly snake, all under the comfortable cover of your shield, as fast as thought and just as safe, but the long sword has to be drawn all the way free of a scabbard almost twice as long. You have to roll your shoulders and raise the rim of the aspis. There's a reason most men don't carry them.

Lucky, or alert to my difficulties, a tribesman slammed into the face of my shield with his metal shield boss while I drew, and down I went, losing my weapon, cutting my hand on my own blade. I fell back down the slope, and for the second time that day my helmet absorbed a major impact – this time, when my head hit a rock.

But Tyche was with me, and my back came up against Nearchus's aspis, so that I got my butt under me and then one foot before the Thracian could finish me, and I slammed my aspis into him two-handed, one hand in the porpax and the other holding the rim. He stumbled back.

I looked down, but couldn't see my Keltoi sword or anything else.

He rifled his spear at me and I knocked it down.

Another thrown spear appeared and I knocked that down, too.

I backed again, still looking for a file partner, and now I was starting to panic – no weapon, and nobody behind me. Had the Hetaeroi really been broken? My helmet cut off my peripheral vision and my hearing, so I really didn't know where the fight was.

I stepped back again. In my head, that meant I'd gone back four steps, and that was *not good*. But my booted heel was on something springy, and that meant my sword.

I knelt, put my right hand down and grabbed the hilt.

A flurry of blows hit the face of my shield. But a full-sized aspis is like a wall for a kneeling man.

A big red-haired man tried to push his spear over the top of the aspis, thrusting *down* into my neck, but I tilted my aspis and pushed to my feet, lifting his spear away and thrusting the long blade under my tabled shield, passing my right foot past my left to ram the thrust home, and he was dead.

I took a shattering blow to the head.

That's what happens when you push forward too hard, or when men leave you. I never saw the blow, and it hit me hard enough to break my nose inside my helmet and leave me barely conscious, and another blow, from a spear, cut across the top of my bicep and by the will of Athena went in the front of my thorax instead of under my sword arm – so I got a nasty and very graphic cut across my pectoral muscle instead of a death wound under my arm.

Really, it should have been the end of me, and I stumbled.

A shield was pressed into my back. It steadied me – both physically and in spirit. Someone was there. It meant everything.

A shield slapped against the lower-left rim of my aspis. Someone was in the rank with me.

My eyes wouldn't focus and I took a scraping blow along my helmet, and Cleomenes called, 'Step back.'

It occurred to me that I'd been hearing that for a long time.

I nodded, rotated on my hips so that my body was inclined away from my opponent and shot my sword forward to cover my step. Cleomenes stepped up on my left, and I felt his shield wrap around my left as he muscled into place and his spear shot forward. And I was in the second rank, with blood running out from under my helmet and into my mouth. There was a lot of blood, a lot of pain.

On the other hand, I was alive.

I knelt and breathed. Spat blood.

Took a drink from my canteen in the third rank. Someone had pushed past me.

I found that I was kneeling by Nearchus. He was breathing, and had a lot of blood on *his* face, so I poured wine and water over his face and he spluttered. I ran my hand over his arm – his sword arm looked bad, with a long shallow cut – and he coughed again and gave a short scream just as I found where his arm was broken.

I got my chlamys out from under my aspis and wrapped his arm as tightly as I dared while he was out of it, and then the whole phalanx was moving. I was better – taking care of someone else is the sovereign remedy for pain – and I got my feet under me and pushed forward.

'Let me through – front rank!' I called. I'd fallen all the way back to the sixth or seventh rank. I pushed forward, replacing men who hadn't fought yet and were – understandably – annoyed.

Some of Laodon's men were in our ranks. I pushed past two pezhetaeroi to get to Cleomenes, who knocked a Thracian off his feet with a pretty move. I put my sword in the man's throat to save Cleomenes the step, but that man must have been the last Thracian in the 'zone', the area where men fight. The rest were drawn up a few paces above us on the slope, throwing spears. When men settle down to throwing spears, the hard fighting is over.

We had held them.

'Exchange!' I croaked at Cleomenes. He shouted a war cry at the Thracians, and then peeked back at me, grinned and nodded, and we did the same dance we'd done earlier, in reverse – he pivoted back, I stepped up, and I was in his place.

Laodon was nowhere to be seen, and Pyrrhus was in the rank next to me, where there should have been a pezhetaeroi. In fact, I could see my own men for four or five files. This sort of thing happens in a hard fight, and with no disrespect to the phalangites of the pezhetaeroi, they weren't trained men like the graduates of the royal pages. And my boys were. And they were eager – for a lot of the 'new' Hetaeroi, this was their first battle – certainly the first big fight on foot, where the heroes walked the earth.

Despite my pain and my wounds, I could feel their eagerness.

We were supposed to hold the Thracians here, so that the hypaspitoi could get around their flanks. If I attacked the Thracians, I'd be pushing them back up the slope, and making Alexander's job harder.

Just then, while I thought about this and while Cleomenes, behind me, pushed against me aggressively and shouted, 'Forward, take us forward', and all the Hetaeroi started to take up the cry ...

The archers got into position, and the shafts began to fall. I couldn't even see the archers – but they had got *past* the flank of the Thracians, and their arrows fell on to unshielded backs. The Thracians began to look over their shoulders.

'Take us forward!' roared the whole right end of the battle line. It sounded to me as if the left end was still engaged, but I could see nothing over there.

There was no one to ask, either.

Cleitus told me later that I was grinning like a maniac. That's not what I remember, but perhaps! At any rate, I stood straight and pointed my sword.

'Silence!' I roared.

The cries stopped as if cut off with a knife.

'Forward!' I called, and I took a step forward, and we fell up that hill like an avalanche. The Thracians stood, and we crashed into them, shield to shield, packed like sardines in a barrel, and then we were pushing – the rear-rank men pushing with their legs, the front-rankers trying to keep a shoulder firmly inside the aspis, so that the pressure from the rear ranks didn't flatten them out and crush them – I'd heard of the othismos but I'd never been in it. We pushed, and they tried to stand, but we practised this and they did not, and in seconds we were pressing them back, and then they were stumbling and the pushing was over – we were cutting and thrusting with spear and sword, and they were tripping, falling, collapsing – and running. They didn't have the cohesion to hold us. Dozens must have died there – men in my rear ranks killed the ones who tripped and fell with their saurouters.

I got an arrow in my aspis – the long iron head came right through the face and scratched my hand. One of our own.

I lowered my aspis slightly, and there was no one there.

I looked left, and the centre of our line was below me on the slope, fifty paces behind. Our left flank was even farther back.

And straight ahead, I saw Alexander leap down from the rocks – now lower and closer – into the rear of the fleeing Thracians, with Alectus and Philip Longsword on either side.

We'd won. Right there. So my new duty was to save as many of our infantry as possible. It looked to me as if the pezhetaeroi on our left were getting the worst of it.

In a flash, I had an idea, even as the hypaspitoi came pouring down from the top of the pass into the rear of the fleeing Thracians.

I pushed back into the middle ranks.

'Forward! Phalanx forward! Half-files – halt and stand fast!' I yelled.

That sent the pezhetaeroi and the Hetaeroi forward on the right – but men from the fifth to the eighth rank stood fast. My men were facing no resistance – they didn't need deep files behind them to help 'hold' the enemy.

Then training told – long training in the snow. The half-file leaders – noble and commoner – stood fast, and as the front ranks peeled away, I had about sixty files of four men each left behind with enough space ...

'Half-phalanx will form from the right files to the left!' I called. This was like rolling a carpet – the rightmost files – four files, to be exact – marched forward and wheeled smartly to the *left*, passing across the front of the new-formed half-phalanx, and every set of four files then wheeled up and joined the column as they passed, until my whole body was marching across the rear of the front files, into the gap opened by our rapid advance, and into the rear of the Thracians facing the centre and right of our army.

I do not claim that this was a brilliant manoeuvre. I merely claim that there was no other army on earth that could have done it.

Once we were clear of our own front files, we formed front – that is, the column formed a new phalanx at right angles to the old phalanx. The Thracians collapsed. It was almost instant, the moment we were formed, as if every Thracian saw the danger at the same moment – and perhaps they did, but an army has a remarkable level of non-verbal communication. They can 'feel' all together. It's like the pressure of your buddy's shield in your back – when it is gone, you 'feel' wrong.

We slaughtered them as they ran by us – packed against the far cliff, pushing with all their might to escape, even shedding their armour to climb the cliffs. More than a thousand of them died – some men say two thousand, a fifth of the fighting strength of their whole nation slaughtered in a few minutes.

Unfortunately, we could not pursue them on horseback. The

downslope of the pass on the far side was too steep, had too many switchbacks, and even in panicked flight, Thracians were a redoubtable foe. Men threw spears, or stood at the bend in the road over the pass to cut at our feet. Had the ground been a little flatter, we might have ended the Thracians as a people for ever. As it was, they died and died, so that the streams that ran down both faces of the pass ran red.

I was carried along with the pursuit for a long way – maybe ten stades, all the way down the pass on the far side to a deep stream with steep banks where one of their princes made a stand with several hundred men in good armour. I could see him – he had a silk standard, some sort of windsock such as the Sarmatians use, and his helmet was covered in gold and jewels. They stood atop the bank on the far side of that icy stream, and we lost as many men trying to push them off the bank as we lost in the whole battle. Three times we crossed the stream, and three times we were thrown back.

Alexander led fifty hypaspitoi across the river farther down, where the water flowed like a torrent and an error meant certain death. He was the first across, and a dozen armoured Thracians ran at him, and he stood his ground, killed one, and then another, and then Alectus was with him.

He was the king. We threw ourselves across that stream to reach him, and the Thracians gave way, and we had all but bridged the torrent with bodies. I ran south, towards where I'd last seen the king, and I found him sore pressed – Alectus with him, Philip Longsword down, twenty more hypaspitoi trying to push him into the rear and fifty Thracians hammering at them.

He was unmarked, and he'd killed a third man, and he had a quiet smile on his face – the smile of a man who's made a fine helmet, or carved a beautiful wood panel of Herakles, for example.

'Ptolemy,' he said warmly as I came up. 'Well done.'

Behind him, the last of the Thracians went down, neither asking nor giving quarter, as half a thousand Macedonians buried them in blades. Alexander stepped up on a big rock as if he hadn't been fighting for his life a moment before.

'Just for a moment, I thought we'd have them all,' he said. He started walking to where we'd fought our way over the stream. The chieftain, their prince, lay pinned to the earth with a pair of spears. His banner lay fallen beside him.

'This one saved all his friends,' he said. 'A true hero. A worthy adversary.'

The man moaned.

Alexander smiled. 'If he lives, sign him up,' he said cheerfully. 'How were the wagons? You look terrible.'

I laughed.

We didn't even rest a full day. That afternoon, we plundered the Thracian camp carefully – it was a rich haul of gold and women and children – and sent everything back to the coast with our wounded and Laodon's pezhetaeroi, who had fought brilliantly and were held to deserve the 'vacation'.

We had about a hundred dead and twice that many wounded – a small enough bill for the victory, but still a visible percentage of our forces. Men were shifted back and forth, and the net result was two larger taxeis of roughly four thousand men each when we started down the mountains on to the plain of the Danube.

All of us assumed that the Thracians were beaten. Even Alexander assumed it. We kept guards and flankers out – we weren't foolish – but as we marched towards the Danube, we assumed we'd broken the Thracians not just for now but for years to come.

We were wrong.

The Triballians retreated in front of us – the survivors of the battle reinforced by other tribesmen – with their livestock and their families – those we hadn't taken at the pass. They retreated, and we pursued, eager to catch them. On the third day, the Prodromoi reported that the Thracians had started a boat lift to move their families to a big island in the Danube.

Alexander threw the hypaspitoi forward, leading them himself.

It was sheer luck that one of our Hetaeroi patrols – under Nearchus – tripped over an *army* of Thracians coming up behind us. They were half a day away, and we'd almost missed them.

The trap was closing. The Thracians behind us now held the pass at our rear and had at least another ten thousand men.

I sent a messenger for Alexander and halted the army, putting out a ring of scouts and dispatching the skirmishers – the Psiloi – to the rear to slow the enemy if they appeared. I asked Philip the Red – remember, I wasn't the commander of anything except one squadron of Hetaeroi – to scout to our rear, and he agreed.

Hephaestion was with Alexander, Antipater was in Pella, and none of Parmenio's precious family had arrived to take command of anything, so that our army had Alexander – and no level below him. In the next few hours, that showed. I was unwilling to take command – it wasn't my job, and I felt the weight of Alexander's displeasure here more than any other place. If I took command, there might be a price.

On the other hand, we *all* knew what to do.

Alexander came back after the sun was high in the sky. He approved all of our joint decisions, and then ordered the entire army to countermarch behind the Psiloi. He put the Prodromoi well out on to the flanks and we moved forward, leaving our baggage to the mercy of the Thracians behind us. I hated that decision, even as I understood it – that was Thaïs being left unprotected. He didn't leave a single slinger behind.

Our Psiloi went forward into another ambush. The force behind us had formed up in a wooded valley that fed into the Danube, right across our line of march, with steep sides and heavy woods to cover them, and as the archers prowled forward along the open floor of the valley, arrows fell on them from the trees, and Thracian noblemen on ponies charged them and killed a dozen before they scattered.

An hour later, I sat beside Alexander as he looked up the pass. I was eating a sausage – I remember thinking how delicious it was, even though every bite hurt my jaw and my nose.

We were all hungry.

Alexander looked at the pass for a long time. It formed a shallow lambda with the point aimed at Pella – to the south.

It would entail a journey of a hundred stades or more, across unknown country, to go around.

'Well,' he said, after a long hundred heartbeats, 'I don't want to attack into that.'

I think we all sighed with relief. It looked like a death trap.

As if to underscore its peril, a Thracian arrow whispered out of the air and fell – well short, but close enough to make Poseidon shy.

Alexander looked around, and his eye fell on Cleitus, not me. 'Cleitus,' he said.

Cleitus grinned. 'Uh-oh,' he said, with mock despair.

Alexander nodded. 'Take the Psiloi forward again. Far enough that they can *almost* cut you off. Make them taste their victory before you let the Psiloi run. Get them to chase you down their precious hills.' He nodded at the rest of us. 'Form in loose order – over here, behind the edge of the downslope. Spears down so we aren't visible. If they pursue Cleitus, we'll charge, and chance it. If we fail – don't go more than a quarter of the way up the pass. Understand?'

Many men didn't. Again, it was a simple plan. The Psiloi went forward as bait, and the rest of us formed a counter-ambush to attack the Thracians if they were stupid enough to bite down.

As with the first battle at the pass, the whole plan was in the details. Most of all, the Psiloi had to go forward with determination and put a volume of fire into the Thracians that would force them to react – and then stand their ground for far too long. It's easy to describe. It's damn hard to do, when you have no shield, no armour and no hope of surviving even a moment of fierce combat – especially when you are a scrawny Cretan looking at gigantic red-haired barbarians with swords as long as your body.

And for the rest of us – well, try hiding a phalanx in the open country by the Danube.

I will say that the magic began that afternoon, because we walked away from that command meeting without a mutter. When Alexander told us to lie down under our shields for the Thracian wagons, we muttered. There were some harsh jokes. But at the Woods Battle, we just went to our posts.

Cleitus went forward with the Psiloi, all the Toxophiloi and some of the Prodromoi, dismounted, as well as a few hundred mercenary slingers and a handful of the new crossbowmen. It is a common enough weapon now, but in the first year of the king's reign, they were virtually unknown and we only had fifty of them. Some said Aristotle invented the crossbow, and others said it came, like all brilliant military engineering, from Sicily. Either way, a bolt from one of these small engines could go two hundred paces and penetrate a good bronze helmet. A Scythian or a Cretan archer could do the same, but took a lifetime to train, and couldn't do either lying flat on his stomach.

Forward he went.

The Thracians let them come.

I had a ringside seat, on the right of the line. All my Hetaeroi were going to fight mounted, if we had a chance to fight. We were to be the horns of the bull. All my troopers stood beside their horses, well over the crest of the low ridge that separated our main body from the wooded valley – the killing zone.

I had climbed up the low ridge with Philip the Red, and we lay under our dun cloaks in the sunshine – sweating profusely, I suppose, although I don't remember. I only remember my heart hammering in my chest as our archers began to shoot into the Thracians – Cleitus had taken them right up the valley, and boldly formed a deep 'v' where both lines of Psiloi had their backs to the stream.

Our archers outranged the Thracian archers, and were better. The Cretans especially were deadly.

I had never seen a contest of shot before. Our men had training and density of firepower, and the Thracians had the protection of brush and woods.

The protection was not enough. I could see men hit in the woods, and other men moving back up the slopes of the valley, and then there were horns blowing high on the crests of the hills, and sunlight glinted off spears and helmets as the main force of the Thracians moved.

Cleitus did not let his men slacken their shots. Nearer to us, we saw the Rhodian slingers begin to pound away at the exposed Thracians in the low, marshy ground at the nearest end of the valley. Archers can't stand tight together to loose, and slingers are worse, needing a spear's length around them; but when a hundred slingers throw all together, their pellets of lead tear at tree branches and pass through brush like a wicked wind. Men screamed.

The archers kept shooting. Philip, at my side, had begun to count arrows, as every archer had twenty-four. The Cretans had loosed sixteen when I saw the glittering might of the Thracian main host start down the ridge.

'We're hurting them,' I said.

Alexander flopped down next to me. 'Of course we're hurting them,' he said. 'We have more archers and slingers than they've ever seen. They have to do something.'

We watched for as long as it takes a slave to start a fire, and then the Thracians began to charge the Psiloi. There was no order, and if anything the trumpet calls were to restrain them. But the wounds – and deaths – were literally driving them down the hill.

They broke cover and took casualties crossing the open ground, because Cleitus – in his first command – held them by sheer force of will for one more volley of missiles. He had so many archers – more than six hundred – they staggered the charge.

Just for a moment, I wondered if the archers could hold the line without us.

Then the Psiloi broke. They all ran together, like a flock of birds taking flight, every wing beating together.

The Thracians were *right* behind them.

Out at the point of the lambda, where Cleitus was, the Thracians caught the Psiloi and killed them.

The rest of the horse came pouring down the hills and into the gap, and our men died.

Alexander lay beside me, counting. 'See the old chiton tied to the bush?' he said.

That bush was less than a stade in front of me. 'Yes,' I said.

'When they pass that bush, stand up and wave.' Alexander got to his feet well to the rear and ran down the slope to where a slave held Bucephalus.

I watched. Our Psiloi were dying in numbers now, running

desperately, tangled up with each other. A rout is ugly, and what starts as a trained flight turns all too easily into a rout.

Thracians continued to pour down the slope. I assume – from the hindsight of history – that their king knew he was committed and decided not to send a half-measure. He sent his whole force.

Now they were flowing through the gap, out of the valley and on to the flat ground, up the shallow ridge that closed the southern end of the valley. The first fugitives were passing the chiton. Then more and more.

Behind me, Alexander had opened every tenth file in the phalanx, so that the Psiloi could run through. But the pezhetaeroi were still, for the most part, lying flat, except the men who had to move to open the files.

I don't think that it mattered any more – the Thracians were committed to all-out attack.

The first Thracians passed the chiton. All the Psiloi who were going to be caught had been caught, by now. The weak. The injured. The unlucky.

I waited a few more breaths, until the main shield line reached the bush, and then I stood up.

I swear that as I stood, the whole Macedonian army rose to their feet. Alexander raised a fist and waved at me, and I raced for Poseidon like a sprinter. A sprinter in greaves and heavy armour.

Polystratus was kind enough to stand at Poseidon's head and give my butt a push as I climbed on to his broad back. I got up in one go and rode to take my place at the head of my wedge.

Alexander raised his arm. Every man could see him – he was two horse lengths in front, and our whole army took up a little less than six stades.

He pumped his arm. His trumpeter sounded the charge.

And that was the sum total of the commands he gave.

We went up the hill in perfect order. And I don't use the term 'perfect' lightly. Every battle has something I remember – every battle is its own mistress, its own dark partner, its own spectacle. For that battle, it was the moment when we emerged from the brush and started up the hill, and two giants could have drawn a hawser, if one were long enough, taut across the front of the phalanx and touched every man's chest at the same time.

Just as we crested the low ridge, the flanks began to get a little ahead.

The Thracians were caught flat-footed, spread over two stades of ground, killing the Psiloi they'd caught in no kind of order. A few noble households were all together, shields locked, but most of them were well spread out and unprepared for ten thousand Macedonians to hit them all together.

Just in front of us, the main force of the Psiloi ran past us, eyes wide – registering delight as they crossed the crest and saw the army and the gaps, and men cheered them. Most of the Psiloi had probably never been cheered. Arms reached out in the phalanx and slapped their backs as they ran by, or pressed canteens full of wine on them. We already knew we'd won. And we knew we owed it to them.

I led my squadron of Hetaeroi from the right. The moment I saw the Thracians spread before me like a battle scene on a tapestry, I ordered the charge and we swept forward. Our wedge was unneeded – the wedge is a deep formation for penetrating an infantry block – and instead we passed through the Thracians left like a hot knife through cow's butter. I doubt that we killed a hundred of them. But Perdiccas and I had the same notion – to get into the entrance to the wooded valley and plug the gap so that the pezhetaeroi could slaughter the Thracians against us, like a hammer against a very small anvil.

We cut our way to the edge of the woods and I wheeled the Hetaeroi right round – try that some time. Great moments in cavalry drill! We got the Hetaeroi around, and formed in shallow blocks – half-files, only four deep. We took up more space that way, and we didn't need to be eight deep – much less in wedge – to kill Thracians trying to get away.

Then we rode forward slowly, into their rear, killing as we went.

I saw the hypaspitoi slam into a nobleman's retinue – there was a cloud of dust, as if a giant had thrown a huge clod of earth at the retinue, and then they were gone, and the hypaspitoi went forward *over* them. The Thracians went from hunters to hunted in moments, but there was nowhere to go except back into our spears, and we killed so many of them that when the fight was over – and there's nothing much to tell about that fight – my hand was *stuck* to my spear shaft, glued with other men's blood, my hand locked closed from hours of gripping the shaft too hard.

It wasn't glorious. But it was professional, and in three hours' work, we'd broken the Thracian alliance at the cost of forty-one soldiers – a dozen cavalrymen from the first part of the charge, and thirty-nine Psiloi, and one – just one – pezhetaeros.

I have no idea how many Thracians we actually killed. I walked over the western end of the field and counted all the dead in one square a stade on a side, and then I measured the battlefield and multiplied by the number in the one square, and got four thousand, two hundred dead Thracians, which seemed high, so I put three thousand five hundred into the Military Journal. See? My handwriting. See the brown smear? I could barely write – and usually we put this sort of info on to wax and let the scribes copy it fair on parchment or papyrus, but that day the scribes were back with the camp and we were too far away to use them.

That evening, I got Alexander's attention by the simple expedient of pushing into his tent, and asked to take the Hetaeroi back to cover the camp.

He had forgotten. He didn't have Thaïs waiting for him. He was Achilles, lying by the fire with his loyal myrmidons all around him. Again, he'd led the hypaspists in person, and they lay around him like mastiffs. Was I jealous?

You bet I was. I missed them.

Alexander looked at me. Nodded. 'Thanks,' he said. He was going to say something more, and then I think the king took over from the man.

I took half the Prodromoi and all my squadron and rode off at the start of the sunset, and by full dark we were riding into our main camp, which we found terrified but sound. They'd seen some fugitive Thracians and been scouted by a mounted force, so I dismounted my troopers and sent Cleomenes back – alone – to warn Alexander. We spent a bad night on guard duty – two war parties brushed us and we held them.

At first light, the hypaspitoi came, led by Alexander in person. He looked at the signs of fighting and led the Prodromoi out himself, and came back two hours later.

'They're still out there,' he said angrily. I think he felt that after two shattering defeats the Thracians might have the good grace to bend a knee and give in.

I was getting a different picture. What I saw was an enemy so diffuse and ungoverned that we couldn't 'beat' them or intimidate them as a group. In effect, I was beginning to believe that we'd have to defeat every individual Thracian – at least once. Or perhaps just kill every one of them.

The next day, the army was reunited with the camp and we moved out to the north, to the banks of the Danube, where by Alexander's usual combination of brilliant planning and ferocious good luck, the fleet lay rocking in the rapid current, tied to giant trees along the bank.

In the middle of the wide river, like a small ocean, lay the rocky shores of Pine Island, where eight thousand Thracians waited with their animals and their treasure. Beyond, at the very edge of sight, lay the far shore.

Right at our feet were the palings of the bridge that Darius had built in the years before Marathon, when he took a mighty army on to the steppes, and lost.

With a sinking feeling, I listened to the king and realised that he intended to march on – to take us on to Pine Island, crush the refugee Thracians there and then across the Danube, like Darius.

'Darius *lost*!' I found myself pointing out, later that evening.

No one else seemed to care, and a lot of wine was drunk. The appearance of the fleet, thousands of stades from home, was like a miracle, and it, combined with two fine victories, raised Alexander's spirits to a fever pitch.

He ordered the cavalry to collect every boat and dugout canoe along the banks for two hundred stades, and I spent the next week riding up and down the river, ducking javelins, arrows and thrown rocks. The woods were full of Thracians, and I was in a fight nearly every day – my sword arm was a mass of scars.

The only day I remember was rainy. I was soaked to the skin when I rode back into camp, fifty canoes richer, and I stripped naked because Thaïs had a bath ready for me. She got me into the bath, helped me scrub the pain away and got the rolled linen off my sword arm in the hot water so that the pain was bearable, and then she told me she was pregnant.

I think that was the only time I'd seen her afraid. She was afraid of the pregnancy and afraid, too, of me.

I was delighted. But I remembered what had happened to Nike, and I was ... afraid. So we had a fight – isn't that what people do when they are afraid?

And in the midst of that fight – me in a tub of hot water, blood flowing from my arm, Thaïs and her woman trying to bandage me while we shouted at each other – Cleitus came in.

'The king wishes you to attend him immediately,' Cleitus said, his face deadpan.

'Tell him I'm bleeding like a fucking sacrifice and naked as a baby,' I shot back.

Cleitus shook his head. 'No, Ptolemy. I will not. Come. Now.'

Things had changed a great deal. There had been a time when no one would have jumped like that for Alexander. We loved him – but we treated him as the first among equals. That was gone, now – even for Cleitus.

I got out of the bath, and Thaïs rubbed the water off me with her own chiton and pulled one of mine over my head. 'Go,' she said.

I really loved her. Then more than ever.

Alexander was sitting on a stool in his tent, with a low table made by two raw boards laid across two more stools – iron stools, taken as loot.

'When I ask for you to come immediately,' he said, and then he raised his head and saw the blood running down my right arm.

'I was having my wound dressed, and having a fight with my hetaera, my lord. I apologise for being late.' I suspect my sarcasm was all too evident.

He looked at me for a long time. His eyes were red, and he hadn't slept, and Hephaestion looked like a corpse with a skull for a head.

'I have fifty more canoes, and I lost three men over the last two days.' I shrugged. 'Aristotle would reduce this campaign to a mathematical equation. If we kill Thracians at this rate, we'll still run out of highly trained Hetaeroi before they run out of ignorant savages.'

Alexander drank some wine. 'You are dismissed,' he said.

I turned and left the tent. I relate this to show that it was not all wine and roses. Alexander had launched four attacks against Pine Island – you won't find this in the Military Journal – and been pushed off every time. The last time he'd got ashore in person, certain that his men would walk on water to save him. Instead, he'd almost been overrun, and twenty hypaspitoi had died saving him. Two full files. Dead.

Alexander probably summoned me to order me to lead the next assault. I was mouthy and he dismissed me and summoned Perdiccas, and he went and got wounded in the arm and the hip so that he was out for the rest of the campaign.

The next day it was Cassander's turn. He went and got knocked unconscious by a blow to the throat that left him unable to speak for days. No great loss.

I brought in more canoes and lost another trooper in the endless fighting, out there in the woods. And I learned from prisoners that the Getae, the largest, fiercest and best-mounted tribe of Thracians – not really Thracians, but a sort of mixed bag of Thracians and Scythians – were present in force on the far bank, with a fortified camp and at least ten thousand horsemen. They were feeding the Thracians on Pine Island.

When I returned, I heard about Cassander, and I went to Alexander's pavilion and was admitted.

'I'm sure you have a great deal to tell me, Ptolemy,' Alexander said bitterly.

I realised that he was drunk. But I told him about the Getae, anyway.

He snorted. 'Barbarians. They won't stop me. I'll have Pine Island, I'll build a bridge like Darius and we'll march across.'

'When do you send Hephaestion?' I asked. 'You've sent everyone else. When is it his turn to try for a miracle?'

300

'You are dismissed. I should never have admitted you,' Alexander slurred.

'You're drunk. That's not your way, lord. And I'm here to remind you that it is not all arete. You have a kingdom.' I was walking a sword edge.

He spat and drank again. 'I am invincible,' he said.

'Just such a prophecy that the gods send to drive a man to madness. There's more ways than one to win a battle.' I shrugged. 'We will never storm that island, not with ten thousand canoes.'

He shrugged.

Hephaestion glared at me. 'I would be proud to lead tomorrow's assault,' he said. 'I'm not afraid of it, like Ptolemy,' he added.

'That's right,' I said. 'I'm afraid.' I shrugged. 'Lord, we need another solution. All the good we've done with those victories is being frittered away with these little actions.'

Alexander nodded. 'Begone,' he said.

So I went.

The next morning, Alexander called all his officers together and outlined his new plan. He was as fresh as a new-caught tuna, and his plan was all daring and no sense. We were going to take the fleet and as many soldiers as could be fitted into the canoes and boats, and we were going across the Danube. His point was that by holding both banks, we would force Pine Island to surrender. They couldn't feed themselves.

It was a fine plan, except that there were ten thousand Getae on the far bank, just waiting for us. It sounded to me like hubris of the grandest kind.

But – it sounded better than battering Pine Island for another week while we ran out of food.

I spent two days gathering another forty boats. The banks were stripped bare. On a positive note, the Thracians had given up trying to ambush my patrols. Even they couldn't take any more casualties.

The army was mutinous. It's hard to believe, now, that Alexander's armies were ever mutinous. In fact, they often were. He had a way of expecting superhuman effort too often, of making plans and not explaining them, or showing childish displeasure when the troops failed to achieve success against high odds – in fact, he didn't understand them. When we were at the edge of battle, he understood them, because men at the edge of battle are more alive, more alert, smarter, better men – more like Alexander, in fact.

But the campaign was wearing them out. We'd marched far, and we were at the edge of the world. We were running out of wine and oil, and those were the key supplies for any army of Hellenes. Most of the cavalry and the hypaspists were fighting every day, in scrubby little actions against teenagers – warriors so young we could take no pride in killing them, but their sling stones and arrows hurt us. And the pezhetaeroi were making daily attempts at Pine Island, and failing. Failure is the canker that eats at an army, and two miraculous victories – as good as anything Philip ever won against the Thracians – were immediately offset by the daily defeats at Pine Island, because soldiers are as fickle as whores and twice as costly.

I tried to tell Alexander that. Twice.

The second time was worse. He looked at me – he had his helmet under his arm, and he was about to take the Prodromoi south to make sure our retreat was clear.

'Are they children, to be cosseted?' he asked. 'See to it.'

'Can we set a date for marching home?' I asked. I managed all this under the guise of the sacred Military Journal.

Alexander was looking at the entries for the last few days, and carefully running the spatulate end of the stylus across the casualties for Pine Island. 'Yes,' he said. He was taking this seriously. He was no fool, and if I'm giving that impression, wipe it from your mind. He was as far above me as I am above most men. He just couldn't think like them, and they were mysterious to him. He looked at me under those blond eyelashes and he gave me that rare smile – the look of his full attention.

'How long do I have?' he asked quietly.

'Three weeks,' I answered, because I'd prayed he'd accept my guidance and so I had an answer ready. 'If I let it be known this morning, I think you'll find the men a great deal more willing to try the Danube crossing. They think ... they think we're going to march off the edge of the world.'

'How well they know me,' he said with a gentle smile. 'Let it be done.' He looked at the Military Journal again and furrowed his eyebrows. 'Every ambassador is going to end up reading this, Ptolemy. Keep that in mind when you write. I don't ask that we seem perfect.' He grinned. 'Merely invincible.'

I must have grinned back. To be honest, I was relieved, myself – first, because we were not wintering here, which I had feared he'd try to do, and second, because *this* was the Alexander I loved. He'd been hard to find since the victories started to come.

That morning I summoned all my adjutants and gathered the entries for the day before, and then I passed the word – three weeks. The Feast of Demeter in the Macedonian festival calendar, and we'd march for hearth and home.

Ever work yourself to exhaustion?

And then eat a meal? And you can *feel* the power going into your limbs – you can feel the lifting of the fatigue? Eh? That's how it was after I dismissed my adjutants. I could feel the change.

We loaded men into the boats. The cavalry went on the triremes, a trick we'd learned from Athens, and the infantry went in the canoes and fishing boats. It took us all day to cross the river, and we spent the night just offshore, a fleet of vulnerable dugout canoes overladen with men, armour and long spears. In the morning, we landed with the dawn, and marched inland through fields of oats and wheat that stood almost as high as a man, and we marched at open order, with every infantry-man carrying his spear parallel to the ground so that the glinting heads wouldn't give us away. The cavalry was last ashore, inside a great square protected by the infantry, and we got on our horses without incident. I led my squadron out to the right. Cleitus had the left squadron.

We came out of the fields about three stades from the riverbank, and we could see their fortified camp in the distance. Our element of surprise was total, and we swept towards them quickly, the cavalry well out on the flanks in extended lines, only two deep and ten horse lengths between men, looking for ambushes.

There were none.

We captured an undefended horse herd, and we overran the little makeshift port where they'd been supplying the island. We took four days' supplies for the whole army and another two hundred small boats. The men loaded up with food and bad wine.

The Getae came out of their camp when we set fire to the boats.

Alexander rode along the line, his cloak billowing behind him, and we roared his name, and charged. It wasn't a complicated battle. In fact, there was very little fighting, and we chased them into their camp.

We milled about outside their log rampart, and then I started to call insults to the men on the walls in my best Thracian.

They sent out a warrior.

That's the trouble with challenging men to combat. Sometimes they take you up on it.

Alexander came over to me while I had my sword arm rebandaged. 'You up to this, my friend?' he asked.

The Getae warrior was sitting on his horse under the walls, shouting insults. On our side, my friends were offering me their swords, their spears and their horses.

I settled my helmet on my head, flexed my fingers and vaulted on to Poseidon's broad back.

'I am, Lord King.' I think I was grinning. I was afraid and elated.

'You'll need to do better than last time,' he said, with a grin. He had a point. Kineas had put me down.

Men slapped my back and told me I was lucky, and then I was trotting over the turf towards my adversary. I took a pair of heavy longche from Polystratus, rather than my usual lance.

I trotted forward and waved to my adversary, thinking we would agree on some rules.

He wasn't interested in discussing anything. He came right at me, drew an arrow to his eye and loosed.

At sixty paces, that arrow went right into Poseidon's chest.

Bless my dear horse, he paused and then sprang forward.

The Thracian was controlling his horse with his knees, and he turned away, fitting another arrow to his bow.

Poseidon was running with an arrow three fingers deep in his chest, but he ate the ground between us as the Thracian turned his smaller horse. I closed – fifty paces, forty paces – and then he turned at a gallop and headed due west, along the front of our army.

Poseidon turned to cut his path.

He turned and shot. It was a beautiful shot, and hit my helmet just above my eyes, but the slope of the bronze and the skill of the maker saved me. Two inches lower and he'd have won that fight, and I'd never have been King of Aegypt.

At ten paces he brought the bow up again, and I threw my javelin. Ten paces is nothing to a trained man, and Poseidon, the best horse I ever had, felt my throw coming and flowed into it, so that I threw on his off foot. I hit my target – his horse – in the neck with a heavy spear, and that horse died before I reached him, and my adversary was tangled on the ground with his broken bow.

The Macedonians cheered.

The man came up out of the wreck limping, and he had a sword. He stood his ground, and I slapped him in the head with the spear-point and knocked him unconscious. Then I dragged him by his own saddle rope, tied round his feet, across the front of our army to where the king sat on Bucephalus.

'Was that better, my lord?' I asked.

Alexander's eyes sparkled. He handed me a cup of wine, embraced me and let me bask in the congratulations of all the other Hetaeroi. Say what you will of the former pages – we all respected success, and no one was ever petty enough to conceal admiration for a deed well done. Cleitus was smothered in it after the Woods Battle, and now it was my turn.

I untied the man and turned him over to Polystratus. 'See if you can revive him,' I said. 'A drag across the turf shouldn't have killed him.'

In fact, my head hurt, and Polystratus took my good cavalry Boeotian, shook his head and showed me the bowl. There was a dent as deep as a man's thumb in the front just above the cranium, and the helmet was ruined. It had saved my life three times.

I lay down for a while but Thaïs, quite wisely, didn't let me sleep, but prattled at me and made me walk about and fed me water and honey. When I could see straight and talk well, she let me have a nap.

When I woke, the Thracians had surrendered, and the sound of the army's cheers brought me back to earth.

They didn't actually surrender. But the Thracians on Pine Island agreed to evacuate and surrender one half of their herds, and the Getae agreed to allow them to come over the Danube to resettle, and Alexander forced them to agree that the lands between the pass and the Danube were his to dispose of.

I suspected that this agreement would be nullified the moment they couldn't see our spears, and I was right, but it made Alexander happy – and we'd shown them that they wouldn't be safe *anywhere*, and that was worth something. To be honest, I'm not sure that it was worth the body count. We lost fifty-eight cavalrymen – mostly Hetaeroi – and almost four hundred pezhetaeroi and hypaspitoi. They were fine men in the peak of training. They died, and we got very little in return.

And yet – looked at another way, we got everything in return, because we were building the reputation for invincibility that was better than ten thousand men.

And we did receive an amazing amount of loot and tribute. When we marched for home, we looked more like a nomad nation migrating than a Macedonian army on the march, and Alexander ordered us – the cavalry – to patrol aggressively, because he feared we were so overladen with beasts and gold that we'd be easy pickings for an Illyrian raid. It had happened to Philip years before – when he fought the Sakje of the Great Steppe. He beat them, but they weren't beaten, and they ambushed him on the road home and took his gear and his cattle.

I'd forgotten – look here, it's in the Military Journal – I'd forgotten the Keltoi. Our last day on the river, when all the deals had been made and all our men were glutted with spear-won beef, and Thaïs and I were, in fact, rutting like a stag and a hind in season in our tent, Cleitus came to our tent – he had the worst timing – burst in and turned as red as a Tyrian cloak. Thaïs was astride me, hands locked under my neck, mouth pressed against mine, and I could see Cleitus ...

Oh, I'm a dirty old man. But I didn't stop, and neither did Thaïs. She just grinned.

'The king wants you,' Cleitus said, staring at a hanging carpet.

'I'm ... a little busy, but I'll ... be along ... shortly,' I said.

'Not too shortly,' Thaïs said.

I used to make Cleitus blush just mentioning this incident – the best killer of men in the Macedonian army, the toughest bastard Alexander had, but he'd blush like a virgin. Hah! Fine man, Cleitus. But a little odd.

When I reached the king, he smiled and said, 'I've been counting the minutes,' and laughed. It was as close to a sexual joke as I ever heard him make, and all the officers around him laughed too.

The embassage of Keltoi was twenty men and as many women. They were tall – in fact, they were huge, many of them a head taller than me, and I'm not small. Most were blond, and all of them had beautiful long hair, wrapped and plaited in gold. The women had the largest breasts and the best figures of any race I'd seen – wide hips, tiny waists and blue eyes.

Their language was truly barbaric, but they had dignity and good manners.

They also claimed to rule an empire greater than ours, stretching all the way to Thule. I was derisive, but Alexander was fascinated.

They flattered him, lauding his victories over the Thracians, although they made it clear they'd smacked the Thracians pretty hard themselves.

Alexander nodded after listening patiently. 'Are you, then, the over-lords of these Thracian tribes?' he asked.

The most noble-looking of the men, wearing a sword worth ten of my farms, shrugged. He spoke through a woman interpreter. She didn't look like the rest of them – she was smaller and darker and very pretty, rather than displaying the normal somewhat ethereal beauty of the Keltoi. She smiled a great deal, too. She listened to him and then turned to the king.

'He says – we are kings and lords to the Triballi, when we will it. Never the Getae,' she added.

Alexander nodded. 'I am now the lord of the Triballi and the Getae,' he said.

All the Keltoi laughed.

Alexander snapped at her. 'What are they laughing at?'

One of the Keltoi women pointed at the sky and said something and they all laughed again.

The interpreter looked as if she was afraid. The smiles were gone.

'What did she say?' Alexander demanded.

'Nothing, lord,' she said.

Alexander shook his head. 'I demand to know!' he said.

She shrugged. 'She asked if you were also lord of the clouds.'

The Keltoi woman spoke again, with vehemence.

Alexander ignored her and turned back to the richest man. 'Are you here to swear your allegiance to me?' he asked.

There was much talk. Then the interpreter said, 'They say – no.' She shrugged.

Alexander pointed at his army. We, as an army, were not at our most impressive, as most of the infantry were busy loading spear-won wagons with spear-won loot, wool and hangings and carpets and furs and some gold.

'You should fear my army, which I can march anywhere in the world,' Alexander said.

The Keltoi talked among themselves, and then the interpreter shook her head and expostulated.

'I think they are saying we should sod off,' I muttered to Marsyas.

Marsyas grinned. In some strange way, it was entertaining to watch these rich barbarians be utterly unimpressed with us.

Finally, the dark woman stood in front of Alexander with her shoulders square as if she was ready to resist torture. 'They say that if you brought an army this small to their lands, they might ignore it. If you brought a real army, they would bury it under the weight of their chariot wheels and the hooves of their horses and the steel of their swords. They say that you have no idea what is north of the Danube, while they know where Pella is and where Athens is. And Rome and Carthage, too, they say. And the queen asks – would you like to swear fealty to her? She says she will be a gentle overlord.'

I burst into laughter. I couldn't stop myself. I slapped my thighs and roared, and Alexander looked at me. His anger dissipated, and he joined me. He laughed, and Perdiccas and Hephaestion laughed, and Marsyas laughed.

And all the Keltoi laughed.

Somehow it reminded me of the visit to Diogenes.

FOURTEEN

‎—⁓—

e marched back over the Shipka Pass with our herds and our loot, and forty days' worth of messages caught up with us all at once, and all the news was bad. The whole western border of Macedon was in arms – the Illyrians had risen, and were coming at us, to a man. Cleitus of Illyria – don't blame me if everyone has the same name – had fifteen thousand men, and he had made a federation with two of the wilder northern tribes – the Autaratians and the Taulantians. According to our intelligence, the two northern tribes were coming down on our route of march.

Let me add that the best of our intelligence was from Thaïs. Thaïs had a stream of couriers, now – letters from Athens, letters from Pella, messages from the Triballians behind us.

'It keeps me busy,' she said. 'It's really no different from organising a party.'

I had to laugh. We were good at tactical intelligence collection – the Prodromoi and the hypaspitoi and the new Agrianian Psiloi were all excellent scouts, and they collected information and passed it back by couriers with professional competence, but at the next level we were still barbarians. Philip had some excellent sources, but they had all been intensely personal – his own friends in Athens and Sparta and Thebes and Persepolis, who sent him news. Alexander didn't run his life that way, and we had to have new sources.

I hadn't even seen the need. But Thaïs lived in the world of exchange of news. She bought news when she was a hetaera – now she merely bought more. And ran some of the sources herself.

Langarus, the King of the Agrianians, met us at the foot of the Shipka Pass. He'd covered our rear for two months, and now he was nervous. He had about four thousand men, and superb men at that – but the Illyrian actions meant that his neighbours might just choose to plunder him on their way to Macedon.

He was, I have to say, a fantastic ally. He stayed and watched that pass while his own crops burned. I'm not sure another ally so loyal existed in all the bowl of the world.

I read all Thaïs's news during a long afternoon while the tent flapped in the early autumn wind, and then I took a stack of scrolls, tally sticks and small notes on papyrus to Alexander. He was sitting with Langarus and Perdiccas and a new man, who was introduced to me as Nicanor, son of Parmenio. He'd come from Asia to take command of the hypaspitoi, and to represent his father.

He glanced at me as I came in and then went back to talking to the king.

Alexander heard him out – he was discussing a point about Asia, of course. And then his eyes met mine.

'It's worse than it looks,' I said. 'I think the Illyrians are getting support from within Macedon.' I started to synopsise the reporting, but Nicanor (as yet unintroduced) cut me off.

'I'll read them when I have time,' he said. 'Carry on.'

I looked at him. And laughed. It was becoming my new way of dealing with everything. 'And you are?'

'Your new strategos,' he said. 'I am Nicanor son of Parmenio.'

Alexander shook his head. 'I'm sorry, Nicanor,' he said. 'I have promised your father that you can command the hypaspitoi, but you will not be strategos. I'll command myself.'

'With all due respect,' Nicanor said, 'this is a time of real peril – not a time for boyish heroics. Pater sent me to put down the Illyrians. Riding about hunting Thracian refugees is not going to help you beat the Illyrians. Lord.'

I didn't have to force a laugh. I could see this would be entertaining, and I sat down.

Nicanor turned and looked at me. 'Who the fuck are you to sit down in the presence of your king?' he asked.

Alexander settled his shoulders against the tent wall and smiled gently.

So be it. 'I'm Ptolemy,' I said. 'If it has escaped your notice – I'm the largest landowner in Macedon after the king. I'm somatophylakes to the king. I grew up with him. And I have no idea who you are.'

'Your insolence is astounding,' Nicanor said.

I turned to Alexander. 'May I smack him around, lord?' I asked.

Alexander shook his head. 'No. But Nicanor, most of the men in this army have earned their rank, through years of hard campaigning. To them, you are a newcomer and you will have to prove yourself. You will command the hypaspitoi under my supervision and direct orders until I say otherwise.'

Nicanor turned red and then white and then red. 'Lord,' he said. He took a deep breath. 'You have been ill advised, if you imagine that you and your boys are ready to face the Illyrians in a campaign.'

Alexander didn't explode. He nodded. 'Would you care to place a wager?' he asked.

When Nicanor stomped out of the tent, Alexander sent Nearchus after him.

'Watch him,' Alexander said. Then he turned and sighed. 'So it begins,' he said. 'Parmenio will never see me as an adult – nor forgive me for outmanoeuvring him. Eventually ...' He shrugged. 'Never mind. Give me Thaïs's gleanings.'

I ran through what we knew, or guessed, about Cleitus of Illyria.

Hephaestion and Langarus had sat through all of this, and when I finished, Langarus made a face. 'I think you should let Ptolemy here take Nicanor's head,' he said. 'That one will make trouble.'

'Perhaps in Pella,' Alexander said. 'Ptolemy, am I right in thinking he'll make no trouble here?'

I nodded. I was glad he was asking my opinion about how the men felt – he needed the help – but in this case he was right. We'd just rolled over the Thracians – the men were worshipping their king like a god. Nicanor was not going to get anywhere with them.

Langarus smiled like a wolf. 'Well – never mind him, then. I'll take the Autaratians – I'll head north in the morning along the old road. You go and take Cleitus, and we'll crush this thing before it spreads.'

Langarus was, as I have mentioned, a pearl among allies.

We sent almost half the infantry home with all our loot and all the baggage. We kept about a third of the beasts – all cattle – to be able to drive our food with us, and we marched before the sun was up in the morning, heading west. We were in top physical shape, and we had just won a string of victories. The defeats of Pine Island were forgotten. We were invincible, and we raced across the Paeonian Mountains at a speed that was unheard of for an army with so many infantry. We'd marched three thousand stades in a month – now it was high summer, and even the high passes were comfortable.

Alexander's goal was to turn Cleitus's flank by rapid marches before he'd heard of us. He wanted to invest Cleitus's capital at Pellium before Cleitus could gather reinforcements – especially from Glaucias of the Taulantians. It was an ambitious plan that required that we march eighty stades a day through mountains, and while we could do it, the cattle could not. Our carts started to break down, and our animals were dying – baggage animals cannot be pushed.

But neither could Alexander. He ordered all the baggage animals slaughtered. We ate for two days. Then everyone shouldered as much food as he could carry – officers and Hetaeroi included – and we marched without baggage. My whole camp went from a tent and three slaves and a cook pot with other pots nesting inside – to a bear fur robe that rolled on the crupper of my saddle, two cloaks and some spare chitons. I kept Ochrid to make my food and sent my other slaves home.

In truth, we looked more like a defeated army than a victorious one, and I worried every day about the weather. Five days of hard, cold rain in the mountains, and we'd have been in trouble. Even as it was, I knew – as keeper of the Military Journal – that we were losing men to desertion and exhaustion.

I had another run-in with Nicanor. There was no report from the hypaspists three days running, and when I approached Alectus, he simply made a face.

So I went to Nicanor.

'You understand the Military Journal?' I asked him, without pre-amble.

He shrugged. 'Send it to me and I'll show you how to keep it,' he said. 'You do it wrong, and it is full of information it doesn't need to have.'

'I keep it as the king commands,' I said. 'You need to send an officer with your reports.'

Nicanor didn't even look at me. 'No. When you serve under my father, you will learn your place. For the moment – don't imagine you can give me orders. I have heard how you fucked up the hypaspitoi and had to be replaced – eh? Don't play with me, boy.'

He had never served in the pages, and in many ways, despite his years of service under his father, he was soft. I threw him to the ground and rotated his left arm until he made a mewling noise.

'I am not a boy. Next time you call me that, I'll kill you and stuff your dick down your throat, understand? Your father is not worth shit here, understand?' I was angry, and spit flew from my lips. 'Your father is all but a convicted traitor, and if you so much as breathe in the wrong way with these troops, you will cease to be. *Do you understand?*' I wrenched his shoulder with every word.

He said nothing. He was going to tough it out.

So I wrenched his shoulder harder, and he screamed. I had a knee in his back, and his Thessalian bodyguards were just a little too late – and Alectus was there, and so was Philip Longsword.

The two Thessalians were induced to stand perfectly still.

'This is not Asia,' I said. 'Your father is *not* the king. And if I rip this arm off, *nothing* will happen to me. Now – order Philip to have an adjutant send reports to the Military Journal, or by Herakles my ancestor, I will make sure the hypaspitoi need a new commander today.'

'Fuck *youuuuaaheeh*!' he said. And then he collapsed. 'Do it – just stop!'

I stopped. Looked around. 'This was a disciplinary matter, and nothing will be said about it unless the king asks,' I said. I let Nicanor go, and stepped away.

As soon as he was with his bodyguards, he turned on me.

'I'll have you skinned alive,' he said.

I walked over to him and his Thessalians, who understood better than he did, and did nothing.

He flinched.

'Go back to Asia or learn our ways,' I said.

Macedon, eh? Tough crowd. And I had a temper, back then. Really, Parmenio made a mistake in not sending his sons to serve as pages. Nicanor would have known better. He'd have been one of us.

He never did learn, and neither did his brother, but that's another story.

Fifteen days over the mountains. Alexander took me to task for beating Nicanor, and I took his admonishment with good grace, since Hephaestion told me in private that Alexander had blessed my name.

We were bleeding men by the time we reached Pellium. We'd come too far, too fast, and we lost more than a hundred veterans in the mountains. Alexander didn't care, and you couldn't make him care. He was on top of the world.

We came down the valley of the Asopus like a torrent, and our cavalry patrols were like a thunderbolt. Cleitus thought we were a thousand stades away.

In fact, I nearly caught him myself. I was leading two files of Hetaeroi in support of the Prodromoi, because the king wanted us to be able to do their job, too – a brilliant idea, really. So we took rotations as scouts, and it was my day, and we were fifty stades ahead of the hypaspitoi when we heard screams.

We were at the head of the valley, and we could see the ripening grain all the way to the foot of the rocky ridge where the grim fortress lurked – a true robber baron, our Cleitus, with his impregnable fort on a high rock so he would never need to fear the revenge of his many foes.

Somewhere away on my right, a child was screaming.

I had fifteen of the best warriors in the world. So I turned my horse and rode to the sound of the screams.

We burst out of the trees to see a ring of richly dressed men – furs, good wool cloaks, gold-mounted swords – and a big natural stone altar covered with blood. There were two sheep's carcasses, and three dead children – two boys and girl. I saw it all in a glance.

The priest had his copper knife at the throat of the fourth child.

In truth, had Thaïs not been pregnant, I'd have captured Cleitus. He was right there, watching the sacrifices to see if the campaign against Alexander would be propitious. But her pregnancy had awakened something in me. That girl – she might have been two – set something off, and my first javelin took the priest high in the breast. He never got to cut her throat, but fell away from her, and she stood there and screamed while Nearchus and Cleomenes and all my lads started to kill the Illyrians around the altar.

Had I been a little quicker, or not wasted my javelin on the priest, I'd have had Cleitus. I didn't know who he was, but he was there – we took a dozen noble prisoners and they all blabbed. He must have run the moment the javelins flew, and he must not have been dressed very well.

We killed a few of them and took most of the rest. I carried the girl back to camp. We had very few camp followers, but Ochrid took her. And of course, as soon as we made camp on the plain below the fortress at Pellium, we acquired hundreds of Illyrian women. Women are attracted by successful soldiers. I picked up a woman old enough to know her own mind and purchased her services as a nanny for the girl, whom I called Olympias for her imperious way with Ochrid. She was a funny little imp, and I liked her.

The problem was, we weren't really all that successful. We occupied the fertile valley easily enough, and when part of his army came down from the hills, we chewed them up. But the bulk of his forces out-numbered us, and he had a heavy garrison in the fortress.

Alexander sent to Pella for siege machines and specialists. A small convoy reached us right away – the light catapults we'd left in the Paeonians came almost immediately, and we assembled them.

But then, Glaucias arrived and occupied the high ground behind us in the passes.

It was, to be frank, one of the worst errors I had ever seen Alexander make. He'd said – back there at the foot of Shipka – that we needed to strike *before* the Illyrians combined.

We failed, and they combined.

They started to eat our foraging parties. Our Agrianians and our archers could hold their own, but the slaves – what was left of them – were taken or killed.

The last of our Thracian cattle were killed and eaten, and we started on the food available in the little valley below the fortress. I knew – it was my job – that we had about five days' food.

Alexander knew. We had an officers' meeting – forty senior officers.

Alexander laid out his plan – a simple one – and we all listened in silence.

Nicanor waited until the king was done. 'This is foolishness, lord. Send me to negotiate. If this army is lost, the army of Asia will have to be recalled.'

Alexander ignored him, and the rest of us saluted and headed for our units. On the way out of the tent, Hephaestion could be heard asking Nicanor how his shoulder was. And if he'd ever worried that the other one might be made to match it.

How Nicanor must have hated us. It still pleases me.

We marched off by regiments, out into the grain fields at the centre of the plain. We only had about seven thousand men, and we filled less than five stades' frontage.

I'd written Alexander's orders down on wax when he gave them, and there they are, copied fair in the Military Journal. We moved in line – eight deep – to the centre of the plain, and then we wheeled by subsections – ten files to a subsection – wheeled to the right to form a column, and then marched a few stades and formed front by inclining our subsections, so that we started in column, moved into a deep echelon, and then as the formed phalanx moved at half-step, the rest of the expended column gradually caught up – a beautiful manoeuvre, with the hypaspitoi on the right and the Agrianians on the left – the new Agrianians, not the ones integrated into the hypaspitoi. The Hetaeroi squadrons were on the wings, split left and right, as usual.

Then we retired from the centre by sections – right/left/right, the phalanx facing an imaginary enemy shrinking and shrinking while the column marched away to the rear – a manoeuvre we practised to be ready for a day of heavy defeat. And to the rear, the phalanx suddenly expanded at the run and faced in the new direction.

It was all well done – and best of all, it was done in total silence. Oh, here and there some awkward sod got struck by his phylarch or his file closer, but the effect was awe-inspiring.

We did it for three hours. We could see the Illyrians, up on the ridges above our little valley, moving around – gathering to watch – wandering down the hills to the edge of the woods. The bolder ones came right out into the fields to watch.

The whole valley was only twenty stades long and ten wide, and every time we changed formation or direction, we eased a little closer to the valley entrance. There was a low knoll there between two steep hills where the enemy had posted some armoured infantry and some archers to stop us from getting out of the valley.

We changed front to the right and then to the left. We faced about. We advanced with ponderous slowness, our lines perfectly dressed, our officers silenced. Even the horses were silent.

And every manoeuvre brought us a few paces closer to the knoll.

We advanced by wings, leaving the centre standing fast, and then wheeled the whole army all the way around, silently, swinging like an enormous and very slow door.

At the completion of that silent, slow wheel, the centre under Alexander was just about two hundred paces from the knoll.

Alexander raised his right arm and pumped it, once, and every man in the army gave the war cry. And then the whole army charged. The spears slammed down into the fighting stance, and the men of the pezhetaeroi charged at a dead run. No ponderous slowness at all. We were on the knoll before the Illyrians could react – and the cavalry rode right up those steep hills.

Cavalry doesn't need cohesion to fight. It's a lesson that infantry get to learn over and over.

I was the first man up the left-hand hill, and it was thick with Illyrians, many of whom were completely unarmed. But more of them were armed, and a lot of them had spears and bows, and we took hits. And every one of us had to pick our way over rocks and steep slopes.

Well – that's what courage is for.

My long spear was perfect for the fight – I could reach up and punch it at a man a little above me on the hill, and it was long enough to pierce an eye socket a horse length away.

Illyrians are brave, and skilled hill fighters, and they tried to get under Poseidon, who was well recovered from his wound. But I used my javelins carefully and then my lance, which I ended up throwing into some bastard who needed it, and then I had the Keltoi sword in my hand, and I was at the top of the rocky hill, and I had beaten Perdiccas, who was still climbing the far hill.

Down in the valley below me, on the knoll, Alexander had the hypaspitoi formed in a small phalanx – now facing the way we had come, because we'd cleared the hills on either side and now, by the grace of the gods and pure luck and daring, the Illyrians were in the valley and we held the knoll.

My men cleared our hill – but we could already see that the victory would be fleeting. We couldn't charge down the hill, and only surprise – complete and total fucking surprise, may I add – got us up that hill. Now the Illyrians were coming to their senses, and their chieftains were arming up and getting their warriors ready to rush us.

I sent Cleomenes down to ask Alexander if we were to dismount and hold the hilltops.

He waved us away as soon as he heard Cleomenes. I didn't need to wait for orders. I ordered my troopers to file down the back of the hill – shallower, and better riding – but some men still had to dismount to negotiate the paths. Despite which, we were down the hills before the Illyrians could come at us, and we formed wedges in the rear of the hypaspitoi.

The hypaspitoi demonstrated the retreat by files from the centre manoeuvre that the pezhetaeroi had done earlier. The hypaspitoi did it in the face of a real enemy, but as soon as their front had shrunk enough to make them vulnerable, I charged from behind them with my squadron. We dispersed the Illyrians and rode over them, past them, and into our camp.

We had almost no baggage, you'll recall, but I was damned if I was losing Ochrid or the little girl. I got him on a horse and her across my saddle-bow, and then we cut our way back through the Illyrians – who were as angry as hornets and just about as organised.

Perdiccas's squadron charged as soon as we were on the knoll, and by the time they came back, the hypaspitoi had marched away. Then Perdiccas retired, and I covered him. It was all just like parade-ground practice, because the Illyrians didn't really have any cavalry and they weren't really interested in pursuit, anyway.

We had no food and no baggage and we'd just lost all our slaves.

It was ten days' march back to Macedon.

But we hadn't lost a fight and we were intact, and I thought that Alexander had done very well indeed.

Just goes to show how little I knew him.

We marched for two days, a little more than a hundred stades through the mountains. We had no reports from anywhere, and that, by itself, was suspicious. Someone was killing our couriers.

Two hours before sun-up on the third day, Cleitus wakened me.

'The king wants you,' he said.

Well – no interruptions in Illyria. I was sleeping in my boots. I got up, pulled my Thracian cloak around me in the pre-dawn cold and followed Cleitus.

For the first time in ten days, it started to rain.

Morale was going to plummet.

The king was standing by a huge fire – a fire made by cutting down three dead trees and lighting a small fire under the intersection. You can warm a great many men that way.

If the fire is big and hot enough, it launches a column of smoke and heat so dense that the rain won't penetrate it. Seriously – you can sleep dry, if you can stay close enough to the fire. And remember, we had no tents of any kind by this time – even Alexander's pavilion had been abandoned to the Illyrians.

'We march in one hour,' he said. It was Nicanor and Hephaestion, me and Perdiccas, and the three remaining regimental commanders of the pezhetaeroi. Black Cleitus was the unofficial commander of the Psiloi.

Cleitus frowned. 'Lord, they are not behind us.' He shrugged. 'We have all the time in the world.'

Alexander grinned. 'We're not going to Macedon,' he said. 'We're going back to Pellium.'

Of course we were. Where had I been?

Alexander gave me charge of the 'new' Agrianians and my Hetaeroi, and we moved as fast as unencumbered, hungry men can march – all the way back up our own trail. The whole valley was deserted. We rode fast, and the tribesmen ran alongside us like hounds. Behind my last files came the hypaspitoi and the other Hetaeroi and the archers, under Perdiccas and Alexander. Ahead of us were the Prodromoi. They picked up or killed every Illyrian on the road – the track, the pair of cart ruts and deep mud puddles that passed for a road in Illyria.

But we moved.

And when darkness fell, we had a new wrinkle. The Prodromoi had spaced men out along the track, with torches – guides – every half a stade.

We kept moving.

All night.

That was new.

I was done in when the sky started to get lighter. I was leading my light riding horse, saving Poseidon for the battle. My legs were like hot lead, and my ankles had twisted and twisted going over the rocks, and my feet were soaked and I had thick crap between my toes, because in the dark you can't see where the worst puddles are.

Nicanor halted just behind me. He was the first man in the hy- paspists, and I was shepherding the rear of my vanguard.

'He's either insane, or brilliant,' Nicanor said. 'And if you try for me right now, I have a sword in my hand.'

I looked back at him. He wasn't afraid of me. None of Parmenio's sons were yellow. 'It wasn't personal,' I said. 'You had it coming. If you obey the king and join with us, the king will accept you.'

'Hmm,' Nicanor said. 'If the king pulls this off, I may be convinced.' He shook his head. 'My pater's going to take even more convincing, though.'

'Fair enough,' I said. It was. I knew the king didn't want conflict with Parmenio's faction. He wanted them to join him, and he was win- ning Nicanor over. He was, after all, the most charming man ever born, like one of the very gods when he chose.

'But I owe you for the shoulder, and no mistake,' he added.

'Think of Pausanias's fate with Attalus, and count yourself lucky,' I said.

We were never friends.

An hour after first light, the Prodromoi reported that the whole enemy army was down in the valley in our old camp, and that they had no guards, no earthworks, no fortifications and no ambushes.

Alexander detached the Hetaeroi, the Agrianians and the archers to hit them immediately, while the hypaspitoi formed in close order on the knoll. Messengers were sent back for the pezhetaeroi, to hurry them along. They'd fallen behind in the dark.

We didn't wait for them, and they were never required.

We fell on them when most of them were still in their blankets. The Agrianians went in first, and then the archers came in from the west, and they were silent and grim. I never saw them, and Illyrians died – throats slit, spears in bellies – without waking. By the time the alarm was given the 'battle' was over. My Hetaeroi charged the camp on horseback, and we were the least effective part of the raid. And the raid turned into the 'battle', because the Illyrians lost their nerve – Cleitus lost his nerve and ran for his fortress, and the silent Agrianian killers ripped his retinue to shreds.

It was horrible work, and we did it without much thought – I wasn't in a single 'fight' and my life was never at risk. I killed men who were running, and I killed men who were sleeping, and I killed a great many men who were simply cowering away from my lance-point with empty eyes.

And then we were done.

It was noon before the pezhetaeroi caught up. They'd taken a wrong turn in the mountains. By then we'd recovered our slaves and camp servants, taken a horde of prisoners and we were mostly asleep. Except that we had sentries, and order.

I was awakened from a brief and exhausted sleep to find the King of Macedon standing over me.

'Something wrong?' I murmured, or something equally banal.

His eyes sparkled, and he seemed to be bursting with energy. 'Everyone's asleep!' he said. By which he meant Hephaestion.

I got up and dusted the pine needles off my chiton. 'Everyone's exhausted,' I said.

Ochrid got up when I got up. He raised a bronze kettle and an eyebrow.

I nodded. Ochrid was an essential part of my life – he knew I wanted something, and he made hot wine and water with spices without interrupting my conversation.

'That was the best battle,' Alexander said, out of nowhere. He was all but bouncing up and down. 'Did you see – did you see me? I was with the Agrianians. I was the first man into the camp.'

I hadn't seen him. It had been dark, and I'd been worried about everything from enemy alertness to my retreat route if it all went wrong.

'I was the first into camp and I killed a sentry. Alectus said I did it perfectly.' He grinned.

These moods were delicate and easy to puncture, and the blackness that followed was worth avoiding.

'Well done, lord. Killing a sentry is the most dangerous task, and deserving of the highest honour.'

'That's just what Alectus said!' Alexander's smile grew wider. 'I wasn't sure you'd understand. You don't always.'

I shrugged. I was looking around for help. This was Hephaestion's job, not mine. 'I don't always agree with you, lord.'

Alexander looked away. 'I'm supposed to admire that in you, but to tell the truth, I'm not sure you are ever right. Sometimes I think you disagree just to be contrary.'

That was scary talk. 'Lord, I try to keep you in touch with the common men.'

He nodded. 'I know you think so, Ptolemy. But I understand them perfectly. They are cattle – but glorious cattle, and I know how to make them rise above themselves. You want them to stay comfortable, down in the mud.'

I want to keep them from cutting your throat, you arrogant popinjay. Demosthenes isn't all wrong, either. I can remember thinking that.

319

'It's all right, Ptolemy. You're the best of my generals – but you can't be expected to understand everything I can see.' He put a hand on my back – too tentatively, not quite the right physical contact, the way a certain kind of boy touches girls – not enough firmness, not enough confidence.

He could conquer the world, but he wasn't all that good with people. Unless they wanted to worship him, in which case he was perfect.

I remember giving him a cynical smile. 'I do my best to keep up,' I said. I pointed at Nicanor to change the subject. 'Parmenio's son is coming around.'

Alexander nodded. Ochrid brought us cups of warm, spiced wine, and Alexander took his and nodded gratefully. 'Thanks,' he said.

Alexander never noticed slaves. It was a sign.

Ochrid almost stumbled. 'My pleasure, lord,' he said.

Alexander beamed at him. Then turned back to me. 'He's a good man, your ... what's his name?'

Ochrid had been serving Alexander for three years. 'Ochrid, my lord.'

Alexander nodded. 'Nicanor will come around in time, but only until his father is here, and then something will have to be done.' He shrugged. 'You know that Attalus handed me all his treasonable correspondence – all Parmenio's, all Demosthenes' – before I had him killed. Yes?'

I had not *known*, but I had had my suspicions.

'Parmenio was in the plot up to the hilt,' Alexander said.

Now, I was no fan of Attalus, and I had little time for Parmenio, but my contrary streak was aching to point out to Alexander that before he killed his father, he'd been the plotter, and *they* were the faithful servants of the king. Luckily, I didn't mention it.

I looked around to make sure no one was listening. 'I think we're facing an organised opposition right now,' I said. 'Thaïs believes—'

Alexander nodded. 'I know what Thaïs believes,' he said.

'Do you have any news from Greece?' I asked.

Alexander shook his head. 'Thebes has already been taught her lesson. They won't rise again.'

I felt like a conspirator. 'They would if they thought that someone else was going to be King of Macedon,' I said.

'Amyntas?' Alexander asked. 'Or Caranus?'

I shrugged. 'If you like.' Amyntas son of Perdiccas was the heir apparent by virtue of being the last legitimate claimant to the throne left alive. He had ties to Attalus and to Parmenio – marriage ties, family ties, office-holding ties and landownership ties.

Caranus – I hope you are keeping track – was Cleopatra's son by

Philip, Alexander's father. He was two years old and unlikely to make trouble for a would-be dynast, meaning that he was the perfect candidate to figurehead a rebellion.

'Parmenio and Attalus and Amyntas were negotiating just four months ago,' Alexander said.

'Fuck me,' I said. I hadn't known, and I wasn't cynical enough, yet. It's amazing how cynical you have to be to keep up with human behaviour.

Alexander nodded. 'When we leave the circle of the mountains, it is at least possible that we march to face Parmenio at Pella.' He looked at the entrance to the pass. 'And it is at least possible that Nicanor is here to watch us and do what damage he can.'

I had little love for the arrogant bastard, but – 'That makes no sense, lord,' I said. 'Parmenio – whatever his faults – loves his sons like he loves himself. He wouldn't sacrifice one.'

Alexander gave me the look of a man to whom all other men were expendable. 'I can't trust to that,' he said.

'The lads need a rest soon,' I pointed out.

'So you always say,' Alexander said.

'We've marched seven thousand stades, according to the Military Journal. We've fought four major actions and two dozen skirmishes.' I raised an eyebrow. 'Lord, that's four years' worth of campaigning in one summer. They're tired. *I'm tired.*'

Alexander finished his wine. 'I'm tired too,' he said, very quietly. 'But we're not done. I can feel it.'

Three hundred stades south of Pellium we found Langarus and his little army of Agrianians marching to our relief. They had won two actions and burned a swathe through the home country of the northern Illyrian tribes, and the Illyrian confederacy was smashed to pieces.

But Langarus had opened the road to Macedon as he came up it behind us, and with him were a dozen couriers, elements of our camp, the siege train, and Thaïs.

Thaïs wasn't showing, and she was riding astride, dressed as a man, with a big straw hat, and only her maidservant, the black woman. I embarrassed my friends by kissing her in public – most of them had no idea who she was in her men's clothes, and the image of me kissing a groom in public was indelibly printed on them. I took a great deal of ribbing.

That was fine.

Thaïs had intelligence – dozens of reports, most of them from Athens. I took her to the king, and left them together.

She told me that he listened to her, read the letters she had and then wrote a long letter to his mother – it took him an hour to write, and he did it entirely himself, with no secretary.

Alexander offered Thaïs anything she wanted – a rich marriage, an estate. She told him that when the time was right, she would ask her favour, and he kissed her and swore by Herakles.

We lay together that night. The sex was emotional but not very athletic. She was distant.

I prodded and pulled at her until she snapped.

'It's all coming apart,' she said. 'And friends of mine will pay. People I like are going to betray Alexander, and he will kill them, and I've chosen sides.' She cried in my arms.

In the morning, she rode back down the hills to Pella, and I sent Polystratus and all my grooms to guard her.

Alexander was wrong. The Greeks had stabbed us in the back.

Demosthenes, that paragon among Hellenes, had arranged for a cloak to be shown, covered in blood, in Thebes and Athens. The story was that Alexander had been killed in a rout in the Thracian hills.

Thebes laid our garrison under siege and some Macedonians were murdered. Athens vacillated – Demosthenes was not universally trusted or popular, and men like Phokion and Kineas's father were powerful enough to stop outright rebellion. But Athens was on the brink.

Sparta was calling up her allies.

But that was not the worst of it.

In Asia, the new King of Kings had finally reacted to Parmenio's presence. He had sent his best general – Memnon, the brilliant mercenary officer – with a largely Greek army to turn Parmenio out of the Troad, a region bounded by the Dardanelles to the north-west, by the Aegean Sea to the west and separated from the rest of Anatolia by the massif that forms Mount Ida, drained by two main rivers, the Scamander and the Simois, which join at the area containing the ruins of Troy.

He crossed Mount Ida and almost caught Parmenio by surprise at Cyzicus, and then slipped past him and took one of his supply bases at Lampsacus. Calas, one of Parmenio's brigadiers, lost an action and had to retire – in the messages, it sounded as if he'd been trounced. Parmenio had given up two years' conquests in Ionia. And worst of all, Darius, this new and powerful King of Kings, had offered Athens and Demosthenes three hundred talents of gold to ally with him and Thebes against Macedon.

Athens and Thebes held few fears for us. Right or wrong, we were sure we could take them. But Athens and Thebes backed by internal rebellion inside Macedon and the Great King – especially if Parmenio was complicit ...

'Look on the bright side,' I said. I was drinking wine with the king, Hephaestion and Langarus. 'Parmenio isn't waiting for us on the plain in front of Pella. He's trapped in the Troad, and he can't even get his army across the straits. The Great King has done us a favour.'

Alexander raised his cup in my direction, as if toasting to me. 'Sometimes,' the king said, 'you and I share a thought. You are a deeper man than you appear, Farm Boy.'

Well, take that as a compliment if you want. Alexander had a way of being at his most offensive when it was his intention to compliment.

We marched next day, from deep in Illyria, almost due south. It was another brutal march, and there's no great story to tell – but if you look at the Military Journal you can see that we averaged a hundred stades a day, in mountains.

That's the stark fact. A hundred stades on mountain tracks – tracks pounded to slush, mud and rock after a hundred men went over them, tracks where no wagon wheel could go and where, sometimes, the cavalry had to go by a completely different route from the infantry. Most nights, we slept without fires in early-autumn conditions, wrapped in blankets, sleeping on rocks.

Sometimes the rocks held the heat of the day. There are some rocks that are quite comfortable. Ask any veteran.

There was no wood.

No grain for horses.

No wine, no oil, too little food and no fire to cook it.

And little things began to spiral into big things. Imagine the wear that our nailed sandals had taken. The thongs that bound them had probably all snapped and been replaced by the time we were south of Pellium, but in the mountains, the soles themselves began to give way. Men's shoulder-bag straps broke. The porpakes on our aspides were bent, deformed, sometimes separating from the wood of the shields. Spear shafts all had a cast to them – every time a soldier leans his spear against a barn, it bends a little. Javelin heads rattled when you picked them up, because successive cold nights and warm days worked the rivets. The beautiful homespun wool of a good soldier's chiton, made by his wife or his sisters, was threadbare and lacked warmth, or worn through to holes; his chlamys was filthy and brown and ragged like a beggar's, and knife blades were dull – or snapped. There weren't a thousand sharp razors left in the army, because men dumped their sharpening stones when they were tired. Swords were like iron clubs.

All of us were as skinny as children in a hill town and most of us had lice.

And we had *won* all our battles.

But we'd been living like this since before winter – and habituated as we were, men's bodies were starting to break down. As an example – I began to pull muscles – in my sides – every day, just climbing and letting myself down the mountains. Just walking. I hadn't had a massage in ten months.

But Alexander was at his best when he was desperate. He communicated to his men that this was a gamble, and that the throne and empire were at stake – and that he took their trust for granted and that he needed them. He went from mess group to mess group every evening, which was unlike him – he wasn't aloof, he listened when common men talked, and he made them promises – promises of rest when Greece was returned to obedience. And promises of loot I didn't think we could fulfil.

We rose in the dark and we didn't get to sleep until darkness fell again. In between, we marched.

Some days, I could look back from where I was near the lead of the column – mostly single file – and down a mountain valley I could see our army stretching back ten stades or more, filling every trail.

Villages emptied ahead of us.

That was just as well, because when we found a village, we looted it down to picked bones, and the bones were broken to get at the marrow.

And that will give you an idea of what it cost to go a hundred stades a day across the mountains.

We came out of the mountains in northern Thessaly. We raced across the Thessalian plain fast enough to shock every man we came across, but slowly enough to feed our horses to bursting on the good Thessalian grain – and grass – every day for four days. Our men ate beef and goat and lamb and bread – ate sausage even as they marched. Thessaly was friendly and had magazines and the king – who had no money at all – had credit there. We ate our way south.

I led the cavalry patrol that seized the Gates of Fire. I knew the way, knew the passes, and I was there and in possession – with a powerful sense that I'd done all this before – and there was no opposition. The grumblers in every regiment began to suggest we were attacking nothing.

We marched over the mountains to Onchestus and no one troubled us with so much as a sling stone.

And then we marched down on to the plains of Boeotia, the dance floor of Ares, and the race was run. The Athenians had not marched to the aid of Thebes, and Thebes did not have a Persian army camped under its sheltering walls.

That night, Alexander received letters from Pella, and a report that our siege train and most of our heavy baggage – including tents – was just five days behind us. Antipater had moved quickly, spending money Alexander didn't have. In a few days, we were going to have twenty-six thousand soldiers.

Alexander dispatched heralds to Thebes. He sent them excellent terms – already, his mind was full of Asia. Or perhaps it always had been, but the spectre of Persian gold at Athens and Thebes brought home to him that Asia was not just waiting for conquest – Persia might, indeed, strike back at him. At every campfire across the Thessalian plain, he'd explained to us that he would be easy on the Thebans if they would bend the knee quickly, because he wanted to get fresh troops across the Bosporus before winter.

In his messages, he announced that he understood that they had been misled – and assuming him dead, had acted appropriately. He simply pointed out that he was not dead. He offered to meet a delegation and *affirm the ancient liberties of the Polis.*

The next morning, we marched early. Once again, I had the Prodromoi and the Hetaeroi, with orders to choose a camp – carefully, and with due *respect* for Thebes.

Well, I had little respect for Thebes, but I knew what Alexander wanted. Despite which, I fanned the Prodromoi out fifteen stades either side of our approach road, and I put strong parties of Agrianians in a chain behind them and kept the Hetaeroi together as a strike force.

Just another routine day, marching through Greece.

Before noon, the Prodromoi officers were reporting near-combat contacts, and parties of Theban aristocratic horsemen who they flushed from cover – olive groves, mostly – with flanking moves and who rode away. Since they had restrictive rules of engagement – in effect, we'd been told not to engage unless the Thebans started it – the Prodromoi just manoeuvred them out of their ill-set ambushes and continued forward. But that sort of thing is exhausting and annoying work, and by late morning, I was being begged for permission to 'make an example'.

I didn't have to. The idiot Thebans did it for themselves. They came at us in mid-afternoon, four hundred cavalry emerging from behind the low hills north of the city to flush my Prodromoi back on the column.

The Prodromoi retreated in good order, very quickly, and broke contact. The Agrianians went to ground and the Thebans never, I think, knew they were there.

I had a long chain of reports, so that half an hour after the Theban attack started, I had all my Hetaeroi in two small wedges facing down a long field of barley, with a hundred Agrianians on each flank.

The Theban cavalry rode into the other end of the field, as I had expected. After all, I was getting a new report on their movements every five minutes.

'Don't even twitch,' I said to my men. 'Let them do it, if they want.'

They rode away.

We rode up to Thebes and I picked a campsite – the same site we'd used the last time. I felt that sent the right message.

Alexander must have agreed, because he gripped my hand at the end of the day. 'Well done,' he said. 'They won't fight now – but you left them no bodies to mourn. Well done.'

I loved his praise, when it was good praise.

I went to bed a happy man, and awoke to the sound of screams.

The Thebans had attacked our outposts in the dark – a huge attack, with twelve hundred hoplites. They came across the open ground in silence, and of course our army hadn't fully entrenched, or anything like it. And Perdiccas hadn't taken the precautions he should have. His outposts were surprised and overrun, and the Thebans killed at least two hundred pezhetaeroi and fifty hypaspists. And then they withdrew, untouched – we didn't find a single body. Of course, they may have taken their dead with them – that's certainly what I wrote in the Military Journal.

Either way, they hurt us and we did nothing in response, and that emboldened the war party. No matter that I'd shown them how toothless their cavalry was – never mind that we had every advantage. When men are determined on violence, it's like a plague, and you cannot stop it.

Philip Longsword was among the dead. Alexander stood by his body in the new light of dawn, and he had white spots on either side of his nose and his lips looked pinched. His face was thinner than I'd ever seen it, and his ram's horns were more pronounced. He looked like a satyr – a very angry satyr.

But despite that, he ordered our troops to dig in, and avoid combat contact.

So we did. The Hetaeroi, being aristocrats, didn't dig – except in emergencies – but we were mounted in armour all day, moving from trouble spot to trouble spot.

The Assembly of Thebes voted for war to defend their liberties.

Our siege engines were three days' march away. And our tents.

It rained. We were wet. Luckily, Greece is dry all summer, but autumn was coming.

The hypaspitoi marched out of camp and spread out, supported by the Agrianians, pillaging the countryside. This was an ancient tradition in Greek warfare. It was a public and somewhat formal statement – it showed the defenders that they could cower behind their walls, but they would lose everything outside them.

We understood from men inside the walls – because many Thebans were supporters of Alexander – that the Assembly was now divided. So, after some hesitation, Alexander had his heralds proclaim at the edge of the walls that any Theban who wished to come out of the city would be allowed to go free – or that if Thebes surrendered the two men who had murdered Macedonians, it could still avoid war. His herald reminded them that Alexander was the hegemon of the League and that Thebes was in violation of her sworn oaths.

The Thebans apparently read this as weakness.

The next day, their herald came out on the walls and called out in a voice of bronze, 'Hellenes! Thebes stands with the King of Kings against the tyrant! Many times before, the King of Kings has aided Greece to throw off the yoke of tyranny and keep their cities free. Let us stand together, war down the tyrant, and be free together! But if the tyrant Alexander will give us Antipater and Philotas, as prisoners, men who are responsible for outrages against the Polis of Thebes, we will let him march away in peace.'

Philotas was Nicanor's brother, and he was thousands of stades away, fighting the Persians in Asia.

I wasn't anywhere near Alexander when the herald came out, but people tell me he went as white as parchment, and that when the man was done speaking, he spat.

No one likes to be called a tyrant. Least of all a tyrant. That was the same day we discovered that Olympias had killed Amyntas and Cleopatra's children and that poor Cleopatra had hanged herself with one of her own dresses.

Macedon, eh? Olympias held the children face down in the coals of a brazier and literally burned their faces off. One at a time.

I didn't need Thaïs to tell me what was in the letters from Alexander to Olympias.

But that didn't make the cowardly Thebans right. Alexander had many failings. But we brought peace to the Greeks, and we made them ten times as rich and prosperous and lawful as ever before. We ended their petty squabbles, and how many women were raped, how many children burned in the endless cycle of wars? How many died when Athens and Sparta danced?

Thebes never had an empire. Thebes never thought beyond the

narrow confines of the plain of Boeotia. Of the great cities, only Thebes allied with Persia – over and over. When Thebes defeated Sparta, they did *nothing* to pick up the reins of Sparta's overseas commitments – and the cities of Ionia, liberated by Athens and supported by Sparta, went right back to Persia. Thebes raped Plataea – the first city of Greece ever *destroyed* by other Greeks. Thebes had a calendar of sins going back to ancient times, and Thebans were the most selfish, grasping and mercenary of all the Greeks.

I never shed any tears for Thebes. Don't you, either.

After the herald's answer, we opened siege lines. The Thebans were cocky, and to be fair, their hoplites were superb. Epaminondas wasn't so long in his grave that their tradition of victory was dead. They raided our lines with panache, took prisoners, put three lines of palisades around the Cadmea to wall the Macedonian garrison off from any support – they were active, brave and professional.

Our siege train arrived, and we set it up. We had engineers – military mathematicians whose work consisted of evaluating defences and planning – scientifically – to reduce them. Calixthenes was the best man – he was young, dark-haired, weedy and small, and he looked like a child in a breastplate, but he was brilliant both at sighting his engines and at predicting enemy counter-measures.

The third day, they released a cavalry sortie, and I captured half of it. It was one of my best actions – one of those actions that make you feel like a god.

When I came on duty, just after sunrise, I set a pair of ambushes well back from the two gates where they might sortie. My ambushes were both subtle – bah, I'm bragging. But I put men in hayricks near one, and in a dry watercourse by the other, with orders to let anyone who emerged go right past them.

Both gates had a small cavalry force at hand, whose sole job was to fake an engagement and then get routed.

The main body of Theban horse galloped out of the Plataean gate a little after dawn and raced for our foragers in their distant fields. My 'small force' of cavalry pretended to attempt to engage them, and then fled before contact, and the Thebans gave chase, pursuing my handful of desperate victims across farm fields, across a dry watercourse ...

Into the main body of the Hetaeroi. We charged them down a low hill and broke them in one charge, and then we hunted them all the way back to their gates, and the Agrianians who had been hiding in hayricks emerged and picked beaten men off tired horses as they fled.

More than fifty of their cavalry broke the other way – towards Athens.

Poseidon was fresh, and the power was on me. I gave chase with anyone who was following me.

One by one, we caught them and captured them, or killed them – ten, twenty, thirty.

Darkness fell, and we were still running them down. None of us had horses to change.

Horses started to die. You can ride a horse to death, if you go long enough and you are sufficiently stupid – or desperate.

They were.

Poseidon ran on. He was magnificent – like a god himself. I overtook man after man, and these their vaunted best horsemen – and they would either beg for quarter, or make a cut at me with a sword or a spear, and I'd ride them down. One man, I remember well, I caught, and all I had to do was grab a fistful of his chiton and pull on Poseidon's reins – Poseidon checked, and I pulled him right over his horse's rump. I left him for slower men to take, and rode on.

Most of their horses foundered all together – ten or twelve in a bunch, the poor animals blowing blood out of their noses where their hearts, shattered by too long a run, had forced it.

They might have run into the woods on Parnassus and avoided me easily enough, but they stood like deer caught in torches and surren-dered.

But one man rode on, and I stayed with him. He had the best horse. He was only a blur ahead, and we were riding in moonlight, and Poseidon had been moving for twelve hours, and I became afraid for him. I was not galloping, or even cantering – in fact, I moved at a walk and then a trot, and I got down as frequently as I dared to give him a rest.

I needn't have worried. He was like a horse of the gods, and as we climbed Parnassus, he seemed to become more powerful, larger, faster ...

I caught my foe at the top of the pass. He turned his horse, raised his sword and charged me.

I wanted his horse. Poseidon felt my weight shift, and he danced a little to the left, and the darkness betrayed us, and we were down – just like that – and a branch hit me on the head as I fell.

I came to and had no idea how much time had passed.

But I had a vast feeling of fear – of impending danger.

Poseidon gave a scream – not a neigh, but a long, loud call.

I got a foot under me, tripped over a root behind me and fell back so fast that the sword meant to cut me missed entirely. The will of the gods – no doing of mine. I fell backwards into the gully that caught the run-off from the narrow track, and hit my head again, and the earth trembled as in an earthquake.

On the other hand, the pain helped steady me, and I could see my enemy against the moon. He cursed.

I tried to get to my feet. The point of my hip felt as if I'd taken a spear or an arrow. It would support my weight, but I wasn't going to execute any brilliant throws from pankration.

I started to climb the gully. I could hear Poseidon, and I aimed my climb at him. He had both my spare javelins, and I assumed that with a javelin in hand I could stand off my attacker.

He moved along the top of the gully and laughed grimly. I could hear his horse – breathing like an ironsmith's bellows. He had his sword in his hand.

'Come up, lackey of the tyrant, and I'll gut you,' he said.

I didn't bother talking.

He came right to the top of the gully.

I whistled.

Poseidon kicked him, and he gave a cry and fell, clutching his thigh. I took his sword and cut his throat.

Glorious, eh?

He had a magnificent horse – a bay I called Ajax. Big as an elephant. His sons are still in my stable – mixed with Poseidon's sons.

But both my horses were done in, and I had to walk back to camp, limping all the way.

As soon as I was back, Alexander sent for me, congratulated me and ordered me to Athens with a small escort of cavalry.

'Take Thaïs,' he said. 'The city likes you, and loves her. I don't care what you do – see to it that Demosthenes cannot raise an army to break my siege.'

Alexander was never bloodthirsty. Far from it – in his mind of wheels and gears, everyone and everything had a purpose and he could never see why people wasted time on anything so inefficient as hate.

And he said outright that if we had to lay siege to Athens, we'd never conquer Asia. 'Athens could take us six months,' he said. 'Thebes I can surround. Athens – we'd need to go home and build a fleet, contest the seas with Lycurgus – at least a year wasted. Perhaps the whole *war* wasted.' He shook his head and drank more wine. 'I hate fighting Greeks. I'm beginning to hate *Greeks*.' He looked into his wine cup.

'Macedonians are better?' I asked.

'Amyntas is dead,' he said. 'There will be no more trouble in Macedon.'

I shrugged. 'Unless Parmenio or Antipater decides to take the throne himself.'

Alexander smiled. 'If I die. Not until. Or am defeated repeatedly in the field.' His smile widened. 'Which is never going to happen. I'm invincible.'

I took my grooms under Polystratus. Thaïs and I had an abbreviated reunion. She did not want to go to Athens.

'I do not want to be treated as a traitor,' she said.

'You have a unique opportunity to save lives in Athens,' I said.

She hit me. It was the only time she ever struck me, but she did it with venom. She meant to hurt me.

She loved Athens.

But she went.

I went with a letter from Alexander demanding that ten leading men of Athens be surrendered to the judgement of the hegemon. I don't think Alexander meant to execute them – well, to tell you the truth, I doubt that Demosthenes would have survived an hour, but there were *so many* of us out for his blood ...

Charmeides and Lycurgus were courageous, if wily, opponents. And they'd have made wonderful hostages. You need to remember the origin of the Hetaeroi – originally, the Hetaeroi and the pages were the sons of captured enemy chiefs and princes – hostages for their father's good behaviour. It was a Macedonian custom to take prisoners and integrate them into our service – and reward them so richly that they became part of us. Charmeides would have done better with us, but he took ship and fled to Darius. Lycurgus lay low. Demosthenes doubtless pissed on his chiton in terror and hid in a basement.

Thaïs was cursed wherever she went. Her house had graffiti scrawled across the beautiful façade, and men yelled obscenities at her in the street.

But Phokion and Eumeles, Diodorus and Kineas and a thousand men like them stood with us, and the Assembly refused to vote for Demosthenes' resolution to send an army to support Thebes.

I'm not sure I helped by being in Athens – in fact, I was hit with a stone on my first day and had little to say for a week – but Thaïs did. Despite her fears and her anger, she was unmoved by the catcalls and the vulgarity. She opened her house and held court – and men came.

And she told them what would happen if Macedon stormed Athens. And she drew them pictures of our siege machines. Athens had a few on the walls. She told them what Alexander had at Thebes.

But her most impressive speech was about Persia.

'Just because Thebes – our ancient enemy – is choosing to waste herself against Macedon,' she said, 'must we? Thebes bragged – I heard them – that they were once again allies of the Mede. Is that who we are? Demosthenes has taken money from the Great King – would Miltiades approve? What about Pericles? Socrates? Plato? Did Athenians die at Marathon so that we could be slaves of Persia? Allies of Thebes?' She shrugged. 'Thebes is not in revolt against the tyrant of Macedon – Thebes has reverted to her truest self, and turned her back on Greece.'

Nice speech. I give it here in full, because I feel she might have been another Pericles, had she been born with a penis and not a vagina.

Her words, in Phokion's mouth – and that was a matter for bitter mirth in itself, because Phokion and Eumeles hated her – and Demosthenes' faction was wrecked.

The Athenians voted to send a delegation of ten men to Alexander to crave forgiveness. They sent Phokion to lead it, and Kineas with a squadron of elite Hippeis as an escort.

We arrived to find Thebes a burned-out husk, with her entire population raped and degraded, huddled in pens, awaiting sale. Later I heard Perdiccas, who led the assault, brag that no woman between ten and seventy remained unraped when the town was stormed. Children were butchered wholesale.

The Theban hoplites fought brilliantly, but they were no match for us. I heard later that they were the best fighters, man for man, of any foe most of the hypaspists ever faced. But as a body, they made mistakes, and a major gate was left virtually unguarded, and Alexander led the hypaspitoi through it and the town was stormed. Most of the hoplites died in the streets.

The Military Journal says that thirty thousand Thebans died. As many again were enslaved.

There were exceptions – a widow of one of the Boeotarchs, an aristocrat, was raped by one of our officers – a taxiarch in the pezhetaeroi. She didn't break or even bend – when he went to take a drink after getting off her, she pushed him into her well and dropped rocks on him until he died. Alexander gave her freedom and all her property.

In fact, he was appalled. His troops had got away from him in the storming, and they were angry. Exhausted. They had marched across the world, in horrible conditions, because of these rebels (as we called them), and they wanted revenge for every boil and every sore, every pulled muscle, every broken bone, every day without food.

I won't say Alexander wept. Merely that, like his father, he would have preferred other means.

But as I say, by the time the Athenian delegation arrived, there were no other means left. Alexander sat blank-faced on a stool and gave many Thebans their freedom – even their property. Many of the temples were spared. Several public buildings were spared. Slaves collected all the dead Theban hoplites and gave them a monument and a decent burial.

But the rest were sold into slavery en masse, and the town was destroyed. Turned to rubble.

Later – during the Lamian War – I heard Greeks claim that the true resistance to Macedon started there, and that Greek unity began in the ashes of Thebes.

Bullshit, says I. Thebes got what was coming to it. A nation of traitors, served the dish they'd ordered. The women of Thebes have my pity. The men died in harness, as rebels, and stupid rebels at that, and they got precisely what they deserved. And no one in Greece gave an obol. Had we done the same to Athens, it would have been war to the end – even Sparta, or Argos or Megara. But Thebes?

When we marched away, the ruins were still smoking, and Plataeans had come all the way across the plain, thirty stades, just to piss on the rubble. They waved at us and threw flowers.

We waved back.

And finally, we marched back to Pella.

Most of us in that army had been on campaign for more than a year. No one had been home that summer, and from the noble Hetaeroi to the lowliest pezhetaeroi, we had fought in at least five actions per man, marched ten thousand stades, killed enemies without count – fought against odds over and over.

We called it 'The Year of Miracles'.

We called Alexander ... king. He *was* king. He was king from Thrace to Illyria, from Sparta to Athens and across Thessaly to Pella. Demosthenes and Darius of Persia had tried to unite with Amyntas and the Thebans to make a web of steel to surround and crush our king, and he had beaten every one of them, all at once.

From the Shipka Pass to Pellium and down to Thebes, no enemy wanted to face Macedon in the field, ever again. And the smoke rising from the yawning basements of Thebes warned potential rebels of the consequences of foolishness.

Tribute flowed from the 'allies'. Everyone in the empire paid their taxes that winter.

As the leaves reddened on the trees, we rode back to Pella. The last morning, Alexander was nearly giddy with excitement at returning victorious, and I suggested we put on our best armour and ride our best horses and make a fine show, and he laughed and agreed.

We spent the morning preparing. Veterans among the pezhetaeroi mounted their horsehair plumes, or their ostrich feathers. I'd gone back to the same smith in Athens and got another helmet – this one covered in gold. He'd delivered it with ill grace – but he'd done a magnificent job, and my helmet had a distinctive shape, with a brim over the eyes and a forged iron crest over the bronze bowl, and a tall ruff of horsehair. It was the kind of helmet men called 'Attic'. It had less face protection, but I could hear and see and, most importantly, it was magnificent, and every man who could see it would know where I was. And the iron crest meant I would never be killed by a blow to the head.

Tirseas of Athens. Best armourer of his day. Hated Macedonians.

We put all our best on – clean chitons, full armour, polished by the slaves with ash and tallow. Swords shining, spears sparkling. Shaved. We were wearing a fortune in armour – brilliant horsehair plumes, Aegyptian ostrich feathers, solid-gold eagles' wings, panther skins, leopard skins, bronze armour polished like the disc of the sun and decorated in silver and gold, tin-plated bronze buckles and solid-silver buckles in our horse tack, crimson leather strapping on every mount, tall Persian bloodstock horses with pale coats and dark legs and faces. Alexander was the richest and the best-armoured – unlike his father, he looked like a god. No one could doubt that he was in command.

At noon, the Hetaeroi entered Pella, and the crowds cheered us, I suppose, but what I remember is riding with the somatophylakes into the courtyard of the palace. Olympias was there, of course – best pass over her – and even the slaves were cheering us.

When we reined up in the courtyard, there was a moment – no longer than the thickness of a hair, so to speak – when none of us moved. We sat on our horses and looked around.

I looked up, to where I could see the marble rail of the exedra, and the double arch of the window of Alexander's childhood nursery. I thought I saw a pair of small heads there, and I wondered if, despite Heraclitus, I could put my toe back in the same part of the river. If I could reach across time to those boys – if they were right there.

Those boys being us – me and Cleitus and Alexander. And tell them – some day, we will do it. *We will be heroes. Fear nothing. We will win. We will do what Philip did.*

But better. And the best was yet to come.

PART III
Asia

FIFTEEN

Pella, 335 BC

W e had no money.

Of course, that's not true. The sale of all the Thebans, plus the loot from Thrace and Illyria, paid the crown of Macedon a little less than eight hundred talents of gold, which didn't quite cover the arrears of pay to the army. Philip had died leaving the crown five hundred talents of gold in debt – in fact, like many an unlucky son, we had new creditors appearing every day, and Philip probably left Alexander more like a thousand talents in debt. A thousand talents. In gold. Remember that the King of Kings tried to buy Athens for three hundred talents ...

We'd been home from our year of miracles for three days when I saw Alexander throw one of the worst temper tantrums of his life. It was horrible. It started badly and grew steadily worse.

I had the duty. There was a rumour – one of Thaïs's sources – that Darius had put out money to arrange Alexander' s murder, and the Hetaeroi were on high alert. In fact, I had Ochrid – now a freeman – tasting the king's food because we'd been away from Pella a year and none of us trusted anyone in the palace.

So I was in armour, and I had just walked the corridors of the palace with Seleucus and Nearchus as my lieutenants, checking every post. I had almost sixty men on duty, and two more shifts ready to take over in turn. Alexander had just promoted almost a hundred men to the Hetaeroi – some from the Prodromoi, some from the grooms and some from other units, or straight from civilian life. They were a mixed bag. Perdiccas and I had shared them out like boys choosing sides for a game of hockey.

Of course we played hockey in Macedon. Do you think we're barbarians?

Hah! Don't answer that.

At any rate, putting my recruits into their places, making sure that every new man was on duty with a reliable oldster – it used up half my evening, and I was late to the great hall.

Olympias was there. I missed what had transpired, but I gathered from witnesses that Alexander had taken her to task for her wholesale massacre of young Cleopatra's relatives, and she had told him to get more realistic about his approach to imperial politics.

As I entered, Olympias had just lain down on a couch – something Macedonian women most emphatically did not do, back then. 'At any rate,' she drawled, 'you need their money, dear. You have none.'

'Money is easy,' Alexander said, and snapped his fingers. 'I'll act, and the money will come.'

Antipater shook his head. 'We've reached a stable point,' he said. 'With the money from your last campaigns, which is just enough to pay most of your father's debts. Disband the army, and we're home free.'

You have to imagine the scene – forty senior officers and noblemen – Laodon and Erygius, Cleitus, Perdiccas, Hephaestion, of course – all the inner circle, dressed in their best, but relaxed, lying about the place drinking too much. We'd gone a year without a break, and the atmosphere was ... festive. Even dangerous. Slave girls walked carefully, or bow-legged. Boys too.

Olympias downed her wine. 'Yes,' she said. 'Disband the army, call Parmenio home where you can keep an eye on him, and we'll be fine.' She smiled demurely. 'I'm sure we can live safe and happy, after that.'

Alexander stood up. Hephaestion knew him best and caught at his hand, but Alexander was too fast. His cup crashed to the floor a hand's breadth from his mother's head. 'I am going to Asia!' he shrieked. 'I am not disbanding my army. I am not releasing *one man.*' He was shaking. 'I care *nothing* for the cost. My men will march without *air* if I march.'

Uh-oh. I knew that the pezhetaeroi had been home three days and they were already muttering about back pay, land grants, new clothes, sandals – all the things soldiers require.

Antipater had been away from the king too long, and had forgotten how to manage him. He took on a pompous tone. 'Eventually, we can consider Asia, lord. But for now, we have to be realistic.'

Alexander stopped shrieking. He turned on Antipater, and his hands were shaking. 'Listen, you,' he said quietly. 'I don't care if I have to have my mother murder every aristocrat in Macedon so that I can seize their estates. I am marching on Asia at the head of a magnificent army – all the allies – the crusade to avenge Xerxes.' He walked carefully over to Antipater. 'Do – you – understand?'

Antipater was shaken. We all were. Alexander had been on the edge of this sort of explosion before, but he didn't actually cross a certain line.

Right then, he had his hidden dagger in his hand, and I thought he was going to kill Antipater. So did Antipater.

Olympias got to her feet – she came up to Alexander's shoulder, or a little more – and took his hand. 'There, there, my love,' she said cautiously but firmly. She took the dagger from him and put her wine cup in its place.

He drank, but his eyes had more white than pupil, and he terrified all of us so much that we didn't talk about it.

The next day, Antipater sent for Parmenio. He did it with Alexander's permission and over the royal seal, but we knew who ordered whom, and again, I was afraid. I suspected that Parmenio and Antipater were now going to murder Alexander because they were afraid of him.

Parmenio arrived two days later. He'd already been on his way – or, as Thaïs suggested, he'd been near by, waiting for Antipater to arrange his arrival. Either way, his timing was propitious.

I'm going to pause in my historical account here to talk about Thaïs. We were 'getting along'. Athens had poisoned something between us. It is difficult to explain, because I understood enough to worry and not enough to make it right. Had she been unfaithful with Alexander? What was unfaithfulness, in a hetaera? And had the situation – loyalty to me, to Alexander, to Athens – unbalanced her? What role had pregnancy played? Pregnant women can be deeply irrational. Men use this as an excuse to describe women as irrational as a tribe – unfair, stupid, vicious, of men, but let's face it. Pregnant women can be very difficult.

Hey, you'd be difficult, too, if you were carrying a baby between your legs in a Greek summer.

At any rate, we avoided *all* these topics. We were like allies, not lovers. We lived together, we were intimate enough. I thought I'd outlast her anger.

Sometimes, I'm quite intelligent.

Parmenio's welcome was tumultuous and magnificent. Alexander spared no effort for him, and he received much the sort of welcome we had received. He had, after all, taken and held the crossings into Asia, even though he'd lost most of the cities to Memnon, who had, let's face it, outgeneralled Parmenio in each of three encounters. Something else you won't find in the Military Journal.

Parmenio was a careful man, a professional soldier and not a courtier. He'd been Philip's favourite, and he and Antipater were, I think, actually, genuinely friends, not just tolerant allies and rivals. As soon as Parmenio arrived and was welcomed, he and Antipater vanished into the part of the palace that functioned as the headquarters of the army and the secretariat of the king – the bureaucracy, if you like. They spoke for four hours, and Parmenio emerged smiling.

I say he emerged, because I was right there. Alexander had ordered me to provide Parmenio with a direct escort. He had a troop of Thessalian cavalry of his own – his 'grooms', if you like, although he was so famous that they were all knights – but they were not allowed in the palace (my new security cordon in effect) and I watched the great man myself.

When he came out of the 'office' wing, he looked around as my guards moved to surround him.

'Young Ptolemy, I think? Last time I saw you, lad, you were naked and playing in the mud.' He held out a hand. But despite his patronising words, he offered me the full hand and arm clasp of the warrior, and held it warmly. 'Your father would, I think, be quite proud.'

'From your mouth to the ears of the gods,' I said. 'The king is waiting for you, sir.'

He nodded. As we walked, he said, 'I gather you and Nicanor had a disagreement.'

I nodded. 'A misunderstanding, I think. My impression is that Nicanor and I are good, now. If not, let's settle it. Your family and mine are old allies.'

'By Zeus, lad, you speak just like your father. "Let's settle it". Herakles' dick, Ptolemy, how do you survive here, if you speak the truth?' Parmenio was like a force of nature. It was impossible – *impossible* – not to like him.

I grinned. 'It's my job. Ask the king. He'll say the same. Hephaestion tells him what he wants to hear and I tell him what he doesn't want to hear.'

Parmenio stopped. 'Like what?'

I saw the pit yawning at my feet. 'Best ask the king, sir.'

He nodded. 'You want to go to Asia?'

Now I stopped. 'Is this a trick question? I command a squadron of the Hetaeroi.'

He shrugged. 'I don't know if we're going to Asia, and I don't know if I'm taking you, even if we go. If this talk is too straight for you, you tell me, son of Lagus.'

'Meaning that I'm no longer commanding my Hetaeroi?' I asked.

He looked at me. 'We'll see, lad. You did a fine job this summer, but you're no veteran. And Antipater wants you.' He looked around – an astounding gesture from a man so powerful. Creepy, almost. 'You are a great landowner, not a penniless mercenary. Think about it.'

340

He nodded pleasantly to me and I passed him through the sentries, to the king.

I came off duty and was summoned to the king myself.

He was papyrus white, and his hands were shaking.

'I am *not* the king,' he said very quietly.

I made a face. 'You are, lord.'

Alexander put his face in his hands. I had *never* seen him do any such thing. 'I am not the king,' he said again. Then, in a voice suddenly more rueful than angst-ridden, he said, 'I don't suppose that you have a secret sister you'd like me to marry?'

I pretended to take him seriously – stared off into space for a little while, shook my head.

'No,' I said. 'Sorry.'

He managed a small smile for my performance. 'Might I marry Thaïs, then?'

I shook my head emphatically. 'No, lord.'

He smiled. 'She's one of the few women I actually fancy. But no – I am Achilles, not Agamemnon. I would never stoop to take your war prize.' He smiled to show it was all in fun – a kind of fun at which he was not very good, and playing far too close to the bone for me. But he was trying to tell me something. I wasn't seeing it.

'Antipater and Parmenio have laid out for me the conditions under which they will *allow* me to cross over to Asia.' He looked out of the window. 'I am to marry and beget an heir.'

I laughed. 'I'm not sure that Hephaestion can bear you a child,' I quipped.

Alexander whirled. 'How dare you presume!' he said. 'Hephaestion is a noble man, not some effeminate.'

Me and my big mouth. 'I apologise, lord. I was attempting to lighten your mood, not to attack Hephaestion.' I shrugged. 'And – your comment about Thaïs hit me hard.'

It was his turn to pause.

He had a scroll in his hand, and he put it down carefully, came over to me and put his hands on my arms. 'I am very fond of Thaïs. I don't know of another woman who, six months pregnant, nonetheless makes me admire her.' He looked into my eyes. 'I have never lain with her.'

I didn't like his choice of words. Too precise. But he was trying to convey ... love, charm, trust – and I wanted it, so I nodded.

Alexander shook his head and let go of my arms. 'I am the womanish one, today. I am sure you thought that was humour. I will try to keep my temper in check. Parmenio has changed every command in the army. That, too, is part of his price.'

I shrugged. 'Well, I knew it was coming. Nicanor to the hypaspists, and Philotas to the Hetaeroi. Coenus? Where's he going?'

'He's to have the Pellan regiment of pezhetaeroi.' Alexander sounded angry, and well he might. The Pellans – the local boys – were the best regiment of pikes – the elite. Alexander looked at the floor. 'But his men – his officers – my father's officers. Asander has the Prodromoi.'

That annoyed me. I'd wanted the cavalry scouts for myself. Not that I'd ever asked.

'You and Perdiccas both lose your squadrons,' Alexander went on. 'I'm *sorry*, Ptolemy.'

I stood silently, my lips trembling. I *loved* commanding the Hetaeroi. And I had done well at it. I didn't want to whine. But this was ... unfair. That adolescent word that adults never use.

'Have I ... failed you? Lord, I ... by Zeus, King of the Heavens!' I turned away from the king. I knew that I was going to cry.

Alexander came and put his arm around me. 'I *know*!' he said. 'I'm sorry, Ptolemy. But I'm paying, too. As soon as I have command – I'll put you all back in your places. But as soon as that man walked into the palace – I was no longer king.'

I held my temper in check, although my stomach did flips and I remember the tears running down my cheeks.

'You are still somatophylakes,' he said. 'And one of my royal hunts-men, for life.'

'I want to hunt Persians,' I said. 'And I'll go as a trooper, under one of Philip's fart-sacks.'

Alexander smiled. It was like the sun coming through clouds. 'You will?'

I frowned. 'Of course.'

He nodded. 'Well, we'll find something for you to do. Antipater wants to keep you home.'

'Antipater doesn't trust me,' I said.

Alexander laughed bitterly. 'The opposite, Ptolemy. We all trust you, and that means you should be left at home. It's the ones I hate that I have to take to Asia.'

The next day, Antipater began to sell the crown lands around Pella – for cash. Alexander wouldn't discuss it.

I had handed all my palace keys to Philotas. He wasn't bad – and neither was Nicanor. They were sitting together in what had always been my room. They rose when I entered. I was in armour.

'My brother says you are like a lion,' Philotas said, and held out his hand.

I didn't feel much like smiling – but remember, my father and their father were old friends, and we all saw Parmenio as the head of our faction, the old aristocrats. I shook hands.

'These are my keys to all the strong places in the palace,' I said. 'They are numbered and have tags on them with the name of the place they unlock.'

Philotas sat and read all the keys. 'Perdiccas has a set as well?'

I shrugged. 'Sorry, sir, you will have to ask him.'

Philotas shook his head. 'Can we *not* have this as us against you? Parmenio's men against Alexander's men? That won't defeat the Persians.'

I folded my arms over my chest. 'You really want to have this conversation?' I asked.

'Try me,' Philotas said.

'Alexander doesn't need you or your father to conquer Asia. You went out there and got your arses handed to you by Memnon while the king was reconquering Greece with a handful of men and the will of the gods. Now you and yours are taking control of an army we created and we trained. So – yes, sir, there is going to be some strain.' I felt much better, having said it.

Nicanor smiled at me. He looked at his brother. 'I told you,' he said.

Philotas shook his head. 'You kids are arrogant, I'll give you that. *We* built this army, Ptolemy. My father and Philip and Antipater. I've been in harness with this army since I was twelve years old. I've trained more pezhetaeroi than you've had shits. I've pissed more water than you've sailed over. You kids have never seen a real battle – never fought an equal foe. And you have the gall to come here and tell me that you trained this army?'

I nodded. 'Yes. That's what I'm telling you. You were never a page, though – so you wouldn't understand.'

'One of Alexander's butt-boys? That makes you *special*?' Philotas laughed. 'Let's just leave it there. I don't want you in my squadrons, however much my brother seems to like you.'

I looked at Nicanor. 'Philotas, I think you are making a real error. I don't think that you understand the king. Or what he can do.'

Philotas shook his head. 'That's what Nicanor said.' He shrugged. 'Doesn't matter, though. He's a figurehead, now. Pater's in charge. As he should be. Pater will fix everything, and we'll have no more of these desperate, amateurish thrusts around Greece or anywhere else – we'll fight like experts. Amateurs excel when their backs are against the wall – I'll give you that. At any rate – you think I'm insulting you, and perhaps I spoke too strongly. You and the king did brilliantly this summer – but Pater would have done it all without leaving Pella. None of those battles needed to be fought. The campaigns cost more than just buying peace would have cost – you know that, right? You work with Antipater – you know that for a quarter of the cost, we could have bought the Illyrians and paid them to fight the Thracians.'

I remember all this – because I had, in my darker hours, thought it all on my own. The king loved war. And he needed it. He needed to be in the saddle every day – he needed to make all those decisions, and make them correctly, and lead us to victory, and be seen to be doing it. It was food and drink and sleep – and sex – to him. When he didn't have war, he had temper tantrums and little addictions and he was on edge all the time.

So yes – we didn't *need* to be in Thrace. Or Illyria. Or Thebes, for that matter. Who cared, in Macedon, if the king was hegemon of the League of Corinth?

And yet, and yet – if you give all that away – if you buy your enemies – if we don't fight Chaeronea, or Thebes …

How long before there's an Athenian army at Pella?

Who knows, eh?

But the king's way was the Macedonian way.

'You planning to conquer Asia that way?' I asked.

Philotas turned red.

Nicanor laughed. 'I warned you,' he said. Although to which one of us, I wasn't sure.

I saluted and left. Later, in my own house, I thought about how Nicanor had, in effect, taken my side against his own brother.

I was worried that Philotas and Parmenio would 'allow' Alexander to be murdered. That it would just 'happen'. So I started a cabal before I left for my estates, and arranged that the two adjutants of the royal squadrons should control the rotations on duty. And I arranged to be notified – in my person as a somatophylakes – if anyone changed this arrangement.

And I told Antipater that I had done it. I walked into his office, smiled and laid it out for him.

He sat behind an enormous table, his chin in his hand, and his eyes burned from under heavy brows.

'So now you distrust *me*,' he said.

'I have reason to believe that there's a plot to kill the king,' I said. 'I assume you will back my preparations.'

'Why not take your suspicions to Philotas?' he asked.

'Parmenio is the most likely culprit and has the most to gain,' I answered.

He tried to stare me down.

'Very well,' he said. 'Parmenio was your father's friend. We expected better of you.'

'It was Pater who warned me about Parmenio,' I said. 'I'm going to tell the king of my arrangements, and then I'll be heading to my estates. As I no longer have a command.'

'Is that your price? You want a command?' Antipater shook his head. 'Why not just say what you want, instead of all this posturing like a boy?'

I sighed. 'I'm not posturing,' I said. 'I don't have a price. I'm too rich to need to have a price. But Antipater – consider this. Attalus crossed me, and died for it. Philip – bless him – died, too. Perhaps you and Parmenio should treat us like adults.'

'If you are declaring war ...' Antipater said slowly – and I could see I'd shaken him.

'I'm not!' I said. And laughed. Oh, the power of it – I had just threatened Antipater and made him twitch.

Court intrigue. Everyone says they are above such stuff, but no one is, and next to war, it is the greatest game.

So I laughed and shook my head. 'I am *not* declaring war,' I said. 'I just want everyone to note that if something happens to Alexander, there will be a general bloodbath – which I am seeking to prevent. But if that bloodbath happens – well, I wish to suggest that neither you nor Parmenio would emerge unscathed.' I leaned forward. 'Or even alive.'

Antipater nodded. 'I understood you the first time.'

I stood back. 'Good. I'm going to see the king, and then, as I said, go to my estates. Glad we could have this discussion.'

Antipater leaned forward. 'He's insane, you know. You must know.'

I shook my head. 'No. He's king. You old men should get that through your heads.' At this point, Thaïs and I had had this discussion fifty times, and we had hammered out a point of view. I shot it at Antipater, a prepared missile. 'You think he's insane because he's convinced he's invincible, and because he can see *right through you* and acts accordingly, and because he says what he thinks. I agree it's not normal – but he is the *king.*'

Antipater raised a hand. 'Listen: you think we are enemies – we are not. May I do you a favour?'

I was instantly alert. 'If you will,' I quipped.

He nodded. 'The king is selling land. We need the money for Asia. I have four farms – all bordering yours. Between Europos and the Axios river – prime land, and twenty stades of royal forest on the river.'

I nodded. I knew the land – farms which actually broke up our holdings along the Axios. They were meant to – to keep landowners like us from becoming regional warlords.

As if.

'For fifty talents of gold, I'll see to it that you own them,' Antipater said. 'It's for the war in Asia – none of it will stick to my fingers.'

That's twelve years of all the profits of all our land, I thought. My lands made me about four talents a year – that's without lots of other profits, like sales of horses and slaves, fish from the river and other projects. In fact, I could depend on a little more than ten talents of gold a year.

'You have last year's accounts for the farms?' I asked.

Antipater shook his head. 'Most aristocrats would just buy them – to have the land.'

'For fifty talents?' I asked. 'Most aristocrats must be fools, then.'

Antipater got up and went to the vast closet of scrolls that represented the tax documents of the empire. Scrolls sat in baskets. Two slaves sat at a nearby desk and sorted outgoing and incoming scrolls.

He pulled down the central region basket, went through the scrolls and shook his head. 'There's no record.' He shrugged. 'Somebody forgot to note it. I imagine the farms and forest are worth … a talent a year. Perhaps more.'

I nodded. 'I'll talk to the king, but I doubt I'll offer more than thirty, and even that is more to help the war effort than because the land is worth it.'

Antipater raised an eyebrow. 'You're going to bargain with the king?' he asked.

I smiled and left him. Again, I mention this because to understand us – me and Alexander and Parmenio and Antipater – you need to understand who Alexander was – and who I was. And how important it was, even when I was in power, to manage my estates well.

The king had all the tax documents, of course. Antipater didn't know the king – I did. If his precious war in Asia depended on finding money, I knew that Alexander would become an overnight expert at funding. And he did.

'Antipater tells me you will buy the Axios estates,' he said, as soon as I was admitted.

Well, well.

'For thirty-five talents,' I said.

Alexander sat back. 'Perdiccas *gave* me ten talents yesterday.'

I nodded – taken aback and trying not to show it. 'What does he get for it?' I asked.

346

Alexander made a face. 'My undying love? And command of a regiment of pezhetaeroi.'

'What're the Military Journal and the Agrianians worth?' I asked.

Alexander nodded. 'You'd have to share with Alectus – who I just promoted to the Hetaeroi, as well. Pater always put the best foreigners into the guards – I'm doing the same. We're going to have ten squadrons of two hundred, and a reserve – Philip's old men – three more squadrons.'

'No wonder you need money!' I said.

Alexander laughed. 'Fifteen talents for the Agrianians and the Journal.'

'Undying love?' I asked.

He looked at Hephaestion, who made a moue. 'As long as you don't make any more jokes about me,' Hephaestion said.

'None? A steep price, but – Done. I'll pay fifty talents for the estates. That's thirty-five for them, and fifteen for you.'

Alexander's tone lightened. 'And I'll have the use of the forest whenever I want it. Yes?'

'For hunting? Done. Put it in the contract.' I grinned, and we shook hands.

I took Thaïs home. Sent Heron with my grooms under Polystratus into Pella with fifty talents of gold – almost the whole of my father's lifetime of savings, gone in an afternoon. On the other hand, Heron said it made him happy.

'I've expected some bandit to come and kill us all for it – for years,' he said.

Thaïs took another talent and poured money out into her spider's web of contacts, and more news came back – more and more news.

Darius had ordered a fleet to combine at Miletus, in Asia.

He knew we were coming.

Memnon was raising a major army.

Darius himself was marching east with his household, to face a rebellion in Sogdiana, wherever that was.

Demosthenes was busy cooking trouble. Theban exiles were the new vector of rebellion throughout the league, and they spread like poison. Thaïs's friends identified them in Corinth and Corcyra and Athens and Miletus.

Thaïs's friends were electrified by recent events. The destruction of Thebes got rid of the mere hangers-on. It tested some loyalties, but others were either hardened as a stick is hardened in fire, or strengthened by fear.

347

But the other side – the anti-Macedonian faction, if you will – was also hardening. And since we were poor and Darius of Persia was rich, the mercenaries were all going his way.

I passed the reports on to Hephaestion. Thaïs stayed with me.

We spent months at the farms. I enjoyed putting my organisational skills to work on the royal farms I'd purchased. They'd been mismanaged for fifty years – no one ever manages a farm for the king as well as they'd manage it for themselves.

I appointed Heron's oldest son to manage two of them, and left him to it, and took the other two for myself. I was determined to breed better horses, and make a killing on them. Or ride them myself. So Poseidon and my new Theban brute Ajax went to stud and passed a very happy winter.

Thaïs and I did too, for a while. She was due after the Winter Feast of Persephone, and she bore me a daughter virtually to the day she'd predicted – but then, she was a priestess of Aphrodite. We called her Eurydike, and she was pretty and plump and had cheeks you just wanted to kiss – or chew on. And thighs – and tiny fingers and toes.

I've forgotten to mention young Olympias, my Illyrian foundling. Thaïs took her into her household, and she grew up as a sort of older sister to Eurydike.

I should also mention that Thaïs and I kept separate establishments. Hers was run by old Chalke, a former smith and former slave, because she'd freed her Italiote, Anonius, and he'd returned to Italy. Chalke was old and tough and pretty much unafraid of anything or anyone – he had an eye gone, scars all over his chest – he was the kind of man everyone fears to meet in a dark alley.

Mine was run by Polystratus. Polystratus and Chalke were not friends – more rivals.

I mention this because Thaïs and I lived very separate lives, even after Eurydike was born, and we were too seldom together even when we wanted to be. She was, in many ways, a great lady – a person of as much importance as I was. Twice that winter she went into Pella without me, summoned by the king to deal with matters relating to her web. If I say she had no secrets from me, it's because she had her private life and I mine. I don't think that she had any other lovers – I know I didn't – but I'd learned my lesson. I wasn't going to ask.

After Eurydike's birth, she informed me that the goddess required that she be celibate for two months, and that if I would join her in this sacrifice, Eurydike would be a healthier child.

Eurydike never had so much as a bad cold as a child, so I'm guessing that Aphrodite's an honest goddess. So Thaïs was not in my bed for months after the birth of our daughter, and I saw less of her by day, as well. So I was shocked one day to walk into a barn on my home farm and find her and Bella lifting weights like men. Why was I shocked? And a month later, I found the two of them at the edge of one of my pastures, dancing to Chalke's pipes, and I lay down and watched them, aching for her and amazed to see the rapidity of her movements, the near perfection of her speed and grace, the coordination of the two women, one black, one white, as they moved, naked, through a bewildering flurry of moves, covered in sweat.

It was truly like watching the gods. I snuck away through the trees. I know now that she was working very hard to get her body back – that this is another tribulation women bear, that they must lose months of conditioning in pregnancy and must train like athletes to return to shape. At the time, I simply missed her.

But two months after Eurydike's birth, just after the early feast of Herakles, she and I shared a dinner, and after dinner, in the midst of a conversation about Menander's latest play, she squeezed my hand. 'I have a hankering,' she said, 'to sleep with a man with a big nose.'

Well, well.

Our whole relationship seemed to be restored in one night of love – not just sex, either. She came to me almost every night, for weeks. But it was rare for her to sleep with me – actually share my bed – never so often as to let it become familiar. She began to use different scents and wore different clothes and once shocked me by having a girdle of gold under her chiton, and another time she was painted – beautiful designs in red and black around her wrists and hips and running down into her loins.

No, I didn't need to tup any slave girls. We'd started something different. We spent time together with our daughter. I remember one day dispensing justice for my tenants, with Eurydike curled on my lap. I was not planning to be my father.

After the Macedonian Feast of Zeus the King, Alexander summoned me to court. I had been gone three months, and I was softer, happier and less exercised than at any time in my life.

Happiness is so much harder to describe than war.

And you won't find that in the Military Journal, either.

Antipater had either forgiven me, or never been offended. He and Alexander had summoned me back to court to help with the logistical planning for the march to Asia. That part *is* in the Journal, so I won't bore you much, but I'll use this opportunity to tell you what the king and Parmenio had chosen to take to Asia.

First, ten thousand pezhetaeroi in five regiments – Elimeotis, under Coenus; Orestae, under Perdiccas, and under Polyperchon the Tymphaeans – all collectively known as *astHetaeroi*, the men of Outer Macedon, as separate from the *pezhetaeroi*, who were in three regiments under Meleager, Craterus and Amyntas son of Andromenes, representing the men of Inner Macedonia. Old Macedonia. To further complicate this, we called all of them – all six regiments – *pezhetaeroi*. Got it?

Nicanor had fifteen hundred hypaspitoi. Alectus left the hypaspitoi for the Agrianians at this time, and took most of the Agrianians with him – not all, but most – and Nicanor drafted the very best men of the 'Asian' pezhetaeroi to replace them. It was a different set of hypaspitoi – but not worse, though it pains me to say so.

The Psiloi – the *professional* light armed troops, made up of men who could have fought in more equipment but were paid for specialist scout services (as opposed to the rabble of freed slaves and lesser men that Greeks used as Psiloi) consisted of six hundred Agrianians and four hundred archers – most of whom were recruited out of Attika and mainland Greece, although you'd never know it to look at them, as they dressed like Sakje or Thrake. But they were not mercenaries, but professional archers serving Macedon and looking to gain land grants and Macedonian citizenship. The archers (the Toxophiloi) and the Agrianians together were the *Psiloi* brigade, which was mine.

Then we had a little more than six thousand Thracians. The conquered chieftains each submitted a band in lieu of tribute – they were serving for plunder. They began to trickle in with the first melting of snow, and they were as excited as children before a feast, and you would never have known we'd beaten them like a drum the year before.

We had about the same number of Greeks – mostly small contingents from the smaller states, three hundred men each from places like Argos and Corcyra. Worth noting here that the Greeks weren't worthless, but they were outnumbered by the Thracians – this in the Panhellenic crusade to avenge the destruction of Athens!

So that was the infantry, with five thousand mercenaries and Parmenio's army in Asia (another ten thousand Macedonian foot in six more regiments). Altogether, we had about forty-two thousand infantry.

For cavalry, Alexander and Parmenio spent the winter expanding the Hetaeroi to almost two thousand five hundred, and we took three-quarters of them to Asia – eighteen hundred men with three horses each and full armour.

We had as many again – Thessalians. They served for pay, but under their own officers, as if Thessaly were a new set of Macedonian provinces, like Outer Macedonia. In effect, they were – they elected Alexander Archon for Life. So – eighteen hundred superb Thessalian cavalry.

Then the one really reliable contribution from the Greeks – six hundred splendid cavalry. Athens sent her best – the lead squadron of the Hippeis, all aristocrats, under my friend Kineas. But the other contingents weren't bad, and they, unlike the hoplites, were friends of Alexander and willing to fight.

Parmenio had another thousand cavalry – mostly mercenaries – and then there were the Prodromoi, now augmented with Paeonians and with Thracians – a little short of a thousand light cavalry. All told, we had at least six thousand cavalry. The army totalled out just short of fifty thousand men, and we calculated rations and forage on fifty thousand, because it was easy, and because a surplus is a hedge against disaster. And besides, if you don't already know it, that army had at least one slave for every soldier – probably more, and certainly many more after we started to gain Asia.

But I get ahead of myself.

Antipater and I went through all these figures, and then we started to draw things. Camps – laid out for one hundred thousand men. Forage – care to know what it takes to feed a hundred thousand men? It takes six hundred thousand pounds of food a day. Thirty thousand animals? Another three hundred thousand pounds of food. Call it a round million pounds of food a day.

Some of that can be found in grass. But that still leaves a lot to find.

And you can't put a month's worth of food in wagons. There just aren't that many farm wagons in the world.

What you do is build magazines, and store food. Philip had started the process, and Alexander had, thank the gods, never stopped spending on his preparations so that the magazines were full at the two ports in Asia and all across Macedon and down the road to the Bosporus.

It was doubly good, because Antipater showed me the accounts. The magazines were full, and the troops were paid, and we had less than thirty talents in the treasury – cash for thirty days' operations.

The men wouldn't mutiny right away, of course – but it would only be a matter of time.

Memnon was reputed to be the best general of his generation, and a brilliant deceiver – and a careful strategist who never fought unless he had to. I began to sweat just thinking of what he could do to us by *not fighting*. Two months of avoiding us and we'd be broke.

*

Alexander flatly refused to marry. He'd accepted all of Parmenio's appointments, and he'd accepted all of Antipater's financial advice, but he was determined to march in the spring, unencumbered, and he referred to marriage in terms that left no one in any doubt of his views that marriage was profoundly unheroic. Achilles was mentioned a great deal.

Parmenio convinced me to talk to the king. On this topic, I agreed with the king's mature councillors. An heir would make the kingdom more stable.

On the other hand, I saw through Antipater and I saw through Parmenio. Both had daughters – both seemed to feel that they would make fine fathers-in-law.

Ochrid was still alive, and no one had attempted to poison the king. My arrangements for his daily security were untouched.

Had I warned them off? Had the warning been a false alarm?

You never know, in this business.

I approached the king and asked if there was anyone he would marry.

He shrugged. 'If Athens had a king, I'd marry that man's daughter,' he said. 'If Darius offered me his sister, I'd consider it.' He gave me his new, lopsided, man-of-the-people grin. 'Otherwise, no.'

I nodded. 'An heir would be good for the kingdom,' I suggested.

'I'd be dead the moment a son of mine put his head from between his mother's thighs,' he said.

I thought so, too.

So I went back to the old general and told him that Alexander would not marry.

He made a face, and dismissed me.

Kineas arrived with the Athenians. He kissed Thaïs, made much of Eurydike, and bought a house for himself and his friends. He was rich in a way that I'd never seen before – he refused all offers of help.

He still adored Alexander, but in private he told me that his father's loyalty to the cause was costing him in the Assembly and in everyday business – that the anti-Macedon faction had unprecedented popularity.

That was sad. Athenians are fools, and democracy is an idiotic way to run a state.

Alectus came down from the hills and learned that we were to share the brigade of Psiloi. He came and had dinner with me, and we embraced and agreed to be good partners. In everything.

'Which nights do I get Thaïs?' he asked with a broad wink at her. In my home, she ate with my friends.

'All the nights I don't want her,' I said.

Thaïs snorted. 'All the nights I don't want him,' she said to Alectus with her dazzling smile.

But I got the better smile, and Alectus rolled his eyes.

'It's the tattoos, isn't it?' he said.

He was sixty if he was a day, and his abdominal muscles stood out like soldiers on parade. She ran a hand over his stomach.

'Some people could learn a thing or two,' she said wickedly.

I went back to training four hours each day.

Alectus laughed. But he always did.

Alexander recruited a small army of non-soldiers. Many were philosophers – men who studied plants and animals, who studied other men, who wrote about government. Their master was Aristotle's nephew, Callisthenes, who had an even bigger mouth than I have and never hesitated to use it. I liked him fine. He made me look good.

Although it was never officially said, all those civilians came under my command – or rather, I was responsible for them. There were more than two hundred of them, with that many again in slaves, and not a fighting man among them, believe me. They had to be cosseted, protected and fed – marched about, saved from predators, kept warm – amid a constant stream of whiney abuse. Once, in the Trans-Oxiana, I wanted to kill them all myself, but that's another story. Alexander was using them to make him famous. What they actually accomplished was, and is, so much more than any of us ever expected – well, that'll come in time. But for the moment – in a way, they all helped me keep the Journal. Callisthenes began a *History* the moment he joined us, and he used to read it some nights. It was tougher than the Journal – sometimes more accurate, but nowhere near as detailed in military information. All the scrolls on the far side of the tomb are my copy of Callisthenes. He was a poor philosopher but a superb historian, and he did a better job than I. However, he was no soldier.

Later, let me add, the corps of scribes, as we called them, or the Philosophoi, filled up with two-obol hacks and con artists out to take Alexander, but at the start, the men who joined us were adventurers as much as we were, and the army had some respect for them. Later – well, later was later. Everything was different later, as you'll see.

In early March, Alexander ordered me – and Perdiccas, Cleitus the Black and Marsyas – to organise a set of games to rival those of Nemea or Olympus. We were given thirty talents of gold to spend.

Perdiccas and I could take a hint – we each added ten more talents, and our games were as lavish as any ever given. We put them on down country at Aegae, and we rebuilt Philip's stadium. We added a triumphal arch, we paid poets and actors from all over Greece – well, to be honest, mostly from Athens – acrobats, dancers – and athletes. The rest of the competitors came from inside the army.

Kineas, for instance, won a crown of gold laurel leaves boxing. He was superb. No one could touch him. He defeated two Olympic champions and all the Macedonian contenders.

We had horse races, foot races, races in armour, javelin throws a-horse and afoot, swordsmanship, spear-fighting and all the usual sports – pankration, boxing, wrestling, throwing the shield. And noble prizes for every one, crowns for the victors, handed out by Alexander himself.

The Homeric imagery was relentless. Alexander was Achilles, Hephaestion was Patroclus and every one of the somatophylakes had a Homeric name. We wore Homeric costumes, and the performers performed scenes from the *Iliad*.

Thaïs, to be honest, planned most of it. She was brilliant at this sort of thing, and it allowed her to bring in all of her friends from Athens and other cities – performers, some free, some slaves. Scene painters – fantastic chaps, men who could make a piece of flat hide look like a mountain.

Her seamstresses made the king his purple tent, large enough to allow a hundred guests to recline in comfort.

She planned the themes, and she watched the rehearsals. Alexander lost interest, sometimes – when the real war in Asia took over his head – but she stayed on target. She would come to meals with a stack of scrolls.

I remember one night, I went to dinner with Antipater. We were working together on the logistics for Asia, and for the games, and sometimes we shared a meal. We went to his house, where he ate in splendour, served by twenty slaves. His wife came through once, heavily veiled, to check on us.

I laughed. I was so used to my establishment, with a woman who had her own work and yet shared all of my life, that the glimpse of a 'real' Macedonian wife made me laugh.

I won't say I hated the work, either. I'll just mention that in many ways I was relieved when the opening ceremonies went off, and I'll note that much of the conquest of Asia was easier. Destruction is much easier than creation. Eh?

And yet, we had fun. I remember a wild party at my house in Aegae, with Kineas and his friends and a crowd of Thaïs's demi-monde friends – slaves and free, dancers, hetaerae, the scene painters, a sculptor and a crowd of actors. Altogether, there must have been fifty of us crowded into my andron.

The laughter went on and on, and Thaïs led them in an indecent re-telling of the *Iliad*, which was hilarious – and which attacked Alexander in a hundred ways, and yet was hugely funny.

Kineas, always a man of immense personal dignity, laughed until wine and snot blew out of his nose.

Diodorus declaimed a long speech with an arm around one of Thaïs's dancer friends. He was playing the part of Achilles, dying in his mother's arms, but he managed to claim, in between stanzas, that as long as she would pillow his head on her breasts, he'd keep declaiming. This reached surprising heights of comedy – he was quite inventive – and every time he looked to expire, she rolled one breast or the other under his eyes, and he'd splutter and go on again, and we'd all laugh – oh, I remember that laughter as well as I remember anything in the whole crusade. I had thought Diodorus merely acerbic before that, but after that night, he and I were friends. We shared some love of laughter that transcended his dislike of Macedon and 'my kind'. It went well for him – look at him now!

And when we had all laughed and laughed, Kineas threw a grape at Diodorus, who was running his tongue along the young lady's flank, and yelled, 'Get a room' and she rose, took Diodorus by the hand and led him away. He looked back at us from the doorway.

'Better a fiery death in glory than a long life and a dull end,' he declaimed as she led him through the curtain.

Damn, that was the best exit line I've ever heard, and I still laugh to think of it.

And when most of the actors were gone, or asleep in the corners, and it was just Kineas and Thaïs and Diodorus and Niceas and, of all people, my Polystratus, sitting over a last cup of wine, Kineas got up (unsteadily) and raised his cup.

'Let's drink together – an oath to the gods, to remain friends always. We will conquer Asia together. Let's drink on it.'

We all rose – no one mocked the notion – and we all drank, even Thaïs. Nearchus was there, and young Cleomenes, and Heron, and Laodon. The cup passed – we all drank.

'I can feel the gods,' Kineas said, in a strange voice – but no one laughed because, as Thaïs said afterwards, we could all feel them.

And indeed, I sometimes think that the gods are as drawn to laughter and happy drunkenness as they are to battlefields and childbirth – and if that is true, we must have had all Olympus by us that night.

The night before we were due to march, Olympias summoned Alexander to her. I was there when the summons came, and despite his love for her and his endless patience with her, he rolled his eyes like any teenage boy summoned by his mother. He was in a state of exaltation that was nearly dangerous – he was about to achieve the entire ambition of his life.

We shouted for him to go and come back, and he waved a hand, pressed Hephaestion to stay and keep the couch warm, and left us. I remember because I passed the time of the king's absence by playing Polis with Cleitus, and I won, and Cleitus, who was drunk and in a mood, punched me, meaning only to give me a tap, but he hit me so hard that I had a bruise for a week, and only Nearchus kept me from hitting him back, or worse.

Alexander came back into the ruckus, and he was white, his lips were almost indistinct and he didn't notice the tension – which dissipated instantly, because no little quarrel was as important as the king's anger. He was angry – or worse.

In fact, he looked terrified.

Hephaestion took a look at him and ordered us all to bed. And we went – Alexander in one of his moods could be deadly.

Of course, nowadays, everyone knows what his mother told him – that he was not the son of Philip, but the son of Zeus Ammon, and that she had been made pregnant by the god.

It's easy to be incredulous and cynical. But in Macedon, we take gods seriously. We're not like fucking Athenians, who think the gods are so far away that they don't exist. In Macedon, we credulous barbarians always believe that the gods are present in daily affairs. And every noble in Macedon is the direct descendant of one of the gods.

And Olympias was no madwoman. Say what you will of her – her only addiction was power, and she played the game better than almost anyone in her generation. She was brilliant, cunning and beautiful, and utterly without scruple, except when it came to defending her son. She used murder, the army and her body with equal facility. She could reason, cajole, threaten, seduce or eliminate. But she was not mad, and if she told Alexander that he was born of a god, it's best not to dismiss the idea out of hand. Certainly Thaïs – a cynical Athenian hetaera – accepted the story at face value. Priests at Delphi accepted it. Aegyptian priests accepted it. It is fashionable now to say that Alexander was not half a god – merely a man. Very well. But I knew him, and I say that there was something beyond the human – something inestimably greater, and yet sometimes less than human, in him.

Regardless, Alexander believed her. The cynic might say that he had to – that having participated in the murder of Philip, he needed to be told that he was not Philip's son. Perhaps – but again, Alexander was never so simple, and I never saw him betray the least guilt about Philip.

What I can say is that from that night, he never again referred to Philip as 'my father'. And that, in turn, had consequences that none of us could have foreseen.

Next morning, we marched for Asia. We marched with forty thousand men, and we had our supplies sitting ready in magazines all the way down to the Asian shores, and Alexander was determined to march along the same route that Xerxes had used. And we did.

We made excellent time, passing from Amphilopolis along the coast route to Sestos in the Chersonese. But the tensions grew every day, and they made the trip harder and harder.

It was all but open conflict between the king and Parmenio.

Parmenio issued orders to the army without any reference to the king. Parmenio summoned army councils and sent the king an invitation. Parmenio changed the route of the march and the intended crossing-point without speaking to the king. Alexander had intended for the army to cross at Sigeon, near Troy, which was in our hands and had a protected port.

I had my own reason for anger. In the first three days it became increasingly clear that I was *not* to have command of the Psiloi. Attalus – another Attalus, one of Philip's men – received the command from Parmenio. I received a verbal message from Alectus, asking me to meet him, and he insisted that we meet outside the camp.

It was a difficult meeting – Alectus got to tell me I'd been replaced, and I didn't know how to respond – I lashed out at Alectus instead of saving my ire for the man responsible.

I went straight to the king, and pushed through his companions – as was my right – to where he was donning armour.

'I have been deprived of my brigade,' I said.

Alexander was just being put into his thorax. Hephaestion was holding it open for him, and he was pulling his heavy wool chiton into folds to pad the metal. 'Good morning to you, too, son of Lagus,' he said.

'Parmenio has given my brigade to another of his old men,' I said.

Alexander nodded. 'I'm sorry,' he said.

I remember the feeling of horror I had as I realised that the king was not going to *do* anything. Either he could not or he would not.

I was reminded of Pausanias, somehow.

'I'm sorry,' he said again. Quietly, he added, 'There's nothing I can do. We are all *young and inexperienced.*'

I stormed out of his presence without asking permission, and I was allowed to go without rebuke.

I considered going home.

Thaïs checked me. 'Sooner or later, Parmenio intends to kill him,' she said. 'Probably on campaign. Will you just ride off and leave him? He'll die without you.'

It was an interesting role reversal, and it did our relationship a world of good. At Thebes, it had been I talking her into staying with the army – with Macedon. Now the situation was reversed, even if the minutiae were wildly different.

'I'm staying,' she said that night, with utter finality. 'Go home if you like. I have sacrificed everything to be there when the king marches into Asia.'

Once I would have reacted to that. I would have attacked her for the suggestion that she had sacrificed *everything*. But I knew better, now.

She came and put her arms around me. 'He'll die without you,' she said again. 'Nor will I be very happy.'

She was in a position to know. With Parmenio in complete control of the army and the scout forces, Thaïs was the effective chief of the king's intelligence service.

I continued to have charge of the Military Journal and attached functions, and what rankled me – perhaps more than anything else – was that Parmenio was unfailingly polite and cheerful, and acted as if nothing had happened. He insisted that his officers supply me with their daily reports, so that the Journal ran more smoothly than ever before. Even officers like Amyntas, who affected to despise me, were quick to send their adjutants to report on numbers and effectives and men sick, ground covered, and all the details that made war possible.

Acting as a glorified military secretary was not what I had in mind, however. It was perhaps four days after I discovered that I would not have command of the scouts, and I was in the headquarters tent, listening to Eumenes the Cardian – he'd been military secretary to Philip, and he was busy trying to take the Journal away from me. I didn't really want it, but basic competitiveness and a deep inner knowledge of how courts work kept me from letting it go – and besides, Eumenes and I got along from the first, so that the struggle was surprisingly amicable and without the drama of some of Macedon's other conflicts. He was a brilliant man, as his later campaigns show – a superb fighter, and a witty, educated man. I liked him.

In fact, I liked a great many of Philip's former officers – some of whom had been my father's friends and childhood companions. It wasn't a simple case of old versus young. But as soon as I warmed to one of them, he'd make a slighting remark – an insistent remark – about Alexander's sex habits or his 'effeminism'. In fact, every day I had revealed to me where Demosthenes' propaganda came from about the king. It came from Parmenio and his men – they had a low opinion of the king, and they weren't afraid to show it. They treated him with a gentle, eternally condescending contempt. And I hated that.

At any rate, three or four days after I lost my command, Parmenio was in the headquarters tent, issuing rapid-fire orders – all simple stuff about our magazines and their replenishment, and tax relief for those districts charged with our food – Eumenes held up a hand. 'Need a minute, here,' he said. 'Lot to write. You need this copied out fair?'

Parmenio nodded. 'As soon as you can,' he said. 'Messenger for Pella is waiting.'

Eumenes went out to get another set of wax tablets, and Parmenio turned to me – ignoring a crowd of taxiarchs and under-officers.

'Men tell me you are angry about the Psiloi brigade,' he said. He held up a hand to forestall anything I might say. 'Listen, lad – it was never yours. The king should stop being dishonest about it. When the king is older and more experienced, I'll give him a share of the command appointments, and I am sure you'll get one. But he does not have that authority right now, and you were a fool to accept such a commission from his hand. That sort of behaviour can lead to discontent and is bad for discipline. Understand?'

This was a glorious opportunity for me to show my hand and tell Parmenio just what I thought of him. On the other hand, if the king wasn't taking him on, who was I to engage him? And Thaïs's comments were ringing in my ears.

And he was still my childhood hero. Let's not forget that.

So I swallowed it, and went back to commanding sixty troopers in the Hetaeroi – half a troop, in the new system. I was in Philotas's regiment. Philotas was not a friend.

On the bright side, all the reports suggested that the Persian command was badly divided – that Darius had all his best troops in Aegypt, and all his personal troops out east subduing rebels, and we were going to land in Asia unopposed.

We were twenty days to Sestos, and we arrived in excellent shape, because Antipater and I had done a thorough job. The men were well fed and their wages were paid up, and the fleet – all one hundred and sixty vessels, the whole fleet of the League – was waiting for us.

At Sestos, Alexander showed his hand. He summoned Parmenio – I was there – and informed his general that he would be taking the elite of the army – the hypaspitoi, the entire Hetaeroi and his elite Agrianians and Thracian cavalry – and marching down the coast to Elaious, where he'd intended to trans-ship, and he requested that Parmenio send us sixty ships from the fleet to cover our crossing. Alexander pointed out that by spreading our crossing, we left the Persians with an insurmountable tactical problem – either force could get behind the flank of any enemy that opposed the other. He also made plain that he intended to make religious sacrifices at Troy.

Parmenio agreed to all of it with a good grace.

'You are the king, after all,' he said.

But an hour later, in the command tent, I heard him talking to many of his older officers. Amyntas made a comment I didn't hear.

Parmenio sneered. 'The boy is running off with his lover to play war.' He laughed.

All the old men in the tent laughed with him. And Philotas spoke up. 'How much longer do we have to put up with this?' he asked.

Parmenio laughed again. 'As long as it takes,' he said.

We rode away with the feeling we were going on vacation.

Alexander rode ahead with his somatophylakes, and we enjoyed the ancient countryside and the monuments. While the Aegema moved into the prepared camp at Elaious, Alexander went and sacrificed to the hero Protesilaeius, reputed to be the first Greek ashore in the Trojan War, and the first to die.

Our squadron of warships arrived on time, and we crossed without opposition, and all the word from the northern crossing was that they were crossing well and on time. Alexander stood on the stern of our trireme and sacrificed a bull in the midst of the Hellespont – no mean feat of logistics and sheer nerve, let me tell you – and then poured a libation of fine wine from a golden goblet and threw the goblet into the water in conscious emulation of Xerxes. And the next day, when the army was ashore, he went off to Troy with his bodyguard and no one else, and he and Hephaestion sacrificed at the tombs of Achilles and Patroclus. It was a massive and expensive sacrifice. Since I wrote the Military Journal, I knew we couldn't afford to do this. We didn't have the funds to pay the troops. Now, Macedonian troops are used to being in arrears, but to launch an invasion of the mightiest empire in the history of the world with an empty treasury argues – well, hubris is not the least of it.

At the Temple of Athena in Troy – reputed to be the field temple that the Greeks set up inside their siege lines – Alexander dedicated his splendid silver and gold armour to the goddess, and left it hanging on the portico. But he took the armour of Achilles – ancient bronze nearly green with age, with patches of heavy gold plate over parts of it.

It was an ancient piece, that breastplate – magnificently made. And it fitted Alexander perfectly. If this was done to impress the army, it did so very well indeed. Soldiers are cynical bastards, but they love a good omen. That the armour of Achilles fitted the king who called himself Achilles seemed to please every man.

And *this* was what Parmenio *didn't* understand. It's funny – he had a far better understanding of the rank and file than Alexander ever did, but he had no sense of drama. Alexander was *like a god*. Parmenio was *a good general*.

Alexander wore the armour every day. It was odd to see him in armour covered in verdigris, but he made it look magnificent. He wore it under a leopard-skin cloak, with a gold helmet that sported the wings of a white bird set in gold on either side of his head.

That evening, he and Hephaestion ran a race around the tombs of the two great heroes. I think it had been years since Alexander ran in public, against a real opponent – and surprising as this may seem, Hephaestion never gave an inch in competition with Alexander. They raced like Olympians, and both of them flew – by the gods, they were magnificent. The Aegema watched them and applauded, and rumours of divine favour and even divine status began to sprout wings among the troops. Alexander won by the length of a man's body over a long course, and afterwards, still naked, he poured another libation to Achilles and grinned like a boy.

I helped him strigil the dust off, and he kept laughing. 'Did you see me run?' he asked me, three times. 'Wasn't I magnificent?'

In fact, he had been superb – but why did he have to ask?

Thaïs had, by this time, heard the rumour of what Olympias had said to Alexander. He'd told Hephaestion, and Hephaestion told some favourite, and the word got around. It seemed to me hubris, at the time, and perhaps blasphemy – but it also seemed possible, at least at a distance.

From Troy we marched north to join up with Parmenio. He'd met up with his own garrison forces in Asia, and together we had almost fifty thousand men.

Memnon, the Greek mercenary, was no longer in command of the Persian forces. Arsites, the satrap of Phrygia, was gathering men, and he placed the brilliant Memnon in a subordinate position.

But Memnon had already done us serious damage. He'd retaken most of the towns of the Asian Troas – Lampsacus and Parium closed their gates to us. We had less than a month's cash on hand, and everyone in Asia seemed to know it. Outside Lampsacus, the philosopher Anaximenes told Alexander and Parmenio point blank that he'd only pay a certain amount of a bribe to get us to leave his city alone – he knew that we didn't have time to lay a siege. And he was right. We took his bribe and marched on, and our army was getting hungry.

Thaïs went to work. That night, with Anaximenes's taunts burning in our ears, she sat by lamplight in my pavilion and wrote a dozen letters to leading men in Priapus, the next town on our route. And she sent Strakos and Polystratus with a dozen men.

It was her first attempt at a clandestine operation, and it ran well enough. They entered the city before the gates closed, and contacted her friends – the men of Alexander's party, or in one case Leonatus, a Spartan exile and one of her personal friends. But this time, they were not simply gathering information.

Polystratus took twenty of my grooms and seized a gatehouse.

Strakos took half a dozen thugs and murdered three men – the leaders of the pro-Persian faction fingered by Leonatus.

The next day, when Alexander rode at the head of his brilliant escort to the town of Priapus, they opened their gates and welcomed him as their liberator. Alexander's mood, already dangerously elated, rose to new heights. He said things – wild things – praised the citizens for their 'Olympian wisdom' and other flights of fanciful rhetoric that left them unmoved and apprehensive that they had backed the wrong horse. Strakos and Polystratus grinned like fiends.

Thaïs looked tired and stressed.

Just north of us, the Persians were gathering an army. Arsites was a capable commander, and he had a good name, and the Phrygians rallied to him in good numbers. Thaïs thought he had thirty-five thousand men, and Parmenio, with lower estimates, still thought he had twenty-five thousand real troops and another four thousand useless levies.

We were apprehensive. There were rumours that the Persian fleet was at sea, and since the Great King had just reconquered Aegypt and had absolute control of Tyre and Cyprus, too, we expected that he could put three hundred and fifty triremes on the water to our hundred and sixty. And his would have better mariners, or better than all but the contingent from Athens.

Worse, the money situation was so acute that we had a hard time buying provisions even with the willing help of the people of Priapus. We were down to ten talents of gold.

Parmenio was suspiciously willing to support the king.

Alexander had one simple answer – we were going to go along the coast by quick marches and force the satrap to battle and pay the troops and the campaign with the spoils of his camp.

It was becoming plain that all the Persians had to do to defeat us was refuse the battle.

What was worse, it began to look to me as if Parmenio was pushing the king to commit to whatever battle was offered. I didn't like the way it was discussed in the headquarters tent, or the undertone of satisfaction to their predictions of doom.

And at the public officers' meetings, to which Alexander was now always invited, Parmenio deferred to the king in everything, allowing him to make the operational decisions and encouraging his wildest flights of fancy. We were meeting on the portico of the Temple of Athena in Priapus when Alexander, looking at a dozen Phrygian cavalry just captured by his Thracians, commented that if these were the vaunted Asians, he could probably rout them with just his bodyguard.

Parmenio nodded. 'Lord, you and your friends are all that will be needed – one gallant charge – like Achilles on the plains of Ilium. Scatter the Medes and win undying glory.'

Alexander flushed, laughed and tried not to look pleased by the apparent praise.

I wondered if Parmenio was contemplating using the Persians as a weapon to murder the king.

SIXTEEN

Arsites chose to await us at the Granicus river.

It was like a miracle from the gods. We needed a battle. If the Persians had retreated and refused battle – well, I assume that Alexander would have done *something*. Or perhaps not – perhaps the gods took a hand, and Arsites, like some actor in a tragedy, had no choice but to stand and fight.

On the other hand, Alexander, for all his flights of fancy, understood the moral vector of war far better than Parmenio. Arsites was the satrap, and Alexander was marching about Asia in his leopard skin, taking cities and threatening to be taken seriously, and that embarrassed the satrap. He wanted to beat Alexander to win glory with the King of Kings. If you look at it, you can see wheels within wheels – our wheels of intrigue, their wheels of intrigue. The gods must laugh.

Their army was considerably smaller than ours, but Arsites had some superb cavalry – easily as good as ours, as you will hear. And he had Memnon – probably the best soldier in Asia, and many men alive today say he was the equal of Alexander in brilliance. Luckily for us, Arsites hated Memnon and ignored his advice.

We had problems of our own.

We got a late start out of Priapus – because Philotas bickered with Amyntas about the dispositions of the scouts. Six hours after marching out of Priapus, near the end of the marching day, late afternoon and the summer sun boiling us in our breastplates and helmets. I was virtually asleep, letting my new mare pick her way.

Suddenly there was a disturbance at the head of the column. Paeonian cavalry scouts galloped up, and their dust moved slowly across us after they drew rein. They were so close to me that I could hear them report that the Persian army was on the move and would probably beat us to the Granicus. The elder of the two reported in bad Greek that the ground was favourable to the Persians, with a ridge dominating the river ford. They reported to Amyntas (who in my book should have been as far forward as his courage allowed) and Philotas together.

I listened with mounting fury as Philotas reacted carefully, after a long conversation with Amyntas about the dispositions of the scouts. They lost minute after minute.

Alexander was too far to the rear in the column, and the column was too narrow and too long for him to come up. I wasn't even sure he knew what was happening. He was with the main body of the cavalry – well back from the advance guard. Simply by the luck of rotation, I was at the front with the squadron assigned to provide an armoured fist to support the light-armed scouts.

It was like physical pain, listening to the cautious 'professionals' debate how to move up the narrow road and where to place the army. In short, Philotas conceded immediately that Arsites would gain the Granicus river line, and began to send Amyntas's scouts to the right and left, looking for ground on which we could camp.

I knew exactly what Alexander would do – what I would do. I wanted to lunge for the river and beat Arsites there. I hadn't seen the crossing, but it was not high water at any of the other streams we'd crossed – and I assumed that we would be able either to get there first, or fight our way across in the face of their vanguard before their main army came up.

Before you consider mocking me – keep in mind that our sense of superiority *was* our main weapon. Still is.

And Philotas and Amyntas were frittering it away.

I turned to Polystratus after fifteen minutes. 'Get Alexander,' I said. 'Tell him he is needed here.'

Polystratus nodded, dismounted and ran off down the column. He was smart – a man can run where a horse cannot walk.

And then I sat and fumed. My nerves were transmitted to my horse, who became skittish and started nipping the other horses. I wasn't on Poseidon – I was on Penelope, my new riding mare, and she had a temper as bad as Medea's, and Polystratus said she should have been called Medusa. Ajax was home on my farms, helping to make little horses.

Philotas turned and glared at me. 'Can't control your horse, Ptolemy?' he asked.

'Like me, she's eager to be moving forward,' I said. See – not so bad. A *gentle* comment.

His face grew red. 'You're as bad as the king,' he shot back. 'You cannot charge everything. Stopping to think is an important part of warfare. Arsites already has the good ground.'

I shrugged. I may have made a derisive noise.

365

Philotas was turning away, and now he whirled back, pulling his horse by the bit in a rather brutish manner. 'What was that, sir?' he asked.

I shrugged again. 'Whatever you like. My horse may have farted.'

The men around me chuckled. The men around Philotas grew as red as he.

'If you have a comment to make, make it,' he said.

'Very well, since you invite it,' I answered. 'If Arsites is moving forward – let's beat him to the good ground. If we lose the race – let's take it from him.' I looked around. 'That's what we call the "Macedonian Way".'

I got approving grunts and a lot of nods.

Philotas was so red I was wondering if he'd turn purple.

Amyntas spat. 'That's why you puppies can't be trusted to command,' he said.

'Oh,' I nodded, 'I'm not very good at caution,' I said. And after a two-beat pause, I said, 'But I'm quite good at fighting. So I don't bother much with caution.'

'One more word and I will send you to the rear,' Philotas spat.

Polystratus appeared at my knee. 'He's right behind me,' he said.

So I held my tongue.

Alexander came up with Parmenio at his elbow – but only because of the press on the road, not because they were together.

'What's going on here?' Parmenio demanded.

'Ptolemy is an insolent puppy,' Philotas said.

'Not pertinent to the tactical problem,' I said. 'Philotas is a cautious old woman who is sacrificing our needs to his pride.'

Parmenio glared at me.

'Arsites is moving up to the Granicus river,' Amyntas put in. 'We're seeing to our dispositions and looking for a campsite.'

'We could beat him to the river,' I put in. Yes – I was a very junior officer. But I was also an important nobleman and one of the king's friends. In Macedon, that made me the equal of any man there. 'Either we win the race and get some Hetaeroi across, or we lose the race and we punch across and take the high ground.'

Parmenio frowned. 'What high ground?'

Philotas shrugged.

Amyntas pointed at the two scouts. 'They say there's a steep ridge behind the ford, with a broad top.'

In fact, they'd said that and I'd heard it, but as I suspected, Philotas had missed it.

Alexander got that look – the look that said he was thinking it out. 'How high is the ridge?'

'Have you seen it for yourself?' Parmenio demanded.

'No, they've sat here talking about it,' I said.

Philotas gave me a look of pure hate.

Alexander looked around. 'Give me the Paeonians, Ptolemy's squadron and ... the Thracians. I'll see what can be done.'

Parmenio shook his head. 'No ...' he began. And then he froze. 'Yes,' he said.

Philotas looked as if he was going to choke.

Parmenio managed a small smile. 'At your command, lord.'

'Send me every armoured cavalryman from the main body,' Alexander said. While he was talking, I changed to Poseidon. Alexander looked around and grinned. 'Right – forward.'

And we were off.

It was quite late – and Philotas had wasted at least a quarter of an hour dithering. Now we pelted down the road with a few hundred cavalrymen. Immediately – in the way of men everywhere – I began to question my own intentions. Parmenio's about-face was suspicious. Was he realising who was in command? Or just betting that we'd go and get killed?

Too late to worry.

We headed almost due south along the coast, and the plain was opening before us. In the distance, less than twenty-five stades away to the south, we could see a great lake spread in rippling fire from the setting sun, and to the north lay the Propontis, the great inland sea between the Euxine and the Mediterranean.

As we came down a low ridge, I could see the Persians moving along the road to the east – and they were already leaving the road and expanding into a battle line, and doing it pretty well, I thought. I could see six ... seven ... eight cavalry regiments, their spear-points flickering like flame. Sixteen thousand cavalry – maybe more.

But their attempt to fan out from the road was slowed by ploughed fields. And while I could see horsemen along the river, there weren't so many.

Just behind their cavalry was a phalanx. It didn't look any smaller than ours, and it was already in formation.

Five stades away.

It was pretty clear to me that our three hundred cavalry, however bold, were too little and too late. Too late by about fifteen minutes.

The ridge the Thracians had described was lower – much lower – than I had imagined. But I could see that determined infantry atop that ridge would close the road, and that the lake to the south would cover

367

the flank of the Persian army, meaning that their thirty thousand men would fill the field from the sea to the lake.

And if I could see it, Alexander was doubtless ahead of me.

He turned – he was ahead – and waved to me. 'I need your Polystratus,' he said.

I brought all my grooms forward.

Alexander reined in, snapped his fingers and a groom came up with Bucephalus. While he changed horses, he issued orders to Polystratus.

'Straight back – find Parmenion. Tell him to march the phalanx to the right by sections – along the line of hills and around the lake to the south. Use the hills to screen the march. I'll buy us some time at the ford and fix their attention there. And tell him to send me all the Hetaeroi.'

Polystratus nodded. 'All the Hetaeroi to you, phalanx to the right, screened by *those* hills and around the lake.' He raised an eyebrow.

I read his mind. 'That's forty stades, lord. They won't make it before darkness falls.'

Alexander bobbed his head. He was up on Bucephalus, and his cheeks were bright crimson with anticipation, and Hephaestion was holding out his magnificent golden helmet.

'If this works, they won't be necessary, and if this doesn't work, we fight tomorrow,' he said. His eyes were fixed on the ford, now just three stades away.

The second and third squadrons of the Hetaeroi were coming up. Nearchus saluted. 'Philotas is ten minutes behind me, lord,' he said to Alexander. 'He's pushing the rest of the Hetaeroi up the column.'

Alexander nodded. 'I won't wait. Wedge!'

We formed behind the king – he insisted on being at the point of the wedge – and after all, he was King of Macedon. I fell into place behind him – with Black Cleitus on his right rear and me on his left rear.

And then we trotted for the ford.

The Persians saw us, but they took for ever to react. I'm going to guess that they didn't expect us to cross. And they weren't formed in a body, but a few hundred Persian nobles spread out across a stade of ground – some were even watering their horses.

We went from a trot to a canter, and our wedge began to spread out. The king was making no concessions to differences in horse flesh. He was watching something – I could see from the tension in his neck under the base of his helmet.

All the Persians began to point. The king was hard to miss. His green-bronze armour and his superb helmet shouted his presence. A messenger dashed back from the forward Persian troops, and they began to form.

We hit the ford. Our horses raised a curtain of spray and Alexander wasn't slowing, so I dug my heels into Poseidon and hung on. Poseidon doesn't love water.

A Persian – a noble in a bronze peaked helmet and a magnificent scarlet saddle – hurtled across our front on a big Nisean horse, moving like a grey streak, and he threw his javelin at the king, and Alexander caught it in the air with his own spear and parried it – a fine feat. Men cheered all along the faces of the wedge.

We started up the far bank. There were fifty Persians there, all throwing their spears, but none of them abided our onset, and they broke before us, and we were across.

Yet as soon as we were up the far bank, I could see that we'd charged into a nest of angry bees. Cavalrymen were coming up from the south and the east – even from the north – as far as the eye could see.

Alexander laughed. It was a mad laugh. He turned and his eyes glittered and his face was white, his cheeks and lips red as blood, and he looked like a dramatic mask – or like a god.

'I think we have their attention!' he shouted, and pointed the tip of the wedge at the nearest formed enemy body, two hundred Phrygian horse preparing to charge us. He raised his spear. 'Ready, Hetaeroi? Charge!' he roared, and my trumpeter picked up his command and sang it out.

The head of the wedge turned less than an eighth part of a circle, and then we were pounding forward up a slight incline, and the Phrygians came down at us with their longer spears. Their files spread as they charged, so that just before impact you could see the sunset between their men.

Alexander did his job as 'wedge leader' perfectly, taking the point of the wedge into the widest gap between enemy files – and he ducked the first enemy lance, a beautiful piece of horsemanship, perfectly judged, so that the lance-point passed a hand's breadth over his back, and then he rose and his spear took the Phrygian on his right just below the throat – killing him and ripping him from his horse in one movement. The king's spear snapped from the impact, and Alexander swung the butt of the spear into the next lance, parrying it off to his left across his horse's head and then cutting back with his whole weight behind the staff – *thunk*, into the head of the second man on the left, and the man collapsed from the saddle – the king dropped his spear haft and unsheathed his sword, his body flat along the neck of his horse to evade the third lance ...

It was beautiful. It made my heart ache to watch him.

And then I was fighting.

I was on the left, and the king had left the front-left man for me – I parried his spear with mine and ran my spearhead along his shaft, so that it slammed into his thorax and he was gone. I kept the spear, turned it and caught the next man with the butt close in – a clumsier blow than the king's, but my man fell too. My horse's haunches bunched and expanded and I was into my third man – Poseidon hit his horse, breast to breast, and knocked it to the ground, and Amyntas son of Amyntas struck me from behind – these things happen in a melee – and we got tangled, and the wedge was slowing – but the king was still pushing ahead, and I put my heels into Poseidon despite the ringing in my ears. I pushed forward into the press – the Phrygians were thickening like lentil soup in the pot, because another squadron had thrown themselves into the fight.

The king had three of them around him. In the glance I got, I saw him thrust his sword into one exposed side, and then, quick as a cat, draw back and flick a cut at the second and carry it around to the third.

He was like a god.

But he needed help.

Poseidon did his bit, pushing forward with heavy, massive, powerful surges from his hindquarters, so that I seemed to be rowing forward.

We were suddenly so close to the Phrygians that we were no longer threading between their files – now we were pushing in close, knee to knee, face to face, horse against horse, and now the horses began to fight each other, and I had to keep my knees all but locked and hang on with my arms to stay with my mount, because he was kicking, biting and *pushing*.

Hipposthismos, I remember thinking, in that way that your brain wanders off in moments of critical danger. Blows hit me – Persian spears – I got a slash across the top of my thigh, below the line of my tassets, and my bridle hand took its usual abuse – that's why it looks the way it does, eh?

Othismos is the pushing and shoving and vicious infighting of the closest-packed melee. So you can guess—hipposthismos is the mounted version.

I came up against an officer – a high officer, with superb embroidery on his cloak and a sword with a hilt of gold – a sword I got to know very well, because he cut at my head, and I parried – sword to sword. Our blades cut into each other – that's why you don't use a sword to parry, lad! – and we bound up, and our horses pressed in, and there we were in a pushing match, hilts in front of our noses, legs crushed together, and I could smell his breath – and he mine.

I reckon he was a good officer, because as we struggled, he looked past me – trying to figure out, as I was, what in Hades was happening in the melee.

I dropped my reins, reached across my body with my left hand, put it under his right elbow and pushed – he twisted to keep his balance and his seat, and I got my hilt free and punched him with it ...

And he was gone in the melee, and I was almost to the king. A blow rang off my backplate – I assume my erstwhile opponent back-cut at me as the melee carried us apart – but it did me no damage, and I was *almost there.*

I had two or three heartbeats to look around – an eddy in the fight – and the Persians were coming at us from every side.

Alexander was putting Persians into the dust with almost every blow, but some of the feline grace was gone from his back and hips as he rode. Grace is the first thing to go as a man tires – we start to make slightly larger motions with the arms, the pelvis – anything to help the muscles work. Alexander was showing the very earliest sign of fatigue.

I got up to him as he caught a Persian spear in his bridle hand, pulled it from its owner's grip and stabbed him with the butt-spike – all in a heartbeat.

My sword was bent. I hadn't noticed it, but my fine Keltoi long sword was bent from the pushing match with the Persian officer, and it had a deep nick – almost a gouge – in the thick metal near the hilt.

I rang it off a Phrygian's helmet, and it snapped.

'Where is Philotas?' Alexander asked, his tone almost conversational.

Here's one of the differences between a normal, intelligent Macedonian and Alexander. I'd forgotten that Philotas existed. I was busy fighting for my life – Philotas was on a different plane of existence.

Alexander pulled on his reins and our horses lined up, head to head. But the Phrygians were done – they weren't running yet, but they were falling back, riding clear of the melee or simply getting shy of combat.

Cleitus came up on Alexander's left side.

He looked across at me, ignoring the king. 'We need to get him out of here,' he said.

I looked over my shoulder. We had Medes – or Persians – behind us, between us and the river – I could see their high hats and their bows.

And their arrows. Arrows were falling on the rear ranks of the wedge, and horses were screaming.

I think that until then we'd lost very few men, if any. We had good armour and excellent helmets – far better than the Phrygians or the Medes. And our horses were big – as big as theirs, if not as good as the Niseans. Our men were better trained in arms – the Persians don't wrestle, and that's a terrible disadvantage in a cavalry melee.

But we didn't have bows, and their arrows were falling on the rumps of our horses. Horses were dying and their riders were left on the ground in a cavalry melee – a terrible place to be.

Had the Phrygians held on for another few minutes, they would have had us. As it was, they fell back, and Alexander ordered us to wheel around – easy enough for a small group of horsemen who had ridden together all their lives, and desperately hard for anyone else. The Medes never imagined we'd wheel – but the whole wedge spun on Alexander, men riding to the flanks in good order, as if this sort of fancy riding in the face of the enemy was an everyday thing. Which it was, for us.

We charged the Medes, and they came right at us – the Medes are the bravest nation on earth, except for ours, and they are never shy about a scramble. Our horses were blown and theirs were fresh, and they shot a flight of arrows at us from close in, and men fell – but nothing touched Alexander, and he had his spear two-handed, the butt clamped under his right armpit, and he wrenched it high just before contact, beating his opponent's spear aside and thrusting. He must have missed – one of his few melee misses, I must admit – and the man's spear rode down Alexander's spear, skipped off Bucephalus's coat and popped up into my line. I got a hand on it, slapped it clear of my body – and my opponent unhorsed himself, because he wouldn't let go of his spear – a juvenile mistake.

Another Mede shot me from arm's length – I had time to put my head *down* and my crest into his shot – it was like being punched in the head, and blackness came before my eyes – a haze at the edges, and another blow rang against the side of my helmet, and then I could see, and my spear had rammed through his chest and my spear-point was out through his back, and the weight of him broke the staff.

And then I was through, Poseidon gathering speed, and Alexander was trying to turn his horse to go back into the melee.

I gave Poseidon his head and gathered the king's bridle in my hand as I trotted past – Bucephalus trumpeted his displeasure as his head was snapped round, but he had to follow Poseidon.

Alexander slammed his spear-butt into my side. 'What ...'

We were in the river. Persian cavalry was coming at the Hetaeroi from all directions, and men were down – at least a dozen, all king's friends. Amyntas son of Amyntas was down, and Lagus son of Perdiccas, and other men I knew.

And Pyrrhus – young Pyrrhus, one of my own. I could see immediately that he was missing from my file, because when I burst out of the back of the melee, all my file followed me like good troopers, and there was Nearchus, and Cleomenes, but Pyrrhus was gone. Damn the boy.

But he was not the king.

I rode through the ford, and Alexander was screaming at me, but I had his reins.

Why, you ask?

Because in my one glimpse across the river I'd seen Philotas. He was sitting on his war horse, and he wasn't moving to our aid. And I thought of Thaïs, and what she had said, and I made the decision – right or wrong – that it was my job to keep the king alive.

The Hetaeroi followed me.

The Medes didn't pursue. They'd lost their prize – the king – and they could claim to have had the best of the melee, in that they held the ground. Another way of looking at it was that we'd broken through the Phrygian cavalry, whirled about and shattered the Medes, but perhaps that's my bias speaking. Heh, heh.

I got Alexander up the Macedonian bank of the Granicus, and I turned to him – well short of the waiting squadrons of Hetaeroi, who looked angry, even at this distance. There was the margin of victory – six full squadrons, fifteen hundred Macedonian cavalry. Sitting.

'Blame me,' I hissed at Alexander. 'Call me a coward, lord, but ask yourself, *why is Philotas just sitting there?*'

Alexander rode past me. He trotted his horse up the bank and turned to look back.

The Persians were still in disarray. But even as we watched, a magnificent regiment came up at a canter – a thousand noble Persians in fine armour – with scales, most of them, that gleamed like a million mirrors, like dancer's bangles in the setting sun. Arsites in person, I assumed. They pushed their own Medes and Phrygians aside.

But they halted at the riverbank.

Our last files got across, pursued only by a handful of Mede arrows.

'Not as easy as you thought, Ptolemy?' Philotas shouted at me.

The king was angry with me, and the army would think I'd been a coward, and Philotas – I should have flashed with rage, but something inside me was tired, and cold. So I rode up the bank and right up to him.

Give him this much – he didn't flinch or quail. I think he hoped I would strike him, so he could order me arrested.

I rode right up close. 'You're right,' I said. I was only as loud as I needed to be for him to hear me. 'But I didn't expect to have to do it by myself.'

His eyes widened a little.

I rode past him and had my Polystratus, now my hyperetes, sound the recall from our place in the Hetaeroi line. I didn't think that the

Persians would come across the stream at us, but it would have been foolish to allow my squadron to continue to mill about in confusion.

We dismounted. All of the horses were blown – even Poseidon was tired.

Alexander left Bucephalus and came over to me. 'I wish to apologise,' he said.

I don't think he'd ever apologised – at least to me. I just stood there with a foolish look on my face, no doubt.

'But we put fear into them, did we not? Did you see me when I went through the front ranks of the Phrygians? I've never been so fast – I felt as if Achilles himself guided my arm.'

I was so relieved to have his forgiveness that I pressed his hand. 'You were ... like a god,' I said.

Alexander's eyes widened, just as Philotas's had, but for the opposite reason. He positively beamed with pleasure. 'Ptolemy! How unlike you!' he teased me, and slapped me on the shoulder. 'And then I missed my stroke against the Mede – did you take him?'

I smiled. In truth, the king's need to refight his actions and praise himself was annoying – the sort of conceit you'd expect from a much lesser man. But I was relieved, strangely happy, even. 'He unhorsed himself,' I said. 'I got his spear in my left hand and he fell off his horse.'

Alexander threw back his head and laughed – a high-pitched laugh that sounded utterly false.

He stopped mid-laugh.

Darkness was falling. And as if he'd become another man, the king suddenly turned his head.

'We should be marching south,' he said. 'Or we'll never reach their flank by morning.'

We'd lost more than twenty Hetaeroi, and in later years the king put up monuments to them. But we were alive, and the king was still king.

If Parmenio had another plan, he didn't try to press it on the king. In later years, he insisted to anyone who would listen that the plan to go south around the lake was his plan, not the king's – that all the king wanted was to ride forward and challenge Arsites to single combat.

Crap.

The king loved to fight, but we went forward to try to steal the ford from the Persians, and we missed by minutes – minutes that Philotas and Amyntas had wasted. To my mind, Parmenio only sent us forward in the hope that we'd die.

That said, though – the king propagandised his version, too. Look at what it says in the Military Journal. No mention at all of the battle at the ford. Eh? Nor any mention of Parmenio, even though it *was* Parmenio who marched the army off to the right behind the screen of hills and got them to the edge of the lake under cover of darkness – and into a cold camp without fires. When we rode into that camp, our horses were *done*, but there were grooms ready to take them, and men handed us cold food and wine and led us to our pallets to sleep – Parmenio had done a magnificent job.

Pyrrhus rode in after dark with four men. He had a claim to having been the bravest of the Hetaeroi, and the king embraced him – it turned out that he'd ridden through the Medes and kept going – with just half a file – sweeping through the Phrygians before realising that no one was behind him. He'd escaped down the Persian bank of the river, and he admitted that he'd been unpursued. The Medes had been shocked by the cavalry action.

We were up well before first light. We crossed the marsh south of the lake on trails marked by the Agrianians and pushed north – crossed the Granicus almost dry shod, where long bars of stony shale lay across the water like piers or bridges.

We were fast and silent, but Arsites was no fool, or perhaps it was Memnon. Either way, the lack of fires probably gave us away, and the Persians sent cavalry probes across the Granicus at first light, and these found us – they on our side of the river, and we on their side. They galloped off, and we couldn't stop them, and the game was up.

So the king led us on faster. I was on Penelope, saving Poseidon for the last possible moment. Polystratus had him in the rear of my squadron. Philotas rode six files to my right – he was commanding the Hetaeroi, and I was reduced to a mere king's bodyguard. He hadn't said a word to me all morning. I'm certain we both had the same thought – no need to quarrel, when with a little luck the Medes would kill one of us.

Arsites formed his army to his own left – which is to say, he now formed with his Greek mercenary infantry on that low ridge, and the far right of his cavalry (the western end of his line) covered by the river, and his left-flank cavalry dangled at the eastern end, but because he had fifteen thousand cavalry to our six thousand, his left flank overlapped our right.

On our far right, in the bushy ground to the east, Alexander set the Agrianians and all the archers under Attalus. Next in line came Philotas with a thousand Hetaeroi, and then the king in the centre of the right, with his bodyguard, and then Arrhabaeus, the scrawny sod, another of Parmenio's old men, with the rest of the Hetaeroi. To our left were the hypaspitoi and then all six taxeis of the pezhetaeroi – ten thousand of them, the largest phalanx I'd ever seen formed in one place.

And on the far side of the phalanx was Parmenio with all the Thessalian cavalry, all the Greek allies, including your father, and all the Thracians.

Opposite us, as we formed, we saw Arsites trot into position facing us. He moved twice, so insistent was he in lining up on Alexander. He had almost two thousand Persian noble cavalrymen – in effect, men as good as our Hetaeroi. The rest of his wing was composed of Hyrkanians and Phrygians, and on their far left they placed six hundred mercenary Greek cavalry under Memnon himself. Thebans, a lot of them, and Thessalian exiles and Athenian exiles – men with every reason to fight well.

Alexander rode along the front of the whole army as it formed, so that we appeared to be in a state of chaos, with regiments spread over forty stades in every direction. In fact, we had a standard formation and we'd practised it almost every day since we left Amphilopolis. Every man and every file knew his place, in rain, in snow, in fog. As soon as the order was given to the marching column to form line of battle, units marched to their places and pushed left or right to make sure they had room. Files opened and closed – cavalry units added or subtracted files to fit into the line.

And as this unfolded, the king rode from unit to unit, calling men by name and shouting encouragement. He didn't restrict himself to units that loved him – he rode to every unit, even the taxeis that had been Parmenio's in Asia, and to every group he called out, 'Tonight we will be rich men!' and they always cheered.

We rode with him, of course, and he rode fast, and I was glad I was still on my riding horse. We cantered from unit to unit, and then, when we'd reached Parmenio on the far left, we halted.

'You ready, lad?' Parmenio asked.

Alexander's head snapped back as if he'd been hit.

'Lad?' he asked. 'I'm your king.'

Parmenio smiled. 'Your first real battle,' he said.

Alexander sat back – spine straight, posture perfect, rein held loose. 'Parmenio, if I win this battle, will you concede that I know my business?' he asked.

Parmenio laughed. 'Relax, lad. Take it easy. We have the numbers, and their Greek foot are no match for our pikes – our phalanx is twice the size of theirs. Nothing to worry you.'

'When I beat them, I'll execute every one of the traitors,' Alexander said.

Parmenio smiled. 'What a fire-breather you are, to be sure. Best get back to your wing. Arsites has decided to come at us.'

Sure enough, Arsites and his wing were advancing.

Alexander looked, turned his horse and we galloped across the whole front of the army.

No one else seemed to know we were late – men cheered just to see the king ride so beautifully, his cloak flying behind him, back straight, as if he were an equestrian statue brought to life. The rest of us followed as best we could – Black Cleitus, me, Nearchus, Marsyas; Laodon and Erygius, and older men like Demaratus of Corinth. In some ways, despite being a nation of innovators, Macedonians are very old-fashioned – in a big fight, we like to see a king go into battle surrounded by his closest friends. I've met dozens of Greeks who accuse Alexander of living like a hero in the *Iliad* – what they fail to understand is that *all* Macedonians live like heroes in the *Iliad*.

We hauled on our reins when we got back to the Hetaeroi. Polystratus was ready for me – I changed horses and buckled the cheek-plates on my helmet, and took my heaviest spear from Ochrid, who gave me a grin.

Arsites and his whole line were a stade away.

The king looked left and right down the line.

He pointed to Arsites, easily visible a stade or less away on a magnificent white horse.

'Blow through them and the battle is won,' he said. 'Thank the gods that they were fools enough to fight.' His personal priest and diviner, Aristander, offered a sacrifice and a libation, and exclaimed at the sight of the liver – he shouted aloud, he was so excited.

'Victory!' he shouted. He waved the bloody liver.

All the time Aristander was killing his beasts, the Persian line was advancing.

They weren't Macedonians. Gaps began to open in their line as soon as they rolled forward. Indeed, the largest gap opened between the wing facing us and their cavalry in the centre. They'd put Paphlagonian or perhaps Phrygian cavalry in the centre – I couldn't tell which – screening the Greek mercenaries to their rear. Why they placed cavalry in opposition to our phalanx I'll never know.

But their cavalry had no intention of riding forward into our sarissas, so the centre lagged behind and Arsites's wing plunged forward, and a gap began to open. An enormous gap.

The king waved to us, his bodyguard. 'Hold here,' he said.

He shouted orders to Philotas and waved at Arsites.

Philotas protested.

Alexander insisted.

Philotas shrugged, obviously angry, and barked orders at his trumpeter. And our entire right division began to move.

Philotas didn't want to do it. It was written in every line of his body – in the way he rode. But I don't know what else he wanted to do.

He rolled forward with half our cavalry, and three horse lengths from the enemy, he flashed his sword and the Hetaeroi went straight to the gallop – a tactic we practised on a thousand strips of grass, in winter and summer – and the enemy were caught by surprise, suddenly turned from aggressive attackers to defenceless prey.

Then I could see nothing but the sudden onset of dust – the battle haze of the poet.

Arsites was no longer opposite us. Something else had caught his attention, and he'd taken his bodyguard out of the line. But we could still see Persian cavalrymen in beautiful tall helmets opposite us. They were rolling into the melee – fighting draws men like a magnet.

Cleitus pressed in close behind the king. 'We should—'

'Silence!' Alexander said. He had one fist in the small of his back and his other hand holding the reins, legs dangling, and he was watching the enemy line where the gap had opened – watching it to the exclusion of all other things.

I watched the Persian line opposite me shred as the line of men threw themselves at Philotas.

The king turned and motioned to Arrhabaeus. The older man saluted.

'Follow me,' Alexander said.

Arrhabaeus saluted again and we started forward. I'd assumed that the king would take us into the flank of Philotas's melee, where the Persians were fully committed, and Philotas was fighting against odds.

But that wasn't the king's intention at all.

He turned to all of us – his friends – and he had the secret smile we all came to know so well – I'd seen it before, and I knew it. 'Now we win,' he said. 'Unless Philotas folds in the next thousand heartbeats, now we win. Follow me, and be heroes, and live for ever!'

I know no other man who could say such stuff with a straight face and mean it. My heart swelled to twice its size, and I felt the power of an Olympian suffuse me. And we went forward.

As soon as the king was clear of the leftmost squadrons of the Hetaeroi, he turned sharply towards the centre of the enemy line – towards the gap.

He was going for the gap.

Ares, we were going to ride *past* their unengaged men and plunge into the open ground between their cavalry line and their infantry.

As soon as the king saw that the Hetaeroi were forming on him and angled appropriately, he sat back and put his heels to Bucephalus and we were off at a gallop.

The Paphlagonians opposite us began to shred as soon as they saw we were going to outflank them. They lacked anything like our level of training, and they couldn't respond in kind – they couldn't wheel to cover the open ground, or extend files, so the end men began to ride back to cover the gap, and in a moment they were in flight, and not a blow had been struck.

I once watched a thatched roof blow to pieces in a wind storm. It was like that. First there was a solid enough line facing us, and then a few men riding to close a gap – and then, as if burned by a flash fire or blown away on the rising wind, the Paphlagonian cavalry was gone, and we were riding for the flanks of their centre division – all those Phrygians, already unwilling to face our pike men.

Arsites saw the crisis. He sent Darius's own cousin, Mithridates, with his bodyguard and the best of his Mede cavalry, straight at us. And to our front, emboldened or perhaps harangued, a few hundred Phrygians suddenly went from vacillation to attack – and came right at us.

That was my last glimpse of the development of the battle. I never saw it, but on our left, their cavalry crashed into Parmenion and threw him back – but he didn't break, and his Thessalians and Thracians gave ground slowly. To our right, Philotas fought against odds – heavy odds. But he had the senior squadrons of the Hetaeroi, men who had fought in the mountains and on the Danube and who believed. They held. They were even pushing the enemy back.

We crashed into the Phrygians, and Alexander killed his man, and then I was fighting, spear against spear – I went high, this time, at contact, and I remember being showered with the remnants of my man as my spear wrecked his head.

Alexander broke his spear a horse length ahead of me, and old Demaratus of Corinth gave his to the king – very sporting. But before we had time to savour our victory, we were fighting for our lives, and the king.

No sooner were we into the Phrygians than the Persians hit the right face of our wedge, and they drove straight for the king – cutting us off from Arrhabaeus.

The first I knew was an arrow in Poseidon's flank. I whirled and saw a man behind me, nocking an arrow, and I didn't have time to make complex decisions, my arm went back and I threw my heavy spear, and it hit his horse in the neck and knocked the horse down.

Poseidon turned on his back feet and I got my borrowed kopis out of the scabbard under my arm in time to parry a spear from a man in gorgeous armour – he might have been the King of Kings, he had so much gold on his body.

His spear scraped across me – it was that close – and he swept past me, even as Poseidon continued to turn – and the world stopped as he drove his spear into the king's side.

Alexander's speed and coordination were legendary among the former pages, and he leaned as far as he could, but the spear was driven hard by a man of great skill, and it hit Alexander's green-bronze cuirass and punched through it, just as Poseidon crashed into the charging Persian's horse.

Alexander reached down and caught the shaft of the spear in his side and pulled it free. Blood spurted.

Alexander took the spear, still wet with his blood, and threw it at the Persian, who was roaring his war cry – 'Mithridates! Mithridates for Darius!' in Persian.

Alexander's throw was perfectly timed, and he caught the man high on his breastplate, where the bronze is thin, and it punched through the hardened bronze and rocked Mithridates in his saddle.

But it didn't go deep – it cracked ribs, but it didn't go deep into the Persian prince's chest. Poseidon had made the Persian's horse stumble, and as Mithridates drew his sword, Alexander swung his own spear – left-handed, no less – and caught the Persian in the face and stunned him.

I got my heels into Poseidon's sides, and he reared over the Persian and I hit him with my kopis – a sloppy shot, but he was stunned and it cut his neck and blood sprayed and down he went.

But in moving to kill the great man, I'd left an opening in the ring around the king, and another Persian – I'd missed him – flew in like a thunderbolt and his back-cut sheared the wings off the king's helmet – cut through the bronze. I *saw* the blade go into his skull.

Alexander reversed his spear, took it just behind the haft with his right hand and rammed it up under the man's armpit – with the man's sword still sticking out of the crest of his helmet.

The Persian screamed.

But the Persian nobles were all around us like sharks around a stricken tuna. Alexander looked back at me – I was facing away from him, trying to stem the rush of the enemy's elite – I took blows in my back, my side, my helmet, but by the grace of Zeus or Apollo or Ares none of them hit my unarmoured arms or face or neck. I backed Poseidon – I don't really remember anything except the blows raining on me, the dust and Alexander looking at me, his mouth working, and the sword stuck in his helmet.

I saw Spithrakes – I only learned his name later – another of their great nobles. He came up *behind* the king in the fight – rode past Nearchus, fighting two men, and put Marsyas down with a heavy back-cut, and then he had the king – he drew back his arm and Cleitus cut it off – one of the greatest blows I've ever seen – that man had the king's life in his hands, and Cleitus saved him with one perfect cut, as if he'd waited his entire life for that moment to save the king's life.

But the Persians were pressing in – another Persian got past Nearchus and his spear blow – sloppy – caught the king in the back and tipped him on to the ground.

We had never imagined that the king could fall.

I had two opponents, and I was not fighting to take them down, but rather to block the path to the king. When he fell, my purpose in the melee changed. Or rather, *everything* changed.

I let Poseidon go forward, and he sank his teeth into an enemy mare's neck and she screamed, and my sword sheared off the top of the man's skull and with my back-cut, I blinded the other horse and spilled its brains, and then, ignoring the press of Persians, I whirled Poseidon on his forefeet and got him over the king's body – looked down, and he was already on his hands and knees, and Black Cleitus was beside me – flank to flank, his horse nose-to-tail with Poseidon, and we had Alexander between us, and we cut outwards into the press.

Bucephalus was the horse Alexander said he was. He pushed in between us to stand by his master.

I cut a man's hands off on his horse's neck, and then I was just trying to stay alive – the spear-points never stopped coming, and I blocked them – up, right, high, anything to clear the iron from Poseidon and the king. I have no idea how long Cleitus and I held them – ten heart-beats? A hundred?

I know that the gods could have made the earth and the heavens in that time, raised a new race of men and made a new golden age. It was that long. It was like the first pangs of love. Like the last moments of severe pain. The intensity and speed of it rose to an intense pitch – there were blades everywhere and my kopis flew through the blocks and parries – I got a spear in my left hand, taken from an enemy or put there by a friend, and I used it to block thrusts at the king, who was off his knees and on his feet by this time, but I couldn't risk a look – or he was face down in the muck and blood and dead. Either way, I had no means of knowing, because to risk a glance would be to die, and I was the last wall between the barbarians and the king.

Faster, and harder. I had never fought so well in my life. I was fighting three men – perhaps four – and holding them.

Like a god.

And then the biggest of my opponents – a giant man on a big black horse with a huge spear – baffled my parry, and I had that sickening moment – the one you get in practice when you know you've missed your parry, and pain is to follow – except this was the end.

His spear-point seemed to come forward slowly – but my attempt to reparry was even slower.

And then a spear came over my shoulder from behind, and the blow meant for my face sheared off into the crest of my helmet.

I rocked back and lost my kopis, but just like that, the fight was over.

The Persians had thrown everything at us – all their cavalry reserve – and while we fought four thousand men, our pezhetaeroi and our hypaspitoi had shattered their centre and our cavalry was gaining both flanks. Their first line was fleeing. Their second line expected the cavalry to rally there – but they didn't, and the only reason I can offer is that three of their senior officers were lying under our horses' hooves.

I sat there, shoulders slumped, looking vaguely at the ground.

Cleitus got a hand on the king's arm and hauled him up on to Bucephalus's back.

His helmet was gone, and there was blood pouring down the back of his neck.

He was looking at Hephaestion, face down in the blood under our hooves. His jaw was slack. I hadn't seen the king's closest companion go down, but he was down, and his horse was dead atop him.

But the pezhetaeroi were cheering their lungs out, and the Persian army was broken. Only the poor bloody Greek mercenaries stood their ground. They could see the king, and they sent us a herald – requesting that they be allowed to surrender.

He picked a bad time.

Alexander raised his eyes from his best friend lying in the bloody dust, and he pointed out the Greeks to his pezhetaeroi, who were close behind us, having to all intents and purposes rescued us from the Persian nobles.

'Kill them all!' he said, his voice harsh.

The pezhetaeroi needed no further urging.

We don't really like Greeks, we Macedonians.

As it turned out, of course, Hephaestion wasn't as badly hurt as the king, who had a cut in his scalp that ran right into the bone. I'd say he missed grim death by the width of a sword blade. Hephaestion had been knocked unconscious.

The Persians ran, leaving their Greek mercenaries to die. But they lost a *lot* of their finest men. They lost Mithridates, widely reckoned their finest fighter – he almost got Alexander.

But I got him. Heh. And they lost Pharnakes, another of their best – Rhodakes, Spithridates, and two more satraps – great men, relatives of the king, trusted stewards of great provinces of the empire. If the king had lost Hephaestion, me, Parmenio and a dozen more like us, it would have been even.

I'll tell you two things about that fight, lad. One is, we voted the king the palm for the bravest in the army. It wasn't some empty compliment. Watching him fight – both days – was inspirational. Ask any man who was there – ask any front-ranker in the pezhetaeroi what it's like to watch your king work his way through a dozen enemies, a sparkling haze of metal and blood as he kills his way to victory. That's what a King of Macedon is supposed to do. That's why farmers from Pella will march to India. It's not for his boyish good looks or his leopard-skin cloak.

He did it with elan. He looked like a god.

And when that fight was over, and he got remounted, helmet gone, blood flowing down his back, they cheered their lungs out and Parmenio could *not* understand why. All Parmenio saw was a reckless boy, foolish, arrogant, who had risked an easy victory for personal glory.

The pezhetaeroi saw a god.

The other is that, in many ways, that fight – those few minutes on the banks of the Granicus – *were* the fight for the Persian empire. The King of Kings lost most of his closest, most trusted warriors. He already had problems in the east, and he'd just lost all the men he could trust.

One more thing.

It was the closest they ever came to getting the king. I hated the bastards – they were the enemy, the barbarians, the Medes I'd waited my whole life to fight, but by all the gods, when they came for us they were heroes, and we were heroes, and it was *the fight* for ever after, around every campfire, in every cushioned hall where the somatophy-lakes lay with the king.

Well – except for Halicarnassus. Halicarnassus was horrible. But mostly, we didn't talk about those awful days. We talked about Granicus.

Which only makes what happened later all the worse.

SEVENTEEN

T he morning after the Battle of the Granicus, Alexander was already master of western Asia.

We took their camp with our scouts after the battle. The Agrianians had superb discipline – remarkable, really, considering their origins – and were probably the only unit in the army that could be trusted not to loot the camp. We rode in the next morning, and discovered that we were masters of thousands of slaves (mostly very attractive women collected from all over the empire), tents, baggage animals (including camels) and a fair amount of gold. Enough gold to pay the troops, anyway.

Polystratus did well for himself, because Alectus and he were friends. Don't imagine that the Agrianians were stupid – just careful, and only their closest friends got first pick of the loot. My share was a beautiful ear-dagger from Aegypt, fine steel and gold and ivory – I have it still – and a new sword in the Persian manner with fine green stone grips. It was beautiful to look at. The dagger was superb *and* a fine fighting weapon – the sword was pretty and broke in my hand, as I'll no doubt tell you later. There's a lesson there, if you like. A parable of some sort.

But the best prizes I received were horses, and a wreath of laurel. Polystratus – always my right arm, especially when it came to practical matters – got the horses of a number of Persian nobles. I was young enough to pretend they were the men I'd put down, but really, I think Polystratus simply rode around the battlefield before the last arrow flew and started collecting horses. I got two Nisean mares *and* a stallion, as well as a dozen lesser horses – lesser, but as good as Poseidon.

Well, that's a lie. As good as Poseidon to look at. Heh – Poseidon. Loved that horse. He was smart like a dog. Horses are dumb – you must know that. But one horse in a hundred thousand is some sort of horse genius.

Its nothing to do with this story, but I put the stallion to the mares the next day and then sent them home with a pair of slaves – Keltoi men, expert with horses – and one of Polystratus's grooms, and they made it all the way to Heron after a dozen adventures, and became the prize of my stud – both threw colts, and suddenly I had a Nisean stud. In many ways, those three horses made me more money than all the gold captured at Granicus. I still ride horses bred from Poseidon, the three Niseans and Ajax, the brute I took on Parnassus.

The Nisean stallion had a mark on his forehead like a trident. And he and Poseidon got along – a great rarity among stallions.

And Heron freed the two slaves for their honest service, and they wandered back to our army and joined the mercenary cavalry, and they ended up serving under your father for years. Andronicus and Antigonus!

Small world, really.

Alexander was beyond elation after Granicus.

The night after the battle he insisted on refighting it, blow by blow. We had an enormous fire in front of what had been Arsites's pavilion. We lay on Persian couches around the fire, and our new slaves served us fine Ionian wines. Philotas was uncomfortable, but Nicanor was already one of us in many ways, and he drank cup for cup with the king, unwatered wine.

Alexander seized a harp from one of our minstrels and struck the opening bars of the *Iliad*, and men fell silent, and he began to sing. He was clever with words – and he was singing the *Iliad*, but it was the Rage of Alexander.

To me, it was like hubris and blasphemy rolled together. But Cassander smiled, and Nearchus, and Black Cleitus could apparently stomach anything Alexander did.

He *had* been the best fighter in the army. I doubt that any man had put so many Persians into the darkness, and he had a wound – almost a death wound – to prove his valour.

But he would not shut up about it.

When his focus was elsewhere, I rose and went off into the darkness to find Poseidon. Polystratus was there, and Ochrid, poulticing the great horse's arrow wound and a dozen lesser wounds, and he withstood their ministrations with the same remarkable intelligence – only men who understand the deep stupidity of many horses can fully appreciate what it's like to have a war horse with intelligence.

I brushed him, where he wasn't wounded, with a pair of marvellous Sakje brushes – woven horsehair – that Polystratus had picked up as part of the loot. Persians love their horses, and have the finest tack and equipment in the world, and next to them, we are mere barbarians.

Polystratus waved away the smoke from the resinated torch we were using and grinned. 'And ten more like it – nosebags of linen, some halters that I think are silk, and horse blankets – beautiful stuff.' He shrugged. 'Seemed better than gold.'

Did I mention that Polystratus was a prince among servitors? And yet, he was no longer any kind of a servant, except where it came to my horses.

I was enjoying the beautiful things – horse things, as I say – when we heard screams. I froze, and then I realised it was the wounded out on the battlefield.

'Scavengers moving in,' Polystratus said.

We'd lost good men at Granicus – almost no infantry, but a fair number of cavalrymen. Seleucus was badly wounded, and I had some nasty cuts – Marsyas was in a coma (although, of course, he recovered) and Perdiccas had a wound, as well. Philip, the commander of the allied cavalry, was killed. So was the commander of the Thracians, one of Philip's old men.

Alexander promoted men in all directions after Granicus. Parmenio's brother got to be satrap of Phrygia, a powerful office that offered comfort and took him out of the command structure. The Thracians went to Alexander of Lyncestis, who'd proved himself relentlessly loyal since betraying his own brothers, and Alexander felt that he deserved it. And Alexander was loyal only to the king and *not* to Parmenio.

Likewise, Parmenio's brother had commanded the Thessalian cavalry, and now that he was out of the way, Alexander gave the command to Philip the Red – Philip son of Meneleus, my boyhood enemy/friend from the pages.

Most of my friends didn't see it happening, but Parmenio knew immediately what was going on, and so did I. Alexander was filling his staff with royalists, just as Parmenio had filled Alexander's with his own people.

It was not a bad policy – a system of checks and balances. Except that this was Macedon, not Athens.

Phrygia fell easily, and we marched inland for Sardis after accepting the surrender of Cyzicus. Alexander led us quickly – the Aegema, which increasingly meant all the hypaspists, the Agrianians and all the Hetaeroi; he left the rest of the army to come more slowly under Parmenio with the baggage (including all the new baggage) and the siege train. Memnon fled the field at Granicus (doubtless muttering 'I told you so') and began gathering forces at Miletus. Alexander proclaimed his intention of following – but we didn't take the coast road.

We raced across the mountains to Sardis. It's a good road, but a brutal trip with an army, and we had minimal baggage and six thousand men and three times as many animals. Any mountain valley was bled white just to feed us. And Alexander cared for nothing but speed, so our movements had the effect of a plague of locusts – and we had the main army behind us.

But fifty stades north of Sardis, Mythrines, the satrap of Sardis, met us with two hundred noblemen at his tail and surrendered the city and the fortress – and the treasury. None of us could believe it – and the next morning, when we rode into our new capital of Asia, our incredulity was downright insulting. I could have held Sardis for six months. It was a richer city than Amphilopolis and Pella rolled into one – I could have fitted both of them into the Jewish quarter of Sardis. The treasury was full of gold, and the magazines were stuffed with grain and oil.

But Sardis's surrender is part and parcel of how Darius failed. Mythrines was no friend of his, and there was very little racial pride among the higher Persians. They were like Greeks in that respect – they were happy to play traitor if it served their own ends. Or put another way, Mythrines hated Darius more than he hated Alexander. And after Arsites killed himself – news of which came to us about this time – there was no commander in West Asia until Darius granted the title to Memnon.

At any rate, Alexander was stunned by the craven surrender of Sardis. It had been his goal since the start of the expedition – he'd spoken of it often enough as the Troy of our crusade. But instead of an epic siege, it surrendered to his advance guard.

The army rolled into Sardis, exhausted and hungry, but the plains around Sardis were fecund, the barns were full and Lydia was almost mythologically rich, and our army ate themselves sick. Probably improved the local breeding stock, as well.

We were a month at Sardis. Spithridates, the actual satrap, died at Granicus, and Alexander didn't trust Mythrines enough to give him the office, so he gave it to Parmenio's brother Asander. Another promotion – another one of Parmenio's old men moved out of the command structure.

But at Sardis we received news that one of the original plotters against the king was at Ephesus – Amyntas, son of Antiochus. And once Thaïs had enough reports compiled, she sent to the king and guaranteed to seize the city in his name if he'd pay the bill – twenty talents of gold.

Twenty talents of gold for the most famous Greek city in Asia.

Parmenio had taken the city a couple of years earlier, but he'd failed to hold it, and Memnon had taken it back without much of a struggle. There was a large pro-Macedonian party in place, and Thaïs fed it with money and hope.

Alexander sat in my house – my borrowed house, chosen and furnished by Thaïs and thus better than the king's borrowed palace, a fine house with a courtyard and a rose garden – his chin in his hand. He was in my favourite of his moods – wry, human and intelligent. 'I want a great siege!' he said. He was mocking himself. Rare indeed. He had Hephaestion with him, and Callisthenes, Aristotle's nephew, his new private secretary.

Thaïs rolled her eyes. 'Play Achilles in your spare time, lord. Achilles didn't set out to conquer Asia. Ephesus—'

'Gives us the port we need,' Alexander said. 'We need a port for the allied fleet. And I need to rebuild the Temple of Artemis.'

Thaïs raised a perfectly plucked eyebrow. One of the most delightful aspects of living with (near, around) Thaïs is that she was many different women and one never had time to grow bored. In the mountains, she dressed in wool and sheepskin, her heart-shaped face and pointy nose peeping out from under a shepherd's hat – the picture of an adventurous woman. But a week in Sardis and her hair had a glint of purple-red from some costly dye, her toenails were solid gold in her golden sandals and her eyes were rimmed with kohl. She smelled like ... the danger of battle and the joy of love all rolled into one smell.

I know I can wax boring on Thaïs, but love is like that. We'd been together a year or more, but Sardis was special. She had provided Alexander with information before, and taken Priapus, but Ephesus was the first time she prepared an action with her own people – and launched it – with his acknowledgement and support. She looked like a queen, and when Alexander smiled at her, she smiled back – peer to peer.

'Give me twenty talents of gold and I'll give you Ephesus,' she said. 'My understanding is that you'll have your Troy at Miletus. You know Memnon has sent his wife to Darius as a hostage?'

Alexander laughed. 'Some men would see that as a double victory – to gain the king's trust and be rid of a wife.' He winked at Hephaestion. Callisthenes winced.

Thaïs smiled, and her smile held a thousand secrets. 'She is reputed to be the most beautiful woman in the world,' she said. 'She or her sister. Some say one and some the other.'

Alexander shrugged. Thaïs was more interested in female beauty than Alexander. 'Why would such a traitor have the veritable Helen?' he asked.

Thaïs crossed her legs and looked away. She glanced at me for help and back at the window.

I cleared my throat. 'Erygius and Laodon serve against their own cities, from time to time. Memnon is Ionian – and African.'

Alexander nodded. 'Oh – very well. Let us buy the damned city. But I assume you'll use the *demos* faction to overthrow the oligarchy – yes?'

Thaïs nodded.

Alexander shook his head and made a face. 'That's contrary to my policy in Greece. I worry that I'll seem fickle.' He glanced at Callisthenes.

Callisthenes frowned. 'The better for us, if you liberate the cities of Asia for democracy,' he said. 'Excellent subject for a panegyric. And perhaps if you made the point that when the mainland cities can be trusted, they too will have democracies?'

Thaïs looked as if she'd eaten bad seafood. She could stomach double-dealing spies, but there was something about the self-serving nature of Alexander's policies that stuck in her throat – or perhaps she was simply enough of an Athenian to be repulsed.

Callisthenes tried to kiss her hand when the king left. He also put a familiar hand on her bottom. 'Are you available only to Ptolemy?' he asked with a leer. 'You must have some spare time.'

Thaïs drifted out of his hands. 'None whatsoever, my lord,' she purred. Her voice was so throaty and seductive that it took him precious seconds to realise he'd just been turned down flat. He flushed, but he was most of the way out of our door.

He turned. 'You whore,' he said, and spat on our step.

'No,' she said. 'What you want is a whore. I can find you one, if that will please you.'

What amazed me was that he said this in front of me, although my relationship with her was known throughout the army. But he was an arrogant pup – and he was as much a fool about men's feelings as the king himself. And the two fed on each other. Aristotle has a lot to answer for.

He made a rude gesture. 'You open and shut like an oyster,' he said. 'And I'll have you whether you like it or not.'

His contempt for her – for all women – blazed like a torch.

Ordinarily, I let Thaïs fight her own battles. After all – that's what she wanted. And she was capable of punishing me for leaping to her defence in any way that seemed to her a slight on her capabilities.

But this had become an attack on me.

So I grabbed him and slammed his head into my doorpost.

Sometimes, the only answer to an arsehole is a good beating. Heh.

His slaves picked him up and carried him out the door, and I wiped my hands on a towel, and then I heard the sound of two small hands clapping. I turned to find Thaïs applauding me.

'I didn't love you for your strength or your temper,' she said, 'but it is sometimes lovely to see a man behave like a man.'

I won't go into details, but we had each other on the spot – court clothes and make-up pots discarded in all directions, until she was naked except for her golden sandals and I except for my Aegyptian dagger. On the carpets in the portico. If our slaves were scandalised, they were discreet. She smelled like danger and love, and she said I smelled like violence.

Oh – Sardis. I remember Sardis through the curtain of her hair.

We marched as soon as Thaïs had a receipt for the twenty talents of gold, and the city opened its gates as we approached. Memnon's garrison marched out through the Miletian Gate as we marched in through the Sardis gate, and Ephesus was Sardis all over again – another magnificent city, this one *grander than Athens*, surrendered without a fight, and even I felt a certain … sadness, if that's the proper phrase.

Thaïs had no such heroic scruples, and though she entered the city with the baggage, on a mule, Alexander sent her a box – inside was a gold statue of Artemis holding a tiny key.

She kept it until she died. I wondered why Alexander found it so easy to admit publicly that she'd taken Ephesus, but couldn't reward Cleitus for saving his life.

Ephesus was more dangerous to us than Sardis. Sardis was an alien, Persian city, and our troops knew they were in enemy territory. Ephesus was Greek through and through, and for all I claim that Macedonians hate Greeks – we love Greece, and we are Hellenes. Women in Ephesus looked like Greek women, and spoke Greek. The temples were to Greek gods. The stalls in the agora sold Greek goods and the shopkeepers spoke Greek.

And the artists and philosophers were Greek. Ephesus was the city of Heraklitus and of Thales – of Hipparchus the Comic Poet, and Archippos his son.

Apelles the Artist was living in Ephesus when we took it, and the purge instituted by Thaïs's democrats had almost killed him. Alexander had the good fortune to rescue him personally from a crowd of democrats who didn't, apparently, appreciate the new taste in art.

For a while, they were inseparable. Apelles was an agreeable man, I confess – and no sycophant, except out of pure sociability. He was an amiable man, gentle, brilliantly educated. Your father knew him.

Kineas had come down from Phrygia with a squadron of Athenian cavalry, because Alexander wanted to garrison the city with Greeks and Ephesus and Athens were old friends. It was the first time Alexander gave Kineas a direct command, as well – Kineas was the son of a great Athenian aristocrat, and as such was the right man to keep the democrats in line and guarantee to the (surviving) oligarchs that the rule of law would be preserved.

It was beautifully done, and typical of Alexander's style. He let Thaïs's partisans get carried away – and they killed almost everyone who might have resisted him. And then he ordered them to stop with a shudder of revulsion and appeared deeply contrite. And summoned his friend, an Athenian aristocrat, to put it all to rights, thus appearing even-handed and just – after ruthlessly exterminating opposition.

Thaïs was disgusted – she'd intended to institute a truly popular democracy. Did I mention my lover was a firebrand? But again, Alexander's brilliance was ahead of her. She loathed aristocrats (myself excepted, I assume) but deeply respected Kineas. She didn't do anything to undermine him – although if Perdiccas (for instance) had been commanding the military police, she might have had a different ... approach.

And of course Kineas did an excellent job. But those few weeks made his career, with us – he dined every night with the king, and never abused the privilege. Only once did I see him anything but perfectly well behaved. One night Seleucus slapped him on the back. 'You're like one of our own officers, Kineas,' he said. 'I never even think of you as Athenian.'

Kineas winced, and his eyes narrowed. 'I am, though,' he said. 'I am *not* a Macedonian, Seleucus.'

Apelles laughed aloud. 'And thank the gods, Kineas!' He raised a kylix of wine. 'No Macedonian could have brought peace to the factions here.'

Apelles had excellent social skills. He did tend to go on a bit about politics, and I sometimes think the king kept him around to make his staff *look* more worldly.

At any rate, we had to wait for the allied fleet to catch us up, and Alexander had detached Parmenio to pluck the rest of Lydia if the garrisons were weak, so we had time to kill, and Alexander spent his time going to parties and getting his portrait painted by the foremost artist of the day. He was drunk a great deal.

Philotas and I avoided each other.

Memnon was gathering an army at Miletus.

Kineas had an increasing number of crimes to deal with – rapes and thefts by Macedonians. He dealt with them as tactfully as he could, but he was also outraged when he found that any Macedonian he turned over to Philotas was released.

And Alexander spent far too much time ignoring all this and sitting on Bucephalus in a tent by the agora, where Apelles painted him in encaustic, carefully coloured wax. I found the new, imperial Alexander a little grating and I had duties to perform, and frankly, I was besotted with Thaïs and we made love as often as I could catch her and get her clothes off – and the success of taking the city had made her as randy as I. We had a fine time, but Ephesus had a certain aura – it was too sophisticated for my taste, and I suspect it actually frightened some of our Pellan farm boys.

At any rate, Apelles finished his military portrait, and I saw it. It was ... accurate. It showed the fire in Alexander's eyes, and the ram's horns where his unruly blond hair rose in rebellion against the brush when he'd been on campaign a week or more. And there were the lines around his mouth that he got in combat, and there were the knuckles, white against the hilt of his sword – and there was Bucephalus, his deeply swayed, broad back accurate in every detail.

Alexander hated it.

By Apollo, I could have told Apelles if he'd asked me. Kineas and I had a laugh about it, and that was *before* the king saw it. It was a magnificent portrait of the King of Macedon at war.

But Alexander didn't see himself as the King of Macedon any more.

I was there when he exploded. I wanted to be there. And besides, had I shown signs of chickening out, Thaïs was going to make me. Everyone in Ephesus knew the king was going to hate it, and everyone wanted to hear what he had to say.

'It is bad art,' Alexander said, his arms crossed, an entirely false smile on his face. 'My dear Apelles – it is trite. You should be ashamed of yourself.'

At the pronouncement, the apprentices at the back of the tent – busy grinding priceless substances to powders so fine they could be used to mix with melted beeswax – guffawed.

Alexander's ear was always tuned to the sound of derisive laughter. His head came up and he looked around, like a stallion hearing a mare. 'What was that?' he asked.

'My apprentices,' Apelles said. 'They are mocking you for pretending to know anything about art.'

Alexander's face grew red. 'I studied with Aristotle!' he said, and Callisthenes nodded.

Apelles shrugged. 'He didn't know shit about art, either.'

Callisthenes had a mouth full of wine, and he spurted it all over the ground.

Good times.

'The likeness to me is good enough, I suppose,' Alexander said. 'I know it's meant to be me.'

Apelles stood stony-faced.

'But Bucephalus is not a swayback carthorse, and my thorax doesn't buckle under my right arm.' Alexander moved around the painting. 'And the light is odd.'

Apelles laughed, and his laugh was unforced and unconcerned. 'My lord, you are the greatest warrior in the circle of the world, and may indeed be the child of the gods, but you telling me about art is like me telling Ptolemy there about horses.'

'Leave me out of it,' I said.

Apelles smiled a lazy, evil smile. 'Why don't you fetch an impartial judge?' he asked the king. 'Get your horse and bring him here.'

The great war horse was brought, and as soon as the horse saw the likeness, he raised his head and gave a stallion trumpet call.

He seemed puzzled when the other horse didn't move. But he looked at the painting for a long time.

'I rest my case,' Apelles said.

'What, your painting is good enough to please a horse?' Callisthenes asked.

'The horse recognises the likeness. Animals live in a natural world – art, to be art, must be natural.'

Callisthenes shrugged. 'Nonsense. Art is always artifice. Any child can copy nature.'

'It is always easier for a pompous fool to imitate a philosopher than other men,' Apelles said to Callisthenes.

Apelles ended up executing another painting, this one of Alexander in the guise of Zeus, throwing a thunderbolt. Kineas, for example, found it horrible. Thaïs laughed and laughed.

Alexander loved it. And so did the troops.

Late summer, and we finally moved. Parmenio had done his usual brilliant job cleaning up Phrygia for his brother, and now he was coming to us with the army. The allied fleet – all one hundred and sixty ships – was riding snug in Ephesus's near-impregnable harbour. But at sea, the Persians had it all their own way, and aside from a few minor ship actions – all won by Athenians – our fleet was too ill trained to risk in a straight-up fight.

We marched to Miletus, and not a moment too soon. Kineas had taken to arresting Macedonians and trying them in military courts without handing them over to Philotas, who was nominally, at least, governor of the city, and the two of them were nearly at war when Kineas executed a pair of pezhetaeroi for rape. Alexander backed him, but Philotas swore to have his head. You can guess whose side I was on …

The fleet anchored between the island of Lade and the mainland, virtually under the walls of the city. There was immense historical value in this – the Persians were anchored over by Mycale, and both places were redolent of past conflict. Here, the Ionian rebels and their Athenian allies had lost one of the greatest naval actions of all time – to treason – against the Persians.

'My ancestor was here,' Kineas said, pointing across the water. 'Arimnestos the Plataean.'

And here, on the beaches of Mycale, the Athenians smashed Persian seapower for a hundred years.

'My ancestor was at Mycale, too,' Kineas said, with a certain aristocratic insolence. He didn't actually *say* 'while your ancestors were herding sheep and sending tribute to Persia, mine ruled the world'. He didn't say it, but he thought it.

He was a fine man, nonetheless.

Heh. Your ancestors, too, lad.

Anyway, we beat the Persians to Miletus by days, and that was pretty much the siege. The Persian commander started negotiating as soon as we got there.

The only battle was between Parmenio and Alexander.

Parmenio had been away, marching around, taking the surrender of Phrygia and cleaning up the corners of Lydia. The king had been in Ephesus, surrounded by admirers and flatterers. Collision was imminent.

The first issue was Philotas. Alexander attempted to fob him off with Ephesus to govern. Philotas had no intention of trading command of the Hetaeroi for one city, no matter how mighty. It's funny, in a way – two years before, when Parmenio took Ephesus the first time, we'd heard rumours that he intended to keep it for his own and make his people into kings there.

But fatter men have greater appetites, or so we say in Macedon. Since Granicus, we'd all begun to raise our eyes to wider horizons. And Parmenio and his family had their eyes on some major prize – although I'm not sure they'd actually named it, even to themselves.

I'll add that the other poison in the mix was that Philotas never bothered to hide that he felt – rightly or wrongly – that his father was doing all the hard work while Alexander was swanning around and flirting with artists.

At any rate, Philotas flatly refused to stay in Ephesus when the army marched. Alexander only accepted him when he'd had a conference with Parmenio – a talk that none of us was welcome to overhear. It must have been something.

But there was worse to come. Parmenio wanted a forward strategy. He wanted to commit the fleet to a major action at Mycale. He was willing to see either of two strategies – a night assault on the beached Persian ships, or a combined attack with the army and the fleet. Philotas marched off with half the hypaspitoi and half the Hetaeroi to close all the stream-heads to the Persians – so that they had to sail a hundred stades around the headland to get water for their rowers.

Parmenio didn't ask the king before sending his son away with half the Aegema, and a bitter dispute arose.

'When I see an opportunity, I act on it!' Parmenio roared. We were in the command tent – a dozen of the king's friends, and most of the 'college of old men', as Diodorus called Parmenio's generals.

'Just as you did at Granicus?' Alexander asked.

Parmenio laughed. 'Boy, you rode off with a wild hare under your arse and almost got yourself killed – as we knew would happen. That wasn't an opportunity.'

Alexander smiled, and his eyes got that glittery look they did in combat. 'Then you are a fool. We could have had Granicus in an hour if your son hadn't wasted so much time.'

Parmenio shrugged. 'I won't debate with you, lord. Men know who won the Granicus, and how it was won.'

Alexander nodded. 'Precisely. You will not dispatch troops without my consent, Parmenio. Not ever again. And these were my own household.'

'They were in armour and prepared,' Parmenio said, but I could tell from his tone that he knew himself bested.

'And I will not risk my empire and my future on a sea battle. The last time the Greeks made a stand here, half their fleet defected. I won't allow it. I don't trust them enough to lead them in person.'

Parmenio crossed his arms on his chest. 'Then we may as well go home. As long as the Persians hold the sea, we're here on their sufferance. Any day now, Memnon will fill that fleet with marines and send it to Athens – and a day later, Greece will be afire behind us and we'll have to march home.'

'Really?' Alexander asked. Again the smile.

'Oh – you have one of your amazing plans?' Parmenio was contemptuous. 'Spare us. Let's get this done. The Athenians are a match for any ten Persian ships. Let's send to Athens for another fifty ships – they'll send them after Granicus. Then we'll have the ships and the skilled rowers. They could be here in two weeks. Less.'

Alexander's smile never faded. 'You can be remarkably un-Macedonian, Parmenio. If we call on Athens for a fleet, whose victory will it be? And what price will Athens demand in the aftermath? And what will the League say?'

'Who gives a fart?' Parmenio roared. 'Lord – you try my patience.'

Alexander's smile broadened. 'Luckily for both of us, I'm the king and you are not.'

It was the first time their conflict was open.

We stormed Miletus anyway. But part of the garrison got away, and Memnon had already shifted his base to Halicarnassus, the best-defended city in Ionia – the birthplace of Herodotus, master of history.

Alexander was determined to follow him. He was tired of men telling him that Memnon was the finest strategos in the world.

So as the autumn rains started to fall on the green coast of Asia, we marched on Halicarnassus.

EIGHTEEN

It was four days' easy marching south from Miletus to Ephesus.

After a long argument with Parmenio, Alexander disbanded the fleet. He kept only the Athenians. The rest of the Greek ships he dismissed, and they ran home as fast as they could. The Persians couldn't believe their luck – without a battle, they had deprived Alexander of his only hope of sea power.

Cynical armchair strategists tell me that Alexander didn't trust them, and that he hated the sea, and that he couldn't afford a defeat, and a dozen other notions. There's a little truth in every one, but the greatest was this – Alexander trusted himself. He had a new plan for the defeat of the Persian fleet, and he was sure that he could effect it. And he didn't understand the sea, and he disliked the extent to which he could not control it. On land, he could walk through the worst weather, the driest desert, the most afflicting blizzard. I know – because he did. Sheer will can overcome weather, on land.

At sea, you just die. Poseidon is, in many ways, the mightiest god, and when you commit yourself to his element, you admit your humanity and your deep helplessness. Alexander was not particularly gifted at such admissions.

But most of all, he wanted rid of the money they cost. Every ship had two hundred skilled oarsmen. The oarsmen cost more than his soldiers, and there were thirty-two thousand rowers to feed and pay. That's why he disbanded the fleet. We were broke – we were literally living from town to town – and he needed to send all those oarsmen home.

Parmenio had learned not to argue that we should quit and go home – but in one season, we had conquered all Phrygia and Lydia and we were poised to take Caria, as well. I'm not sure that it was unrealistic of him to suggest that we march back from Miletus to Ephesus and take up winter quarters.

'You seem to have liked it well enough,' Parmenio said. 'And you found that nice city site – wouldn't you like to be there when they start to build?'

Alexander had, indeed, found a pretty site while hunting. I was there. It's Smyrna, now.

But Alexander just shook his head.

'All Caria,' he said. 'I will face Memnon now.'

Kineas and his squadron of Athenians were assigned temporarily to the Hetaeroi. This sort of thing happened all the time – we built temporary brigades for scouting, for flank guards, for night guards – all sorts of purposes. After Miletus, Alexander wanted to have all his Athenians together – where he could see them, I expect, because the most obvious strategy for Memnon was to spark revolt in Greece, as I've said.

And we didn't make the march to Halicarnassus in four easy days. We made it in ten brutal days, because we didn't take the coast road into Caria. Oh no.

We marched east, into the mountains.

Armies live on rumours, and as soon as we marched on a sunny early autumn day, I heard veterans suggesting that we were marching on Susa or Persepolis. We were obviously going east, and into the mountains – hence, to many soldiers, this must be the great march.

I couldn't fight the rumour because, despite being a friend of the king, I had no more idea where we were going than they did. I knew that Parmenio was angry, and I knew that Philotas had attempted to block my very temporary promotion to command of the scouts. I had half the Agrianians and my Hetaeroi and Kineas and his Athenians, and we scoured the country ahead of the army, a broad 'W' with the Agrianians in the centre and the cavalry on the flanks. A 'W' is a superb way to counter potential ambushes – enemy troops close to a road or defile are caught by your outflung wings and exterminated.

Nothing like that happened. We entered the mountains and the arms of our 'W' came in closer and closer to the column, and eventually we halted and switched roles, with the hardy Illyrians out on the wings, climbing the ridges above us, and the cavalry close in.

Kineas loved it. He loved scouting and careful, professional cavalry work – he excelled at little details of tactics, such as keeping a file of horsemen over the crest of a ridge so that they were invisible as they moved. He was a keen hunter on horseback, and he used the skills from hunting very well.

Up and up, ridge after ridge, switchback trails on which the horses had to go two abreast – sometimes one abreast. And cold. A taste of winter.

Where in Hades are we going?

Up and up, and then down into a high valley – a magnificent valley that rolled away into an infinite distance – a hundred stades of high valley, with magnificent hills on either side, some already snow-capped, and beautiful farms laid out all along the valley floor.

The valley had a side door – a spur of the valley floor that ran off to the south, back towards the coast.

Locals called it the land of Herakles, in their own tongue. It looked remarkably like the best parts of Macedon, or southern Illyria.

We marched up the road, and came after two days of climbing to the mountain fortress of Alinda, reputed to be the strongest place in Caria, and perhaps in the world. The entire fortress was of stone – two outer walls, each the size of Pella, and separated by a bowshot, so that men on the high inner wall could support troopers on the outer wall, and then, towering over the inner wall, a great citadel like the stern of a ship rising over the so-called Carian Gate, itself protected by a pair of towers and with a magnificent carving over the lintel of an enormous lion snarling at visitors, very reminiscent of the stone over the lintel at Mycenae.

From the plain, we looked up and shuddered. I could see from the valley floor that the walls were too high above the plain for even our largest one-talent machines to reach them with enough force to dislodge stone.

'What's he thinking of?' I asked Thaïs, who rode between me and Kineas.

Thaïs smiled. 'He isn't going to lay siege to it,' she said. 'He's going to make love to it.'

She was at her most witty when she was enigmatic. So I smiled at her and kept my scouts moving.

I needn't have bothered. Not a Carian mountaineer troubled us. The most excitement we had was when the Agrianians smoked a nest of bandits and we massacred them – good fun, but hardly a contest.

We camped below the citadel, and every Macedonian lord – certainly all the highlanders – looked up at it with something like lust. Alinda, the fortress, was a fine hold, and the man who had it would be comfortable, safe and powerful for ever.

It turned out that Thaïs and Alexander had been negotiating with the commander for weeks. Not quite the commander – rather, the semi-exiled queen of Caria, Ada. She had a few troops – all mercenaries – and she held the lower two circuits and had the Persian commander holed up in the citadel.

Thaïs took me with her when she and Alexander went to meet her. She was in her late thirties, and she had brown-grey hair, fine eyes

– really startling, widely spaced and large – and was athletic rather than beautiful – slim-hipped and small-breasted.

How can I tell this?

Alexander fell in love with her. Right there, before my eyes.

She did have something of Atlante about her. She wasn't shy, and she was not particularly feminine – she'd been in the field much of her life. She rode well, walked with purpose, and the word among her troops was that she was a fine sword-fighter and a good wrestler. She was twice the king's age, or near enough.

I've done Alexander a disservice if I've made him sound like an effeminate. No Macedonian army would have tolerated such a man, and he was not, except in the propaganda of farts like Demosthenes.

Nor did he prefer boys to girls. The truth – a hard truth that men never wanted to believe – is that he was above such things. He didn't particularly fancy *anyone*. Oh, a perfect beauty like Calixeinna moved him to possession and sexual satisfaction – but that was really a conquest, not a lust. He didn't *look*.

I know. Despite being besotted with Thaïs for years – for most of my life – I look at every woman I see. If a woman bends over to pick up a basket, I'll look at her breasts. If a woman walks away into the sun, I'll look at the whole outline of her figure. Really – it is one of the joys of life. Women are always beautiful.

I've even seen beautiful men – a few. They don't move me the same way, but there's something truly admirable about a good body – hard and well trained and ready for war. Not as interesting, perhaps, as a woman's body – but worth a look.

Alexander never looked. You could see it in him, if you took the time. You could parade hetaerae by him all day, and he'd only react to the beauty with a certain fascination – never with an obvious head-turn of the *man*. He was not a man.

He was more, and he was less.

But Ada, in her slim-hipped, hard-bodied, older and wiser way, pierced him.

There was an element of rich comedy to it from the first. She was a practical, unromantic woman, as hard as a sword blade, deeply suspicious of this foreign conqueror. Her face was more handsome than beautiful, aside from her eyes – her nose was too long, slightly curved in an Aramaic way, her skin was dusky and her lips were thin. She kept Alexander at a distance, distrusted the lot of us and tried to negotiate.

Alexander gave her anything she asked for.

Since she was neither romantic nor yet a tease, she had no idea of

400

the effect she was having, and his besottedness confounded their negoti-ations.

Thaïs and I laughed ourselves to sleep, that first night.

Thaïs grabbed me and put a finger on a very sensitive place. 'You have to help him,' she said, stifling a giggle. 'The goddess has him, and he can't think.'

The things I've done for the king.

Next morning, I had the duty anyway. My little command had been broken up – we were clearly camping in this rich valley for a few days, and Philotas had the next turn on point. So I was back to bodyguard duty. I presented myself in armour.

Hephaestion was in a pout.

Alexander was having his hair brushed. 'I want to look my best,' he said to me as I came in. 'Hephaestion's being difficult, Ptolemy. And you could look better – when did you last polish that thorax?'

I made a face. 'I think I was fourteen,' I said. 'Since then, I've had slaves to do it.'

That got me a smile.

'Thaïs told me to have a talk with you,' I said.

Alexander nodded. 'She's the most intelligent of women. Although Ada ...' He smiled again. 'I keep saying her name.'

Hephaestion rolled his eyes.

I made a small motion with my thumb. Hephaestion read it and got to his feet. 'I'm going to go and curry my horses,' he said sulkily.

It's funny. As I tell you this story, I keep insisting that Hephaestion and I were never friends, but I find that we cooperated awfully well – at least in the early days.

At any rate, he went out to the horse lines, and Nearchus – who was becoming the kind of yes-man who stands too close to the man in power, so close that the term 'henchman' comes to mind – Nearchus got the message and went out, looking back all the way, hoping to learn whatever deep secret was about to be related.

I took a cup of herbed wine and water from the duty slave. 'Go and have a rest,' I said. 'Don't come back for ten minutes.'

The slave beamed. And vanished.

Alexander looked around at his suddenly empty tent. 'This is about Ada?' he said, ready, I think, for a quarrel.

'Yes,' I answered. 'Thaïs says I should tell you that this is falling in love, and you have no defence for it, and she'd like to take over the negotiations, please, before you make her Queen of Persia.'

Alexander spluttered.

Really, it was like talking to a stranger. He spluttered, he stammered, and he hadn't a thing to say.

I put an arm around his shoulders. Alexander wasn't much for human contact – but he submitted to my embrace. 'She's quite ... handsome,' I managed. 'And I think she likes you.'

'Really?' he asked. 'I feel like a buffoon. I talk too much, and she must think I'm a boy.' He looked at me. 'She's so ... mature. Almost godlike in her wisdom – when those eyes fall on me, I'm afraid I'll babble.'

There was a gentle tap at the tent door, or rather the poles to support the door, and in came four slaves, all Hyrkanians, carrying two bronze kettles. They bowed very deeply, lifted the lids and the oldest man proclaimed, in a sing-song voice –

'The queen sends these, the best food of her table, to her young friend. Eat, and be joyful!'

He bowed again, and withdrew.

Alexander needed no second urging. He ate.

I ate too. It was stewed antelope with raisins – delicious – and with wonderful bread.

We ate well, and I had our slaves take the cauldrons around the duty Hetaeroi as well – there was food for forty.

Thaïs met with the queen, using a pair of slaves as interpreters, and in two hours they hammered out an agreement. Ada became Alexander's vassal, but more, she adopted him as her son.

Thaïs smiled. 'She wanted to marry him,' she said. 'I knew she would. And he'd have done it.'

'Zeus, god of kings,' I muttered. 'A forty-year-old barbarian queen? Blood everywhere. Civil war.'

'Adoption seemed better,' Thaïs said.

That night, we celebrated with a feast, and Alexander gave her two hundred men from the hypaspists to help her take the citadel after he marched away. She turned and kissed him.

We had sword dances, and Queen Ada danced the Pyricche with some of her soldiers. She danced very well.

Alexander drank far too much. I tried to stop him – he was drinking unwatered wine at the speed I was drinking it with three waters.

Finally I took the cup from him. Ada was gazing into his eyes and laughing. Wine made her far more feminine.

Alexander turned and looked up at me, and Ada rolled away and went decorously down off the dais – I assume off to piss. It was quite a party.

'Give me my wine cup, Ptolemy!' Alexander commanded, and then he giggled.

'Planning to take her to your bed?' I asked.

He blushed. Here's how fierce his blush was – even in firelight, you could see it.

'You can get drunk, or you can get laid,' I said. 'But you will almost never get drunk and do a good job of getting laid.'

Alexander shook his head. 'So vulgar. Wine ... has truth in it! Makes me happy. *Please* give me my wine.'

'Let's dance!' Ada said, returning.

Some of the men were none too happy to see women at a dinner – Philotas, for example – and he spat. 'The King of Macedon does not dance!' he said.

Alexander would not have danced, otherwise. But he got up – barely able to walk.

'I will dance,' he said.

Then nothing would do for him but he must dance the Pyricche, and in his own equipment. So Ochrid was sent for his harness and spears, and then Ada admitted, coyly, that she had her own harness – gods, it was all I could do not to giggle and retch at the same time.

Philotas got up. 'You're making a fool of yourself with this old hag,' he said. And stumbled off to bed. Macedonians had a habit of speaking their minds, especially when drunk.

But the musicians struck up the Pyricche, and although the Macedonian version was very different – and far more practical – Ada learned it as fast as I can describe the movements to you. She was imitating the king by the third cycle of the dance – leaping, ducking, menacing with her spear, hiding behind her shield – which was itself full-sized.

I was impressed. Even Thaïs was impressed. Ada could dance, and she had the kind of mind that perfectly controlled her body.

'Is she a woman-lover?' I asked.

'How would I know?' Thaïs said – with the slightest downturn of her lips. Indicating that this was none of my business.

Ada stamped, turned, clashed her spear on the king's shield – and launched into doing the dance in opposition, the way I'd have done it if I was dancing with the king, so that instead of two dancers in perfect unison, now she thrust when he ducked, parried when he thrust, leaped in the air when his spear whirled low.

He was drunk, and she was untrained, and they were magnificent. They were so good that the musicians began to play faster.

Alexander seemed to grow with the music – he began to stretch himself. He was a superb warrior, and he knew the dance intimately, and now he began to embellish every movement with subtle additions – the sort of things that old Cleitus used to encourage us to do, to help us remember what the Pyricche was for – to make us better fighters. So Alexander began to make his cuts steeper and more dangerous – rolled his hips to snap his shield forward.

Ada copied him, and added a sinuous martial element of her own.

I only ever saw one other woman who struck me as being a real warrior – a fighter, the way I am. Perhaps there would be more if women weren't so busy making babies, but Ada was the real thing, and she was breathtaking to watch.

I was afraid one of them would be killed. They were competing, now, to strike harder and faster, and the music was *flying*. Everyone was clapping. Sweat was pouring off them both, and their spears left trails of fire in the air. Remember that he had taken a cut to the head that bit into his skull at Granicus, and that we'd been marching for days.

I walked over to the musicians, my heart in my mouth, and made a spear-point with my fingers. The flautist nodded sharply.

They played through the tune once more at speed.

The pipes whirled, and they played more slowly, and then more slowly, the tide of the music rising to compensate for the decreased speed, and both the dancers drew back together; both cocked their spears back, together ...

And as the music ended, they fell together, giggling, in a clash of armour. Thaïs took my hand. 'Come,' she said.

I followed her, and we caught the king and Ada, still leaning on each other, and we led them to the tower's guest chambers. Slaves had taken the king's clothes when he put his armour on, and they lay on a cedar chest.

I got his thorax off while he laughed, and his greaves, and I towelled him myself as if I were his slave. He ruffled my hair.

'That was pretty good, wasn't it?' he said.

I hate being cast as a sycophant. On the other hand, it had been ... magnificent. Almost unearthly. 'I've never seen anything like it,' I said. Then I thought – Athena sent me the words – *be generous. It was magnificent.* 'It was magnificent,' I said.

'What I love best about your praise,' the king said, 'is how unwillingly you give it.'

He had new bruises where his thorax bit into the top of his pectoral muscles.

A voice at the door said, 'Wine for the king.'

I turned to find Thaïs, handing me wine. 'Come!' she said. 'Leave him!'

So I handed him the wine. 'I'm sure you can dress yourself,' I said.

Thaïs reached through the door and pulled at my arm, and I fled, but not before I'd seen Ada come in the other door of the chamber, naked. Alexander had stopped noticing me, by then.

'You are a wicked, wicked matchmaker,' I muttered to Thaïs.

She laughed. 'He's not going to marry her – so what's the harm?' She laughed. 'Wine makes men randy – even the King of Macedon.'

'Even Ptolemy,' I said, catching her against a wall hanging. I loved the feel of her naked hips under her chitons – there was something about lifting her skirts that always made me wild, even when I could have her naked. I was hard in a deep breath, and we were as busy as the king and the queen in another.

She laughed into my mouth, my busy little plotter.

And the next day, we marched for Halicarnassus down the high passes. We had to climb the mountains behind Ada's castle, and we made Labraunda by dark the first day, Mylasa the second – days were getting shorter. The third night we were at Iasus on the coast, which had submitted to our Athenian flotilla, and where Alexander guaranteed their 'ancient rights' (the ink was not yet dry), and we met a young man who was considered a prophet of Poseidon. He was sixteen, and he could talk to the dolphins – they swam up to him eagerly. I saw this with my own eyes. One dolphin in particular followed him all over the town's inner harbour. And my horses adored him – when he came (at my invitation, as Poseidon is my special god) to my tent for a cup of wine, Polystratus hurried in to see what had happened, because all the horses had begun to whinny.

He was a very special young man. His name was Barsulas, but we all called him Triton. I took him into my household as a priest. He could read and write, and to get ahead of myself, Thaïs had me send him to the Temple of Poseidon at Sounnion in Attika, and we sent our young foundling, Olympias, with him. We trusted the boy, and with good reason. They were, in many ways, like our family. We sent him to Sounnion to be trained as a priest of Poseidon, and we sent her to the Temple of Artemis to learn all the dances of the Bear. I made good donations to both temples, and they were only too happy to admit my 'children' and Thaïs's.

Our daughter was eight months old, and Thaïs had a pair of nurses for her, because running Alexander's special intelligence section was now a full-time job. And at Iasus, we were one day's march from Halicarnassus, and she had no report to make.

I was at that meeting.

Thaïs hated to be defeated, but none of her agents had emerged from

Halicarnassus to report. She'd sent three or four. We had friends in the town – by then, every town in Ionia had a faction who wanted Alexander to liberate them.

That night, Parmenio had another try at reasoning with the king. I was starting to change sides, by then. There was a nip in the air – autumn was coming. It had rained intermittently all day, and as usual we were ahead of our tents, so that our men were camping in fields – wet.

'It takes three years to make a good soldier,' Parmenio said, after dinner. We were in the local Temple of Ares, using it as a headquarters. 'It takes three nights of rain to kill him. Lord, it is time to call it quits. Ada was a brilliant conquest. You will be lord of Caria in no time – well done. But let's get back to Ephesus and get the troops under cover. You'll want to send all the pezhetaeroi home for the winter – it's their right – and you must be as tired as I am.' Parmenio chuckled smugly.

Alexander shook his head. 'No,' he said. 'I'm not tired, and I'm going to take Halicarnassus from Memnon.'

Parmenio shrugged. 'As you will, lord. But the weather is turning and this is not a fertile area. There's not much fodder here, and little wine and less olive oil. What will the army eat, while we lay siege to Halicarnassus?'

'We have a magazine at Miletus,' Alexander said. 'We can send convoys along the coast road.'

'For water?' Parmenio shot out. 'You've never been to Halicarnassus. I have. There's no water – all the water's inside the town. We have thirty thousand men. They drink a great deal of water.'

Alexander looked around at the rest of us. 'Anyone else of the same mind?' he asked.

His voice gave away his opinion. He wasn't asking. He was looking at dissent.

No one spoke up.

That made Parmenio angry.

'Listen!' he said. 'Tomorrow, when we head up the coast, we're going up against *Memnon*. He's not some hill chieftain. He's not the commander of a soft confederation and he's not going to make any easy mistakes. He's going to meet us on a battlefield of his own choosing, where he has a fleet at his back and an army of mercenaries – expendable men. You've sent our fleet away. He can get reinforcements – and food – whenever he likes. And if he doesn't like the odds, he can sail away. *And you won't be able to stop him.*'

Alexander took a deep breath. He nodded very slowly.

Some of the older officers began to let out their long-held breaths in relief.

'I guess we'll just have to be on our best game, then,' Alexander said. 'Because in the morning, we march for Halicarnassus.'

Philotas had the advance guard. His version was two hundred Thracian Peltastoi and a hundred Thracian cavalry, well spread out in front, backed with two full squadrons of Hetaeroi and two hundred archers. Philotas didn't like my 'W', and he used a more linear advance-guard formation.

We entered the mountains again at Bargylia, with Mount Lyda on our left and the sea below us on the right – a road well cut, an old road, and one that offered no cover at all. Twenty stades south of Bargylia we left the sea and started overland on the last leg of the road, through a valley pass that climbed slowly, and was at least broad enough for the advance guard to shake out into formation.

It was raining. I felt old – my hand throbbed, and all my wounds hurt as if they were new, and Thaïs and I had had a fight – about Queen Ada. A stupid fight.

I was riding with the royal escort, well back in the column, and Parmenio was well behind us – pouting, or so it seemed. Seleucus was finally healed from his wounds at Granicus, and he was back with us, in armour. Nearchus was there, and Marsyas, and most of the rest of the old guard. Kineas was with us.

'I wish Ada could see this,' Alexander said.

'Aphrodite's tits, I'm tired of Ada,' Hephaestion said.

'You know I do not like blasphemy,' Alexander said coldly. 'Or vulgarity.'

'Ada has tits,' Hephaestion said reasonably. 'I assumed that you'd want to hear about them.'

Alexander turned to glare at him.

'Well, she does!' Hephaestion insisted with his usual foolishness. 'I mean, they're not much bigger than mine, but she *does* have *tits*.'

Nearchus started to laugh, and Black Cleitus, and Alexander reined in.

'Shut up!' he barked, and raised his hand.

Hephaestion, always happiest with an appreciative audience, ignored the king. 'And arm muscles! Bigger than mine!'

Alexander struck him. He had a riding whip – as long as his legs – in his hand, and he hit Hephaestion in the mouth – not hard, but fast. 'Shut your foul mouth and listen,' Alexander said.

Hephaestion put both hands to his mouth. 'You bastard,' he spat.

By now I could hear what the king was hearing. 'They're fighting!' I said.

Alexander put his heels to his riding horse. None of us was on war horses, but we raced up the top of the pass, crowding around the hypaspists and the second Hetaeroi squadron.

'Arm!' I shouted as we pushed by. 'Shields! Armour!'

Only the advance guard marched armed for battle.

We went over the top of the pass, and below us we saw Philotas entangled with an ambush.

There were enemy hoplites, immediately identifiable by their big, round shields, in among Philotas's archers, and farther ahead, archers were dropping arrows from high above on the Prodromoi and the Thracians.

The Thracians panicked and broke, running back along the column, just as Alexander and Seleucus and I started to get a counter-attack together. It was my squadron of Hetaeroi, after all. They were to hand, and they were good, if I don't say so myself.

Alexander watched the Thracians break, five stades away. He looked around.

Calm as a man in his andron – calmer – Alexander looked off to the north. 'Philotas was not ready for this. Now, if Memnon is the great man people say he is, he'll have cavalry. And cavalry can only be ...'

Alexander was looking right at the low hill that dominated the craggy heights to our left, and as sure as cats make kittens, just as he said this, fifty Greek cavalry emerged from behind the hill.

I had maybe twenty of my own men, and Polystratus and a few grooms.

The Greek cavalry didn't come at us pell-mell. They formed in a neat rhomboid a stade away, and Cleomenes had time to buckle his breastplate.

'They look professional,' Kineas said. He pulled the cheek-plates down on his helmet. Quietly, he said, 'Shouldn't the king go to the rear?'

I smiled. 'He should,' I agreed. 'But he won't!'

They came forward at us, and we had about the same numbers. Alexander took the point. There was no stopping him. He saw Kineas and smiled. 'More Athenians over there than here,' he said.

'Quality over quantity,' Kineas said. He grinned at the king.

Alexander threw his head back and roared. 'By the gods, you are a man after my own heart,' he said. He tossed his javelin in the air and caught it. 'Oh, I am *alive*.'

As soon as we started forward, I realised that the big man with the dark skin who was coming right at me had to be Memnon himself. And these cavalrymen would be his Theban exiles.

We smashed together at a fast trot. Neither side had time to get to a gallop. But because we were so slow, both sides were perfectly ordered, and we *crashed* together as if we were hoplites on foot.

Fights like that aren't about skill, but about horse size and riding ability. We were evenly matched, and we were suddenly in our hipposthismos, pushing and cutting, and my spear was broken – I can never tell you how, it always just seems to happen.

I was sword to sword with Memnon – or rather, he cut at me with his kopis, and I blocked with the ash staff of my busted spear. I forced him to parry high, and I got my bridle hand on his elbow and started to push, and quick as a viper he put his head down and rammed my face with the crest of his helmet. But my nasal held, and he didn't break my nose or my face. I went for my dagger, rammed it into his side and missed my blow – he caught my dagger in his bridle hand and disarmed me.

He was good.

'Let me at him!' Alexander shouted at my right hip.

I'd have laughed, if I hadn't been so busy.

Memnon now had my right wrist and I had his. I had his with my left thumb *down*, so I started to rotate his hand by main strength and leverage. My riding horse didn't help – too small and light for this kind of work, but she had lots of heart, and as she backed away from Memnon's bigger stallion and took a bite to the face, she reared, and for a second I had the purchase, and I stripped the sword from Memnon's hand, getting a slash across my neck in exchange.

He slashed a dagger at the back of my off leg, and scored deeply. When I tried to throw him to the ground, he punched me in the neck, under the helmet, and by luck, his instinctive punch was with the pommel of the dagger and not the blade, or I'd have had to end this story right there. I sagged back, and suddenly – without warning – the whole lot of them were cantering away from us, and it was all I could do to sit on my horse and breathe.

I'd never been hand to hand with another man who could wrestle on horseback as I can.

Kineas had a long cut down his sword arm, but he'd taken a prisoner.

Alexander slid from the saddle and picked up the sword at my horse's front feet. 'Memnon's sword!' he said. 'An omen if ever there was one.'

Aristander proclaimed the omen throughout the camp that night, which was good, because the omen I saw was that Memnon's ambush had killed a hundred archers, as many Thracians and more Hetaeroi than died at the Battle of the Granicus. And we found six bodies of his men, and Kineas took a prisoner. The worst of it was that his tiny cavalry force had only charged us to cover the rest of his ambush as they broke contact. I wasn't an old veteran, back then, but I knew enough to be chilled at the professionalism of an ambush force that struck – and vanished. They didn't hang around to let us bring up reinforcements – the failure of most ambushes.

Kineas's prisoner was a Megaran aristocrat, and thus, by League law, a traitor to be executed. But all agreed he'd fought well – even when unhorsed – and Macedonians, unless their blood is up, don't really hold with killing prisoners.

Kineas bowed to the king that night. 'Lord, I can't make him a slave. He's a gentleman.'

Alexander nodded. He'd enjoyed the fight, and his mood was much better. 'Recruit him, then,' he told Kineas.

And that's your friend Coenus, young man.

Fighting Memnon was the best training that the Macedonian army ever received. He was like a slap in the face – a lesson from a particularly nasty teacher.

It was good for Alexander. At the time, it was a nightmare.

We set our camp for the siege, and that night a hidden battery of engines rained rocks on us for half an hour while our camp dissolved into chaos. Memnon's Greek engineers had time to break the machines down, burn the wood and carry the bronze parts back into the city. Only about a dozen Macedonians were killed – twice that many wounded and twice again in slaves lost – but the panic was incredible.

The second day, Memnon sent a daylight sortie – a *daylight sortie*. Everyone knows that you only sortie at dawn, dusk and in the light of the moon. The besieged – brave but doomed – sneak out a postern gate and try to set fire to a siege engine or two. It never works.

Memnon had two of Athens' best commanders – Ephialtes and Thrasybulus – in his service. Thrasybulus took the picked hoplites of the garrison, waited for our noon guard change to be about one quarter complete and charged out the *main gate*.

I was a stade away, sitting on horseback with Kineas and Cleomenes. We were off duty, and we'd decided to go for a hunt in the hills. I'd never seen such a barren place, and I was minded to find another camp-site – a place where the cavalry could camp closer to water, for example.

We'd just left the camp when the assault started – the noise alerted us. I saw the Greek hoplites teem out of the gate and slam into the pezhetaeroi, who were strung out over five stades of ground in no kind of formation. Guard duty was a formal thing. No one worried about fighting by day, in a siege.

They had fire in pots, and in moments a half-built siege tower was engulfed in flames, and a row of torsion engines went next.

Cleomenes cursed. Those were all the machines we had. The Athenians and the transport fleet had the rest of the siege train, way north at Miletus.

Kineas laughed. 'That's Thrasybulus!' he said. We were close enough to see helmet crests. Yellow with two red side plumes. Thrasybulus. 'Alexander ordered him executed.'

I must have made a face.

Kineas shrugged. 'Would you want a Macedonian exile to prove a coward?' he asked.

The pezhetaeroi were completely defeated, and the Greek hoplite force formed up and marched back into the city, singing a hymn to Athena.

That stung.

Next day I took my grooms and rode cross-country to Miletus with orders for the fleet. The fleet, which consisted of twenty Athenian triremes and forty transport ships, against roughly four hundred Persian warships.

Nicanor, the fleet commander, made a face. 'The Athenians don't love Alexander,' he said, as if I needed to be told that. 'And all those oarsmen have relatives serving on the walls at Halicarnassus.'

'The king needs the siege train,' I said.

Thaïs and Alexander and I had cooked up a plan. Each of us contributed something, although I'm sure that Alexander thought of it as his plan and I'm quite sure it was really mine.

Thaïs arranged for a prisoner to escape with news that our fleet was going to raid Cos – a large island off the coast still loyal to Persia.

Alexander tried to assault the walls four nights in a row. It cost him men, but it kept Memnon busy – too busy to brew mischief.

Nicanor sent the Athenian squadron to appear off Cos and then sail south, as if going to Cyprus or Tyre or one of the other Persian bases.

And then, naked as a babe, the transports sailed before dawn on the fourth day from Miletus with our entire siege train – nipped round Point Poseidon and landed at Iasos. Did our brilliant trickery play any role? Who knows. But the Persian fleet left Halicarnassus and sailed – to Cos – and our siege train moved down the coast unmolested.

Day seven of the siege, and we were ready to start in earnest. We built the engines well to the rear, where no sortie could reach them, and the whole army spent two days moving earth – the miserable, sandy, scrubby soil of Halicarnassus – in sacks from the more fertile regions to the west. It was brutal, and because it was brutal, we all did it. Alexander made a point of carrying sacks of earth.

Parmenio did not. He was openly derisive of the effort.

Day eight – see here, in the Military Journal? At least this part is honest – four days of rain. Autumn had come, and the wind blew, and most of our precious soil was washed away. That taught us to keep our dirt and sand in sacks. Of course, the sacks for sandbags had to come from somewhere. Sieges are a delight, I tell you – a logistician's dream.

Memnon, damn him, had everything – bags, quarried stone, full magazines, water, oil. His engines were as good as ours and a little higher on the walls – our first earth platforms were too low, because we hurried. His engines had our range to the dactyl, and before a stone was launched we'd lost engines to his engines.

But we were learning. We put all our earth in sacks, with every camp follower and whore in the army sewing like mad, and our next artillery platforms were higher than the walls and better sited, and in two more days (days eleven and twelve) we'd blown a breach in the wall.

Day thirteen – an exhausting day bringing more earth from the west and north. Every piece of fabric between Miletus and Halicarnassus was now in our earthworks, and Ada had sent us the whole cloth inventory of her realm – thousands of pieces of woven stuff, some quite costly.

And it rained.

And we built new mounds for the second battery.

The thirteenth night of the siege, the rain stopped a little after midnight. There was no moon.

Memnon came out with his picked men, all with their faces blacked, and they burned more than half our engines. The sentries were asleep. There was no one to punish, because they died to a man.

See what I mean about training? It was as if Memnon's job was to punish us when we failed. His scouting and intelligence were excellent.

Thaïs began to worry that he had a spy in our headquarters. Her immediate suspect was Kineas.

'Or you,' I pointed out. 'You are ideally placed, and Athenian.'

She nodded. 'If I'm a traitor, you'd already be dead,' she noted.

Both of us worried that Parmenio was so angry at the king that he'd sell us out just to get the campaign to end. It was hard to know what exactly Parmenio was playing for. I suspected him of plotting to be king, but if so, he was far more cautious a plotter than I would ever have managed. Thaïs felt that he only plotted to defend himself against the king – that he assumed that, in time, the king would try to kill him.

Macedon, eh?

*

The king moved our batteries to the south side of the city and we started all over again, with fewer engines tossing their stones against a narrower front of the wall. We worked all day on the fifteenth day and all day on the sixteenth, and on the morning of the seventeenth we started to pound the southern walls, and by nightfall we had four breaches.

We stood guard all night, waiting for the inevitable attack, because we'd blown huge holes in the walls and Memnon had to do something.

He did not.

I smelled the rat, but no one would listen to me, and at dusk on the eighteenth day, we formed up to assault the breaches. Alexander was going in person, and I was going with him – all of us were, all the king's friends.

Dusk. The sun had burned all day, but in autumn, the evening has a bite in it, and the tireder you are, the colder it seems. My arms hurt, my abdomen hurt – I'm a cavalryman, by Poseidon! Not a dirt carrier. My thorax seemed to weigh fifty pounds, and my wrist bracers were like stones. My helmet weighed down on my neck.

And the start of the assault was slowed because Perdiccas's taxeis was late getting into their assault positions.

Alexander stood near our bit of parapet, outwardly calm. When he saw Perdiccas's men cutting across the 'no man's land' between our works and the city wall, he frowned.

'They're announcing we're coming,' he said, and then, I could see, he was clamping down.

He kept looking up the steep ramp of rubble at the breach, which seemed to tower above us. But the breach seemed empty of men, so our surprise was still intact.

We were going first, of course. Right up the breach, all the way to the top. In one rush, with no rest and no slacking, in fifty pounds of armour.

Try it – climbing over pulverised rock in iron-shod sandals going up a forty-five degree slope into fire.

Their archers took a long time to wake up. That much of the plan worked. And Alexander had fires set – wet grass, brought from the hills to the east – and the smoke covered us for a while, although I, for one, choked on it. I threw up on the ramp. War is glorious.

So I was well behind Alexander at the top of the wall, but since he's told me the story a hundred times, I can tell you. He was the first into the city. There was no resistance.

A dozen archers on the wall shot down into us. Men fell, but not many, and even they were only wounded. It's awfully hard to kill an armoured man carrying an aspis with a missile from above.

Alexander ran over the rubble, light-footed as a god, spear at the ready, crested the breach and started down into the town. There appeared to be a row of houses in front of him, so he turned along the alley and ran south, towards the sea, with a dozen men at his heels. About this time I'd made it to the breach, and the pezhetaeroi were coming up the ramp behind us in big numbers, the sprinters already three-quarters of the way to the top.

Alexander was afire with the thought of being the first into the town – a great honour among Macedonians, and indeed among all Hellenes. I saw his helmet plumes ahead of me, going south, and I pushed through the hypaspitoi to get to him. I wasn't worried about Memnon's garrison – more fool I – but about murder. By then, I was convinced that Parmenio meant to kill the king.

I went south along the alley. I picked up the smell of new masonry – the smell of new-laid mud brick and mortar – as I ran.

Someone had walled up those houses – perhaps five days before.

We were in a cul-de-sac, and the whole attack was an ambush.

I ran as if my legs were powered by ambrosia and the gods were lifting my feet.

Alexander was standing at the head of the southern end of the alley, staring at a wall of new masonry and sandbags three men high. He only had a dozen men around him.

'Trap!' I screamed. 'Run!'

That got their attention.

Hephaestion got his aspis up in front of Alexander's head, and Nearchus put his over the king's shoulder, and then the first volley of arrows hit – fired point blank from a few horse lengths.

Men went down. That close, and the Carian and Cretan longbows with their very heavy arrows punched through bronze. I took an arrow two fingers deep into my left shoulder and it stood clear of me like some sort of banner.

Alexander was hit four times, despite his friends covering him. There were that many arrows, and Memnon had predicted that he would be there. Memnon's whole plan, in fact, was to kill the king.

I fell to one knee – I probably screamed. The pain was intense, and the sight of the king battered by arrows broke my heart.

I won't soon forget that moment – the taste of vomit in my helmet, the searing pain in my shoulder, the sharp rubble under my knee.

Alexander stood straight as a blade. 'Form the synapsismos!' he called. There were hypaspitoi and pezhetaeroi mixed together in the breach and the alley behind it, but the king's voice impelled instant obedience, and men formed ranks even as they died in the arrow storm.

The closer they formed, the more shields there were to cover them, and the safer they were – but the requirement for discipline was incredible.

And they rose to it. There must have been a thousand men packed in the trap, and Alexander saved them – most of them.

'Back step!' he ordered. 'Shields up!'

Step by step. I was in the second rank, with the arrow sticking out of my shoulder until Nearchus saw it and pulled it free. The barbs, thanks to Apollo, had caught in the leather lining of my shoulder armour and had not passed my skin.

Nearchus had a small, very sharp knife inside his thorax – we all did – and he used it to cut my pauldron free of my thorax even as another volley of arrows tore into us, but the gods were with me, or too busy elsewhere to care, and I was not taken.

I got my aspis on my bleeding shoulder, and the spirit of combat filled me and kept me from fainting, and we backed step by step across the rubble with their arrows pouring in on us and Alexander calling the step like a taxiarch. Step by step.

It took for ever. I still have dreams about it – the feeling of the rubble under my sandals, the grit *inside* them and inside my thorax, the feeling of blood and sweat turning cold in the morning air, the pain, and the king's voice carrying us down the ramp a step at a time.

Memnon's archers shot at the king. He was easy to spot, and they showered him with arrows, but the hypaspitoi and a few old sweats from the pezhetaeroi covered him with their shields and died for it. And no chance shaft killed him. He was hit again and again – I saw one shaft hit him square in the helmet crest and stick – and he continued to give orders as if on parade.

We got down the ramp, and the hypaspitoi gathered around him and carried him away to where his personal physician, Philip of Acarnia, waited with hot tongs and boiling water. Alexander had four wounds – three from arrows and a fourth where a friendly spear-tip had ripped across the back of his neck.

We all wore scarves – rolled tight and tucked into the top of our thoraces to catch the sweat and to pad the necks of our armour against our skin. When Philip pulled the king's neckcloth off, an arrowhead fell with a clank to the wood floor of the tent. I saw this with my own eyes.

Every man present gasped. That arrow had penetrated the cloth of the neck pad, and somehow stopped against the king's neck. There wasn't a mark on him.

His four wounds were less onerous than my one. As soon as Philip had seen to the king, he put me on the table, gave me a leather billet to bite and cauterised my shoulder wound after cleaning it. That made me scream. But he had a light touch with the iron and his slaves were famous throughout the army, and I was on my feet the next day in time to see the King of Macedon send a herald to Memnon requesting permission to retrieve the corpses of our dead.

It was the only time Alexander ever had to do so, in all his life. In the Hellenic world, it was an admission of defeat – it entitled the other side to set up a trophy of victory. Memnon had beaten us, and worse, he'd killed three hundred veterans in the breach and rumour had it he'd lost just three men in exchange.

That morning, Parmenio openly proposed that we break the siege and march for Ephesus. 'We can't take this town this winter,' he said. 'Possibly not ever.'

He didn't push it, however. In fact, to me, he sounded as if he was egging the king on, pushing him by teasing him. Perhaps I wronged him, but by then I had ceased to hold any affection for Parmenio.

The argument in the headquarters tent went on for hours – and was bitterly acrimonious. It was so nasty that it occurred to me that Alexander was king only by virtue of victory. I had never thought it before – but what I heard in that tent convinced me that if the king were to take a major defeat, these bastards would leave him in a moment. I was shocked, for a while.

The truth was, as usual, that Alexander's near-inhuman perfection had a flaw. The flaw was that men doubted it, and waited to see him fail. In some perverse way, many men wanted to see him fail. And by the time of the siege of Halicarnassus the strain was beginning to show. Some of the pezhetaeroi were openly mutinous, being forced to serve past their appointed time. The harvest was in back at Pella, or nearly, and they weren't home on their farms.

And the aristocrats were starting to realise that, under Alexander, there would only be war, followed by war. None of the delights of peace – such as plotting the king's overthrow. They'd realised that he meant what he said – he meant to conquer all of Asia.

For four hours they yelled at each other, and then Perdiccas went off to set the guards – the two junior regiments of the pezhetaeroi.

I was not paying very close attention because my shoulder hurt, and I had reached a level of fatigue and injury that left me dull. I just knew that I'd had too much wine, my wound was throbbing, and suddenly most of the officers had left the tent, leaving Alexander and Hephaestion and Parmenio and Philotas.

Alexander stood with his arms crossed. 'I'll stay here all winter if that's what it takes to take this city,' he said.

'You'll burn the cream of your infantry and leave us nothing,'

Parmenio said, mixing his metaphors like mad. 'Memnon is reading you like a book, boy.'

'You are not welcome to call me *boy*, Lord Parmenio. Take yourself to bed. You are drunk, sir.' Alexander spoke carefully. I thought he was a little tipsy himself.

'I may be drunk, but you are *young*. The first duty of any strategos – never mind the King of Macedon – is to protect his army. To keep it alive. To fight another day. Halicarnassus is not a fair trade for the army your father and I spent twenty years training.'

Alexander shrugged. 'Yes it is,' he said. 'I'll do what I can for the pezhetaeroi, but I'll trade them all for defeating Memnon. There're more boys in Pella who can carry a sarissa.'

I would have shut him up if I'd been well. Hephaestion didn't care – he shared the king's delusions of grandeur.

Parmenio turned red.

Philotas spat. 'Maybe if you had to train them yourself, you'd take more care with them.'

Alexander shrugged again. 'At least I wouldn't squander them in ambushes,' he said.

Philotas reached for his sword, and even though I had no time for him, I managed to pin his arms against his side.

Alexander looked at him, and at Parmenio. 'Did your son just reach for a weapon in the royal presence?' he asked.

And I shook my head. 'No, lord. He did not. Nor would I say he did in front of the Assembly.' Cases of treason and lese-majesty were always tried in front of the Assembly of the freemen of the army.

Parmenio threw me a glance of thanks.

I didn't want his thanks – I wanted the king to stop being an arse.

Alexander looked through me.

Parmenio did the right thing, took his son and his Thessalian officers and got out of the tent.

Alexander watched him go. 'I didn't expect you to side with Parmenio,' he said to me in a chilling voice.

'Lord,' I said, and I turned on him, 'I don't need to protest my loyalty to you, do I? You risk an open breach with Parmenio in the middle of this siege. Is that what you want?'

'Eventually I must clean my house,' Alexander said.

I had missed it. He was drunk. He was telling the truth, as men often do, in their cups, but he was drunk.

'Not right now, I think. Not while we are in the face of the enemy – a very competent enemy.' Marsyas said that – bless him. The only courtier with enough balls to agree with me in the face of the king's drunkenness.

'Parmenio cannot be trusted,' Hephaestion said.

I nodded, glad that I, at least, was sober. 'Parmenio cannot be trusted,' I agreed. 'He may even try to kill the king,' I added quietly. 'But he is the second most powerful man in the army, and he has the loyalty of many, many men – men we need to conquer Asia. Now is not the time. We might have civil war.'

Marsyas nodded, and Black Cleitus looked at me carefully. But Alexander turned his back on me, leaned on Hephaestion, and walked from the tent.

About six hours later, while the sun was just a hint of orange-grey in the sky over the sea to the east, Memnon struck.

He sent a thousand men with buckets of pitch and blackened faces out of a secret postern gate. They ran silently across no man's land, overwhelmed the young men on guard duty and plunged in among the war machines. Their pitch buckets and fire pots went straight to work, and in minutes they had all the engines on the north side of the city aflame.

It was brutal, and grim, and in those flames we read our doom. We had lost our entire siege train in fewer minutes than it takes words to tell it.

The pezhetaeroi rallied to counter-attack over the batteries and men formed up with buckets of water – scarce water, many men using what was in their canteens. The pezhetaeroi stormed forward in the dark, and met a fierce resistance – the black-painted men fought like demons. The pezhetaeroi were spear to spear and shield to shield with many of Greece's best men, and it was dark. In many ways, the situation favoured the Greeks fighting for Persia.

When the pezhetaeroi bogged down – still well short of retaking the battery platforms – Memnon sprung the second part of his trap, and released *another* sortie from the *main gate*. Again. We still weren't ready to see troops coming out of the main gate, but they did – a major force of hoplites and a handful of cavalry, led by the two Athenian strategoi. They slammed into the flank of the pezhetaeroi, catching them at open shields, and the execution they inflicted was horrible.

And then the gods took a hand.

It was at this point, when all was lost, the machines burned and Memnon's masterstroke was unveiled, that I arrived on the scene – in armour, thanks to Polystratus's and Thaïs's efforts. My shoulder was stiff and painful and I ached all over, but the sound of disaster

418

is unmistakable. I ran for the fighting, with my grooms and a dozen friends at my back.

I found Alexander in the gloom. He was waiting for the hypaspitoi to form up. He was watching the fighting – listening, perhaps.

Alectus was forming men as fast as they piled out of their tents, and I put my grooms and any man I could lay hands on in the ranks with them and ran to Alexander's side.

'Good morning, Ptolemy,' he said.

'How bad is it?' I asked.

'Oh – terrible. But not insurmountable. Memnon has made a mistake. Very unlike him, but a good lesson to all of us.' Alexander turned to me, and he was smiling. 'Memnon is really very, very good. When this campaign started, he was a better general than I, but by the time we're done, I'll have learned what he has to teach. He does everything by misdirection. Brilliant. We Macedonians too often bludgeon. Memnon always cuts with the fine knife.' He nodded.

I could hear the pezhetaeroi dying.

'Memnon's made a mistake?' I asked.

'He has. His raid burned our engines and his masterstroke killed our counter-attack to rescue them.' Alexander was, as always once the fighting started, calm and detached. 'Had he broken contact at that point, and got his force back behind the walls, we'd have lost here. And not just here. Memnon's strategy is brilliant – to wear me out here and then take his fleet and go to Greece.' Alexander watched the fires of the siege engines burning, his dreams of conquest going up in pitch-soaked flames and the fires reflected in his eyes and the gold of his helmet. Behind us, Alectus was roaring at stragglers.

Alexander pointed with his chin towards Parmenio's tent on the left of the army. 'What he cannot understand is that we are fighting for Greece, right here. If Memnon leaves us defeated here – we're done. Most of you cannot imagine how vast the Great King's empire is. Nor how many times we'll have to defeat it.'

'Ready, Lord King,' Alectus reported.

Alexander pointed at the gates. 'But Memnon elected to commit his troops to his victory, and even now, more and more of his precious Greek hoplites are pressing through the main gates on to a chaotic battlefield where it is as black as pitch. On to the killing ground.' He raised his voice so that the men behind him could hear. Next to us, a battalion of old men was forming. They weren't even all from the same taxeis – it was a formation of veterans. Philip's veterans. Hundreds of them.

Alexander pitched his voice appropriately, as he was always able to do. 'They have burned our engines, but they have now sent so many of the garrison outside the walls that we have it in our power to win the city on the battlefield. The pezhetaeroi have fought like young lions – have not broken. Now – you veterans of Philip – go and show them what you learned from Phokion and Charmides and on a hundred other battlefields. We are not in Asia to survive. We are in Asia to conquer.'

The veterans let out a growl like a cheer and went forward, led – in person – by Parmenio. It was odd, and more than a little ironic. The very best thing he could have done for his own plans would have been to stay in his tent. But he was not that man. He was Parmenio – the best general in Macedon – and he led his veterans to save the day because that's what he did. Most men – and women – can plot and scheme evil, but when it comes to the day and the moment, they will be staunch to what they believe in. Thus Parmenio, in that hour, could not leave his men to die to serve his policy of humiliating the king.

He roared the king's name, and his phalanx answered, and they went forward into the firelit darkness.

We went farther north, skirting the fire. Alexander was sure there'd be another sortie out of the gate facing the new works, and he led the hypaspitoi there. I had Kineas the Athenian on one side of me and Hephaestion on my other side, and we went into the ditch that surrounded the city and caught the Persian levies that Memnon had been using as a labour force, now given weapons and released to cause havoc. We caught them leaving the gate and we slaughtered them.

I take no joy in slaughter. I like a good fight, now and then – I like to win and I hate to lose, but I like the fight to be ... interesting.

This was a butchery of peasants, and it went on too long.

And then we pressed forward into the dark, with Alexander's golden lion helmet burning like a beacon in the light cast by the flames from the walls and the burning machines. He glowed with power, and we ran through the night, falling over logs and stones, cursing the darkness.

The fight at the main gate was locked in stalemate. The old men – Philip's men – had saved the phalanx and steadied it, but they could not beat the hoplites, who, man for man, were as good or better. And darkness aids no man. Darkness robs the best swordsman of his skill and the rawest recruit of his wits. Dawn was coming up, somewhere far to the east – Athens was probably already lit by sun, and Pella was at least burning pink, but under the walls of Halicarnassus, it was still as black as new-poured pitch, lit only by fires.

We slammed into the Greeks. We didn't really catch them by surprise – the Athenian captains had turned to face us – Ephialtes himself, I heard later, one of their best.

But our arrival had an effect nonetheless. The Persian levies were dead or broken, and their survivors were glutting the gates in terror, and now we threw in our last reserve – and Memnon, who also had an elite reserve, couldn't get men through the gates blocked by his useless peasants.

Don't think the irony was lost on any of us, lad. We were saved – Macedon was saved from defeat by Athens under the walls of a city in Asia by the cowardice of Persian levies.

The fighting was desperate. All fighting is, but this was made nightmarish by the darkness. Inside my helmet, I could see *nothing* once I was engaged, and the worst of it was that our rear-rankers had no sense of the combat and kept pushing forward, grinding me relentlessly into the ranks of the hoplites I was fighting, so that I couldn't fully control my weight or balance. More than once, an unintended shove from my file partner sent me to my knees or worse.

But unlike most men, Kineas and I were in full armour. I had greaves and a heavy breastplate, a full helmet, an aspis and a heavy spear, and Kineas was armed the same way, and details – long 'feathers' covering our upper arms, a full yoke covering the back of my neck in bronze – were lifesavers, because none of us could see a blow coming. I don't know how many times I was hit, but I know that the next day I threw my beautiful helmet into the sea – too dented and cut up to be saved. Only the thickness of my cap and my hair saved me from death – there were shearing blows that penetrated the thick bronze.

I don't remember a single fight. There's nothing to remember – no vision to cling to – just the relentless weight of the men behind me and the ringing blows on my shield and all too often on my helmet. I took a bad blow – something, probably a spear shaft, hit my spear hand and suddenly I had no weapon and was almost weeping from the pain.

Pyrrhus and Kineas covered me while the tears flowed out of my eyes unbidden and I flailed about on the bloody ground for a weapon. My sword was gone, my spear was gone, and by the time my hand closed on the shaft of a spear I was disoriented. But I got my feet under me and found myself under Pyrrhus's shield, safe – I got a breath in me and got my spear and shield up, and I was alive.

That heartbeat of complete disorientation on the dark battlefield with death all around – it still visits my dreams, like falling from a great height. That's terror.

And then the Greeks began to back away.

In fact, I suspect they'd been backing away for some time, and I was just too busy to notice. But now I was moving forward at a brisk pace – by the standards of infantry combat – tripping over bodies and without someone's spear trying to poke out my eyes.

Memnon ordered the main gates closed while more than two hundred of his hoplites were still trapped in the darkness. It was the correct decision, but it doomed them to death, and they knew it, and the whole combat developed a ferocity that I have seldom seen equalled. It is not for nothing that strategoi speak of the 'Golden Bridge' – the easy path of retreat we offer to a defeated enemy in most circumstances. Trapped men with nothing to lose are ferocious.

Those Greeks were monsters, and many of us died.

Of course, they *all* died.

Alexander was in the front of it, and his spear flashed like the bolts of Zeus, and he didn't hesitate to go shield to shield with those raging monsters and slay them, and where he led, we followed, shouting his name.

But when the last Greeks were dying, we were still under the walls, the gates were still locked and they were pouring red-hot sand on us.

The Military Journal says that we lost one hundred and twelve pezhetaeroi and found six hundred bodies of the enemy.

In fact, we lost – dead and badly wounded – a little over nine hundred men, and we found about five hundred corpses.

Our machines were all burned, and we would have to start all over again.

In the morning, Memnon asked for a truce to retrieve his dead. This pleased Alexander immensely, as it meant that he could claim to have won a victory. He was difficult, that morning – elated, brash and far, far too talkative. Parmenio looked at him with something that seemed to me like loathing.

He was never his own best friend, Alexander. On the battlefield, he was solid, calm and brave, but afterwards, he was like a boy after his first girl – all bragging and no substance. How could the god become so very human?

He went on and on, that day, tiring every one of us – even Nearchus grew tired of his recitation of his own triumphs. He may well have killed the Athenian captain, Ephialtes, himself – he certainly claimed he had, and we found the body – but when he told the story of the fight with *Iliad*-like embellishment, we all knew he was a liar. No one among us could have seen a single thing, and his description was like a piece of theatre. The theatre of the inside of the king's head.

Hephaestion tried to shush him, and failed.

Philotas left the tent, disgusted, and Parmenio walked out a little later. I was trying to pretend I was somewhere else – perhaps someplace involving a bath – when Parmenio came back.

'You have won a *noble* victory,' he said with rich sarcasm. 'Come and see, *great* king.'

Alexander, when he was like this, didn't even notice his sarcasm. He followed Parmenio out of the great tent, and up to the top of one of our northerly engine platforms.

Memnon was abandoning the city.

He was ferrying his entire force to the three island citadels that dominated the harbour mouth, and the Persian fleet was putting to sea.

He was keeping his army intact, and slipping away to fight another day. And we could do nothing to stop him.

Alexander nodded. Looked around, expecting approval. 'We beat him,' he said. 'Every city in Greece will know we took Halicarnassus from Memnon.'

Parmenio watched his nemesis slipping away, and all we could hear was the sound of the slaves digging graves in the thin soil. The only smell was smoke, because as he left, Memnon set fire to the city. It burned for three days, and there was nothing we could do to stop it.

'He intends to bleed us until we drop, and then destroy us,' Parmenio said.

'We made him ask for a truce to bury his dead,' Alexander said.

'We have no fleet!' Parmenio said, disgusted.

'I will deal with that. One victory at a time,' Alexander said, his voice a little too bright.

'Ten more victories like this one and we will have no more Macedonians!' Parmenio shouted.

'Calm yourself,' Alexander said.

'He is not beaten! He still holds all the citadels and he's left the city an empty shell! By the gods, are you insane? Stop this! We cannot conquer Asia!' Spittle flew from Parmenio's mouth. 'Even if by the will of the gods we were to war down Persepolis, we will never hold it all!'

Alexander looked around. 'How many of you feel the same?' he asked, ingenuously. You had to have grown up with him to know what mood he was in.

About half of the officers present raised a hand.

Most of them were older men, Parmenio's friends.

'Then I recommend you go home, every one of you.' Alexander shrugged. 'We'll just have to carry on without you.'

NINETEEN

———

Parmenio took half the army and marched away.

Alexander gave me four thousand Greek mercenaries, my squadron of companions and Kineas and his Allied Horse, and left me to reduce the coast to obedience and complete the conquest of Caria and Cilicia.

He had a small ceremony to mark the occasion. As was his way, I had no warning – suddenly I was summoned to the command tent and given an independent command. I knew that this was a result of Parmenio marching away, and I knew that I was being given troops from Parmenio's command. And that I was facing long odds – equal or greater numbers in fortresses for which I had no engines, or on islands I could not reach without ships.

But I accepted his commands without hesitation. He put a circlet of gold on my head and girded me with a new sword, and promoted Polystratus to the companions, which I greatly appreciated and which made Polystratus a nobleman. It was only fair – the man had been my hyperetes all campaign, and had charged with the Hetaeroi at every engagement. But it was a great reward. And this is one of the things that makes Macedon – and Greece – great. Polystratus was a good man, and now he was an aristocrat. His children would not be the sons of a freed slave, but the sons of an aristocrat. His daughters were going to have dowries and would marry the sons of other minor aristocrats. In Persia, they would live and die as slaves.

The truth of it was that our losses were heavy enough – not just battlefield losses, either, but dysentery and other sickness, accident, weather – that most of us who had brought our own grooms were not above putting them in dead men's armour and using them to fill our ranks. The sort of distinctions that mattered enormously in lowland Macedon – birth, horse quality, armour – either mattered not at all in Asia (such as birth) or were gone (horse flesh and armour). We were all mounted on Asian horses and almost every Macedonian cavalryman regardless of social status now had a full thorax, a good helmet, a lance and a couple of javelins, a sword – and like as not, gold on his bridle and silver in his scrip.

Polystratus's promotion mirrored mine. I arranged for all of my grooms to be formally taken into the companions, and Polystratus was then formally my hyperetes, as Niceas served Kineas. And my troop returned to near full strength of over a hundred riders. I got Coenus's troop, as well – he was going home to Macedon with the newly married men, a move that restored the king to popularity with the rank and file, because it looked normal – the married men were *supposed* to go home every winter.

In fact, I was beginning to fear that the king didn't really care what happened in Macedon. War in Asia was self-perpetuating – we were making about as much money as we needed to maintain the army, and even to increase its size. We were locked in a competition with Memnon for the service of all the mercenaries in the Greek world, and we were fighting for our lives, and Alexander loved every heartbeat of it. Why go home? What did Macedon have to offer?

Also worth noting is that as long as we were fighting for our lives in Asia, no one was going to plot against the king – well, except Parmenio, and he was right there where he could be watched.

And Olympias was a long way away, too.

Coenus marched away with the married men, and Parmenio marched away with the left wing. He went back to Sardis, as he had wanted to all along – paid off some mercenaries, and then took the rest with the siege train and began a leisurely mopping up of mountain tribes north and east of Sardis.

Alexander marched away along the coast, bypassing strongholds still held by Memnon. He had the hypaspists, the Aegema and the un-married pezhetaeroi, and the scouting cavalry. I heard from him quite regularly for about four weeks – he seized Telmessus by a stratagem, and gave it to Nearchus to hold.

I like to think that Alexander had tired of Nearchus's constant syco-phancy, but it's worth noticing that he'd sent me away, too.

I had four thousand men and plenty of slaves – I had seized the best portion of the city and had my men rebuild the houses. I inspected the work every day, and in two weeks we were the best-housed army in Asia. Then I kept them at work, rebuilding the temples and other houses, and after another week surviving citizens started to return.

I also sent Kineas to find the Athenian squadron and beg or borrow some engines and an engineer.

By the gods, he did me well. He came back in two weeks with ten heavy engines – or rather, the bronze parts for them – as well as Helios, a freed Cyprian slave, who had all of the problems of Pythagoras in his head and knew how to construct ... well, almost everything. He'd been serving the Athenians as a dock builder, and he was bored. I offered him the Macedonian rate of pay as an engineer, and he signed on the spot. He was short, very short for a man, and his skin was deeply tanned, almost the colour of old wood. He had curly blond hair – hence his name – and a pleasant face. He'd been well born, but taken by slavers as a boy and treated badly.

He looked at the three island citadels off Halicarnassus, and shrugged.

'Three ways to take 'em,' he said. He ticked them off on his fingers. 'Build a fleet and storm 'em, starve 'em, or grow wings and fly there.'

I nodded. 'I agree,' I said.

He grinned. 'Good. I was afraid you expected me to make something out of nothing.'

I shook my head. 'My plan is to start with the easiest and move from there. Caunus and a town called Knidos.' I shrugged again. 'Never seen them myself, but they *have* to be easier than this.'

In fact, Thaïs had people in both, plotting revolution.

It was great fun, the two of us planning a complete campaign together. I've known men to freeze in high command, and it is different, but it wasn't my first time, and she liked it too, and it was something we did together. And because she was working for me, and not for the king, I began to see *how* she ran her net of informants, and to watch the details of her intelligence-gathering.

For strategic intelligence – the news of politics, of the thoughts and intentions of great men and cities, of the Persian court, of the satraps – she had her web of letter-writing friends. They didn't think of themselves as spies, and in fact she called them her Epistolaroi. And the greatest and most important of the Epistolaroi was the Pythia and her priests at Delphi.

For tactical intelligence – the immediate collection of information on local troop movements and enemy intentions in the near term, our scouts did most of the collection – most, but not all, because by this time, after almost a year in the field, Thaïs had a corps of spies she called the Angeloi, the heralds. Strakos led them, and they were mostly freemen. Their characteristics were unarmed anonymity, and superb horses. We knew every one of them by name and by sight, so that they could come and go from our lines without passwords. They seldom carried weapons openly, and they rode far and fast, gathering news. Every one of them had funds to buy information, and most of them had the personal skills to recruit their own informers on the spot.

And above all of them was Thaïs. She read every report, spoke to the returning cavalry patrols, interviewed the Angeloi, read the letters from the Epistolaroi and answered them. It was an enormous workload, but she had a secretariat of slaves and freemen, most of them taken at Granicus – slaves who read and wrote Persian, or Thracian, or Aegyptian, or Carian. All told, her establishment had a hundred people working for it, men and women. It was *not* a miracle of efficiency, because it was more like art than science, but her information was reliable and quickly gathered.

In the fourth week, I took a cavalry reconnaissance down the coast, with the Angeloi out in front and detailed reports on the towns already in my head, and Caunus looked the easiest, on paper and in fact. Knidos sat on the end of a 250-stade long peninsula with a mountainous spine. Riding cautiously along the coast road, or rather the coast goat path, I could see an ambush site every five stades. By pure good luck and with some tips from Thaïs's friends, we caught about a quarter of the garrison of Knidos outside their walls and captured them. And then, reversing Alexander's policy, I hired the lot of them, and didn't execute them. I wanted to make it *easy* for men to surrender, not hard.

Caunus, on the other hand, sat three-quarters surrounded by land – flat, well-earthed land. Helios got off his horse in the dawn – we were moving fast and light – and crawled right up to the city wall, and he returned convinced that he could tunnel under the walls in a week.

We got back to Halicarnassus late in the evening, after dark, soaked and very cold. I rode into the courtyard of my house and found it in near panic.

Queen Ada had come into my house in Halicarnassus without being announced. The cold rain poured down the gutters of the house and spat out on to the ground, and I was in a surly mood – I wanted to throw Thaïs on a bed – or a warm floor – and I didn't want to deal with this woman.

It *was* as bad as I feared.

'Why has he not written to me?' she demanded as I entered the room.

Why indeed? Because he was done with her. Because sex with her made him feel like a mortal, not a god.

Thaïs spoke to her rapidly in a low voice.

'You are my strategos, Lord Ptolemy?' the queen asked, more pleasantly.

In fact, I was the absolute lord of Caria. It said so on my warrant. But Alexander had promised her independence, when it suited him, and now I was left holding this particular bag. Love, sex, war, politics. A nasty brew.

'I command all of the king's troops in your kingdom,' I said, as precisely as possible. 'I will complete the task of reconquest.'

She nodded. 'When will he return?' she asked.

It was pitiful – sad, awful. When I'd first met her, I'd been impressed with her vitality, her youth and her complete mastery of the situation. She was a tough woman and a warrior.

Now she was an adolescent girl at the well, begging for news that her beloved still loved her.

She looked old and she sounded foolish, and she knew it herself.

Thaïs was equal to the situation. With a long glance at me – a hopeful one, I felt – she took the queen off to the baths, and I was left with two male slaves and a basin of tepid water.

I got clean, and had them oil me. I was lying on a heated slab – Halicarnassus was a civilised city, and we rebuilt the best parts – and the masseur was pounding my back and then running the sharp edge of the strigil over it – a wonderful, clean feeling. He went on and on, and then the strigil began to scrape harder, and the wielder poked the bent front of it sharply into my armpit and I was fully awake.

I thought he'd slipped, and he did it again – this time the thing prodded me just over the hip and I jumped like a skittish horse.

'Hey!' I said, and rolled over to find that Thaïs was bending over me with mischief in her eyes and a string of pearls wound into her hair – as her sole ornament.

By the gods, life can be good.

It took me a year to reduce the strongholds of Caria. I won't say it was hellish, but it was exacting, hard work, and it changed my relationships with the men under me, with Kineas, with Helios, with Polystratus, with Thaïs. I had had commands before, but this was *my* army, and these were *my* orders from the king. Like Antigonus One-Eye, I had a major command and no help whatsoever. Each of us had to make our own way. That's what the king expected.

Unlike One-Eye, I was in the face of the real enemy. Memnon retreated from Halicarnassus only to seize Cos, just a few stades from the end of our peninsula. Thaïs's people said he had received little opposition there, and in fact Ionia was already a little tired of Alexander. He was rather too much like a conqueror and rather too disturbing. These weren't enslaved Greeks clamouring for freedom – they were rich, settled men and women looking to get on with their lives. He also took Mytilene on Lesbos, and all of Chios. He had a base facing us across the water – and the first stepping stone towards moving his fleet to Greece and Macedon. He had four times the number of troops I had, and the entire Persian fleet – four hundred ships. So I had to be very careful when I moved. In the whole year I was in Caria, I feared – every day – a brilliant descent on my beaches, a dashing attack on a marching column. I scouted everything.

It made me a better soldier. Memnon was to my generation and your father's as Phokion was to Philip – fighting him made us better.

One advantage we had was the empty city of Halicarnassus. Memnon couldn't spy on me there – there was no population base, and as they began to return, Thaïs's people were ruthless in searching out his agents. Her finest hour came at midwinter, when she detected one of his men – a Greek soldier posing as a merchant 'returning' to his city. Instead of hanging him, she planted a slave on him – a slave who was, in fact, one of *her* own men. For the rest of the winter we fed him carefully written reports – he suborned slaves in my headquarters and bought scraps of parchment and stolen wax tablets from them, and we spent some amusing hours drafting these forgeries.

First we fed him a cheap victory. I had hired a pair of shipwrights from Miletus and they were building me a pair of triremes down the coast, but either they were charlatans or their workmen were useless. Either way, what they ended up with weren't worth a pile of horse manure, so we allowed news of them to get to Memnon and he obligingly landed a force and burned them. That proved to us that our man was working, and also built his credibility.

Then we allowed Memnon to know of a grain ship heading for us. I had plenty of grain. He seized it, and our tame agent was delighted. Then we allowed Memnon to know that we were so terrified of his intelligence network and his fleet that we were barricaded in Halicarnassus.

And then, on a cold, rainy night, I slipped my little army out through a postern gate and raced for Caunus.

We missed storming the place by surprise – by a blade of grass. But the closing of the gates caught a third of the garrison outside the walls, gathering new bedding, and we took them prisoner. I didn't even summon the town to surrender – I constructed my ten engines from the abundant local wood, and my first stones were flying before the sun set on the first day of the siege.

The town offered to surrender on the third day, but informed us that they could not surrender the citadel, which was in the hands of Memnon's troops. I accepted their surrender and moved my machines up, all in one day. In the face of the outrage of the citizens, I had my slaves demolish a whole (rather rich) quarter of the city, and I used every slave in the town and many of the poorer citizens to move earth so that my platform was done in three days – to the same height as the top of the citadel wall.

They were Greeks. They didn't expect it to be so fast. On the fifth day, my machines were smashing the parapet. It was a small citadel, less than a stade on a side, with three steep, rocky sides, but the fourth was merely a steep slope with a high wall, and I blew that wall to Hades in a day – mud brick on a stone base.

They went to work building a new wall behind the rubble of the old wall.

Before they finished it, Helios's mine, started on the first day, reached the point he thought was correct, and we fired it, and the whole north face of their acropolis crumbled.

Helios, the former slave, accepted success and victory with a calm equanimity that made me love him. He thanked every slave and free digger, and he freed three men whose efforts had been spectacular.

And then I packed up my army, put a garrison under Pyrrhus in the town and raced back up the coast to Halicarnassus. As I expected, Memnon landed a counter-attack, but his attempt to cut the coast road missed me by a day, and I was safe in the walls of Halicarnassus when his army got back in their ships. They tried to retake Caunus by *coup de main*, but Pyrrhus was ready and they failed.

That was the easy one. But every man in my force knew we had beaten the great Memnon. I had thousands of Greek mercenaries – men who might, but for the chances of Moira, fate, Tyche, have been serving Memnon and not me. I needed some victories to convince them that I was the better boss.

Somewhere south of me, the king was marching through the snow of the high mountains. I had no idea what he was doing – or why. I knew that he intended to take every city in Asia Minor before he went inland – to cut the King of Persia off from the sea. Queen Ada fretted, and sometimes I did too.

On the other hand, Thaïs and I had a wonderful winter. I had enough campaigning to keep me busy, and I enjoyed – I still do – administration. They don't call me Farm Boy for nothing. I made sure that the city was rebuilt, and I built Ada a mint. When bandits plagued her main road, I sent Kineas and his Athenian Hippeis and they destroyed the bandits and burned their camp.

Locals told Thaïs and her people that there came a two-week period in late winter when the storms die away and zephyrs blow. It seemed worth a try, so I collected light boats – fishing boats, which could carry ten men. We collected several hundred of them, causing grumbling and mutiny all along the coast, which moved me not at all.

When we'd had two days of golden sunshine and light winds, I put all my cavalry into the boats with the best of my Greek mercenaries and we flew under sail across Keramaeios Bay – eighty stades of pure terror, where a few big waves might have done me in. I'm no great fan of the sea. But I knew that Memnon would be insane to risk his naval supremacy at this time of year. I felt it was worth the risk.

We landed on the rocky beaches east of Knidos in the last light of evening, and we spent a hard night on the rocks north and east of the town. I got lost in the darkness and there was no moon, and we were an hour late to our rendezvous when we found Strako and his lieutenant, Anarches, waiting beneath the walls.

But after that, it went like a play. Strakos pounded his spear-butt against a low postern gate – and it opened.

He grinned at me. 'And it didn't cost an obol!' he said, and that was that.

By the gods, that one was sweet. There is a special feeling when you take a great risk and pull it off. I sent a message to Kineas to send me a garrison – by land – and waited to see who would reach me first – Memnon or Kineas. I sent Strako to Thaïs with the same message and a note of thanks for a job well done.

Perhaps Memnon was too busy taking Mytilene, or perhaps he made an error, or maybe, just maybe, Thaïs's precious agent and his false information about the size of my garrison kept him at home.

However it worked out, I took Knidos with no loss, and ten days later I left Kineas there with his Athenians and four hundred mercenaries.

We heard – from the captured garrison – that the king was in Pamphylia. Whatever the truth of it, he wasn't communicating with me or with Ada, and he moved so fast that Thaïs didn't know where he was.

I got quite a nice note of congratulations over the mountains from Parmenio. It was as flattering as the source was unexpected. He wrote from Sardis, praised my energy, diligence and success, and asked me to bring my part of the army to a rendezvous at Gordia in the late spring. The letter informed me that the married men and new recruits under Coenus would meet us there, and the king, as well.

That left me with only the three island forts to deal with.

The problem was that each fort occupied the entirety of its island, and I couldn't lay siege without a fleet. So I once again hired naval architects – this time with input from Helios and other men to make sure I wasn't cozened – and I started to build a quinquereme and three triremes – at Queen Ada's expense. Caria had once been a naval power, and she fancied the idea. Helios felt that this was the smallest squadron that would give us a chance. And we built a mole under the walls of the city – a fortified mole with engine towers, to cover our ships. And to bombard the nearest island, less than a stade off the coast.

Spring burst into flower, and my mole brought my ten engines in range. Over the water, on Lesbos, Mytilene was still holding out, which gave us hope, and Mythymna promised to rebel against Memnon when we gave the word. I suspected that now that the sailing weather was here, as soon as Mytilene fell Memnon would come and try to take Halicarnassus back. And he would, too – but I might hold him long enough for Alexander or Parmenio to swoop down on *him*. I dreamed of such a victory.

Just after the Athenian spring feast of Demeter, Mytilene fell after a heroic resistance. These days, when men speak of the ease of Alexander's conquest of Ionia, I want to spit. Men died – good men – fighting for Alexander or just fighting for their own beliefs and freedoms. Mytilene helped us almost as much as victory at Granicus.

A week later, Memnon had seized Miletus, too, and all the other port cities in Ionia and Aetolia hurried to surrender to him.

In three weeks, all our gains of two years were reversed. Memnon had cut Alexander off from mainland Greece, and the rumour that Thaïs's agents had was that he was going to use Mytilene as a springboard to go to the island of Euboea off the coast of Boeotia, near Thebes, where the population would welcome him as a liberator from Macedonian oppression.

It wasn't a 'brilliant' plan. It was merely an excellent plan that he'd worked out carefully, and he had the money, the logistics and the fleet to make it work.

Antipater had a powerful army, and Macedon had a fleet in the Dardanelles. And Athens, bless them, wavered – they had three hundred triremes in the water, thanks to Lycurgus, and Demosthenes was demanding that his city join Memnon every day.

We were one bold stroke from ruin.

I saw no reason to stop what I was doing, so I sent a message to Parmenio telling him that I would come to the rendezvous at Gordia when I'd finished the task set me. Then I sat in my chair in the warm spring sun and watched my ten-talent engines chip away at the nearest island's walls.

I had to pretend I had all the time in the world. It really was the most leisurely siege ever – the defenders were sure they'd be relieved, or even become the attackers, in just a few weeks – they had abundant supplies, and I had no fleet. I, on the other hand, had an inexhaustible supply of stones and ten heavy engines and a proper platform for them.

I turned their walls to rubble, and then I went to work on their inner works – or rather, Helios did. We spent forty days pounding their walls, and by the end of it, my artillerists were probably the best shots in the world, and I needed new machines – I'd worn even the crossbars to flinders.

That night, with blackened faces, my companions and I stormed the *farthest* island – the one out of range of my machines, the one whose garrison hadn't had a scratch. They had no idea I had four ships, no idea that I could reach them. Helios had built high ladders on to the triremes – and lashed two of them together. We ran them in under the island's cliffs and ran up the ladders straight to the top while the sentries tried to figure out what was happening. One sentry – a gifted fighter – killed the first three men on to the wall.

Kineas put him down with a thrown javelin.

And then we were in, and the butchery began.

I thought that perhaps, after the shock of that, the other two islands would surrender, but they did not, and now I had wasted my surprise. Or – not precisely wasted. I could now bombard both islands. I tried a daytime maritime assault on the nearest, and lost fifty men and got an arrow in my behind as a memory. That hurt, and I had scant sympathy from Thaïs. I lay there for five days, feeling like a fool, and Thaïs came and went, and mocked me gently when she had time.

It was growing hot, and the ground was dry. The campaign season was opening, and I had lots to worry about.

Thaïs came in – I remember this vividly. She was skipping like a girl, and she beamed as she took my hands.

'Memnon is dead,' she said.

I was speechless, and she laughed.

It took me a moment to realise what she wasn't saying.

'You killed him?' I asked.

She shrugged. 'I tried to. I assume that I succeeded.'

I sat there with my arse hurting and shook my head. 'Brilliant. Don't ever let Alexander suspect.'

She looked at me with the pity that women use on men who state the obvious.

Memnon died north of Mytilene, of a curious stomach complaint that came on suddenly. The nut of the Strychos, ground fine. It comes from India, and Aristotle taught us about it. Thaïs had her own sources, of course.

Over the next weeks, as Helios cast bronze parts for new torsion engines, as his smiths pounded iron to make new frame supports and as trains of oxen brought timber for new frames from the mountains, we watched Memnon's plan shatter. There was no successor to his office as the Great King's strategos. There was no man who could hold his plan, or his army, or the fleet, together.

His death changed everything.

And still the two islands wouldn't surrender.

Memnon's death rendered my presence in Halicarnassus somewhat unnecessary. Now there was no threat from the sea. Now there would be no relief of the garrisons. In effect, I had won, or rather, Thaïs had. Game over. No further need even to hold Caria, really. No threat to Macedon.

At the end of the planting season, we heard from Thaïs's people that Coenus was marching the new recruits and married men by rapid stages across Thrace. And we heard that Charidemus – another Athenian-born professional – had advised the Great King to send him to Ionia to carry out the invasion of Greece. According to our source – a damned good source – Charidemus dug his grave with the truth, telling Darius that he didn't have the troops to face Alexander in the field and shouldn't try, but should leave the fighting to Greeks, who could bear the brunt of it.

He was a brilliant fighter, or so men said. I heard he was a good general. Whatever the truth of it, Darius had him executed and started raising an army, and the last of the Persian fleet across from us at Chios broke up and sailed away, and the two garrisons asked to meet me in an hour when we shot news of his execution into their positions.

Both garrison commanders were Athenians. Most of the best mercenaries were Athenians or Spartans, and the latter were as good or better. I gave them wine and told them what I knew.

Isokles and Plataeus, they were. Older men, almost Parmenio's age. Plataeus was a true believer – one of Phokion's men. He hated us, and all our ways. But he hated serving Persia, too. I knew all this from Thaïs.

I talked to them for an hour, and they surrendered their islands and I let them keep everything – their loot, their pay, their armour and weapons. Isokles joined me. Plataeus sailed away for Athens.

Pharnabazus, the last Persian friend of Memnon's still trying to do any work, threw a major garrison into Mytilene, and ordered all the mercenaries and citizens captured there in arms to be used as forced labour rebuilding the walls. I suppose it was better than executing them, as Alexander did, but not much better. Thaïs got her agents in among them, and recruited a dozen to report to us on what was happening in Mytilene. Most of them were ignorant men, but one was literate and so gifted at spying that by the time the last garrison surrendered after the summer feast of Demeter, he himself was running a dozen other agents and had refused to be 'rescued'. He remained in place until the city fell to us later, leading the life of a slave, leading teams of saboteurs, scouting for weak points.

I wouldn't mention it, but that's your friend Philokles. I never met him, until we fought along the Jaxartes river. But I'm sure it was him. It was a huge war, and yet it seemed like a very small world, and it still does. And the irony of it – Philokles hated Alexander, but he loved liberty, and he loved both Mythymna and Mytilene. And a woman, or so I'm told. It's his story. Ask him.

At any rate, with Memnon went his intelligence-collection apparatus. We never lost another agent. Now we had the better information, and the networks in place to get the earliest reports of changes in policy. It was clear that Darius meant business. He was raising an army. He was levying troops, and raising rebellions where he could.

I sent Kineas to Parmenio with his Athenians and the promise that I would march in three weeks, when Caria was secure. Then I moved fast, south, clearing the coast road as far as Kallipolis. I gave Queen Ada the keys to her own capital, and left it ... well, better than I might have. She was a bitter woman. But returning to her earlier armour of doubt, and probably healthier for it.

On my march north, I collected Thaïs and all my baggage, and all my men. I had been king in all but name for almost a year. I think I did pretty well. I certainly enjoyed it.

It was a happy time.

I found, as I marched north, that I hadn't really thought of Alexander in a year.

TWENTY

When I rode into Gordia, I found something more – and less – than an army camp. Gordia in high summer is a nasty place, where waves of gritty dust roll on the slightest breeze and the sun pounds down like a white-hot aspis held a few arm's lengths from your face. There's not enough water and not enough greenery and everyone smells.

I had four thousand men behind me on the bad roads, strung out over fifty stades. My cavalry was at the rear, preserving their horses. I had plundered Caria for horses – with Queen Ada's willing support – and my Hetaeroi had two or even three chargers apiece – and I meant to keep it that way.

The army camp was vast, reaching across the rolling valley to the north and west. At a glance I thought there were more than thirty thousand men in the valley.

And then there was the other camp.

I rode along the edge of it with the taste of grit in my mouth. There were more than two hundred great pavilions, towering edifices of canvas and silk.

Thaïs sneered. She had a very pretty sneer. She was dressed as a man and riding at my side, our preferred method of travel. With a scarf over her hat, she was invisible to most men. These days, she sometimes led her Angeloi in person, dressed this way.

'Look at them,' she said.

They were a new breed of courtiers, a breed of vermin never before seen in a Macedonian army camp. Artists, musicians, actors, prostitutes, politicians from twenty rival cities and every faction in Greece and some in Asia.

Thaïs shook her head. 'Alexander must be winning,' she said. 'These vultures are usually in the Great King's camp.'

*

I found Parmenio at the north end of the town, under the great ridge that rose above it. He was standing in the middle of a dozen Macedonian officers, watching two female slaves fight. They'd torn off most of their clothing and they were hard at it in the dust, and they both meant business.

To the Macedonian mind, this is about the highest form of entertainment.

I slid from Poseidon's back and hobbled over to the old man. I'd been in the saddle for twenty days and I wanted wine, bread and oil, in that order. A massage. A bed with Thaïs in it, if she was clean.

Heh. Anyway, I got to Parmenio, and he turned at my approach and surprised me by throwing his arms around me.

'There's a proper Macedonian,' he said.

Apparently we were few enough on the ground that we all loved each other. I filed that away.

'Coenus has a letter for you from Antipater, and another from your factor.' Parmenio held me at arm's length. 'Well done with Queen Ada, lad – brilliant campaign. When we heard that Memnon was landing troops, we wrote you off!'

I grinned. Praise is praise, and he was the greatest strategos of our day, for all that I thought he wanted to be rid of the king.

We even embraced.

'I think all the troops I have are yours,' I said. 'I didn't lose many and I picked up about eleven hundred. They'll need a place to camp.'

'So how many?' Parmenio asked.

'Five thousand foot, and five hundred cavalry. You already have Kineas back, eh?' I said, looking around for him.

Parmenio flashed a grim smile. 'There's a good soldier. A little too Greek for my tastes, but a damn fine officer.'

Philotas shook his head. 'Fucking Athenians think they're better than us. All of them.'

I wondered what was going on in Thaïs's head. She was standing right behind me.

'I'll assign you a campground. I'm delighted to have my mercenary infantry back. What did you think of them?'

I nodded. 'First class, really. As good as the pezhetaeroi, in most cases. There's a new officer – Isokles. I had him from Memnon. He's Athenian, and a damn sight better than that clown Casides you left me with.'

'Casides is a Spartan!' Philotas said.

'I doubt it, and if he really is, he's from the bad side of Sparta.' I made them laugh, always a good sign. 'Anyway, they're all yours again.

Isokles will be here in an hour. I have the cavalry at the back. Where do I camp?'

Parmenio looked at Philotas, who frowned.

I couldn't help but notice that Philotas was wearing a fortune in clothes – a silk chiton that must have cost the value of a good farm, Boeotian boots in red and gold with ivory eyelets, a scarlet felt hat. He had a brutish face with a pair of burning blue eyes that showed how smart he really was, and he always stood with his hands on his hips.

'Why do you have your grooms in with your Hetaeroi?' he asked. His tone was ignorant. He was looking for a fight.

So much for my homecoming.

'The king gave me permission when he gave me my commission for Caria,' I said.

Parmenio gave me an odd glance.

'You provided me with some good information, last winter,' he said. 'I appreciate it.'

I nodded. In fact, Thaïs sent her best tidbits to both Alexander and to Parmenio, and I was, for once, privy to all of it, which was fun.

'Your troop should be camped in my area,' Philotas continued, as if his father had not spoken. 'But I have no more space. Go and camp to the east.'

His tone was so disobliging that I couldn't ignore it.

'Philotas, I'll camp where I please, if you take that tone with me,' I said.

Philotas spat. 'You need to learn to obey your superiors, lad.'

This from a man only ten years my senior.

I held his eyes and shrugged. 'Never seen the need so far,' I drawled. 'Except the king. He has the right to give me orders.'

'Fuck the king.' Philotas spat again. 'Being his butt-boy doesn't make you immune to discipline.'

I looked to Parmenio for help. Parmenio slapped his son – pretty hard – on the arm.

'What are you thinking, boy?' he said. 'If you treat your officers like this, you'll have no friends.'

'I don't need friends,' Philotas said. 'Only obedient slaves.' He ended the comment with a smile to me.

I started to tremble. I wanted to punch him, but I knew where that would end. So I shook my head. 'You have neither, with me,' I said. And turned on my heel.

My next stop was Alexander's tent. He had a whole compound, now, I saw – five red silk tents all together, and the starburst of Macedon on every one in gold.

There was a low but solidly built palisade all the way around his enclosure, and there were four hypaspitoi on duty in full kit. I saluted, but they barred my way. I didn't know three of them, but the fourth I did.

'Bubares! I don't know the password, I've been on detachment.' I waited for the black man to recognise me. 'I'm somatophylakes, and I've had a bit of a morning.'

He saluted. He met my eyes, and he was trying to tell me something. 'You'll have to wait for an equerry. It's orders, and I don't want to be beaten.' He said this so quietly I wasn't sure, at first, that he had spoken.

After ten minutes, a young man in a spotless white military chiton and boots appeared. He had a stick under his arm. He looked at me.

'Yes?' he asked.

'Ptolemy, son of Lagus,' I said with exaggerated courtesy. I knew him – he'd been a page until last year, and his name was Simonides.

'You may not come before the king unless you are clean,' he said. 'Indeed, I'm surprised you would even—'

That's as far as he got before I put him in the sand with a throw. Then I kicked him in the arse for good measure. Then in the balls. Then I raised his chiton, showing his bare arse to the camp.

Bubores laughed. When the young man had run for help, Bubores let the laughter take over. 'I've wanted someone to do that for a long time, boss,' he said.

'I'll come and have wine with you,' I said. 'How's Astibus?'

Bubores positively glowed. 'Alive, and well enough. Got himself a Persian girl at Granicus – he's besotted.' He bowed past me at Thaïs, who had watched the whole exchange impassively from mule-back.

'My lady,' Bubores said.

She laughed. 'Most men can't even tell who I am,' she responded.

Bubores tossed his head a little impatiently. 'I can hunt a fly on the ocean,' he said.

Alectus appeared in armour, with twenty men and a rather rumpled royal officer. When he saw me, he laughed and we embraced.

He escorted me around the compound, and I saw more slaves than I thought existed in the palace at Pella, and more courtiers than soldiers, and a tent full of scribes busy writing, with Callisthenes, Aristotle's useless nephew, leading them. Then I found the king, and walked in.

He was being massaged. Hephaestion was arming. He smiled when he saw me.

'Look who's back,' Hephaestion said.

Alexander raised his head and smiled. 'Ah,' he said. 'Ptolemy. Well done. A little too well done. I dangled you to draw Memnon, but instead of drawing him, you singed his nose and then he died.' Alexander smiled, and put his head back down. 'Why did you go to Parmenio first, Ptolemy?'

'I had his troops, and I needed to have a place for them to camp,' I said.

'You see?' Alexander said. 'Always an excellent explanation.'

I didn't like that. 'If I wanted to dissimulate, I'd tell you that it is difficult to gain access to the king. I was refused entry at the gate.'

Alexander raised his head again. 'Then how is it you are here?' he asked.

'I cut the comb of a rooster who needed it,' I said. 'The hypaspitoi all know me.'

Alexander lay getting his back pounded for a long minute.

'I will let this pass this time,' he began.

I laughed. 'No, my lord, *I* will let this pass this time. I am somatophylakes, and I have the right of access to you at all times of the day and night, and even you cannot restrict me.'

Alexander sat up. 'Leave me,' he said to the masseur. When the slave was gone, he frowned at me. 'This is not Macedon,' he said.

'I can tell, because your tent is full of Greek prostitutes masquerading as politicians,' I said. 'But this is the army of Macedon, and we have laws. Parmenio wants to let you run free, lord, so you will let power go to your head and become an oriental, so he can depose you. Or so Thaïs and I think his thought tends.' I shrugged. 'I won't let you drift, and neither will Hephaestion. You are not the Great King of Persia. You are the King of Macedon.'

'I am your king, and I may decide who comes and goes from my enclosure!' he said. He was angry, and red spots were forming on his cheeks.

I nodded. 'Yes – with the exception of your closest friends and bodyguards.' I shook my head. 'This is foolishness, lord – I am, of course, your willing servant and officer, and you may strip me of my rank in a moment. But even you must obey the law.'

'A few months of independent command have only increased your arrogance,' Alexander shot back. 'You are insufferable.'

'He's in a bad mood,' Hephaestion said.

'Fuck off!' Alexander said.

'Why?' I asked Hephaestion, as if the king weren't right there.

'He's going to face the prophecy this morning, and the whole camp is coming to see him do it,' Hephaestion said. 'He swore he could solve it, and everyone expects he can, and now he's touchy—'

'Get out of my sight, you ingrate,' Alexander barked, and he was on the verge of tears.

'Darius has sixty thousand men moving on the Euphrates, and he means business,' Hephaestion said. 'Although you must know that, since we had it from Thaïs. We don't have that many men, and Darius has a whole second army forming in Ionia to hit Greece if we lose. Our supply lines to Macedon are largely cut by Pharnabazus and his fleet, and there's nothing we can do about it. Athens is teetering on the brink of open rebellion, which will be the end of our fleet. But Golden Boy here had to mistreat their ambassadors yesterday, just to show them who's in charge.'

'Leave me!' Alexander roared.

'No!' Hephaestion roared back.

They glared at each other.

'Lord, your camp is full of vultures in silk and you have boys at your gate keeping men at bay. That needs to be fixed. It makes you appear weak.' I bowed my head.

Alexander was crying.

Cleitus – Black Cleitus – caught me outside the pavilion and embraced me.

'What in Hades is happening here?' I asked.

He shrugged. 'I just obey,' he said. 'He's getting harder and harder to handle and he has all these new friends and a lot of useless tits.' He looked around, clearly afraid he'd be overheard.

'And he swore to everyone that he'd solve the Gordian Knot, today. The prophecy says that he who solves it will be Lord of all Asia,' Hephaestion put in.

I made a face, and Thaïs giggled.

Cleitus looked at me. 'What?' he said. 'It's the prophecy.'

'Was Cyrus the Great Lord of Asia?' I asked. 'Darius? Xerxes?'

Cleitus nodded and looked around. 'Oh. You know, sometimes you remind me of fucking Aristotle, Ptolemy. With your snide laugh and all.'

'I'm not well loved today,' I admitted. 'Was that Callisthenes I saw in the Military Journal tent?'

Cleitus nodded. 'We call it the "School of Lies".'

Ouch.

'The Military Journal is now for public consumption in Greece and Macedon,' Cleitus said bitterly. 'So its contents now reflect our unvarying path to victory.'

'Make that up yourself?' I asked.

Cleitus barked his laugh.

'Come on, and I'll find you a place to camp,' he said. 'Maybe now that you're back, everything will be all right.'

Cleaner and more richly dressed, I was in the middle of a long procession of soldiers, sycophants and priests processing up the ridge to the temple at the top. At the head of the procession was Alexander, who looked as scared as I'd ever seen him.

My invitation to attend had come too late to allow me to be up at the front with the other philoi. I assumed that was done on purpose. But Alexander looked *so* bad when I saw him that I began pushing forward through the crowds on the steps. I had Polystratus and his new sidekick Theodore at my heels, and we pushed pretty effectively. Most people got out of our way.

I caught up with the king at the base of the temple steps. His eyes passed over me without recognition. The whites showed all the way around his eyes, and if he'd been a horse, he'd have been on the edge of bolting.

Hephaestion caught my eye, and he was desperate, somehow.

I pushed through to the king's side.

Alexander looked at me. 'Ptolemy!' he said.

I touched his shoulder. He didn't always like to be touched, but sometimes he did, like a nervous horse when you need to get a pebble out of his hoof. When he didn't flinch, I put my arm around his shoulder.

'Cyrus the Great,' I said. 'Xerxes,' I added softly.

He looked at me.

'It's all horseshit,' I said. 'Something to draw the credulous.'

Alexander had the oddest habit of clinging to superstitious nonsense – as if his mighty brain took rests from reason.

He glared at me, but I smiled resolutely, and he finally returned my smile and straightened his shoulders. I took away my arm and he looked around. In a moment, he was through the great bronze doors and into the temple.

Well – you know the story. Everyone does. There must have been five thousand men and women there to see it, crushing so close we could simply have trampled the Gordian Knot.

The old wagon – it wasn't a chariot at all, but a four-wheeled wagon – had a long draught pole attached to the harness bar by a massive and very complex knot. The knot was done in an ancient rawhide, and whoever had done it – about eight hundred years earlier, was my guess – whoever had done it had had a lot of skill, and both ends of the rawhide strip were buried in the knot, and the rawhide, like all rawhide,

442

shrank as it dried, so that the fastening was almost like a solid lump of rawhide, shiny and dense.

The king looked at it for a long time, and people began to mutter.

Alexander was no longer nervous. Of course not. In his head, this counted as combat, I'm sure. Now he was cool and professional.

'Tell me the prophecy again,' he said, aloud.

'He who opens the Gordian Knot shall likewise be Lord of Asia,' a priest intoned.

There was a buzz from the crowd. Alexander, the performer, waited it out.

They fell silent.

'So it doesn't really matter how I open it,' he said. His eyes glittered.

The priests talked among themselves.

Alexander turned, drew his sword and slashed down, as hard as he would in cutting an armoured opponent.

The ancient rawhide shattered into a thousand dry fragments, and the yoke-pole crashed to the floor.

Alexander lifted his sword. People looked stunned, and he smiled. 'I do not intend to take Asia by my wits,' he said, 'but by my sword.'

That night, I attended my first command meeting in almost a year. Parmenio was there, and Coenus and Philotas, but many men I knew were gone. Nearchus had his own command in Phrygia, Seleucus was sick, Alexander of Lyncestis was under arrest, Antigonus One-Eye was off in Paphlagonia.

There were new officers and, for the first time, Asian officers – mostly Phrygians, mixing with the Greeks and the Macedonians.

Alexander came in and we all saluted, and then he went to the head of a table on which lay a set of itineraries for the roads to the coast.

'Darius is in the field with sixty thousand men,' he said. He smiled. 'It is my desire to bring him to battle at the earliest opportunity, smash his army and lay claim to Asia. One field battle, and we will be the masters here.'

There was an almost imperceptible murmur.

'I'm sending Amphoterus to the coast to take command of the fleet in the Hellespont,' he said. The gentleman in question bowed. Alexander smiled at us, and I knew he was about to say something meant to shock.

'And then I'm cutting the cord, gentlemen. The way to defeat the Persian fleet is to hold all of their land bases. We've made a good start. This summer, we're going for the coast of Syria. If Darius remains as indolent as he has been, we'll work our way down the coast to Aegypt

443

and close the sea to him for ever.' He looked around, expecting opposition.

He got it. Parmenio shook his head. 'You'll be out of touch with Macedon, and if Amphoterus is beaten, we could lose Pella. What if Athens rises? Sparta? What if—'

Alexander's grin was a wolf's grin. 'Pella is not worth the effort of defending if we can win Asia, gentlemen.'

'It's our home!' Philotas said.

Alexander shook his head. 'It is a huddle of mud huts at the edge of the wilderness. We have Ephesus. We have Sardis. We have Halicarnassus.'

'We *had* Miletus,' someone said aloud.

'We have Gordia, too,' Parmenio said. 'Lucky us.'

Alexander looked around. 'We are here to conquer Asia. I have every confidence that Antipater can hold Macedon behind us, and in the worst case, if he fails' – and here Alexander's confidence sounded more godlike than brash – 'if he fails, well, we'll return and take it back next season.'

Parmenio shook his head. 'Syria? How do you plan to get there?'

Alexander's smile grew softer. 'Ankyra – and the Cilician Gates.'

Parmenio put his hands on his hips. Now I saw where Philotas got that habit. 'It cannot be done,' he said. 'A goat path through tall mountains. Fifty men could hold us for days.'

Alexander nodded. 'It will be glorious,' he said.

We lingered at Ankyra while the Prodromoi went far to the east, looking for Darius, looking for news, and while contingents from all of western Asia came in to make terms with the conqueror. I found their terms too lenient, and most of them were allowed to go with little beyond a promise of submission. The king was in a hurry, and when he was in a hurry, he didn't bother with minutiae like the conquest of eastern Phrygia.

I took my Hetaeroi south and east, on to the broad, dry, dusty Cappadocian Plain. We moved fast, with no baggage, and we slept under the stars, with saddlecloths for pillows. Thaïs's beautiful skin grew tanned, and she claimed that it would ruin her complexion, but she was developing a new persona, Thaïs the Amazon, and her Angeloi were developing into a miniature Prodromoi, complete with spears and swords. Our daughter had her second birthday in Asia, carried on a mule.

I had Philotas to my south and Kineas, of all people, to my north, and we swept east and south, looking for enemies and for news.

In every town, either Thaïs had people, in which case they reported to her, or she didn't, in which case her Angeloi bought some. And she was teaching us – a few of us, Calchias of the Prodromoi and the Paeonian commander, Ariston and Cleander, from the so-called mercenary cavalry. Teaching us to use this network of spies carefully, to integrate it into our scouting. Thaïs knew a little of how to handle a cavalry patrol, and none of us knew how to suborn a town official, but together we made a powerful combination – the more so as we learned from each other.

As an example of how this might work, let me offer the race across the Plain of Cappadocia. It was Parmenio's operation – remember, the king was still in Ankyra, and was determined not to march until he could move all the way to the Cilician Gates with his flanks covered. Given that we were abandoning our communications with Macedon, this seemed sensible.

I had the middle route – south from Ankyra, then south-east along the axis Gorbeus–Mazaka. I was confident that this would be the army's actual route, but by sending Philotas along the southerly route and Kineas along the northerly route, we spread the most confusion and we gave the king options in the event of logistical or political troubles – water shortage, or hostile tribes.

On the second night, three of my best rode into Gorbeus with Strako and a half-dozen of the Angeloi – the town was six days by pack train from Ankyra, and still imagining itself safe from us. The next morning at dawn, Thaïs's friends opened the gates and my whole squadron came in at a canter, raising dust all the way. The garrison – forty Persian archers under a drunken aristocrat – surrendered on the spot.

That's how it was supposed to work. But the news was all good – the satrap of Cilicia had only three hundred men in the Cilician Gates. Arsames was raising his men on the other side of the barrier. Thaïs's people said he was considering outright surrender.

'Oh, if I were a man,' she said bitterly. 'Someone should go.'

We sent Polystratus with the former garrison commander's signet ring and an offer – a thousand talents of gold to let us have the Gates without a fight. It was insanity – the gates were a hundred and fifty stades of goat tracks that even Persian levies could hold against us – but it was always worth trying Thaïs's way.

In the morning, we were off across the parched plain, all volcanic rock and thin soil and people living so close to starvation that the girls were old hags at twenty-five and the men looked like bent-over old men.

I lost touch with Philotas and pushed on. A day out of Gorbeus, and there was no more water. Nor local people to help us.

We pushed on. Our canteens were full and we had packhorses. My two-year-old squawked a lot – she wanted more water than we had to give her.

Thaïs and I had the worst fight of our lives. She told me that I was a typical man and a poor father, because I would not send her back to the last water source with a detachment. I couldn't spare the troopers, and she knew it.

For the first time I could remember I slept alone that night, and it was cold.

And my mouth was dry, for several reasons. I slept badly. I considered what would happen if my daughter died in the waste. What would die with her. How much I loved Thaïs.

In the morning I made her a public apology, and sent Polystratus's sidekick Theodore and twenty men back to Gorbeus with Thaïs and our child. I was selfish. I loved being out on patrol with Thaïs, and at some remove I was jealous of the daughter that seemed to take up all her time.

But the desert is full of tests, and Thaïs kissed me before she left. 'You are better at admitting you are wrong then most men,' she said.

North of Mazaka, we ran into our first Persian cavalry patrol. They were good, and they'd laid an ambush for us at a waterhole. We, on the other hand, were exhausted and our horses were done in.

But we'd been fighting Memnon. No one gets sloppy against a master. The Angeloi – men dressed in local cloth, riding local horses – picked up the ambush a day in advance.

I triggered it myself, with fifty men in full armour, heads down against the sun. We rode over the ridge that defined the northern edge of the watered area and they hit us immediately. Poseidon was so far done that he ignored the fight and went for the water, which we could see – blue as blue in the distance.

We lost two men. I got Poseidon to see reason with some hard kicks to his ribs, and we turned into the attackers, most of whom had bows. They were shooting our horses, trying to dismount us for easy capture.

Then Pyrrhus appeared behind them with the rest of my force, and they didn't stop to think about it. They were well trained. As soon as they saw their ambush broken, every one of them broke contact, changed horses and they were gone. We killed six and captured four more, all wounded.

We lost over a dozen precious horses and got none in return.

I didn't bother pursuing them. They were desert men themselves, and I expect that they had a second ambush pre-prepared. I would have.

I was very cautious moving up to Mazaka, but I didn't make another contact. Thaïs's resident there refused to meet any of us – there's the real world of spies, afraid of their own shadows – but a small boy brought us two parchments, covered in dense Aramaic, and one of my grooms, a Babylonian Jew named Jusef, read it well enough. It was an itinerary of the Cilician Gates, with notes of distance and troop locations, and it was just ten days old.

I sent it back to the king with Pyrrhus and ten troopers, and then I sat in Mazaka and waited for Philotas. He came up the next day, and I was happy to see him, and he to see me. Things are different, once the fur begins to fly.

Kineas was four more days, and all his horses looked as if they were going to die. He'd gone as far east as Tyana and had made two contacts with the Persian scouts coming over the mountains from the Euphrates Valley, far to the east. The Persians were closer than we hoped, though farther than our worst fears. Just like war.

Philotas wanted to go for the Gates with five or six hundred horse, but I restrained him gently. I appealed to his fear of failure.

The king crossed the desert in three days. He did it with night marches – always easier in the desert – and forward stores of water.

When he was a day away and we were in contact with the Prodromoi, Polystratus came back with a gold ring and a promise.

'He's a right bastard, and that's no mistake, lord,' Polystratus said. 'He wants to play both sides – said he won't openly go against the Great King, but that he'll keep all but his advance guard out of the Gates and it's up to us to get through them.' Polystratus shrugged. 'And that's what we get for a thousand talents.'

But Alexander agreed like a shot, and then he sent the Thracians, the Agrianians and a company of hypaspitoi through the gates. The Cretan archers and the Macedonian crossbowmen moved along the high ground, slowly but thoroughly, and the Thracians tripped anything they came across, and the army marched in behind us – I was with the archers. Alexander was so confident that the advance guard didn't even leave a day in advance. We moved at a slow walking pace, and we surprised the poor bastards at the break of the second day. It was red slaughter, professionals against amateurs. When the Thracians broke them, the Agrianians harried them along the ridges and the archers shot them down.

We were beginning to see what two years of Memnon had done to us. We had a team.

Three days of careful movement, advancing from one strong-point to the next, the two groups on either ridge supporting each other, and we were through. The plains around Tarsus were so green they seemed to *burn* green, and I could see the sea in the distance. Behind me, the army began to shout, 'Thalassa!' like Xenophon's hoplites, and men hugged each other.

Arsames was burning the plains, scorching the crops to deny us food.

We picked up a bunch of angry peasants who claimed he was going to burn the city.

Parmenio was commanding the advance guard himself, and he told us to go for it. His assumption was that if the local people viewed us as liberators, the worst we'd get was a bloody nose.

Alexander was in the rear. Rumour was that he'd drunk too much the night before with Parmenio, and could barely ride.

Kineas's Athenians were the first into Tarsus, because he went by road while I covered his flanks and two heavy troops of Thessalians covered mine. We found Arsames just north of the city and had a sharp skirmish, but he had no confidence, or he was a traitor, or whatever happened inside that kind of man's head, and his troops ran. Kineas secured the north gate – more, he said later, by happenstance than by plan.

We took Tarsus intact, granaries and all. And Arsames rode off to the east to join King Darius, whom he had just betrayed, either by crass incompetence or by greed.

Alexander was one of the last men into the city. He'd spent the day, unaware we were fighting, driving the stragglers across the last of the desert and up into the Gates, making sure that no one lay down and died. It was noble of him, but when he came in through the north gate, he was tired, hot and surly, because we'd fought a nice little action, taken prisoners, seized a town, and all without him.

And we were through the greatest obstacle in Asia.

But he brightened up when he heard the tale, and he gave Kineas his hand and thanked him. Kineas adored the king. He didn't see the flaws beneath the surface. To Kineas, Alexander *was* the hegemon of the League, leading us to revenge against Persia. And the hegemon's thanks made him glow with joy.

Alexander rode along with Philotas, Kineas and Parmenio. I trailed behind. He rode down to the river, which flowed icy cold from the mountains we'd just traversed.

Kineas put his hand on the king's bridle when Alexander moved to dismount. 'I lost a horse to that river this morning, lord,' Kineas said.

Parmenio laughed. 'Don't be such a nursemaid, Athenian! In Macedon, we swim in ice.'

The king stripped off his chiton and boots and dived into the clear water and surfaced, spluttering. Hephaestion leaped in after him, shrieked and swam back to the bank.

He crawled out, laughing. 'Zeus! My balls are gone.'

We all joined him. I was stripping off my own chiton when I realised that the king wasn't there. Everyone else realised it at the same time, and we charged into the water – me, Philotas, Seleucus, Black Cleitus, Philip the Red and Kineas. We found him floating just under the surface, and we hauled him to the bank. He was having some sort of fit, and his skin was dead white. He'd taken in some water, too.

Everyone assumed he'd breathed too much water, and we did what men do for a drowning victim – a blanket, and Hephaestion forced air into his lungs, and he breathed.

But an hour later, he was no better.

By nightfall, he was speechless and his eyes were closed and his breathing was rough.

Parmenio took command. Thaïs had agents here, and they reported that Darius was just ten or fifteen days to the east. We were too close to break off in safety. Parmenio held a command council the first night of the king's illness and told us that, while he doubted the wisdom of facing the Great King, he was going to accept battle if he could get it on his own terms.

Perhaps I defame him, but I heard a man making his bid for the kingship. If he defeated Darius, no Macedonian would stand in his way. I think we all knew it.

After the meeting, I went to the king's tent. The vultures were gone. I wondered if they were already clamouring for Parmenio's attention.

I gave the password to the guards and entered the tent. Alexander was awake. He was pale in the lamplight, and only his head showed. His eyes were wild, and his hair was plastered to his forehead.

I sat down, and Hephaestion got up with an ill grace and made room for me.

'I must get up,' Alexander said.

I shook my head. 'Parmenio is no fool. He'll fight.'

But Alexander shook his head, and his whole body shook. 'This is the battle!' he said, with so much force that they must have heard him in the streets of Tarsus. 'This is the battle. Not for Parmenio! For me!' He all but writhed.

'He just keeps saying that,' Hephaestion complained. 'I can't get him to sleep.'

I took his hands. 'There will be other fights, lord,' I said. In fact, I had my doubts. The odds were long, and if we won, and Parmenio led

449

us – well, I've said before that Alexander's popularity with the troops was based on godlike demeanour and unbroken victory.

'My battle!' he said, and his eyes rolled back in his head.

Parmenio took the Thracians, all the light cavalry and his precious Thessalians and rode east. I should have gone, but Thaïs convinced me that Parmenio meant to kill Alexander with poison. Or that, rather, it was possible enough to warrant caution. But the king drank only water and ate only bread, and I didn't see how he was getting poison.

Five days of this and the king was obviously losing weight, and his stomach had swelled in an odd and very bad way. His gut hurt all the time. He didn't scream, but he lay on his camp bed and made grunting noises when he thought we couldn't hear him.

He insisted on hearing every report, so that he knew that Darius was marching towards us by easy stages, a confident commander eager for battle, and that Parmenio had seized Issus.

There are only two passes over the mountains on to the plains of Cilicia from the headwaters of the Euphrates – the way the Great King was marching. To the north, there are the Amanic Gates, a good pass even for a large army and to the south, there is the pass of the Syrian Gates. Parmenio put scouting forces into both passes and then lay in wait at the Pinnacle of Jonah to see what Darius would do.

The news that Darius had a pontoon bridge over the Euphrates drove the king into a fever. He raged at his doctors, and none of them could agree what was wrong with him or how to fix it. And as more and more men suspected poison, the Greek doctors grew more and more afraid to take any action.

When Darius was estimated at five days' march away, Parmenio came back for the army. He had the Great King where he wanted him, and he was ready to set his battlefield. He gathered all of us in the command tent, and laid out his plans of march. Like most of his plans, it was a simple one.

He was going to take the army to the Pinnacle of Jonah, with tripwire forces in both passes, and wherever the Great King went, Parmenio was going to meet him – in the pass where his superior numbers would be no match for our superior infantry.

I raised my hand. 'Why would he fight us under those conditions?' I asked.

'Why does your foreigner do anything? Pride, foolish pride, young Ptolemy.' Parmenio nodded. 'Anyone else?'

Then he sent all the cavalry commanders away – except his sons. He

450

kept Craterus and Philotas and Nicanor and Perdiccas, because this was to be an infantry fight.

I didn't like it. I didn't like the secret meeting, and I didn't like the notion that Darius was a fool and would dance to our tune.

I went to the king's tent, and found the king's own physician, Philip of Arcarnia.

'I won't,' he insisted as I entered the tent.

Alexander, remember, was in love with medicine. He'd studied it extensively under Aristotle, and if it had been one of us on that bed, he'd have been ordering concoctions by the cup.

Philip was standing with his arms crossed. Cleitus looked as if he'd been weeping, and Hephaestion had his jaw set.

I looked around.

'I am your king. Do it.' Alexander's voice was so weak it barely registered.

Cleitus looked at me. 'He's ordered Philip to make him a powerful emetic. Kill or cure, he says.'

Alexander turned his head in my direction. I didn't think he could see me. That's how far gone he was.

'Darius is five days away,' he said, as clear as the sound of distant swordplay. 'Parmenio will fail. I will not. This is my battle, and the Lord of Contagion will not keep me from it.'

Philip shook his head. 'This is powerful, dangerous medicine,' he said. 'You will probably die.'

'But if there's something evil caught in my bowel, this will move it. Yes?' Alexander said.

'If you survive the experience. Yes.' Philip sounded wary.

Alexander nodded. 'This is my order. Do it.'

Philip looked at Hephaestion.

Hephaestion bit his lip and looked at me. But before I could say anything, he nodded. 'It is what he wants,' Hephaestion said.

He could be a nuisance, and a drama queen, our Hephaestion, and he was at best an average cavalry commander, but he made the right call that night.

Philip bowed. 'You all heard him,' he said.

The physicians were terrified, you see, because Darius had offered a fantastic reward – ten thousand talents of gold – for Alexander's death. This is the same Darius who had tried to bribe Athens for three hundred talents, not three years earlier. Our price had increased.

Even old veterans in the pezhetaeroi openly joked about what they could do with ten thousand talents of gold.

It was such a staggering sum that it made me look at every man as a potential regicide, and I watched every flask of water, every pitcher of wine, every loaf of bread. I took samples from every one, as well. Thaïs wrote the labels for me.

I fed things to stray dogs.

The evening passed, and Parmenio came to visit the king.

'Tell him I do not wish to see him,' Alexander whispered, and Parmenio went away, but Hephaestion returned with a note.

'Open it!' Alexander urged me.

I still have it, right here, in my copy of the accurate journal. There's the original, in the old man's handwriting.

'We understand you have urged Philip to make you a purge – it is poison. He has been bribed by the Great King. We beg you to throw out his medicine and order the false physician's death.'

Alexander blinked a few times.

'Damn,' Hephaestion said.

'I don't believe it,' Cleitus said.

'Take no action,' I said, and fled the tent. I went straight to Thaïs, who was writing in her tent, and gave her the note.

She took it, read it and then put it down with a sigh. She looked away from me.

'Do not put this burden on me,' she said.

'So Parmenio is the traitor,' I said.

'You are far too intelligent for your face, Farm Boy,' she said, and touched my hand. 'That is why they always underestimate you. Yes. To me, this note merely proves that Parmenio poisoned him in the first place, and now fears that the king's superhuman constitution, aided by some medicine, might yet triumph.'

I kissed her, and ran back to Alexander's tent.

He was quite calm. I handed him the note, and he gave a slight smile. 'What does your hetaera say?' he asked.

'She says that Parmenio is wrong,' I answered.

Alexander took a deep breath, and released it slowly. '*You* know what that means, I think.'

I leaned over the king. 'I think that right now, today, in the face of the enemy, it means nothing,' I said.

Alexander gave a slow nod.

Philip came in with a horn cup.

Alexander sat up with Hephaestion and Cleitus to help him. Both of them stood as far from Philip as they could manage.

Philip didn't like the atmosphere of the room. 'I do not want to do this,' he insisted.

I, for one, believed him.

He set the horn cup down on a side table.

Before I could pick it up, the king had it.

'Let me test it, lord,' I said.

Alexander smiled enigmatically and gave Philip the note from Parmenio to read.

Philip's eyes all but bulged out of his head. His hands shook. But he stood straight and his voice was steady, by the gods.

'I swear I would never harm you or any other man or woman, in the pursuance of my art,' he said. 'If you take that cup, it may kill you, but not by my will. You and I both know the risks. That would be dangerous medicine for a man in the peak of fitness.'

Alexander raised the cup in a mock toast, like the guest at a good Athenian symposium, and drank it off.

Then he took a deep breath, and screamed.

It was three days before the shit poured out of him with the sweat, and he fouled the bed three times in as many hours. Those were bad days, and I've no need to describe them. Our cavalry was in contact with the Persian cavalry all along the line of the passes, and we were going to fight, and the king lay in a sweat, unable to talk.

I put Polystratus on Philip, to protect him.

But mostly he stayed with the king, massaging his abdomen and groin and putting cloths on his head.

And then the fever broke and the king rose, smelling slightly of his own excrement, and walked.

TWENTY-ONE

—⟊⟊⟊—

The king spent three more days in bed while the Great King of Persia sat on the far side of his mountains and held exercises for his army, and then Alexander marched *north* against hill tribes that threatened his communications – subjects of the Great King who were waging a very successful guerrilla war against our supplies.

He was as weak as a new colt, and on the second day of that small campaign, I saw him fall off a horse for the one and only time in his life. But he laughed and got back in the saddle, and the tribesmen saw their villages burned, gathered their flocks and retreated north of the Taurus mountains – unbeaten, but less of a threat to us. The last two thousand of my troops marched along the coast road from the west, with Asander and Queen Ada at their head, and Alexander decreed three days of games at Tarsus. He sat with Ada throughout the games, and she smiled a great deal. On the last day, he distributed prizes, money and crowns. Ada presented him with a magnificent chariot, with four beautiful white horses and harness-work all solid gold, and he embraced her in public, something he had never done. He told me later it was the finest present of his life, and he loved driving it.

I was astounded to find that I received a gold crown as reward for my victories in Caria. Asander received one, as well. I had the right to wear the crown on any public occasion. It was the highest award a Macedonian could receive. Parmenio had three, but Philotas, for example, had none.

And – perhaps the joy of my life – he gave me a phalanx of my own, ostensibly Macedonian, although more than half of my two thousand men were Isokles and his Athenians whom I had captured. Craterus, who I thought disliked me, embraced me on the platform, and Perdiccas thumped my back.

Local commands could come and go, but in Macedon a phalanx command was for ever. My phalanx would bear my name. I could only be displaced by death or treason.

454

Old Parmenio took both my hands, the bastard, and embraced me. 'You deserve it, boy. *Now* you are good enough to have a command.'

The temptation to put my fist in his eye almost spoiled the occasion. But it didn't. I don't have Alexander's need for praise, but it is pleasant, and the unforced admiration of my peers – the men I'd marched and fought with for eight years already – was a heady wine, and I drank it Scythian-style.

Thaïs lay next to me that night, stroking my crown of gilded oak leaves. 'What does it mean?' she asked.

'Glory!' I said.

She shook her head.

I laughed. 'You, my love, killed Memnon. You stormed the Cilician Gates. It's really your crown.'

She smiled sadly. 'Will you remember that when my belly is round and my breasts are flat and I have wrinkles?' she asked.

I sat back and appeared to consider. I took a long time about it, until she gave a little shriek and rammed her thumbs expertly into my armpits. Much later, she told me that she was pregnant again.

It may not have been the greatest day of my life, but it has few rivals.

TWENTY-TWO

I should tell you about the manoeuvrings before Issus, but I'll have to keep it to a few sentences, because suddenly I was a taxiarch and not a cavalry officer. I wasn't scouting, or running a temporary battle group just behind the scouting line – I was in the cloud of dust, plodding along the road with my men and their baggage carts. It's a different view of war, I can tell you.

Of course, I had served on foot before, but the responsibility for two thousand pezhetaeroi was enormous and complicated, with everything from internal promotion to daily food, muster lists for the Military Journal (oh! how that boot was suddenly on the other foot!) and reports to Craterus on the progress of training.

In a way, I was lucky in that I had no predecessor. I've found that when you inherit a unit, either the man before you was a god, and you are constantly compared to him, or he was a fool, and you are constantly compared to him. Often both at the same time. Men do not really like to be disciplined – men detest taking orders. It's easiest to focus that discontent on the man in charge, unless he has enormous talent, great wealth, good looks, charisma or birth. Best to have all of them, like Alexander, or Kineas.

Or me. I didn't have the looks – but I had money, even by Asian standards, and a fair reputation, and I was getting a new taxeis, just raised from recruits and 'mercenaries' who were considered close enough to being Macedonians – Thessalians, Amphilopilans, men of the Chersonese. I was their first commander.

I spent my first day in command wandering around the army, looking for officers. I had Isokles, and he was first-rate, although as an Athenian he was widely distrusted. I had Polystratus, although I left him mounted. Marsyas was bored as a file leader in the Hetaeroi and an apprentice on the Journal – I made him a wing commander in the taxeis. Pyrrhus followed me as a matter of course, and Cleomenes was back from his wounds and bored as a trooper, and I gave him the other wing.

456

In fact, I ended up with more battalion officers than anyone else. I liked to subdivide, and I liked to have the ability to break my units up. So I had four companies – Isokles, Pyrrhus, Cleomenes and Marsyas – each a little shy of five hundred men. Every company commander had a tail of mounted men as messengers and a hyperetes with a trumpet.

Isokles had some excellent notions of drill. One was that his men should drill every day, the way we had in the hypaspitoi. He became our drill master. He was a professional who had fought everywhere, and he knew tricks I'd never seen – like reversing your deployment in camp so that when your column of files reached the battlefield, they could deploy left to right instead of right to left. I admit it's an esoteric trick, but it had never occurred to me that I could reverse the order of my deployment just by 'about-facing' my men in camp and leading with the back of the column. I never won any battles with it, but there's a habit to thinking outside the accepted drills – and that applies even to something as apparently rigid as the close-order drill of the phalanx.

By the fourth day after the games, we drilled well. Our recruits were above average in height and in strength, because the fringe districts where they'd been recruited were new ground to the recruiting officers. And our Athenian former mercenaries (every one of whom could now swear by Athena he'd been born in Amphilopolis, a former Athenian colony, and thus evade the prohibition on foreigners in the ranks) were excellent soldiers with as much experience as Philip's veterans – some of it gained fighting them.

The truth was that the king was running short on troops. Our Asian campaign was killing men at a great rate – as I've said before, dysentery killed more than enemy action, but not a day passed in my taxeis that someone didn't break an arm, a leg, fall off a wall, fall into a well, get sick, desert, run mad, get trampled by a horse – Zeus, the list goes on for ever. And the original nine recruiting districts couldn't keep up, even if Hermes had been willing to pick up every new recruit at the door of his farm and fly him to his new duty station in the phalanx. Even if transport had been available, even if our rear areas were safe, even if we had rear areas – we were using men faster than Macedon could supply them, and on top of that Antipater had his own troubles with Athens and now with Sparta.

More and more non-Macedonians were put in the phalanx. Or rather, the definition of what made a man a 'Macedonian' became more and more flexible.

But I digress. We drilled hard every day – marched fifty stades, made camp, cooked and drilled. The army was rolling east. Somewhere far ahead of us, Parmenio was watching the mountain passes. We could *just* see the mountains on the fourth day of march, and we knew that Darius and seventy thousand men – probably more, by now – were just over the mountains.

It was interesting to go from Viceroy of Caria – ultimate power, with lip-service to Ada – to unemployed 'friend of the king', in which capacity I got to watch every decision made – to pezhetaeroi commander, with a view of the world limited to my baggage carts, my drill field and the cloud of dust in which I lived. That dust – the dust raised by marching feet – was the symbol of our lives in the infantry, because we couldn't see out of it. Unless it rained, we ate dust, slept in dust, marched in dust ...

I think I've made my point. Horsemen eat dust too – but they *can* ride out of it.

We marched east to the Amanus mountains and then south to Issus. Parmenio took a Persian cavalry patrol, and the officer knew all the details of Darius's campaign plan – and confirmed the rumour we'd heard from the peasants that Darius would come across the southern pass, which was the kind of slow, conservative move that we expected from Darius, who always seemed, like all Persians, to act to best protect his own communications.

Let me just pause here to note that when I gained high command, I always acted to preserve my communications. Some forms of conservative behaviour just make sense. A starving army is no army at all.

At Epiphaneia, the coast of the sea turns sharply south and the terrain starts to change, from the austerity of Cilicia to the relative richness of Syria. Just a day's march south of Epiphaneia, the king ordered all of us to leave our baggage and our sick at Issus, a very pleasant small town on its own river. That night, in Issus, there was a general officers' meeting, and for the first time I attended as a general officer, as opposed to a king's friend.

Parmenio argued that we should camp on the green plains around Issus and wait for Darius to cross the passes.

He talked for too long. I could see Alexander's attention wandering, and I'll just mention here that one of the things that stood between them was that neither of them could really speak to the other in his own language. Parmenio spoke to Alexander as a man speaks to a boy, which robbed even his best arguments of worth. Alexander, on the other hand, always spoke of glory, of religious duty, of omens – he phrased his strategies, which were often as brilliant as Parmenio's, in the heroic terms of the *Iliad*. That's how Alexander saw the world – through the *Iliad*. Parmenio had, I swear, never even read the *Iliad*. No, I mean it.

The result should have been lethal to us. I can only suppose that the internal divisions and miscommunications of the Persians were worse.

At any rate, Parmenio argued for putting the army between the passes, sitting and waiting for Darius to make his move. With our backs to the sea and our supplies intact, we had the rest of the fighting weather to wait – all autumn, if Darius hesitated. We had the wages to pay the troops, and we were holding his terrain. In effect, from a moral standpoint, Darius had to come to us.

Like most of Parmenio's suggestions, it was sound, unexceptional and virtually guaranteed success.

Parmenio further argued, in a monotonous voice that put many officers to sleep, that on the narrow plains this side of the mountain, our flanks – both of them – would be secure, and the Persians' numbers wouldn't matter.

But somehow, in his summing up, Parmenio managed to offend Alexander. I watched it happen. He said that our army could not hope to triumph against the Persians in the open field.

Really, that doesn't sound so bad, does it?

Alexander reacted like a horse given too much bit.

He leaped to his feet. 'If we cross the mountains, Darius will be forced to fight, and his army will be at the disadvantage of knowing themselves the lesser men. Our boldness will disconcert them and make up for any disparity in numbers. We know from the prisoners that Darius was going by the southerly, Syrian Gates. Let us go to the Gates and force our way through before he seizes them, and the whole plain of the Euphrates is before us.'

Like all of Alexander's visions, it was bold to the point of madness. The young men were fired by it and the old men shook their heads. His voice rose with emotion, the more so as he was not yet fully recovered and his hands still shook when he got excited.

Parmenio shook his head. 'Lord, this is folly.'

That was waving a red flag. Sometimes I thought that Parmenio did this on purpose, to drive Alexander to recklessness and defeat, but none of the old man's other behaviours tended that way. Perhaps he couldn't help himself. I've seen parents make the same error with a wayward child. In fact, I've made it myself.

Parmenio was shouted down, and we marched before light in the morning, headed south for the Syrian Gates. We were outnumbered two to one, but this, we all knew, was the battle for Asia.

If anyone worried because the king's eyes glittered or his hands shook, they kept that to themselves.

*

The rains started two days south of Issus, and they battered us like a living embodiment of Poseidon pouring himself on the land, and men offered sacrifices – the sea was so angry, over to our right, and we passed very slowly through the Pillar of Jonah. Men were lost to the waves, and baggage animals. We had to march virtually single file, and when the water rose too high, we just had to wait. You don't know it? Well, there's a point south of Issus where the coast road has to go down the cliffs and across the beach. Just for a few stades – and the beach is wide and easy – unless Poseidon is angry. When we crossed, it was as narrow as a cart track in the mountains, and the penalty for slipping was drowning.

Then we marched farther along the coast, taking Myriandros. There, at Parmenio's insistence, we sent Philotas with six hundred cavalry into the passes to make sure we could get across before Darius did. That much caution the king accepted.

I was summoned to the command tent in the morning, at which time I was standing on a wagon bed holding my morning orders group. I had just managed to get all of my phylarchs to laugh at a fairly weak witticism when Black Cleitus appeared behind me, spoke to Polystratus and literally ran off.

That caught my attention. I turned to Polystratus, who was mounted.

Polystratus was laconic. 'Trouble,' he said.

Such was my trust in Alexander that I assumed it was trouble between Parmenio and Alexander, or medical trouble. I left Isokles to command the troops and I jumped on Medea (a new Medea, a beautiful Arab palfrey with a small head and a wonderful stride), and cantered across the camp to Alexander's pavilion. At the palisade gate, there were forty men – disfigured men, most of them blinded, many with other wounds. Prisoners? I passed them, thinking on the fates.

No one was talking when I entered. But every officer in the army was there. Parmenio's face was white and red – blotches of red. That meant rage.

Alexander was smiling.

No one was saying anything.

Craterus was my brigadier, so I went and stood with him and Perdiccas, and he gave me a nod.

'What's up?' I asked.

Perdiccas caught my eye and I followed him out of the tent.

'Darius tricked us. He's already behind us – has retaken Issus and all our baggage. He ... blinded most of our sick and wounded, except a few he left with one eye.' Perdiccas shrugged.

'Ares,' I breathed. Now Darius had us. He was on *our* communications. He'd outmarched us.

Darius, the slow, conservative Persian.

I followed Perdiccas back inside.

Parmenio was busy apportioning blame. 'I told you!' he shouted as I entered. 'Darius will pick a river – the one with the steepest sides – and he'll entrench on the other side, and we will *have* to fight through him. We're going to have to attack an entrenched army that is double our size.'

Alexander's smile never wavered. 'I agree,' he said. 'The greater the difficulty, the greater the glory. And now Darius is committed to fight. He won't be allowed to slip away.'

Parmenio was about to go on with his (perfectly accurate) rant, but Alexander's comment brought him up short.

'You don't get it, do you?' Parmenio asked. 'This is not a play. This is not a game. If we fail to break Darius, we are *done*. We will have *lost.*' He was so angry that spittle flew from his mouth.

Alexander's smile was like the grin of a satyr. 'Then we'd best win, hadn't we?' he said, and his confidence was both infectious and offensive, all at the same time.

Two more days of rain, and we came *back* to the Pillar of Jonah. Darius could have held it against us for ever, but that wasn't his style. He wanted a field battle as much as Alexander did. So we began to pass it, led by the Agrianians and the Thracians and Paeonians, who went through as fast as men could swim and run, and then spread out on the far side to give us some cover.

That night, we camped on the heights north of the Pillars, and we could see Darius's fires like a carpet of fireflies. The weather was mild in the evening, but around midnight the rains returned, drowning out Alexander's attempt to make a burned offering on an ancient altar in the hills.

I doubt my men were dry, but here's the value of an old sweat like Isokles – he'd spent time training the new men to build shelters. Recruits build shelters that trap water and soak their cloaks – and then fall down at the first touch of wind. Veterans tend to build tiny, snug shelters that will last out a hurricane and have room for five men as long as the men don't mind lying atop each other. Warm men can sleep, even if they are damp. Our men built some remarkable shelters that night – I remember them – my favourite of which (remember we were camped on a steep hillside) was a shallow cave with stakes driven deep into the sandy soil at the back – and then the file's shields carefully laid across the stakes to form a roof of solid wood and hide. With some cloaks and some stolen cloth to pad it out, it was as dry as a bone and warm in there. I know, because that's where I ate breakfast in the morning. With the rain still pouring down.

I had some old friends to breakfast, because we'd made camp late and were all camped together on the ridge – pezhetaeroi and Agrianians and hypaspitoi and Hetaeroi, too. So Bubores and Astibus shared my hot wine and honey, my barley with local yogurt – and those were a general officer's provisions, gathered by expert foragers like Ochrid. We were in trouble, and everyone knew it.

Later, I gathered that the yogurt cost me a gold daric. The cost of a good donkey, at home.

Bubores was delighted by the provender, and deeply troubled. Astibus was less concerned, but he kept looking at the rain as he chewed his three-day-old bread, and both of them were damp and less than lively company.

Polystratus made room for Strakos, who pushed in under the shields like a dancer, carefully avoiding putting undue pressure on the supports or shaking water off the shields.

'What news?' Polystratus asked the Angelos.

Strakos laughed. 'Darius has a huge army, and it is still raining,' he said. He got his cloak off and threw it out into the rain.

Bubores looked at me from under his eyebrows. 'It's the wrath of the gods,' he said quietly.

Astibus rolled his eyes. 'Don't start that crap again,' he said. 'It's bad weather, and it is just as bad for the Persians.'

Bubores shrugged. 'I know what I know,' he muttered.

'What do you know?' I asked. Bubores had a reputation in Aegema as a seer and a bit of an astrologer – self-taught, but still respected.

He rocked back on his heels. He could sit on his heels more comfortably than any man I'd ever seen. 'There's a blood offence against the gods,' he said firmly. 'It must be expiated.'

This wasn't just bad morale. This was a serious accusation. Ignoring this kind of thing is what got Parmenio into trouble. 'Have you spoken to the king?' I asked.

Bubores shrugged. 'It is the king's to answer,' he said in his deep voice.

Astibus slapped his shoulder. 'You and your dark premonitions! At Halicarnassus, you said—'

'It's the rain,' Strakos said. 'The Thracians are openly mutinous. Last night I heard a group of them preparing to desert to Darius.'

Polystratus nodded. 'There's men among the Paeonian cavalry who are suggesting the same.'

Polystratus handed me a cup of hot wine, and I drank it – rich with honey, the nectar of the gods. I passed it around. It was my job to tell them that this was all nonsense, and we'd be triumphant in the end, and I was just framing my reply when Cleomenes pointed to the beach below us.

'Look at him,' Cleomenes said, awe in his voice.

Alexander had ordered that his four-horse chariot be hitched on the beach. The horses were restless in the rain and thunder – but even in the rain, they gleamed with gold and animal magnificence.

Alexander was practically at our feet – as I say, we were eating our barley in a dry cave on a steep hillside in the first light. The rain lashed us, the wind blew straight out to sea from the land, and the king's pavilion was directly below mine.

Alexander emerged from it naked except for a wreath of gold. He had a good body – his legs were a little short for perfection, and his shoulders were a little narrow, but he was always in top shape, every ridge on his abdomen perfectly defined, and he never minded being seen naked. Now he leaped into his chariot and whipped his horses along the beach, and as he drove them along the front of the army, men stood up, despite the rain, and cheered him.

By the gods, he was the king.

He looked like a god, and the rain didn't change that. Had he driven in a sodden purple cloak, he'd have looked like a fool, but naked he looked like Poseidon's son, or Zeus's, as much a creature of the weather as the horses.

I will never forget the sight. He was a god. What more can I say?

From the far end of the beach – the end closest to the Persians, about twenty-five stades away – he turned the chariot and drove it back along the army at a dead gallop, the wheels throwing sand, the horse's hooves shaking the earth, so that we could feel his passage upon our ridge. His hair blew out behind him despite the rain.

And then he turned the chariot – right into the sea.

He drove his chariot, horses and all, until the horses were swimming. The weight of their harness dragged them down. They panicked when they were too deep to save themselves – there was a steep drop just off the beach, and the whole chariot, car, team, gold and all, vanished into the dark line of water just off the beach.

The whole beach was stunned into silence. We sat there. Thirty thousand men. Men coughed, and it disturbed the silence. That's how quiet we were.

The rain *stopped*.

And just beyond the line where the dark water met the light water, a blond head, dark with wet and crowned with bright green kelp, surfaced.

The *sun broke through the clouds.*

I was there. The sun came out, and turned his hair to a fiery gold as he walked up the beach.

It was the greatest, most perfect sacrifice I have ever seen, and Poseidon gave us his favour immediately. I think of it every time I make sacrifice. Impiety is for the foolish, lad. *I was there.*

The army stood as one man, as if it was drill, and bellowed our cheers to Apollo Helios and to Zeus, and to Alexander, son of the gods, crowned by Poseidon.

Bubores was beaming like the sun, pumping his fist in the air, with Astibus pounding him on the back, and even Strakos, who never betrayed emotion, was grinning from ear to ear.

And then, in the light of the warm sun, we donned our sodden equipment and we marched towards Darius.

We marched out of the defile where we'd camped in a column of files. Alexander's plan was as simple as one of Parmenio's, with the difference that Alexander played with his plans constantly, so that a string of messengers altered our dispositions all the time.

I was at Issus, but my Issus was utterly different from everyone else's. I've heard Alexander's tale of the day, and Philotas's, and Parmenio's and Kineas's, and Niceas's – by Ares, I've heard a hundred versions and heard most of them told fifty times! And never heard the same story.

Darius was, as Parmenio expected, waiting for us at the Pindarus river. He had brought his finest troops, mounted and foot – we hadn't had to contend with them at Granicus. He also had almost twelve thousand Greek mercenaries. They were *not* the very best men – we had most of the best men in our army by then, or they lay dead. They were lower-class Greeks wearing the panoply, or Asians trained to look like Greeks. But they had Spartan and Athenian officers. Since everyone knows what happened at Issus, I won't ruin my story if I say that those second-rate 'Greeks' almost wrecked our centre, and had they been Memnon's men led by Memnon, I'd be dead. And so would everyone else from Macedon. Even as it was ...

We went forward from camp in a column of files. We could see the Persian line by mid-morning, formed right across the beach where the beach and the farms of the plain were about twenty stades wide from the steep hills to the sea on our left. As the plain widened, the king kept ordering us to form to the right, and to double out into our battle formation. My taxeis was right in the middle of our line – the most junior position – and so we formed thirty-two deep by sixty wide early in the morning, when we were clear of the narrowest bottleneck; by the time we reached the Persian line, we were in normal order and just sixteen deep and one hundred and twenty wide.

Around noon, we were less than five stades from the Persians, and their line glittered with gold.

Alexander ordered us to halt and cook lunch. We had lost our baggage, remember – we'd lost all our slaves and all of our heavy equipment. What we hadn't lost was our mess kettles, and old soldiers know that a hot meal matters, so most of my men, for instance, had gathered a dozen sticks before stepping off, and tied them inside their shields. We had food in minutes, our fires rising like sacrifices – or pyres.

The Persians didn't even cross the river to scout us.

That made them seem cowardly. In retrospect, Darius had a polyglot army and he didn't trust his commanders to cooperate, and now that I've had that experience, I feel for him, but at the time it made us confident.

Off to our right, in the low hills, there were a great many Persian light troops, and the whole front of their army was covered by more – I don't want to guess how many ill-armed peasants the Great King had. It's by counting this skirmisher cloud as soldiers that men come up with the ludicrous numbers the Persians supposedly had against us. I think he had fifteen thousand Psiloi, but there wasn't a soldier among them, and they weren't like our Thracians or our Agrianians, who could be counted on even when the fighting got stiff. These were peasants, and they had pointed sticks and light bows, slings, bags of rocks.

Still, there were an awful lot of them, and Alexander, who ate his sausage with me, was increasingly concerned about them and finally sent Cleitus with the Agrianians and a battalion of hypaspitoi to clear the ridge to our east. Alexander continued to eat. I was having a hard time eating.

It was not like Granicus. I had lots of time to look and see just how many Persians there were – a sea of them filling the beach. And to remember just how terrifying Granicus had been. This had never happened to me before, and is an essential part of being a veteran. Raw men fear what they do not know. Trained, experienced men fear what they *do* know. I knew it was going to be horrible. The Persians were not foolish, not effeminate. Win or lose, we were going to wade through our own guts to beat them.

After lunch, a lunch I wanted to vomit up but could not, I rode forward with Anander, Perdiccas and Craterus to have a look at the part of the plain where we'd be going. All along the line, Macedonian officers rode forward to scout the enemy lines.

What I saw chilled my heart.

Right in front of my position, the Great King's bodyguard stood, with their six-foot spears tipped in long steel cutting heads, and instead of sharp iron or bronze saurouters, or butt-spikes, every spear had a solid silver apple at the base of the shaft, making them fearsome weapons. I had never faced one, but Kineas's father had one on the wall of his andron, as I've mentioned, and I knew what a deadly weapon it could be.

And I assumed that the Great King's bodyguards would be the best.

And worst of all, the banks of the Pindarus, right there where my lads would cross, were *five feet high*.

Craterus looked it over, turned to me and said, 'Well, you're fucked. Better hope I can do better on your flank.'

And Perdiccas wouldn't meet my eye. No one would. We rode back to our battalions, all of the other officers treating me with the gentle regard friends pay to a dying man, or one condemned for a crime.

Here's how it was, five stades out. We were on a plain. It was flat – but rose steadily from the sea on our left to the steep hills on our right, so that every unit in the line was slightly uphill of the unit to its left and downhill of the unit on its right. I had Coenus to my right and the hypaspitoi just visible beyond – and past them were the king and Philotas and all the Hetaeroi. That's where the king's mighty blow was going to fall.

On my left was Craterus, and beyond him Perdiccas – and beyond him, Parmenio with the rest of the army. The king started with the Thessalians but sent them quite early, round our rear to help Parmenio. I missed all of that. I was busy.

Each of us had a front of roughly one hundred and twenty files. Each of our leftmost men locked shields with the rightmost man of the next taxeis in one continuous phalanx, but we all knew that would go to shit the moment we hit the river, because the river turned twice and the banks were all different heights, and some parts of the riverbank were heavily brushy.

Alexander, now dry and magnificent in his gold and green patina'd antique armour and leopard-skin saddlecloth, his lion-head helmet, his purple Tyrian cloak, rode along the front – back and forth. Every man I know says he gave a different speech.

Opposite my men, he reined in and grinned at me, gave me a little mock salute and made his horse rear, and the men roared.

'Asia!' he yelled, pointing at the glitter of gold. 'Ours for the taking!

Now we avenge Greece. Now we make ourselves masters of the greatest empire on the wheel of the earth. Now we make all that they have, ours – by the spear. Our gods are with us. Poseidon crowned me in the dawn, and I feel Athena at my shoulder, and before the sun sets, we will drive this rabble like sacrificial animals into the sea. And avenge every indignity, every burned temple, and the betrayal of Xenophon and his ten thousand!'

That's what I remember, anyway. And when he mentioned Xenophon, my lads – half of them Athenian street kids – cheered like madmen.

He swept off to the left, towards Parmenio, and we started forward, and the cheering followed him.

Four stades, then three. Then two. Now Alexander was coming back down the line from the left, his cloak flying behind him, the sun gilding his fair hair, and the phalanx roared for him, a wall of sound like our wall of shields. At a stade, we all halted at a gesture from the king – he held his hand out, and the army *stopped.*

It was magnificent, a word I use too often.

He rode off to the left, to the head of his cavalry, and the trumpets blared, and we went forward.

At that point, I dismounted. Being on a horse gives you a fine view of a battlefield, especially when everyone else is on foot. But Greeks and Macedonians expect their taxiarchs to lead from the front, not from the middle or the back. That's just the way it is.

I took my aspis from Polystratus, and my favourite spear, about twice the height of a man, heavy as a tree, of old ash, tipped in heavy steel at one end, quite a long blade, and tipped in bronze at the other, quite a short saurouter. Every man to his own taste. My spear was a man's height shorter than a sarissa. The sarissa is a recruit's weapon, anyway.

Half a stade on. Twenty horse lengths, and we could see their line as clear as anything, and individual helmets, and the precipitous drop to the river bed. I wanted to panic, but I was too busy yelling for my lads to close up and trying to get my cheek-plates tied together. My hands were shaking too hard, and if I stopped walking, the line would leave me behind – or stop with me.

I remember every one of the last fifty paces before the Pindarus river. We had the worst ground to cover, into the face of the most dangerous men on the enemy side.

And then there was a mighty blare of trumpets from the Persians, and arrows flew from their Psiloi line. I assume that every man shot something, and fifteen thousand arrows were launched and fell in a hail as dense as the morning's rain. I got six in my aspis.

The trumpets blared again, and another volley flew.

We'd shuddered to a stop under the barrage. I'd seen it before – men can be shot to a halt. We had a lot of men down. Some would rise again and many wouldn't.

I remember saying 'Fuck it' aloud. I didn't think of Thaïs, or Pella, or my farm, or any of that. What I thought was that I wanted to get it over with.

'Follow me!' I roared, and ran forward into the arrow storm.

I could tell you a lot of stories I heard from other men, but I'll be honest – that's all I remember of the Battle of Issus, until Perdiccas's taxeis broke. Obviously we went forward into the river, but I don't remember a moment of it. We went up the far bank. I know that the enemy guards officers made a stupid mistake and defended the river-bank from the very edge, as if it were a wall, and that meant that our spears went into their legs, at first, and they lost men, and we pushed them back. But when they learned to stand a horse length back from the bank, they started killing our front-rankers as soon as we got up the sandy bank.

As the fighting went on, that bank started to collapse. It was sand and gravel, fairly sharp cut in the early fighting, but after an hour it was a ramp of dead men and collapsed gravel, and I imagine somebody thought we'd fight our way up it in the end.

Not me. I was cut down twice, both times by those terrifying silver apples that could knock a man unconscious right through a good hel-met. Both times, my men pulled me out of the fighting.

When I came to the second time, I was woozy and I vomited, over and over, and my head felt soft and spongy and there was a lot of blood in my hair.

My taxeis was standing in the river, and the Persians were standing on the far bank, jeering at us, and my men weren't even pretending to push forward. Once in a while, a Persian officer would lean out with a bow and shoot one of my officers or file leaders. But that was better than trying the ramp of dead again.

Isokles was holding my shoulders, and Marsyas was holding my hair.

I drank a lot of wine from Polystratus's canteen. As in, the whole canteen.

Hope you're getting the picture.

Polystratus leaned in close. 'Things are going to shit by the hypas-pitoi,' he said.

So I mounted his horse and rode about a hundred feet, my head pounding and my limbs uncertain.

It was like watching a dyke break when a river floods.

I don't know where they came from, but there were thousands of Greek mercenaries, and they'd broken through, and they were coming into Perdiccas's flank. And Perdiccas's men had had enough. They were running. I couldn't see the hypaspitoi. I didn't know that Alexander was, even then, trying to kill Darius, or that he'd broken the enemy line. All I saw was dust and the collapse of our centre.

And let me tell one thing from where Perdiccas stood. He says he never knew how Greeks penetrated our line. His men were stuck in like mine, and unable to break through, just like mine, and suddenly they were struck in the flank by a battering ram of well-formed infantry. It was so bad that most of his front-rankers *died*. Virtually a generation of leadership in a veteran phalanx, dead in heartbeats. My namesake, Ptolemy son of Seleucus, died there. Parmenio's bastard son Attalus died there. We lost good men at the rate of water draining from a pool.

I rode back to my taxeis – just a few horse lengths, and lost in the battle haze.

Thank the gods for the horse.

'Back-step! March!' I bellowed.

Back-stepping is when the hoplite backs from the enemy but with his face still looking the enemy in the eye. Only the best troops, like the best horses, can do it. But my lads were only too happy to leave the killing zone between the banks of the river. And we'd worn both banks to ramps. I'm sure it was bad enough, backing up the near bank, but they got it done.

When the right file leader (the one who should have been next to me) was at my left foot, I ordered 'Halt!'

Isokles came running out of the haze of dust.

His was the rightmost company.

'Form to the right,' I said. 'We're about to be hit in the flank.'

I'd backed the taxeis far enough that he could simply wheel his thirty files to the right. Then Marsyas marched – the Spartan way – by files to the right and reformed his front – to Isokles' left. Wrong place in the line, but we had practised this – and every other possible disaster. Thanks to Isokles.

'Go to Parmenio and get a squadron of cavalry,' I said to Polystratus. 'I don't care who they are. Tell him the whole centre is going to collapse and Perdiccas is already gone.'

And then the Greeks hit Isokles.

That's all the time we had. Perhaps the time a man takes to make a speech in the Assembly. But all those brave men – Meleager son of Neoptolymus, Parmenio's bastard; Ptolemy of Selucus and Leon son of

Amyntas and all of them – they died to buy us those fleeting heartbeats, and we honoured their deaths by using the time as best we could.

The Greeks hit us, and Isokles' men gave way ten paces. Marsyas's men went back far enough that they disordered Pyrrhus's company where they stood ready.

There were so many Greeks. I remember my heart falling as I realised that we had lost the battle.

I dismounted and ran to the rear of Pyrrhus's right file.

'About face!' I roared. Maybe I squeaked it. But they brought their sarissas upright and faced about – a terrible muddle – fighting all around us, and Marsyas's rear files being pushed in among us.

'Follow me!' I yelled. Pyrrhus was ten men away, and his men were not in any order at all, but the Greek formation was wider than ours by half as many again, and I was determined to fight the turning motion of the overlap with an attack of my own.

As it turned out, all of Pyrrhus's men and all of Cleomenes' assumed the order was for them, and the whole lot of them – more than five hundred men – followed me into the Greeks, leaving *no one* facing the Persian guards across the river.

Nor were we in any order at all. We were a mob.

But victory disorders as thoroughly as defeat, and the Greeks had been victorious twice, once against the hypaspitoi and again against the flank of Perdiccas, and they were spread over a stade of ground, and suddenly ...

It was all man to man. Vicious, brutal and utterly devoid of tactics. Had these been Memnon's men, we'd have been dead. Praise Ares, the only veterans of Memnon's were in *my* ranks, at *my* back.

I remember crashing into a very young Greek, knocking him flat with my greater weight, and putting my spear into him. That never happens in a line fight. But here – it was every man for himself in the dust.

The sarissas were useless, and most of my veterans simply dropped them for their swords. The sarissa is a fine team weapon, but has no use at all man to man.

Then it was just fighting.

We lost.

They seemed to have an inexhaustible number of Greeks and Ionians. It was incredible – slow, almost nightmare-like. The initial shock of the open, confused fighting gave way to a gradual, almost glacial collapse into a line fight.

We lost, but we lost slowly. Cleomenes quite wisely sent his mounted messengers down the line to Craterus to tell him what was happening, and we lost ground, step by step, and the Greeks kept pushing our flanks and driving south, away from the river, trying to turn us.

We died.

Let me tell you how war works. I had, at the start of the day, about eight hundred veterans of Memnon's and about nine hundred Macedonian recruits. At the end of the day, I had about seven hundred veterans of Memnon and about three hundred Macedonian recruits. The young die, and the old fight on.

Back and back we went.

Praise to Ares, some of Perdiccas's men – and he himself – joined us on our southern flank. But every time we tried to stand, we were pushed back by numbers.

Over the next hour, we lost two hundred paces.

But now I'll tell you what didn't happen.

The Persian guards didn't charge us in our exposed flank. I don't know if they didn't want to get their feet wet, or they didn't know what was happening, or they were worried for their own king, who even then was being hunted like prey by Alexander – but they had it in their power to win the battle – one killing blow at us, and the centre was gone.

That man – the commander of Darius's foot guards – lost Issus.

I was wounded – really wounded, a thrust from a spear that went through the top of my thorax and lodged in my breastbone – about the time that Craterus arrived with the rear files of his taxeis to try and steady mine. It *still* wasn't enough. But his timing was good, because about twenty heartbeats after he slapped my shoulder and told me the king was coming, I was on my face in the blood and sand.

And that, for me, was the end of the Battle of Issus.

I suspect you know what happened, but here it is – Alexander launched his blow at the first roar of the trumpets, smashed through the line facing him and made straight for Darius, intending to kill him. Say what you will, it was a fine plan. It was a fine plan because it mostly worked.

Darius hadn't planned on a fast battle, but on a long, slow slogging match. Darius made two mistakes – he didn't keep a big cavalry reserve, and he assumed that we wouldn't fight along the river front. What happened is that our failed phalanx attack still had the effect of locking all his drilled troops – his Greeks – in place while Alexander rode across his rear.

At some point, some bright Greek realised that Alexander's charge had left the flank of the hypaspitoi hanging in the air, and the Greeks turned our flanks. Callisthenes did some very careful writing in the

Military Journal to suggest that we'd lost so many officers – more than a hundred – in *winning*. We lost all those men – and their followers – in losing.

But Darius lost faster than we lost. I've heard Kineas's version, and I've heard Amyntas's version, and Parmenio didn't really do all that well – in fact, it's one of his poorest performances. Cleitus openly said – much later – that Parmenio left the king to get isolated behind the Persian lines and die, and kept his men together so he could retreat in good order.

I don't buy that, either.

What really happened is that Alexander, let loose in the rear of the enemy, spread panic while chasing Darius – he got so close to the Great King that Darius's left-hand dagger scored our king's thigh.

The irony is that it all came down to culture.

In our culture, the king is king while he is winning. He's worthless if he is losing. So our king attacked and kept attacking.

In the empire, they'll do anything to protect the Great King, and when he is threatened, they hustle him out of danger. So while the battle teetered in the balance – when, in fact, those Greek mercenaries had it in the bag – Darius was dragged from the field by his cousins, and Polystratus reached Alexander. That's right. Polystratus ignored me. He didn't go to Parmenio. He went to Alexander, right through the gap in the Persian lines.

According to Polystratus, Alexander looked back at the dust cloud over the river, spat and said, 'By Zeus my father, do I have to do everything myself?'

But he came back, crashed into the rear of the Greeks and the day was ours.

I wasn't there. I was halfway along the road to Hades.

It took me five days to recover enough to leave my beautiful Persian bed – we took their camp and got all our baggage back, although not our slaves, of course. Now we had all new slaves.

I missed all the fun. I missed Alexander meeting Darius's wife and mother, which I gather was worth seeing – the older matron, perhaps the most dignified woman I've ever known, managed to assume that Hephaestion was the King of Macedon, and who wouldn't? He was taller and handsomer and didn't look like an insane street urchin, which our king always did, the day after a fight.

Give the old lady credit. Our army was mad with victory, and every woman in that camp got raped. Hideous, ugly – I'm no fan of rape – but that's what happened. In Persia, a raped woman can be

472

executed for adultery. That's fair, eh? Lucky them. So when the king and Hephaestion and a dozen other men came into their tent, they assumed that they were for it – especially as the lot of them were as fair as any group of thirty women on the face of the world. Forgive Sisygambis her error. But I gather that it was fantastic theatre.

And Alexander kissed her gently and said, 'Never fear. For he, too, is Alexander.'

Alexander visited the wounded, handed out the prizes as if we were the Greeks before Troy (and never doubt that under those blond curls, he thought that we *were* the Greeks before Troy) and praised everyone. Kineas was made bravest of the allies – he'd fallen across the river, deep in the Persian ranks, and lots of people saw this act of insane heroism. And he lived, the lucky bastard. And a dozen of us who fell holding the centre got garlands, as well. I got one. Perdiccas got one. My young Cleomenes got one.

We had a lot of dead. Alexander held a moving funeral, complete with oration, and we burned the corpses.

We were rich. Every man in the army got enough loot out of that fantastic camp to retire. We were done. Victors. We had done it, and beaten the Great King.

Alexander let us believe that for three days. I knew better immediately, of course – Thaïs was by my side (in later years, she said it was to keep me from the Persian girls) and she already had reports of Darius gathering troops in the eastern valleys. He was a tough fighter. And he was not beaten.

TWENTY-THREE

———

The greatest victory in Greek – or Macedonian – history earned us a week. Then we were off down the coast road, headed for Syria.

To say that Alexander was insufferable doesn't do justice to his behaviour. He retold the story of his daring charge and his chase of King Darius, of their brief struggle hand to hand, of Darius's attack with a dagger after his sword broke, of his own brilliance in overcoming the captain of Darius's guard while simultaneously holding Darius himself at bay.

It was all true. He had a hundred witnesses, and he liked nothing better than to make Philotas, for instance, tell how he, the king, had rescued Philotas when his horse went down and he took a wound. He insisted that I tell how and why I had sent for help, so that he could explain how he had come into the rear of the enemy Greeks like a god from a machine in a play.

It was his first victory that was all his own, against the Persians. He had triumphed – with his own feats of arms, his own battle plan, an army that followed him. Parmenio played a very small part in the battle, and that Alexander couldn't let anyone forget.

We were weeks travelling south along the coast, through the mountains and back to the coast of Phoenicia, and every night I heard the story of Issus again.

One afternoon, when I was with the king, we rode off the road in answer to a summons from Ariston, who was commanding the advance guard. We went north from the road a stade or two, and there was a statue. It was magnificent and barbarous all at once, in black basalt.

It depicted an ancient king in a high crown, with his fingers raised on his right hand. I had to look at them from several angles before I realised that he was in the act of snapping his fingers.

I laughed.

The king shrugged at Ariston.

Ariston had the look of a man who had tried to play the courtier and please his king, and failed. He shrugged. 'The peasants said he was the greatest king in the history of the world,' he said. 'I thought you'd want to see him.'

Alexander made a face.

'Who is he?' he asked.

Ariston spoke briefly to a Syrian, who cowered in the dirt. The man raised his face, like a dog expecting a bone. His Greek was halting.

'He is the Great King Ashurbanipal,' Ariston said.

'What does the inscription say?' Alexander asked. 'I know who Ashurbanipal was. He ruled the world – or enough of it that it didn't matter.'

Ariston spoke to the cowering Syrian.

He laughed, slapped his thigh and turned to the king. 'According to this peasant, the inscription says, "Eat! Drink! Fuck! And the rest is not worth this!"'

'What rest? Is not worth what? Foolish old man. Worthless!' Alexander shook his head. 'There's no greatness here. A village bull might say the same.' He looked at me, because I was sobbing with laughter. 'What's up with you, Ptolemy?'

I couldn't decide what was funnier – that Ashurbanipal had raised a statue to proclaim this message (and the rest is not worth the snap of my fingers) or that Alexander didn't get it.

Later, I thought that if only he'd mentioned war, the king would have found him worthy.

There was another change. Until we marched into Cilicia, we were liberators. It was in the official letters, and in the Military Journal, too. We had come at the behest of the League of Corinth to avenge the burning of Athens and to liberate the Greeks of Ionia and Aetolia.

That was now done. It was shown to be rather hollow by the fact that less than a month after Issus, Halicarnassus and Miletus were back in Persian hands and their fleet continued to dominate the seas.

The truth is, all we won at Issus was time. Darius had a new army within hours, and we actually *lost* ground after the battle.

And we only truly owned the ground under our feet. More and more, the king had to send detachments – like the one I had led, like Antigonus, like Seleucus – to hold key cities or to put down the endless rebellions in our rear. I use the term 'rebellions' advisedly – I didn't work for the Military Journal any more, and I disdained their jargon and still do. *We* were the foreign usurpers. Why should we have expected loyalty of the satraps? They would make submission to us, but as soon as Darius showed his teeth, they all flocked to his banner. Including a great many Greeks.

On our side of the struggle, once we marched south into Phoenicia, we were conquerors, not liberators, and that had an effect on the army that I didn't like to see. The younger men revelled in it – especially relatively new recruits fresh from the farm. Their peasant myths of their own superiority were played out. They had licence to slaughter – aye, and rape and steal – because we were Macedonians!

But the older men saw it differently. I never heard one put it just this way, but my feeling was that until we liberated the last Greek states in Asia, the old veterans could pretend to themselves that this was Philip's son completing Philip's crusade, and then we'd all go home.

After Issus, Alexander bragged openly that he intended to make himself Master of Asia. King of Kings. And all the veterans knew what that meant.

It meant thousands of stades of marching and a lot more fighting, that's what it meant.

Morale plummeted, and between atrocities committed on the civilian population and suicides among the older veterans, the signs were obvious.

Phoenicia should have been easy. I can still grow angry just telling this part of the story.

As we marched south, the cities surrendered one by one, and the Persian fleet lost base after base. Granted, in the north, they had retaken about a third of Ionia, and most of the islands, which, if you consider it, suggests that Alexander's strategy was utterly hollow. The only thing that kept the Persians from counter-invading Greece and Macedon was lack of a strategos and Athens' continued prevarication. Men like Kineas's father did more to help Alexander than he did to help himself. That whole autumn and winter, had Athens come over to Persia, we'd have been cut off from our homes.

Sparta did, in fact, join the Persian cause, but in their own special Spartan way, they left it too late and bungled it. That happened later, of course.

We marched up to Sidon, the second-greatest city in Phoenicia, and they made submission gracefully enough, and Alexander was munificent in rewarding them for their choice. Then we marched down the coast to Tyre with four thousand Sidonese marines in our ranks.

Again, it should have been easy.

Alexander's demands were very easy – the usual tokens of submission and a payment to the treasury to cover the cost of their submission

– the costs of conquering them, so to speak. And taxes, of course. But Alexander was far too wise to impose a foreign government over them – he usually left a military governor with a few thousand troops to watch a whole region.

With Tyre, which was a city associated with Melkart, the Syrian version of our Herakles, Alexander had an additional desire – a pothos, a heroic craving. At Tyre, Alexander wanted permission to worship and sacrifice (lavishly) in person at the Tyrian Temple of Melkart. Tyre was an island fortress, a set of rocks of two stades or more forming a promontory, and the temples were magnificent – but no man might enter without the leave of the city fathers.

Alexander wanted to sacrifice there.

I was present for the negotiations, and I watched the next year of my life vanish in poor judgement.

Azemiticus was explaining that he had no interest in fighting, and Alexander was smiling away, already marching on, in his head, to our next prey, when the Tyrian shrugged.

'As to making sacrifice at our temples,' he said with that mock ruefulness you so easily detect as a falsehood that you know you are being mocked – then paused. He meant to offend. 'That is the privilege of the Great King and no other.'

Alexander's head turned as rapidly as if he had been struck. 'There is no longer a "Great King". I am your king, and I will worship there.' He smiled, his lips tight – those who knew him understood what this meant. 'All the better that it is a privilege reserved for kings alone.'

Azemiticus spread his hands wide, to indicate that it was beyond his control. 'The ancient temple is in the ancient city, here on the mainland,' he said. 'Really, you should content yourself with that.'

How did this man get to be the leader of one of the most powerful cities on earth? No wonder translators so often lie about what their principals have said. Had the fool Syrian merely suggested that the land temple was older and more sacred than the island temple, we would have been done. Consensus might have been reached. Alexander might easily have been convinced that the older temple was the more important.

But the word 'content' and the contempt with which it was uttered settled the matter.

Alexander's smile didn't waver. 'Your temple in the city, or I storm it,' he said.

Azemiticus stood. 'Try, barbarian.' He grinned. Then he turned and left. I think he always meant to – I think he wanted, like so many other men, to be the man who stopped Alexander.

To be fair, Tyre was a hideously hard nut to crack and Alexander didn't want to do it, so after a stormy council meeting with Hephaestion and Craterus and all of us, we sent three officers to the city with new terms. The king was to be allowed to sacrifice at the altars of Melkart, but in every other way, Tyre paid less gold and got less interference.

Azemiticus had all three young men executed. He stripped them naked on the walls where we could see, had spears rammed into their anuses until the spearheads came out through their mouths, and then threw them into the sea.

What a fool. In so doing, he condemned his city to death. With whom did he think he was dealing?

Diades was Alexander's foremost engineer, after Halicarnassus. He was a pupil of Aristotle's, not brilliant but careful and conscientious, and best of all, he was very good at making Alexander understand him. Alexander was too impatient for a siege, and it didn't suit his temperament. Diades was a patient man.

He got a small boat and had himself rowed all around the walls. Tyre was on a large island – in fact, I've been told it had once been four small islands, now linked together by generations of mortar and stone. The walls facing the mainland were quite high, but some of the walls were not.

Tyre had its own fleet, and recalled a large portion of it from Persian service to face us – almost a hundred triremes, and a dozen larger ships. We had no fleet to speak of, so their sea power not only eliminated any chance that we might land troops on the lower parts of the walls, but guaranteed that they would be supplied whenever they wanted them. In fact, quite early in the siege, before we'd even begun our engineering efforts, a Carthaginian fleet arrived with food and left carrying all of the city's women and children to safety. Carthage had the largest maritime empire in the Inner Sea, and the knowledge that they would come to the rescue of their mother city was a blow to us. Watching the ease with which their thirty-ship squadrons sailed in and out enraged Alexander, who responded with a declaration of war against Carthage. Against Carthage! Because we didn't have enough enemies!

The third night after the assassination of our envoys, Diades called the military council together to make his report.

He was a short, thick man with arms like old cables, and men called him 'The Smith'. Other men called him Hephaestus. He was not old, but he was so careful in his speech that he sometimes sounded like a man of Parmenio's generation. He had my Helios as an assistant, and Helios grinned at me when he set up the easel on which Diades arranged his drawings.

Diades rubbed his beard and waited for silence.

Philotas threw a bread pill at his brother, who responded by throwing a grape at Philotas. It missed and hit his father, splashing purple-red on Parmenio's spotless uniform chiton. Nicanor paled.

Parmenio walked over with the grape and slapped it into his son's hair. Then he rubbed it in.

Nicanor just allowed it to happen.

Alexander wasn't the only man with a bad temper, let me tell you.

At any rate, after a great deal of throat-clearing, Diades held out his hands.

'Tyre,' he said. His voice came out in an odd, loud, strangled way, and in the old temple – which we were using as both a temple and a meeting room – it was so loud that he frightened himself. He went on in a voice so soft that men behind the first row could not hear him.

'Speak up!' Alexander said.

Diades glared at him.

We all laughed. That seemed to help him. He steadied, looked around and rubbed his beard with his left hand.

'You know how it is,' he asked, 'when you start a project and you don't know if you can finish it? Those are always the hardest projects. Because you fear that all your work may be in vain. Whether that project is the pursuit of a woman, or the conquest of Asia, or the making of a fine gold seal – in every case, the uncertainty of completion is more of a limit to success than any limits to our skills – whether seduction, conquest or craftsmanship.'

I told you – Aristotle trained him. He was a brilliant thinker, when he put himself to it.

'The siege of Tyre will be an extreme example of such a project. There is only one practical way of approaching the city, and that way will bring us into contact with the highest and stoutest portion of the wall. By my estimation, it will take us seven months merely to reach a point where we might say that the city is under siege. Until then, we will merely be building – building a causeway. And the citizens of Tyre will laugh at us. We won't interrupt their food supply. We cannot even slow their trade! We cannot build engines whose stones will hit their walls, we cannot throw fire into the city itself, we cannot open trenches, we cannot undermine. We cannot storm the city, because we would have to walk across the ocean bottom to reach it.'

Alexander made to interrupt, but Diades, who knew his man, drove on.

'But we *can* take the city. We will need to build a mole – a causeway – three stades long and half a stade wide. The amount of earth and stone required will make the building of this mole a greater labour than any performed by Herakles, and the gods may be jealous, because if we succeed, that mole will endure for ever. But my lord king, and all of you – if we persevere, we will succeed. Engineering is a science, not an art. If we work hard and move earth, the mole will grow a little each day, and eventually, we will have them. And if you choose not to build the mole ...' He shrugged. 'We will *never* have them.'

He went and sat.

Alexander rose. 'You are talking a siege of a year.'

Diades nodded. 'At least a year, unless a fortuitous event happens, or the gods take a hand.'

Alexander shook his head. 'We have triumphed thus far by the speed of our advance and our reputation as invincible. How will that look if we take a year to storm one city?'

Parmenio sneered, 'We have bypassed cities before.'

Callisthenes shook his head. 'Not cities that have defied us. Not cities that have murdered our ambassadors.'

He directed the Military Journal, and he decided what the Greeks should be allowed to know – and he wrote the florid reports of our victories. His carefully doctored lies were essential to the way the Macedonian army was perceived. More and more, he worked directly with Thaïs, whom he affected to despise, and her information and his often worked together.

I disliked him. But in this case, I agreed with him.

'I took the Halicarnassus island forts,' I said. 'Or rather, Helios there, by the easel, took them. It took us seven months. Until the last three weeks, none of the garrison even thought that they were in danger.'

Diades nodded his thanks to me.

Cleitus fingered his beard. 'If we fail here ...' he ventured.

Diades slammed his fist on the table. 'We do not need to fail!' he roared, no longer timid.

Alexander looked around. It was not like him to be so cautious, but he had been shaken by the killing of the ambassadors. The very impiety of it stung him.

'Parmenio?' he asked.

'Oh, you want my opinion?' Parmenio asked. 'Delighted to give it. March away. Always bypass strength. Except that in this case, your whole strategy is that we can take any city along the coast that can offer a harbour to the Persian fleet – isn't it? So your strategy requires that we take this city – and every other city from Ionia to Aegypt.' He

480

sighed theatrically. 'Of course, we could just march home. We're richer than Croesus. We hold the best part of the empire. And my soldiers are tired, Alexander.'

Alexander nodded. 'My soldiers, Parmenio.' He looked past the old general to me. 'Ptolemy?'

'I lost half of my new levies at Issus,' I said. 'I've had eleven suicides and four murders in the last month.' I looked around and saw a great many heads nodding. 'I'm concerned that while we sit here, Pharnabazus is retaking Ionia behind us, rendering our efforts meaningless. But ... I agree with Diades – if we put our minds to it, I'm sure we can do it. I would only hope that once we decide on a course, we set that course in stone.' I stood up. 'Again, let me mention the Halicarnassus forts. It will take a long time. But like many tasks, it is the task never begun that is impossible.'

Alexander frowned. 'Do I ever change my mind, once I am set on a thing?' he asked.

Like many men, Alexander had a vision of himself that was at odds with the reality. Some men see themselves as timely, but are forever late. Other men see themselves as great lovers, and women tell a different story. So with Alexander, who thought that he possessed a will of iron.

Parmenio guffawed. 'You change your mind like a woman,' he said.

Very helpful.

Diades alone stuck to his message. 'We can build something worthy of a descendant of Herakles,' he said. 'Perhaps greater than any labour of Herakles.'

Alexander looked at him. Looked at Parmenio.

He was silent for a long time. And then he stood straight like a sword blade, and spoke like an orator.

'Friends and allies,' he began, and his full charm was on. 'I see that an expedition to Aegypt will not be safe for as long as the Persians retain the sovereignty of the sea, nor is it a safe course for other reasons – and especially looking at the state of matters in Greece – for us to pursue Darius, leaving in our rear the city of Tyre itself. I would be precipitous if I were to advance with our forces towards Babylon and in pursuit of Darius and allow the Persians to reconquer the maritime districts – and with them in hand, to transfer the war into Greece with a larger army, considering that the Lacedaemonians are now waging war against us without disguise, and the city of Athens is restrained for the present rather by fear than by any goodwill towards us! But if Tyre were captured, the whole of Phoenicia would be in our possession and the fleet of the Phoenicians, which is the most numerous and the best in the Persian navy, would in all probability come over to us. For the

Phoenician sailors and marines will not put to sea in order to incur danger on behalf of others when their own cities are occupied by us. After that – well, Cyprus will either yield to us without delay or it will be captured with ease at the mere arrival of a naval force – which then prosecutes the war with the ships from Macedonia in conjunction with those of the Phoenicians.' He looked around.

Alexander seldom made long speeches, and when he did, with his face shining, his whole attention on his audience, he was virtually impossible to resist. Even Parmenio was nodding along.

'Once Cyprus is in our hands, we shall have the absolute sovereignty of the sea, and at the same time an expedition into Egypt will become easier for us. After we have brought Aegypt into subjection, no anxiety about Greece and our own land will any longer remain, and we shall be able to undertake the expedition to Babylon in safety with regard to affairs at home and at the same time with greater reputation in consequence of having cut off from the Persian empire all the maritime provinces and all the land this side of the Euphrates. And at Tyre, we shall have shown the world that we are worthy sons of Herakles!'

Sons of Herakles. As Diades intended, the very challenge fired him, and he, in turn, shot it at us. Because the men of Macedon see themselves as the heirs of Herakles.

The siege was on.

Diades rode around the countryside for ten days while the Tyrians jeered at our lack of effort. When he returned, he sat with Alexander for most of a day.

I sat with Thaïs, who was deeply depressed because she was pregnant, and because the Tyrians had executed one of her agents in their horrible way and dumped his body in the sea. I tried to console her that they'd executed three other men who were not her agents. 'If they kill three of theirs for every one of ours, we will win the siege in a month,' I joked.

She raised her eyes. 'Leave me,' she said. And she meant it. Never make a jest about defeat or death.

I wandered among my troops, watched a dice game, watched two men beat a slave, watched two more men butchering a lamb. The pezhetaeroi were sullen and didn't want me in their camp. I went to sit and drink wine with Marsyas and Cleomenes, but they were screaming at each other like prostitutes fighting over a customer in the streets of Athens – and on the same subject.

'She was *mine*,' Cleomenes shrieked.

'She's not a slave. You cannot own a woman.' Marsyas spoke in the sneering way that poets have when being superior, always the very best way to incite a riot.

Two of my officers, standing in the street, fighting over a woman. With half a thousand of their own men watching.

Cleomenes reached for the dagger he always wore. Really, we all wore them. I grabbed his hand from behind and then had to kick Marsyas in the crotch as he had drawn his and in his rage seemed to think I was pinning Cleomenes' arms for him.

Macedon. I tell you.

As Marsyas the Poet fell forward, I slammed his forehead into Cleomenes' forehead and the two fell together to the ground.

I didn't feel any better, but I'm sure that I helped to preserve discipline, which was going to Hades already, and we were on the day *before* the start of a year-long siege. Bubores, passing by, helped me take them to their tents.

'We had a murder this morning,' he said sullenly.

As I left Cleomenes' tent, I couldn't help but note that the men going on guard were drunk.

However, the finest anodyne to soldiers' behaviour is work. And suddenly, the God of Work, with his high priest Diades, descended from the heavens. And none too soon.

He had divided the areas around the landward end of his proposed mole into districts, and he'd assigned one each to all of the pezhetaeroi commanders. We were to employ our men as labour, and gather stone and wood.

Craterus held a meeting and suggested that we refuse.

'You have to be kidding,' I said. I remember laughing at him. 'It's better than my lads deserve. I intend to work them like slaves. Until I trowel off the fat and the bad attitude.'

Perdiccas nodded. Perdiccas and I had always been rivals – but having reached high command, we were, somehow, allies. He rubbed his chin and drank wine and then nodded. 'If I enforced the king's law about harming civilians,' he said, 'I'd have no phalangites. Last night, some of my men were sending children into the hills so they could *hunt them*. I need this *work*.'

Craterus breathed a sigh of relief. 'Thank Ares,' he said. 'I expected you all to be angry, and I was ready to back you. But in truth, there's been too much loot and not enough discipline.'

'Every man in camp has his girl,' Perdiccas said. He looked at me. 'I don't mean you – yours does a job of work.'

'Even Philotas has a beauty.' Amyntas laughed. 'And he affects to despise women.'

'He despises all of her,' Perdiccas laughed, 'except when he's on top of her.'

The next day, we began working. I mustered my full strength – we'd had some levies, so I had a little more than fourteen hundred men. With Perdiccas, my men were assigned the old city of Tyre, which we were to dismantle, stone by stone, and move to the seaside.

I stood on the bed of a four-wheel wagon and gave my orders, district by district. Isokles and I had already put out coloured tape – Tyrian red linen tape, used for marking, worth a fortune at home – to mark what streets were to be demolished and by what company.

Marsyas and Cleomenes stood well apart from each other. They both looked a little green.

I marched the taxeis over to the old city, had them strip and put them to work. One man in fifteen went into an army-wide pool to weave baskets. Every man who could handle a donkey went to the baggage train. Every man who could do fine carpentry or forge metal went to work directly for Diades.

The siege of Tyre ran on manpower. We had four hundred oxen and a little over a thousand donkeys and perhaps two hundred mules at the height of the siege, but most of the digging and most of the rubble fill was 'mined' by men and carried by men in baskets woven by men who needed a new basket every couple of days.

We had about twelve thousand pezhetaeroi and twice that again in slaves. Thirty-six thousand men, each needing a basket the size of a market basket every two days. To give you a notion of the scale of the siege of Tyre, let's imagine the requirement for brush to weave baskets, at eighteen thousand baskets per day. Just for the sake of easy calculation, let us call that eighteen thousand mina of brush a day. Three thousand talents of brushwood, every day. Roughly the weight of a completed trireme with all its oars and all of its sails and equipment and fully laden with men – *every day, just for baskets.*

Of course, I exaggerate. Of course not every man wore out his basket – nor did the basket-makers ever keep pace. Men were lost from the work to repair their own baskets – indeed, at one point, I had almost a hundred of my own men making baskets to keep the rest at work, and Diades came and took the whole draft – slaves and soldiers as well.

Brush came from close by – for the first few days. After that, the local brush was gone, and the foragers had to go farther and farther afield, slowing the whole process. By the end of the siege, our brush was being brought from Kana and Sinde, east in the hills and down the coast in Galilee.

And then there was food, water, forage for animals, heavy beams of wood, whole trees and stone. Wine, oil, water and food for fifty thousand men. Every day.

And every man thus served could carry perhaps two hundred baskets of fill a day, if he was fast and devoted and fit. Care to guess how many men fell into that category? And men had to be detailed to destroy as well as to carry – to pull down the old houses and get at the stone in their foundation courses, or the base of the walls, the pillars of old temples. On and on.

After just six days, it seemed normal. After ten days, I joined in, because that's how you lead troops, and stripped naked and carried a basket on my head all day. I never made two hundred, either. And two days later, my whole body hurt, but I kept at it.

We rested for major feasts, so on the nineteenth day of Mounikhion, by the Athenian festival calendar that dominated in my taxeis, we celebrated the feast of Olympian Zeus. I ordered five oxen to be sacrificed, and we feasted on them amid the rubble of Old Tyre. I gave games for my men, and pitted company against company. I couldn't help but notice how well muscled everyone was.

In Greece, women are forbidden the games, but in the field, all the camp followers watched, and Thaïs was no exception. Thaïs also had young Antigone, the girl who'd caused Cleomenes and Marsyas to come to blows, living in our cluster of tents. The two officers were perpetually trying to outwork each other – there was an endless amount of guilt they felt they had to expiate. I used it against them shamelessly.

At any rate, she had chairs brought for the women of the taxeis – all the women, Syrian and Jew, Greek and Persian, slave and free. They all had stools on which to watch, and our phalangites, exhausted by the labour of the siege, ran, fought, wrestled and sang, naked, while the women giggled and roared their approval. They were *very* fit.

When Marsyas wrestled Cleomenes, the two stripped in front of us, and Thaïs rubbed her thumb along my forearm. 'My, my,' she said.

I determined to improve my own physique.

We feasted for two days, and then went back to work. My body no longer hurt, and while I did not carry baskets of rock every hour, I made a point to get in several hours a day. Every day.

One day, the slim man ahead of me took his own sweet time dumping his load on the towering rubble pile at the edge of the sea. The idiot had stopped to watch the construction work on the mole with his basket still on his shoulder.

I kicked the back of his knee.

He fell and spilled his load. Then he got to his feet and came after me, face suffused with anger. Of course, working naked, we had no badges of rank.

Which was good, because the sunburned bastard trying to kick me in the nuts was Alexander. I ended up dropping my basket and holding him, and after I yelled my name a few times, he dissolved into laughter. And when the men around us realised what had happened, they stopped betting on the outcome and laughed with us.

Out on the end of the peninsula, meanwhile, Diades had built a framework of heavy timbers – superbly heavy timbers, the roof-trees of the largest houses in Old Tyre and some new-cut cedars. There was a low isthmus of sand and rock just under the sea – we were going to use it as the spine of our mole. And that day, two days after the feast of Olympian Zeus, we started to fill the frames with crushed stone and rubble.

And then the mole seemed to leap forward.

It took almost three weeks for us to use up all the rubble and stone we'd moved forward, but after the Thargellia, the feast of the children of Leo, we saw the mole grow every day – and we carried our baskets straight out to the end of it and dumped them in the frames. If we had doubted, we doubted less, now. The mole crept forward, and the sound of the taunts from the other side grew distinctly more strained.

Alexander grew distinctly more strained, as well. In the heady weeks after Issus, he'd sent Parmenio off to try and take Damascus. It was a gamble – Darius had sent his whole treasury to Damascus before the battle – but the gamble paid off and Parmenio had scooped the entire hoard. As well as all the families of Darius's senior officers, and the Athenian ambassadors to Persia, the Spartan ambassadors – it was a good piece of theatre, I can tell you.

Parmenio also got Memnon's wife, Barsines, and her sister, Banugul. They were identical twins, both beautiful, blond and sophisticated. I was there when they were brought from Damascus.

Their arrival set their tone. Barsines rode in an ox cart with screens against the dust, the whole cart painted elaborately with flowers and scenes of the life of Aphrodite. Barsines, as I have said, was Memnon's wife. And she was said to be the most beautiful woman in the world, although some said her sister was her rival. They were both reputed to be descended from Aphrodite, but in fact their father was the satrap of Hyrkania.

Banugul rode a horse – a Nisean stallion of which she was the master. She rode beautifully – like a Scythian, with her legs well up and her knees bent.

Hephaestion had arranged to meet them as they entered camp. I think it was now part of the king's policy to heroise his better opponents. Memnon was now praised regularly – now that he was safely dead. And Alexander loved to appear chivalrous.

But I don't think he'd listened to the gossip, and I know he was unprepared for the sisters.

He stood, looking at Banugul as if he'd been struck by lightning. She was dressed from head to foot as a Persian nobleman, and all the male attire, the loose trousers, the burnoose, served only to accentuate the slimness of her limbs, her athletic build, her straight back and neck – and her breasts, which defied the masculine clothing.

She leaped from her horse, leaving the reins to Tyche, and threw herself down before the king in full proskynesis. We had seen it before, of course, but we'd never seen a woman throw herself in the sand before our king.

She did it with grace, and a complete lack of submission. Somehow, she did it seductively, and yet she didn't waggle or wiggle. Nothing gross.

The king reached out and took her hand, raised her to her knees and looked into her eyes, and then he kissed her hand.

And the gate to the ox cart opened.

If Banugul was the Queen of the Steppes, Barsines was the Queen of the World. She stepped out of the ox cart as if, rather than travelling all day, she had been lounging in the Lyceum, listening to men recite the poets. She was dressed as a Greek woman, in a white chiton with a perfect Tyrian purple border itself edged in gold. The chiton was linen, and transparent, and the body beneath it was as perfect as the cloth of the chiton and as hard as any phalangites labouring under the walls of Tyre.

And she, too, lowered herself into the dust.

The king was transfixed. And it was as if he had taken two arrows – his eyes went back and forth between the two women.

Hephaestion cleared his throat a dozen times, and I began to wonder if the king might need rescuing.

But he raised her from the dust as elegantly as he had raised her sister, and kissed her hand. He said something, and she smiled – a perfectly genuine smile.

Her eyes were as big as a man's hand, or so they seemed.

The king took each of the sisters by the hand and led them to his pavilions.

So many women – and men – had tried to set their hooks into the king that we, as his friends, had begun to look forward to watching them fail against his lack of interest. I have said it before – he did not look at women – or men – the way most men do. Beautiful women would come to camp, arrange an invitation to meet the king and end leaving with a small present, and he would shrug and wonder aloud why they wasted his time.

But the twins were different. Was it that he saw them as children of the goddess? As peers? They were witty, engaging, seductive, serious, well read, giggly – they were any woman he wanted them to be, with noble birth and descent from the gods thrown in. But I was there, and he was besotted instantly.

It is worth noting that, at the same time, we had Darius's wife and her women in camp and she, too, was a great beauty. Alexander treated her with great gallantry – but it became obvious, as the siege went on, that gallantry alone was not holding their relationship together. She was a beautiful, powerful woman who had been deserted by her husband. What could you expect?

Thaïs lay with her head in the crook of my arm one night, and sighed. She sighed a great deal – it was as hot as the bowl of a helmet being forged, even at night – a horrible wet, sticky hot, that hurt a pregnant woman more than anyone. She had taken to swimming in the sea – scandalising older Macedonians – if only to have relief from the weight of the child and the heat for an hour every day.

So she lay with her head in the crook of my arm, and all the rest of her posed strategically as far from my body heat as she could arrange.

'Alexander has discovered women,' she said.

'Alexander has discovered the siege of Troy,' I said. 'And that Helen has an identical twin sister.'

The army speculated endlessly that he was having both of them at the same time, an impractical fantasy that appealed to every Thracian, every Greek mercenary and every Macedonian – every man, and some of the women, too.

A week or so after they arrived, I entered my pavilion to find both of them sitting with Thaïs, drinking sherbet in the Persian manner. Thaïs looked beautiful, despite her pregnancy and even because of it – pregnancy enhances some things, and not just breasts – hair, and skin.

Barsines sat next to Thaïs, and Banugul closer to the door, and a pair of slaves fanned them while Bella, my love's Libyan, brought food and wine.

I was wearing a soldier's chiton over a naked body. I had been carrying rocks. I imagine that I smelled.

Both women rose to their feet and offered deep curtsies. I returned them – I'm a gentleman, despite being dressed as a slave.

Thaïs stayed seated. 'My lover, the taxiarch Ptolemy,' she said in a matter-of-fact manner.

Both women curtsied again.

Bella brought Eurydike into the tent, and Thaïs gave her a big hug and a kiss, while Eurydike looked out from the safety of her mother's embrace at the two women. 'Ooh!' she said. 'Real princesses!' She had just begun to speak well. She was a little more than two, and she was never shy.

The two women laughed easily, and Barsines reached out for the child, who came to her quickly enough – an amazing thing, if you know children.

'You are blessed,' she said, touching our child.

Thaïs nodded.

Banugul turned to me. 'You wanted a son?' she asked.

I suppose that I frowned. I wanted Eurydike. I couldn't remember a time when I had wanted anything else. 'No,' I said.

'You *are* blessed,' Banugul said, in her seductress's voice. It wasn't human, that voice. It was the sound of man's desire for woman made flesh. But she was speaking to Thaïs.

And her sister kissed our daughter on the forehead. 'I never had a child by Memnon,' she said, with what sounded to me like genuine sadness. 'You are very brave. Yes?'

Thaïs shrugged.

Women can be such cats to each other. But these two seemed to be above such stuff. Barsines leaned forward. 'I was afraid to bear him,' she said. And then looked confused, because she had said too much. 'I loved him – too much.' She looked at the rug on the floor of the tent.

'Memnon?' Thaïs said. And I realised that she had killed this woman's husband – that Barsines, for all her seductive ways, had loved Memnon – it was graven on her face – and that Thaïs was just now understanding what every soldier learns – that every corpse you make had a sister and a brother and a wife and some children.

Eurydike had had enough of the strange princesses and came to me, and then raised her head. 'You smell,' she said. And giggled, aware that she was the centre of attention, and happy about it.

'And you will have another child,' Banugul said. She was openly curious. 'You, who were reputed to be as beautiful as we?'

Thaïs laughed aloud. Whatever she had been thinking, the sheer hubris of Banugul's comment didn't gall her – it amused her. 'I don't think I was ever as honey-golden-beautiful as you,' she said, coining a fine Greek word like any good poet. 'But I do hate being pregnant. And yet ...' She took Eurydike back. The child glowed, put her arms around Thaïs, and said 'Mummmmmy', in her too-cute-to-live little-girl voice.

Thaïs rolled her eyes, and all three women laughed.

'Beauty fades,' Thaïs said.

Barsines nodded. 'I try to make myself ready,' she said. 'Because I do love it.'

Banugul laughed. It was a laugh of bitterness.

Thaïs clutched her child. 'I'm sorry,' she said suddenly to Memnon's wife.

Barsines had tears in her eyes. 'Whatever for?' she asked.

She's sorry, now that you prove so human, that she killed your man, I thought.

The next day I donned a good chiton and military sandals and went to attend the king. He'd received a formal letter from the Great King of Persia. He presented it to us – a plain letter on good papyrus, not a purple parchment with golden ink, as I'd been led to expect by Herodotus, but such things are often exaggerated.

Darius referred to Alexander, not as a fellow king, but in a slighting manner, and asked for the return of his wife and mother and his eldest son, and he offered to cede to Alexander about a third of the empire. It was a curious letter, full of false pomp and oddly arrogant for a man who 'begged' for the return of his wife.

We debated the letter after a fine dinner, the way Athenians debate the role of love after a symposium. As you might expect, it broke down into an argument – a nasty argument – between the two factions. The older men, Philip's men, were for agreeing to its terms, and the younger men were for rejecting them out of hand. Despite the slowness of the siege, every one of us was sure we'd take the place. It would take time. But we were winning. The Persian Empire was beginning to shred itself – satraps were negotiating through Thaïs's people, or directly with our king. Athens continued to sit on the fence.

Alexander stayed carefully silent.

When everyone had had too much wine, Parmenio rose to his feet and raised his cup. 'If I were Alexander, great King of Macedon, I would accept this offer, and be done with war – victorious King of Asia.' He raised the cup and drank.

Alexander took the cup next and smiled into Parmenio's eyes. I thought for a moment that he meant the two of them to be reconciled.

He raised the cup. 'If I were Parmenio,' he said with careful malice, 'I would accept.' He drank the wine, and Parmenio's face flamed with humiliation.

I helped draft the letter to Darius. A group of us did – Hephaestion, Amyntas, Nearchus, who was down in our camp for a visit.

But Alexander set the tone.

'Your ancestors invaded Macedonia and the rest of Greece and did us harm although we had not done you any previous injury. I have been appointed commander-in-chief of the Greeks, and it is with the aim of punishing the Persians that I have crossed into Asia, since you are the aggressors. You gave support to the people of Perinthus, who had done my father harm, and Ochus sent a force to Thrace, which was under our rule. My father died at the hand of conspirators instigated by you, as you yourself boasted to everybody in your letters, you killed Arses with the help of Bagoas and gained your throne through unjust means, in defiance of Persian custom and doing wrong to the Persians. You sent unfriendly letters to the Greeks about me, to push them to war against me, and sent money to the Spartans and some other Greeks, which none of the other cities would accept apart from the Spartans. Your envoys corrupted my friends and sought to destroy the peace that I had established among the Greeks.

'I therefore led an expedition against you, and you started the quarrel. But now I have defeated in battle first your generals and satraps, and now you in person and your army, and by the grace of the gods I control the country. All those who fought on your side and did not die in battle but came over to me, I hold myself responsible for them; they are not on my side under duress but are taking part in the expedition of their own free will. Approach me therefore as the lord of all Asia. If you are afraid of suffering harm at my hands by coming in person, send some of your friends to receive proper assurances. Come to me to ask and receive your mother, your wife, your children and anything else you wish. Whatever you can persuade me to give shall be yours.

'In future whenever you communicate with me, send to me as King of Asia; do not write to me as an equal, but state your demands to the master of all your possessions. If not, I shall deal with you as a wrongdoer. If you wish to lay claim to the title of king, then stand your ground and fight for it; do not take to flight, as I shall pursue you wherever you may be.'

Humble, really. That was Alexander in full stride.

Outside, the mole got longer, and in his tent, Banugul, or Barsines, or Darius's wife – perhaps all three at once – lay on his couch.

TWENTY-FOUR

———

I spent a significant portion of my life at Tyre. None of it is in the Military Journal.

After about six weeks, the Tyrians saw what was going to happen, and they became active in their defence. They flooded the sea in front of the mole with small boats, and shot arrows into the work parties. Cleomenes took an arrow through the bicep, and Marsyas stood over him with a pair of nested wicker baskets and kept him from death, and they were friends again. Thank the gods, they'd been tiresome as enemies, and Thaïs's best efforts to reconcile them had failed on the twin rocks of pride and fatigue.

The next day, under fire, men from my taxeis, in full armour and with more men covering them with great hide-covered shields, erected two tall towers and built a wooden wall across the end of the mole. During the night we put heavy bolt-shooters into the towers, and by day the low wall was lined with Diades' own specialists, the bowmen carrying gastraphetes and oxybeles, two-man crossbows.

The next time the Tyrians came out in their boats, we shot them out of the water. It was very satisfying, but it didn't get the mole built, and now we had to push the towers forward every time we advanced the top of the mole any distance. That was harder than it sounds, and the towers had to be taken down in the dark and rebuilt, and Diades, who had the painful honesty of the professional engineer, reminded us that in a month we'd be in the range of their most powerful engines on the walls, and then they would be able to hit us while we worked and to cover their boats – and perhaps even batter down our towers.

Before that, however, the Tyrians tried their first serious sortie. They came at us in the dark. I wasn't on the wall – I was sound asleep in the arms of exhaustion. Thaïs was in her eighth month and slept in a separate tent with slaves fanning her all night.

There was a rumour that Banugul put on armour and served in the ranks.

The Tyrians sacrificed a pair of ancient triremes, filling them with flammables and ramming them ashore against the mole before setting them alight. Then they bombarded the mole with showers of hot sand and gravel – red hot, glowing hot – so that we couldn't fight the resulting fires.

I was awakened to light in the sky and screams. I slipped my sword belt over my head and ran for the head of the mole, with Isokles and Polystratus behind me. I ordered the taxeis to stand to, with phylarchs in armour and everyone else ready to work.

By the time I reached the mole, the end was an inferno. The Tyrians had packed those ships with oil and resin and old cloth and cedar. They burned so hot that they set the timber frame of the mole on fire, and it burned, and suddenly, about an hour before dawn, four weeks' work collapsed. The end of the mole simply fell away into the sea with a massive cloud of steam that cut off the stars and then an explosion as the superheated rocks of what had been the surface of the mole fell into the water and shattered.

There was *nothing* we could do.

In the morning, we looked out and the mole wasn't there any more. There were blackened timbers and occasional glimpses of rock. But we'd lost the work of two months in as many hours.

Alexander vanished into his tent. I didn't see him for a week, and during that week, I heard discouraging rumours. Then, as the clean-up was under way and Diades was replanning the framework of his mole, I was summoned to the king's side.

'Ptolemy!' Alexander said, as I entered. 'How well muscled you are. I see too little of you!'

False bonhomie was never a good sign, with Alexander.

'The mole takes all my time, lord,' I said.

'When we ride, I insist you ride with me so that we can catch up,' Alexander said, as if I didn't serve in his army. About what could we catch up? The minutiae of my taxeis?

'Are we to go hunting?' I asked.

Alexander bit his lip for a moment – then smiled. 'No – I've decided to give up the siege. It's dull, and it won't get us anywhere. Tyre is not that important a city – and if we build even a small fort here on the mainland, we can deny them the ability to forage on the mainland, and they won't be able to keep their fleet here, which is all I need.'

Well, I hated the siege, and I was considering just letting go, but I've never been good at keeping my mouth shut. 'They can keep their fleet supplied in Tyre,' I said. 'They're doing it right now. They just sail around us. Merchant shipping can keep them supplied.'

Alexander looked at me, and his mouth worked like a fish's.

Hephaestion glared at me. 'The king has made up his mind,' he announced.

I shrugged. 'Well, I could make an argument that we're screwed either way. If we march away, Darius can say we're beaten, and if we stay, we let Tyre soak up our efforts while Darius rebuilds his army.' I gave the king a mocking, lopsided smile. 'I know that I'd rather march away. Even if the siege is good for my physique.'

Alexander was looking at Hephaestion. Hephaestion was giving me his angry drama-queen look.

'They will use ships to resupply their ships,' Alexander said. 'And be astride my rear when I march into Aegypt.' He slumped. 'Curses on this place. If I take it, I'm going to kill every person in it, free or slave.'

I didn't like the sound of that – Alexander prided himself on being merciful.

We played dice for a while. And then we played Polis, and I entertained them with the tale of Marsyas and Cleomenes.

Hephaestion glowered. 'Women only bring trouble. There should be *none* with the army. Nasty creatures, that dull a man and sap his strength.'

That sounded personal.

Alexander made a face. 'Now, Hephaestion,' he said, gently reproving.

'If you spent less time between certain thighs, you'd be doing a better job prosecuting this siege.' Hephaestion was all but pouting.

I chuckled, because it was funny, and the two of them turned to me as if their heads were controlled by one string.

'It's true!' Hephaestion said, between anger and whining. 'Ask him where he was the night the mole burned? Eh? Ask him.'

There're times when it is best to think of another errand, but I was with the king, and I couldn't think of an excuse to leave.

Alexander turned to me. 'Do you think I'm avoiding my duties, Ptolemy?' he asked, his voice as mild as a mother's to a newborn.

What is the old joke? Have you beaten your wife, lately? Much the same.

'That is too serious an accusation, lord,' I said. 'And I wouldn't know. In fact, of the three of us, only *you* know whether you are fulfilling all your duties.' There – the biter bit, and all that. Aristotle would have been proud.

When I left the tent, there was a very pretty boy in perfumes and powders waiting in the anteroom. I gathered from a chance-heard comment that he was a pet of Barsines, come to beg the king to attend her for music.

There was, too, a eunuch from the Queen Mother of Persia, also waiting.

When I emerged into the full heat of day, I noted that there were at least a hundred men and women waiting outside the command compound for audiences with the king, and not one of them was anyone I knew – or anyone to do with the army. Most of them were vultures.

We must be winning, I remember thinking. We must be winning, because all these useless mouths are following us.

I related the whole scene to Thaïs, to pass the time, because she was in the eighth month and distinctly unhappy. I don't think any woman, no matter how well beloved, loves her heaviest month, and for Thaïs, one of the world's beauties, to have to face Barsines every morning over sherbet – Banugul on her way out to riding with the king ...

Thaïs was only human.

But that morning, I remember that she heard me out and sent for Barsines. I had no inkling of what she was after, so I went about my work.

It became clear in an hour that we needed a new source of timber and a great deal more rock. Helios showed me the numbers, and begged me to get Diades an audience with the king. Or even with Hephaestion.

Diades was afraid it was over. Everyone was.

I took both of them with me, picked up Perdiccas and Craterus for support, and marched the lot of them to Alexander's pavilions, where the hypaspitoi admitted us without delay.

Astibus caught up with me as we crossed the Aegema's parade square. 'He has the Persian slut with him,' he said. 'One of them. The Greek one.' He shrugged.

In fact, I'd have sworn that Astibus was jealous.

I brushed him off and we went to the door of Alexander's pavilion. Hephaestion was standing *outside*, which never happened. I made to speak to him, but he raised a hand brusquely, and then – lest I be offended – cupped his ear.

He was listening.

'I am not interested in your protestations of love,' Barsines said. The words floated out of the tent, and her magnificent voice was as hard as rock.

Alexander sounded plaintive – a tone of voice I had only ever heard him use with his mother. 'I seek only to please you,' he said.

She laughed. 'Then take Tyre,' she said.

Alexander was haughty. 'I will choose to take it or not to take it as my strategy dictates.'

'When a woman changes her mind on a whim, she does not pretend it is a strategy,' Barsines shot back.

'You go too far,' Alexander spat.

Gods, he sounded just like a man. Not at all like a god.

Even the sentries were smiling.

'You know nothing of war, nothing of strategy and nothing of how my mind works,' he continued.

Barsines' voice was a steel sword in a silk sheath. 'My lord, I know none of these things. I only know that *if my husband, Memnon, had set his mind to take this city, he would have taken it.*'

Silence fell.

After a long, long hundred heartbeats, the most beautiful woman on the face of earth swept by me. She flashed me a small smile.

I turned my party around and marched them back out of the royal precinct.

'Not a good time,' I suggested to Helios and Diades, who were both deeply shaken.

But several hours later, as I went over Helios's notes on wood consumption, Hephaestion poked his head into the command tent and grinned.

'Back on,' he said. He had the good grace to shake his head – he'd wanted to end the siege, but he was as much of a hero-mad fool as Alexander, and he did occasionally like to see the king taken down a peg.

And just like that, we were back to work.

We spent two weeks gathering new materials from new sources, and after the Athenian feast of Plunteria, we were back to work on the mole, and it went faster than before, because there was a broad base of gravel and rubble just below the surface to receive our work. It took us just two weeks to push the base of the mole out to where it had been before, and then we had a new enemy with which to contend. Because a stade short of the walls, the underwater ridge we'd used as the basis of our mole ran out, and we were now flinging rubble into deep water. It sank away out of sight, and after five days, we didn't see any change.

Divers measured the distance to the bottom and said that it was over ten man-heights deep.

Diades rode away for three days while we stockpiled baskets and rubble and large stones, and he returned, gathered all the oxen and rode away again with a large force of Hetaeroi.

We worked. Alexander worked with us, and Hephaestion. Parmenio took 'his' half of the army and marched away south to clear more coastline. There was a rumour that Alexander had ordered him north, to reconquer Ionia, and Parmenio had refused the duty. Thaïs was days from delivery, and she wasn't paying any attention at all.

Diades returned with four hundred great trees, all with their limbs and branches intact.

He had a plan, and it wasn't what I expected at all. I sent him fifty men with bronze axes, and he sent them back. And then, in one long day and night, he threw all four hundred trees into the water at the end of the mole.

And we levered several thousand talents of gravel and rubble on top of them.

The Tyrians pounded us with their machines, because we were within a stade of the wall. But despite the work of their machines, we got the trees in the water. We'd pin each one we put in with rubble, and then put in another. We worked fast, and men died – men were pinned in the water by trees, or pinned to the mole by arrows. When it got dark, we worked by firelight.

The Tyrians landed parties on the beach behind us in tar-blacked boats and killed men going with empty baskets for more rubble. But I had ordered my phylarchs to come out each night in armour, and Craterus and Perdiccas did the same, and after the third night, the rest of the phalanx taxiarchs did the same, and the enemy raids slackened off.

The fourth night after the trees went into the water, I was leading a work crew on the edge of the mole itself. Every night, Diades begged us to work one more night without the protection of siege towers. His reasoning was excellent – as long as we could keep it up, we had men working on the whole forward edge of the mole – perhaps a stades wide, or the width of a hundred men lying on their backs, head to toe. As soon as we put up the towers and the wall, everything slowed down, and we had all seen how the mole narrowed because men didn't like to work directly beneath the towers, which drew the most fire – so every few days, the width men worked got a little narrower. It was like tunnelling, in reverse.

The Tyrians came at us in boats – straight on. Thirty boats fired arrows into us – the thickest salvo of arrows yet, even in the dark, and my men fell. But another dozen boats full of marines rushed the head of the mole.

I had forty men in armour – all phylarchs, all veterans. I told the workmen to run as soon as I saw the boats come forward. Then the rest of us locked our shields.

It was ironic – in a deeply Olympian way – that we outnumbered

497

the Tyrians about fifteen to one, but that there on the mole, they out-numbered us at least ten to one.

I remember it because it was bad fighting on bad footing, but also because I gave one of my best battlefield speeches. Remember, they weren't all my men – we all took shifts, so I had men from every taxeis.

I said: 'Remember that every man you kill here cannot face you from the top of their wall when the mole is done. Remember that we have thirty thousand Macedonians behind us, and we have only to hold these bastards for five minutes and we'll have done a finer thing than any men have since the siege started. And remember,' I shouted, as the boats grated against the mole, 'that the only choice besides victory is death. I am betting victory is better!'

I received a heartening cheer. The worst feeling in the world is going into action with men who have no heart. These men cheered, and that gave the Tyrian marines pause. Then they started to form up.

'Charge!' I called to my own. Always better to be going forward, especially in the dark.

Our charge shattered them, even at odds of one to ten. About a third of them were out of their boats, and the arrows had stopped. What – did they think I'd just stand there and let them unload?

We crashed into the centre of their line, with only two ranks of our own. We didn't have sarissas – most men had a pair of javelins, and a few had longer spears, like the Greek dory. They were on the bad footing where the rubble was fresh, and we had them with their backs to the illumination of the fires they had lit on their own walls.

Speaking only for myself, I have seldom killed so many men in a single fight. The first man I faced flinched at the contact and I rammed my new kopis over his shield – had I mentioned my new kopis? – and into his helmet and he was dead. There's no coming back from that wound.

He fell off my sword and there were three of them facing me, but body posture said only one was a threat, so I put the knee of my greave down hard on the stone – one of the best reasons to wear greaves in a fight – and cut low. He cut high, and sheared my crest, and I cut right through his ankle bone and severed his foot and he screamed like a soul in torment – perhaps he was.

A really showy, brutal death can shake inexperienced troops, and that's what happened to the Tyrians. The men on either side flinched away and I followed them. One fell back, into the water, and the other missed his footing, slipped and got my kopis in his throat.

All along the front, my men had pushed the Tyrians into the water – literally. And there were corpses everywhere. I think I've said it before, but in a night fight, armour and discipline are everything, and we had more and better of both. These men were marines and lightly armed.

And they had no place to run.

When I saw that their centre was gone, I left the fight with Polystratus at my heels and half a dozen other men who could think on their feet, and we ran for the northern flank, where it seemed that the Tyrians had the upper hand. We hammered into the flank of their charge, a wedge of eight men, and it being dark they never saw us coming, so that each of us downed a man or two from behind before they knew what was happening – and then they ran, pure panic, given the circumstance. Armed Macedonians were pouring on to the mole, and for a few ugly moments we hunted them around the surface like so many rabbits in a field. And we killed every man who had made it on to the mole.

But while we were butchering their marines, the enemy engineers were putting grapples into our underwater trees and pulling as hard as they could, with ships and from the wall. As soon as they realised that we had slaughtered their marines, they started to pound the mole with thrown gravel and red-hot sand and fist-sized rocks. We were too thick on the mole and we took hits. Red-hot sand – even when it has crossed a stade of cool night air – is horrible – it burns into your skin, so that Thaïs had to pick each grain out with tweezers, and all of the skin infected, which in salt air is horrible enough.

But we were Macedonians, not cowards. I saw the ropes and felt the mole move, and Diades was there, and Helios – and Alexander. And Craterus and Philotas, and together we led men with axes forward into the hail of stone and sand. Hephaestion was badly burned, and Craterus took a stone to the shield that broke his arm – but we got two of the ropes cut, and then Alexander got hit, and it was all we could do to keep him alive.

Those moments – in the dark, with a helmet on my head, the haze of the red-hot sand as it fell, sometimes still twinkling, the steam from the fires and the salt water and the screams – Alexander down, and Craterus screaming – they seemed to go on for ever. I just held on, my shield pressed against his body, my head covering his head, as more shit fell on us. It would have to go through me to get to him. He was the King of Macedon, and he was not going to die here, in the dark.

Sometimes, the gods send me this moment in my dreams, and I am stuck there, for a long time. In a dream, as in reality, you can *tell* yourself that it will end. But you don't really *know* when it will end, and it seems to go on and on and on.

Then the hypaspitoi were coming up, and Bubores and Astibus came and dragged us off the king and got their shields over him, and we were all pulled clear of the killing zone. Alexander was alive, and virtually unhurt. I was covered in sand. The Tyrians mixed dog and pig shit into the sand to make it carry disease, and I missed the next month of the siege from the burns and the infection that came with them. Hephaestion was never quite so handsome again.

In fact, although I was screaming with the pain of my burns and didn't know it at the time, they got their grapples deeply into the trees and dragged several of them from under our rebuilt mole, and caused almost half of our new work to collapse. They also managed to burn the machines we'd built on the mole, and a separate group of raiders burned the towers where they sat on the shore ready for deployment.

As I say, I missed all that. My recovery was slow, and our second child was born dead – just as I was starting to recover. The pregnancy had not been a good one; Thaïs had been depressed, anxious and sick, and her delivery was painful and hurt her in more ways than just the loss of blood and tissue ...

And I was not really there to help. In fact, we were on two beds next to each other for a week. I was aware that she was hurt. But that was about all I could manage.

My fever broke eventually. I had lost a lot of muscle and a lot of weight, and my beloved was lying in a bed next to me, with a fever so hot you could feel her body from an arm's length away. I fussed about uselessly, got in the way of Philip of Acarnia and a pair of midwives who were actually trying to help her, and eventually stumbled out of the tent into the brilliant sunshine of a late summer day in Syria.

Isokles found me immediately, and took me by the hand.

'We were worried about you,' he said. He gave me a wry smile, as if that was too much of a compliment and he thought I might bite him. 'Hey – I'm an Athenian in a Macedonian army. No one likes me when you aren't around. Except Kineas – and we try not to spend too much time together. It's like committing adultery. You don't want to give people ideas. Actually, it's more like *not* committing adultery, but having your wife suspect you anyway.'

We walked from the officers' lines across the camp. There was a heavy series of dust clouds running away north and east.

'More trees?' I asked. The dust made me cough, and the light made me blink and I was already tired. Everything seemed odd – off kilter. I'd been wounded before, but the hot sand – and the infection – was different. I felt weak.

Craterus was directing operations on the mole, and he embraced me carefully. 'How are the burns?' he said. 'Lucky for you – you never had any looks to lose.' He laughed.

People say the damnedest things.

He shrugged. 'Hephaestion got sand all over his face,' he said.

Then I understood.

I looked at the mole. There were four towers across the far end, and from where I stood in the heat shimmer, it seemed to be touching the walls of the city.

'But we're there!' I said.

Craterus shook his head. 'We haven't made a yard in the last week. Rebuilding was hard enough. Alexander marched away, and both Hephaestion and Barsines taunted him for cowardice.'

I looked around. 'I would like to have seen that,' I said quietly.

Craterus shook his head. 'No, you wouldn't. Anyway, Diades kept us at it, and we rebuilt what we lost. But now there's a deep channel – so deep our divers can't find the bottom, and we've dumped … I have to think. Ten thousand talents of gravel? More? And trees, dirt, huge boulders—'

'Where's the king?' I asked.

None of the officers on the mole would meet my eyes. 'Hunting,' Isokles said; because he was an Athenian, he didn't have to care.

'Hunting? As in, not here?' I asked.

Men nodded.

'Ares' spear!' I cursed. 'With Barsines?'

'Barsines is tending to Hephaestion,' Craterus said, with a world-weary grin.

And then I fainted.

It was three more days before I left my tent again. I couldn't take a great deal of sun, because of the burns on my head and arms. So I sat with Thaïs, whose fever had broken, fed her tea and learned a little about embroidery. I read to her – at first, the *Iliad*. But after a day, she looked at me, gave me a wonderful, sad smile and said, 'No more war, love. Not the *Iliad*. I'm … living in the *Iliad*. And it isn't so beautiful, from inside.' She drank some iced water – provided by Philip.

So I began on the plays of Aristophanes, and we laughed ourselves silly over *Lysistrata*, the more so as Thaïs claimed descent from the lady herself – the high priestess of Athena in Socrates' time. Laughter heals, too.

We were laughing – we'd just read:

Lysistrata: *By the holy goddesses! You'll have to make acquaintance with four companies of women, ready for the fray and well armed to boot.*
Magistrate: *Forward, Scythians, and bind them!*

Lysistrata: *Forward, my gallant companions; march forth, ye vendors of grain and eggs, garlic and vegetables, keepers of taverns and bakeries, wrench and strike and tear; come, a torrent of invective and insult! (They beat the officers.) Enough, enough! Now retire, never rob the vanquished!*

Magistrate: *Here's a fine exploit for my officers!*

Lysistrata: *Ah, ha! So you thought you had only to do with a set of slave-women! You did not know the ardour that fills the bosom of free-born dames.*

Magistrate: *Ardour! Yes, by Apollo, ardour enough – especially for the wine-cup!*

And for various reasons, the magistrate (that would be me) was laughing too hard to attend to the door of the tent, and the king came in.

Thaïs stopped laughing. Her look made me glance over my shoulder.

Alexander was angry.

'In all my camp, there are only two voices laughing,' he said. His voice was like ice, and his disdain was obvious. 'And I find you reading that hateful play. Disgusting.'

I had to laugh.

His face flamed.

'Is it hateful because it is *against war*?' I asked.

'Perhaps,' Thaïs said, 'it is the notion of women seizing political power?'

Alexander ignored her. 'If you are well enough to read to her,' he said, 'you can be with your troops.'

'Oh, I'm a well-known malingerer,' I shot back. 'I just lie around avoiding my duty, eh?'

It occurred to me that if I was sick and Hephaestion was wounded and Nearchus was up north ruling Lycia, there was *no one* supporting the king. Or keeping him out of trouble.

Alexander was so angry that I knew he would say anything – *anything* – to make me hurt. That's how he was, when the darkness came on him.

'Since this bitch came into your life, you have more time for her than for your duty,' he said.

'Is that what Hephaestion said to you about Darius's wife? Or was it about Memnon's women? I can't remember.' I smiled. I was good at this – I'd known him since birth, and if he wanted to trade insults, I was happy to oblige. 'And how is Barsines? Or is it Banugul this week?'

He hit me. It took me by surprise and I crumpled into Thaïs's chair, and the chair broke under us.

The left side of my face, where his blow landed, was where I'd got a patch of sand – so it was pebbly, shiny and painful. His punch sloughed off some flesh and I began to bleed.

Alexander stood there, and all the life seemed to go out of his eyes. His shoulders slumped.

I stood up and got Thaïs on to the bed. He turned and strode out of the tent. As soon as I saw that Thaïs was well enough, I pushed my feet into boots and followed him, pushing past Ochrid where he stood with some cowering slaves, throwing a light chlamys over my shoulder. It was hot – Thaïs and I had been sitting naked.

He was moving fast, headed for his own tent. Once there, he would, I suspected, order the hypaspitoi not to admit anyone, and go into the dark.

So I ran. I called his name – once, and then again, and heads turned all over the camp.

He all but ran away from me. He pulled a corner of his cloak over his head and got in between his guards, and Alectus stopped him, clearly meaning to ask him something – the password of the day, no doubt.

I came up.

'Alexander!' I shouted at him from an arm's length away.

'Do not admit that man!' Alexander yelled.

I pushed right past the spears. Alectus was utterly loyal – and used enough to the wonderful ways of Macedon that I'm sure he saw me as capable of regicide. So he drew his sword and put himself between me and Alexander.

'By Olympian Zeus, lord over kings and men, Alexander, if you do not turn and speak to me, I will go home to Macedon and leave you here!' I shouted at his back.

He paused.

'I will apologise,' I said. 'You should too.' I paused. 'You will feel better if you do.'

He turned. 'Why don't you say that I *must* apologise?' he asked, his voice crabbed with disjointed emotion. 'Tell me!' he insisted.

I shrugged, through Alectus's sword. 'You are the king. No one can *make* you apologise.'

Alexander let his cloak fall from his head. He stood up straighter. But he couldn't meet my eye. 'It was unworthy of me to ... hit a wounded man.'

I laughed in his face, pushed past Alectus, who didn't know what to make of us, and threw my arms around him. 'That is the lamest apology I've ever heard,' I said. 'I am sorry that you are in such a piss-poor mood that you had to come to my tent and vent your spleen on a wounded man and his mistress – both of whom have served you loyally every day for many years.'

He struggled to be offended. I could see it on his face. But my embrace enfolded him, and it is very difficult to be really angry with someone who is holding you. Try it.

I was, however, waiting to feel Alectus's steel grate against my spine. It may have looked as if I was rushing the king. Darius had put ten thousand talents of gold on his head.

Many loyalties were being tried at the same time.

But suddenly, his arms were pounding my back, and he was crying. We stumbled a little, as men will do when locked in an embrace, and he cried on my shoulder, and I ... looked over his.

I was in his private tent, of course, not his receiving tent. And there was the table he used as his desk, and on it was a letter written in golden ink on purple paper. I didn't have to be a genius to realise that this had to be the original of Darius's letter. Nor did I have to be a scribe to be able to read the first three lines, in which Darius greeted Alexander as 'My brother, the King of Asia'.

Alexander began to make tearful apologies to me – for claiming that I was malingering, for causing me to fall on Thaïs, for a host of things for which he suddenly felt the urge to apologise. But he didn't mention that he had falsified the letter from Darius. As I read it over his shoulder, I realised that the forged letter – for surely this was the real one – left me not angry but curiously empty.

Alexander means to fight for ever. I had never formulated the thought before, but here, in his arms, in his tent, I realised that it was not a simple pothos – he was not fighting to be lord of Asia, or King of Kings. He was fighting because war made him something that peace could never make him. What he wanted was war.

Not conquest.

Merely ... war.

I accepted his apologies and made some of my own, my daimon all but extinguished by the same realisation that many of my pezhetaeroi had made months before.

There would be no end.

TWENTY-FIVE

t took me two further weeks of training to get enough meat on my
bones to consider leading men in combat. I wrestled with Meleager,
fenced with Craterus and practised hoplomachia with Isokles, who
had charged fees to train men in the armoured fighting when he was a
young man in Athens, and was truly expert. Meleager was older than
I and no great wrestler, and he took it ill when I threw him so that I
needed a new companion, and I took to wrestling with Kineas's friend
Diodorus, who was a fine wrestler and a good weight for me – then
and even now, though I've gained weight and he's stayed slim, the
bastard!

I noticed – perhaps because an illness is like a visit to another country
– as I say, I noticed on my return to duty that there were changes
throughout the army, and some of them were deep – some were changes
in individuals and some were changes in the whole identity.

I think that Meleager was my key to the whole set of changes. He and
I had never been friends, particularly, but we had got on well enough,
and when I found that he had set up his pavilion near mine and liked
to get his exercise at the rising of the sun, I thought it natural that we
exercise together. But after a few mornings, he made excuses and began
to exercise elsewhere. The man I had known ten years before – my
superior, I would add – would have cared nothing for a little sand in
his face – or would have offered to box with me, or fight with sticks or
clubs and arms wrapped in our chalmyses until I was black and blue.
But the older, more powerful Meleager didn't want to take risks. Or if
he did take risks, he wanted to take them under different circumstances.
There was no 'private exercise' for Meleager. He was a public man. He
cared deeply whether his subordinates saw him thrown to the earth.

My second lesson in this change was several days later, after my first
bout with Diodorus. I was wiping the sand from my face – Diodorus
threw me quite regularly, until I gained some muscle and some much-
needed skill – and Craterus, who watched us, took me aside.

'Do you think,' he asked me cautiously, 'that you are wise to let men see you be bested by an Athenian?'

I spat sand, and shook my head. 'Herakles was a fucking Theban, and I'm pretty sure he'd put my head in the sand, too. And I'm pretty sure men would cheer.' I gave him my best farm-boy grin. 'No one minds if I get thrown. Who cares? It's what I do when the bronze is shining that matters, isn't it?'

Craterus smiled, and that smile was false. 'Oh – of course. Absolutely.' He withdrew, and I saw that we had changed as a group. We were keeping up appearances.

But the siege of Tyre was not about appearances, thank the gods, and by now we had machines on the end of the mole, throwing stones as big as my head – two a minute, all day, and a rank of spare machines ready for whenever the brilliant engineers on the other side managed to destroy one of ours.

Summer was becoming autumn, and the feel of the breeze had changed when I went back into the line. It was a late summer evening, and the heat of the day seemed to flow upward into the sky, and the breeze that came with the setting of the sun was like balm on wounds, and seemed to blow right through my leather-backed shirt of scales to cool my body.

I was right forward, in the line of engines, watching the teams load and loose them with a terrible precision, when there were cries – and screams – from the forward edge of the mole, and I assumed we were under attack. By this time, Alexander had forced virtually the entire servile population of Syria into our work crews, because so many slaves had died at the hands of the Tyrians – perhaps, by this time, as many as fifteen thousand or more. I had been told that armed soldiers were required now to whip the slaves forward with their loads, and to kill any who attempted to desert. And I was told that soldiers no longer worked on the mole – only slaves.

No wonder we'd slowed to a crawl. Slaves love work the way a rat loves a cat.

At any rate, I went forward with fifty men as the slaves fled in panic, shouting in five languages – Greek, Aramaic, Syriac, Phoenician and Persian. I couldn't understand them, so I pushed a few into the water as I shoved my men forward through the machine line and then past the towers – four towers, now.

I made it to the very end of the mole, and came to an abrupt halt. The Tyrians were casting red-hot sand, and the smell of it – the look of it in the air – almost made me puke.

But what I saw was far, far more horrible and awe-inspiring than red-hot sand.

There was a sea monster.

It was enormous – as long as five men. Perhaps as long as ten men. A day after the event, I had a hard time recalling exactly what the monster looked like, although hundreds of us saw it. Even as I watched, this spawn of Poseidon seemed to throw itself on to the mole. Its enormous teeth seized a slave who stood rooted in fear, and he was gone – dismembered and stripped to bloody fragments – by those rows of teeth in less time than it takes to tell it.

I was the next man closest.

I'm told that I bellowed the name of Poseidon. Good for me – all I wanted to do was get my head under the covers and wet myself.

But I saw its eye. And it saw me. Something passed – something old, something incredibly alien. And yet, it *saw* me. I swear to you, in that moment, I was changed by the regard of a god. An old sea god, perhaps disturbed by our mole – perhaps merely investigating the latest piece of human hubris. One of Triton's offspring, or one of Amphytrites', perhaps. Some bastard child of Thetis of the glistening breasts, or perhaps some titan sent to the water for some long-forgotten crime, but that god was older than man. It was in his eyes, the way you can see all the horror and torment and combat a veteran has seen in one blink, sometimes, eh? You know what I mean. *It was there.*

I like to think it was a true son of Poseidon, a mighty hero of the deep. I like to think that, because he *nudged* me aside with his face, rather than ripping me to shreds with the mighty engine of his rows of teeth – nudged me, rolled a little and slid effortlessly back into the water, and vanished into the deep next to the mole.

There was a pause, for as long as a man's heart might beat sixty or eighty times. The world was silent.

And then the Tyrians began to loose their engines at me.

They missed.

We spent weeks discussing the sea monster. No two men saw the same thing, and of those who saw it, every man had a different theory of what it was and, more importantly, what it portended. Alexander's seer declared that it was a god, Poseidon's only son, and he came to show us the way into Tyre.

Well, I don't have much time for his ilk, and even though his prognostications fitted my own desires, I didn't like him any better for them. Alexander had *not* seen the monster, and seemed curiously dismissive of the event.

When I told Thaïs of this, she smiled. 'He doesn't believe there's room at this siege for more than one god,' she said.

She had not returned to her former work collecting information since her delivery. She wouldn't discuss it with me, but more and more her work devolved on Callisthenes and his people. It was interesting to see the difference. She had started her work to please me and to help Alexander, and had based her collection of information on the wide circle of her friends and former lovers and partners and clients – and the Pythia.

Callisthenes used Aristotle's circle of friends, for, as Thaïs said nastily, he had none of his own. But he was more inclined than she had ever been to spend money on information, and he was less interested in examining it, weighing it and measuring it before he sent it on to Alexander. Or rather – and we saw this almost immediately – his principal interest was information that fitted seamlessly with his own worldview and his own expectations. And Alexander's.

In just a few weeks, Alexander's view of the world began to narrow perceptively.

Ironically, in the way that the gods move, Thaïs's last great triumph came in such a way that Alexander was made to realise what he had lost. A few days after the sea monster, I went into my pavilion to find Thaïs deep in conversation with a handsome, older man with a salt-and-pepper beard and large blue eyes. He wasn't tall, but had a magnificent bearing, and he sat in my tent as if he owned it. I was prepared to hate him on the spot, but he rose graciously, took my hand and thanked me courteously for his wine and the use of my couch.

He was, in fact, the King of Cyprus – absolute ruler of more than one hundred triremes. Thaïs had been making overtures to him for more than a year, and like a fisherman with a small boat who catches a big tuna, she'd spent all that time bringing him carefully ashore.

I was sent for by the king. He was sitting with Callisthenes, getting the news of the world. I loathed Callisthenes, who neither told the king the truth nor managed to be a decent lickspittle, but played both harlot and harridan. But he paid in the end. He was a poor philosopher and a sad comment on Aristotle, although I've heard men say that Theophrastus was Aristotle's real favourite, although no blood relation. Perhaps.

To me, though, Callisthenes, even at the height of his power with the king, was a paid foreigner, not a soldier or a man of account in any way. So I brushed past his protests and crooked my finger at the king. 'A matter of some urgency,' I said quietly.

Callisthenes stood up.

'Just the king,' I said to him.

'Who is it that sends for me?' Alexander asked.

'Thaïs,' I said. 'A matter of some urgency. And delicacy.'

Callisthenes shrugged. 'Oh, then I *must* come,' he said. 'Anything of hers is my business.'

I caught Alexander's eye, and he nodded. 'No,' he said to Callisthenes. 'Wait here.'

We walked out together. I ignored Callisthenes' outrage – I cared little for him then, or ever. As soon as we were clear of the guards, I said, 'Thaïs has won over the King of Cyprus. He's in my tent. He wants only your word on certain matters, and his whole fleet is at our service.'

Alexander stopped, looked at me and then gave me a brief embrace that hurt my burns. 'A fleet!' he said. 'By the gods! Poseidon's gift! A fleet!'

He went swiftly to my tent, embraced the King of Cyprus and the thing was done.

Afterwards, and many times, Callisthenes claimed that he had *turned* the King of Cyprus.

And it was the last political act of Thaïs's life for a long while.

The Cypriot fleet changed everything. Alexander kept it hidden, up the coast, and put Craterus's taxeis aboard as marines, and went aboard himself. Several evenings later, another beautiful late-summer evening, and the Tyrians descended on the end of the mole with fifty boats, grappling hooks and a barrage of covering fire from their engines on their walls.

Alexander sprang his trap, and the Cypriot fleet raced for the entrance to Tyre's island port – a passage the length of a trireme wide, between two enormous stone towers bristling with engines.

We cheered like madmen as the king's galley raced into the setting sun, but the Tyrians were canny, and they fled from the mole. We only took five of their ships, but dozens of their marines were left on the mole in the panic, and we killed every one of them.

At the command meeting later that night, I pointed out that neither of the towers had loosed so much as a rock at our ships.

'The towers were empty,' I asserted, and Diades nodded. And thumped my back.

The Tyrians were running low on men. Or rather, when they put fifty ships to sea with full rowing benches, that stripped their manpower.

And what that meant was that their fleet would never dare put to sea again. We had mastery of the sea.

Diades and Alexander put it to use that very night.

Boat raids. Twenty men in the bow of a trireme, or five men in a smaller boat, rowed up to the walls, attached grapples and the crew of the trireme tried, by rowing away, to force a section of wall to collapse. In other places we set fires, or tried to scale the wall.

Helios refitted pairs of triremes with huge platforms between them – like monster catamarans – mounting large siege engines. We'd done this at Halicarnassus, and now he did it on a larger scale. We built six of them, floated them and parked them opposite the weakest portion of the wall, just about a quarter of the circuit around the wall from the mole. In two days, they brought a section of wall down. We boarded ships for an assault, but the weather worsened and we had to abandon the idea, and the next day they had rebuilt the wall.

Two more days of pounding away, and we had to rebuild all of the engines on the ships while the enemy rebuilt their wall. And then we were at it again, and with a rush, their whole line of new masonry went down, despite hoardings, and the cover of great oxhides and a dozen other contrivances.

That afternoon, however, a pair of Cypriot triremes ran across a pair of Carthaginian triremes and they fought each other to near extinction. One of the Carthaginians limped away, and both of the Cypriot vessels were turtled, although both were reclaimed later and restored to service.

Now Alexander had to fear the appearance of a great Carthaginian fleet. We might lose our mastery of the sea at any moment. The mole was pressed forward. A man could almost jump the gap. The fleet was brought in close, and Diades had four of the oldest triremes brought up to the mole so that they could be filled with stones and sunk in the channel to act as piers for his mole.

But that night, a storm hit us like no other I had experienced. It lasted three days, and every tent in the camp blew flat. I had to rescue Thaïs, still weak from the loss of our child and still so depressed that she would take little or no action to save herself. I moved her to Isokles' tent, and then, moments later, that too collapsed and I had to lift her out through more sodden silk and canvas.

The next day was no better, and the only standing shelters in the camp were the ones built from lashed boat sails spread over heavy timbers – and tied down by sailors. And that night, when the storm hit its height, even those fell, and we huddled together, taxiarchs and strategoi and pezhetaeroi and slaves, all together in our shared fear and misery. The gods have the ability to make one feel very small, when they wish. A good storm is humbling.

When we awoke on the third day, I followed Diades down to the shore to see what had happened.

The mole was gone.

Perhaps that is an exaggeration. Certainly, the sea was breaking over something, so the bulk of the earth and wood was still there, but the sea flowed over it, and it was enough to break your heart. His precious ships – full of stones, ready to be moved into position – were all gone, capsized and sunk in shallow water north of the mole.

'Poseidon's fury,' he said.

'And now we have it all to do again,' I said.

Diades shrugged. 'I have already stockpiled more stone than we had when we started,' he said, with a grim smile. 'It will go faster this time. But only if the king does not despair.'

That night, we had the stormiest command meeting I can remember.

The factions were fully developed. Parmenio, his sons and the older officers – men like Meleager who owed their careers to Parmenio, and men who were midland Macedonian landowners – and men who were tired of war.

The truth is, I should have been with Parmenio's faction. I knew what was in the king's mind. An abyss of endless war – a sort of infinite *Iliad*, with himself cast as Achilles, where an endless procession of enemies threw themselves on his heroism and his genius – and perished.

The other faction was no longer the 'Young Men'. We were no longer so young – no man faces battle eight or ten times and counts himself young. Perdiccas and I – to name two – had the scars of men twice our age. My shoulder hurt as if pierced with ice every time the weather changed, and my hands – I awoke every morning, at age twenty-six, winter or summer, with hands that hurt enough that I often had to warm them in hot water before I could make them obey me.

This is not the life of a 'young man'.

What distinguished us from Parmenio's party was that we loved the king, and had grown to adulthood with him. It is not that he could do no wrong – indeed, the paradox was that we were the ones who expressed our doubts openly to Alexander.

That night after the storm, Parmenio and Alexander locked horns like two bulls.

'We have stood here for seven months, and we have nothing to show for it.' Parmenio didn't trouble to hide his contempt. 'I told you that we couldn't take the city. We cannot take it. We have lost a year's worth of gains and all the treasure of Issus – squandered to take this pile of rock.'

Alexander was at his most difficult – conceding nothing, absolute in his righteousness. He simply smiled. 'Anyone else?' he asked.

Philotas stood. 'Lord, there is no point – if we start the mole again, we'll face another disaster and another. For what? We don't need the city. The strategy of taking every sea base on the coast is no longer valid – it is now we who have the larger fleet.'

Alexander's smile was fixed. 'I asked if anyone else wanted to speak,' he drawled.

Philotas's face flamed. 'My father has led your armies and won your battles, lord. Your treatment of him is ungrateful and mean!'

Alexander nodded. 'Let us stick to the matter at hand,' he said.

Amyntas, the current favourite, rose to his feet. 'We can take Tyre in four more weeks. Given the time we've put in, and the treasure, as Lord Parmenio has so eloquently put it, should we not finish what we started?'

Alexander's expression did not change.

Parmenio glared at him. 'Why don't you speak your own view, Alexander? Instead of letting your "friends" do it for you?'

Alexander shrugged, every muscle in his body speaking contempt. 'I am the captain general, and I will speak last.'

Parmenio crossed his arms.

'Craterus?' Alexander said.

Craterus looked at the carpeted floor of the tent. 'Let us march away. Let us march *home*.'

Alexander looked at me. 'Perdiccas?' he asked.

Perdiccas looked at me, as well. He made me feel like a ringleader. A role I did not fancy. 'Lord, I will stand with you whatever you choose.'

'As if I would not?' shouted Nicanor, son of Parmenio. 'By Zeus who judges all oaths, I swear that none of us have suggested that we will not follow the king! How dare you suggest such a thing?'

'Meleager?' Alexander said, but his eyes were still on me.

Meleager mumbled something.

'Speak up!' Alexander spat, sounding very like a hoplomachos on a drill field.

Meleager took a deep breath. 'Finish the siege,' he said.

Parmenio looked like thunder.

Alexander's eyes flicked back and forth in surprise. I was surprised too. I no longer had to cast the tying vote, to allow Alexander to settle the issue. Which he clearly wanted. Now my vote would decide the issue. Not that, as king, he couldn't just order us to do it. The democracy of the council was more apparent than real.

Alexander nodded to me. 'Ptolemy?' he said.

'Finish the siege,' I said. Not because I believed in it, but because I was his friend.

Diades went to work immediately, the next day, and from our 'stores' of rubble and rock, we rebuilt the mole in two weeks. We had ships to cover the head of the mole and ships to move bulk rubble and ships with engines to attack the enemy batteries, and the coordination of the ships grew better every day.

Diades built superstructures for the ships so that a pair of triremes, lashed together, could hold a tower with ladders inside – the assault troops protected by wet hides and wooden hoardings.

In days, we had our own engines clearing the wall from the end of the mole.

In a week, the city must have seen that the end was near.

Two weeks to the day after the storm, a pair of Cypriot cruisers picked up a Carthaginian trireme that failed to outrun them. The ship carried a message, sealed in a bladder.

No further help was coming to Tyre.

We shot the message into the walls, and that night, in a brilliant piece of seamanship, the Cypriots sank two old triremes in the deep-water gap – both full to the gunwales with rocks. The next night, under a protective hail of stones, they performed this feat again.

Six engine ships pounded the southern walls day and night, turning every repair to rubble. Sixteen engines on the mole launched larger stones at a shorter range, so that the tallest walls on the island, those facing the land, began to crumple under the weight. Alexander was heard to joke that at the rate we were throwing stones, we were raising the level of the city and providing them with years of building material.

On the feast of Herakles, Hephaestion donned armour for the first time in a month, and we cheered him. And then we boarded assault boats and the trireme pairs with the great scaling towers.

I took the picked men of my taxeis – two hundred men in the best armour we could scrounge – and we boarded two pairs and filled the decks and the towers. Remember, a trireme ordinarily carried ten, or at most twenty, marines. With the double hulls and the towers, we could carry a hundred, but it made the ships ponderous and very, very slow. We needed near-perfect calm and bright moonlight to move and assault.

Alexander had chosen to lead the assault from the mole. The sea was never his element.

The first fight after a wound is always hard, like getting back on a horse that has thrown you. At the head of my ladder, swaying wildly, or so it seemed to me at the very top of a tower between two big ships, I had hours to consider the feel of the red-hot sand as it poured down my body and was trapped against me by my own armour, and the smell as my flesh scorched, and the feel of heavy rocks on my shield, on my helmet, on my thorax.

The sea stank with eight months of refuse, garbage and human filth from the siege – uncollected corpses, offal, carcasses from all the sacrifices, excrement. The enemy engines were loosing as fast as they could be loaded, and we could hear as heavy rocks or long spears struck our ship, and once, quite early in our manoeuvring, a ballista bolt tore through the hide covering and killed three men where they waited on the ladders. There was shouting, screaming and, in the distance, the constant sound of massed prayers – hymns to Melkart. Thirty thousand voices singing together – an eerie sound.

About midnight, all of our engine ships began to launch all together. First they threw baskets of heavy gravel to clear the walls, and then multiple salvos of great rocks, chipped round by slaves, and then more gravel.

By that time, my ship was quite close, and I could see individual men on the walls. And they could see us.

A disc – like an aspis, but flung sideways so that it spun, and full of red-hot sand and burning dung – hit our tower. The sand fell harmlessly into the sea with a hiss and a burst of steam, but the burning shit stuck to the hides and they steamed.

When I peeked over the top of the tower, I could see that we were coming up against a pair of huge wooden wheels with paddles attached, almost like mill wheels placed on their sides. They turned very fast, and even as I watched, a huge bolt struck one – and was deflected by the rotation of the wheel and the struts.

But a heavy rock from one of the distant catapults struck the wheel edge on – as if striking the top of a chariot wheel's tyre – and something gave. The wheel began to break up as it turned – pieces of wood showered off it like sparks off a sharpening stone.

By the will of the gods or ill luck, my tower would be the first to reach the walls. Despite all the engines throwing rocks, the hail of small stones and all the fire being cast, the fires burning in the city beyond and the ships afire under the walls – despite all of it, the enemy had gathered a large force where my tower would reach the wall – more men than I could count.

A wind blew a charnel-house stench – hot with furnace air from the fires in the city – over our faces, and then our tower took another direct hit from one of the discs full of hot sand, and the hides burst into flame, and archers on the walls immediately began to sweep the tower. We were a horse length from the wall – less every heartbeat. Men on the wall with huge tridents mounted on gimbals stabbed them through the leather walls of the tower and into the troops waiting inside, causing panic on the ladders.

We had six archers at the head of the steps – Cretans armed with longbows. They stepped out on to the platform of our tower and in that moment I thought that they were the bravest men I'd ever seen – unarmoured, facing all that fire.

They flicked arrows down on to the wall faster than I can tell it – the smallest of them was the finest archer, and he emptied his quiver before we reached the wall. Two of them were hit, but they struck back – they made me feel better, because we weren't just standing or crouching and taking hits, we were killing the enemy, as well.

It was all I could do to hold my sword. I had a pair of heavy javelins, and when the tower touched the wall, I cut the cord that held the great gate and it fell across the gap, giving us a ramp *down* into the enemy defences.

I was hit twice before I got on to the wall – both stones, probably our own, and one all but knocked me senseless – and that after hitting my crest. A big rock. But I was *on the wall* and I threw my javelins – I don't even remember throwing them, just that my right hand was suddenly empty – and I snatched my sword and moved against the nearest tower.

One of my phylarchs fell victim to a bucket of red-hot sand and died horribly, screaming and thrashing, and he pushed men off the wall. Another phylarch cut left and right – cut beautifully with his kopis, dealing death, but a defender caught him with an axe, a murderous weapon, and the blade went in at his neck and cut through to his crotch, so that he opened like some evil flower and his guts exploded on the men around him, who flinched and died.

The defenders were not beaten. They gave us the wall, or rather, the pile of rubble that had been the wall. Behind it, they had a second wall, about the width of a street – like Memnon's trap at Halicarnassus, and I had fallen for it. I went to the edge of the breach and shouted for ladders. We had them, lying along the planking of the upper deck, lashed to the gunwales.

I felt my men were being sluggish coming up the ladders.

I remember roaring, 'Damn it, come on!' at the ladder men, and then I took a blow to the back and I was fighting for my life against a counter-attack. There were very few Macedonians alive on the rubble of the outer wall. The first fighting had gone against us.

But then the Tyrians made an error. Whether on purpose or because of a misunderstood order, their engines swept the wall with stones and red-hot sand. Their own men took the bulk of the punishment, and their own reinforcements refused to come at us. By the will of the gods, none of the eight or nine of us holding the breach open was hit.

My men were just as unwilling to come up those ladders. There were corpses all through the ship – our pair of vessels, as the first in, had drawn more than our fair share of missiles, and men had to climb over the wreckage of former men to get up the towers. That's always hard. And some men had gone for more ladders, and then used that as an excuse to stay below.

There was a huge cheer from the centre of the city, and then another cheer from the mole – whether ours or theirs I couldn't tell.

The fighting in the breach was sporadic, deadly and man to man. A few Macedonians continued to join us from the ship. I was exhausted by the time I realised that the tide had turned at the top of the ladders, and that we now held the breach in strength.

Isokles found me in the dark. 'Lads don't like this a bit,' he shouted. 'We need to go forward!'

Some brave men had come up the outside of the tower with two ladders – plain scaling ladders – and we put them against the new wall from the breach, with archers in towers virtually all around us shooting down into us. But we got the ladders up and we went up them. I led the way. It is my job.

I was first up the first ladder on the inner wall, and two big men tried to push the ladder over with tridents, but my men were pressing against the base of the ladder. The ladder itself bent and groaned, and I raced up it as fast as my arms and legs would carry me, and I didn't wait on the ladder to make my cut – I jumped in between them and cut back and forth – low is always better in the dark, although low cuts are an invitation to a head-cut counter in daylight. And then more or more men were beside me on the wall – Isokles, and Polystratus, and Cleomenes.

We heard more cheers – and they were absolutely *not* Macedonian cheers – coming from the direction of the mole.

I looked back and saw that the second ladder/tower ship had been sunk where it had rested on the waves, and that a pair of triremes were rescuing the rowers and marines. That meant we would not have a second wave.

The Tyrians rushed us. We had about sixty men on the inner wall, but we were between two towers and we didn't have anywhere to hide. They shot us with arrows and then charged, but they'd left it too long and we were ready, and we blunted their attack with javelins and then gutted them as they came up the inner face of the wall.

I turned to Isokles, but he was dead at my feet. So I looked for Cleomenes and shouted, 'Time to go!'

The pezhetaeroi caught my meaning immediately. Most of us didn't wait for the ladder – we jumped down into the breach, because a turned ankle was a small price to pay for your life, and then we fled down the tower ladders to the ship below. Cleomenes and I managed to get Isokles' corpse between us – we threw it down into the breach and then carried him down into the tower, the last men off the wall.

Of two hundred men I took up the ladders, I lost fifty, including four phylarchs and Isokles.

And we lost.

The next day, in camp, you could feel the burning hatred, the dull, red-hot resentment.

No one spoke of abandoning the siege. From the pezhetaeroi to the hypaspitoi to the Agrianians to Alexander himself, what every man wanted was revenge. But there was little love for the king.

That night, Hephaestion invited me to take wine with him and of course, Alexander was there, with Amyntas and Nicanor son of Parmenio, which I took for a positive sign.

'Welcome back to the land of the living,' I said to Hephaestion.

His arm was in a sling. He pointed at it and said, 'I should have waited another day.'

Alexander shook his head. 'Patroclus would never say such a thing. You were brilliant on the wall, my friend. We simply needed ten more like you.' He shrugged at me. 'We almost died. Men were slow up the ladders, and the resistance was – magnificent.'

'Magnificent?' I asked.

'Aren't things better when they are difficult?' Alexander asked. 'When we take Tyre, our names will live for ever!' He grinned. 'I feel as if I am living in the *Iliad*.'

He was all but bouncing up and down. I had left fifty men dead in the breach, and Isokles' body was burning on a pyre beyond the horse lines, and my king was living inside the *Iliad*.

He had a cut across his face where a Tyrian had no doubt died trying to kill him – the sort of cut that tells the informed observer that the victim came within ten or twelve hairs of dying.

Sometimes, I wondered if he was insane.

He handed me a cup of wine. 'Not you, too? Infected with the Tyrian rot? Wake up! We've almost taken the place, and we'll do it in a matter of days. Three more assaults – four at most.'

I drank the whole cup of wine. It stiffened my spine and gave wings to my thoughts. I had an angry exhortation ready – but when had anger ever moved Alexander?

What I wanted was to get the siege over with – as quickly as possible, and with the minimum casualties. Because if he spent men like water to take Tyre, he was going to have a mutiny, or something very like it.

I drank more wine, thinking on Alexander and the *Iliad*.

Alexander was praising Nicanor for his work with the hypaspitoi. Indeed, they were superb, and I joined in the praise, which obviously surprised Nicanor. The lines of faction were beginning to run too deep – to resemble lines of fracture. In truth, in my experience faction usually breeds in the absence of power, but sometimes it can breed right under power's nose.

When it came to me, it was as obvious as anything in the *Iliad*.

I took another cup of wine but did not drink it straight off. 'If we were to abandon the siege,' I said, 'what would be the first thing that would happen?'

Alexander shrugged. 'I have no intention of abandoning the siege.'

I held my arm out strongly, like an orator. 'I speak as wily Odysseus, not Farm Boy Ptolemy.'

Alexander laughed, and Hephaestion laughed, and Nicanor nodded. He hadn't played our boyhood games, but he was in much the same mood I was in.

'I assume they'd land to burn our engines – if in fact we didn't burn them ourselves when we retreated.'

He looked at me.

'And take the stockpiles of food, firewood and materials we have all over camp,' Hephaestion said with a shrug.

'We'd destroy all of that, too,' Nicanor insisted.

'Not if we had to march away suddenly,' I said. 'To fight Darius with a fresh army, coming up behind us.'

Alexander turned to me. 'No one would believe such a tale.'

But Hephaestion shook his head. 'Desperate men would believe it. Men with nothing left but hope would believe it.' He nodded.

'And look, there's little risk except the loss of some time and some machines. We spread the rumour that Darius has marched. The Syrians with our own army will take the news into Tyre. Then in two days, we vanish. We march for four hours and double back. Send the Cypriots to sea. Catch whatever's ashore in late afternoon and slaughter them. And launch an *immediate* assault. It is, if I may say so, only a variant on the Trojan Horse. When they come to burn our machines and take our grain, we gut their land forces and cut their hope out from under them. Any lover knows that a hope destroyed is far worse than no hope at all.'

Three days later, we marched in full armour, with all our baggage, leaving heaps of supplies for man and beast and most of our engines – although the engines had been moved away from the mole and well inland, forcing troops bent on their destruction to pass a cornucopia of logistical delights.

It was early autumn.

The wind was fair, and the Cypriots sailed with the dawn, even as we marched.

I had the satisfaction of seeing the Tyrians rush to their walls to see the sight. The end of the siege.

We marched inland less than ten stades, and then the Prodromoi and the Paeonians, Thessalians and Thracians continued, with brush tied to the tails of their horses to raise more dust, while the rest of us ate in the shade of a low valley full of olive groves. When the sun had started to decline, and the sky was a deep-blue bowl, we marched back – ranks open and men loping along. We were in top shape – we'd had seven months of carrying rocks.

Ten stades can be run in half an hour. But we were cautious, taking on a half-moon formation to envelop as many of the enemy as we could catch.

These things either work or they don't. On this occasion, it worked better than we might have ever imagined, and we caught a tiger. The Tyrians were out in force – virtually their entire garrison was in the field, at least eight thousand men. But the very size of their force spelled their doom – they could not possibly get back into their boats in any kind of order.

They had spent a great deal of energy on the mole, without much effect, and on burning our engines, which they had done with more jubilance than efficiency. As soon as they had warning of us coming back, they began to form – when they saw that they faced all of Alexander's infantry, their despair was writ in their faces, and just as we engaged, when the Cypriot ships came in behind them cutting them off from the town, some actually committed suicide.

Craterus faced the bulk of their marines, all formed up in the centre of their line. He did so because neither Alexander nor Parmenio was with the phalanx. And that day, my taxeis was not with the phalanx, either. As Craterus, Amyntas and Perdiccas rolled forward to combat the disorganised Tyrians, the hypaspitoi and all my taxeis boarded the Cypriot ships.

Alexander always improved any plan he was offered.

We went straight for the walls. The virtually undefended walls.

They'd been breached in four places, before our machines stopped firing and we marched away. And the Tyrians had done some repairs, but conditions inside the city after seven months of siege were quite desperate. Very little work was done. Everyone was hungry.

The end might have been anticlimactic, except that our thirst for revenge outweighed any sanity.

Alexander was at the top of the ladder this time, but the enemy machines fired only sporadically, and every Cypriot ship was packed with Macedonians – ninety ships, sprinting for any place they could get a lodgement on the walls.

We had a theatre-seat view of the back of the Tyrian army as it collapsed under the weight of our phalanx and the Hetaeroi. The people on the walls – what must they have felt, in those last hours and minutes, as their marines died – pointlessly – just a few stades away? As they saw the shiploads of Macedonians coming for them.

I hope they felt terror. I hope they despaired, and cursed their gods, and tore their beards and hair. They had killed every prisoner they took. They had defiled our ambassadors and murdered our people, and they, if any, were the original aggressors against Greece. And they had burned me with sand, infected me with shit and killed Isokles and my unborn child.

Alexander leaned down off the top of the ladder, and called to the men inside the tower: 'No quarter. Kill everyone in the city, save those who take refuge in the Temple of Herakles.'

I was as bloodthirsty as he – despite the fact that I knew that in his mind we were in the depth of the wooden horse, and were about to sack Troy. It occurred to me to ask him if he was now Neoptolemus and not Achilles. If his presence didn't change the scene.

I doubt that Alexander would even have laughed.

I said when I started to tell the story of Tyre that it needn't have happened. That there was arrogance and foolishness on both sides.

And there was horror.

We had little to fear – the walls were virtually empty, the mighty machines didn't, most of them, throw a single rock, and when Alexander sprang out of the tower on to the rubble of the breach, it was almost like walking on to the stage of an empty theatre. The only enemy soldiers were archers – they had been left behind by the marines, and they shot as fast and as accurately as they could.

But they could not hold even the towers, and we swept from wall to wall, using short scaling ladders to get down into the streets beyond or into the low towers on either hand.

Very quickly, the defence collapsed. I had seen some sieges by the time I reached Tyre. I knew the signs. The enemy no longer thought he could resist. Men fled – usually to their own homes, to die in the doorways of their own houses.

And die they did.

I would like to say that I remember nothing of it, but I remember it all too well. I was with beasts – I was a beast. I killed men, and I killed women, and I killed young children. I killed a goat that passed in front of me. I killed anything that was not a soldier of Macedon.

There were few women, because most of them and their children had gone to Carthage at the start of the siege. But those that there were went to the roofs and threw tiles down on us – no laughing matter, when a piece of terracotta the size of your fist hits you on the head.

Our engineers knocked a hole in the land wall of the city facing the mole, and even as we butchered our way through the streets, Diades connected the city to the land, opened the wall and led the victorious phalanx into the devastated city to finish off any rats trapped in their homes.

And at the end, when they knew that there would be no quarter, the population turned and fought like rats facing dogs. Such rats often give the dogs a bad bite or two before they die, and sometimes the bites infect. The simile is apt. The Macedonian army triumphed at Tyre, but the price was high, in blood, in pain, in spirit, and the results took years to play out.

But for Tyre, the price was higher. Because before the sun set, every man, woman and child in the city was dead. Every dog was dead, every donkey, every mule, every cat. We killed everything except the handful of lucky families who took refuge in the Temple of Melkart.

Alexander dragged them out and let them live – as slaves. Then he had the temple *purified*. And he made his sacrifice there, just eight months later than he had expected.

But what I remember best is walking out of the gap in the walls, climbing down Diades' breach to the mole, and looking back in the red sunset – the purple-red that men called 'Tyrian Red' after the murex dye. A haze of dust and smoke sat like a toad atop the city, and fires burned throughout, and you could smell death everywhere.

But what I will never forget as long as I live is the sight of blood – red blood – leaking out of the foundation stones of the walls, and mixing with the seawater, so that sharks and other sea creatures began to beat themselves against the walls in the last light, as if Poseidon had turned on the town, or as if there was a portent to be read in the angry battering of the fish and the blood.

I stood there, full of rage and hate and the kind of sick guilt that a man can only gain when he sacks a city and behaves like a beast. My hands and arms dripped blood and my feet were sticky with it.

If I had wanted revenge, what I had was my nauseated fill of it.

And that was Tyre.

TWENTY-SIX

---*vvv*---

Gaza is just six days' marching from Tyre, and stands on rock about twenty stades from the sea. We marched there four days after the fall of Tyre. Four days. That's the rest we had, and two days of it were given over to a mass parade of the army and a set of games in honour of Herakles. My phalanx looked terrible at the review – exhausted men slumping, poor armour, threadbare chitons. Only a few of my decarchs – file leaders – had coerced their men into polishing their dented helmets. In fact, only about two-thirds of my remaining men *had* helmets. The rest had leather Boeotian caps. My only consolation was that the rest of the army – except the Hetaeroi – looked as bad or worse.

The approach to Gaza is sandy and the sea near the city is everywhere shallow. The city of Gaza is large, built upon a lofty mound around which a strong wall has been laid. It is the last city you meet, going from Phoenicia to Egypt. It is situated on the edge of the desert. When we arrived near the city on the first day, we encamped near the spot where the wall seemed to Diades most easy to assault. The engineer ordered his military engines to be constructed – those that we had with us. Most of our best and heaviest gear was still at Tyre, under repair, with Helios sending out still more parties for still more wood. But the Jews came to our aid – they had no love for the Persians, and now that we'd taken Tyre, we had a flood of support from Palestine.

As at Tyre, Alexander and Diades and all his engineers spent two days in careful examination of the city and all of its approaches, while we stripped the countryside like a host of armoured locusts for brushwood, for food and for manpower. Tyre had made us expert in what we needed, and it was all too clear to every footslogger that Gaza, even without the sea, was another tough nut and one for which digging and engineering were required in order to crack it.

The army was tired and surly, and we needed drafts from home to fill the places that disease, malnutrition and overwork had carved in our ranks. Recruits play an essential role in the long-term life of an army. They may be clueless, useless men who can't start a fire or cook their own food or dig a decent latrine, but they bring a spirit of emulation that veterans lack – or rather, they restore a spirit of emulation and enterprise. The veterans have to work harder to show the recruits what fine men they are. The recruits band together to prove themselves worthy. We hadn't had any recruits for a year, and I put out the word – and some gold, as a recruiting bonus.

The Persian commander in Gaza was Batis, and he rendered the siege very different from the siege at Tyre. It is worth noting that the rest of Palestine and Syria surrendered to us, but Batis, for whatever reason, determined to keep us out of Aegypt by holding Gaza.

Probably the most significant difference was that he was a professional Persian officer, a loyal servant of King Darius, and not the 'king' of a semi-independent town. He had a powerful garrison, thousands of troops, most of them veterans of Issus and other campaigns, and he had an excellent reputation with the local people – for justice and mercy.

Callisthenes' propaganda got us nothing at Gaza, and his agents provided nothing from inside the town. It was, to all intents and purposes, a Persian town. And the hill on which it sat was tall, rocky and looked, to the casual eye, impregnable. Gaza was the first city we faced without Thaïs's networks, and the difference showed immediately, at least to me. We didn't even have a former Gazan citizen on the staff to help show us the strengths of the walls.

Callisthenes' shortcomings showed in other ways, as well.

Far off in Greece, the Spartan king, Agis, had finally taken the bit between his teeth and declared war on Macedon. He took fistfuls of gold from the Great King and provided a haven for parts of the Persian fleet, and one of his first acts was to seize Crete, which neatly balanced our alliance with Cyprus and threatened our communications with home. He summoned home every Spartan citizen, and extended citizen's rights to many who were not citizens, in order to prepare for war. We needed information on Sparta's intentions and her plans, and we had nothing, because Callisthenes hadn't seen it coming and had no sources prepared. Nor, we quickly saw, was the Pythia willing to communicate with Callisthenes. No more priests of Apollo appeared in our camp.

Sparta wasn't our only trouble. Athens was vacillating, considering new alliances and a stab in the back to Macedon. Even there, Callisthenes had fewer sources than Thaïs had had, and he didn't even trouble himself to make use of the Athenian officers in our army, a shocking omission.

But Kineas mentioned to me, one day when we were sparring, just as Diades began to have our horde of barbarian slaves raise the siege mound, that he thought Agis had waited too long.

'If he'd struck before Issus, there's many in Athens – supporters of Demosthenes – who'd have put aside their hatred for Sparta and marched on Macedon.' He paused – we had a habit, when sparring, of falling into conversation, and when we did, it had become our custom to relax our stances deliberately so that neither would feel threatened. He smiled, perhaps ruefully. 'But now? Most Athenians hate Sparta more than we hate anyone. Their cowardly behaviour in the great war – their lickspittle toadying to the Great King. And look you – no sooner does Agis declare war on Macedon than he accepts a great subsidy from Darius and welcomes his fleet!' Kineas shook his head. 'Even the lowest classes – even the most hardened thetes, even the most corrupt democrat – would hate to betray the heroic dead of Marathon and fifty fights with Sparta – just to have a go at Macedon.'

I prayed he was correct, because still, and again – even with Tyre in our hands and Cyprus – Athens was the key, and if Athens, with her three-hundred-ship navy, chose to go to open war with us, the crusade in Asia would be over.

We opened our lines on the third day – a nice phrase, which means we began serious operations. By coincidence, it was the day Aristophanes – not the comic, but the statesman – became Eponymous Archon in Athens. The sun was high and the heat was brutal. The slaves – many of whom had, a few days before, been free farmers in the region around Gaza – began to dig.

I get ahead of myself. When the slaves were collected, and the brushwood, and all the digging tools brought up from Tyre (but not the siege machines, most of which were still under repair back there), Alexander summoned all of his friends and all of the officers and allies. We expected to have a command meeting – I certainly knew from my conversations with Nicanor and Philotas that their father was fit to explode over the fact that we were settling down for *another* siege that might take another year.

But what we attended, instead, was a sacrifice. Alexander was waiting for us, at the top of the slope that led to the ground on which his first siege mound would be commenced. The town of Gaza seemed to tower over us from here, and the garrison was shouting insults – or at least, I assumed they were insults. Thankfully, Alexander couldn't hear them.

A pair of gulls were fighting in the air above us. There were gulls everywhere, because an army leaves a lot of garbage about, and near the sea, the gulls outnumber the other vermin. Their cries were louder and more raucous than those of the guards on the walls, but in the same tone.

Alexander was dressed in a pure white chiton of beautiful, shining wool, with a narrow gold border. He cut the throat of his ram without getting a speck of blood on the chiton, and as the ram slumped and the king stepped back, a gull screamed and something struck Alexander on the head and he fell to one knee.

Every man present rushed to his side.

The gulls had been fighting over a bit of flesh attached to a bone – perhaps a dead lamb from another sacrifice – and the bone, falling from high above, had hit the king on the head, driving him to his knees. It had left a smear on his left shoulder and on his left thigh, as well.

He waved us away, but he was shaken, his eyes wild. Aristander, that wily charlatan, stepped forward and raised his arms. 'An omen!' he cried, as if we needed a priest to tell us that we'd seen an omen. 'The king will triumph here, but he will risk his body to accomplish the deed. Take heed, O King!'

Alexander was spooked. I had seen him this way as a child, especially when his witch of a mother told him peasant tales from her home, terrifying tales of children lost in the woods and being eaten by human creatures that sucked children's marrow bones – I'm not making this up, Olympias had a thousand of them, and she revelled in them. I suspect they helped make Alexander what he was.

Whatever he was.

At any rate, I hurried to his side, exchanged glances with Hephaestion and we hustled him to his tent.

For the next week, Alexander stayed well clear of the siege lines. It took the full week before the first comments began to reach me. I had spent so much time wounded at Tyre that I was using the siege of Gaza to re-establish my place with my pezhetaeroi. I was lucky enough to get two hundred new men – mostly Ionian hoplites who willingly enlisted and could claim, at least loosely, to have relatives in the Chersonese or Amphilopolis. They were the last fruits of Isokles' reputation and persistence in recruiting.

I was a rich man, too, and I began to lavish some of my loot on my regiment. A number of the best armourers, with large, well-trained shops of slave and free artisans, in Athens and elsewhere, sent representatives to the army. I arranged the purchase of helmets – not matching, but all similar enough, in tinned bronze – so-called Attic helmets, small, fitted to the head, with a tall crest and long cheek-plates that hinged back in hot weather but covered most of the face in combat. Many of Memnon's officers had such helmets and I had ordered one for myself

– in gilded bronze, of course, with a red, white and black crest and a pair of ostrich plumes in gilt holders.

And I paid for my front-rankers to have matching shields – the newer, lighter Macedonian aspis, because that was more practical for men who had to march every day and carry their own shield, without a slave to carry it for them – but with strong, bronze faces on the shields and ten coats of bright red – Tyrian red – paint with the Star of Macedon in the middle in white. I hung the sample from my tent, and men admired it. I announced that the helmets and shields were my treat.

On such little things rest the twin rods of command and discipline. I also paid for twelve hundred new wool chitons, and twenty-four hundred pairs of iphicratids, the sandal-boot that the great Athenian general (whose own father, so I'm told, was a shoemaker) invented.

My taxeis played kerētízein against Perdiccas's men and then against Craterus's taxeis. It is a game played with a stick shaped like a club or horn, and a ball. The players can only use the stick to touch the ball, although when men play the game, they often use the sticks on each other. But despite the broken heads and broken ankles, the games, and a certain amount of wine, did much to lighten the load of a second siege. I was learning how to take my men through – because I could see that Alexander was now in love with sieges.

In love, but for perhaps the first time, afraid. The mounds grew; Diades had outdone himself this time, envisioning a ring of earthworks that would seal the town in from supplies and then raising the works until our machines, coming up from the coast, could easily dominate the enemy walls.

The siege mounds grew every day. After Tyre, where we had built the mole ourselves, Gaza and its army of slave labourers seemed like a vacation. The mounds grew, and the enemy killed our slaves, and our troops dreamed of new helmets and good hockey games.

There is something intoxicating about a siege, if you are an officer. You can plan, and watch other men do the sweaty part, and it is like being a god.

Batis was, as I have said, a first-rate officer, and he was no more interested in killing our slaves than he should have been, so in the third week of the siege, just after the sun had set, he came out of three gates at the same time in a massive raid on our siege lines.

His raid was completely successful. He burned the handful of machines we had with us, and his raiders burned the wooden shoring under our most advanced siege mound and got the whole edifice to collapse. More than a hundred Macedonian soldiers were killed and a party of hypaspitoi under Alectus himself was routed. Alectus was badly wounded, and Batis got a dozen messengers through our cavalry screen.

I think that the most remarkable thing about Batis's raid was that it had no effect on the morale of the army. For men who had fought for three solid years in Asia against Memnon, Darius and Tyre – we had seen our share of bitter mornings and brilliant enemy raids.

By the time the sun was well up, the burned pilings had been removed and replaced, and later that evening, the siege train came up from the coast, so that two days later, Batis's men faced the full power of our artillery.

Gaza, for all the bravery of its defenders, the brilliance and charisma of Batis and the magnificence of its rocky eminence, was not Tyre. Tyre's walls were solid stone, and Gaza's were mud brick on a stone socle. Once our machines started lofting rocks, the city was doomed. Or so we thought. I was with Alexander while the first battery opened up, and we cheered together to watch the engineers (in excellent practice since Tyre) strike the walls on their third casts, resight their batteries and commence effective barrage – in minutes instead of hours. And every stone that struck the wall brought down a section, so that the battery seemed like the invisible teeth of a giant, gnawing away until the cloud of dust thrown from the shattered mud bricks obscured the target.

Diades kept throwing rocks, all day and sometimes at night. He had a new stratagem, using the stone-throwers to keep the enemy engineers off their own walls, so that repairs were either perilous to the most skilled men, or the walls didn't get repaired.

In the fifth week of the siege, Alexander scouted the walls and ordered an assault. The town still loomed above us, almost impossibly high, but the walls were battered down in four places, and in each place it was possible for an armoured man to go up the mound and then climb the breach, because our engineers drove the poor slaves forward with whips into the arrow fire of the besieged with baskets of rubble to fill the ditch. The top of our siege mound stank from the number of corpses that were buried in the forward face and the ramp up to the enemy wall.

The first assault on Gaza – the only memorable thing about it is how badly we were suckered and how the army felt when they discovered that the king was *not* coming. I don't think we'd ever assaulted anything – gone into action anywhere – without Alexander at our head. That's what kings of Macedon *do*.

It is typical, I guess, of Macedonian soldiers that no man – not even the king – was ever any better than his last performance. It took them a few weeks to forget his brilliant courage – his virtually maniacal courage.

I heard it all while I buckled on my battered cuirass, once a brilliant glare of gilded bronze and now a dented, scraped and battered remnant of its once proud self, missing both silver nipples and with ring-ties replacing the hinges I had had and which had been ruined by the hot sand. I had new armour coming, too.

My thorax reminded me of a statue we had had in the gardens when I was a boy. My father loved it, but it had been taken to the barns to be cleaned one winter, and somehow dropped. That's how my thorax looked, and my helmet was worse, and I was a *taxiarch*.

But I digress. I had to replace Isokles as company officer and as my second-in-command. Marsyas was the obvious choice. He was a friend of the king, and his brother, Antigonus, was an increasingly important man – he had just won us a fine victory over Phrygians in the north, and without him our supply lines would have been severed repeatedly and no new recruits would be reaching our army. Marsyas himself was a fine officer, if you took into account that he had his nose in the air *and* his head in the clouds.

He loved Thaïs, though. So I made him swear to her by Aphrodite, his chosen goddess, of whom Thaïs was a priestess, that he would never let a woman come between his duty and his men again. And on his own account, before the end of the Siege of Tyre, he went to Cleomenes and apologised for his hubris, and they were reconciled – indeed, like proper gentlemen, they were better friends than before.

Ahh. I am avoiding the first assault on Gaza. I will digress again and again. Here, pour me some more wine, there, boy.

Marsyas told me that men were complaining that the king was sulking in his tent, or worse. And moments later, I heard the same from Cleomenes.

And with that in my head, I went to the king's pre-assault briefing. It was dark, and despite the summer, cold. All the army's senior officers were there, and they gathered in two distinct groups. That had never happened before. One group around Parmenio, and the other around Hephaestion. Ugly.

Alexander was not in armour. It's true – perhaps he was damned either way, but as the only man not in armour, he accentuated the fact that he was not going up the ramps and we were. Or rather – Philotas was not going up the ramps, and neither was Attalus or Amyntas, but they were in armour, as if to indicate their support.

As it happened, when the king moved to the centre to discuss the assault, I could smell him and he reeked of spikenard. I had never known him even to experiment with perfume, and he smelled – very strongly.

Diades had drawn a view of the city on a large board in charcoal, and the king pointed out our assault positions and the timing of the assaults. It was all routine, and yet somehow, every word he said struck us as odd – because he was perfumed and clean and wearing clothes more suited to a bedchamber than to the field. Hephaestion was in armour – a panoply that had once been at least as magnificent as my best, and now looked as bad or worse.

Alexander dismissed us without a smile or a speech. In fact, his thoughts seemed to be elsewhere. And then he went back into his tent, and we went to our units.

I remember the first assault well. My pezhetaeroi were in the first wave on the southernmost ramp, and we went as soon as we had light to see the uneven footing. That uneven footing saved my life, too. I was the first man up the ramp, and I went fast – determined to be the first man on the wall, because if you must lead an assault on a city, you have no choice but to be a hero.

I must digress, again. In Macedon – in Sparta, in Athens and even in gods-cursed Thebes – officers led from in front. The wastage among Athenian strategoi was always incredible. Men in front die. Macedonian taxiarchoi had a better survival rate only because we wore lots of armour and trained as pages to overcome anything in hand-to-hand combat. But one of the things I remember about the pre-dawn minutes at Gaza was the fear. My men were afraid, and I was afraid, and my recruits were jittery, even the many among them who were themselves veterans. I didn't want to lead the assault. I wanted to go and join Alexander and wear perfume.

My hands shook.

I had a great deal of trouble getting my cheek-plates tied together.

My knees were weak, and my forearms felt as if I'd spent the night lifting weights.

Because, like my men, I'd done too much. Tyre was too close behind us. Alexander owed us a rest, and we hadn't had one.

Off to my left, a red flag was lifted from the tower that was closest to the king's command pavilion.

I sprang up from rock to rock, and the arrows fell like sleet in the Thracian mountains, and my big aspis was hit again and again, and my poor old helmet took another battering.

I took one quick look when I was almost at the base of the socle. I wanted to hit the base of the breach *just right*. There were a dozen men just inside the breach, with heavy bows, shooting as fast as they could, and even as I looked, another arrow thudded into my aspis and I stumbled, and my left foot went into something that cracked under my weight and suddenly I was down, my left leg deep in the dirt and stone of the ramp, and something went over my head with the sound of summer thunder – or the sound of a sheet of papyrus being torn asunder by an enraged merchant. Whatever it was snapped my neck around and tore the crest right off my old helmet.

Pyrrhus, who had been with me since he was a child, simply exploded. An arm and his head flew off, and behind him, a dozen more men died in a hideous fleshy mess.

There was a ballista in the breach. Even as I tried to pull my left leg free, the men in the breach were cranking the great bow back into position and the men on the walls above the breach were throwing boiling linseed oil into our faces. I only caught a little – perhaps a cupful – on my shoulder above my shield arm, but the pain spurred me and I got my left leg free and almost vomited, because my foot had collapsed the ribcage of a corpse and my leg had slid into the body cavity – a mass of corruption and maggots – and the smell of death stuck to me like glue.

And I went up the breach anyway, because after Tyre ...

I reached the ballista well before it was loaded, and threw my light spear into the nearest man and then my heavy spear – not really meant to be thrown – into an archer, and he and the loader fell across the enormous bow, and I drew my sword – a heavy kopis – from under my arm and continued the draw into a cut – to the rope holding the bow wound against its drum. The men on the bow screamed as the bowstring slammed into their soft bodies.

A wave of Macedonians joined me in the breach, and we killed every man we found there. And then we went down the rubble on the far side of the breach into the town.

At Tyre and Halicarnassus, the defenders had built mud walls behind the breach, to channel our attacks and make the breach a trap, but Batis had gone one better.

He let us into the town – he had more town to use for depth – and had built little battlefields for his garrison to use to fight *inside* the town. The houses were heavy and often stone-built, and between them there were barricades across the narrow streets – low enough to tempt assault, and high enough that such assaults weren't worth much – the more so as every barricade was flanked by the towers of the tallest houses on the street, and every pair of towers had a small garrison of archers and slingers. Some of the barricades had a ballista. And some of the houses had assault groups waiting for us to pass them.

It was a nightmare.

When you assault a town, you know that the easiest way to achieve victory is to break the enemy's will to resist. There comes a point in an assault when the town has so many soldiers flooding it that the defenders either surrender or simply allow themselves to die. The expectation of every man in an assault is that it is his duty to penetrate as deeply into the town as possible to cause panic.

Batis used all that against us. Our men came up the breaches like heroes and went into the town, where he wanted us to be – inside his defences, and far from the support of our dominating artillery. His defenders had superb morale, and they faced us resolutely, no matter where we met them in the town. And indeed, early on, they abandoned some positions – I assume to lure us deeper into the web of streets.

I am proud of my performance as a taxiarch that day, because I didn't lose my head. Oh – I was fooled. I may have penetrated as deeply into the town as any Macedonian. I know that I was enraged by Pyrrhus's death and I killed my way over a barricade despite a hail of stones. But as we overwhelmed our second barricade, losing a dozen good men in the process, I began to look around.

I had about a hundred men with me, and far too many of the officers – good for my group, bad news for my assault as a whole. I remember killing my way over the second barricade, and pausing to drink water from my canteen. I found that my strap had broken, or been cut, and I turned to Cleomenes and stopped him – carefully, as his blood was up.

'Water, brother?' I asked, and because I had to pop my cheek-plates to drink, I could hear and see when the enemy ambush began to filter into the street behind us.

'Ware!' I bellowed, and all the men on the barricade turned, and we made a shield wall – fifteen or twenty of us – and we held them. Please do not mistake me – the Persians and the Nabataeans at Gaza were brave men and well led, but they were never a match for us in combat. They lacked the armour, and they lacked the mettle. They hit us and we broke them and then we chased them back down the alley.

And now I really had time to look around, and what I saw was that we were not actually taking ground – that every stone house had defenders, and we were receiving a constant and deadly barrage wherever we went.

The problem I had – the problem every strategos always has – was information.

I gathered the men I had and we stormed a house. The fighting was bestial – kopis and xiphos against short spear and knife in rooms no larger than a large himation laid on the ground, through doorways so narrow and so low that a child would have to stoop to enter, and up steeply turning stairs that rotated to the right to cramp a fighter. At every check, the enemy put an archer or two behind a few swordsmen.

I couldn't take more than a room or two at a time, and then I had to exchange out of the front rank. It was true of every man – fighting inside a city is a terrifying thing, every blow is a death blow. But as with fighting at night, discipline and armour make all the difference.

In the end, we stormed the tower and exterminated the garrison at the top, throwing the last bodies to the street below.

Now I could see.

There were fires throughout the town, and the dirt streets – the alleys – raised clouds of dust, so that a pall seemed to hang over the town, lit red and yellow by the flames in the early light.

It was actually quite beautiful.

But the pattern leaped to the eye. We were not penetrating the town. We were being funnelled down four corridors for the convenience of the garrison – a corridor for every breach – and each corridor led to a maze of alleys and barricades.

I stayed there for a long time. Long enough to catch my breath. Long enough for the sweat on my abdomen to start to dry. Because I had to be right.

Then I ordered my hyperetes to sound the recall.

I was the first. I remain proud of my decision.

Alexander did not feel the same way.

'You what?' he asked, his arms crossed. 'You *ran*?'

I stank of death, and I was covered in soot, and I had two wounds. I had prepared myself for the encounter, and when I was clear of the breach, I ran – ran – all the way around the wall to Perdiccas to find him in his breach, and he, too, was coming out. And I promised him I'd explain to Alexander. I had set my mind to it as I climbed back up our siege mound, and I went straight to his tent.

And I was still not ready. I had my logic all prepared, and the king needed to know what Batis had done.

He smelled of spikenard, and he didn't have a mark on him. He shrugged. 'Perhaps I have grown used to uninterrupted victory. Or perhaps I simply cannot expect as much when I'm not there in person. I know what fear is, Ptolemy. You are forgiven.'

I suspect my mouth opened and closed like that of a fish. I don't remember that part. What I remember is my head screaming at me to keep my mouth shut.

'Fuck you!' I roared at him. Alas. 'You weren't there – Lord King. You have no idea what we faced, and you think I *panicked*? You're fucking right you should do it yourself. Because if you continue to talk like that, you may have to!'

Wise, carefully considered words they were not. I turned on my heel and walked away. But he had it coming, and then some.

The thing is, Alexander was ... Alexander. God, monster, man, inhuman – all of them in one body.

So while Thaïs washed the crap and blood from my body, and my rage simmered and I tried – tried hard – not to turn it on my lover – Alexander came in. He had four Hetaeroi with him, and he was in armour.

He had a baton in his hand, and he put it carefully on my camp bed and came immediately to my side. He sniffed, made a face and sniffed the wound in the top of my shoulder, where you could see the white fat oozing out through the blood.

'Do you have a wound gone bad?' he asked. 'You stink like a bad wound.'

'I stepped in a corpse,' I said, my tone carefully neutral.

'Ah,' he said. He took a cloth from Thaïs and cleaned my shoulder wound with what I can only call tender ruthlessness – he was as quick as he could be. He was very good with wounds.

It was all I could do not to cry out, or just cry.

When he dipped the cloth into the hot water, he said, 'I am sorry, Ptolemy. Not fighting – I cannot do it. I cannot cower in the rear. It makes me a woman. In too many ways.'

Thaïs sniffed and muttered something about childbirth.

Alexander ignored her. 'I should have been there. But I'm told it was a trap.'

'A well-laid defence – a trap if we were foolish enough to come into it.' I began to breathe more easily. My first thought when he entered the tent was that I was to be stripped of my command.

'And perhaps, had I led today, I would have died.' He shrugged. 'I will lead the next.'

'Tomorrow?' I asked. In truth, I felt weary to the bone. It was still early morning, and I wanted to sleep.

He shook his head. 'This was bad. We lost – three hundred pezhetaeroi, and perhaps more. I will let our men rest. Five days. And then I'll take the Hetaeroi and the hypaspitoi.' He smiled.

I knew what men would say in camp. That my men hadn't been up to it. But neither could we assault every time, and my men didn't have anything to prove. I took two breaths to fight down the urge to demand to participate, and then I nodded. 'Bless you, Lord King, for coming to me.'

He put a hand on my good shoulder. 'I love you, Ptolemy. Even when I behave thoughtlessly.' He kissed me on the cheek and left the tent.

Go ahead. Hate that.

I couldn't.

I don't remember how many days passed – ah, here it is, in the Journal. Three days.

I probably slept for two of them.

My taxeis came out of the siege lines at midnight. Morale wasn't bad – the new armour was coming in any day, I'd just given a small pay rise to all the married men in my regiment and I'd bought meat far away at Jerusalem and had it driven on the hoof into our camp, and every man knew he had a dinner of lamb to look forward to. In fact, I was spending money as an orator spends hot air, but my men needed it or they were going to collapse. All the taxiarchs were doing all they could.

I heard Parmenio, playing Polis with Craterus, mutter that the best thing that could happen to us was that Darius would get up the nerve to attack us, because that would put spine back in the pikemen. Parmenio was deeply depressed. His shoulders slumped, and he spoke slowly and very seldom, and he and his sons had become isolated.

At any rate, we were filtering down off the siege mounds north of the city, far from the breach that had killed seventy of my men, when we heard the unmistakable sounds of combat from all the way around the city.

I was already down at the base of the siege mound, on the road that Diades had built and kept clear for rapid troop movements. I had a habit of forming the men every night before dinner, to 'pass the word', as we used to say, and that night it stood me in good stead.

'Files from the left by fours – to the left – march!' I shouted, and ran to their head. Each group of four files marched forward to the road and then wheeled in fours to the left, forming a column four wide on the road from a phalanx eight deep. Simple stuff – if you drill every day.

As soon as the first fours were on the road, I trotted to their head. 'At the double! Follow me!'

It was six stades around the wall to where we heard fighting. We were not sprinting, but we made it in time.

When we came up to the southernmost siege mound – territory we knew all too well, as it is where our own assault had jumped off – there was a vicious fight – a dust cloud, darkness falling and several thousand enemy troops engaged on the front face of our siege mound. They'd clearly made it into our works, because one of our batteries was aflame, and the smell of naphtha was in the air. Amyntas's taxeis was broken – I could see his phylarchs rallying men to my right. And the hypaspitoi were fully engaged. I looked for Alexander.

I couldn't see him.

The hypaspitoi were being pushed back, step by step. The Persian assault was ferocious. I didn't know why, yet. I just saw disaster looming.

So did Perdiccas and Craterus, both of whom were forming their taxeis as quickly as they could on the parade ground, just two stades away. But the time was right then, or never. The Persians outnumbered the hypaspitoi four to one or more.

I led my men *down* into the no man's land between the siege works and the town, and halted a spear-cast from the flank of the Persians.

'Form your front!' I ordered.

The first four halted. All seven men in the four files halted, as well.

The next block of four files came at a run and fell in next to them. Now eight files wide.

Then four more files to the right and four more to the left.

In heartbeats, we were thirty-two files wide. I didn't wait. Marsyas could bring up the second half as he saw fit – the darkness was growing, the growl of the Persians was deadly and I was already afraid that I had waited too long.

'Spears down! March!' I ordered, as the files closed up.

The Persians had had minutes to prepare for us, and they had a body of armoured bowmen loosing into our front ranks, and men fell, but shafts that went over got lost in the forest of spears, impetus broken. The archers didn't await our onset, and there were no spearmen to resist us, and we tore right into the side of the Persian force and men fled us. This was the eternal problem for the Persians – without good Greek infantry, they had no foot who would abide us.

I was in the front rank, and I saw the man who I later learned was Batis cursing his men and wielding an enormous long sword with one hand. He was as tall as a small tree and as wide as a rock. His arms were the size of my legs. He swung at me, I put my aspis into his sword and he caved in the face of my aspis, crushing the bronze, breaking the wood underneath and causing the wooden ribs to splinter. His blow was so powerful that it hurt my shield arm, although the edge of his sword never penetrated the bronze or I'd not be here to tell of it.

I thrust my spear at him, and it glanced off the long scale tunic he had, and I stepped in and slammed my spear butt into his head even as he reversed his sword and slammed his pommel into my head. I caught some of his blow on my spear and my helmet took the rest and I was knocked flat – conscious, but knocked straight off my feet.

He stumbled back from my blow, and my file partner, Stephanos, once one of Memnon's men, pounded his spear-point into Batis's chest. Again his scale and his luck held, but now he fell backwards into his own ranks, and I was on my feet again, my ears ringing. In fact, my nose was leaking blood. But that didn't matter, because Batis was being carried to the rear, and now his men couldn't be held – they were back-pedalling as fast as they could go.

Except in one place. Even as I struggled to reach it, another surge of Persians – led by some Aegyptian marines with big shields – pounded into our hypaspitoi over to my right and farther up the hill.

I had no idea why the Persians were so tenacious, but they were pushing the hypaspitoi back, and the hypaspitoi were literally dying in place.

So I started cutting my way towards them. As I say, the bulk of the Persians didn't want to face us. A gap opened in their line. That happens, on battlefields, and I ran into it, and part of my phalanx followed me and the other part stayed behind and kept rolling the Persian main body back. Not according to the drill field – but on a real battlefield, you can't stay with the textbook. I counted on my files following me, and they did.

We slammed into the Aegyptians. The fighting was chaotic – my phalangites were in no real order, just following me in a mob – the Aegyptians were trying to lap around the hypaspitoi, and were caught in the flank or rear, but they themselves had reinforcements coming up behind, and catching my men in the shielded flank.

In the time it took me to break my spear on a hippopotamus-hide shield, the fighting was man to man, and neither my flanks nor my back were safe. I hit my opponent over the head with the butt of my spear, used as a club, and then crushed the skull of another Aegyptian through his leather cap with one blow to the side of his head – my bronze sarouter made a powerful mace. A blow caught me from behind, but the bronze of my thorax held and I stumbled forward into the enemy ranks – an enemy marine swung at me and our weapons locked, and he slammed his shield into mine, roared at me and cut at my head – I could see down his throat. I bashed his fingers with my sarouter-club, and he lost his sword and threw himself on me, arms wide, shield flung aside, and I stopped him on my shield, shoved him to unbalance him and punched the pointed end of the bronze butt into his throat.

Then I almost died at the hands of a hypaspist. He shot his spear forward with the power of a desperate man, and my shield – crumpled like a trireme that's been rammed – didn't really turn the blow, and it slammed down into my left greave.

'Macedon!' I yelled at him.

He stabbed at me again.

'Macedon!' I roared, and he flinched. Then he thrust powerfully into another man, and I had the pleasure of hearing him mutter – I didn't catch what he said.

I turned my side to him and backed into the ranks of the hypaspitoi. My back foot, my right, was on a corpse.

The Aegyptian marines made *another* rush. I needed to be sure of my footing and glanced down, and saw that I was standing over Alexander. He had an enormous spear – I learned later it was the bolt from a ballista – in his shoulder. He was screaming, eyes blind, and the ground was wet with his blood, and there was a *pile* of dead hypaspitoi around him. Perhaps as many as fifteen or twenty. Even as I looked, a man grabbed his ankles to pull him, he screamed and the man with his ankles got an Aegyptian spear in his guts and fell atop him.

Zeus Soter, I thought. *He's going to die right here.*

Yet even as that thought tickled my mind and the marines hit us again, my phalanx fell on their rear. There was a moment – a flurry of blows, an unendurable pressure on my chest and my shattered shield, my blows seeming too feeble to make a difference – and then they were running, abandoning their magnificent hide shields to run down the hill, and my men killed fifty of them in as many heartbeats, and we had held.

Even as the Aegyptians broke, the hypaspitoi had lifted the king. His shield – a full-sized aspis – had taken the ballista bolt. It had struck through his shield – through all seven layers of bull's hide, wood and bronze – into the meat of his left shoulder and out the back, so that when they lifted him I could see the red-black shimmer of the metal like some obscene thing projecting from the pturges of his arm armour.

He was done screaming. His eyes were open, and they locked on mine, just for a moment. He *smiled*. In that moment, he was a god.

And then he screamed with the pain, again.

Philip of Acarnia removed the ballista bolt, cutting the head off and then oiling the shaft with olive oil – pouring the oil right on to the wound – and then pulling it through. Then he slathered the king's wound with honey and bandaged it. I watched, and held Alexander while he screamed, cried and shat himself. I helped clean him, and I helped carry him to his bed. He weighed very little.

The doctor filled him full of opium, and he went off into a drug-hazed sleep. I sat in his chair and watched him for a while, with Perdiccas and Hephaestion and some of the others.

He looked small and vulnerable and very pale.

Later that night, a pretty girl with hennaed hands and feet came to Thaïs to ask for news of the king in a very shy voice.

Thaïs came for me. 'Memnon's women sent her. They must be terrified – if Alexander dies, all that seductiveness has been wasted.' She
smiled, a somewhat catlike smile. 'I feel for them. They're likely to be
passed from hand to hand if he dies,' she said. 'Will he die?' she asked
suddenly, her voice changed.

'You are kind to them,' I said. And whispered to her, 'I fear for him.
But we must not say it.' Thaïs kissed me and nodded.

I went to the girl, who threw herself on the ground and hid her face.
'Great lord!' she said.

'Tell your mistress,' I began.

The serving girl shook her head. 'Please come, lord. Please?'

Well – it is always pleasurable to have beautiful young women call
you *great lord*. I followed her to her tent, and met a queen, sitting quite
calmly on a couch.

'You remember me, Ptolemy?' she asked, voice husky, without pre-
amble.

Banugul must have been eighteen or perhaps nineteen. I hadn't been
alone with her.

I almost couldn't breathe.

I had Thaïs in my bed every night – widely accounted the most
beautiful woman in the world.

How do we measure these things?

Banugul had, as I have described, skin and hair the colour of honey,
green eyes that slanted a fraction from her nose to her temples, and fine,
arched feet. The rest of her was robed in splendour.

And the only thing I could smell was spikenard.

I managed to tell her that the king would recover. She thanked me
very prettily, and I left the tent, still alive.

Thaïs laughed at me for most of the next day. I would have laughed,
too, except that war was everywhere, and Ares, not Aphrodite, had us
in his fist.

Hephaestion led the second assault. I watched them go up the hill, in
the first light of dawn, watched the engines and the boiling oil kill their
share, and watched Amyntas and Philotas race each other like heroes at
Troy to make the northern breach first.

They lasted about the same length of time we lasted. Perhaps an
hour.

Batis met them inside the town and killed them. On the south side,
his men actually held the breach – the assault never penetrated into the
town. This time, according to Amyntas, who was wounded twice, Batis
had concealed pits, ditches and spiked caltrops waiting for the assault

troops, and local counter-attacks to cut the lead elements of the assault off from the reserves.

Hephaestion returned covered in dust and other men's blood. He was taller and better-muscled than Alexander, and looked more like I imagined Achilles to look than any man I ever saw.

He threw his aspis on the ground, grunted and went into his tent to drink and sulk – just like Achilles.

Parmenio appeared out of nowhere and took command of the army. He did it without fuss, without asking for anyone's approval and there was no loss of momentum or discipline.

Groups of silent men gathered outside Alexander's tent – every morning. They never fussed or made noise, merely waited to see if Philip would emerge and tell them something of the king.

On the fifth morning after his wound, the king came out into the sunshine in person, blinking in the sun.

The cheers started from the men by the tent.

Alexander smiled, and waved with his right hand, and the cheers spread as flame spreads in a dry field, until every man in that camp was roaring, 'Alexander! Alexander the king!'

I was with Diades, watching slaves raise the battery platforms yet higher. As the cheers spread, and we understood their cause, *even the slaves began to cheer.*

About an hour later, Parmenio summoned me to the king's tent. I expected the command council and found only the strategos and the king.

Parmenio nodded when I stood before them. There was something curiously formal about the situation, so I remained standing, battered helmet under my arm, and gave them a salute.

Alexander was as pale as lamb's parchment, and Parmenio appeared like an automaton. No emotion at all.

'Gaza will fall to the next assault,' Parmenio said. 'I want your troops to spearhead it.'

I looked back and forth between them.

'Batis is losing men as fast as we are, and we have deeper pockets.' Parmenio shrugged. 'He can't keep it up. I mean to fake an assault this evening and then pound the breaches for half an hour with stones to kill his defenders. Tomorrow I expect to move the batteries forward to the new platforms. Then I'll pound the walls for two days while Diades pushes the ramps higher and makes the footing better.' He looked at Alexander.

Alexander smiled.

'Then I want to go in with all six pezhetaeroi regiments, all together.'

Parmenio nodded. 'I want you to lead it. I can't afford to lose Craterus, and Perdiccas is too young.'

It was, in many ways, the most sincere and heady praise I ever received.

So I did.

I won't bore you. It was anticlimactic, like the ending of a bad play. Parmenio, the professional, had it just right. The endless barrage of the last two days had broken the garrison's spirit, and our six assault columns coming up long, shallow ramps that were virtually paved with brick ate their souls. The men facing me shot their arrows and fled while my men were only halfway to the breach, and when we got to the rubble, the two ballistas there were smashed to flinders by our barrage. In the streets beyond, we went cautiously, linked up with the other columns at the wall and refused to be channelled. It was all very slow and methodical.

In the centre of the town, there was a big open square. We surrounded it – they had fortified the square like a reserve citadel.

Batis sent a herald asking for terms.

I was, for once, unhurt. I looked around at our men, and then I looked down into the square – I'd once again stormed a house to get into its tower for the view.

Batis had about four thousand men still prepared to fight, facing twice that. And he had little food and no water.

The herald was terrified. We were the evil enemy he'd heard so much about, and he wasn't a real herald but some Persian nobleman's son – proud, brave and polite.

I shrugged. 'Tell the noble Batis that he will have to surrender without terms. I have him either way.'

The boy gulped. 'I ... I was charg-ged t-to say th-that—'

'I won't eat you, lad. Say your piece.' Someone brought me a bunch of grapes and I started devouring them.

'We will fight to the end-d if y-you won't promise us our f-freedom.' He stood straight. 'W-we won't be slaves!' he said suddenly.

Alexander had enslaved all the Greeks after Granicus. All those he didn't massacre. I nodded. 'That's up to the king, lad.'

Batis, after some deliberation, decided on the better course, and surrendered. I marched his men out of the city immediately, lest he change his mind – out of the main gate and down on to the plain, surrounded by Macedonians.

Batis led his men in surrender. He was a mighty figure and a noble one, unbowed by defeat. And what a defeat! Two months, toe to toe with our entire army. I found it difficult to hate him, now that he was walking behind me. He was canny, but not mean-spirited. He released to me all of our wounded that he'd captured – he hadn't cut their hands off, he hadn't blinded them. He'd seen to it they had doctors. He'd actually saved twenty of my own men – men I loved and valued.

We marched out on to the plain of Gaza, and Hephaestion came with the king.

Amyntas, who was expert at currying favour, had brought some sample plunder out of the town. It was a rich town, and my troops were going through it with ruthless efficiency even as we accepted Batis's surrender. But Amyntas found the prize – a royal chariot, possibly even one kept for Darius, sheathed in gold. He found a team to draw it, too. He led it down on to the plain, rather than driving it. And he presented it to Alexander when the king emerged from his tent.

Alexander embraced him carefully – his shoulder must have hurt like fire – and mounted the chariot. With a strange team, in front of twenty thousand men, he drove the chariot effortlessly across the sand to where Batis waited.

Batis stood as straight as an old tree. Other Persians fell on their faces. Batis looked at his conqueror with neither fear nor fawning.

Alexander stopped the chariot. Two files of hypaspitoi joined him.

He looked at me. 'What terms, my friend?' he asked.

That didn't sound good. 'No terms,' I said. 'But I would ask for their lives.'

Alexander nodded curtly. Now he turned and looked at Batis. 'Say something,' he said.

Batis locked his eyes with the king's. He was a head taller.

He crossed his arms and stood negligently.

Alexander walked up to him. 'I can order your garrison massacred – or sold into slavery. You are not a soldier of Darius, Batis – you are a rebel against me. You understand that? Darius is no longer King of Asia.'

Alexander was angry. His spit flew into the Persian's face.

Batis didn't even seem to blink.

'I have summoned this town to surrender five times,' Alexander said in a loud, clear voice. 'And I was mocked each time.'

No one moved. Batis allowed himself the smallest smile of contempt.

Alexander made a motion with his hand, and the hypaspitoi seized Batis and threw him to the ground.

'Strip him,' Alexander said. He took a spear from another hypaspist – a dory, twice the height of a man – and snapped it in two in the middle.

Batis remained silent. Two hypaspists pinned him while a third cut his clothing off with a sharp sword. He bled. He began to struggle and Alectus slammed his fist into the Persian's temple. Batis thrashed and Alectus hit him again.

'When you resist, you waste my time,' Alexander said. He took half the broken spear – the half with the head attached – and walked over to Batis. He thrust the spear into Batis's leg, near the foot – I thought he was just prodding him, but then he leaned his weight on it, and Batis grunted, the cords in his neck showing like ropes as he struggled not to scream. He was a brave man.

Alexander punched the spearhead out through the other side of the leg at the ankle, and thrust again, against the whole weight of Batis's thrashing leg, with superhuman strength, and his blow was sure. He penetrated the other ankle, at the back near the heel.

Batis moaned and gave a strangled cry.

Alexander looked up from his task. 'You read about Achilles doing this,' he said, conversationally. 'But you have to wonder what it's like to do it – and now I know.' He kicked Batis's near ankle and pulled the spear shaft through so that the spear penetrated *both* ankles, with several feet of haft emerging on either side.

A slave held a towel while the king wiped his hands. Hypaspitoi tied the spear shaft to the back of the chariot.

The king looked at what they'd done and shook his head. 'You need knots *outside* the ankles,' he said, conversationally. 'Otherwise, he'll slip off, and we'll have to do all this again.'

He smiled at Amyntas. 'My thanks for the chariot. A god-sent opportunity.'

Batis coughed and choked – a very brave man struggling not to scream, knowing that when the first one came out, he'd never stop until he died.

In every life there are things for which we do not forgive ourselves. I cannot forgive myself for not stepping forward and putting my spear into Batis. He deserved a hero's death.

Alexander smiled at Batis. 'You wanted to be Hector. And now, you are!'

He cracked a whip and the horses moved, and Batis screamed.

And screamed.

And screamed.

Alexander drove up and down until the Persian was dead. Then he stopped the chariot in front of us, stepped down and nodded to Hephaestion and Parmenio, who stood as stunned as I was. The army was cheering him.

He didn't look at me. He beckoned to Parmenio.

I knew what he was going to do. I watched, unable to make myself act, with revulsion and a certain weariness, the way I used to watch when he would go out of his way to make Philip his father unhappy, or to embarrass Aristotle.

'Kill them all,' Alexander said, waving his hand at the town. 'It's time they learned not to waste my time.'

Parmenio glanced at the garrison. 'All?' he asked.

Alexander made a face. 'No, keep all the eunuchs with two left feet alive. Yes. All! Everyone!'

And then he turned and walked across the sand, surrounded by hypaspitoi. Back to his tents. And left us to the blood, and the killing.

TWENTY-SEVEN

In the aftermath of the capture of Tyre, I heard a great deal of ugly grumbling from the friends – the inner circle – about the last year. The murder of Batis shocked us all. The manner of it – the bloody-handed tyranny of it – shocked the aristocrats and the army's leaders.

For the first time, I heard it suggested openly that the king was insane.

I didn't think he was insane – if he had ever been sane by the standards of normal men, he still was. But the enormous wound he'd taken and the drugs Philip must have put into him to keep him on his feet – by Apollo's bow, I still look for any excuse to cover him. He ordered almost fifty thousand men and women killed between Tyre and Gaza, and for nothing. Everyone else had already submitted. There was no *example* to be made. And the killing of Batis went clean against his code – except that more and more frequently, he seemed to be set on the annihilation of all resistance, rather than the honourable combat and complex warrior friendships of the *Iliad*.

It was a paradox – the kind on which Aristotle thrived – that Alexander seemed to want to create the world of the *Iliad* – a world of near-eternal war and heroism – and yet seemed to want to destroy all of his opponents so that they could not continue the struggle.

The public killing of Batis galvanised aristocratic Persian opinion, and any Persian who was not a snivelling lickspittle determined to resist Alexander to the last arrow. I hesitate to give voice to this theory – but it is possible that the king wanted the war to go on, and feared that the Persians would simply murder Darius and cave in. It is difficult for me, even as one of his closest confidants, advisers and perhaps even his closest friend – to say what went on inside his head.

The priests here in Aegypt are quite expert on matters relating to what happens inside a man's head. They claim to be able to discern hundreds of illnesses that afflict a man and yet are invisible. Some are obvious – one man can drink wine all his life, get drunk when it pleases him and otherwise live a normal existence, while another man craves the drink in unseemly ways and ruins his life.

Others are harder to sort out, and I've met a priestess of Hathor who claimed that the sort of paradox I mentioned can drive a man to madness. Perhaps.

I think there are other factors. In all the years I knew Alexander, I never heard him once say the words 'my fingers hurt'. Hurt fingers are the ultimate commonplace among soldiers. Every soldier hurts his fingers – the wooden sword catches them sparring, the fingers hurt from the jarring of constant use, they're the first things injured in a fall. Soldiers bitch about them all the time.

Mine hurt every morning by the time I was twenty-one. And every morning, I pissed and moaned about them to my peers, who did the same in return. Add in shoulders, backs, hips, thighs when riding, old wounds, new wounds ...

Aside from sex and money, pain is probably the third most common topic among veterans, rivalling the availability of wine and easily beating anything to do with warrior skills or tactics.

I never heard the king mention any of his wounds, or any other pain. Not true – on two occasions, I heard him mention his wounds. Both times he was virtually unable to speak from the pain. When he stood in his chariot, rolling across the plain below Gaza with Batis being dragged to death behind him, every bump of the bronze-clad wheels must have sent a lance of fire through his left shoulder. When he pushed the spear through the enemy's ankles, the action must have torn at his wound, nearly blinding him with pain.

I say this not to excuse him – you will see my views more and more – but to explain why we did not rise as a body and murder him as unfit to be king. I, for one, was still absolutely loyal, and when men questioned his sanity and his fitness, I shouted them down and questioned their loyalties and their love of Macedon. What else could I do? If I had joined those questioning, where would I have gone from there?

I had a greater worry than the king's sanity, and Hephaestion shared it, as did Parmenio. All three of us had begun to wonder what would happen if the king died.

The king's sickness at Tarsus and his wound at Gaza revealed that the army would – with grave reservations – take orders from Parmenio. It would not take orders from Hephaestion. Or rather, everyone would obey orders from Parmenio up to a point, and the point was commitment to battle.

If Alexander died, we were going to melt away like snow on Mount

Olympus in high summer, and all our conquests were going to be like smoke from a sacrificial fire – beautiful to smell, and gone on the first wind.

The pezhetaeroi cared nothing about it. Neither did the mercenaries. But from the time of the wound at Gaza, a few of us began very quietly to discuss the future of Macedon when the king died.

When, not if.

A last word on the subject.

Mazces surrendered Aegypt without a fight. Mazces was a worm where Batis had been an eagle, but as I have said before, it was never possible to look far into the labyrinthine corridors of the king's godlike mind. Alexander killed fifty thousand at Tyre and Gaza. But Aegypt surrendered without a fight – Aegypt, the most populated place I'd ever been. While I grant that their soldiers – excepting only their superb marines – were not very good, had their populace chosen to resist, we'd still be fighting there.

But they did not. It is possible that the wholesale murders helped break their will to resist. I doubt it. The king might have thought so, but Thaïs's letters suggested a country that was going to fall into our laps like a ripe grape. And so it proved.

We marched south from Gaza after a four-day rest. If any man in our army was sleeping well, I didn't know him. I know that the night before we marched, Marsyas and I sat and got very drunk.

The fleet was waiting for us at Pelussium seven days later, and Mazces was waiting a few parasanges farther on to offer submission. We marched to Memphis – some of the army went downriver by ship and boat, and Alexander marched cross-country. He was starting to recover from his wound, and as the drugs wore off, he was surly and difficult.

Three weeks after the fall of Gaza, I happened to have the vanguard. We were two days out from Memphis, according to our scouts, and the country had submitted – but we'd learned from experts, and we took no chances. I had a double screen of light cavalry – I already had fast-moving parties in every village on the river for two or three parasanges in either direction, and behind these patrols and the thick screen came my pezhetaeroi in a three-sided box covering the archers and Agrianians ready to pounce on an ambush.

All routine, of course.

Alexander was driving his chariot. The roads in Aegypt were excellent – some of the best I'd ever seen – and the chariot was ideal for a man who wanted to be active but still suffered a lot of pain.

I trotted Medea over to the king. We were making a long march – a hundred stades – and the men were starting to flag. The same men, let me add, who had been in continuous combat for seventeen months.

'Lord,' I said, with a salute. There had been a time when the king's friends didn't need to salute, but I found that, since Gaza, I needed to show respect. Lest some draw the wrong conclusion.

Alexander looked up through the dust and nodded. 'Ptolemy,' he said.

We rode along for a stade or two – I offered him wine, he drank it. I got the impression that he was clamping down very hard to control himself. I suspected that the wound from Gaza still hurt a great deal more than he let on.

'When are we celebrating some feasts?' I finally asked. I had worked on a dozen methods of manipulating the king into this conversation, but although he virtually refused to speak, I wasn't going to let go.

He looked at me, his brows furrowed and the lines around his eyes as stark as writing on paper. 'Feasts?' he asked.

I leaned down. 'The army is exhausted,' I said. 'They need a rest.'

Alexander looked at me. I'm not one for reading into expressions – I like men to speak their minds, and women, too – but Alexander's face was haggard.

'You are driving yourself rather than give in to pain,' I hazarded.

'I am above pain,' he said. The lines around his eyes contradicted him, although his voice was *perfectly* controlled.

'Save it for the troops,' I said. 'The appearance of effortless control costs you. But they don't know that. If you will play at being a god, they will take your sacrifices for granted. And curse your name.'

He looked away.

'It is openly said that you are insane,' I said.

His head shot around with the speed of a falcon's.

'I am *not* insane,' he said. 'All I do must be done.'

Well, well, thought I.

'The army needs a rest,' I insisted. 'Don't take my word for it. Ask Black Cleitus. Ask Hephaestion. Ask Parmenio.'

I watched his face close down.

'You are dismissed,' he said.

I'm sure we'd both like me better if, at this point, I offered him some more home truths, but sadly, I didn't. I went off to make a show of tending to my advance guard.

Two days later, we arrived at Memphis. The king announced that he would take the elites upriver, and the rest of us could sit at Memphis for a month-long rest and sacrifice to Amon and Apis. He purchased every sacrificial animal in the city and gave them to the army, as well as a 'donation' that amounted to a little less than three months' pay per man.

His status with the army changed overnight. Every wine shop and brothel in Memphis was packed to the rafters. The women of Aegypt were short, with short legs and heavy breasts and tawny skin, and they did not age well at all – peasant girls were young at twelve and old at twenty-four. But they were plentiful and warm and very alive – they could dance and sing, and a third of the men in the army acquired a wife, many through actual services conducted by the priests of Hathor. For we had seldom been welcomed as heroes before, but in Aegypt, among the common people, we were their liberators. Greeks had a fearsome, but in the main wholesome and heroic, reputation here as preservers of the people's liberties, and we benefited from years of Athenian meddling.

That's a convoluted way of saying that the women welcomed us with open legs. It is possible that some men were pleased, as well, but none of my soldiers was paying any attention whatsoever.

Thaïs and I wandered around the palaces. Alexander went to sacrifice to Apis as king, and we were invited to attend – women have greater participation in Aegypt than elsewhere, and Thaïs could attend as her-self and without prejudice.

I'm a pious man, as soldiers go. I worship the gods, and I have learned to respect the gods other men worship, as well. As an Indian once told me, there is more than just one truth.

But at Memphis, I experienced the divine.

Oh, Aegypt, the land of gods.

We entered the temple of Osiris, which was old when Heraklitus taught, and old when Homer wrote, old when Troy fell, old when Herakles walked the earth. It chilled me – chilled us all, even in the blinding heat of Aegyptian summer – to feel the sheer age of the temple, and see the stains on the warm red-brown stone where thousands upon thousands of feet had trod the surface to perfect smoothness – a rippled effect that said more about worship than all the images of men and gods with the heads of animals around me.

The gods of Aegypt have the heads of animals – I expect you know that by now. Seen safely from a distance, this can be ugly or merely disconcerting – alien. But seen in rows, hundreds upon hundreds, or seen in colossal repetition, as in the great temple complex at Memphis – it forces you to ask the obvious question.

Why not the faces of men?

Or rather, are men any the less animals, when compared to the gods?

Apis is different. Apis has many statues, but all of them are men. Or many are men, and some are bulls. Some are bulls that walk on all fours, and some are bulls that walk erect like the Minotaur, and some are bull-headed men. And some are men. Those are the kings of Aegypt, who, through the mystical powers of Ptah and Osiris, rise again as gods – in Memphis they say Osiris-Apis, or Oserapis, as we say in Alexandria.

Thaïs was walking from statue to statue, touching every one in reverence, and the priests gathered around her – she was an acknowledged priestess of Aphrodite, which can be a joke among Greeks but gave her a very serious status in Memphis.

A senior priest walked beside Alexander, answering his questions.

His questions were concerned with exactly how reincarnation and rebirth worked.

'Why only kings?' he asked.

The priest shrugged. 'Kings are part god from the first,' he said.

I was leaning on the plinth of a statue, and when Alexander passed me to lean over an incised decoration on a tomb, I stumbled – sheer farm-boy clumsiness – and put my hand on the gold-encrusted hide of a mummified Apis bull.

Without warning *I stood on an infinite plain. My first impression was desert, but there was no desert – simply blinding white light and an infinity of it, and no horizon.*

A voice spoke in my head, a strong voice. 'You will be king, here. Do what is right.'

I awoke with my head on Thaïs's lap, and Alexander massaging my wrists. I was embarrassed, as any man is who shows weakness, and perhaps most remarkable, it was some time before I remembered what I had seen and heard, so that at first I imagined I'd just passed out.

Looking back, I have a difficult time recalling the dream, but no trouble at all recalling the deep confusion it engendered in me. Although I worship the gods, no god had ever spoken to me so directly. Indeed, when I saw Alexander sacrifice his chariot on the morning before Issus, I thought of *that* as the supreme moment of my religious life.

And now, an alien, foreign god had reached out and touched me.

I stumbled along through the rest of the tour.

The Apis bull is chosen from a herd of very ordinary black and white cattle. They'd look odd in Macedon, but not so odd that they wouldn't fetch a decent price at market. However, it is different in Aegypt, where from the whole herd, one bull is chosen and taken to the temple, where he becomes *king* or, as they say here, *pharaoh*. That bull is king for twenty-eight years, and at the end of his reign, he is sacrificed – usually by the pharaoh and in the presence of the priests. Sometimes an older pharaoh orders a champion to do the deed for him, but then all of the priests and the king eat the flesh of the slaughtered bull and this ceremony, very secret and sacred, is symbolic of the renewal of life that Apis offers. The slaughtered bull is called 'Apis-seker-Osiris' and the Aegyptians call him 'Living dead one'.

Pardon me for this Platonic lesson in cosmology, but what happened cannot be understood unless you know what Apis is.

When we had toured, and sacrificed, a Greek priest of Zeus was introduced to us – a pilgrim, come from the shrine of Zeus at Lampsacus to visit the shrines of Aegypt.

He bowed deeply. 'Great King of Asia, I am Anaximenes of Lampsacus!' he said with a flourish.

It is not often a man can combine the pomposity of a horse's arse with the false humility of a false priest, but Anaximenes did both at the same time, to which he added a brilliant mind, a wit razor-sharp in the service of flattery and an actor's ability to be all things to all men.

Hush, let me tell you how I really felt about him, the shite.

Alexander loved him.

And well he might. Anaximenes it was who knew that the Apis bull was due to be slaughtered – that, in fact, it was but two weeks until the ceremony was due. Anaximenes knew that Darius had forbidden the ceremony.

In hours, we were preparing to take part, and Alexander spent money like water to have his vestments and crown as the Great King of Aegypt prepared. The priests leaped to serve him, eager, I think, to have a king who might be their ally instead of their enemy, as the kings of Persia had been. He invited me to participate, and I was drawn to it, and I noticed that one of the priests – not the Greek, but one of the smooth-headed Aegyptian priests – seemed to follow me with his eyes.

While the details of the ceremony were discussed, a priest came to Thaïs, and after a brief conversation, she squeezed my hand and vanished. What followed was a secret – I will not tell you, even now, although if you, in your turn, should by the will of gods be a king, I cannot recommend to you too highly the worship of Apis – and we spent a long evening learning our roles.

Later, unfed, I fretted alone in the palace. I had sumptuous rooms, and they had the most remarkable furnishings – Aegypt was, and remains, the richest country I had ever seen, and even the palace guest rooms to house a foreign, barbarian general were superb. I summoned slaves and ate in solitary splendour, missing anyone – Marsyas, Cleitus – who might share the tolerable beer.

Unsummoned, a pair of attendants came and took me to a bath – a remarkably ugly bath, but enormous. It was as if someone had heard of a Greek bath but knew none of the details, and used sandstone rather than marble for the fittings. On the positive side, I emerged clean and fresh, and the towels were superb. On the negative side, I was not oiled, and so left the bath chamber feeling dry and scratchy.

I walked back along the corridors of the palace to my rooms, flanked by four bath attendants, and it was curious that there were no other men or women in the corridors. It gave the experience a slightly dream-like air.

And Aegyptian architecture is heavy – to the point of ugliness – and I had a moment when I experienced something almost like vertigo, when I wanted to see something familiar – a Greek shape, a Greek column ...

And then I was in my rooms.

Thaïs was sitting on a rather formal chair. It took me three heartbeats to know her, as she wore the disc of Hathor on her head and Aegyptian garments, with kohl-painted brows and lashes and henna on her hands and feet. Her eyes seemed huge, the whites white, the pupils enormous.

She stood and smiled at me. 'I have had the most glorious experience,' she said, and for some reason I bowed to her.

I must digress, because you are so young. When you fall in love, your lover is the most beautiful thing in all of creation. You cannot get enough of her. Her feet, her hands, the inside of a thigh, the perfume of her, the scent of her breath ...

When you have been partnered for some years, neither of your bodies has any secrets left, no surprises, no wonder. This is not the death of love – far from it – but it is possible and human to long for that sense of wonder, that desire so strong it can bend steel.

My partner was reckoned, even after two pregnancies, one of the world's most beautiful women. She added to that – her natural beauty – training in music, dance, singing, rhetoric – and sex. She was a superb horsewoman, and a fine archer.

And yet, I would lie if I say that either one of us excited the other then as we had in the first months we were together. We pleased one another. No woman I've ever lain with had pleased me as she could, or as easily, and I dare say I knew her as none of her other partners ever had.

And yet ...

I bowed because, in her Aegyptian priestess's costume, she was herself, and yet she was someone else. Her dignity – always asserted – was even more evident, and elegant.

And in that moment, I remembered clearly what the voice had said.

552

It hit me – again – like a bucket of seawater on a hot day.

I think I stumbled.

She tilted her head a little to one side. 'You, too, I think,' she said.

I sat in the chair she had been in. It was still warm from her. 'I ... touched ... the gods,' I said. Indeed, as I said the words, I thought them. I had not allowed myself to think about it, simply walled it away.

She pursed her lips. She had some sort of wax, almost crimson, on her lips. I wanted to lick them.

'A voice,' I said. My voice was deepening, hoarse with emotion. 'Told me I would be king here. And that I should rule well.'

And even as I spoke, and my voice grew hoarse with emotion – thickened – I felt a pressure on my body like the very personification of lust, and I pulled her lips against mine.

My hand found that she had nothing under her gown, and with a shrug, she lost it – but not her crown, not her regalia, not her paint.

I have never experienced anything like that night, and I will tell you no more. Except to say that it was not sex, but the sacred. Or perhaps all sex is merely another contact with the sacred.

Two priests instructed me the next day in every aspect of my function, because, owing to Alexander's wounded shoulder, I was going to be his 'champion' and sacrifice the bull.

Hephaestion, it turned out, would not do it. He saw it as sacrilege. He wanted nothing to do with foreign gods.

Cleitus refused on other grounds. He was a man who feared failure more than he wished for success, and the notion of killing the sacred bull in front of an audience of a thousand, with the king's success riding on his stroke – Cleitus passed.

I knew I was the king's third choice. And the thought of performing it gave me the same shakes that it gave to Cleitus. But I was driven, a mere tool of the god. Nothing like this had ever happened to me before.

Those were two happy weeks. Something entered into my love of Thaïs – or returned to it – that had been lost with our second child. She once again looked at me with her secret smile lingering almost invisible in the corner of her mouth. She sang. I croaked back at her.

She teased me, and parodied my bad Aegyptian accent when I practised my lines, and when I reached to tickle her, she did not run shrieking like a young fool, but took my hands in her grip of iron and put me over her hip like an old and wily pankrationist, so that I had to roll on the floor. And dug her thumbs into my armpits until I bleated like a lamb, and we lay together ...

Good times.

And other times, I left her to her new friends – and she had quite a few, the priestesses of Hathor – and I went into the lower town and drank expensive wine and cheap beer with Marsyas and Cleomenes and Alectus and Cleitus.

I remember one night, I had a slave from Marsyas inviting me for wine – Greek wine – at a tavern by the river. I dressed simply and left all my expensive jewellery and my good cloak, left a note on the cheap and available papyrus for Thaïs and ran down the palace steps like a schoolboy going on an adventure.

The slave led me to the rendezvous, and it was well lit, with oil lamps hanging in rows so that the walls seemed to have their own star fields. It was hot, and most of the patrons sat outside in the night air. The river smelled of silt and ordure – but it was a smell you got used to quickly, like manure in springtime. Men sat on benches and drank, played dice or knucklebones – a few barrack-room intellectuals played Polis or backgammon.

I was early, or the others were late, and I found myself sitting at a small table reserved, I expect, for those who looked likely to pay more, but wedged between an enormous potted plant in an urn carved from stone, and probably three thousand years old – and a trio of pezhetaeroi. Not mine – men of Craterus's taxeis.

There was an old one, a middle-aged one and a young pup straight from the fields around Pella. I tried not to listen too hard, or look too hard, as they would recognise me and grow stiff and formal, and the last thing a good officer wants to do is to rain on the fun his men are having.

I had a scroll – Xenophon's 'On Hunting'. It fitted nicely in my bag, so I left it there, and sitting alone in a tavern in Aegypt with a bowl of wine that had cost me a day's pay for a soldier, I leaned my stool back, tucked my shoulder into the enormous stone urn and read about boar spears.

If, in spite of javelins and stones, he refuses to pull the rope tight, but draws back, wheels round and marks his assailant, in that case the man must approach him spear in hand, and grasp it with the left in front and the right behind, since the left steadies while the right drives it. The left foot must follow the left hand forward, and the right foot the other hand. As he advances let him hold the spear before him, with his legs not much further apart than in wrestling, turning the left side towards the left hand, and then watching the beast's eye and noting the movement of the fellow's head. Let him present the spear, taking care that the boar doesn't knock it out of his hand with a jerk of his head, since he follows up the impetus of the sudden knock.

''Scuse me?' the oldest man was asking. He was polite – nodding at me, and pulling at his chiton. Drunk as a lord. ''Scuse me? Damme, you look familiar.'

I laughed, perhaps a little bit self-conscious.

'Except it's like this, see? Dion says that this chit, here,' and the grizzled veteran of Philip's wars caught the wrist of a serving girl, 'has the best tits of any girl in this fine establishment.' He nodded sagely. 'Which she may, or may not.'

Like many Aegyptian women, the server had no garment north of her belly button, so modesty was hardly an issue. She wriggled. It was more than just an automatic gesture, and thus very winning.

I gave the veteran a smile and then looked at the woman's breasts.

They were young and well displayed. Not a patch on Thaïs, but comparison is odious.

'Lovely,' I opined.

Veteran nodded. 'That's a fine answer. See? He's not too hoity-toity to look at tits, now, is he? I said to them – he's an officer, but he ain't above us here.'

The youngest one shook his head. 'I'll take him off to bed,' he said apologetically.

I made a face. 'Why?'

Veteran nodded. 'Exactly. Why? I may be fucking dead in a few days, if soldier-boy-the-war-god gets a hair up his arse and marches us to Hyperborea. Why can't I sit and look at her tits? They're fine, and she won't come to no harm from me.'

The middle-aged soldier just glowered. Finally he said, 'What're you reading?'

I had to smile. 'Xenophon. On hunting.'

Veteran roared. 'You're a fuckin' officer. Look, lad – that's a *girl*. For a tenth of the cost of that scroll – a hundredth – you can have what she offers. Feel alive.'

Middle-age shook his head. 'The scroll gives him something for ever. That girl will be gone in the morning.'

'At her age? She'll be gone in ten minutes – off to another garlic-eater, eh? Moving from sausage to sausage?' He laughed at his own witticism. 'Who cares? When I sit and think—'

'You fall asleep, old man,' said Middle-age.

'Yeah?' Veteran shot back. 'Who put the fucking Syrian in the dust when somebody was on his back at Gaza? Eh?' The older man got up, and just for a moment he wasn't a drunk fuck – he was a vicious predator with thin limbs and a grizzled beard, and eyes that burned with malice.

Then he subsided. But the other two had flinched.

He tossed a gold stater on to the table and laughed. 'I'm all blather, boys. Don't let me piss on your evening.' His eyes flicked over to me, and I realised he wasn't as drunk as he let on.

The serving girl came, her eyes drawn by the gold. When her hand reached out for it, Veteran pinned it to the table with his own, and pulled her on to his lap and neatly tucked his tongue inside her throat.

She put her arms around his neck.

He came up spluttering and laughing, and gave her the coin. She skipped away, and he shook his head.

'Where did it go?' he asked. 'A gold daric – where'd she put it? Eh? I ask you, gentlemen. I gave her a gold coin, and she *made it disappear.*' He laughed, drank off his wine and got to his feet, and I realised that I'd been wrong again – he could barely walk. 'Well, friends, I'm off to find it. If she hid it where I think.' He leered. Looked at me. 'You're Ptolemy, I think.'

I nodded.

He nodded back. 'King's friend?'

I nodded again.

'Tell him from me he can suck my dick if he thinks I'm doing any more forced marches in the desert for fuck all. Eh? That's Amyntas son of Philip, phylarch of the third company of the taxeis of Craterus.' He winked. 'You think I'm kidding, eh?'

I shook my head. 'No. I think you're serious.'

'You're not bad, for an officer.' He was swaying, and the girl, who, when bought, apparently stayed bought, had come back and caught his hand. He clasped hers. 'He's made us do some bad shit, eh?' he said suddenly. 'Storming a town's one thing – right? Officer? Whatever you do in a town that refuses to surrender – that's between you and the gods, eh?'

He spat.

'But what we did at Gaza ...' He looked at the girl. 'I killed one just like you, honey.'

The other two were taking his arms. I thought he might cry. But he didn't. He grinned. 'Fuck me,' he said. 'Let me go.'

'Let him go,' I said.

The girl pulled his hand, and he laughed. It wasn't a good laugh, but neither was it the laugh of a broken man.

'Let him go,' I said again.

He came back at me. 'Give me a hug, eh, officer boy?' he said.

I stood up, because I thought he was serious, and he was. He put his arms around me. 'What's it about, eh?' he whispered in my ear. 'I just want to know what the *fuck* it's about, eh?'

Then he pushed himself away. 'Sorry. I'm drunk. You smell good, officer. But not as good as my little friend here, who's waited. Aphrodite, she stayed!'

He smiled at all of us, but most of all at her, and took her away into the dark.

Middle-age shook his head.

'He's saved my life ten times,' he said. 'Please – don't report him.'

I sat back down. 'Relax!' I said. I caught the attention of another girl, whose breasts, to be frank, were not up to the standard of the first. 'A krater of wine,' I said. And then made gestures. Finally I showed her a large silver coin, and she bit it and smiled and ran off, showing her flanks very nicely.

A day's wages for *me.* Wine for three.

Bad wine. But I poured for the two of them, as if they were guests in my house, and we drank.

'He's a great man, really,' Middle-age said. 'But he needs to go home.'

I shot my mouth off, too. 'He can't go home,' I said. 'Unless you want him to die as a bandit in the mountains. It would be like caging a wild boar.'

Middle-age nodded. 'That's what war has made him. It's all he knows. All I'll know, soon, too.' He drank.

'All they do is complain,' the farm boy added. 'It's glorious serving the king. My pater served Philip and he was in *two battles.* I've already been in two great sieges and a battle.' He shook his head. 'Who gives a shit if we kill a bunch of barbarians?'

Middle-age shrugged. 'You will, boy. Or you won't. We have both kinds in the phalanx. Except that if you don't give a shit about them, like enough in time you won't care about anyone. Not even yourself. And then – you'll die.'

'You're just old and burned out,' Youth said.

'Talk to me in twenty more fights, boy.' Middle-age looked at me. He was half my age again – but I'd been fighting a long time. 'If you live that long.'

Youth took a big drink, anger written on his face.

And fear.

I bought another round. I seldom thought much about my longevity, or my future. Despite Aristotle and Heron, I lived from day to day.

Some day, I would be King of Aegypt.

That hit me again, and I sat there drinking, my scroll forgotten.

Veteran came back, his girl in tow, and perched her on his knee and drank my wine. He was mellow now, and the girl ran her hands idly over his chest.

He looked at me and laughed. 'Good hug,' he said.

I pointed at the girl. 'She does have the best tits in here,' I agreed.

He laughed and laughed, and he was still laughing when Marsyas came in. He had Cleomenes and Philip the Red with him, and Kineas and Diodorus, and we embraced as comrades do, and then my three companions tried to escape.

'They're good companions,' I said. 'Let's stay and drink with them.'

Marsyas, it proved, knew all of them, and their names – Amyntas son of Philip (one of a dozen I know) and Dion, and Charmides. Marsyas was a poet, and a drinker, and a rogue, and he knew everyone. And we sat and drank, and watched the girls.

That was Memphis.

I worried myself sick about the sacrifice. When it came, it was sacred, but my nerves fell away as if the god touched me, and perhaps he did.

The bull stood, undrugged, in the middle courtyard of the great temple, tethered to a ring but otherwise unconstrained. I had met him three times, so he would know my smell, and I walked up to him, and the crowd of priests and royal advisers and Alexander's entourage – and Anaximenes, of course – knelt. All except Alexander, who stood just behind me, the only man standing.

The bull saw only me. He moved his head, and I walked very slowly up to him. Dignity has this added benefit – movement with dignity is an excellent practice for calming an animal, whether a horse or a bull.

When I was at his head, I drew the sword I had brought, purified by the priests and fresh from a night on Osiris's altar, wiped clean to perfection with a cloth provided by the priestess of Hathor and smelling very strongly of Thaïs.

I drew it very slowly, and he rolled his eyes, and I wondered how many kings and champions had been lost this way. And I wondered if the high priest, if he disapproved of the pharaoh, or his champion, arranged for the bull to be in a mood. I wondered at a great many things, and then the tip of my sword – a heavy kopis – cleared the scabbard throat and I slowly raised the blade, placed my left hand on the great beast's head just behind the horns, slowly rotated my hips and passed the sword back into the overhand guard position you see so often on vases. It's there for a reason.

The bull raised his head, stretching his neck, and roared – a trumpet noise that made me jump, but with his neck muscles stretched like that ...

I severed his head.

He fell forward on to his knees and pumped blood for a moment, and then sank to the ground and fell over, and the earth shook, and Alexander slapped my shoulder with his right hand.

'Perfect,' he breathed.

I felt empty. Hollow. And from the eye of the head on the floor came a last ... something.

Rule well.

No one cheered, but many, many faces wore a broad smile. And men came to touch me. A priest – the one I had found staring at me, weeks before – came and took my sword from my hand. 'It must be destroyed,' he said, apologetically. 'It has killed a god.'

I guess I understood.

That evening, Alexander gave a party. We drank too much and played stupid games, and Alexander treated the pages much as his father had treated us – which is to say, not very well, with some hard teasing and some innuendo that would not have made their mothers happy.

Anaximenes rose and toasted the king as the son of Apis, the God of Aegypt, and men roared. Bull gods are always popular. Hephaestion looked away in distaste.

'Lord, I have spent months here, looking into the origins of Apis – and Zeus, and Amon.' He paused, and his false humility was like bad incense – it choked me.

'It is said in Greece that your mother claimed you as her son – by Zeus!' he said, and I thought, *What a charlatan. Alexander will have him gutted.* And the silence at the party was so thick you might have thought a beautiful woman was naked.

But Alexander merely nodded.

'Lord, the chief shrine of Amon is close – well guarded, and secret, but in Libya, across burning sands where no mere mortal man could survive the journey. But with you to lead us, we might go to the shrine of Amon. And there learn something of your parentage. With the benison of Apis upon you, and the most favourable sign he has vouchsafed to you ...' He threw his arms wide. 'Your light be revealed to the *world* as the divine son of Zeus.'

I choked on my wine. In truth, I had no trouble seeing my king as a god. In many ways, he was greater than human, and in others, like the gods, he was merely *inhuman.* And yet, paradoxically, I also *knew* that whatever troubles Philip and Olympias had had, and they were legion, the bedchamber had not been one of them, and they had romped like bull and cow for many and many an afternoon and evening, until the lady was pregnant. I wasn't there – but my father was, and many other men I knew.

Hephaestion turned his head away.

Black Cleitus frowned.

But Alexander nodded, his odd, eager smile coming to his face. Pothos again.

'I have a gift to make to Aegypt,' he said. 'And then I will go and see my father, Amon.'

Every man knows the story of the founding of this city of Alexandria. I won't belabour it. Alexander laid it out himself, and he used sacks of barley. The site was superb, and still is – and his eye took it in in one go, just as he saw battlefields, with an Olympian precision of thought that was not like other men's. He looked, and saw, and thought, and the thing was done – the map of the streets was in his head. I know, because he told me.

He left the army at Memphis – to eat off the priests, he told us – and took only the elites north. But he asked me, because the ceremony of the sacrifice of the bull was important to him, and suddenly I was back in his inner circle. I wasn't aware of having been excluded until I was put back. Running a regiment is a job that requires the same dedication as being a parent.

And Thaïs came downriver with us and sailed from Naucratis to Athens. She told me that she had to go – she wanted to see our daughter and our adopted boy, and she needed to sell her house in Athens.

I did not want her to go. I felt her loss keenly, and something told me I would never see her again. Despite which, I gave her ten talents of gold to spend on horses and equipment for me in Athens. New spears – new swords. Anything, really, to reawaken my interest in war, which, by the time the army reached Memphis, sickened me.

We marched from Alexandria – what *would be* Alexandria – and along the coast over sixteen hundred stades, and our horses grew thin, and the Hetaeroi grumbled as loudly as the Agrianians. We ate like a swarms of locusts, leaving the inhabitants rich with gold and destitute of grain wherever we travelled. Eventually, we had to send for the fleet to bring us food.

Having marched so far that some men expected to see the Pillars of Herakles, we turned south into the desert with native guides to lead us to the shrine of Amon.

We marched for ten days, until all of our water was gone. And then we marched for two more days, and the guides admitted they were lost.

Alexander rode bare-headed, the sun grilling him, his hair bleached almost white, while Hephaestion looked more and more like a statue of bronze, his skin and hair matching perfectly. Alexander roved the column on horseback until his horse died, and then he took my Medea. I offered her – he was the king. And he rode her to death, too.

And then we ate the horses and drank their blood, and marched again.

Sometimes, the blind faith that you are the son of a god is a good thing.

'I am being tested,' he said on the twelfth day. He smiled. 'I won't let you die,' he added cheerfully, and rode away.

On the fourteenth day, men started to die – good men, hypaspitoi who had survived a dozen campaigns. I was marching with Alectus, and I had Bubores and Astibus off to my right – we were four abreast in the sand, and even the hypaspitoi were losing their formation, stumbling along, and the hot sun burned even our feet as we trudged, and the gravel got into our sandals and hurt like spear-points. None of which mattered a damn compared to the lack of water.

Men gave way to despair. There were suicides.

I had no unit, so I had returned to the hypaspitoi of the Aegema, where I lived, ate and soldiered. But after that night, I wandered among the men, because the only way to prevent despair is through action.

Alexander was everywhere.

'Rest!' he told the hypaspitoi. 'Get sleep. We will find water, or it will come to us.'

Men said he was insane.

And the next day, it rained.

In the desert, in summer.

Two days of rain.

And when the rain cleared, priests from the shrine, led by portents, found us and took us to the oasis and the shrine of Amon.

Sometimes, I had to doubt whether it was Alexander who was insane.

It is hard, in retrospect, to choose when Alexander changed. I used to argue the point with Cleitus, and with Kineas. Each had a different answer. For Kineas, Alexander's change began after the pursuit of Darius, while for Cleitus, it began as soon as he won Granicus.

Both are right, and both are wrong. To most of us, the change began some time before his sickness at Tarsus. Or perhaps at Tyre. But the change became set, like the hardening of concrete or mud bricks in the sun, during the visit to the shrine of Amon.

TWENTY-EIGHT

—◦⁀◦—

Alexander went to the oracle alone. The oracle of Amon was famous in the Greek world, as well as in Aegypt, and was ancient – as ancient as Delphi or older.

Anaximenes says in his book that Alexander asked if all of the murderers of his father had been punished. If you consider that – if you look carefully at the question, and the man asking it – you have to face what a paradox Alexander lived. If Alexander didn't wield the dagger himself – if Olympias arranged it without informing him – that was the very best he could claim, and I know better.

To ask such a thing from a sacred shrine – what can I say? Is it gross impiety, or a reckless craving that the past might be changed to suit the present? Alexander sought *not* to be a patricide. Not to be Oedipus, but Achilles.

Again according to that toad Anaximenes, Alexander was told that his question was impious. *Because his father was Amon, Zeus Amon, and could never be killed.* Was that what he was told? That's what the lickspittle says.

Or was that what Anaximenes and Aristander cooked up when Alexander was told that his question was impious?

Or was the entire show managed from the first, so that Alexander could go on a quest to discover his parentage?

I cannot see clearly into his mind. I often try – and did then. Sometimes on matters of procedure, or war, or building, as with Alexandria, he would explain to me how he thought. But on something like this, I was left to guess.

And the paradox of the patricide seeking to avenge his father was not something I could understand, despite years of trying.

The only effect of the visit to the shrine of Amon was a hardening of Alexander's resolve to be viewed and accepted as the son of a god and a god in his own right.

And the introduction of Anaximenes as a favourite.

*

We marched from the shrine of Amon with carts full of water skins and we made the coast and the fleet in good order, without any more deaths, as if, the drama done, Alexander needed to hurry. We reached the building site at Alexandria, and we had been gone only four weeks, but Alexander was angry that so little had been done. I think he had imagined that Zeus his father would build him a city in the desert while he visited Amon. I have no idea.

I wanted Thaïs, and now that I was not going to die in the desert, I thought about her constantly. But we marched from Naucratis upriver to Memphis, moving fast, as if the King of Kings was behind us and this was a desperate race.

In fact, I gathered from the grumblings of Callisthenes, who was considerably less happy with Anaximenes than the king was, that Darius had, in fact, used the year's respite since Issus to rebuild his army. I had heard – through Thaïs and her endless network, and through military sources close to the king – that when we had entered Asia, the Great King had serious troubles on his own eastern frontier, far off in the lands we knew only by repute, such as India and Bactria.

Now it appeared that by concession and temporising, he had brought his eastern barons to heel, and we were, finally, to face the whole might of Persia.

Parmenio and his faction openly questioned the king's strategy, and while they were loyal, their carping damaged morale. It is possible that, had Alexander plunged eastward after Issus, we might have taken Babylon and ended Darius, but as events were to prove, the empire remained the property of Darius for as long as he lived, and his bodyguard and his cousins were too realistic to leave him to die on a battlefield. And had we marched on Babylon from Issus – with the Persian fleet still alive behind us, with Aegypt as a base, with all the taxes and riches of Aegypt to support them – we might well have found ourselves cut off, alone and surrounded.

Whereas now, as the king gathered his forces at Memphis, we held all the ground west of the Euphrates. There were hold-outs and rebels, as Antigonus and Nearchus could attest. But in the main, we held the field, and we had continuous supply lines all the way back to Pella.

Which Antipater demonstrated by sending part of the fleet from Amphilopolis with fifteen hundred recruits for the various pezhetaeroi, a paltry six hundred more mercenaries and four hundred excellent Thracian cavalry, as well as more Thessalians. We divided the recruits among all seven taxeis, at about two hundred men each, which was excellent for me, and I took two hundred of the 'mercenaries' as well.

563

They were a mixed bag of brigands, Peloponnesian defectors and other scum – all the good troops were fighting alongside Antipater – or fighting against him. Or we already had them with us. The truth was, every professional hoplite in the world of the Hellenes was in harness.

I cared, but not much, because my taxeis was as close to full strength as I could get it.

We marched by easy stages up to Pelusium, and then back to Gaza on the coast road, and then along the coast to Tyre. I dined with Alexander every night – with Craterus, Perdiccas and a dozen others from my boyhood. The king was more natural than I had seen him for a year. The only false notes were Anaximenes and Aristander, who were infinitely more obsequious than the most toady-like of the Macedonians – Nearchus, let us say.

When we were alone – almost alone, that is – when it was Alexander and Hephaestion, or Alexander and Cleitus – we talked about a final shake-up of the command structure of the army. Parmenio was never included in these discussions, which troubled me.

While we speak of paradox, let us remember that the whole army was in a state of paradox. Alexander commanded, and Parmenio was his second. When Alexander was sick, or wounded, Parmenio took command, and the reins slipped into his hands easily. And he never hesitated to hand the king back the reins when he rose form his sickbed.

And yet, by this time, they cordially detested each other. And as far as I could see, each schemed carefully for the destruction of the other – while, at the same time, acknowledging that the army and the kingdom were *better* for the continued existence of the other.

And if the Macedonian army seems to you a mighty thing, a monolith of military efficiency, let me tell you that inside the monolith, the edifice was plaster and wood, not stone; rats were gnawing at the thin ropes that held all the other stuff together. We had a lot of very mediocre mid-level officers, many of whom were Alexander's friends and had been given commands owing to their loyalty to him.

And Alexander had reached a point where friendship with the king was not enough to secure command. I approved, but of course, I didn't get the sack, either.

At Tyre, we had a long halt for the spring rains. Alexander had acted with foresight – we arrived to find a camp built by slaves and hired labour, vast magazines of food, and tents – new tents of heavy Syrian flax.

Alexander had actually thought about his army.

There were stockpiles of sarissas, well made by good smiths, and swords.

But mostly, there were water skins, baggage carts and barley. I whistled as we examined the stocks, and the horde of rats that came with them, but Alexander was angry.

It's worth examining why, as an indication of how fast his mind was.

The grain stocks were held in sixteen enormous stone granaries, each of which was so new that you could smell the mud brick and the mortar. I was looking at the nearest in something not unlike awe, and Alexander said, 'He's short by a thousand mythemnoi. Perhaps five times that.' He pursed his lips. 'Get me the satrap of Syria,' he said, grimly.

'He' was Menon, and his successor in office, a local man. Satrap of Syria. The man responsible for bringing in the grain as taxes and building the granaries. It was nothing to Alexander that he had built this camp, arranged to receive the shipments of everything from linen to weapons, hired the workers to build the granaries – all a miracle of organisation, by Eastern standards. Inside Alexander's clockwork brain, what mattered was that he was more than a thousand mythemnoi of grain short for his projected march to Babylon.

He sacked the poor bastard on the spot, ignored his protests and appointed a new man.

And with that, I must digress again. The farther into this story I get, the more often I see, with my finger on a line of the Military Journal, that I have left out an important subplot that will suddenly emerge to bite me.

I have said almost nothing of Harpalus. He was a page with us, a young man with us, and he was fanatically loyal to the king. He was sent into exile when many of the rest of us were, and he was, for a long time, Erigyus of Mytilene's lover. He was, like Marsyas, a fine fighter but a better brain, and had, quite early, taken to mathematics. He almost never accompanied us on campaign in the early years.

But he was, almost from the first ascension of Alexander to the throne, his chief treasurer. He was good at maths, but more importantly, he was expert at talking men into making donations, and he seemed to be able to conjure gold out of the air, so that, in the early days, he stood as a barrier between the king and his very real poverty.

In fact, I haven't mentioned him because ... how can I put this without seeming a cuckold? He never hid his admiration for Thaïs. And she liked him in a way she didn't like me – as one brain to another, I think. They shared jokes – gossip – and secrets. Together. Without me.

To say I hated him is to do all three of us an injustice. But I confess that most of the time I tried to pretend he didn't exist.

But he did.

While Alexander was sick – at Tarsus – he defected. He took an enormous sum of money, and left us – for Athens and Sicily. To me, it was good riddance.

Thaïs was pregnant, you recall, and delighted to be so. I was newly promoted to a taxeis, and all was well.

But when I spoke of him as a traitor, Thaïs would look at me – a look that always meant, 'You are better than that.'

It made me think. After a while, I stopped referring to him as a traitor.

At Amon, the king included Harpalus, *by name*, in his prayers and sacrifices.

He was in Athens. And about the time the army arrived at Tyre, I realised that he was in Athens, and so was Thaïs.

There were two ways for me to read it. I could see the love of my life as despicable – capable of running off with another man, without so much as telling me where her feelings lay.

Or I could go back through all the conversations I'd ever had with either of them, and sort through for some facts.

I was, and am, intelligent enough to see that Thaïs was not the woman to behave that way. If she had left me for Harpalus, she'd have said so. Or so I had to believe, despite the recurring notion that her spectacular appearance as a priestess of Hathor was a form of farewell.

But the heart can be a dark place, and I could not conquer the image of Thaïs lying in his arms. In Athens.

We'd been camped at Tyre for a week when three ships came from Athens – the Athenian state galley *Paralus* and an escort, as well as a private ship, with them – Stratokles of Athens in his first *Black Falcon*.

I was drilling my taxeis on the wide plain when they came in, and an hour later, Polystratus rode up on a beautiful mare – a new one – and saluted.

'The Lady Thaïs has arrived from Athens,' he said. 'She has a shipload of your goods, and requests your immediate presence.'

Polystratus slipped from the horse's back while he spoke. 'And this divine filly, and a pair of geldings for you. You lucky bastard.' He patted her back. 'Don't keep the lady waiting.'

I could have kissed him. Instead, I vaulted on to the horse's back – what a sweet horse – no war horse, but beautifully trained and responsive. A little small for me, but all heart.

I rode her down to the beach, enjoying every minute.

There was Thaïs.

With Harpalus.

566

I almost choked, but I am not a fool. If *any* of my unworthy suspicions were true, then they would not be standing on a beach together laughing. Or rather, they might, but only if Thaïs was a different woman.

So, not without effort, I dismounted, gave Harpalus a civil bow and opened my arms.

Thaïs moulded herself to me. There is no other way of describing what a woman can do with the man she loves, so that as much of the body is in contact as can possibly be managed. She raised her face and I kissed her. I think it was the first time I kissed her in public.

She laughed into my mouth.

Harpalus looked at me with a certain bewildered jealousy. I thought him a traitorous, fickle, high-strung idiot, and he, I suspect, thought me a clod. Still thinks it, I suspect.

There we go, then.

'I have a few things for you,' she said. She introduced me to Stratokles – father of the current politician – who looked at me with distaste. With him, and Harpalus, was a soldier – I knew him in a moment as one – well dressed, in the Athenian way.

'I have all your armour,' Thaïs said, delighted by her own success. What can be more wonderful for a man who has doubted his mistress than to watch her, in turn, be pleased at her ability to give pleasure? I didn't need to hear the story to know that she had worked hard to get the armour shipment together.

I sent a slave to get the taxeis down to the beach. I had arrangements of my own to make – I needed a man to replace Isokles. I had asked Kineas, but he – and Diodorus – refused to leave their precious aristocratic Athenian cavalry. I wanted an Ionian or an Athenian to help me with the prickly sods I had from Memnon, but no one was forthcoming.

I digress, because of the association of ideas. The man with Harpalus and Stratokles the elder was Leosthenes, who had been elected an Athenian tribal general twice, and was as near a mercenary as you could be without carrying the name.

I was introduced to him. He looked familiar.

'You served with us at Issus?' I asked, as soldiers do.

He shrugged. 'In the second line. Your king always puts men like me in the second line.'

He had the kind of charisma that Alexander had. It burned from his eyes. And he had a nice Ionian accent.

Thaïs laughed. 'I brought him for you, dear. He goes with the horses.'

Leosthenes blushed. 'I don't like to seem a supplicant,' he said.

Thaïs put a hand on his arm. 'He has helped do the king a great service in Athens, and he needs a home for a few months.'

I held out my hand. 'I need a company commander, and an Ionian one is ideal. I don't suppose you have any way of qualifying as one of us? A Macedonian?'

Leosthenes laughed aloud. 'My mother is Thessalian. The Athenian Assembly never tires of reminding me.'

By that time, Polystratus and Marsyas had brought the taxeis down to the beach, stripped to chitons.

I ambled the mare over to them and raised a hand for silence. 'Listen, gents. I have spent a fair amount of gold to get you lot some new kit – so you can look like proper princesses when you go to the dance. Unload it from the ship, and we'll have a feast tonight in the old way, and share it all out. This is my gift, lads – not an obol from your pay.'

Unlike Alexander, I knew what appealed to soldiers.

We unloaded that ship before the sun went down, and while we did, the regiment's slaves built a dozen bonfires on the beach, and Leosthenes showed his skills by getting up fifty baskets of lobster. Just try to make fifty baskets of lobster appear. It takes skill and the will of the gods.

The slaves built the fires high and burned them down to coals, and we buried the brutes in the coals and roasted them. There were anchovies so fresh that some tried to get back into the sea, and Thaïs had brought wine. I suppose – no, I know – she brought good wine for the campaign, but I handed it all over to the troops, save a few lonely amphorae for us, and she rolled her eyes, but held her peace.

We had almost four hundred bales of goods, every bale wrapped in cowhide, with a layer of tallow, and then a couple of layers of linen canvas. When we had eaten, with all the mess groups in circles by their fires, and the officers all together – Marsyas and Cleomenes, the senior phylarchs, with the addition of Leosthenes, and Thaïs sitting with us as if the presence of a woman at a camp dinner was the most natural thing in the world – I took a sharp knife and started to open the bales.

By luck, I got the helmets first. They were Attic in style, as I had requested – but with a brim over the eyes, a close-fit skull and hinged cheek-plates that adapted to the shape of the face. They were good bronze, and every helmet had a crest box and a horsehair crest.

There might have been fifty men in the taxeis with better helmets than these, but I doubted it, and I started to give them out, starting with phylarchs, then demi-phylarchs, file closers, and on and on, so that senior men got them first – I had no idea how many there might be, and as this was the work of seventy or eighty armourers, I couldn't make head or tail of all the bills of lading.

The officers joined me, and soon we had men formed in files, and we had all the bales open – men took their new thoraces, their new sandals, their new chitons. The helmets were magnificent, but the sandal-boots came in for the most comment.

It was a fine occasion, and we went to our tents late and full of good wine, and Thaïs and I cuddled and kissed and fell asleep. I imagine I told her that I had missed her a thousand times. She laughed.

That was her way.

Just before she fell asleep, she put a hand on mine. 'You know that Darius's wife is pregnant,' she said, as if this was the sort of thing we discussed every day.

I was half asleep. It took me a moment to realise that Darius's wife was in a tent not far from me, not in Babylon with the King of Kings. And that only one man could have made her pregnant.

But it didn't really seem that important.

Maybe Harpalus was right. Maybe I am a clod.

Alexander arranged games. He put money and effort into them, and we had tracks and fields marked out in advance, and marvellous prizes – magnificent cloaks, gold cups, whole panoplies of fine armour.

I ordered my men to store their new equipment. The new chitons were fitted, sewn to shape and put away. There was some grumbling, but I promised we'd have a promotion parade before we marched and wear it all. Games are hard on equipment, and I wanted them to go out in their old gear. I fought with spear and shield in my battered helmet, and Alexander, while commenting on my skill, managed to take note of the helmet.

'You are, I think, one of the richest men in the army,' he said. 'Treat yourself to a new helmet.'

Thaïs had brought it from Athens, and it sat on my camp bed – thickly plated in gold over iron and bronze, the same Attic design as my men's helmets, but with blue and gilt over the whole outer face; the cheek-plates on springs, the brim a little more peaked and with a pair of bull's horns flanking the rich crest.

I wasn't sure what I thought of the horns.

Thaïs shook her head. 'For the bull. See?' She smiled. 'I spent four *days* in the Chalcidean's shop, making sure that the engraving was as I wanted it.' Indeed, the entire cycle of the bull was on the helmet, and a depiction of Zeus enthroned on Olympus, but with bull's horns.

I loved it for her, as I thought that it was a little more gaudy than I needed. But the thorax matched, with white leather pturges.

I like fine gear. What soldier does not?

She'd brought me a dozen spears, each finer than the last, all fine steel work with long heads and long sockets, elegant saurouters, some with pierced work, some gilt, and all with fine silk tassels at the base of the socket – to keep the blood off your hands.

As I say, I fought in the hoplitomachos. I was the only one of the taxiarchs to do so, although they were all excellent fighters. Perdiccas was always my match. Craterus, ten years older than I, was faster than most men.

It was odd, because despite the prizes, many of the contestants were mercenaries and professionals, and few of our hypaspitoi or our pezhetaeroi chose to match themselves. I suppose it was not so odd. We were the best fighters in the world, but few of our farm boys had the formal gymnasium training in wrestling and pankration that was the essential underpinning to being a truly formidable single fighter.

In the second pool of fighters, I faced Draco of Pella. He *was* one of ours. In fact, he was a pezhetaeros of my own taxeis, and, despite his youth, a canny, thoughtful fighter with long arms and a heavy hand. When his spearhead struck my shield, he cut pieces from the cover, or took chips from the rim, or bent the bronze. But I got past his spearhead and threw him to the ground and rested my saurouter on his thigh and he grinned at me.

And while I helped him up, I promoted him to phylarch.

I faced Leosthenes, as well, and he bested me. I never saw the blow that clipped my old helmet and tore my crest away. I had never faced a man so fast.

We put the judges in a quandary, because I had more wins than anyone in the competition *except* Leosthenes, but we were in the same pool. Or the judges were loath to disqualify a taxiarch and friend of the king. These things happen.

Either way, we both went on to the last round on the third day. I was elated because one of my many Philips had won the garland for the stade sprint, bringing honour to the regiment, and another man, an Ionian, had placed second in the wrestling to Kineas's friend Diodorus. Kineas won the boxing easily, as the sport was not well known in Macedon. I lost the pankration fairly early, as the competition was worthy of the Olympics or the Nemean Games. There were big, well-trained men, such as Demetrios of Halicarnassus, and he dropped me on my head about as fast as I could tell it, although, like a good comrade, he held my feet so I didn't injure my neck.

Alexander came and watched the final bouts of the hoplitomachos. Many men I knew were there, such as Kineas, wearing his garland, and Diodorus, wearing his.

The herald assigned every one of us a little metal badge, each one of which had a sign of one of the gods on it. I drew Zeus.

I prayed to Zeus-Apis. That's how far my change had gone. Before, I would have prayed to Herakles before any contest, or perhaps Poseidon.

Zeus-Apis denied my prayer, which was that I *not* face Leosthenes.

We were matched immediately.

Let me tell you how you fight a man who is better and faster than you are.

You take your stance well out of reach of his spear, and you manipulate the measure – the distance – to mislead your opponent into making one of his lightning-fast attacks while still out of range.

We circled for so long that men started to hoot and call suggestions. Leosthenes knew perfectly well what I was about, and he tried to push me, but I kept circling, using the angle of my movement to keep my distance while never getting backed against the wands that marked the edges of the competition area.

Round and round.

Had he been an impatient man, I'd have had him.

Leosthenes the Athenian was never impatient.

Let me add that we fought with bated spears, twice the height of a man. They hurt when they hit, but they didn't punch through flesh.

I grew impatient.

Not the sign of an expert fighter, but I am a taxiarch, not a champion.

I shortened my grip, sliding my hand to the centre of my weapon, and I stepped in.

Leosthenes' strike came like a levin-bolt, and I didn't raise my shield. Instead, I caught it on my spear, near the tip, turned it into my shield and leaped forward.

Fast as thought, he leaped back. I wanted to close inside his spearhead, and he wanted to hit me in my rush. He didn't want to fight me close in.

His feet crossed, and he fell. But even as he fell, he rolled on his shield shoulder and never let go of his spear, and he was as fast as a god. I closed the distance, but his roll changed the angle, and I had to brace, and he was on his feet. He thrust, and I caught his off-balance shot on the rim of my shield – *Zeus, he was fast.* I passed forward, sure I had won the fight, but he recovered his spearhead in the tongue-flick of a serpent, and he backed off two steps, as fast as a dancer at a symposium, avoiding the grabbing hands of clients – perhaps faster – and his spearhead licked out again, and *just* tagged my helmet.

I ducked my head and stepped in, spear across my body, and reached out to push him to the ground ...

And stopped. It took a moment to realise he'd hit my helmet.

But I knew it.

I turned to the herald. 'He hit me,' I said.

The herald bowed.

The crowd began to roar.

Leosthenes bowed to me. 'My back foot is out of the ring,' he said. He spat the words, but by the gods, he was an honest man that day.

My rush had pushed him out of the limits.

The question we all had was – which happened first?

Alexander came down from his dais, and walked the sand with the heralds. He called the two of us together.

'Leosthenes of Athens, you stepped out twice – two steps in a row.' The king shrugged. 'You are a brilliant fighter. Tyche was against you.'

I raised my hand. 'Lord King, may I use this moment to crave a boon? May I ask that Leosthenes of Athens be considered a Macedonian, that I may have him as an officer in my taxeis?'

Alexander smiled one of his rare smiles of genuine amusement. 'Is he at least as Macedonian as your Isokles?' he asked.

Leosthenes stripped off his armour and went to stand with Kineas, whom he idolised, while I went on to win my next three fights. None of the other finalists was anything like as good as the Athenian.

Which the king acknowledged when he gave me my garland. Because he summoned Leosthenes and presented him with a garland as well, rather than the man who was, by points, the second.

Alexander could be fair, just and astute, when it suited him. As the judge of games, he was easy to love.

Alectus slapped me on the back when I received my garland. 'He'd have killed you, if it was real,' he said. 'Don't get cocky.'

There you have it.

But praise from peers is sweet. Bubores came, and Cleomenes, and Kineas, and a dozen other friends, and they poured wine over my head and slapped my back, and then a dozen of them picked me up and carried me to the beach and flung me into the sea – the sea that, a year before, we had dyed red with the blood of slaughtered Tyrians.

Alexander held a parade – one of the few I remember in any detail, although he held enough of them, in emulation of Xenophon's *Anabasis*. My men looked forward to it eagerly, the last day of the games, because they *knew* they were going to dazzle the other pezhetaeroi, and even the hypaspitoi, with their new splendour.

Nor were we wrong. Leosthenes, Callisthenes, Marsyas and I worked overtime to arrange how to get ourselves and all our soldiers into our kit without the rest of the army seeing us. We put the kind of planning into it that we would have put into a military operation, and Leosthenes revealed what a cunning bastard he was in his brilliant misdirection plan.

In short, we were late for parade. All the taxeis competed to be *first* on parade, and we were deliberately last.

We had the front left file closer – Leosthenes now – carry a sarissa with every wreath and garland we had won as a body in the games tied to the spearhead with superb cloth-of-gold tape that Thaïs provided. We had a pair of slave aulos players, whom I freed for service.

We marched on, crossing the back of the parade to the tune of our flutes, marching in step.

We could hear the muttering in the ranks; 'awkward sods' was about the nicest thing we heard.

And then they saw us.

Heh. Another great moment.

There was no body of troops in that army of fifty thousand men who had matching helmet plumes, matching armour, matching spears, new chitons that shone like snow. We glittered.

And when I called 'Ground your ... spears!' fifteen hundred saurouters crunched into the gravel with a single sound.

Alexander glanced at me. I had on my new panoply. I smelled like new leather and Thaïs's perfume – I think she'd kept the armour awfully close during the sea voyage.

The king grinned.

Then he rode away to the head of the Royal Squadron, and we passed in review, marching past the king sixteen files wide, and in step, in a way that never really happened on the battlefield, and yet was a practical test of a regiment's drill.

We marched up and down, and we marched past the king. And as the head of our regiment drew even with him – he was deep in conversation with Hephaestion – he touched his heels to Bucephalus and rode out to us.

'Men of Outer Macedon!' he shouted. Technically, that was our taxeis – the Taxeis of Outer Macedon.

He waited a moment or two.

'YOU LOOK LIKE GODS!' he roared.

They were still shouting his name when we went back to camp. They were willing to die for him, then.

Sometimes, he was easy to love.

*

Harpalus brought us detailed information on the war with Sparta and the threat to the League of Corinth in Greece. The night of the great review, when Craterus had pretended to punch me in the nose and Perdiccas had demanded that I tell him the source of my wonderful helmets (I told him), we discussed the war behind us – what Alexander later referred to as a war between mice.

They were dangerous mice. The Spartans were nothing like in their prime, but man for man they were still magnificent. And their king, Agis, understood strategy better, I think, than Darius. He struck immediately, and where we felt it most – he put a fleet to sea and took Crete, as I've mentioned above. Had we *not* won Tyre and Aegypt, Agis's strategy would have crippled us, cut us off. So much for Parmenio's views of the world.

But Tyre fell and the Cypriots came over to us, and the world changed faster than Darius and Agis were prepared for, and once again, Alexander was a step ahead.

As usual, *everything* depended on Athens. During the winter, while Alexander went to the shrine of Amon, our entire campaign teetered on the edge of extinction. Athens had three hundred ships. If Athens had joined Sparta, we would have faced a general uprising of all the states of Greece, and Antipater notwithstanding, the war would have been fought at sea, and in Macedon.

But Athens stayed loyal. Actually, Athens seethed with discontent, but stayed just the right side of betrayal. Or, as I have said before, the thetes couldn't stomach siding with Sparta and Persia at the same time.

What role Harpalus played, I can only guess. His role was never vouchsafed to me. But Thaïs's trip to Athens while Alexander went to the shrine of Amon ... at the time, I never guessed it. She had apparently withdrawn from politics and spycraft, during her second pregnancy. Callisthenes took over her duties and ran her agents.

When I look back, now, I realise that she controlled Harpalus's false defection, and ran him as a fisherman plays a fish. She was his lifeline and his paymaster, and the five thousand talents he 'stole' were used to bribe Athens. It was a brilliant move. I wish I could be certain whether Thaïs thought it through herself, or whether Harpalus designed it, or whether the king did – all three in concert, I think, but somehow, it has his stamp. Alexander's mind ...

Last year, I saw a device at the house of Ben Zion – a device that had been ordered by the Tyrant of Athens. It was a bronze and steel machine for predicting the movement of the planets. Have you seen one? If you rotate a lever, you can see the moon spin on its axis as it moves around the earth, passing through her phases, and you can watch

Ares make his remarkable movements – forward, back, forward, like a man dancing the Pyricche.

You've seen one of these machines? Yes?

That is how I see the mind of Alexander. Except with an infinite profusion of those cogs and levers, calculating, calculating, so that unless his agents of information betrayed him with false data, he could see forward, not by prescience but by calculation, on the battlefield, in politics and perhaps even in friendships. So that, just as Demetrios of Phaleron's machine could calculate a thousand years of eclipses, so Alexander's mind could calculate three years of campaigns in Asia and all of Darius's responses.

How dull the rest of us must have seemed.

At any rate, Harpalus returned, and the king felt his rear was secure. He restructured his commands to suit his campaign, and Parmenio didn't quibble.

The two of them had a meeting, in private, with no witnesses. I can only guess, but I will. I think that the king promised him an honourable retirement and the satrapy of Persia proper. And Parmenio accepted, secure in the knowledge that he was being given a huge command and the Royal Treasury – and thus, that he could continue to provide patronage for the officers in his 'family'.

Hephaestion was given his first large command. He took the elite cavalry – the Hetaeroi minus the royals, the Paeonians, the Thracians and some of the allies – such as Kineas – and the Agrianian skirmishers, and he vanished into the desert. He had what appeared to be a siege train. That accorded badly with the speed his column was supposed to maintain, but rumour said he was out of the area covered by the Prodromoi in a single day, so he must have moved like lightning.

You've no doubt heard the story from Diodorus, eh? How they raced to the Euphrates, and threw a pontoon bridge across.

Mazaeus, the best of the remaining Persian commanders, was there with three thousand horse, and the two forces fought every day – skirmish after skirmish on the banks of the Euphrates, up and down as Hephaestion sought to outflank Mazaeus, like two skilled men fencing with sticks. And Kineas won the day, racing south, finding a ford, fighting his way across with his Athenians in the face of a determined enemy, and turning Mazaeus's flank, so that his whole force was rolled back and Hephaestion got the bridges across. That's where your father won his magnificent Nisean stallion, and he rode that horse for years.

If you know your *Anabasis*, you know that Cyrus's army took the same route we were on. And having won the crossings of the Euphrates and built a pair of bridges, we might have turned south towards Babylon and lunged at the Persians.

That's what Mazaeus expected, and what Darius wanted us to do – march down the east bank of the Euphrates. Like Artaxerxes before him, Darius had ordered the land between the rivers scorched, the grain removed and the most populous place on the wheel of the world depopulated, so that when Alexander made his move for empire, he would have to cross a battlefield stripped clean of food and forage.

When we marched from Tyre, it was late in Hecatombion by the Athenian festival calendar, but we marched fast – up to two hundred stades a day. The men were fresh and well rested, and well fed. And even eager. We had water with us, and we marched across dusty plains at the height of midsummer.

When Kineas rolled Mazaeus up and forced him back on the road to Babylon, the rest of us – the main army – were virtually a dust cloud on the horizon. The next day, my taxeis and the hypaspitoi marched across the bridges yoked like oxen, carrying water, and behind us came the whole army. Mazaeus retreated south along the east bank of the Euphrates for two days, and Hephaestion, on what was probably the best day of his career, pursued just the right amount, and they fought another inconclusive action in the dust.

I was still marching.

We didn't turn south to Babylon.

The wheels of the king's mind had turned, grinding this campaign down to a few problems, and here's the solution he reached, as best I understand it.

If we marched in spring, as soon as the ground was dry, then the rivers would be in spate, and crossing either the Euphrates or the Tigris would have been very difficult indeed. The marching would have been better for the soldiers, but that was never a great concern of Alexander's.

But if the rivers were full to flood – if the spring rains came late – and the countryside was empty of crops, as every set of farms on earth is empty in late spring, when all the stores have been consumed – then we might reach the Euphrates bank and starve, or be trapped between the rivers.

As it was, although I think most of the army never saw the plan, his campaign worked better than he imagined. We shot east, crossed the two bridges mere hours after they were completed, and Mazaeus, by the sort of luck that comes with good planning, was pinned back south and couldn't explore our dispositions. Two days later, when Hephaestion had withdrawn, Mazaeus's elite cavalry came pounding north.

And found the crossing deserted, and our army – gone. Gone to the east.

By luck, good planning and the godlike far-sightedness of Alexander, we had broken contact, and our entire army was loose in the plains of Iraq.

Mazaeus raced south, leaving his best men to try and find us. Mazaeus had a head on his shoulders – he went in person to tell the Great King that Alexander had just shredded his operational plan and was now *somewhere*.

In fact, we marched for twenty days, moving as fast as men and horses could move. We were north of Darius's scorched earth, and we were in the cool foothills and not in the Mesopotamian plains, and while 'cool' is a relative thing to a foot soldier who has been marching for ten hours with the sun pounding him like an enemy, we were not losing men.

The best of the Prodromoi swept south in small groups – ten or twelve men under a trusted officer or phylarch, covering huge distances with six or eight horses per man. By the time we reached the Tigris river, we were receiving the first reports of Darius's army, as scouted by Agon's men.

Alexander flatly refused to believe what he heard. Because what he heard was that Darius, the despicable and defeated Darius, had almost a hundred thousand men covering miles of ground, and that his army outnumbered ours nearly two to one.

The speed of the army was not good for everyone. The animals suffered in the heat and dust, and the women suffered worse than the men, even when they rode in litters, and one pregnant woman suffered worse than the rest.

I was with the main body when I heard her scream.

We had reached the Tigris river the night before, and our lead elements – today, Perdiccas and the Agrianians, backed by Thracian horse – punched across against no opposition. The Tigris, contrary to Callisthenes' sensational account, was about four fingers deep over the rocks, and we scarcely cooled our feet in it as we went.

We were flanking the baggage, and I had the rotten job of making sure that the baggage carts made the crossing in good order. I was watching my officers check the cartwheels – because any old ones would break in the middle of the river, and any loose ones would come off. And the Great King's wife began to scream.

I can't pretend I knew who it was, but I was the officer in charge, and I rode to her cart – more like a broad pavilion mounted on a wagon bed.

There was so much blood that it was coming through the baseboards of the wagon.

I sent Polystratus for Thaïs, and then I climbed into the wagon. She was screaming, and her mother-in-law was holding her head, and two eunuchs tried to prevent my entering the wagon and I threw one out through the door.

'You cannot enter here!' the other said, desperately.

I ignored him and looked at Sisygambis, the Queen Mother. She didn't meet my eye.

Leosthenes had been checking wheels. He popped his head in.

'Fetch the king,' I shot at him, and his head vanished.

Thaïs came. The eunuchs continued to try to remove me, but Sisygambis said something and they desisted. Thaïs put a hand on the woman's forehead, reached down and flung the blood-soaked sheets back and caught my eye.

Miscarriage. I'm a country boy. I knew the signs.

Philip of Acarnia came first, and then Alexander. I'd have left the wagon, but I couldn't get out, trapped in the press. Philip looked at her, felt her pulse and exchanged a glance with Thaïs. That was the worst thing – the conspiracy of silence. The poor woman. Imagine – trapped with fifty thousand enemy soldiers, pregnant with Alexander's bastard and marching *towards* your husband, who will have you executed when he sees you. With only your mother-in-law and her ladies for company.

Then Alexander came.

Philip was blunt, as he always was. 'Say your goodbyes,' he said. 'She won't recover.'

Indeed, the poor thing was bleeding at such a rate that it didn't seem possible a body could hold so much blood.

She cried out.

Alexander turned his head away in revulsion.

She flung her arms out.

Alexander stepped back.

'She is unclean,' he said.

'I am cursed!' the Queen of Persia cried out. 'Oh, God of Light, why must I endure this!'

Alexander shot me a look of disgust. 'Why *exactly* was I summoned?' he asked.

'You got her with child,' I shot at him. I don't think I had ever been so angry with him.

He didn't meet my eye. This had never happened before, save once.

He turned and left the wagon.

Philip of Acarnia all but spat.

The Queen of Persia died in his arms, with Thaïs holding her hand and her mother-in-law holding her head.

Later, Callisthenes put it about that she died in an accident, and that's the official version.

I followed Alexander from the wagon. I had her blood on my left hand and I let it dry there. I mounted my pretty mare, now Medea like the others, and I rode her hard to the head of the column, where Alexander sat with Hephaestion, watching the last of the main body cross.

I might not have done it, but Alexander turned as I came up. 'The baggage is falling behind, and we have to move,' he said.

I reached out and wiped her blood across his face. She was nothing to me – I had scarcely met her, and she openly despised us all. But I was his friend, not his slave, and no man worth a shit treats a woman like that.

He had no trouble meeting my eye. He held out his hand, and a slave put a towel in it. He wiped his face.

'I gather you feel that needed to be done. I have other things on my mind than the troubles of women,' he said. 'Now get the baggage moving.'

Sometimes, he was easy to hate.

TWENTY-NINE

—~~—

We turned south.

We started to intercept spies – they weren't very clever – with offers of vast riches for the murder of Alexander.

Darius was willing to do anything to avoid the trial of battle.

To cap his other efforts, he sent a deputation of nobles to try and make a treaty. This time, he was clever enough to make it very public indeed. This time, Alexander was not going to change the wording.

They offered him everything west of the Euphrates and a royal wife.

Again, Parmenio suggested we accept.

Alexander didn't deign to reply. But later, we heard that he allowed the head eunuch of Darius's wife's household to escape with the embassy.

Because the news that his wife had been unfaithful with Alexander drove Darius into a rage of madness – a paroxysm of jealousy, or so I understood later, when most of the Persian officers were my own officers – the sort of frustrated rage that all men experience when nothing seems to go their way.

Just as Alexander intended.

And then there was no more talk of peace.

The War God was riding to Babylon.

Darius concentrated his army at Arabela, and offered battle on a plain of his own choosing, which he had his engineers improve with labour gangs of slaves until it was as flat as a well-wrought table.

We heard about this battlefield when we were still hundreds of stades to the north, and as we marched closer and the rumours of the enemy's army size became ever more inflated, we were more and more derisive. The mere fact that Darius had attempted to negotiate showed how weak he was. Our best estimates from all sources suggested that even with some help form his eastern barons, he'd have a hard time gathering twenty thousand cavalry and as many infantry. Ariston nearly lost his job for reporting twice that many on a daily basis.

And then Darius moved north from Arabela, suddenly closing the distance with us.

It's easy to fall into hubris. Easy to forget how smart an opponent is. Darius outgeneralled Alexander before Issus. He'd planned a fairly subtle campaign this time, too, and Alexander had outmarched him – something that all of our opponents always underestimated, as we could march roughly three times as fast as anyone we ever faced. But even faced with our speed, he changed his campaign plan and moved his army – and did unexpected things.

In an afternoon, we went from deriding Darius to the knowledge that he was a day's march to the south. Reliable men reported that his army was 'uncountable'.

Kineas of Athens came in person to tell the king that Darius's army covered a hundred stades of camp.

The tone of command meetings changed.

Late that evening, the army moved up a low ridge. Scouts told us that the ridge we were occupying was less than two dozen stades from Darius's new battlefield.

Alexander summoned the old crowd to ride out with him. There was Craterus, and there was Perdiccas, and there was Black Cleitus and there was Philip the Red. And Parmenio, and Philotas, and Nicanor.

And me. He came to my tent, as in the old days, and called me by name.

A dozen of us rode out of the camp, up the ridge.

The ridge rose well above the plains, and had a good view. Perhaps too good a view.

It looked as if the Valley of the Tigris was on fire.

I will *never* forget the sight of Darius's army. Their camp filled the earth – as far as the eye could see to the south and east, there were fires.

'Zeus my father,' Alexander muttered.

Parmenio looked for a long time.

Then he shook his head. 'We're fucked,' he said.

No one disagreed, and then, after a silence, he went on, 'Throw Hephaestion out with the cavalry as a screen, and let's get out of here. We can vanish into the mountains. We'll lose some men, but not what we'll lose if we go down on to that plain.'

What I remember best is the feeling that Darius had led us the way a pretty girl can lead a drunken soldier. The ugly feeling that we'd been had.

Alexander was white. And silent.

Twice I saw him touch his forehead, where I had smeared her blood.

He was terrified. I hadn't seen it often, but often enough to know.

Terrified not of dying, but of failing.

I'd love to say that I offered a brilliant plan, but I was terrified too. We'd outmanoeuvred Darius, but in the end it was like a little man dodging a giant. The giant doesn't care about all that dancing around, because eventually, when it comes to the clinch ...

When we rode back to camp, there was still a streak of summer light in the sky, red-pink and angry, and Alexander ordered the duty taxeis to dig in. Amyntas's men – and they didn't love it. Nor did mine, on duty next. We worked half the night, and we kept men awake.

Because I had the night duty, I knew that the king was awake. There was light in his tent.

But I didn't go to him.

I've heard a hundred legends about that night, but I was there. He didn't summon a council. He didn't consult the auguries. He didn't feast, and he didn't drink wine.

Nor did he summon Barsines or her sister.

What he did was to lie awake, silent, on his camp bed, staring at the ceiling of the tent and the flies.

At some point, according to Hephaestion, he fell asleep, and son of god or not, he snored. We all heard it.

There is something immensely reassuring about the sound of your warrior king snoring in the face of the enemy.

I was about to rotate the duty with Alectus of the hypaspitoi when Ochrid came and told me that the king wanted the duty officer.

I entered his tent. He was awake.

'Ptolemy,' he said. 'I'm glad it is someone intelligent. I have written down my dispositions for the morning. Please see that the army is formed. I will no doubt sleep late.'

The arrogance – the bored assurance – of his voice would have angered me at any time – but just then, his arrogance was rope in the hands of a drowning army.

'Formed' could only mean one thing. I nodded and took the parchment, and he smiled at me and lay down on the bed and was almost instantly asleep.

I cast my eye over the dispositions. But they only confirmed the word 'formed'. We were going to fight.

We were going to fight.

My hands shook as I left his tent.

And yet – I took his orders to Parmenio, left them with a slave, disarmed myself and lay down with Thaïs, and I was asleep in a few heartbeats.

Odd.

THIRTY

Other men have told the story of that morning. Read
Callisthenes, or read the Military Journal, if you must.
He really did sleep late. He left the forming of the army
to Parmenio. I think it was drama – I think he was awake and armed,
awaiting his moment to come onstage. But perhaps not.

He formed us in a very similar manner to the traditional, Philip of
Macedon formation. The phalanx was in the middle, with cavalry on
the flanks and a strong second line posted to our rear.

The differences were subtle.

The second line was very strong.

The cavalry was equally balanced in numbers, but the right flank had
our best shock cavalry *and* our best skirmishers.

And perhaps most interesting of all, we refused *both* flanks as soon as
we began to march out of camp.

The old man did his part. Parmenio was up with the dawn, out with
his own Thessalians, riding Darius's carefully manicured battlefield. He
dismounted and walked, counting his paces across the frontage that the
field would have.

It was like fighting on a good wool blanket. It was *flat*. However, on
Darius's side of the field there was a patch of ... I wouldn't call it brush,
but let's say unmanicured ground that stretched from the ridge on our
right down towards Darius's centre. To be honest, on most battlefields
it would have been considered good going, but here, where slaves with
heavy rollers had rolled the anthills flat and other slaves with shovels
had filled in the holes, the patch of untended ground leaped to the eye.

Darius's left flank was going to rest on it. As if it was actually bad
ground, brush or marsh. We could see that even at first light, because
Darius, who did not have an army as well trained as ours (by a long
shot), had unit markers already in place in the warm yellow light of
early morning.

Parmenio counted off his frontage. He turned and looked at me. I was riding with Nicanor, because I was up and it soothed my nerves. To the south, a dozen Prodromoi covered us, and a little farther south, as many Persian cavalrymen watched them the way hawks watch distant prey.

Parmenio stopped walking.

'Anyone have a tablet?' he asked, and I did. That made me their secretary.

'You here to spy on us?' Parmenio asked.

I shook my head. 'I'm here to fight Darius,' I said.

Philotas chewed on a blade of late-summer grass. 'If we lose here, none of us will make it home,' he said quietly.

I shrugged. I wasn't going to share my opinions with Philotas.

Besides, Parmenio began to call out numbers, and I scratched them in the wax.

My taxeis, at normal order, is eight deep and two hundred men wide, each man using about three paces, giving a frontage of six hundred paces. Roughly three stades. And we had seven front-line taxeis.

They alone took up twenty-one stades at normal order. If we closed to our tightest order, of course, we could almost halve our frontage.

But the Plain of Gaugamela is vast, a carpet of bronze-burned summer pasture grass and naked ochre earth that rolled away to distant ridges – room for all the soldiers in the world to fight, if the gods ordained it. The Greeks might have called Boeotia the dance floor of Ares, but the Plain of Gaugamela was surely laid down by the gods for war, and Darius had *improved* it.

When we reached the nominal position of the right marker of my taxeis, I dismounted and built a small cairn of stones.

Polystratus, mounted on a pony behind me, spat. 'Fucking dust,' he said. He pointed to where his plodding pony's hooves were raising puffs of fine grit with every step the animal took.

'This field will be one impenetrable cloud of dust from horizon to horizon as soon as we march on,' I said.

Polystratus spat again and nodded. 'I said that. You just used more words.'

It took us two hours, from sun-up to breakfast, to measure the battle front. Philotas calculated unit frontages, Parmenio paced them off in the dust and I marked the unit down with the final measurement on the wax. The wax got softer and softer as the sun climbed, until my stylus started to strip the wax off the boards.

When we reached the last nominal position on our left, we all turned our mounts and stared across the plain.

Our leftmost unit would match up with the centre of Darius's right flank, to judge from the positions of his markers. Put another way, his right flank would overlap our left by at least six stades.

Parmenio looked back at me. 'Still here to fight Darius, boy?'

I wrote down the last figures. The wax was growing too soft to hold the letters, and the morning was young.

'Yes,' I said.

'Good looks and luck won't win this,' Parmenio said.

It is one of the oddities of my make-up that I could flare into rage at the slightest provocation from the king, but Parmenio never affected me that way. I merely shrugged.

'He's insane,' Philotas said, suddenly at my elbow.

Medea fidgeted, and I curbed her.

'He's insane and he's going to get us killed here,' Philotas insisted.

Parmenio looked away, as if carefully detaching himself from the scene.

Polystratus coughed.

'You don't think any better of him than I do. I saw your face when the Persian woman died,' Philotas said. 'For the love of all the gods, Ptolemy! He's not our king any more. He's becoming a monster!' Philotas read in my face that he'd gone too far. 'We do all the work, and he'll fuck it away,' he said bitterly.

I glanced at Polystratus, who looked mad enough to punch Philotas, which wouldn't have gone well.

'We wouldn't be here on this plain, ready to fight for the dominion of all Asia, unless Alexander brought us here,' I said. 'And the very power that renders him able to conquer Asia contains the set of flaws that make me angry at him.' I turned from Philotas to Parmenio. 'You, sir, are as blind as he, if you cannot see that he is leading this army and you are not.'

'He makes messes, and I clean them up,' Parmenio said angrily.

'I'll copy this fair for you,' I said. I was done. They were edging towards treason. I would shout myself blind at him to get his attention, to find the spark of a *man* that he must still have burning, but I wasn't going to side with the weasels.

'He'll destroy all he has built,' Parmenio said. 'Or rather, he can only destroy. He can't build. He's a war god, not a king.'

'Tell them in Alexandria,' I said.

I gathered my officers and we rode back to the battlefield. I had a bag of hot sausages across my thigh – the fat burned me. I ate them anyway.

And Polystratus had pomegranate juice – gods know where he got that – and I drained his canteen.

I took them to my little cairn of stones, which itself took me five minutes to find. While we sat on our mounts and talked, Polystratus and Ochrid and a dozen camp servants built it up into a cairn that could be seen for two stades – waist-height, and broad. They put a spear into it, with all of our wreaths from the games at Tyre.

Leosthenes put his hands on his hips and turned slowly through a full circle.

'Nothing to cover our flanks,' he said.

Cleomenes looked at the Persians, slowly filtering on to the field. Alone of all their troops, their Greeks marched on, singing. The rest didn't march – they just strolled to where their markers were waiting, and sat.

It was ... odd. In a few hours, we'd be killing each other. At the same time, it seldom made sense to interrupt an enemy's dispositions, as he'd just run away, and the whole thing would have to be done again.

I'm pretty sure Memnon would have sent cavalry to disrupt our planning.

'We are in the centre,' I noted. 'Almost exactly in the centre. We have the hypaspitoi on our right and Craterus on our left.'

Callisthenes smiled. 'We've moved up in the world.'

It was true. Alexander's dispositions suggested we were now the most trusted of all the pezhetaeroi, standing between the hypaspitoi, the household and the rest of the sarissa-armed infantrymen.

Marsyas stole a sausage. 'Maybe he just thinks we'll look the best next to the hypaspitoi,' he opined. 'So – why are we here?'

I nodded at the cairn. 'Dust or sun or pouring rain, when we reach this part of the field, I want to have to touch that cairn as I march through, because then all our dispositions will be right. If I'm already dead, you three make sure we hit it.'

They nodded.

'We're the one thing Alexander can absolutely count on,' I went on. 'We can beat his second-rate Greeks and we can eat his levies for break-fast. We must grind forward. It is the relentless advance that panics the Persians, and the knowledge that they cannot fight us to the front. Given the king's dispositions, I think it is safe to say that he needs us to keep going forward. If I fall, see to it that the lads go forward. He's going to spend the cavalry like money in a brothel to keep our flanks secure. Don't get distracted. Keep rolling forward.'

I was solemn, and slow, and it would have been much more

impressive, as a speech, if I hadn't been so hungry that I chewed sausage constantly, and so nervous that I farted every third line.

But they got it. We all four clasped hands, and then we rode back to our camp. I saw Kineas and his friends ride by going the other way – probably on the same mission I'd just accomplished – and I waved.

Diodorus waved back, and then it was time to put my panoply on.

Beautiful armour is always a pleasure to wear. And on the day of battle, when your guts turn to water and all your body is ready to shake, a beautiful panoply is worth every obol you spent. When I was armoured, I looked, and felt, like a war god myself. And the shakes stopped.

Men are simple animals, really.

We marched off from our camp by companies on an eight-file front, and wheeled into line at double depth – one hundred wide and sixteen men deep – and formed on Craterus's taxeis, already in line.

I was still mounted on Poseidon, who was still a fine horse, and that day had more spirit than he'd shown throughout the whole campaign. I rode over to Craterus and explained about my cairn, and he nodded.

'Good thinking. We'll march off from the right – so you'll be at the head of the pezhetaeroi. Line up on your cairn.' He smiled. It was a forced smile, but that's what you get on the day of a battle. 'One less thing about which I get to worry.'

And then, like soldiers since the world was born, we waited.

We were ten stades from the battlefield. We had offered no sacrifice, nor read the omens. The sun was rising in the sky. The whole army was waiting in parade formation.

If nerves had been visible, they would have been a pall of sparks, like the cloud a bonfire shoots out in the last light when men celebrate the feast of some god, and our line, all twenty stades of it, would have been lit like the Milky Way.

And we waited.

Some of Perdiccas's men began to sing. We had a song – Philip's men had coined it, long ago.

It is sung to the tune of the 'Homeric Hymn to Ares', and it sounds very martial, but the words are:

Why are we waiting?
Why are we waiting?
Oh, why are we waiting?
NOBODY KNOWS!

Perdiccas's men started it.

My men took it up, and so did Craterus's men, and even the hypaspitoi and some of the Hetaeroi. The sound filled the air.

It must have sounded scary, to the Persians.

It made us laugh, and laughter makes scared men relax.

We sang it again.

And Alexander came. In truth, he appeared none too pleased. But he brightened up when men started to cheer. The word was that Parmenio had had to go to his tent and wake him. As I've mentioned, that may be true, but his grooming was spotless, his armour was perfect and his hair, sometimes a grizzled mass of blond curls, was straight and well brushed, except that his forward curls over his ears had been teased up to look even more like horns, and he had his magnificent lion's-head helmet on his saddle-bow. His cloak and his saddlecloth were leopard skin. All the fittings on his armour were gilded, and his scales had been buffed like a thousand mirrors. He rode bareheaded to the centre of the army, and so he was all but nose to nose with me.

'Asia!' he shouted, his voice perfectly pitched to carry. 'Asia dangles at the end of your spears, yours for the taking. Darius has nothing but peasant levies and the same cavalry you have beaten before, many times. Carve your way through and Asia is ours. Fail, and we all die here in the dust.'

He drew his sword. 'I know which I'd prefer,' he said, and tossed the sword high in the air. I watched it, but I needn't have worried. He caught it by the hilt. 'Kill Darius, and the day is ours,' he said, and they cheered him as if Zeus Soter had descended from Olympus.

He trotted Bucephalus over to me. He was calm, almost detached, but he managed a smile.

Parmenio trotted his horse over to us. He was old – I'd never seen him look older. The night had worn him, and the morning was ageing him before our eyes.

'Have a good sleep?' Parmenio said, and his tone betrayed his anger. 'More importantly, do you have a *plan*?' He looked around. 'The army is restless. You plan to fight? Aren't you just a little afraid?'

Alexander didn't sneer. He turned his horse, ignoring me, and extended a hand to Parmenio. 'Afraid? Parmenio, when we were marching around the northern part of the country, I was terrified – lest Darius refuse battle and hide behind his burned crops. This morning, he is *right there* and he has no possibility of retreat.'

His eyes sparkled.

He laughed, and his laugh carried conviction. 'Darius is offering *me* a pitched battle. Herakles has put him in my hands.'

Parmenio hawked and spat. 'Very well, son of Zeus.' He made the soubriquet sound like a curse. 'We'll be outflanked – badly – on both sides. What *exactly* do you expect us to do?'

Alexander shrugged. 'Is the arrowhead outflanked when it enters an enemy's flesh, Parmenio? I expect you to fight your wing and avoid defeat, while I do the work and win the battle.'

Parmenio glowered. 'When this is over, if we survive—'

Alexander laughed. 'You are less a threat to me than Darius, and he is no threat to me at all. Listen, Parmenio! Is there one voice here shouting for you?' He reared his horse, and my men roared his name, and the other phalanges took up the cry, so that I couldn't hear what he said next, but Parmenio did, and his face grew red.

Alexander laughed. Then he turned his horse and rode over to me. And embraced me – one of perhaps five or six times I can remember when *he* embraced *me.*

'I wish …' he said. His hand slapped the back of my thorax. The soldiers roared his name.

That was the measure of the morning. Alexander needed a hug from a friend.

I never learned what he wished. But I count it as the second-to-last time I saw the man I loved.

He rode off to the left and we heard the volleys of cheers follow him, and then he rode back. His trumpeter sounded 'All Officers', and we rode out to him. He was in command of himself, and us, but by the time the sun was high in the sky, it was the war god who was among us, and not Alexander. Alexander was gone.

He didn't even trouble to look around, or smile. 'Gentlemen,' he said, and he pointed at the Persians, 'I intend to march directly to the fight – to form our front from a column, rather than forming it here and allowing gaps to develop. We will advance from the right on full front-ages – I expect this to be done with no fuss. I'm leaving the Thracian Psiloi to cover the camp and I'm sending the Paeonians to screen us and raise some dust – Ariston, see to it that you do not use up your horses, and that you *come back* to the line.'

He looked around. 'We will advance directly to contact. Unless something has changed, Darius will feel rushed by the speed of our advance and will attempt to encircle our flanks. We *want* him to encircle our flanks. I'm leaving Cleitus with the rear phalanx. He will reinforce our line and cover our rear – if necessary, he will face his phalanx to the rear and we will make a *box*, like Xenophon's men in their retreat, except that we will attack – we will attack relentlessly. *Whatever you do, if your men are advancing into the Persians and killing them, you are doing my will.* We, not they, have the moral advantage. We have beaten them like a drum – they have never beaten us. We have a phalanx of bronze and they *do not*. Behind our phalanx is another! The *phalanx* will win the battle by pushing forward without pause.' He looked around. 'Do you understand?'

We did. It was, after all, something that we'd looked at a hundred times. And it would be executed using drills that the rawest new pezhetaeros had performed every day he had been in the ranks.

Aristander, dressed from head to foot in shining white wool and crowned in gold like the Great King himself, rode to the front of the army in Alexander's chariot and offered sacrifice. The Persians were grilling in the sun, standing in their ranks, their army about two-thirds formed. Our men sat to watch the sacrifices, and grounded their spears.

Aristander was a greasy hypocrite, but he managed the sacrifices with sure-handed expertise. And that's not nothing – try killing an animal with a knife while forty thousand pairs of eyes watch you. He didn't flinch that morning, and he killed two rams and a bull – a great black bull. He held the bull's heart above his head, and the blood ran down his arm, and the symbolism was obvious.

As one, forty thousand men rose to their feet and screamed their approval.

And then we marched.

It was daring, to manoeuvre in a column of regiments in the face of the enemy. Even more daring, Alexander made the first of several changes to his battle plan before the army had marched off from camp. He rode past me to Parmenio and told him something, and Parmenio immediately marched off in a parallel column led off by Craterus. And then Alexander rode to Cleitus, with the mercenaries, and he began to form a *third* column.

Columns are deceptive. The problem is that, like a xiphos, their deception is double-edged, because they can deceive their own strategos as effectively as they deceive the enemy.

The enemy really only sees the head of the column. Part of this is the problem of battlefield visibility. With cavalry raising dust, on a flat plain with no ridges or handy hills, the enemy strategos has a hard time seeing past the front five or six ranks. And unless he's a magical combination of oracular wizard and mathematician, he cannot imagine how much space your column will eat when it turns into a line.

There's the double-edged part. An inexperienced strategos can misjudge the width of his own line, which makes forming his line a disaster, as one end or the other collides with a river, a hill, rocky ground or some other obstacle and the whole line is disordered.

Multiple columns that have to fit together?

I'd never even seen it tried before.

Alexander rode back to me, his leopard skin already covered in dust. 'You understand?' he asked.

It's good to be good at your job. 'I understand that I'm now the linchpin in linking up with Craterus,' I said. 'We'll form front by advancing obliquely?'

He gave me a curt nod – in terms of his present plan, what I asked must have seemed obvious and even impertinent.

'I built a cairn on the plain to mark the point to which I should march,' I said.

He turned and looked at me. Nodded. 'Good,' he said. 'Well thought of. Leave the column the moment you see it and march on it, and the rest of the wing will conform to you.'

I mention this, because details such as this decide battles as surely as the sword arms of heroes.

We had twelve stades to march to the cairn, and they flew by. Time – I have heard a hundred philosophers say that time flows the same for all men. I saw Callisthenes, a year later, put a stick in the ground and mark off the quarters of the day, and time – the chariot of the sun – could be seen to pass in an orderly manner, from left to right, every quarter of the day the same length as every other.

That's all very well, but the morning of the Battle of Gaugamela proved the opposite. Time crept by during the speeches and the sacrifices, and then we began to march, and I thought twelve stades would never pass, and then, five stades out, we could see the entire length of Darius's line, and the army almost stopped marching. At five stades, the Persians were like a thick rope across the plain, a rope that lived and moved.

Most of us had never seen an elephant before. Darius had a dozen. Scythed chariots sparkled in the front rank of his centre. He had more cavalry over there than we had men in our entire army.

It took our breath away.

No one had ever seen such an army.

And despite the rate that a marching man may seem to accomplish on a normal day, that morning we seemed to *hurtle* at Darius's line like a thunderbolt – a small, weak thunderbolt.

I managed to work up a good set of nerves about finding my cairn, and I left the column and rode out in the dust, alone. The Paeonians had already covered the ground and raised enough dust to mask our advance, and it took me some heart-pounding minutes to find the cursed rock pile with its gaudy spear.

Polystratus laughed at me.

I left him to watch the rocks and galloped back to the column. From two stades away, the column was nothing but a thin line of bronze and a haze of steel spear-tips in a dust cloud.

I rode back to my taxeis. 'At my word, we will incline together to the left!' I called out. I rode up and down my files until every man had heard me. Awkward sods on the left files began to incline and had to be swatted back into their spots with cries of, 'Wait for it, you dickless fuck!'

I trotted back to the head of my part of the column. 'Taxeis of Outer Macedon! To the left! INCLINE!'

I left Leosthenes in charge and rode back to the front until I could see Polystratus. Then I halted. Leosthenes knew his job – he guided the right front phylarch – another Philip – to moderate his incline step until he matched perfectly with my line and Polystratus and the cairn, after which he ordered them to face front and march forward.

Then I galloped. I put my head down and raced for the head of the right flank column. I found Hephaestion – Alexander was gone on another errand.

I pointed well behind him and to his left. 'See my lads? They are on line.'

Hephaestion nodded. 'Column! Halt and form front to the left! Look for Ptolemy's taxeis to dress on!'

My men were marching forward all this time, so that they were already halfway from the rear of the right column to the front, a stade or more to our left. They were easily visible in their magnificent armour.

Hephaestion held out his hand. 'This is it,' he said.

I clasped his hand. 'He'll do it,' I said.

Hephaestion nodded.

And then time sped up again.

I was back with my taxeis, and I sent my Poseidon to the rear and my view dwindled – the height of a horse makes an enormous difference on a flat, dusty plain. And then – then we were so close to them that I could see individual men, horses, helmets.

We were opposite the Persian Royal Guard. Again.

And the last time, they'd held us.

Well, the last time they'd had a man-high riverbank to help them.

Polystratus rode up and handed me my greaves, which I snapped on my shins while walking. I'm sure I looked like a clown, trying to get them on while walking, bouncing on one foot and then another, but only a fool goes into hand-to-hand combat without greaves.

Then I ran, and sprinted across my own front. We were, just in that moment, the very point of Alexander's arrow. We were the lead element, and our right flank echeloned away to the right, so that the hypaspitoi were a little behind us but perfectly formed on our flank, and the Aegema – the household companions and then all the rest of the Hetaeroi – were formed on them, each squadron a horse length to the rear of the one before, and then, far out in the dust, I could see more horses, each squadron back from the last – less like an arrowhead than a bent bow, but from where I was I could see the men, the horses, or their dust.

We were two stades from the enemy, and Darius was getting his first look at our formation.

By Herakles, it was beautiful.

Of course, had some unit cocked it up, we'd have had a hole in our own lines.

I got a few yards in front. 'Friends!' I roared. 'In a few moments, we will have the pleasure of ripping the guts out of Darius's Royal Guard. The same bastards we saw at Issus. NEED I SAY MORE?'

And then Darius let loose his scythed chariots.

I've heard stories about those chariots. So here's what I saw.

They were useless.

The speed of our approach caused somebody – probably Darius himself – to misjudge the moment of their release. Horses take time to get to a gallop, and horses won't gallop at a solid wall of spears. They would have had to start while we were farther out in the plain – but then, of course, we weren't a solid wall, we were in parallel columns, and there was nothing for the chariots to hit.

Moreover, our echelon allowed us to form gaps – quickly, and without fuss – in any direction, because each unit was ahead of or behind the next, so that we could all move to the flank. That scarcely mattered, because all the chariots on our front – the moment their drivers bailed out, and many jumped before their chariots were even moving – headed for the gaps that already existed, between the taxeis.

Craterus took the worst of it, because his taxeis was echeloned well back, giving the horses time to reach their gallop, and because bad manoeuvring by the taxeis on either flank left him with no place to go. Even there, however, he dropped four files to the rear – a brilliant manoeuvre – and another pair of files lay down with their aspides over their heads, as we had fighting the Thracians. Some men had arms broken. Two men died.

Two. Not to belittle their sacrifice, but Darius unleashed a storm of war horses and flashing bronze, and we lost two dead and about forty injured.

And most important, we paused, took the stroke and *marched on.*

We were picking ourselves up and dusting ourselves off – remember, I couldn't *see* what happened to Craterus's phalanx, I had to wait for word. The dust was as thick as smoke in a burning house.

Alexander came out of the dust, with his staff behind him.

'Darius has a gap between his centre and his left,' Alexander said, as if we'd been together all afternoon.

Never mind how he knew. The Paeonians must have reported it.

I wanted to say something like, 'Hello to you too', but he was too intent on the battle.

'I am about to charge it,' Alexander said. 'The hypaspitoi will follow. You must hold the ground they give up. Cover our front. And press forward, or, at worst, give no ground.' He glanced at me. I was not Ptolemy, his boyhood friend. Merely the commander of the Taxeis of Outer Macedon. Truly, I don't think he could have told anyone my name at that moment.

I wanted to protest that my men would have to double their front-age. That we would be at most six deep, to fight Darius's finest infantry.

But I was sure that my men could do it. And so was he. So there was no point in complaining.

'Halt!' I roared. 'Right division – half files to the right! Turn! March!'

I tucked half my taxeis in behind the hypaspitoi. Now my men were six deep – four deep, in one place. I had expanded my front by one third.

While my phylarchs readjusted their files to balance the numbers and close up, so that we were as ready as we could be in this shallow formation, the Persians stood close enough that we could see the silver apples on their spears. But they didn't loose an arrow.

And they didn't charge us.

Listen, I could tell you what happened on the rest of the field. But I wasn't there. On our left, Bessus, of whom more anon, led his Easterners in a well-timed attempt to turn our flank left. He sent his Sakje to raid our camp, which they did with ruthless joy.

On our right, Persian and Mede noble cavalrymen, backed by Bactrians and led by Scythians, tried to turn Alexander's flank; racing to the edge of the unlevelled ground and then curving out and around our Paeonians and our veteran mercenaries under Menidas, they closed in. But they didn't charge home – they came in as a skirmisher cloud, shooting their bows.

Menidas charged them, because he had no other choice. He kept his ranks closed up, took serious casualties in men and horses and dusted them back into the bad ground, and then the Paeonians pursued them.

In time, the reckless pursuit of the Paeonians was punished by the Scythians and the Persians, but it took time.

On the left, Bessus and Mazaeus were more determined and more reckless, and Parmenio was a little too cautious. But when the Albanians and the Armenians were in the rear of the second line and threatening to turn Craterus, who had had to halt to prevent his flanks from being penetrated, Kineas and the allied horse under Coeranus countercharged. Their triumph was short-lived. But it bought Craterus time, and it bought Parmenio time.

Of course, I knew none of this, but a god, watching from above with a magic helmet that allowed him to see through dust, might have noticed that the king's battle plan was still intact. Our army would have looked like an embattled crab – with Persians *almost* all the way around us.

That's what was happening elsewhere.

Here's what happened where I was.

Alexander charged. But there was nothing simple about it, and while the troopers no doubt thought that it was all hard fighting, I could watch it unfold, and to me, it was all about precise manoeuvre.

As at Issus, he had formed two thousand Hetaeroi into a single wedge with himself at the head, sixty ranks deep at the centre, sixty files wide at the rear base of the triangle. The most manoeuvrable formation that you can achieve with cavalrymen.

Then he danced with it. The gap was off to his right, and Alexander faced his wedge to the right and *trotted* there, faster than the Persians could respond – possibly before anyone had noticed that the charge of the Persian left flank, intended to envelop our right, had opened this gap.

To genius, Alexander added patience and craftsmanship. He didn't race to the gap and charge. He trotted *past* the gap and wheeled his wedge back, so that it formed an arrowhead pointing through the gap and *back towards Darius.* Alexander wasn't just going to break the line. Alexander intended to kill the King of Kings. Himself. Just as he had told us.

I had time to watch it all. And I had time to watch the hypaspitoi under Nicanor wheel off by divisions to the right and reform.

My rear files then closed to the front on my line.

The hypaspitoi charged first. It is remarkable that every account – even the Military Journal – suggests that Alexander led the first, last and only important charge. I think it is a comment on what a bunch of subservient flunkies we became after Gaugamela that every man within

595

a stade knew that Nicanor led the charge and Nicanor had his orders from the king.

Nicanor slammed into the Greek mercenaries – the best infantry Darius had, except possibly his Immortal Guards. His attack was executed faultlessly, at the double – the most difficult speed for formed troops, but devastating if delivered perfectly, and the hypaspitoi were the essence of perfection that day. They struck the Greeks, who were waiting at a stand, crumpled their front ranks and shoved their entire phalanx *back* ten horse lengths.

The Greeks held. But only just, and as soon as the pushing started, they were at a disadvantage – literally, rocked back on their heels.

Now every man in the Persian ranks opposite my taxeis was looking to his left, watching. Because suddenly the Persian Immortals were naked – their own left flank now hanging in the air.

I stepped forward. The Immortals were lofting arrows, but from a stade's distance, they were more an irritation than a threat. And it told me that the Immortals were shaken.

'Ready!' I bellowed like a bull.

Sixteen hundred voices roared.

'Spears! Down!' I ordered. Two hundred and fifty files, covering more than a stade – only four or six deep. But the spears came down from the high carry to the attack.

I tucked myself back into my place. Latched my cheek-flaps. Now my view of the battle was cut again – from the panorama of the dusty line to the tunnel that led from me to the sun disc standard of the Immortals. Under their standards, they stood in perfect rows – sons of noblemen, in fine scale armour, with heavy spears and beautiful recurved bows; their alien trousers tucked into boots made of the finest leather; every man had on him enough gold to pay a file of Macedonian phalangites for a year. The officers had long beards like old-fashioned Greeks, and a few had them hennaed bright red.

'Front! March!' I called.

Opposite me, orders were being roared in Persian.

To my left, Coenus was matching his front rank to mine. He was eight deep, and would be more fearsome. His men overlapped the Persian guards and were facing more Greek mercenaries.

A few arrows came in, and then a volley, all loosed together – someone had fucked that up, as we were still well out.

'At the double! March, march!' I roared. I had not, until that moment, intended to duplicate the prowess of the hypaspitoi and charge at the double. But the early, sloppy volley of arrows gave me a slight edge. If we hurried. Perhaps Apis inspired me, or Herakles, my ancestor.

Had even one sarissa-man in the front rank tripped over a rock, or taken an arrow in the throat, it might have unravelled our front rank.

Ten horse lengths out. You can see men's faces under their helmets.

Five, and all you feel is the gravel under your feet. There are no more thoughts, no more observations. You are no longer hot or cold, nervous, terrified, or even calm.

You are the spear. And the moment.

Men tell wonderful tales of combat. I do myself. Most of it is lies and impressions gathered up by the mind after the fact, with the lies of others added in for good measure. But I remember two parts of that fight.

Our line was well formed when we hit. That, by itself, was a miracle. So I was neither ahead of nor behind the rest of the rank when I struck, and because we slightly overlapped the end of the Immortals' line where the Greeks had been shoved away from them, I *passed* the end of their line, ran a few paces and watched my men crash into the Immortals like a mighty wave on a calm beach which heralds the coming of a storm. Five or six files were with me, and we wheeled – an orderly not-quite-mob – into their left flank. A man's left flank is his shielded flank, and ordinarily, this flank is not particularly productive to strike – especially as we were so few, just thirty men, and we couldn't strike deep.

But the Immortals had kept their bows in their hands too long, and were still getting them back in their cases, and someone had ordered the rear ranks to keep shooting.

I had my best new spear in my hand, overhand as on the old vases, and I was killing men before I reached their line – shieldless men with too little armour. The overhand spear thrust comes down from above, into the throat, into the top of the thigh, into the breastbone, into the helmet. Without a shield, a man is all but helpless before it.

We were just thirty men, but we must have put twice that number on the ground in the time it took Perdiccas's men to give our charge and Coenus's three cheers. The Immortals were already jumpy – the Greek mercenaries had recoiled again – and they flinched from our attack into their flanks, and the front didn't stand its ground.

I still had my eyes on that great golden disc. I didn't know whether it was the king's or just the banner of the Immortals, but I killed my way towards it.

I had a wonderful new sword – my favourite, I think, of all the swords I'd ever had. Thaïs gave it to me. It was a simple kopis, neither long nor short, not even fancy – but magnificently balanced, so that it felt like a feather – a deadly feather – in the hand. And yet, whatever

I hit, parted. Flesh, leather, bronze – at one point, my beautiful sword cut *through* the iron rim of a Persian shield.

My Ionians were singing the paean. I had forgotten – we Macedonians don't usually sing it after we leave camp. But it was beautiful. And the brashness of it killed the Persians as thoroughly as our spears.

A big man came out of the dust. A man with a hennaed beard – an officer with more gold on him than Thaïs wore as an Aegyptian priestess, and his first blow took the head off my best spear, and he hammered me with a long-handled axe, and his blows began to destroy my aspis.

I made myself push forward into his blows, but a blow from outside my field of vision knocked the sword from my hand. I got a hand on his right elbow and shoved him – turned him – hammered the rim of my aspis into the small of his back and he roared, and I got a leg behind his as he cut back into me, put his arse against my hip and flipped him with my sword arm, over my hip and into the dust – kicked him, and then fell on him with my dagger from my side, and he was leaking in the sand and I was up and moving.

Another man – smaller, with a hooked sword that scored past my dented aspis on my greave, but didn't penetrate – hurt anyway – and I left my dagger in his guts. And by sheer luck and the will of Ares, or Zeus-Apis, my Athenian sword was lying so close to my feet that I all but cut my foot on the blade. I reached down and she came to my hand like a lover. I stood straight and looked around.

I'd left all my men behind. I'm a good strategos but sometimes a poor soldier. How often did phylarchs tell new men never to leave the ranks?

But the disc of the golden sun was *right there.* It was as if I could hear the king telling me: *Whatever you do, if your men are advancing into the Persians and killing them, you are doing my will.*

Off to the right, behind my head, the earth trembled. Two thousand horses went from a walk to a gallop, aimed at a gap only slightly wider than the base of Alexander's wedge – but the shoulder of the gap was held now by the hypaspitoi, and the Persians could no longer move front-line men to fill the gap.

I've used this metaphor before – but it's like that moment in a match, in pankration or wrestling, when you know – *you know* – that you have made an error, and it is going to hurt. You have bought a feint, or you have missed a hold, and now, before your heart beats again or you can do anything, his elbow is going to slam into your head. You know?

That's what Darius must have felt. The battle proper was still less than half an hour old, and Darius must have known, right then.

*

The rear ranks of the Immortals were a bloody shambles, but they were game, and every one of them was struggling to push back the front-rankers, stabilise the formation and save the standard. My moment of calm was past, and I was all but buried in opponents. Spears rang off my aspis and my helmet, and I staggered.

But combat is a complex dance, and what can I say? I was lifted above myself. A blow pushed my helmet back against my face, and the pain transformed the fight – in an instant, I was a little faster for the rage, a little stronger ...

My aspis swung at nose height, flat like a plate, and two men took its force, their faces crushed, and I was into the hole like water through a breaking dam, my kopis like a predatory bird taking insects at the edge of night, and I was above it, in it, through it. I remember no one cut, but the aggregate – for a few heartbeats, *I was a god*, seeing each opponent, seeing his intention, seeing his eyes, the minute shift of weight, baffling with my cloak, my shield, lying with the tip of my sword or telling a final truth with the blade or the grip. I suppose that blows fell on me but I didn't feel them, and Coenus claims that he could see me move through the Immortals the way you can watch a mole moving underground. I love the metaphor, even though I suspect he was as busy as I was and didn't see a fucking thing. It makes one hell of a good picture.

Under the disc were two giants.

I was alone.

I remember thinking, *I can do this.*

I swayed, like a child trying to evade his father in a game. Then I leaped forward to the left, and my two opponents failed to follow my movement, and now I had them aligned – not both facing me at once.

I hate fighting big men.

I had a sword that was too short to let me snipe, and my immediate opponent had a spear, and he rifled it at me. But his contempt betrayed him, and when he drew back and thrust again, I cut at the spearhead, swept his spear wide and powered forward under it, and my back-cut went into his greave and his knee, and he fell like a tree in the forest, bellowing – and I got the sword clear of his leg, and the blade rose, I turned it edge on, where his partner was cutting at me, and severed all the fingers of his spear hand; they were like a shower of thrown grapes at a party as his point went past my head. Again I powered forward, and my back-cut went through his crestless helmet and into his brain.

The great golden disc fell with a barbarous clang in the dirt, and they were on their way to Hades. It was like that. It was as if they stood still. Apis granted me that moment, and Herakles my ancestor. I had never been so good before, even before I took my wounds at Tyre, and I was never so good again.

But oh, the glory of it!

For the space of a hundred heartbeats, *I was a god*. And in those hundred heartbeats I learned what it might be like to be Alexander. What made him incomprehensible to other men was revealed to me – not in that moment, when there was nothing but the moment, but later, when I knew all the things I hadn't thought while I was a god. I hadn't doubted. I hadn't cared. I had *known*.

My time of grace ended as the great golden disc crashed into the dust.

But by Apis, it was glorious.

Up until that moment, I'm not sure that Darius had made a mistake. It hadn't all gone his way, but despite Alexander's perfect timing and godlike assurance, our army was in mortal peril. We were, to all intents, surrounded. The Sakje were already sacking our baggage and razing our camp.

Thaïs was calmly shooting Sakje from their saddles with her bow, shooting out of the door of our tent. She received a Sakje arrow through her calf in return fire, but they gave up our sector of the officers' lines as a bad job. Three hundred Thracian Psiloi and a thousand terrified, angry camp followers with spears and rocks were sufficient to keep the enemy out of the baggage wagons and the herds.

But the hypaspitoi and the Taxeis of Outer Macedon and the Taxeis of the North under Coenus crushed the front of Darius's centre *so fast* that he chose to stabilise his front rather than counter Alexander's cavalry charge.

A natural reaction, because when his horse guards charged me, I could see him, and he wasn't so very far away. Alexander must have seemed like a distant threat.

They glittered and shone like all the flowers of the fields in the Hebrew book. Like every hero of the *Iliad* gathered into a single magnificent regiment. They were red and gold, purple and gold, black and gold. The only silver was the steel in their hands, thousands of folds of perfect steel, magnificent weapons that made the Athenian kopis in my hand look like a crowbar.

The best men of the whole empire.

Darius sent them into my taxeis, and I was standing about two horse lengths in front of my men, who were in no kind of order. We were in those last moments of a melee, when the losers die and the winners swirl in, faster and faster as the losers no longer have friends and file partners and men to watch their backs, and it all comes to an ...

'Cavalry!' I roared.

Zeus, I was exhausted.

I set my feet. I didn't even have a spear.

Some mighty Persian lord got his spear on to my aspis and knocked me flat, and then they rode over me.

By the will of the gods, I didn't take a kick.

They had less than a tenth of a stade in which to launch their charge, and they were hampered by Coenus's men and the hypaspitoi coming at them, and so they were – most of them – not much above a fast trot. And like good men the world over, they cared about their own kin in the Immortals, and so they rode too carefully.

That didn't spare us much. But it might have been the edge between destruction and survival.

I lay in the dust and there were hooves all around me, the screams of frightened horses and maddened horses and war cries, and when they began to pack in together, I rose above my fear and the dust, got my legs under me between two horses and started cutting – heavy cuts, underhand, into the bellies of the animals and the legs of the lords.

I've heard versions of this story from other men – when you are deep in the enemy ranks, they are virtually defenceless. I got my feet under me, and men were off their horses and on their faces before they knew what had killed them.

Their formation was too open, as well. I went under horses' bellies, got bitten on the thigh and kicked – a splendid bronze thorax ruined in one blow. The hoof of that horse collapsed the careful forming of the bronze-smith, and it then stayed in its new form.

I pissed blood for two weeks. At the time, I fell to my knees and urine ran from me into the dust, and I coughed blood – all from one inglorious kick from a big horse.

Above me in the melee, a Persian leaned down and thrust his spear at me, and the point skidded across my back and dug into my hip between the pturges.

That's what happens when you are alone.

I retched. I couldn't help it – the pain of the horse's hoof was too much. And then I was flat on my face, and I had dust in my mouth – something hit me, or a horse stepped on me.

I lay there and waited for the end. I couldn't see the wound on my back, but the blood coming out of my throat suggested that I was done. I felt clear-headed, but I couldn't move my legs.

Clearly, through the forest of horses' legs, I could see the golden wheels of a chariot.

I remember thinking – perhaps my clearest memory of the day – *Fuck, I'm that close to Darius.*

And the earth trembled.

The *tone* changed.

I can't tell it any other way.

My legs moved.

The Persians above me in the melee had stopped raining blows on my corpse. They were looking somewhere else.

The earth shook.

The war god was coming. I could feel him.

I knew. Because I was almost under the wheels of the Great King's chariot – Alexander was coming *right here.*

I got to my feet like an old man, but no one contested the ground with me.

Someone – someone who glittered – was shouting at the man in the chariot, and the man in the chariot, who had the look of greatness, calm, dignified – was remonstrating. The man who glittered tore the reins from the Great King's hands. He was bellowing like a bull, demanding, begging, cajoling.

I had no idea what he was saying, but I'd guess he was begging the King of Kings to get the fuck out of there before the war god ate him.

And I imagine that Darius was yelling – But I'm winning! I'm collapsing his flanks!

He was, too.

He was fighting his cousin for the reins when he saw me.

One Macedonian. Two horse lengths from his offside lead horse. It was a four-horse chariot, and I could, if I'd had a spear, have killed one of the horses with a cast. And saved us all from tragedy, or not. Saved five years of my life, I suspect.

I didn't even have a dagger.

Darius looked into my eyes. I looked into his. We were about as far apart as a man courting in Pella and his lady-love above him on the balcony of her exedra.

And in that moment, Marsyas got his shield over my exposed side and said, 'You fuckwit.'

Cleomenes got his shoulder into my back, and his spear went over my head.

Leosthenes came up on my left and locked up on me.

And Darius looked at us, and his eyes moved from us to our right

– to where the war god, heralded by the storm of hooves, was coming. He let his cousin take the reins, and raced for safety.

The Persian horse guards rallied, and charged Alexander.

And Alexander cut through them like a sword through straw. I saw it, while Polystratus put a bandage on my hip – that's a nice way of saying that he ripped the chiton off his body and stuffed it, sweat-soaked, under my broken thorax to staunch the blood.

We weren't doing much fighting, you'll note. There was no need; Alexander swept past us, and we roared our approval, and then, so close I could almost touch Bucephalus, his wedge slowed in the thickening sea of Persians and I saw his rage – the lion baulked at his kill by a tribe of hyenas was never so outraged as Alexander cheated of Darius.

Even from the ground, I could still just see the golden wheels of Darius's chariot slipping away in the press.

Alexander swung his sword like a priest cutting up the sacrifice – heavy, professional strokes without a lick of mercy. He didn't shout any of his battle cries – no prayers to Zeus, no imprecations to Athena or Herakles or Amon.

He roared – in his curiously high-pitched, leopard-like cough – 'Darius!'

And again.

'Darius!'

And he locked his knees on his horse, cut a Persian nobleman almost in two from his eyebrow to his ribs – a superhuman stroke – rose to a position where he almost stood and roared so that his voice sounded over the whole battlefield.

'DARIUS!'

Alexander was – in that moment – greater than mortal. He was not a man. Bucephalus was not a mortal horse.

'FACE ME, DARIUS!' filled the air.

Darius rode away, leaving his empire.

Alexander killed men as if he had the fire of the gods in him and had come to scorch the earth. But though he cut a swathe you could follow with your eye, Darius was clear of the melee, and the chariot was moving faster.

'Ptolemy? Lord Ptolemy?' sounded from behind us.

My men were in no sort of order. I seemed to have very few casualties. I was a mess, and couldn't think.

It sounded like Diodorus the Athenian. He was pushing his horse through my ranks, shouting hoarsely for me.

Polystratus roared back, 'Here! Here!'

Ranks parted. Men were trying to get back in the right file, or trying to find the spear they'd left in some Immortal, or trying to get that damned sandal lace where it should have been all day, or drinking all the water in their canteens. They were behaving like soldiers who have survived hand-to-hand combat.

Diodorus became visible in the battle haze, which was as bad to our rear as to our front. 'Where is Alexander? Where is the king?' he asked.

Polystratus gave him wine. Diodorus looked like I felt.

'The left is collapsing,' he said.

I pointed and Cleomenes said, 'He's in the thick of it – right there. In front of us.'

Polystratus grabbed my shoulder. 'Can you ride?' he asked.

A pezhetaeros brought me Poseidon, and I mounted – it took two sets of hands pushing my arse, and I screamed at one point when I had to bend the wrong way. But no one in the Hetaeroi knew Diodorus very well. And everyone knew me. Blood was flowing from under my cuirass.

'Come,' I said. 'Leosthenes – find Coenus, link up, wheel to the left and push.'

All three of my officers saluted. It still makes me smile.

Men don't salute on battlefields. Mostly they grunt.

I don't know how long it took me to reach Alexander, but he'd halved the distance to Darius by the time we reached him. Darius was changing from the chariot to a horse, and we could see him.

Alexander spared me a single glance, and then looked back, anger written clearly on his face. 'What?' he asked. 'Another spear!' he shouted back at his immediate companions.

His arms were both bleeding. I doubt he knew, or cared.

Bucephalus was a pale golden horse, and his legs were coated in blood to the top of his fetlocks. Alexander had fought for some part of the action with a spear held high in a two-handed grip – and his arms were coated in blood to the elbow. When he cut a Persian in half, the man's insides had exploded over him, and he had blood on his face, his chest was coated in it and his thighs were matted with ordure.

He was the carrion god in person. Ares, come to earth. Why did Alexander *ever* imagine himself the son of Herakles or Zeus?

Even on that battlefield, I could smell the blood on him, copper and shit mixed together. And over all of that, his eyes glittered like blue ice.

'What?' he demanded of me again.

'The left is collapsing,' I said.

Diodorus said, 'I come from Parmenio,' and started to fall from his horse.

Philotas caught him.

Alexander looked at me. He might have been Darius a moment before – because he said, 'But I've won the battle.'

I was on horseback, and the Persian horse guard was mostly dead, covering the flight of their king, and as far as I could see, the Persian centre was done for. And I could see a fair way – we were out of the worst of the battle haze and in the rear of the Persian line.

But even from here, you didn't need to be Alexander to see that the enemy right wing was not in line with the enemy centre, and that the battle haze had a distinct kink in it.

There was a hole in our line.

If I could see it . . .

'Fuck him,' Alexander said, in a terrible voice. 'My curse on him.'

He didn't mean Darius.

He meant Parmenio.

The Hetaeroi were still under control. The wedge was still recognisable, and despite the fact that Darius was slipping away, no one was leaving the right face of the wedge to run him down.

Alexander looked. I had seen how very quickly he could read a battlefield, all my life since we were first in the field together, and I know he read that one ten times, looking for an alternative.

My men, and Coenus's men, and the hypaspists, were changing direction – slowly, like a grain ship under oars. Hoplites can go forward quickly, but when they move to the flanks, by files or by wheeling, it is like watching a glacier move on a mountainside.

He turned his head back towards Darius.

Then his face set.

I hadn't meant to join in, but Poseidon and I were swallowed by the wedge, and I was in the place just behind the king.

It was all I could do to ride. Blood was actually running over my saddlecloth. Philotas, who had no time for me whatsoever, looked concerned.

'Follow me!' he called to his wedge. Turned it decidedly to the right, angled back towards Parmenio.

Alexander looked back at me, and the smile on his face, the elation in the whole set of his body, outweighed his frustration at failing to get Darius. 'Don't you feel alive, when the trumpet sounds?' he asked me, and then we were away.

We charged into the flank of Mazaeus's triumphant cavalry just as they closed the noose around Parmenio's throat.

How bitter the Persian must have been, as he ordered the retreat.

*

There are a thousand ironies to the Battle of Guagamela.

It is ironic that the Persians killed so very few of us, because they were moments from massacring our entire left and with it, perhaps, the whole rear phalanx. I expect that had Alexander been ten minutes later, Darius's defection from the field would have been meaningless.

It is ironic that to Bessus and Mazaeus, Darius – their king – betrayed them by running. Ironic as I had watched him struggle to stay and make a fight of it. I can say with assurance that had Alexander botched his final attack, Bessus would have won the battle. Darius lost his empire when he turned and ran, and he would never have been king again after that moment.

It is ironic that Alexander blamed Parmenio for costing him his pursuit of Darius, because Parmenio, in my opinion, had the weakest part of the army, faced the cream of the Persian cavalry and fought for as long as anyone could have expected, and then for a while longer – long enough to ensure that Alexander won the grandest victory of his life, and did it well enough that the battle flowed almost exactly as the king had predicted. Yet the king never forgave Parmenio for his *failure*.

Ironic that in victory, Alexander was so powerful that his opinions were like laws. Even men who had served in the left flank said that Parmenio had *failed.*

And hubris? It fell from Alexander as blood runs from a mortal wound.

About the time that Mazaeus cursed the name of his king and ordered his victorious cavalry to retreat like dogs whipped off the corpse of a lion, I was one rank behind the king, deep into a melee with the aristocracy of Babylon and Mesopotamia. They had beautiful armour and they weren't much as fighters, and I suspect that they could read the wind as well as Mazaeus. Given our reception in Babylon, I'm not even sure they were sorry to see the golden disc of the sun fall.

But one of them, a mass of gold and bronze with armour all the way down his arms and scale mail that covered his face, exchanged sword cuts with me, and his mate drove a spear through Poseidon's neck. Poseidon didn't fall – by his namesake, he rose on his back feet, snapped the haft of the spear, and his mighty iron-shod forefoot crushed the chest of his killer before he slumped to the earth. And I crashed down on the same hip that had taken the wound earlier, and as Homer says, darkness covered my eyes.

PART IV
King of Kings

THIRTY-ONE

I f you've come to listen to the end, young man, you must know that most of the glory has gone out of the story, and only the tragedy remains. Have I convinced you, yet, that Alexander is not the king you should seek to emulate?

I will.

Guagamela was Alexander's masterpiece. He realised the plan, and he executed it perfectly – with brilliant, lightning-like changes of direction and purpose that marked his genius – instant response to the changes on the battlefield.

I am an excellent general, and I have won my fair share of battles. I could have *planned* Guagamela. But through all the dust I could not have seen the moment when the King of King's centre had drifted from his right, and thrust into it.

I awoke to pain and stupor – I'd been given poppy. Thaïs and Philip were waiting on me personally. My eyes opened, and Thaïs looked at me and a smile lit her face.

That's a good way to come back from the edge of death.

Philip leaned over, looked into my eyes and nodded. 'No concussion,' he said.

I was in the king's tent. The red-purple tinge, like fresh blood, was unmistakable. Outside, the sun must have been high in the sky, and the tent cast a wine-coloured pall over everything.

Somewhere to my right, I could hear the king.

'Oh,' he said. 'And immediately after I shattered their centre – could you see? There is no feeling like riding at the point of the wedge. The power! And the danger! Did you see it?'

Murmurs of appreciation.

Thaïs made a face. 'Please wake up and recover,' she said. 'I've had two days of it.'

Philip's lips made the slightest twitch, acknowledging – and agreeing.

It all came back to me in a single piece of memory. The fight in the dust. The message. The wedge.

Poseidon was dead.

'What's the butcher's bill on my taxeis?' I asked. 'Could you get me Isokles?'

Thaïs wiped my mouth. 'Isokles has been dead almost a year,' she said.

'Of course,' I answered, confused momentarily. 'Pyrrhus, too.'

'Yes,' she said, and looked away.

'Callisthenes, then?' I asked.

She shook her head. 'He died here,' she said.

'Marsyas?' I asked. 'Leosthenes?'

'Leosthenes is badly wounded and in the surgeon's tents. Marsyas is collecting Persian women and writing poetry to them.' Thaïs nodded to Philip. 'I'm going to move him.'

Philip nodded back.

Marsyas came to see me a day later. I assume he'd tried and been turned away, but he'd done all that I could have done – he'd arranged burials, sent letters and even managed to retrieve and bury mighty Poseidon.

He told me that the Taxeis of Outer Macedon had lost two hundred and thirty dead and wounded not expected to recover. Other taxeis had fared worse. Craterus had lost almost five hundred men, and altogether we'd lost almost two thousand infantry, most of them from the taxeis with Parmenio.

Marsyas wasn't going to tell me, but I saw through him.

'Our taxeis is being broken for replacements, isn't it,' I said.

Marsyas nodded.

And that was like the death of a friend. Another death. I hadn't started to mourn Callisthenes yet.

The rest of Babylonia fell without a fight.

That took months to play out. The welcome did not.

I was back to being a Hetaeroi. Because of my place in the battle, I was in favour, and because of my wound, I was still fevered, and I confess in advance that it added to the intensity of the experience. I was perpetually light-headed, and the sun had a quality to it that is hard to explain. It was brighter than I have ever known it, even in the endless Gedrosian desert. Even in Aegypt and Lydia. It burned into your eyes, and the grit – not really sand – rose to suffocate you, and the green of the trees was so green as to seem lurid. And the smell of human excrement, which they used for manure, fought the stink of naphtha fires and the omnipresent smell of incense. Men say that Aegypt is priest-ridden, but Babylon is god-ridden. They have gods everywhere, and they worship them to distraction.

Incense and naphtha. Smoke at the back of your throat, grit in your clothes. All the way south from Arabela to Babylon.

There was another kind of grit in my throat, and that was Mazaeus. Somehow, while I was recovering from my wound, he had come into our camp and made peace with Alexander, and he was suddenly the favourite – so much so that Hephaestion rode with *me*. Mazaeus had been one of Darius's most trusted officers, and his defection *was* important. Because of him, Alexander received the homage of dozens of important Persian and Mede officers, and our way was made smooth.

Darius had fled the field – again – and I found it almost melancholy to hear from Mesopotamian peasants that they no longer considered him king. Greek peasants, I'm sure, would have maintained their allegiance a little longer.

Or perhaps not.

At any rate, Mazaeus was tall and handsome and dignified, long-limbed, a beautiful horseman and a fine warrior. He wasn't ingratiating or obsequious.

But he did throw himself on his face every time he entered Alexander's presence – the royal presence was suddenly becoming the Royal Presence. Because of his age and immense dignity, Mazaeus made the rest of us seem like clods, and he clearly thought we were – except Alexander, who he found a way to love.

Really, I have a hard time remembering how it all started. We didn't go to war, on Alexander's staff, about proskynesis and Persian customs for *years*. And yet, the whole argument, the whole cultural disagreement, could have been read on every Greek and Macedonian officer's face, the first morning that Mazaeus made his reverence.

We rode south, away from Darius. I thought it was a mistake, and so did Parmenio. I felt that we needed to have Darius's head on a spike, or we weren't done. Parmenio agreed.

The old man was in a state of shock – not utter shock, but a sort of euphoric disbelief. He hadn't expected us to win the battle, and he clearly hadn't expected to *survive* the battle, and in the aftermath, he was quite naturally a little aloof, a little diffident, and genuinely generous to those who had played a role in the rescue of his wing – Diodorus, Kineas and the king. He was not hesitant in describing how desperate the situation had been.

This was not politics. This was just an honest old man thanking the team that saved him.

But Alexander's faction didn't hesitate to capitalise on his admissions of weakness, and Parmenio's sons, who were *not* thankful and felt that Parmenio had been hung out to dry, so to speak, were in turn angered.

Two days out of Babylon, with rumours rife that the city would resist, that Darius had another army forming behind us, and that Bessus, the senior satrap who had escaped Arabela, was still in the field with all his cavalry – a force still larger than our army – Alexander ordained that all the officers would dine together.

A symposium.

I remember, because he had just promoted Astibus and Bubores to company commands in his recently expanded hypaspitoi, and they were on the next kline to mine. They were crowned in wreaths of gilded laurel. So was I, and so was Marsyas, who shared my couch. Kineas shared a couch with Diodorus, also crowned.

Whether by intention or not, half of the great circle wore crowns of valour. And the other half did not. Philotas did not have one, and neither did Nicanor, although he had led the hypaspists with flair and reckless bravery. The older men, the partisans of Parmenio, had no crowns.

Parmenio was on a couch to my left, well within earshot, and he shared the couch with Philotas.

On the third bowl of wine, Philotas sat up. 'Why no crown for Mazaeus? He fought well enough!'

I must confess, I laughed too. It was funny. He was so ill at ease with us, in his long flowing robes. He'd probably never eaten lying on a couch, and he was desperately uncomfortable sharing his with Cleitus the Black, who glowered at him.

There were other Persian officers present. They did their best. It is almost impossible to be conquered with dignity, but they did it well enough.

But Philotas couldn't let them go. 'Why the long faces?' he called. 'We'll all be in high hats and long robes soon enough.'

This quip was not greeted with the enthusiasm that his earlier jibe received.

The wine went instantly to my head, even well watered, and I went off to Thaïs and bed. After I left, the Persians were heckled until the king ordered the verbal attacks to stop.

Just one big happy family.

Babylon.

The morning after the symposium, we formed the entire army in battle order on the plain of Mesopotamia. Despite dykes and irrigation ditches, we could march unimpeded. Indeed, Mesopotamia was the ideal ground for infantry – three thousand years of tillage had levelled it as flat as a skillet.

We advanced on the city in battle order, and we made camp the next night within sight of the place, a great mound twinkling with lights in the middle distance. It had an air of unreality.

Babylon was, and is, one of the mightiest, if not the greatest, city on the wheel of the earth. No one knows how many people live in its mighty compass, but I have heard that it has a million inhabitants. The girdle of walls, mud brick, fired brick and stone has a greater circumference than that of any other city walls I've ever seen, and despite that, the suburbs spill out of the city gates like wine from a drunkard's lips, so that there is a further girdle of intense habitation all around the city, many stades thick. The dense population is only possible because Mesopotamia has some of the finest soil and farmland in the world, and the two great rivers – the Tigris and the Euphrates – allow the produce to be floated directly to the city, which is also at the head of navigation, so that ocean-going ships can depart straight for the eastern seas from Babylon.

Babylon has ten times the population of Athens, the greatest city of our world.

Babylon could, all by itself, field a mighty army. Only sixty years before Marathon, a king of Babylon had challenged the whole might of Persia by himself, fielding a magnificent army of armoured cavalry and chariots. He had only narrowly been defeated.

I had a hard time sleeping. The fever was on me – the mosquitoes were like nothing I had ever seen. In god-ridden Mesopotamia, they didn't have a mosquito god, which I found surprising. I would have done a great deal to propitiate such a god.

I eventually got to sleep, only to have a dream that took me high over the Great Pyramid at Chios, and then, as if driven by a catapult, I did not so much fall as was driven down and down, into the very top of the magnificent structure, and I awoke covered in sweat. I threw off Thaïs's leg and my military cloak and stumbled out into the oppressive heat.

The only peace from the flies was by the fires, where the heat was worst.

A fever, high heat and bugs. I don't think that man can know a greater torment, unless it is the pain of a bad wound and the sure knowledge of coming death.

I settled by the smoke of a fire. I had lost my way in the camp. I was lost, or uncaring. Even now, I scarcely remember it.

But Philip, the veteran phylarch of Craterus's taxeis, came and sat by me in the smoke. He had wine, and I drank some.

'Fucking bugs,' he said. 'I hate 'em.'

After some time he pointed at the distant, twinkling lights. 'Think they'll fight?' he asked me.

'No,' I said. Thaïs was sure they wouldn't fight. Her sources were new and untried, but we had the feeling that the Babylonians, inscrutable in their religious bigotry, hated the Persians far more than they hated us.

But a city of a million men could field an army of a hundred thousand. And again, as at Gaza, the army was tired. Victorious, but tired. The elite cavalry units had been in continuous combat since midsummer, and everyone – every single unit – had been engaged at Arabela.

I wasn't exactly afraid.

Neither was Philip. He fingered his beard. 'I'd rather they fought,' he said.

'Who?' said another veteran, who plonked himself down by the fire and coughed in the smoke. 'Fucking bugs. Ares, where do they come from?'

'Farted out of Hades' arsehole,' Amyntas son of Philip said. A gross impiety, if you like, but it summed up what we all felt.

The other man held out his hand for the wine. 'May I?' he asked, and I recognised Draco, the man I'd faced – and lost to – in the pankration at Tyre.

We passed the wine and he drank, coughed, drank again. 'Who would you rather we fought?'

'Not we, damn it. I want to fight the Babylonians. I hear they aren't worth shit as fighters, and if we fight them, we get to sack their city.' He grinned. 'Sack Babylon. Just think of it.'

Draco roared. 'Good thought. Let's sack it anyway. The king will forgive us eventually.'

'What if it's too big to sack?' Amyntas son of Philip asked.

'Let's try!' Draco said. 'I've never fucked three women at once, either, and I might not be able to do it.' He grinned. 'But it wouldn't hurt to try.'

The wicked old man glanced at me.

I was being teased. I was an officer, in their space, and they were having a little fun.

I sighed. 'I don't think we'll get to sack Babylon,' I said.

Draco nodded. 'When exactly do we all get rich and march home?' he asked. 'Babylon? Susa? Persepolis?'

He grinned, but I thought he meant business.

I shrugged.

'Well, if you don't know, strategos—'

'I don't, friends. We'll go home when Darius is beaten, I suppose, and the empire is ours.' I noticed that there were a dozen men around the fire. We cycled almost unconsciously through the smoke – in, out, duck the bugs, get overheated, back to the bugs.

But their faces started to swim, and I began to see men who weren't there – who couldn't be there. Pyrrhus. Isokles. A dozen other men who had been my tent companions or my officers.

'When will we go home?' Pyrrhus asked.

'My wife expects me for the planting,' said a young spearman with a spearhead-sized hole in his chest.

'What's she planting, eh?' asked Draco, with a laugh, and Isokles roared and slapped his thigh just below the groin, where blood flowed.

They were laughing, and my head was spinning . . .

Polystratus put a hand under my elbow and another under my arm and he got me on my feet and walked me back to my tent, where there wasn't the hint of a breeze, and I lay in a wine stupor until I fell asleep.

I awoke to a pounding head, a face full of bug-bites and the thought that perhaps we had an army of our own ghosts following us across Asia, waiting to go home to Macedon.

Somehow, Ochrid got me up and dressed and armoured. I threw up twice – once the remnants of the wine, and again some bile. There was no cool water, and Ochrid didn't like the smell of the water that the slaves had brought in the night before. I drank a little of the tepid local beer and kept it down.

And then I mounted my second war horse, a big gelding named Thrakos, and said a prayer to Poseidon. I missed the horse every time I rode. Intelligence is the most precious ability in horse or man – Thrakos was as dumb as a post.

We formed by camps, and we covered two parasanges, a great line with the cavalry wings thrown slightly forward and all the baggage in the rear. Remember, we'd taken all of Darius's baggage at Arabela.

We marched on Babylon, and as the sun climbed the dome of the heavens, we saw a vast army forming to receive us – an unbelievable multitude that filled the horizon.

Alexander had the 'All Officers' sounded on the trumpet, and I responded without thinking. In fact, I was no longer commanding a phalanx; I had no command. On the other hand, no one tried to stop me.

Alexander was in full armour, with his lion's-head helmet, and he sat on his charger's back, hand on his hip, and watched the Babylonians with impatience.

'Let's get this over with,' he said. 'If they had an army worth anything, they'd have won their independence from Persia.' He shook his head. 'This is a waste of our time and manpower.'

The vast sea of enemies was coming at us across the endless plain of Mesopotamia.

We rested our right flank on the river and refused the left, under Parmenio, and began to move forward.

The Prodromoi went out to scout the face of the enemy army. Because we were already in formation, there was nothing else to do.

Ten stades apart, and the number of the enemy was unbelievable. They were deeper than we, and their main body was as great as ours. And they seemed to have three or four more bodies of like size, as well as dust clouds behind them as far as the smoke of the great city.

I was close to Alexander when Strakos rode straight into the command group and saluted. He was all but naked on his horse – like a Babylonian – deeply tanned, weaponless. I hadn't seen him in a month. The Angeloi continued to function, although these days they mostly reported to Alexander's permanent military secretary, Eumenes.

'They aren't armed,' Strako called.

Immediately, Alexander stopped talking to Hephaestion and cantered to meet the Thracian. 'What?' he asked.

'There are companies of armoured cavalry among them – but that's not an army. It is' – Strako grinned – 'a welcoming mob, lord. We're in contact with the high priest, who is with a great many dignitaries under that banner in the centre – you see – the huge red cloth? He hopes to meet you in person.'

I think we all breathed a little better.

No battle.

No fight for Babylon.

If Amyntas son of Philip was unsatisfied, he was virtually alone. You could hear the news spread through the ranks – you could see the ripple of spearheads as the men heard that there was not to be a battle.

Some men wept.

That's where the army was.

And then we marched forward, into the welcoming arms of a million Babylonians.

Every citizen and slave in the city must have been in the fields awaiting us. I don't think any of us had ever seen so many people together in one place in all of our lives, and it was, in its own way, terrifying. I rode next to Hephaestion, and as we passed into the belt of suburbs on a street wide enough for the phalanx to enter sixteen files wide despite the absolute crush of people, he turned to me and gave a thin smile.

'If every one of them threw a rock, we'd be dead in a few heartbeats,' he said.

It was true.

The sheer *number* of people in the streets and the fields transformed my idea of conquest. It occurred to me – for the first time – that conquest has an element of social contract to it. It was obvious to anyone there that the Babylonians outnumbered us fifty to one. Our army *vanished* into the city.

Who was conquering whom?

The city itself was like a feverish dream – a riot of plants and bright colours. Every house had great urns of trees and roof gardens, streets had shade trees and every available surface was plastered and painted garishly, or fired and glazed. Expensive houses were built of fired brick with the glazes fired in, amazing patterns that baffled the eye, or towering figures of their gods that filled a wall in shiny perfection.

And then we entered the walls – by the main gates; they were twice the height of the walls of Athens, with great gates of cypress and bronze that shone in the omnipresent sun, and the waves of cheering pounded at my head – on and on.

Alexander met the priests outside the city, and insisted that they walk with him in procession.

The men were tall, well fed and prosperous, tending a little to fat, with broad shoulders and tawny skin. The women were shorter than Greek women, and showed a great deal more skin, and wore gold ornaments in sufficient profusion to pay for the army for many days, and there were tens of thousands of bejewelled women.

Alexander rode with the priests through the heart of the city to the ruins of the temple of Bel, where he mounted a rostrum that had been provided by the Angeloi. They were very much in evidence in Babylon. They had prepared the way.

Alexander mounted the steps of the platform.

He took off his helmet.

He threw his arms wide, a sudden, sweeping movement that made his armour glitter in the sun, and the crowd roared like a living thing – a great beast with a million heads.

The army kept marching. The Prodromoi, by this time, had their orders, and the army wasn't going to be camped in the midst of the city. But the Aegema stayed by the king.

He waited until the cheering died away. That took a long time.

'I have come,' he said, in a beautifully controlled voice, 'to free Babylon from the Medes. And to restore your gods.'

At his side, Strako stood with the high priest of Bel, who spoke – loud, clear and high – to the crowd in Sumerian. They didn't even let him finish, but roared and roared – the roars became chants, and I was deafened. My horse became skittish, and all around me the Hetaeroi had a hard time keeping their mounts under control.

They began an odd, keening chant. I think it was the name of Bel, sung in a high, nasal voice by a million throats, and it sounded – terrifying.

But it affected Alexander like a drug, and he seemed to grow in stature. Again he lifted his arms, and again they roared their approval.

Naphtha and incense. And shit.

That was Babylon.

The next day – we stayed in the royal palace, which effortlessly accommodated a thousand hypaspists and as many Hetaeroi and grooms – Alexander met the hierophants of every temple in the city. He confirmed every ancient privilege and restored the rights of the temples that had been taken away by Persia.

Babylon was utterly ours. While I'd lingered in fever, I now understood, Eumenes the Cardian, Alexander's military secretary, had outmanoeuvred Callisthenes for control of the Military Journal, and Thaïs supported him. Harpalus was involved somehow, as well, and Babylon was their shared triumph. They had the priests from the first – Eumenes won over the nobles, and Harpalus brought the commons. I still find it interesting that the treasurer, the secretary and the hetaera took a city of a million men without a fight. I thought about things that Aristotle had discussed with us, things I'd relearned on the couches of Athenian symposia. About the contracts between governed and governing. About what victory and defeat are, in war.

But those were my private thoughts.

The next day, Alexander went to visit the temples. They were incredible – as old as those at Memphis, or older, and if Aegypt sent chills down my spine, Babylon was just scary. That day, at the Temple of Bel, Alexander was shown the scribal entry for the Battle of Arabela. It pleased him immensely, because, as the priest noted, until that date, Darius had been called 'King of all the Earth'. But in that entry, Alexander was called 'King of all the Earth'. And henceforth would be known as such, in Babylon.

Marsyas stood with me and with Black Cleitus. We were all staggered, by everything, but Marsyas's intense curiosity never flagged. He walked over to the priests. The youngest was actually writing with a bronze stylus in clay. The hierophant stood with the king.

'How far back does this record go?' Marsyas asked, pointing at the rows of tablets that literally ran off into the dark, shelf after shelf running off to the north in the foundations of the great temple.

'Ah!' the hierophant said, his pleasure at the question evident. He was a great man – spoke Greek and Persian, Median, Aegyptian and Hebrew. Later – as you'll hear – when I was laid low by fever, he helped tend me, and asked Thaïs thousands of questions about Athens and Greece and Aegypt.

At any rate, he led us off into the cavernous rooms under the temple – room after room, and in every room he lifted his torch so that we could see the neat baskets of clay tablets that lined the walls. After ten rooms, the baskets were so old that the tablets had deformed them. In twenty rooms, we saw new baskets.

I forget how many rooms there were, but by torchlight, in that endless undercroft, itself oppressive and musty, like some man-built intellectual Tartarus for burying old truths – my fever was returning, and the place terrified me, and still haunts my nightmares – eventually, the high priest raised his torch.

'The First Room,' he said to Alexander. The king nodded. This sort of thing engrossed him.

The hierophant walked along the shelves, looking carefully into the baskets at the left end of the top shelf, until he found what he wanted, and pointed to the last basket.

'First Basket,' he said. His own awe was evident.

'But how old is it?' Marsyas persisted. This had all taken what seemed like hours.

Reverently, two junior priests took down the First Basket and extracted the tablets, which were laid carefully on a portable table that was painted with images of their gods.

To the best of my feverish ability, I stared at the three tablets. I was alive enough to note that the style of the squiggles was identical to those on the tablet the youngest priest was inscribing out in the main temple.

'This is the First Tablet of Record,' the hierophant said, and he kissed it. 'It records the events of the year, as it should – the rainfall, and the maintenance of the irrigation channels.'

'How *old* is it?' Marsyas asked. 'Is it five hundred years old?'

The hierophant leaned down. He traced some marks with his fingers.

'This was written down three thousand, four hundred and nine years ago, by the priests of this temple.'

'By Zeus, that is before Troy!' Alexander said.

Marsyas drew a deep breath. 'That is before Troy was *founded*.'

The hierophant shrugged. 'It is not our oldest record. Merely our oldest record in writing that is part of the Yearly Almanac. We have records of weather and river floods at least a thousand years before that.'

Babylon had a way of making all of us feel small.

Except Alexander, I think. And I think that seeing his name as King of all the Earth in that temple did ... something.

Two days later, while the king held a review of the Hetaeroi for the Babylonians, I fell from my horse in a dead faint. When I returned to the world, a month had passed, and I was being tended by Marsuk, the hierophant of Bel, in person. He and Thaïs had become friends – they remained correspondents until his death. And there's little doubt in my mind that he saved my life.

Alexander took the army east, headed for Susa. I missed an entire campaign, lying on my bed in the city of the hanging gardens. I lay about for almost three months, eating, making love to Thaïs and recovering. I read a great deal, and thought some deep thoughts. And talked them over with Thaïs. A very happy time for me.

Not part of this story, though.

When I was recovered, I took a party of recovered wounded, as well as sixteen hundred recruits and Greek mercenaries, and marched towards Susa. The rumour was that Alexander had stormed the Susian Gates, and was pursuing Darius through the Elymais hills.

As we moved up to Susa, recrossing the mosquito-infested marshes and the dry, dusty plains of southern Babylon, we began to encounter the wounded from Alexander's attempt to storm the Susian Gates and his disastrous repulse. Another thousand phalangites lost; Marsyas wounded, and on his way to Babylon to recuperate.

I had left Leosthenes in Babylon, and he never rejoined us, for reasons that will become evident. My command was completely broken up, and I assumed – hoped – that the party of recruits and mercenaries I was taking up to Susa would become a taxeis.

I had forgotten what happened in the hours after the death of Philip. I had been away from Alexander for three months.

I caught up with him at a tiny village called Shakrak on the edge of a volcanic lake. Cleitus was the officer of the day.

I reported to him. He saluted me, embraced me, held a snap inspection of my reinforcements and immediately split them up among the existing taxeis. He didn't ask Alexander, and he didn't ask me, and when he was done and it was too late to do anything about it, I snapped.

'That was my command,' I said. I had intended it to sound humorous – it came out the way I really meant it, as bitter.

'You don't have a command,' Cleitus said. 'Neither do I. Nor do most of the old boys.' He glanced around. 'Ask yourself why. Or don't. But don't be surprised if you don't hold any more commands.'

I tried not to shoot the messenger. 'I'll find the king,' I said.

Black Cleitus shrugged. 'Your funeral,' he said. 'But I wouldn't.'

I did, anyway.

My timing was poor. I had entered Alexander's marching camp on the heels of a dust cloud, and that cloud was the harbinger of a troop of Prodromoi with a pair of Persian traitors. The commander of the city of Persepolis – the very capital of the Persian Empire, no less – had offered to hand the city over to Alexander.

I entered the command tent. Alectus saluted me and smiled. Hephaestion looked up to see what the interruption was, and even he managed a smile.

Alexander was facing two handsome Persians. The one wearing a pound of gold foil was apparently named Darius, and he was the son of Tiridates, the commander at Persepolis.

'My father says come now, and come quickly,' the boy insisted. 'Before there is looting.'

Men were turning – Philotas gave me a little wave, and Perdiccas grinned at me. Alexander looked up. His eyes went to me – and slid right off me.

'Silence, there,' he said. 'Will your father recognise me as King of Kings?'

The young man gave Alexander the strangest look. 'No. You are not the King of Kings, are you?'

Remember, Persians value telling the truth above all things. They don't prevaricate well.

Alexander flushed. 'I am the King of Kings. Are you Persians blind as well as deaf and dumb? I *am* the absolute master of Asia.'

Young Darius stepped back a pace. 'My father,' he said again, 'bids you come as quickly as possible.'

Philotas shook his head. 'Let me go, lord. It could be a trap. Where better? Their terrain, every peasant is one of theirs, and only this boy's word on it.'

Alexander glanced at him. 'Never fear, Philotas. You will go. With me.'

The Persian boy leaned forward and spoke quietly into Alexander's ear.

Alexander's eyes grew wide.

'Stop!' Philotas said. 'Tell all of us!' He was obviously angry, and just as obviously distrusted the Persians.

Alexander turned on him. 'Desist. Do *not* give orders under my roof. Go to your tent – I will send for you.'

And Philotas went.

Zeus Soter, the world had changed while I was gone.

Alexander didn't stop to greet me. He assembled his household cavalry and prepared to ride off to Persepolis.

But technically, I was still a troop commander in the royal Hetaeroi, and I mounted my horse – it was bitter cold, the very edge of a two-day snowstorm in the mountains. My troopers looked at me and laughed, or slapped my back – they were all men I knew. Polystratus took the trumpet from the troop hyperetes, and no one said a word. Philip the Red had been commanding my troop, and he simply clasped my hand and fell back a rank.

It touched my heart.

We rode like the wind. The bridge over the river gorge was gone, destroyed by Darius. We stripped a village of roof trees – in the depths of winter – and prepared to build our own bridge. A troop of enemy cavalry hovered on the far side of the winter torrent, but they only watched us. We put a line of horses across the stream to break the current, and then men – knights of the royal household, aristocrats and veteran soldiers – stripped naked and waded in, bellowing at the cold, carrying the roof trees of the stripped village on our shoulders. We got that bridge across in two hours, and not a single arrow was lofted at us.

We built big fires, warmed ourselves for half an hour and mounted up.

The cold river did something good for my hip and pelvis. I'd been in pain every mile of the ride through the hills, and now, suddenly, the pain was gone. At the time, I thought my balls might be gone, too, but they remained intact.

Up and up, into the hills.

Just before darkness fell, my troop was in the lead – the most aristocratic Prodromoi in history, I suspect. I had Polystratus and Theodore and all his former grooms – all of whom were Hetaeroi now, of course – prowling every track we passed, but it was snowing hard enough that I had reached the point old soldiers reach too often, where I didn't particularly care if some enemy troopers wanted to ambush me. I was too cold and tired to care, and the snow was piling up on the shoulders of my thickest cloak and starting to melt through, so that trickles of freezing water snuck down my neck and back under my breastplate. You cannot get warm once that starts to happen.

Up and up.

No one ever thinks of Persia as cold.

And then, across the track in front of me, there were three men, like ghosts, or like some horrid set of masks. The light was odd – early sunset in heavy clouds and snow, an amber light with a grey edge to it, cold, hard and evil.

Polystratus reined in, but he'd missed them, or they were supernatural. He was past them.

Here we go, I thought. *An ambush.*

But the supernatural remained uppermost in my head. There was something *wrong* with them. I was half a stade away, and with the snow and the light, they looked like corpses. Closer and closer and the wrongness grew worse. The hair rose on the back of my neck. I checked the draw on my kopis.

I retrieved my spear. I had tucked it under my leg so I could keep my hands warm, and now I put it in my right hand and looked around.

Three horse lengths, and they *still* looked like raven's food come to life, and my hands were shaking. Philip the Red, at my back, was praying, and he was not a pious man.

Polystratus turned his horse and came cantering back, his horse's hooves throwing snow.

He was too late.

The middle figure raised an arm.

The arm had no hand, only a stump.

Close up, I saw that he *did* look like raven's food. Neither he nor his two companions had either noses or ears.

I reined my horse in so hard that he reared.

'Pardon, lord!' the central figure said in Athenian Greek.

I was fighting to control Medea, who was spooked.

'Greetings!' said the next figure. Zeus, they were hideous.

They seemed excited. Even happy.

They spoke Greek.

'Please say you are Greeks!' the leader said.

I got my knees, frozen through, locked around Medea's barrel and restored her to order. 'Greek enough,' I said. 'Who might you be?'

'I am Leonidas of Athens,' the leader said. He raised a hood from his cloak and hid his face. His right hand was intact.

He moved carefully. The swirling snow made him more hideous than he might otherwise have been.

I realised that one of his legs was made of wood.

'You—' I began.

'Artaxerxes ordered that all of us who had taken arms against him be mutilated,' he said. 'I have my lips. Many do not.' He took Medea's bridle in his good hand. 'So it is true. You are here! Alexander is here to avenge us!'

'Zeus!' I muttered. 'Were you taken in arms against the Great King?'

He nodded. 'Most of us were taken in Aegypt,' he said. 'The old king kept us here. He would come to our village and watch us.'

He was crying by this time, and he tried to embrace my horse. My horse!

I cannot do justice to how hideous he appeared, and how his tears and those of his two wretched companions made him look worse.

'It is true!' he cried.

I dismounted, and forced myself to accept their embraces. They were not lepers. They were brave men who had fought the same enemies I fought, and had come to this bitter end.

I sent Polystratus for the king. I sent him with strict orders to warn Alexander what lay ahead, so that he was not taken by surprise.

The Greeks had built fires, and they took us forward to their village, which lined the Royal Road. They were despicable beggars, to the Persians, but they had prepared fires and food for us.

I warmed myself, and made myself accept the embraces and the thanks – the thanks! Of a hundred miserable wretches with no eyes, no lips, no noses, no ears, no hands or feet.

I watched them tend each other. They were like file mates – the man with no legs depended on his mate with two to fetch for him.

The king rode out of the snow.

He dismounted, threw his arms around Leonidas and walked through them, embracing these wrecks of men, and promising them that their troubles were over.

He did it well.

I thought it possible that these men would die of joy. I had never seen men to whom pleasure was so very painful.

And eventually, Alexander made his way to me.

'You did well to send me word,' Alexander said to me. He nodded. 'This – it is for this that we march to destroy the rule of Persia.'

The falsity of his speech sickened me. I had never heard him sound so openly pompous.

Whatever passed over my face, he missed it, but Hephaestion didn't. He looked at me with a special kind of pleading. The way a parent looks at another parent, begging that a child *not* be told something.

So I let it go.

In the morning, we rode on, to Persepolis.

*

Tiridates surrendered it. When we marched through the passes to the city over the next day, we couldn't believe he hadn't made even a token effort to hold it, but of course Alexander had massacred almost every man who held the Susian Gates, and that may have broken Tiridates' will to resist.

We rode into the city of the Persians, and I couldn't believe my eyes. I had seen Aegypt and Babylon – I don't use that phrase lightly.

The magnificence of the city rolled on and on, so that the eye couldn't drink in all the splendour at once, and skipped from detail to detail. It wasn't like Athens – which I love – or Memphis – which I dream of – or Babylon. All three cities have a magnificent central focus that draws the eye and holds it, and any man or woman watching the sun set on the Acropolis has to ask if mere men built the Parthenon, yes? And the same with the temple complex at Memphis, or the Temple of Bel in Babylon. And Athens was ancient when Hector died at Troy, and Aegypt was ancient when Herakles walked the earth, and Babylon – by the gods, Babylon is just ancient.

But at Persepolis, there's more than you can see at a glance, and so you try to look everywhere. Or you did. It is no longer a problem.

And it was all new-built, like the house of a parvenu rich man. The oldest building was perhaps two hundred years old.

The lower town populace stayed in their houses. A hundred Persian cavalrymen met us outside the gates, led by the traitor in person. We had almost two thousand cavalry with us, and Alexander ordered Philotas to take the gates with his personal troop.

And then we rode in.

I remember that at some point, after most of the column had passed the ceremonial gate, I looked back to make a comment to Philip the Red. I can't even remember what I meant to say. But behind him, one of my gentleman troopers – Brasidas, a highlander – fumbled his helmet and dropped it. It struck the stone street pavings with a hollow clang that sounded as loudly as a hundred temple bells.

That is how silent Persepolis was as we rode through the streets.

I still do not understand how it was that Darius chose to leave it intact. Or why he abandoned his treasury.

We rode to the palace. And Alexander threw the reins of his horse to the slaves and grooms as if he were the owner, and walked into the palace, led by Tiridates, who took him to the throne room.

I knew what Alexander intended. Apparently, Tiridates did not.

Alexander went to the throne – the great throne, with the winged lions supporting it. And sat. He had to get a table to climb into it. I helped carry the table, and two Persian servants standing by, shocked, burst into tears when the alien usurper sat on the king's throne.

Alexander turned and looked at them.

'Now I am your king,' he said.

The silence inside the palace was thicker, if anything, than the silence in the streets.

'Now take me to the treasury,' Alexander said.

Our footsteps were loud. And the palace was immense.

It was utterly different from Memphis. At Memphis, enthusiastic priests led us from room to room of a living palace.

Despite the presence of the full staff at Persepolis, we were looking at the corpse of a palace, and I could feel the hate from every servant, every eunuch – even the slaves.

We crossed the complex to the double tower that acted as the royal treasury. A pair of eunuchs made trouble, and then subsided, and their keys were taken from them. And the doors were opened.

I walked in, one of perhaps eight or nine men behind Alexander. I looked at him. He had stopped, transfixed, in the midst of a marble floor inlaid with black basalt. He had a look – like the Greeks. Raw joy. Hunger.

I lifted my eyes from him, and saw it – I can testify to what it looked like.

It looked like all the gold in the world.

A talent of gold will feed a peasant for his entire life.

We launched the invasion of Asia with forty talents in our war chest.

A hundred thousand talents was, in a very real way, all of the gold in the world. Every treasure that the Persians had taken from every empire that they conquered – from the Assyrians, the Babylonians, the Jews, from Thrace, from Euboea in Greece, from Athens; from India, from the Saka, from the desert tribes of the East, from the hill tribes – here it was, the product of two hundred years of ruthless war. Melted down, refined, stacked in bars that reached to shoulder height in front of us and vanished on either side into the murk of the vault, with chests of jewels, swords, armour, mirrors of silver, nets of pearls, the tribute of a hundred kings to the might of Persia.

Alexander made a sound like a moan – the sound of a woman in the joy of love. In that place, a hideous sound.

In that moment, Alexander ceased to care about Macedon. Macedon was an appendage of his treasure room.

Because the veins of Ares are not full of ichor, but molten gold. War requires gold as a horse requires hay and grass. War *consumes* gold.

We had all the gold in the world, and our king moaned with pleasure to see that he could make war *for ever*.

We were four months in Persepolis. The army moved up to us, and then the baggage moved up, little by little.

The soldiers began to grumble. They knew the scale of the treasure we'd just seized. They wanted some of it. The older veterans – especially Parmenio's oldest men – made it obvious that they thought it was theirs.

I was adapting to my lack of place with the king. He scarcely seemed to recognise me when I attended him, and I was never summoned to council. He did say my name from time to time – but usually only to put me in my place.

I might have been bitter, but I had lost my heart for it. There was a busy crowd around him, fighting for supremacy and power. Viewed from the outside, it looked … obscene.

But the near mutiny of the old soldiers was being ignored at every level. Men like Craterus were obviously afraid to bring it up with the king. You'll note there's not a whisper about it in the Military Journal.

I sent a note to Hephaestion, requesting a cup of wine with him. He was, as far as I could see, the last of the old crowd still close to the king.

I dressed carefully. I had a feeling that this was very important. That appearances now mattered more than reality. That somehow, we were *becoming* Persians, with their elaborate rituals and their empty honours.

When I entered Hephaestion's tent, he wasn't there, and his servants gave me a cup of wine and did not offer me a place to sit.

I waited for a long time.

It is odd how waiting affects you. I grew angrier and angrier, of course – who does not? But the oddest part was my inability to decide whether I should sit or not. The only place to sit was on Hephaestion's bed, and it was not at a good height for sitting. I couldn't help but think what I'd have done to Hephaestion if he'd kept me waiting when we were young.

But I remained standing.

My knees grew tired.

My hips hurt.

Eventually, he came into the tent, reading a scroll. He looked at me. He was puzzled, and then shook his head. 'Oh – Ptolemy. Of course. I can give you two minutes. What do you want?'

We were only a few feet from Alexander's great red-purple tent, and suddenly I heard the king's voice. He was angry.

'What do you mean, *you will not?*' he shouted.

I knew that tone. He was enraged.

'I *am* the Great King. I *demand* that you hold the spring festival.' He was spitting – I could hear it.

Hephaestion glanced at me. 'What do you want, Ptolemy?' he asked brusquely.

I had had an hour to consider how I was going to put this, but all my good resolutions fell away.

'I want the king to get his head out of his arse,' I said.

That got Hephaestion's attention.

'Some of Parmenio's men – most of the phylarchs in the four senior taxeis – are on the verge of mutiny,' I said. 'Do you know about it?'

Hephaestion froze.

'The king has taken all the loot of Asia that you may remember he promised to the troops – soldiers don't forget that sort of thing.' I stepped across the tent towards him, and the bronze-haired bastard flinched. 'He's fucking around with some Persian festival and he's bribing the magi – the Persian priests – and he's all but told the army that we're marching east, not west.' I was close to Hephaestion now. 'And none of you useless *fucks* seems able to tell him. They're going to refuse to march. And the troops will back them.' I was looking into his eyes. 'Someone might decide that the easiest way to go back to Pella is over the king's corpse.'

Hephaestion looked at me, took a breath and behind him the king screamed, 'You will have the spring festival, and I will walk in it and take the part of the Great King, or by all the gods we both hold sacred, I will destroy you.'

'The king has other troubles just now,' Hephaestion said blandly. 'Leave my secretary a list of the ringleaders and I'll see it's dealt with, and see to it you get appropriate credit.'

There is a difference between living a story and telling it. Even as I tell you this tale, I know that I foreshadow, I embellish and I explain. So that moment, when Hephaestion treated me as a minor court functionary – I have probably made it seem natural. I have probably prepared you for this, and you nod, and say, yes, the king has started to behave as a tyrant.

But I was stunned. 'Hephaestion – there are no *ringleaders*.' I remember shaking my head. 'We are talking about – I don't know – a thousand men. The very heart of the army.'

Hephaestion took a deep breath, and released it. 'Very well,' he said. He met my eye. 'You tell him.'

And so I did.

Hephaestion took me to the king's tent. The magi were nowhere to be seen. He was on his couch, staring at the roof.

'Patroclus, why do the gods send me fools—' he began. And then he saw me.

'Ptolemy has news he deems serious,' Hephaestion said carefully. Hedging his bets.

'Achilles, sulking in his tent,' I said.

Alexander sat up. He opened his mouth.

I shook my head. 'Your veterans are on the edge of mutiny,' I said. 'Pay is late, and you have just seized all the gold of the empire – a mountain of gold. You made them help load the mules – they know to the talent how much you gained.' I looked at Hephaestion, but he was no help. 'They are talking mutiny in the streets.'

'I asked him to give me the names of the ringleaders,' Hephaestion said.

'There *are no ringleaders*,' I said. 'Nor are there any dissenters.'

Alexander nodded, once, decisively, as he did on the battlefield. He assimilated what I was saying, matched it to other data and agreed that I must be right – as ruthless with his own notions as with enemy troops.

'I see.' He nodded. 'Yes. And you will, as usual, tell me that I have been blind,' he said, looking at me with a disarming smile.

But by the gods, a false smile, like an actor in a mask, or worse.

He nodded again. 'Very well. We shall give them a bone, and perhaps send a warning to other quarters at the same time.'

'A bone?' I said. 'You need those men. They are the officers and file leaders of your army.'

Alexander shook his head. 'No,' he said. 'I don't need them. I can buy any army I want.'

'Didn't work for Darius,' I said.

'Darius was not me,' he said. 'Your concern is noted. Gather an army council, son of Lagus. And you have my thanks for this timely warning.'

It was still winter in the mountains. Hephaestion gathered all the spears of the army – all the Macedonian citizens. They came with spears, and with torches. They came ready, I still believe, to mutiny.

Alexander stood before them in the white and gold of a Macedonian king. He'd had a few hours to prepare, and he had with him on the besa a half-dozen of the disfigured Greek veterans.

'Men of Macedon,' the king said. 'The time has come to avenge these men. Look at them well. Professional soldiers – men of Amphilopolis and Pella, of Athens and Sparta, of Ionia and Aeolia. Tortured and mutilated by the Persians. *Look at what Persia really is.*'

Even as he spoke, the poor miserable things shuffled through the crowd, and more of them emerged from behind the king to stumble or push themselves or drag themselves in among the Macedonians.

'Don't flinch!' the king said. 'Look at them. Had we been defeated at Issus or Arabela, we would have shared this fate. I would be dead, or I would have no lips and no ears. That is the *peace* we would have earned from Persia. Ask a Euboean. Ask an Athenian!'

He had them, and they had never even voiced their discontent.

'Persepolis is the richest city in the empire,' he said. 'I give it to you, my loyal troops. I reserve only the temples and the treasury and the palace. Take the rest. Kill the men, and take the women for your own, and let every house be looted and the spoils shared as is the custom of the army.'

We had lived among these Persians for six weeks. Eaten their bread. Laughed at their children and tickled them.

But these men were Macedonians.

They roared.

And then they went and raped Persepolis.

I helped massacre the population of Tyre. I did not help at Gaza. But at Persepolis, I actually stood aside.

The hypaspitoi moved into guard positions around the treasury, the palace and the temples. The magi were carefully protected, as was our growing camp of collaborators.

Every other man in the city was butchered. Perhaps some escaped. I never met any.

It must have fallen like a bolt from Zeus. As I say, we'd lived among them for six weeks. And then, one night, with no warning, their town was sacked.

There was an orgy of destruction. I did not watch it.

But I'm sure you can imagine, if you put your mind to it.

And the next day, most of the lower town was burned flat. The temples and palaces remained untouched, somehow yet more noble for the ruins at their knees and feet. The wailing of women – the cry of absolute degradation and horror – could be heard everywhere in the temple complex. And in the palace. It was as if Persepolis itself wept.

Two days later, when Thaïs arrived with the mules returning from carrying the great treasure down to Susa, the town still smoked and the women were still weeping.

I embraced her, buried my face in her neck and kissed her, but when my hand sought the pins on her chiton, she pushed me away.

'Raped women are an offence to Aphrodite,' she said coldly. 'I will not make love, even with you, while they weep for their dead and their virtue and the sanctity of their bodies outside my tent.'

What could I say? I nodded. Stepped back. 'I took no part,' I said.

'Did you take action?' she asked.

I turned away. 'It is probably my fault,' I said. 'I wanted Alexander to see what the soldiers thought. Instead, he told them what to think – made them beasts, and rewarded them for it.' I drank wine. I was drinking too much, in those days. 'And all to pressure a handful of recalcitrant priests into holding some festival.'

'The Festival of the New Year,' she said. 'I am sorry, Ptolemy. But my body cannot love while I listen to all that hate and despair.' She crossed the tent to me and kissed me. 'Why does he imagine that he will be allowed to celebrate the New Year festival?'

'It's about being the Great King,' I said. 'It is like Tyre. Only the Great King may accept the sanctity of Ahuru Mazda. If he's allowed to celebrate the festival, that makes his rule legitimate.' I shrugged. 'Aegypt accepted him as Apis. Babylon accepted him as Serapis.'

She smiled. 'Aegypt is older and wiser, and Babylon is the whore of cities.' She motioned for me to pour her wine. 'Persepolis has never been conquered before.'

'We have a thousand Persian noblemen with us now,' I said.

She shook her head. 'They will collaborate only until there is an alternative,' she said. 'Because Alexander thinks himself the ultimate power on earth, he cannot imagine the strength they can derive from their culture and their god. I have met with magi in Susa and in Babylon. They mean to resist.'

I shrugged. 'He has done everything he can to appease them, and the Queen Mother.'

Thaïs shook her head, this time vehemently. 'She hates him, now.' She began to fiddle with her leg-wraps, and I knelt to help her get them off – we were having this conversation when she was no doubt cold and saddle-sore. She sat back. 'I have missed you, son of Lagus. It's harder and harder to get good help.' She smiled at me. Then turned away. 'He must be pushed away from the lure of Persia. If he makes himself Great King in fact, he will be a monster beyond the rich imagination of Plato or Socrates.'

A month in Babylon, and Thaïs had never been so direct.

Persepolis is where it all happened.

I was invited to 'court' more and more frequently. As if, having proved my usefulness again, I was welcome back once more. As if . . . nothing. That's what had happened every time I left, and this time, my eyes were opened to the process. Out of sight, out of mind. In sight, rewarded.

It was chilling to talk to him. He had forgotten who I was. He spoke to me as if I were a stranger – with a false charm and a manicured sociability. In fact, he wooed me.

I didn't want anything, and that made me dull.

Weeks passed, and I attended parties. Thaïs came and played her kithara. I tried not to be jealous that sometimes, when he'd had enough wine, the king treated her with the mixture of respect and mockery with which he'd once treated all his inner circle.

He no longer had an inner circle. Callisthenes was careful to flatter him, but increasingly, I think, disillusioned. Anaximenes was such a blowfish that he continued on his own path of subservience. But the former pages, such as Cleitus and Philip, and the older men, such as Craterus and especially Parmenio, found themselves alienated.

I had some excellent dinners with Kineas and his friends – Gracchus, Niceas, Diodorus, Coenus – gentlemen all, and we went hunting in the former royal parks. Alexander went hunting almost every day, but he took only his Persians and Hephaestion and some of the younger pages.

I found that I could not discuss the changes in the king with foreigners, even with Diodorus or Kineas.

And then the date of the Festival of the New Year approached.

Alexander stopped hunting in the hills.

A dozen talents' worth of royal costume arrived by mule from Susa – rich vestments encrusted in gold, and a pair of towering headdresses, from the same priests who had made the costume for Darius.

I saw them on him. He modelled them for us, explaining with precision what each garment represented, how it symbolically linked the wearer to the sun god and to the ceremony.

He was still confident that the priests, the magi, had received the message of the destruction of the lower town.

They had.

On the morning of the festival, the complex was silent. Of course it was silent. The town was gone, and in its place was a population of soldiers.

When hypaspitoi went to the temples to fetch the magi, they were gone. Except the six chief magi, who had committed suicide.

For the first time in the history of mighty Persepolis, there was no feast of the new sun. The New Year was not praised. No King of Kings rode the sacred way, nor wore the high crown.

'Bah!' the king said. 'Get me my friends. We'll celebrate a feast of Dionysus, instead!'

But he fooled no one. His rage was as vast as his power, and unlike lesser men who succumb to rage, he had the power to act it out.

I saw that his hands shook, and his face was blotched, red and white.

632

He ordered couches brought to the high temple, where hours before the magi had stabbed themselves to death. And he assembled a hundred of his officers, and most of them were ordered to bring their partners – from great ladies of Macedon or Aegypt to prostitutes grabbed from the camp. Not a single of the new Persian officers – even the most trusted ones – was invited. In fact, I was present when Hephaestion ordered Nicanor to post men at their tents.

But every Greek in the army was invited – every Greek officer, Athenian, Ionian, Spartan and Megaran and Plataean, all the way down the ranks to phylarch. Kineas was invited. He brought a beautiful girl. I had seen her at parties – a girl who was somewhere between a prostitute and a courtesan, and Thaïs had invited her to our pavilion for wine, discussed her profession, admitted her to the lower priestess rank of Aphrodite. She was called Artemis, I remember, and she was slim and sharp and moved like a fighter.

But I digress, like an old man. Except I will tell you, lad, that the memories of beautiful women outlast all the foolish battles. Ashurbanipal had something, whatever Alexander said. Eat, drink and fuck. The rest is not worth a snap.

We ate venison and mutton with foreign spices, and we drank Greek wine. The Great King had vats of good Greek wine. There were stacks of barley rolls, as if we were in Athens.

Alexander knew what he intended from the very first. I suspected, but I don't think anyone else did. But the theme of the dinner was *revenge*, and he ordered the entertainments to goad every officer attending.

The mutilated soldiers had couches, and they assembled at the beginning of the dinner – a truly hideous regiment – to receive grants of land and taxes to ease the burden of their lives.

Then Artemis rose and danced the Athenian Pyricche in armour. Every man was on his feet cheering her. She was magnificent. When she was done, she read from Herodotus, of the destruction of the temples of Athens.

When she had finished, Thaïs rose with her kithara, and played. She played the song of Simonides, about Plataea, and she played the lament for Leonidas, and she played the opening lines of the *Iliad*, and suddenly the king was weeping.

She finished, and every man there roared his approval, and all the Greek women, as well.

I suspect that Alexander had coached her, and Artemis, on what to do. Because the purpose of the entertainment, there amid the barbarian splendour, was obvious. The women said, 'This is who we are. We are not these foreigners. We are Greek and Macedonian, and our ancestors were Hellenes.'

Women are the guardians of culture. And often, only women can say these things.

When she was done playing, Thaïs rose and walked from the chair, but the king leaped to his feet, the garland on his head askew, and put out an arm to stop her. 'Ask me for anything, and it is yours,' he said.

She smiled into his eyes, and I felt a pang – more like a dagger-stab – of jealousy. But she was what she was. The greatest courtesan of her generation.

'You have offered me *anything* before,' she said.

He was not used to being mocked. 'Well?' he said, puzzled. 'I offer it again.'

She nodded.

Silence fell. Silence fell whenever anyone showed a sign of winning the king's favour – or losing it. No one knew which Thaïs was doing, and so the silence was absolute.

'Burn it all,' she spat. 'All this barbarian splendour. For Athens. For Euboea.' She nodded. 'For me. And most of all, Lord King, for yourself. Burn Persepolis, and let the flames have her. And march home.'

Alexander laughed. I'm sure all this was planned – to me, it had the feeling of bad drama, but others I know – Kineas, for example – were sure it was extempore.

Thaïs and Alexander wanted the same thing. Nor had she watched him from the shadows for five years for nothing. She knew him. She knew that he could not resist a challenge, nor refuse a dare, nor take back a favour. He had to be like the immortal gods.

He strode to the central brazier, where slaves roasted the ritual meat and lit new torches. There were fifty tallow torches waiting in neat stacks on the ground. Alexander seized one, put it into the brazier and lit it.

'Burn it all!' he shouted.

And we did.

Persepolis wasn't really a city. It was really a monument to Persia. A symbol of triumph, of ten generations of struggle and victory. The entire place was a monument in stone.

But the roof trees were cedar, and they were dry.

We were just two hundred people, but we danced through the great and silent palaces, and as we passed, we took turns setting the hangings alight. That was all it took. The magnificent tapestries were like the wicks of a great candle – sheets of fire rose up them to the rafters and caught, and the floors caught, and the great square and rectangular buildings were like chimneys roaring their throats out to the gods in the heavens, and the fires rose higher and brighter – the royal palace, the shrine of Ahuru Mazda, the Chamber of Records – on and on. Before the beams fell in on the royal palace, we set the last of the buildings afire, and Persepolis burned like the sun.

I still do not know if he acted from policy or impulse. I only know that while Thaïs won the round, and her revenge as a woman and an Athenian, Alexander did not march back to Pella.

We destroyed Persepolis, and the fires in the temples there were the funeral pyres of Alexander's ambition to be recognised formally as Great King.

Darius was preparing to throw the dice again in battle, to the north, at Ecbatana.

We marched, leaving ash behind us.

Again.

I began to be part of the inner circle again. This time, I didn't crave it. In fact, I began to crave another command – for the independence, and because I enjoyed the exercise of authority. I was good at it. I helped keep my men alive and happy.

Not one of Alexander's concerns.

All the way to Ecbatana, he forecast that the army was about to undergo another reorganisation. He'd done it at Tyre, when we marched to finish Darius off, and now he was preparing to sack several satraps and replace them, as well as changing the command structure of the army.

Darius was north and east of us, with nine thousand cavalry and four thousand veteran Greek infantry. Ariston rode in with a dozen Prodromoi, having made a broad sweep towards Ecbatana, to report that Darius was still gathering troops from the east.

I noticed that the Queen Mother was no longer travelling with us.

Thaïs asked around, and could not discover where she and her ladies had gone.

Thaïs couldn't find her. So we assumed that Alexander had had her strangled, and all her ladies. Certainly, we never saw or heard of her again. Later we understood that they'd had an argument, but Callisthenes insisted that she and her whole family were in secluded retirement, receiving instruction in Greek.

Sure.

At any rate, about the time that Sisygambis went missing, Ariston returned from his cavalry sweep. I was there, sitting at my ease in the king's tent. Polystratus was at my elbow, using tow and olive oil and some fine pumice from Lesbos to take a stain out of my good kopis.

I was sewing on the leather lining to my scale shirt. There were slaves aplenty – but one of the things that drove our new Persian comrades to drink was the Macedonian habit of doing things ourselves. Do you really want to trust a slave with your armour? Your weapons?

Ochrid was serving warmed wine with spices. Hephaestion was working on a papyrus scroll that he was keeping from me, and I was trying to seem uninterested, although I was pretty sure that it was the army reorganisation. Callisthenes came in and sat in the entrance – a cold place to sit, but Callisthenes could pretend to be humble, when required.

'Ariston is here with his report,' Callisthenes said. He was scooping Eumenes, and he wanted everyone to know it.

Alexander had been reading the *Iliad*. He glanced up – bounced to his feet.

'Well! Bring him in!' he proclaimed. He took wine from Ochrid and reached down to tap my shoulder. 'Like old times, eh?' he said.

I didn't think, by then, that Alexander even remembered any 'old times'. I had begun to suspect that in the corridors of his mind, all the time before the death of Philip had been erased. He *never* referred to his childhood, or to his time with the pages.

But I smiled. I was happy that he was happy.

Ariston came in, covered in snow, red-cheeked and with a fresh cut on his bridle arm. He had Kineas with him, and a Persian, bundled in wool. Kineas spent as much time scouting as he could – it was a form of warfare he loved, and at which he excelled. As we were to learn!

Alexander offered them wine, Achilles to his very speech patterns. He had, after all, been reading the *Iliad*.

Kineas gazed at him the way a boy watches his first love. He annoyed me – I admired Kineas, and I wanted to tell him just how hollow his hero was, but I didn't want to be the parent telling the child that fairies don't come to take teeth, so I held my peace.

'Darius has taken seven thousand talents from the treasury in Ecbatana and marched away,' Ariston reported. 'This gentleman has had enough of Darius and hopes that you will make use of him. Kineas picked him up – he's called Cyrus.'

Cyrus bowed. 'I was looking for your Greek army. I am indeed called Cyrus, after the great Cyrus who is my ancestor. Darius has forfeited the diadem. He will not fight you again. He is a broken reed, a torn scroll. He is over.' The Persian knelt and then bowed to the floor.

We'd all seen the Persian proskynesis before, but it was a bit of a shock, right there, in the mountains, and in the midst of our attempt to reacquaint Alexander with Macedonian informality. He'd left Mazaeus behind as a satrap, and our other Persians were not causing trouble.

I smiled at the king. 'I'll bet *that* didn't happen in the *Iliad*,' I said.

But Alexander looked thoughtful. 'You may rise,' he said, holding out a hand to silence me.

Cyrus rose to his feet. He did it with dignity. This was a superb example of the way customs influence every aspect of culture. In Persian clothes, with trousers, the prostration can look elegant and refined. In Macedonian or Greek clothes, wearing only a chiton, a man usually looks as if he's baring his buttocks – volunteering to take the woman's part in sex. That's the nicest way I can put it. The chiton rises up as a man lies down, and there he is – bare-arsed to the world.

Cyrus had none of those problems. He nodded. 'Darius is fleeing east with Bessus. Bessus intends to betray him.' Cyrus shrugged. 'I will not be a part of it.'

Kineas nodded to the king. 'I can attest that he came in of his own will, with fifty armoured horsemen and twenty more mounted archers. Diodorus met them and brought them to my camp under guard. They have not been any trouble.'

Alexander looked at Kineas. 'You will vouch for him?' he asked.

Kineas looked at Cyrus. 'Yes,' he said slowly.

Cyrus let out a breath.

Alexander turned to look at Hephaestion. 'Aegema. And Kineas's Athenians. Let's grab Ecbatana and see what we get.'

He was elated.

He glanced at me. 'I *am* the King of Kings,' he said, and grinned. It was his old grin, but it had a new purpose, and one I could not like.

Alexander enjoyed seeing men bend their backs.

We rode like the wind. It's a saying men use too often, but it was true of the race to Ecbatana. We had fifteen hundred cavalry on appalling roads. Every man – even the Athenians – had a pair of horses, and we moved two hundred stades a day despite the mountains and the treacherous rains.

We took Ecbatana by riding in. The treasury was looted, but the apples were in baskets along the road, waiting for the tithe-takers who never came. I remember stooping from the saddle and grabbing one, eating it as I rode under the marble lions.

There were Persian noblemen everywhere. They had come, not to fight, but to make submission.

Four thousand recruits and mercenaries reached us from the coast, having come up the road from Susa. Cleitus went back to Susa with the return messages, because he was so sick.

The word was that Darius was going to hold the Caspian Gates against us, up north, almost to Hyrkania. He was raising Hyrkania now, with Bessus. But increasingly, the Persians told us that Bessus meant to make himself king. Remember – Darius had faced revolt in the east before we ever came over the Hellespont. Now, after three lost battles, the east had had enough of him.

Alexander read the dispatches that came in from Greece and Antipater, and for the first time in a long time, I shared them, standing in yet another superb palace, under tapestries made so beautifully that you might have thought the figures would turn and speak to you. The kind we'd burned at Persepolis.

He frowned.

'Antipater has defeated the Spartans,' he said.

Hephaestion's eyes widened. 'Wonderful!'

Alexander's eyes narrowed. 'Nothing wonderful about it. We're conquering Asia, and Antipater is conquering mice. Sparta is *nothing*.'

I winced. Nothing was allowed to compete with the king's accomplishments, lately.

Thrace was in revolt. Under a Macedonian.

Zopryon, the satrap for Pontus, was, without consulting Antipater, or just possibly with his connivance, marching north to the Euxine coast.

'Idiot,' Alexander said. 'He'd better win. If he loses I'll have his head.' It wasn't clear whether Alexander meant Antipater or Zopryon.

After a three-day pause to move up some baggage carts and collect water and pack animals, Alexander left the rest of the army – just marching in through the western gates of the city – and we were off again.

We raced north and east, across the low hills to the east and down into the saltpan and dust of the Iranian plateau.

It was a nightmare. We never had enough water, and our horses suffered. My 'new' Medea died on the saltpan, and I had to switch to a country mare – the ugliest horse, I think, that I ever rode. But she got me to Rhagae, where we heard from Kineas, who'd managed to sweep north despite the lack of water, that Darius was three days ahead and going hard into the mountains of Hyrkania.

There was a Persian royal stud at Rhagae, and Polystratus looted it for me while I rode in on my hideous horse. By the time we had organised water and I'd gone back with fifty Hetaeroi to rescue the stragglers in the saltpan, Alexander had pressed forward, got lost in the mountains and come back – another day lost. I rode in on my mare, angry to have been left behind but happy enough to have found seventy men alive.

That's when I discovered that I had Barsine's sister riding with me.

I'd had a long day, and one of my troopers was sitting in the agora of the dusty town, while all the rest of them – aristocrats every one – dismounted and watered their horses.

I tossed my reins to Polystratus and walked over to the one man too proud to water his own horse. I need not mention at this point that although we all disdained trousers, every man of us now wore light Persian cloaks and headcloths against the sun.

'Are you lazy, or stupid?' I asked.

The man turned his head away.

'Lazy or stupid! Get down from your mount this moment or I'll throw you off.' I put a hand under the rider's foot. I meant business.

The rider turned back to me. 'If I get down, every man here will know who I am,' Banugul said. Her face was wrapped, so that only her eyes showed. Those eyes.

'You!' I said, or something equally witty. Now that I could see her legs, her sex was obvious, and I couldn't believe I had been fooled.

Her eyes smiled. 'Me,' she admitted. 'You know that we are Hyrkanians, eh?'

In fact, I didn't. I might lust after her body – it was impossible, despite my deep love for Thaïs, not to look at Banugul without some lust – but I'd scarcely noticed her otherwise.

'The king needs a guide. I need some help from the king, too, so I'm hoping we can arrange an exchange of favours.' Her eyes smiled again, and I tried not to imagine what she might have in mind.

'I will take you to the king,' I said carefully. 'But I cannot guarantee his reaction.'

'I would be in your debt,' she said. Her voice was level, and offered no seduction.

Alexander was bathing. Two slaves were attending to him with sponges.

'What do you want?' Alexander spat at me.

'I have recovered the stragglers, as you ordered,' I said. 'I also picked up Barsine's sister, who wishes to see you.'

'Splendid,' Alexander said. 'Send her in.'

Another man might have leered, or made a gesture, but Alexander didn't see the world that way. I doubt that he ever flirted in his life. His own nudity was neither here nor there.

'She is Hyrkanian,' I said. I'm not sure why I was inclined to help her – perhaps the oldest reason in the world.

Alexander turned to me for the first time. 'By Zeus Amon my father! Of course she is! Well done, Ptolemy son of Lagus!'

No thanks for a day in the desert, chasing water mirages and finding men near dead of thirst. But for bringing him a guide for his latest pothos ...

And of course, I had done nothing.

'Your servant, Great King,' I said. I was mocking him, and he didn't acknowledge it. Or perhaps even then, he took it as his due and missed the mockery altogether.

Banugul entered. She made a noise.

'Greeks don't worry about nudity,' I said. Everyone's friend, that was me.

She unwrapped her hair and face, and fell on her knees, and then did the full proskynesis.

Alexander nodded. 'You may rise, sister of Barsines. How may I help you?'

'Reconquer my kingdom for me, lord. And I will guide you through the mountains.'

'Are you bargaining with me?' he asked, voice silky.

'Never, lord. I answered your question. I will guide you, regardless!' She sounded breathless, insistent, and very, very intense.

But Alexander's horses were wrecked, and the hypaspitoi were at least a day behind us across the saltpan.

Alexander looked at Banugul – the coolest, most appraising look I suspect she had ever received, from a man. 'How long to Hecatombion?' he asked. That's where our scouts and the Persian turncoats reported Darius to be.

Banugul pursed her lips. 'Four days. Better to travel at night.'

'You could guide me at night?' he asked.

She simpered – you could see on her face that she was reaching for the sexual innuendo, and then realised that he meant none, and her face changed – a fascinating glimpse into her mind. 'I could guide you blindfolded,' she said.

He nodded. 'Ptolemy?' he asked, without taking his eyes off her.

'Lord?' I answered.

'I need you to fetch in the hypaspitoi. Go fast. Take your pick of men and horses. I'm sending Coenus south for water and remounts.' He finally turned. 'I need to leave here tomorrow night. But I need men, animals and water.'

As he ordered, it was done.

I rode out before the sun was up, with twenty men – Polystratus and my own former grooms, most of them now remounted on the best Niseans, fresh from the royal stud, as well as Cyrus the Persian and ten of his best men. Kineas went north, with fifty of his men, and Philotas took the very best of the Hetaeroi and went due east.

I found six more men alive, on the trail, and left a party to bury three more I found dead. Before the sun was high, I'd made fifty stades, and I found Nicanor. I had forty water bags, and his men shared them – forty bags among a thousand men – and we marched.

I spent the day riding up and down the column, telling desperate men that they had a few stades to go and no more.

And falling in love with my new horses. Tall, strong, beautiful Niseans, both steel grey, both tall like goddesses, fast – I had never been so well mounted, though it was disrespectful to Poseidon to say as much. And there in the desert, when I stopped to change – for the tenth time – I spread my arms wide and sang the whole hymn to Poseidon, and cut a lock of my hair and burned it.

Cyrus watched me. He made me uneasy – he was so silent – but despite that, I was prepared to like him.

The column had escaped while I made my prayers, and we rode along at a fast walk – anything faster might have endangered the horses, in that vast and dreadful desert – moving as fast as we dared to catch up.

Cyrus turned to me after a few minutes. 'That was religious?' he asked.

I nodded.

He frowned, but nodded.

'This is the first time I have seen a Hellene pray,' he noted.

I shrugged.

'Hmm,' he said. After a stade, we caught up to some stragglers sitting, defeated, in the desert, and I swore at them and got them moving.

I was afraid that if I rode past them, they'd collapse again. One of them was one of my men from the first days – Amyntas son of Philip – and I was not going to let him die.

So we rode slowly behind the three men.

'You worship the horse?' Cyrus asked.

I shook my head.

He looked at me, annoyed. 'What, then?' he asked.

'Poseidon,' I said. 'Lord of horses. I had a wonderful horse. A godsent horse. He died in battle. These are the first good mounts I've had since the battle, and I was thanking the god.'

We rode on for as long as it takes a man to make a brief oration.

'That is good,' Cyrus said. He rubbed his beard. 'Yes.'

I left him to watch the three end men, and I rode up the column, and I felt as if I were on a Persian flying carpet – one of their legends. The pace – the gait – of the Nisean is like flying.

I found Nicanor, also by the end of the column. He looked terrible – grey-faced and tired, and he admitted to me that he spent far too much time vomiting. Like Cleitus. There was something nasty going around. Apollo had shot his deadly shafts into our army, and men were dropping fast.

But when I told him we were less than five stades from the town, he showed his mettle, pulled all his men together and made them march. Men who had been shuffling their feet, barely alive, suddenly raised their eyes and saw the town at the edge of the heat shimmer.

They began to sing. Bubores was there, at the head of his company, and Astibus.

Have you any idea
What we're like to fight against?
Our sort make their dinner
Off sharp swords
We swallow blazing torches
For a savoury snack!
Then, by way of dessert,
They bring us, not nuts, but broken arrows, and splintered spear shafts.
For pillows we have our shields and breastplates,
Arrows and slings lie under our feet, and for wreaths we wear catapults

We marched into Rhagae like the elite veterans we were. Alexander emerged from his tent, and smiled.

He gathered all his officers an hour later. Nicanor looked as if he was going to die. The rest merely had sunburn. Water had restored them.

'I have twelve hundred good horses. I need to go for six to ten days with no sleep and very little food so that we can carry enough water to keep going.' He looked around. His eyes glittered with excitement – he was deep in the game he loved, overcoming tasks with Herculean strength and daring.

'I need the very toughest men. The very best. Nicanor – three hundred of your best. And Ptolemy – choose me three hundred of the Hetaeroi. We will leave in four hours, and ride at night.'

I thought he made sense. Craterus and Philotas thought the risk was insane, but chose not to say so aloud.

I did not find this idea insane. Burning Persepolis – yes. Chasing Darius – well, we were close to the end. We were going to finish the last act, and be finished with Asia. We wanted to catch Darius, and our latest turncoats said that Darius's army was on its last legs. Mazaeus's son – Mazaeus, who was already a satrap for us in Mesopotamia – had come in while I was in the desert, surrendered, offered the proskynesis and told us that Darius had been deposed by Bessus.

Alexander had the oddest reaction to this. The fight between them – Darius and Alexander – had been very personal. Darius had wounded Alexander at Issus, and Alexander had sought across the battlefield at Gaugamela to avenge that – because he was living in the *Iliad*, if you ask me.

And now he vowed to avenge Darius, on Bessus.

It was difficult to credit, really. I couldn't decide whether it was an act for our growing force of Iranian nobles, or whether Alexander had some deep fellow-feeling for Darius, or a mixture of both.

It's worth mentioning how Cyrus's arrival among us symbolised, to me, the change in the Persians. Up to a point, despite our victories, the Persians who came over to us were opportunists – traitors. Scum. And then – starting with Mazaeus, to be fair – they started to represent a different type of man altogether. The true Persians resented Bessus and his easterners. They didn't all prefer Alexander but many did, and for a while we benefited from an ancient division – an east/west split in the empire – and the westerners – Lysians, western Persians, Phrygians – began to side with us of their own free will.

At any rate, just before darkness fell, we were off – six hundred men, twelve hundred horses. We had twenty carts with virtually every water skin the vanguard possessed, and we moved *fast*.

When we left Rhagae, Darius and his army were six days ahead of us, already through the Caspian Gates at Hecatombion.

We rode for three days. The less said about them, the better. We moved fast, and men died, and horses died. I looked after my own.

On the fourth day, we came across a dozen war bands still in a camp that had obviously held an army. They surrendered to Alexander as soon as he rode in, and told us that this was the camp where the king had been betrayed by Bessus. The Greek mercenaries had stood by Darius and offered to protect him. The irony of this threatened to make me vomit.

Kineas picked up the Great King's interpreter, who was seventy years old and badly dehydrated. He told us the story of the betrayal.

Alexander grew angrier and angrier.

I began to think that, at some level, he identified with the king. Was it their shared role? Was Darius his other self? Priests talk of such things. I cannot fathom them.

But we rode on. We were making a hundred stades a day through mountains and salt desert, and now, without resting, we went straight on, all day, reminding me powerfully of the Year of Miracles. Men who hadn't been there commented that we were attempting the impossible, but Hephaestion and I laughed. Even Alectus, by now one of the oldest men in the army, laughed.

By noon, when we stopped to change horses and drink water, there were fewer than two hundred men with the king.

I decided that it was time somebody spoke to Alexander. I left my horses with Polystratus and walked to him, where he lay between Banugul and Hephaestion.

'The raven of misfortune,' Alexander said, 'come to croak at me.'

I shrugged. 'You know that we're down to two hundred men,' I said. 'You know that, ten days ago, Darius had twenty-five thousand men.'

Alexander shook his head. 'His army is breaking up – running for cover, like fish from a shark,' he said. 'I can feel it. No one will stop and fight now.'

I rubbed my chin. I had stubble at the edges of my beard, my face itched and, perhaps worst of all, Banugul looked every bit as perfect, tanned, fresh and beautiful lying in the dust beside the king as she did in a tent on the Syrian plains.

'Lord, if they turn on us, your capture loses us *everything*.' I shrugged. 'I had to say it. I won't shirk. I won't stop. I'll go where you go. But this is past daring.'

Alexander grinned – not at me, or Hephaestion, but at the Persian girl. 'I know exactly what I'm doing,' he said.

So we were off again.

Three hours later, we were sixty men on a hundred horses.

When darkness fell, we were fifty men on sixty horses, and Banugul stopped and threw up.

My two Niseans paced along, light as air. Poseidon bless and keep them.

Polystratus kept up, and Cyrus, and Kineas and Diodorus.

I had the strangest thoughts. I watched Craterus carefully, and Philotas, because it occurred to me that with this few men, anyone could kill the king.

At dawn, we were in a valley and we had a stream to water our horses. We had forty-six men left and one woman.

At noon, we came to a village. Bessus had come this way – the villagers had seen him.

Alexander sat on his charger, dejected – that rarest of his moods.

I saw Banugul master herself and ride to his side.

In five minutes, we were moving again. I had missed what had passed, but we turned off the road, with its sad trail of broken wagons and dead animals. Bessus's retreat was easy to follow, and, exactly as Alexander predicted, the enemy army was disintegrating.

I could barely think. I drank a cup of water that a village elder offered me, filled my two canteens and rode off after the king.

We rode all night.

When the sun rose, we crested a ridge – our fourth ridge of the night. We had, by then, perhaps twenty Macedonians with us. But as we rode down the east side of the knife-back, we could see Bessus's army spread before us on the plain ...

Thousands of men.

Tens of thousands of camp followers, beasts and wagons.

From the height, we could see that they had come around the flank of the ridge and split into three columns. And we could see all three, extending from our very feet to the far horizon.

I reined in, took my canteen and drank. Spat. My water tasted of mud and defeat. We had *failed*. Darius had escaped – again. As with Issus, as with Gaugamela, as at Ecbatana. We couldn't pursue into the plains with twenty men.

Alexander rode up beside me. Looked over the plain, sat straight and smiled.

'Got him,' he said.

He turned and beckoned to Philotas. 'Get the stragglers,' he said. 'Bring them here and await my orders. The rest of you, on me.'

We attacked Bessus's army.

We had twenty men, and one woman.

And once again, Alexander was right.

We hit them the way a flake of snow hits a mountainside – that is, it is the flake of snow that begins the avalanche. We rode down the ridge, changed horses and struck the nearest column, hitting the stragglers in the tail, and before anyone's sword was red, we had a hundred prisoners and the column stampeded like cattle in a storm.

We rode down the column, picking up prisoners, demanding to know where the king was. Alexander's only interest was Darius – I think that, had we found Bessus, he would have been killed. For whatever reason, it was all about Darius.

All morning, we went east, harrying the column – if twenty men can be said to harry fifteen thousand.

By noon, Philotas had five hundred more men together, and he joined us. It shouldn't have made a difference, but it did, and we spread our nets wider. Exhausted, bedraggled Persians and Hyrkanians threw themselves on their faces – it was incredible to see. At one point,

Polystratus, Cyrus and I captured so many men we couldn't imagine why they didn't take *us* prisoner.

We ranged farther and farther from the king – up and down the columns. The southernmost column was already gone – it held together better and moved too fast for us to follow, and the two northern columns were slowed by their own chaos. We rode unopposed through the final ruin of the Persian empire. Not an arrow threatened us. The squalor of the retreat was sickening in a way that even the slaughter at Gaza had not been sickening. Perhaps it was the utter abandonment of hope. Perhaps it was having Cyrus at my side – perhaps it was my growing respect for him, which made me share his humiliation that his country had come to this.

It was late afternoon when Polystratus sent a boy for me. I was sitting under the overhang of a ruined posting station, drinking water from the well. The boy was Hyrkanian, very blond and very dirty, and he all but crawled.

I mounted my new horse and followed him. It will give you an idea of how far gone we were that I was *alone*.

I rode through the rout. This part of the northern column was mostly slaves and servants, and they simply trudged on, waiting to be threatened or killed. No one challenged me, and no one tried to surrender. Mostly, no one even raised their eyes.

We crossed a main flow of refugees – perhaps six hundred people. And then climbed down the shallow slope of a stony gully. At the base of the gully was a big wagon, with six dead oxen. The grass here was so poor that Polystratus's horse was not bothering to eat it. Blood dripped from the base of the wagon bed in slow, gloopy drops. Flies gathered in the blood. I could *feel* a curse in the air.

Polystratus's head emerged from the wagon. A dog barked. 'Send the boy for the king,' he said.

I went and looked into the wagon. There was a man lying on his back, and the wagon bed was full of blood. He had two javelins in him.

I knew him at once, even though I'd only seen him at a distance.

He was Darius.

I looked at Polystratus. 'Go and find Alexander,' I said. 'Cyrus should be at the posting station – less than a stade up the ridge. Look there first. Hurry. This will be very important to the king.'

Polystratus left me without a word. He grunted, once. He spat when he left the wagon bed – a Thracian way of averting a curse.

I took the King of King's hand.

He gave my hand a squeeze.

Even an enemy is better company than dying alone.

I had wine and water. I offered him both, and he took a little and gasped.

I had some Persian, by then. So I understood when he thanked me.

I took off my officer's cloak and did my best to bind his wounds. Removing the spears would kill him. So I did what I could without moving him much, and I gave him more wine. He'd lost so much blood that it flushed his face.

Cyrus came in.

He took the king's other hand.

He kissed it.

I didn't think less of him. It's one thing to see that a cause is lost. Another thing to leave the *man* who led it. I think Cyrus loved Darius, the man.

At any rate, the next one into the wagon was Alexander.

Darius was barely alive. And drunk. But he had been waiting. I know that. I don't know exactly *how* I know that, but I could feel him waiting, holding the spirit in his body.

Alexander came up, and I wriggled back to make room for him.

Alexander was weeping.

So was Cyrus.

I waited by Darius's feet.

Alexander looked at Darius. He took his hand. 'I will avenge you,' he said.

Darius gave a minute shake of his head.

Alexander bent low. 'I would give *anything* for you to live. I ... what will I do without you?'

Darius had the will to smile. It set him very high in my opinion. He smiled, and his face had a gentle strength. 'So ...' he said, very clearly. 'So you are Alexander.' His smile stayed, and he sighed, and with that sigh, his soul left his body.

'No!' Alexander screamed. 'No! You will not slip away again! Damn you, Darius! What is there after this? What can possibly be worthy or great, after this!' He was weeping, speaking wildly, and he took Darius's head and held it in his lap. 'Is this the end? The end of the story?'

I got out of the wagon.

After a time, Cyrus slipped out, too. He didn't meet my eye.

And when Alexander came out, I wiped the blood from him, and we said nothing. But he put his arms around me, and cried. For once, I understood. Memnon had slipped away, and now Darius. That's not what happens, in the *Iliad*. In the *Iliad*, Achilles is filled with rage, and he kills, and feels no remorse. When he hunts Hector round the city, he kills him, and drags him behind his chariot, and feels no remorse.

Only when faced with Priam, Hector's father – and with the reality of his own death – does Achilles feel anything.

Draw your own lesson. I'm a king, not a philosopher. Alexander loved the whole game. And when Darius died ...

After a time – I couldn't tell you how long – he stopped weeping.

'Ptolemy,' he said. There was a question in his voice. 'Is this ... all there is?'

Sometimes I wonder if he actually asked me that. Sometimes, I think that I read it into his tears and the tension in his body.

But I'm pretty sure he asked.

Because if he didn't, then what I didn't say wouldn't still be stuck in my head, rattling around. I should have said it. I should have told him true.

I should have said, *You've traded friendship and love for adulation and power. What did you expect?*

THIRTY-TWO

We straggled back into Ecbatana. Which occasioned the first time that Alexander himself altered the Military Journal.

Alexander wanted to pursue Bessus immediately. But despite our success – and taking Darius, even dead, was a victory, because we immediately inherited most of his loyalists, by the law of 'The enemy of my enemy is my friend' that rules all civil conflict, all *stasis* – despite our success, our army, such as it was, was wrecked. The Hetaeroi were mostly dismounted, or their horses were ruined by the pursuit. The hypaspitoi were spread from the plains north of Ecbatana all the way beyond Hecatombion and into the Hyrkanian mountains by the pursuit, by fatigue, by the need to garrison the villages that were our lifeline to the rear.

And Alexander was barely functional. It was terrifying, because he didn't have a mark on him. He ranted at Craterus about pursuing Bessus, and then sat on his horse and issued no orders.

None of us was senior. In fact, among the men who'd ended up on the point of the spear, the concept of 'rank' was meaningless. We were the king's friends, his companions, and we didn't agree about much except that we were king's men.

I convinced Philotas to retreat. And when he went down with the dysentery, I led the retreat.

It was my only taste of what it must have been like to *be* Alexander. Now *I* had to ride up and down the column, looking for stragglers, issuing orders, seeing and being seen. Pretending to be calm and unruffled when in fact I was terrified that Bessus would turn and bite us – or that Alexander would snap out of his funk and kill me. He had ordered us to advance, and we were retreating, and that was my decision.

Ecbatana was twenty-five hundred stades behind us when we started. But that's where the main army was, and to summon them forward with no preparation would have been foolish.

Or so I maintain.

649

We didn't all retreat. I used our new Iranian allies and a hard core of hypaspitoi to hold every oasis and every village, to start building up water supplies and depots of baked bread, grain and water.

Craterus backed me up, and when we fell back on Rhagae and finally had enough healthy troops to fight if we had to face a force larger than twenty raiders, Craterus took command of it. I was exhausted.

Alexander continued to be silent. He made comments, and for some hours seemed to be in command.

But the only person he spent any time with was Banugul. Even Hephaestion was shut out.

At Rhagae, he recovered. It happened all in an hour, when dispatches came in from Ecbatana. He read them, shared them with no one and started firing off orders – mostly to do with Darius's funeral.

He never mentioned the retreat, except that several days later, when we were already preparing the main body to march up-country *from* Ecbatana, and Darius had had his burial, I was adding my notes to the Military Journal, because Eumenes was still with the headquarters back in Ecbatana.

Alexander came into the tent. He nodded to me, went to the main copy of the Journal and leafed through it.

He took a knife and cut the scroll at the death of Darius, and joined it to blank papyrus with a strip of linen. He did this himself. He looked at me, threw the scrap with fifteen days of retreat into the brazier, and walked out.

Read it yourself.

He'd never done it before. But he started to do it more and more.

Darius was dead, and the crusade in Asia was over. That was the tenor of the king's message, and he gave a speech to the army that was not particularly moving and raised a great deal of resentment.

The long and short was that he was sending the allies home. Most of them were richly rewarded, and a great many of them were offered superb bonuses for staying on without their officers as *our* troops. Kineas, for example, was heartbroken. Alexander actually singled him out at a command meeting – a Macedonian-only meeting – when Parmenio, of all people, asked that he be kept on or even sent to the Prodromoi.

Alexander shook his head. 'I need friends in Athens,' he said. 'And Kineas is *not* one of us.'

Further, he actively recruited the troopers – the rank and file men of the allied contingents.

He released the Thessalians. Parmenio's household troops. Men who had served Philip and Parmenio and Attalus since the first light of

Macedon's dawn. Alexander gave them rich rewards, but he sent them home. Next to the Hetaeroi, they were our best cavalry.

I was at the staff meetings, and I knew the agenda – Alexander was clearing the army of rivals, and was preparing to function as the King of Kings. The Greeks – even Kineas – were the most intransigent about who they were, about *being Hellenes.* They had come to Asia to make war on Persia. To destroy the Persian Empire.

But Alexander was getting ready to *become the Persian Empire.*

He rid himself of dissent.

And he destroyed Parmenio's power base. He paid off the veterans – with rich bonuses. He bought mercenaries. And he paid every pikeman who stayed with us a bonus – a two-talent bonus. Two talents of gold. Per man.

For old men like Philip, who asked *where is my reward,* this was the answer.

The army of Macedon – ably assisted by the Greek allies, backed by mercenaries – took Persia and conquered Asia.

The army that marched away from Ecbatana was *Alexander's army.* It had no loyalties but those it owed to him. He was lord, god and paymaster.

I never saw Kineas go. He took his men and his gold and his horses and all the wreaths he'd won and packed and left. Polystratus saw him go – hugged Niceas, sent a letter home to his Macedonian wife. And Thaïs held the prostitute Artemis in her arms while the younger woman cried and cried. Because she wanted to follow the army to the ends of the earth. She didn't want to go back to Athens and face ... well, face an aristocrat's family.

Thaïs sent letters home by Niceas, too. Letters asking that our child and our priestly ward be sent to us.

It's worth noting that Athens stood firm – or at least stood hesitantly – and Sparta died alone, their gallant hoplites outnumbered by Antipater's mercenaries. Their king died gloriously, but he died, and the revolt, if you can call it that, was over. And so was Sparta.

Alexander sent rewards to Athens, and treated her like the queen of Greece, which, in many ways, she was. But like Darius's wife, she'd served her turn, and as we were all to discover, Alexander was done with her. And when he was done with things, he let them fall.

The last night in Ecbatana. We had a dinner – a magnificent dinner. Four hundred Hellenic officers and almost that many Persians – that is to say, Iranians, Cilicians, Carians and Phrygians. Medes. Aegyptians.

I had not received a command in the new army allotment. But I had received orders – to add Cyrus and two hundred Persian nobles to my troop of Hetaeroi, doubling it in size. In fact, we lost a great many Hetaeroi at Ecbatana, and on the pursuit of Darius. I'll backtrack and say I tried to recruit Thessalian gentlemen from the disbanded regiments, and Athenian gentlemen from the Athenian contingent. I got a few.

Cyrus and his men were superb horsemen, well mounted, with fine armour and good discipline. But they were Iranians, and Philotas, for one, didn't trust them at all.

As soon as I took Cyrus into my troop, I began to walk a knife's edge, and because of it, I have more understanding of what the king faced than most men. The common story – Callisthenes' story – is that the king was seduced by Persian tyranny and became a Persian tyrant.

Well – that's not entirely untrue. Alexander was always impatient of limitations on his power, since he knew, with absolute certainty, that he was right about all decisions of rulership and the making of war. So Persian-style lordship appealed.

But by the time we rode out of Ecbatana the second time, I understood *exactly* why he did as he did.

Persian gentlemen were such excellent soldiers that you had to ask, after two weeks, how Darius had ever lost. Cyrus and his men were far more obedient than my Macedonians, who, being Macedonians, plotted, fought, lied, cheated, back-stabbed, sometimes literally and spent their spare time questioning every order I issued.

And they hated the mirror that the Persians held up to them, which quickly translated into hatred of the Persians.

I had a few Macedonians and a handful of Greek troopers who saw it differently – who made friendships across the line, or who found the time to listen. But I also found myself trying to be two different people – the fair and honourable commander of Cyrus and his men, and the quick-witted, argumentative king of the hill that the Macedonians expected.

I had four hundred cavalrymen.

Alexander had thirty-five thousand men.

There are things he did for which I cannot love him, but his attempt to rule Persia while remaining our king was a noble effort, and he did the very best with it that could be done. He made an effort to be all things to all men – an effort that he had made since he had been a boy, in many ways. Callisthenes and some of the other Hellenophiles argued, almost from the first, that Alexander was being *corrupted*.

I agree. He was being corrupted. But it wasn't Persia that corrupted him. It was war, and the exercise of power.

*

The army rallied at Hecatompylos. Those were the next words in the Military Journal after the death of Darius, and they left out three weeks of supply-gathering and slow marching. And yet remained true. The contingents that Craterus, Philotas and I had left spread across southern Hyrkania were there still, and the hypaspitoi had remained well forward of the army, so that we might have been said to have 'concentrated' at Hecatompylos.

But despite the bribes and the bonuses, Hecatompylos was where the army discovered that we were marching east, to Bactria. Until then, most of the troops thought we were going to crush the mountain tribes. A fairly solid rumour said that we were going to restore Banugul to her little kingdom – as a lark – on the way to the Euxine and ships for home. And even Hephaestion, who usually read the king better than this, told me confidentially one night that we were going to march north into Hyrkania and then home via a campaign against the Scythians of the Euxine.

But at Hecatompylos, Alexander sent two full squadrons of the Hetaeroi and Ariston's Prodromoi *east*, trying to re-establish contact with Bessus's retreating columns.

It wasn't mutiny, but by the gods, it was close. Our second morning in the clear air of Hyrkania, and I was awakened by Ochrid to be told that the pezhetaeroi were packing their baggage for the trip home. That they had voted in the night to march away and leave the king.

Once again, I was the one who warned him. Artemis – who had been Kineas's lover, and left him to stay with the army – came to Thaïs in the night and told her that the pezhetaeroi intended mutiny. And old Amyntas son of Philip came to me at first light. He didn't name names. He didn't really meet my eye.

'They mean business,' he said. He shifted uncomfortably. 'I can't … I can't stomach it. Though the Undying know I agree with 'em. The king's mad with power. Ares. Ares come to earth, he is.'

So once again I went to Hephaestion.

Who took me to the king.

Alexander wasn't angry. He was frightened.

He called the taxeis commanders one by one to his tent, and he interviewed them. Craterus knew everything, and Perdiccas. The others knew less, or admitted to less.

When they were gone, it was dawn. Alexander sat back on his stool and looked at me. 'Any remarks?' he asked.

'You need to talk to them,' I said. 'Yourself. And not give them a town to pillage.'

He shrugged, as if he regretted the absence of a town to pillage.

I saw red.

'They just want to go home!' I said, suddenly. 'They've crossed the whole gods-created world at your behest, and we're in the arsehole of the universe, Hyrkania, and it's going to go on for ever, and they know it!'

He laughed. 'I love it when you, the aristocrat, remind me of what the common man wants,' he said.

I shrugged.

He ordered Hephaestion and Philotas to form all the Hetaeroi. And then he summoned the taxeis, all together, and we met with them in a great stone bowl cut in a Hyrkanian hillside.

They stood muttering, and the stone carried their angry whispers like evil spirits. I stood close by the speaker's pnyx and every whisper seemed to come to me from ten thousand men, and again, as at the fire by the Tigris, I felt as if I was listening to the dead as well as the living, fifty thousand corpses demanding to be taken home.

Perhaps I still had a touch of fever.

And then he came up the steps, bounding up two at a time. The whispers stopped.

He came up to the pnyx, in armour but without a weapon or helmet.

'Friends!' he shouted, and his voice cut across the whispers – smashed them flat. 'I understand that you all want to go home!'

A roar greeted him.

'What a simple lot you are, to be sure!' He smiled. 'You think that, because Darius is dead, the war is over? How many of you marched through Babylon? Through Susa? The Medes and the Babylonians will *crush us* if we let them out from under our heel. Even now, Bessus rides to the east with four times our number of cavalry. Do you want to see him facing us on the plains beside Pella? Do you want your sons to have to face the same foe – march over the same ground?'

He waited.

'Now! Now is the time!' he said, slowly but clearly.

Silence.

'Now, when they feel beaten, we will finish them. I will follow Bessus to the ends of the earth, and I will kill him, and then – then, when Persia has no army but our army, and when all of this is ours – then, my friends, your farms are secure, your sons and daughters are secure, and then we can rest. But you owe it to your sons to finish this enemy now. We are *so close*.'

Some shouts, and some hoots.

'Friends – do you hate me? Have I not led you to victory after victory? Have you *ever* been defeated when I was in your ranks?' Alexander seemed to grow larger. 'Are you ingrates, to forget what I have given you? The suzerainty of the earth – the mastery over every man and woman you will ever meet, the lords of creation! You were farmers in Pella and Amphilopolis, and now you stride the earth like giants! Will you go *back* to being peasants?'

Now they shouted. 'No!'

'Will you deny me my hour of triumph? Your king? The moment when I am undisputed master of Asia – a moment for which I have sacrificed everything and taken every risk?'

NO!

'Or will you tuck your tails between your legs and leave a beaten Persian army to follow us, gnaw at our tail and take the war across the sea to *our* homes?'

NO!

'Or rather, will you follow me again to the ends of the earth to preserve the virginity of Macedon – to keep her inviolate, to put fire into the homes of our enemies and steel in their breasts until we, and only we, rule the world? Will you?'

YES.

They shouted – they chanted his name.

And he turned to me, and smiled.

It wasn't what he said. It was that he said it at all. He'd been even more distant than usual since Gaugamela, and that morning, he treated the pezhetaeroi like men – like his men.

Their opinion of themselves, and of him, soared.

Thaïs said it made him more human. I thought that it was all making him think he was a god.

Three things happened in Hyrkania – four, if you count Banugul.

We took the capital. Or rather, we marched into it. Banugul's father had been satrap of Hyrkania, and she received troops and support to go and reconquer it. Hyrkania means the 'Land of Wolves', and the only wolves I saw there had two legs. They fight endlessly, but not very well, and Banugul retook her city with three thousand mercenaries, many of whom had just joined us – Darius's last loyal men.

The vizier who helped murder Darius awaited us at Zadracarta, the capital, if such a dreadful place could be called capital of anything. Banugul left us, and Thaïs informed me that she was pregnant by the king, and I took that at face value. If she had influence with the king, I never saw it – he liked her, and she pleased him, and that had lasted a few months and no more.

But Nabarzanes, Darius's vizier, received a full pardon in advance, and then joined us, and he brought Bagoas to replace her. He – I never checked, but I assume Bagoas was formed as a man – was the most effeminate man I have ever seen. He was beautiful – I loathed him, but I could see the beauty – and he moved with a carnal grace I had only seen until then in women. He knew exactly how to use his body. He was not a handsome man – he was a beautiful, wilful woman trapped in a man's body. He had been Darius's catamite, and now, in hours, he became the king's.

By Ganymede, he was a horror. He blatantly manipulated the king's generosity and his desire to be 'godlike', seizing money and small political powers for himself as fast as he could. Nicanor, Parmenio's son, shared a couch with me one night, and he took a sip of wine, watched the Persian boy writhing next to the king and spat.

'He sucks power with the same greed he sucks dick,' Nicanor said.

I almost choked on my wine. And when I repeated it to Thaïs, she shook her head. 'Men always make sex sound like a financial exchange,' she said crossly. She was angry with me for a day.

Now, from the lofty height of my advanced years, I realise that it was the wrong joke to make to a courtesan.

But on balance, despite the number of men who maintain that Bagoas was directly responsible for all kinds of sins – the king's increasing attraction to things Persian, the king's occasional lapses of judgement, the king's open flouting of his willingness to bed the boy – while all these charges are, at their base, true, none of them mattered. They were the grousing of a tired, battered army on the edge of mutiny, looking desperately for a reason that their king was suddenly alienating himself. Bagoas was no worse than any of Philip's minions – he was prettier, anyway, and no less bitchy or demanding. Macedonians had a tolerance for such things. The king used the boy as a vacation from reality. The trouble was, the soldiers didn't get the same vacation, and it was just too far to home.

Alexander retained genuine affection for Bagoas, and the boy returned it, so that years later, after India, their affair was renewed. That speaks a little in the boy's favour.

But mostly, he was a horror.

Philotas led a set of punitive raids against the Mardians – mostly to seize remounts. Alexander grew bored with waiting for Ariston to return and led one of his own.

I went with him, because I was determined to separate him from Bagoas and keep his mind on his job – odd, and you'll note that I was trying to make him function as god-king and keep him from being human, which was not my usual role.

We burned some villages, killed some women and children and got ourselves some fine horses. Our third night in the high valleys, and the Mardians raided *us*. They took Bucephalus. No other horse. Just Bucephalus.

Alexander sent us out to bring in prisoners. I brought in two, and Philotas six.

Alexander gathered them, had them bound and then stood over them.

'I want my horse back,' he said. He was not calm. He could scarcely breathe, he was so angry. I think he meant to make an elegant speech, but he couldn't get it out. He stood there, breathing too fast, and finally, in an odd voice, he said, 'If I don't have my horse by this time tomorrow, I will kill every man, woman and child in these hills. I will use my entire army, and I will wipe your pathetic little race from the face of the earth. I won't let my soldiers rape your women, because any children they had would allow your kind to continue to walk the earth. Do you understand?'

The interpreter, another former officer of Darius, was so scared that his voice shook and his knees trembled.

Coenus, on the other hand, merely laughed. He thought that Alexander was finally growing tired of the locals.

Bucephalus was returned immediately.

At Ecbatana, Alexander had left Parmenio as his satrap of Persia. While this seemed the ultimate honour, the army that marched into Hyrkania didn't have Parmenio as chief of staff and planning officer, and we felt it. Little things seep through the cracks – just as an example, Bucephalus was only taken because no one had given the night guards a password, for the first time in about forty years.

Before we marched east after Bessus, Alexander divided the roles that had been Parmenio's three ways. Craterus would become, to all intents and purposes, his deputy commander of the Macedonians, but for the moment he was far to the south, collecting reinforcements. Hephaestion continued to command the Aegema on occasion, but he became the de facto commander and liaison with the Iranian and satrapal forces – an increasingly important part of our army.

I became the chief of staff. I didn't outrank either Coenus or Philotas or Nicanor or Hephaestion, but I could handle the mathematics and the planning. And Alexander trusted me – again. Who knows what clicked in his head? But it was odd – and almost eerie – to move my folding desk and my old wax tablets back into the striped tent that housed the Military Journal. Many years had passed since I had held this post, or one like it.

Immediately, I had to start laying out the route and the depots for the march east, into Bactria, which up until then was merely a name. I arranged for Ariston – for all scouts – to report directly to me. This, too, had a feeling of irony – there was Strako standing at my desk with his reports from the Angeloi, and there were Prodromoi I'd worked with on the plains of Caria.

They had, once, reported directly to Parmenio, and Alexander had taken that power from him – because we all feared Parmenio would use the scouting reports against the king. But I no sooner held the logistics in my hands than I realised how much I needed the scouting reports.

We had outrun Thaïs's network of friends – they ended at Babylon. But she knew how to organise information, and she was bored. And she had worked with the Prodromoi before Tyre, with great success, and I encouraged her to take part.

The first news she brought us was that Satibarzanes, satrap of Aria, was ready to defect. We checked and double-checked with couriers and agents, and then we laid out a march route to Susia, sold the king on the plan and marched.

This was the way to make war. Our information was spot on, and our scouts covered our movements, our advance parties had water and food, and despite the terrain … Alexander's army was used to terrain. There are mountains everywhere – or at least, everywhere Alexander wanted to go.

We marched off the edge of the world.

And we moved fast.

Whatever Satibarzanes may have thought, or planned, we were on him too fast for him to change his mind. Our cavalry seized every approach to his capital and then we 'arrived'. It was Alexander's plan, but Coenus and Hephaestion and I executed it, and I still look back on it with pleasure. Everyone was fed, everything moved on time and no one died. Good soldiering.

Satibarzanes was a snake – the very kind of Persian that Craterus and his Macedonians expected every Persian to be. Thaïs had enough evidence to hang him, but Alexander was in a hurry and he confirmed the man as satrap – when we had all his troops in our power.

That night, I lay beside Thaïs in my new pavilion – a magnificent tent of striped silk with a tall separate roof that held its walls up on wooden toggles – superb work, a piece of engineering as much as a bridge or a tower.

It is lovely to make love to your own intelligence chief – it makes staff meetings more secret and much more fun. We were both still breathing hard when she said, by way of love talk: 'Satibarzanes will turn on us as soon as we turn our backs.'

I kissed her, and agreed.

'I need money to spread around,' she said, rubbing her hand down my legs and over my belly.

'You know,' I said, and I paused, unsure of whether my joke would be well received – 'you know, I owe you four years of your fee as a hetaera.'

Her hand slipped along my thigh, over the hard ridge of muscle and then along the crease between groin and leg – the most ticklish part of my body. 'Pay up, old man,' she whispered.

'I could marry you, instead,' I said. I was perfectly willing. It came into my head just then. I was one of the most powerful men in the world, and I didn't have to give a thought to the opinion of anyone but my peers and my soldiers.

She laughed. 'To save money, you mean?' she said, and that was that.

But two days later, I was planning provisions for the advance guard as Ariston scouted us a march route east. Into Bactria. And writing out a receipt for ten talents of silver to Thaïs.

Eumenes the Cardian came into the Military Journal tent. 'Everyone out but Lord Ptolemy,' he ordered.

The slaves fled, and Marsyas looked at me. He had a fine hand and an excellent understanding, and I used him as my own chief of staff. He gave me a long look, but I shook my head. He picked up the scroll he was checking and left.

Eumenes and I had got along for years without a skirmish, but I didn't really know him at all. He was Greek – now that Kineas was gone, he tended to lead the 'Greek' faction on the staff. He'd worked for Philip, as I'm sure I've mentioned, and Alexander had taken a long time – a *long* time – to trust him. Hephaestion still viewed him as a spy for Parmenio.

He poured wine from an amphora at his own desk and put the krater down between us.

'You have a reputation as a straight arrow, my lord,' he said. He drank and passed me the cup.

I raised it to him. 'As do you,' I said. I drank.

He nodded. 'Good. Let us try and do this the man's way. I don't want to give up the Military Journal. I intend to prove myself to the king and get a military command of my own, and this is my office.'

I thought about that. 'Agreed,' I said carefully.

He brightened. 'Yes? Then the rest is details.'

I must have brightened, too. 'You thought I was after the Journal?'

He shrugged. 'Callisthenes is still trying to get it back. You ran it very well – for an amateur. I've read all your entries.'

He was older, and he'd been Philip's military secretary. So there was no need to take offence.

'What about the collection of intelligence?' he asked. 'I've noted in the last ten-day that you have all the scouts reporting to you. Now, you are a king's friend, an officer of the Hetaeroi, one of the inner circle. Of course they take your orders.' He paused. 'But it's my job, and I *need* the reports, as you know.'

I thought about that. You have to appreciate his honesty. Instead of having a typical staff cat-fight – they can go on for years – he was laying it out.

I nodded. 'I need the information. I plan all the march routes.'

'So we need it together. Can we get it together? And on days when one or the other is busy, can we collect notes and pass them?'

This may be boring you, lad, but this is staff work. Eumenes was offering to help me, if I would help him. This is how we conquered the world – good logistics, good intelligence, good staff work.

I nodded.

He leaned forward and looked into my eyes. 'Who is the chief of intelligence for the king?'

I smiled. 'Thaïs,' I said.

Eumenes shook his head. 'No, I am. Thaïs gave the position up – if it was ever truly hers – back at Tyre.'

I began to grow angry.

'If your paramour wants to run some agents, she can do it through me,' Eumenes said.

'No,' I said.

He sat back. 'Well, you're honest.'

I crossed my arms. 'What have you ever done, in terms of actual accomplishment? Thaïs gave us Memnon, took cities in Asia Minor and opened the Gates of Babylon.'

Eumenes narrowed his eyes. 'I've never heard of any of these operations.'

I smiled.

He laughed. 'Fair enough, Ptolemy. But we can't have two separate intelligence services.'

I shrugged. 'Why not? We have all the money in the world. And Thaïs says that two sources of information are always better than one.'

Eumenes turned away, and I could see he was on the point of a nasty verbal cut. But I've seen this before – mostly with rational Athenian gentlemen at a symposium – a man takes a verbal hit, and before he can shoot back, he absorbs the content, thinks it all through – realises the point is valid. Only a mature man or woman can do this.

The Cardian took another sip of wine. 'Who collates the intelligence?' he said.

I leaned forward. 'Honesty for honesty. I can imagine that you and some other man might vie – racing to Alexander's side with your latest scrap – the best traitor, the open gates,' I said. I took the wine cup. 'But Thaïs doesn't need Alexander's ear, and I have it all the time. So if you give credit where credit is due, I think Thaïs would be happy to send her news through you.' I shrugged. 'I'll have to ask her.'

'I would like to meet her,' Eumenes said. 'I've seen her at dinners. We've never spoken.'

'And if you try to go behind her back ... well,' I said with a smile, 'I see the king six times a day.'

Eumenes shook his head. 'I know that,' he said, a little peevishly.

'Come and have dinner with us,' I said. 'Let's talk this out together.'

And that was that. Five minutes of straight talk, and we avoided a clash. After that, I got steady reports from Eumenes, and Thaïs shared all her information with him. And we became friends – real friends. His wife was not always with the army, but when she was, Athenais became Thaïs's closest female friend.

You have the look that all boys have when they find that war runs on gold and grain and rumour and intelligence, not blood and honour. Listen. In all of Aria there was *just barely* enough surplus grain to feed our army for three weeks. We could not linger. We needed to get out of the endless hills and down on to the fertile plains. That's how war really works.

So we marched into Bactria. We had a flood of defectors, many of whom were the last of Darius's loyalists who would never go over to Bessus. But some had just waffled – because they had fresh reports from Bessus, who was across the Oxus river, raising troops. He was rumoured to have forty thousand cavalry.

Alexander wasn't just low on grain. He was genuinely worried that, having marched off the edge of the world, he was going to get stuck in a fight he couldn't win. But he was elated – Bessus was proving to be a foe, and a foe meant challenge, opposition and conquest. We summoned the main army – Cleitus with the rest of the pezhetaeroi – and marched east.

*

Nicanor died two days east of Aria – he'd never grown stronger after the illness, and when the king gave Parmenio the satrapy, Parmenio made his two sons swear to hold their positions with the army. Nicanor commanded the hypaspitoi and Philotas commanded the household cavalry, and that meant that Alexander was still, to some extent, in the power of Parmenio.

Nicanor's death was sudden. There was no reason to expect it – he was sick, but he was tougher than scrap bronze.

Alexander didn't even halt the march, and when Philotas broke down – Nicanor was *his brother* – Alexander shook his head.

'Stay and arrange the funeral, if that's what suits you,' Alexander said. 'Bessus isn't going to wait for us to hold games. Ptolemy – get them moving!' he called to me, and we marched off.

I never had any time for Philotas, but Nicanor and I had long since made our peace and become friends. I left Polystratus to make my contribution.

Alexander gave me command of the Hetaeroi. I thought it odd – Philotas couldn't be more than a day behind us.

But we were tired, hungry and I had all I could handle just getting the food arranged ahead of us. We were living day to day. Not the way the planning staff likes to live.

But two days after we entered Bactria, it was obvious that Bessus had the troops to stop us, and we had other problems. Craterus was twelve hundred stades to the south, marching with Black Cleitus and the four taxeis of the reserve army, and Bessus had more men. And worst of all, bloody Satibarzanes revolted, and so did his cousin in the south, Barseantes, the satrap of Drangiana.

Alexander took the Aegema and turned back. He sent me to lead the main army south, to the edge of Drangiana, to link up with Craterus's column. Hephaestion went with him.

We smashed the two attempts Barseantes made to stop our march. Behind us, the king drove Satibarzanes across the Oxus and caught most of his army on a wooded mountain. Alexander surrounded the base of the mountain and set the woods on fire. It was brutal, but I can't disapprove. He was in a hurry, had no rearguard, no base of operations, and he needed a quick victory with no losses.

I had troubles of my own, and I got a taste of what the coming years would hold, moving the main army over brutal terrain full of hostile – or sullenly apathetic – villagers, most of whom were hardy and dangerous. After just two weeks, I gave up on the notion that I could hold open a route to the logistics heads in Iran. I lost men trying to patrol the roads behind me, and leaving garrisons – well, if you have twenty thousand men, and you leave a hundred men each day in small towns in the mountains to watch your rear, how long until you have no army? You do the maths.

In the third week, I halted, recalled all my garrisons and then pressed forward. The next morning I had a staff meeting.

When I entered the Military Journal tent, Eumenes called 'Attention!' and most of the officers present snapped to their feet and stood as stiff as statues. It had never happened to me – although we'd all done it for Parmenio. And the king.

Cyrus bowed deeply, and so did his son and a handful of other Persian noble officers.

I decided to think about the implications later. 'At ease,' I called. 'Listen up.' I walked to the middle of the tent. Eumenes had an easel set up with a sheet of local slate. I had a piece of chalk, the kind tutors in Athens and Pella used to teach children in the agora.

'First thing,' I said. 'We no longer have a road home behind us. All we have is the ground beneath our feet. All forward troops need to assume that every contact is a hostile contact. Rearguard, too. At the same time, foraging and logistics purchases will go better if we can form a market every night and get locals to come in of their own free will and sell us produce. Understand?'

I wrote the words *Firm But Fair* on the slate.

'I need the Prodromoi to operate a day ahead of the army and I need the Angeloi two days ahead. At least. I need the Prodromoi to scout a box ...' I drew a rectangle on the board. 'And then we can move from box to box. The Agrianians will handle security inside the day's box, the Prodromoi scout the next one. Any questions?'

In fact, there were a hundred questions, but that became our doctrine for movement in hostile country. It changed a great many things – for one thing, Strako and the Angeloi began reporting directly to the Prodromoi, not to me – but it made our march routes far more secure, and it meant that even as we fought a battle, we already knew where our next camp would be, and it was already secure.

We fought six actions that summer, and the scouting units were in action every day or two. This sort of warfare is terribly wearing on troops, and after just two weeks, the Angeloi were exhausted and the Prodromoi had taken losses of a third and were no longer an effective unit. Again, the mathematics of war are relentless – if your scouts lose one man a day, even from bad water or accident, and there's only a hundred of them ...

So Eumenes began to rotate men, and later whole units, from the main body into the scouts. It was an excellent programme, and it allowed him to begin taking small commands himself. He was an honest man, but he was still a wily Greek.

We pulled all three columns together in early autumn, on the shores of Lake Seistan. Craterus and Black Cleitus came up from the south, and brought us our daughter and our newly made priest of Poseidon, fresh from Sounnion.

Olympias was fresh and lovely and just eleven years old, and she scarcely remembered us after two years in the Temple of Artemis. But that night she was curled in her foster-mother's arms, and Thaïs was happier than I had seen her in a year.

The truth is that the woman who had sent her away to be educated was a different woman in many ways from the mother who welcomed her back. And I was a different man and a different father. I wanted them to have stable lives, but I wanted them close.

Barsulas was tall and handsome and very sure of his relationship with his god. Sounnion had sent him to us with a letter to the king.

So I promised him an interview with the king when he caught up with the 'main' army, and that night we talked for hours about the gods. About Zeus-Apis in Aegypt – about Poseidon.

Athenian notions of good conduct and the rational had not changed the inner boy. The boy who swam with dolphins. He was very easy to love.

But Olympias, after just a week in camp, threw herself at my feet one evening.

'Please, Pater!' she begged. Young Eurydike, our daughter, followed Olympias the way an acolyte follows a priest, because the young priestess was on the very threshold of adulthood and thus the ultimate object of Eurydike's ambition. At any rate, when Olympias threw herself at what had once been a beautiful pair of Boeotian boots rather than a cracked and tangled mare's nest of leather repairs, my daughter Eurydike threw herself down next to the older girl.

I tried to calm them both. Olympias's tears seemed dramatic, and Eurydike's were completely false – to me. Shows how little I knew about being a parent.

'Please send me home!' Olympias begged. 'I hate it here! The Virgin Goddess will desert me here! There are no olive trees – no grass – men – all men ...' She wept.

My younger daughter beat the floor of my tent – a local rug, as I remember – and wept, too.

I thought this might pass, but Olympias was at it, day and night, and Thaïs was beside herself. Bella undertook most of Eurydike's care, but

Bella had no authority with this lovely young girl with the assurance of a well-bred Athenian aristocrat.

Thaïs lay next to me – it must have been a week after the first outburst. 'The obvious answer is to marry her to someone,' she said. But she shook her head against my chest. 'She does not want to marry. And my life started with a marriage I did not want.'

I stared at the lamp burning above me in the roof of the tent, where it hung from a chain, suspended from the cross-beam. 'She desires to be a priestess,' I said.

'And a virgin,' Thaïs said. She said it with a sob that was half-laugh and half-cry. 'She called me a porne – a prostitute.'

Yes. Children. Even the adopted kind.

The army had marched three thousand stades south from Sousia and Hyrkania, and Alexander gave them a rest while we poured scouts into the east and tried to find routes into Bactria that we could scout, hold open and supply.

I was busy stockpiling food – the harvest was coming in, all over the empire – when I realised that Cleitus's arrival meant that Parmenio's command had been stripped of troops. That struck me as odd – he was the satrap of Persia, at the centre of the vast web of the old empire, and while the 'Persian' satraps all seemed to be in revolt, Parmenio held the centre.

That night, I was again cuddling up to my intelligence chief, and I said – by way of small talk – that I wondered why Alexander had taken all the new Lydian and Thracian troops as well as all the taxeis under Parmenio's command.

Even as I said it – my hand reaching for one of Thaïs's breasts – I realised why Alexander had done it.

Thaïs frowned at me and moved my hand. 'Parmenio's days are numbered,' she said.

'You've said that before,' I accused her.

She shrugged, which was very attractive, given the circumstances. 'Perhaps. But in the past, he was a threat. Since Aegypt, he has offered no threat. After Arabela, he couldn't have toppled the king with Zeus by his side.' She turned her head. 'I have no love for him. But there is something ... poisonous about Macedon. And Athens. Why cannot old men be allowed to retire? Why must we kill them?'

Two day later, Philotas rejoined the army, having buried his brother.

He was a difficult man – given to dressing like a king, flaunting his riches and his father's political power, and far, far too addicted to telling us that he and his father had made the king who he was.

He was also a brilliant officer, who could control a cavalry reconnaissance from the saddle, simultaneously riding, fighting and working
out his campsites and his supply routes and his watch bill. He was
foul-mouthed and he hated the Persians, whom he openly derided.

Cyrus hated him, and he hated Cyrus, which made Eumenes' job
of running the scouts more difficult, as more and more Cyrus and his
Persians served directly with the Hetaeroi.

The day he returned to the army, I was coming in from the east with
Cyrus, and Philotas had discovered that I commanded the Hetaeroi in
his absence and came to find me.

He waved. 'Ptolemy,' he said. 'Tell your Persian butt-boy to fuck off,
and we'll talk.'

I put my hand on Cyrus's bridle. 'Cyrus is my deputy,' I said. 'He
serves the king.'

Philotas grunted. 'Any way he can, I bet. He understand Greek?
Hey, Persian, sod off, understand me?'

Cyrus's face grew darker.

'You are a fool, Philotas,' I said. 'Go and see the king.'

'When I'm ready. I see you have *my* command.' He spat.

I raised a hand. 'Let's try this again,' I said. 'I'm sorry Nicanor died.
Has his shade gone to Elysium? Did you bring me Polystratus?'

Philotas looked away. Then he turned his horse and rode away without another word.

I went to the king, but he was with Bagoas.

I went to Hephaestion. 'What's happening with Philotas?' I asked.
'He wants his command back. I'm perfectly ready to give it up. I have
all the grain to get in.' I gave a bitter laugh. 'The wily Odysseus, reduced
to tracking grain shipments.'

'The mighty Patroclus, reduced to writing orders for Achilles,' he said.
He had four papyrus rolls open. 'You know that fucking Zopryon has
managed to go and lose an entire army? To the Scythians?' Hephaestion
shook his head. 'It defies belief.' He raised his head and put his stylus
down. 'I'm not at liberty to discuss Philotas.'

An hour later, as I sat by lamplight with Polystratus, Ochrid and
four slave scribes, Black Cleitus came to the door. We had a long, warm
embrace.

'Missed you,' I managed to say. I remember being proud of myself
for getting it out. He grinned. Then he sobered. 'I have orders for you.
For the Hetaeroi.'

He gave me two papyrus scrolls. By then, all orders came out in
Persian and in Greek. I read the Greek.

'Go and get Cyrus. Get all the troop commanders.' I shook my head.

Polystratus, who hadn't seen his tent in four weeks, shook his head back and ran for the officers, and my new hyperetes, Theophilus, a Paeonian gentleman who had come to us with the Illyrian reinforcements, sounded 'All Officers'.

I was ordered to turn out the whole force of the Hetaeroi; Macedonian, Greek and Iranian – almost four thousand cavalrymen. And they were angry at being hauled from their sacks of straw and angrier when they found that we were marching east on a pointless two-day patrol. A four-thousand-man patrol? Leaving in the dark?

We marched an hour later, and we slept hard and ate worse, because even the army's logistics chief cannot conjure grain out of the air, in late autumn, in country already picked clean.

Just before noon on the third day, I led them back into camp.

Cleitus met me at the edge of camp.

Philotas had been arrested for treason.

Alexander arraigned him in front of the whole army. When Philotas was brought out, he shredded the accusation. I heard him. It was all nonsense – that Parmenio had plotted to sell them all to Bessus. There were boys involved, and sex – there's sex in any plot that Macedonians make – but the charges as laid were absurd, and Philotas, in his flat drawl, mocked them, and the king.

Alexander grew angry.

Hephaestion took him away.

Craterus then shocked me by making a speech reminding the army of what a snob Philotas was, and how often he'd done petty things to get his way. It turned the assembly into an ugly popularity contest.

For Craterus, it was an excellent speech.

And now I could see why I'd been sent away, and why I'd had with me every man in the army who might have stood with Philotas to prevent his arrest.

I'd been used.

That night, I lay with Thaïs and listened to a man being tortured. He was being tortured in a house not far from mine, and his screams rose and fell, not unlike the sounds of a woman giving birth, if the same woman might have had to bear six or seven children in one night. Thaïs held me hard – so hard her fingernails left marks on me.

The next day, when the army assembled to consider sentence, we had another shock. Philotas – the ruin of Philotas – was brought out on a stretcher.

He'd been tortured – he was broken. Utterly wrecked.

Years later, I heard from a former pezhetaeroi that Philotas was tortured for twenty hours, and after just two was begging Craterus and Hephaestion to *just tell him what he needed to confess.*

Hephaestion certainly conducted the interrogation, and now he led the case against the accused. Philotas was accused of treason – a capital crime that had to be tried in front of the full Assembly.

I was horrified. And the horror didn't stop. Alexander got the army to execute Philotas – by stoning. And he threw them his cousin, Alexander of Lyncestis, who had been under arrest for years but never prosecuted.

The death of Philotas was the end of reason. The end of the rule of law. Macedonians acted under the law to kill him, but the charges were foolish and the accusation was spurious, and the army knew it. And the army knew that Alexander had used Philotas's greed and vanity against him. It is an interesting aspect of human behaviour; a leader can manipulate people to his own ends, but the people are perfectly aware when they've been manipulated.

I didn't know it for weeks, but Alexander also sent a messenger to Parmenio. When the messenger arrived . . .

The old general was murdered in cold blood.

Let me speak a moment, boy.

Had the king done such a thing at Tyre, or Gaza, I'd have understood. To the best of my knowledge, Parmenio plotted actively to remove the king, or at least limit his power. To the end of his days, the old general thought we were all blind, and that Alexander was a parvenu boy, an amateur warrior, an actor playing at being king.

But when Alexander killed him – he did it without any justice, after the old man's fangs were pulled, and he acted through a man who thought he was the king's trusted friend, a man Alexander ordered tortured.

It was ugly.

And I'd like to say that after Lake Seistan, nothing was the same.

But nothing had been the same for a long time.

It was late at night. In my memory, it was the night that we heard of Parmenio's assassination, although to be honest, that whole period is a blur in my memory – a blur of betrayal, anger and drama, not least of which was Olympias's attempt at suicide.

I was standing with Eumenes, and we were determinedly *not* talking about Alexander. We were, I remember, looking at a local bow – a very fine example, picked up by Ariston's patrols that afternoon. It was lacquered blue and green, and had gold and silver leaf, or perhaps paint, in intricate patterns all along it. It seemed to bend the wrong way, and we had to call one of the Saka slaves to string it.

Sake make terrible slaves, but that's another story.

She came in, and her face was like a mask of rage, and her chiton was torn, and she had a dagger in her fist.

'On your head be my death!' she screamed at me.

She brought the dagger down.

Now, one of two things is true. Either she knew I'd stop her, because I am a professional soldier and she was an eleven-year-old girl, or she absolutely meant to kill herself. In fact, I suspect that both were true at the same time.

I caught her hand, disarmed her and Eumenes threw her to the ground.

She roared her tears, and Thaïs came hurrying from wherever she'd been, and Olympias struck her.

'You whore! What do you care how many men rape me!' Olympias screamed the words.

But Thaïs only hugged her the more fiercely, and Eumenes and I left her to it like the cowards men can be.

The stars were out when Thaïs reappeared.

'A soldier put his hand under her chiton,' Thaïs said wearily.

'Bound to happen,' Eumenes said with a chuckle.

'If that's all you have to say, you can say it somewhere else,' Thaïs spat.

It is interesting – I might have said the same thing myself, and with the same leering chuckle – soldiers are soldiers – except that hearing it from Eumenes, it sounded ugly, and pat.

'I told her we'd send her back to Artemis,' Thaïs confessed.

'Ephesus,' I proposed.

Eumenes fingered his beard. 'Well thought,' he said. The Ionian cities all bore watching. Alexander had offered to rebuild the temple at Ephesus. It wouldn't hurt us to have family there. And you *have* to think that way, when you are both a parent and the god of war's chief of staff.

A few minutes later, Thaïs brought Olympias to us, and she held my knees and wept and begged my forgiveness for her outrageous behaviour.

Why on earth did we name her Olympias?

At any rate, I promised to send her to Ephesus with the next convoy going west, and she kissed us both.

When she left us with Bella, we all three breathed a sigh of relief.

Eumenes watched her go. 'I'm sending my children to Athens,' he said quietly.

Thaïs and he exchanged a glance.

I was often the slowest of the three of us – people don't call me Farm Boy for nothing. 'What?'

'Alexander had Parmenio killed,' Thaïs said slowly, as if she were speaking to Eurydike.

I nodded. We all glanced around. It was like that. We had heard – that day, I guess.

I still hadn't taken it all in.

Thaïs leaned forward. 'Alexander sent Polydamus – that little snake – to Cleander and Sitalkes and told them to kill Parmenio immediately. They stabbed him to death in his bed.'

Polydamus was a junior officer of the Hetaeroi, and he even looked like a snake. The king used him for confidential missions.

Eumenes looked at me. 'Hephaestion and Cleitus get the Hetaeroi,' he said. 'You get Demetrios's spot in the bodyguard.'

I shrugged. I had been somatophylakes for years. The king tended to emphasise it at times, and forget it at others. It was absurdly symbolic that at this point he was going to announce my *promotion* to the army.

Parmenio was dead. I couldn't really get it through my thick skull.

THIRTY-THREE

espite the army-wide depression that set in after the execution of Philotas – forty men threw javelins at him and the other conspirators until they died – we continued to plan a thrust to the east. I assumed the king would march in the spring, when there was grass in the valleys.

I was wrong.

At midwinter, we heard that Satibarzanes was back in Aria raising rebels, and Alexander sent Erigyus – recently returned to us. The Lesbian mercenary not only crushed the rebellion but killed Satibarzanes in single combat. In doing so, he won the praise of the army – and lost Alexander's friendship.

A sign of things to come. Alexander could no longer stand to have any sign of competition.

It was five months since I'd had command of the main body of the army and rationalised the scouting system, but one afternoon Alexander came into the Military Journal tent and began reading through the entries from the days he'd been off in the north with the Aegema – that is, the entries Eumenes had made while I was in command. He paused and looked at me.

'I gather you allowed the officers to salute you, while you were in command,' he said. His tone was mild enough, but I'd known him from childhood.

I just held his eyes. I knew how to handle him, as well as any man in the world except perhaps Hephaestion.

He glared.

I looked back at him.

'Well?' he asked.

'Well what?' I asked.

He stood there.

'If you don't trust me with the army,' I said, fairly caustically, 'then leave someone else in command.'

He shrugged.

I considered mentioning Parmenio, but I was smart enough not to. But when Craterus came with recruits, I sent Olympias *and* Eurydike – and that hurt – away to the coast. To Ephesus. To be safe, or at least, harder to use as hostages.

At any rate, as soon as we had word that the revolt was beaten, Alexander ordered us to march – midwinter.

We struck like lightning, and we had manoeuvred Bessus out of his impregnable position astride the Oxus river by the time the first grass was growing in the valleys. That is a strategist's way of saying that we marched over four high mountain passes in heavy snow and lost almost a thousand veteran soldiers to weather, poor supplies and bad guides; to hubris and hurry.

To be fair, fighting Bessus for the passes would have cost us more, and I know – *I know* – that we did all we could to prepare.

We took Aornos. So many men were snow-blind that you could see a man leading another man to the army market by the hand. I gave up trying to supply the army – Alexander outmarched all supplies I'd arranged, dumped my carts, ordered my mules eaten.

But Bessus lost Bactria without a fight, and his Bactrian tribesmen deserted him in a wave, and suddenly *we* had a Bactrian army.

We pressed on into Sogdiana, across another desert. I sent Thaïs back to Susa, and she was happy to go. She handed over her networks – such as they were – to Eumenes. We stood together for a long time – she dressed as a man for riding, as straight as an arrow, her beautiful face lit by the dawn in the clear mountain air.

'Don't let him kill you,' she whispered. We kissed, to the delight of the cavalry escort, and then she was gone.

I'd have gone, too, if I had thought I could leave the army without being murdered.

Alexander had never cared much for his troops, but that march set a new record. He himself changed horses daily, and he moved with the Prodromoi, covering more than a hundred stades a day to the Oxus. Men died so fast it seemed as if a plague had hit us. Men who'd been weakened in the snows died in the desert, or died of drinking too much water when we reached the Oxus. All told, from Lake Seistan to the Oxus, Alexander lost more pezhetaeroi and Hetaeroi than he'd lost in all of his battles combined, and when we reached the Oxus, we had fewer than twenty thousand men, and more than half were barbarian auxiliaries that even I didn't trust.

And many men had had enough. None of the veterans had been allowed to go home – home to Pella – for the winter. Of course, home was so far away that if they'd marched on the usual autumn Feast of Demeter, they'd still have been marching west on the date they were due back – but that's not how angry soldiers think. And the army had just heard of Parmenio's murder, as we lay on our sunburned backs along the Oxus and wondered how exactly the king planned to get us across.

The Thessalians – those who were left, including a dozen troopers I'd convinced to stay with the Hetaeroi – demanded their pay and marched for home. Over a thousand veteran pezhetaeroi did the same.

Alexander was so shaken he let them go. Or so uncaring. Every day, local chiefs brought their barbarous retinues in to join us. These weren't Persians like Cyrus. These were utterly barbarous northerners who hid their womenfolk, swore oaths for everything and lied when they breathed.

They were excellent light cavalry, though.

Alexander made up his numbers from them. Then he ordered all our leather tents stitched into bladders, and we used them to float ourselves across the Oxus. It was midsummer, and terrifying, but the survivors of the army were by this time not so much hardened as indifferent.

You can still find some of those pezhetaeroi – in my army, or on the streets of Alexandria. Look at them. Ask them.

By the time they reached the Oxus, they no longer expected to live. They marched day to day. They didn't even grumble. Nor did they drill, and discipline became a real problem, even in the elite corps. Officers were murdered. When recruits came in, they were treated brutally and ignored. The older veterans didn't associate with them, or help them. In fact, mostly, the veterans just waited to see which of the new boys would die first.

My old friend Amyntas son of Philip found me one day, just after we crossed the Oxus. I was trying to convince Ariston and Hephaestion to give me a thousand local cavalry to use to gather forage from the west, where we hadn't been yet.

They left me to find Alexander, and I was standing under some kind of tree – something alien to me, anyway. A thousand Macedonians were washing their chitons in the river, or swimming, or simply lying on the rocks watching the water trickle by.

Philip came and saluted. He'd never saluted me before. I clasped his hand, and he smiled.

'You never know, these days,' he muttered.

'What's on your mind?' I asked. 'I won't ask how you are.'

'Hah!' he said. 'I'm alive, that's how I am. Alive to walk the earth.' He sighed. And was silent.

I offered him some wine, which he drank.

'How's your little girl?' he asked.

'Fine,' I said. 'I hope that she's safe in Ephesus by now. Hermes protect her, and the Virgin Goddess stand by her side.'

Philip smiled. 'I love to hear you speak Greek,' he said. 'Virgin Goddess.' He crossed his arms and hugged himself. 'I'm too far from home,' he said.

'Don't you think the gods see us here as well as in Greece?' I asked.

He shrugged. 'I don't really think they care. But here?' He looked around – at the patches of scraggly grass, the rock, the barrenness, the trickle of water.

My adopted son, despite his status as a priest, had become a passable cavalryman, and he was serving me as a messenger. He had a pair of fine horses – local stock. Horses loved him.

I digress. Barsalus smiled at old Philip. 'Of course the gods are here, friend,' he said with his usual complete confidence.

Philip nodded. He didn't agree. 'You know the recruits Craterus brought us?' he said.

I nodded. Amyntas son of Philip looked away.

'The old boys stripped them. You know that? Took all their equipment, and made them take ours. They had good chitons and good spolas. Now we have them. And we beat the ones that complained. And Amyntas and his friends are wagering on them – on what they'll die of, and when they'll die.' He shrugged. 'I'm wagering, too. Fuck it all. He's going to kill every one of us.' He looked around. It was the new epidemic in the army – fear. Hephaestion, men said, had organised a corps of pages and serving soldiers as secret police. Myself – I had trouble believing it. But later, it proved to be true.

When Amyntas son of Philip looked over his shoulder, I did too.

That's how it was.

In effect, the army that had left Ecbatana ceased to exist. Alexander had yet another new army – a central Asian army with a few Macedonian and Persian officers. He made a new army out of the air, and we crossed the Oxus, again outmanoeuvring the supposedly mobile Bessus.

Bessus's nobles deposed him. In the East, men ruled by military competence, and Bessus had failed them three times – in Hyrkania, in Bactria and now at the Oxus. Many abandoned him, and his lieutenant, Spitamenes, offered to betray him and make submission to the conqueror.

I was sent – with a major portion of the army – to take Bessus from Spitamenes. In fact, the wily bastard handed over a whole company of troublemakers – his former commander, a dozen untrustworthy chiefs and some captured Saka, including three women.

One of whom was your mother, of course. I had no idea – I just saw trouble. I didn't even find her modestly attractive at the time. Her glare of hate was enough to render her more murderous than beautiful, let me tell you. And she tried to escape.

More than Bessus did. I dragged Bessus back, and at Alexander's orders, he was tied naked to a post by the side of the road, and the entire army marched past him.

I doubt most of the remaining pezhetaeroi even noticed him as they trudged on towards the horizon.

With the submission of Spitamenes, even I thought we were done. Alexander was fascinated by the *Amazons*, as he insisted on calling them, and Hephaestion, who was growing more inhuman by the day, took one and tried to rape her into submission, and was badly injured as a result. No tears from me.

But Alexander wanted to see what was north of us, and he had a notion that he could remount the Hetaeroi on the superb Saka heavy horses of the steppe. At the time, we thought – some men still do – that we were close to the Euxine. Our patrols had begun to spar with eastern Massagetae, the Saka that Cyrus the Great died fighting. Since we knew from experience that the Assagetae – your mother's people – lived north of the Euxine and were cousins of the mighty Massagetae, the philosophers, like Callisthenes, came to the conclusion that we were close – that the Hindu Kush connected to the Caucasus mountains, that Hyrkania and Bactria were much closer than they were.

We were wrong, but Alexander believed it, and your mother's appearance seemed to clinch the deal – a western Assagetae in Sogdiana. We went north towards the Jaxartes, to gain the submission of the Saka, and a tribute in horses that we could use, so Alexander claimed, to conquer India.

There comes a point when hubris is raised to an art form.

We marched north.

Spitamenes felt betrayed. We were, in effect, doing what we'd just told him we wouldn't do – we were marching into his tribal areas.

He didn't withdraw. He raised an army, and attacked.

THIRTY-FOUR

A nyone who served with Alexander that year calls it the same –
the 'Summer of Spitamenes'.

Go down to the waterfront, find a soldier's wine shop and
offer to buy a round. Then ask the men with grey hair from Macedon
who was the most dangerous enemy we ever faced. Memnon was brilliant, and daring. Darius was cautious, capable and resilient.

To my mind, Spitamenes was brilliant, daring, capable and resilient.
If he had known when to be cautious – if he had had any reliable
troops ...

It was the year Cephisophon was archon in Athens. We had beaten
every army in the world from Sparta to Persia.

And then came Spitamenes.

Just in time. Let me explain.

We took Marakanda without a sword being loosened in its scabbard
– the first town worthy of the name we'd seen north of the Oxus, and
we were happy to use its markets. It was a major entrepôt, too, and I
received two letters – long, lovely letters – from Thaïs, full of love and
information. Olympias was safely ensconced in the great Temple of
Artemis at Ephesus, and enclosed a note begging my forgiveness. Thaïs
was at Babylon, with a house and forty servants and all my treasure,
bless her.

I went out of my tent, I remember, and I built an altar with my own
hands, out beyond the horse lines. Polystratus helped me, and Strako,
and Eumenes the Cardian came when I was done. I invited Astibus
and Bubares, Theophilus of the Hetaeroi, Philip the Red, Amyntas son
of Philip from Craterus's taxeis, and Ochrid, now not only a freeman
but the head of my household, my steward. My son sacrificed a white
ram in the dawn, and I swore to wed Thaïs if I made it alive back to
Babylon. I swore to Zeus-Apis to build a temple in Alexandria to his
glory, and I have not been a laggard in that, have I? And the others

swore similar oaths. It made every one of us feel closer to home, and Barsulas spoke to us in the new light as we roasted our shares of the ram over the ashes.

'You think the gods have forgotten you,' he said. 'But they are here, all around us, every day, I promise you.'

I think he was right – but I know he put heart into every one of us. Even the king loved him – and consulted him often enough that his seer and his other priests became jealous.

But enough of my life. Our supply lines now ran from the coast of the Persian Gulf upriver and over two mountain ranges. A recruit coming from Macedon had to march from Pella to the Pontus, cross on a ship, march to Babylon, then down to the gulf, take ship to Hormuz, then march upcountry to the king. New armour, good swords, decent spearheads, long ash hafts for sarissas, any kind of olive oil, letters from home – everything had to crawl up this lifeline.

Alexander was aware of it. He left four taxeis under Craterus, with ten squadrons of local cavalry, to hold Bactria behind us and he took the rest of the army north and farther east, to explore the northern borders of the Persian Empire.

It made me happy just to hear him say the word *border*. A border implied a limit, and if we had a limit, then perhaps some day we'd all march home.

The nightly drinking had reached epic proportions. It had started after Darius's death – in fact, Alexander had always drunk too much when the mood was on him – but the last year, he was drunk every night.

In fact, he was bored, in the first weeks of that summer.

In a way – a distant, godlike way – it was interesting to study him when he was bored. He became increasingly irritable; he tended to focus on things of no importance whatsoever, which confused men who didn't really know him, such as Callisthenes and Aristander. His focus could suddenly fall on exercise, on medicine, on the power of prophecy, on the colour of a man's excrement as influenced by food. And then, for days, that focus would consume him.

We were south of the Jaxartes, in the brownest country I have ever seen. Thirty of us were lying on portable klines by a bonfire – it was the little Heraklion, and we'd had a day of contests. I hadn't won anything, but I had that pleasant level of fatigue that comes with the agon.

Hephaestion came and lay down on my couch. I had avoided him since the torture of Philotas. He knew it. But he lay down.

'Philotas was never one of us,' Hephaestion said.

And at some horrible base level, that was true. I knew what he meant.

He meant that he didn't owe Philotas the kind of emotive loyalty that he owed me, or any of the other men who'd survived childhood at Philip's court.

It was an olive branch.

'No,' I said. That was my dove back to him.

He nodded. His head was on his arms, and he was watching a trio of lewd slave girls writhe. They weren't any good – they'd been used too hard, paid too little and they assumed men were brutes. It is one of the delightful, horrible complexities of the human condition – soldiers want girls who want them, not whores. They'll take whores, but only if the whores behave as if they want the soldiers.

Makes you laugh, in a nasty way, doesn't it?

Ares, you're thirteen. My apologies, lad.

At any rate, he watched them. And then he grunted. Rolled over.

'I need help,' he said. 'I'm trying to manage the king all by myself. He needs ...' Hephaestion made a sign of aversion – the peasant sign, with two fingers.

'*O phile pais*, I've known Alexander since he was five,' I said. Hephaestion had seldom asked me, or anyone else, for help before. So I put an arm around his shoulder and he let his head sink on his arms. 'What's the matter?'

'The matter?' Hephaestion looked at me, and his eyes held more rage than sorrow. 'He's fucking cut himself off from everyone, and doesn't know how to get back.'

'Does he *want* to get back?' I asked.

Hephaestion hid his head. 'No,' he admitted. 'He just wants to be god.'

Hephaestion must have manipulated the king, one way or another, because I was promoted from king's friend to the Persian equivalent of somatophylakes a day later, and suddenly Alexander wanted me to ride with him.

We were on the Oxus, and the day before I'd met a Sakje while on patrol and bartered a fine mare for a superb bow and fifty arrows in a gorytos. I'm not much of an archer, but I loved a thing well made and I'd just determined – back then – to write a book about my travels. I had my journal and the Military Journal, but I was not so different from the king, and I, too, wanted to know – *Is this all there is?* The idea of writing a travel book made me happy.

Perhaps you have to be fifteen thousand stades from home for this to make sense.

And the conversation with the Sakje man made me happy, perhaps because he met me with a grin, chose to trust my patrol and no one was killed. I had become so inured to killing every fucking stranger I came across that sharing the white horse milk that the Sakje think is delicious *was* fun. He ate our onion sausage, we ate his deer meat and he rode away richer by two horses and without one of his bows, and Cyrus, who was at my side the whole time, actually laughed. Out loud.

Never mind. You have to make war for a long, long time for a man's laugh to seem alien. But these are the things that stick in my head.

I left my squadrons with Polystratus. He was an officer, now – increasingly, a trusted officer. No one doubted that he was an aristocrat. Think of it! From Thracian slave to Macedonian cavalry officer! Mind you, he was a superb officer – but such a thing would never have happened if our lines hadn't been so long. Ochrid, my steward, now routinely gave orders to fifty slaves. He often helped me with the logistika and would casually order out a patrol for forage. No one doubted his place, although he had started out as my slave. What seemed like a lifetime before.

I rode along with the king, and he affected to be delighted to see me. By luck, his latest passion – dice – had burned itself out.

'Nearchus is on his way to us,' I said. I was handling the incoming letters. Eumenes was trying to establish even the most basic level of intelligence collection in Sogdiana and Transoxiana, and he had – in one of those role reversals impossible to enemies and simple to friends – asked me to run the Journal for a few days while he tried to get a network of agents in Marakanda.

'Nearchus?' Alexander looked at the mountains to either side for as long as it takes a man to breathe three or four times. 'Ah! Nearchus!'

For a moment, you see, the king didn't know of whom I was speaking.

'Remember shooting bows, lord?' I asked. My false innocence was glaring to Hephaestion, and he looked at me, but Alexander noticed nothing.

He glanced at me.

'Look at this,' I said, and held out my new bow.

He all but snatched it from my hands.

For nine days, we shot everything that moved. I gave him my fine bow, and Cyrus, bless him, took a patrol north of the Oxus and exchanged a dozen local horses for five good bows, so that the inner circle all had them.

The king had a dozen Sakje hostages, and he brought a woman out to see her shoot. He was intending to mock her, and he was already shooting well, although his forefinger and thumb were bleeding from the Sakje release, which Cyrus taught us. Cyrus used a leather thumb ring and had a thumb callus as deep as a coin, but Alexander was above such things.

'Amazons!' he laughed, as we rode along.

The woman who joined us, between two guards, was heavily pregnant. She was beautiful – in a deadly, feral way, and pregnancy neither softened nor diminished her. And she rode like a satyr – which is to say, the horse seemed part of her. The king had met her a dozen times, and she'd famously threatened to geld Hephaestion, which made her a bit of a favourite among the inner circle.

She spoke beautiful Greek – accented, but pure Athenian. Well, we both know why, don't we?

The king had set a dozen targets by the trail – we were well in advance of the army, moving south along the Jaxartes. The first was about ten horse lengths from the rocky road, the next was a little farther, and so on, until the last was easily a hundred paces to the south of the road.

The king came up to the Sakje woman with her two guards – both, as it happened, men from Philotas's former squadron.

'My apologies, lady, but the guards say you begged to be allowed to ride.' He smiled. 'I thought perhaps you could show us some shooting.'

Hephaestion was smirking. This was for him – she was being humiliated to please the bastard.

Well, I know she was your mother, but at the time she was just some barbarian captive, and if that's what it took to keep the king happy, I was willing enough.

She looked at Alexander with contempt. I suspect that wasn't a look he received often. I wonder if the novelty of it drew him to her. She held out her hand for the bow he carried.

He held it out, but snatched it back, and we all laughed at her eagerness. Macedonian humour.

'You want to kill us all,' he said. 'Please remember that we have your other ladies. They would not survive any dramatic performances. And neither would you.' He pointed to where a pair of the army's engineers stood with their crossbows.

She shrugged. He gave her the bow, and she flexed it. 'Heavy,' she said. And held out her hand for his quiver.

Alexander gave it to her with unaccustomed hesitation. 'You will shoot the targets, and only the targets,' he said. 'Let's see how many you can hit. Show us how the Sakje shoot. And perhaps – perhaps I'll send you back to your husband.'

He smiled at her. He was used to the responses of men who lived and died at his whim, so his smile was expectant.

She laughed. 'It amazes me that a man so foolish could have conquered so much,' she said. And took his quiver.

She put her heels to the barrel of her horse the moment the strap of the gorytos touched her palm, and her horse – a small gelding – went straight to a gallop. And she screamed – a long, ululating yell. As she rode, she twisted her body, and the quiver fell down her arm and she buckled it into place, riding at a full gallop with no hands, the bow pinned under her right knee, and then it was back in her hand and an arrow leaped from her bow and shot *through* the king's first target.

At that point, we'd been shooting that bow mounted for a week. None of us had even considered loosing arrows at a gallop.

Her second arrow went into the second target.

Her third arrow went into the third target.

She hit every target.

Then she turned her horse and rode back to us. Men were applauding, and Hephaestion had the good grace to join them.

She was coming at us at a gallop. I noticed that she had arrows in her fingers.

Suddenly, she angled her horse a little to the north, turned – remember, she was eight months pregnant.

She was shooting backwards.

Her first arrow was shot at the *most distant* target.

She drew and loosed, drew, loosed, drew and loosed, so fast that I couldn't follow all the movements of her arm. She was still riding *away* from the targets at a dead gallop.

Drew and loosed and drew and loosed.

Her horse turned under her – a sudden turn on her bow side – and she loosed the arrow on the bow and drew and loosed again.

And again.

I was holding my breath.

Her first six arrows struck. She'd shot from farthest to closest, so that *they all struck at the same time.*

She cantered her gelding across the rocky slope, to the side of the king.

'Good bow,' she said, and handed it to him.

Later that same afternoon, a Corinthian athlete offered to demonstrate his skills as a hoplomachos. He'd made a claim about what a good fighter he was, and the king was in a foul mood, overheard the boast and ordered the man to dismount right there, strip and fight.

He looked around, and his eye fell on Coenus.

One of our very best.

Coenus dismounted and summoned a slave to help him take off his armour, but Alexander spat. 'If he's so very good, this Greek, he can fight naked with a club. Like Herakles. And you can wear your armour.'

The Greek was all but weeping with frustration. He was prepared to apologise, but the king was in no mood. The archery had ruined his day – he'd ordered the woman and her companions to be taken to Marakanda under escort.

Coenus was uneasy. He could be a brute, but the Greek – despite a superb physique – was not a big man, and he looked inoffensive – naked, with a club. Coenus looked at the king. The king shook his head. 'Just kill him,' he said.

The naked man was an Olympic athlete who had come all this way to train Alexander's soldiers.

Coenus – our Coenus, not your father's friend – wouldn't have lasted this long if he hadn't been absolutely obedient. He turned, drew his sword and set his shield.

The naked boy came forward, edging crabwise.

Coenus struck, thrusting his shield into the man's body and cutting hard, overhand.

The Greek slid inside the cut, broke his arm and knocked him unconscious with his club in one blow.

Fight over.

Alexander drew his bow from the gorytos, nocked an arrow and shot the Greek. The arrow went in just over his kidneys, and he fell screaming.

His screams pursued us down the ridge.

Hephaestion looked at me, and I just shook my head at him. I couldn't think of what to say, or do, but for the first time, I considered two things.

Riding away from the army and taking my chances with the king ordering me killed.

Or killing Alexander.

That night, six of us had a secret meeting. It was a conspiracy – we all knew we could be killed for having the discussion. I swore never to repeat what we said, or who was there. It was a desperate hour, and a desperate oath. So I won't tell you – except that we discussed options.

When we were done, Hephaestion held me back. 'Barsines or her sister,' he said. 'Bagoas turns my stomach, but he'd do, too.'

Well, it was better than regicide. I nodded. 'But we have to get through the weeks until he finds a sex toy or we can import one,' I said.

Hephaestion shook his head. 'We need something as good as the bow was. And we need it to stay beautiful.' His bronze hair glittered in the firelight. It was already cold in the mountains.

'Horses? Playing Polis? How silk is made?' I was talking to hear myself. I wanted Thaïs. I wanted to drink wine with Polystratus and Cyrus, or Marsyas. I wanted to stop being afraid.

Hephaestion shook his head. 'He's close to the edge,' he said. 'What do we do?'

I didn't have an answer.

I went to bed.

Polystratus wakened me while the stars were still turning overhead. 'Listen!' he said. 'The king wants you.'

I got out of my cloak, wrapped it back around me and ran for his tent – terrified, in a sleepy, cold way, that he'd done something. Killed Hephaestion.

But they were sitting together.

He was smiling, his face easy and unlined, his eyes glittering.

'Listen, Ptolemy!' he said. 'Spitamenes is in revolt, and he's slaughtered all seven of our new garrisons.'

Hephaestion looked at me. His eyes said *everything*.

Alexander went on, 'He's raised the whole province while we were playing at archery – and he's cut us off from the main army. We're surrounded. And our supply lines are *cut*.' He fingered his beard. And smiled.

Hephaestion smiled.

Hades, I smiled myself.

Alexander looked up from the dispatch. 'Gentlemen, I think we might have a war on our hands,' he said.

We were saved.

THIRTY-FIVE

～～～

A
lexander's reaction to Spitamenes was planned in one night and ran like lightning over the plains. He sent a relief column to break Spitamenes' siege of Marakanda. Alexander placed Pharnuches, a skilled speaker of Persian and several of the Bactrian tongues, as commander; he got a troop of Hetaeroi, three hundred Macedonian pezhetaeroi mounted as cavalry, and two thousand mercenary infantry – good men, mostly Ionian Greeks. Alexander also gave him all the Amazon captives to escort into Marakanda. Spitamenes had sold them to us in the first place, and Alexander thought they might be useful as bargaining counters. He expected that Spitamenes would negotiate.

We marched for the Jaxartes. And we went hard and fast.

We took four forts in three days. In each case, we took the fort by storm, and the garrisons were slaughtered in the storming action. Alexander made it clear to the Bactrians that there were to be no survivors.

In every case, Alexander led the storming party in person.

This was not misplaced Homeric heroics. We had added thousands of barbarian auxiliaries to the army, and we were so short on 'Macedonians' that Illyrians and even Thracians had begun to seem like close friends. And morale among the Macedonian troops was low. Alexander made it clear that we were to lead from the front, and when the assault parties went in, the entire front rank of a taxeis might be, for instance, Hetaeroi officers.

That's what it was taking to get our men into combat.

It was bloody work, but the Bactrian levies did their part, and that meant that they were ours. After killing their cousins in Spitamenes' service, they weren't going to go back to the steppe or join the revolt.

The Bactrians were better soldiers than any of us expected. They had enough tribal feuds and remembered hatreds to get them going, and they were still in awe of us. The problem was that as the Bactrians began to outperform the Macedonians, the bad feeling, already present, began to escalate.

There's a belief, common among the sort of generals who fight their battles in the baths or lying on a comfortable kline at a party, that men who have fought in a number of battles are *veterans* and thus better soldiers. In the main, this is true. Veterans don't die from preventable accidents. Veterans get fewer diseases, know how to dig a latrine and know how to find food. So they can indeed wager on how new recruits will die, in the field.

Veterans have learned a few things, and one of the things they learn is that people *die* in war or are horribly mutilated, and that the way to avoid these fates is to be careful and not take risks. Sometimes, in combat, the raw, unblooded troops are the better fighters.

The fifth of Cyrus's forts on the Jaxartes – the one we called Cyropolis – was the worst.

Alexander had been wounded the day before, storming the Dakhas fort. He'd taken an arrow right through the shin – Philip had it out in no time, but it left the king out of the next action, against a fort that had a garrison of seven thousand men.

So there I was, with most of my friends and my own retainers. I had set out from Macedon with twenty grooms, and I had six left. Polystratus was now a gentleman and an officer – a phylarch. His second, Theodore, was now a hetaeros, a half-file leader in a gold-plated helmet. Ochrid, who had begun our campaigns as my body slave, was now my steward, as I have noted, and about this time started to serve as my mounted groom, and usually fought with the Hetaeroi, and any day now, I was going to have to put him in the ranks and add him to my roster. This is not a complaint – Ochrid was, it turned out, a warrior to his fingers' ends. Most men are, if they are well led. Rather I mean it as an example of how desperate our manning problems were. The lines between master and man, between 'Greek' and 'Macedonian', between 'mercenary' and 'professional', were hopelessly blurred.

As the numbers of Greeks in our ranks increased – even in the Hetaeroi – the older Macedonians grew less and less inclined to accept the Bactrians and the Persians, as if the line had to be drawn somewhere.

But I digress. Cyropolis. The fort was two hundred feet above us, and I was standing in the front rank between Polystratus and Marsyas. I had four thousand men formed behind me, and another thousand Bactrians under Cyrus, ready to go up a dry gully to the south of the place. As far as I could see, the dry gully would get them within fifty paces of the position and the useless amateurs guarding the fort had missed it. I certainly hoped so.

My four thousand were all veterans. They were a mix of mercenaries and one of Parmenio's former taxeis – Polyperchon's Tymphaeans. Polyperchon was down with one of Apollo's shafts in him, and his men – some of whom were survivors of Philip's campaigns – were none too happy to be used as assault troops.

I could hear them behind me.

'Let the fucking Medes do it,' one old man said. 'They seem to like it.'

But soldiers always said such things before a fight.

It was a calm, clear morning. I could smell the sharp smell of our morning fires, and while it promised to be hot, the early-morning air was still quite pleasant. The river made a low growl off to my right, and we had so many horses in our army that they made more noise than the enemy.

But not more noise than a battery of war engines. Twenty engines loosed their bolts and baskets all together, about a stade to my left, and their noise drowned the river and the horses – the whip-crack of the torsion engines, the louder, deeper thud as the catapults released their heavier payloads. The engineers had opened breaches the night before and kept the range, despite the workings of temperature and dew on the torsion ropes. Dust rose all along the top of the breaches, as the gravel and the larger stones struck home. Someone was hit – he lay in the breach screaming.

An archer on the wall tried a long shot. He must have been good – his first shaft struck a horse length from my right foot. But his second shaft fell shorter yet, and he stopped.

We weren't exactly going to surprise them.

I exchanged embraces and arm clasps with my friends in the front ranks. Then I turned to the pezhetaeroi.

'Let's get this done,' I said. Perhaps not my best speech.

All I got in return was a low growl, but that was fine. Professionals.

I looked at Laertes, another former groom who now carried the trumpet and acted as my hyperetes, because Theophilus had been promoted to decarch.

He nodded once and sounded it, and we were off.

I didn't see any reason to hurry, since my real attack was going in with Cyrus, and the trumpet was his signal to start up the dry gully. We marched quite well. My shield hurt my shoulder. I was reaching an age when the accumulation of my wounds had begun to bother me almost every day. Thaïs had made me concoctions – they didn't all work, but the thought was there. Now I had nothing but what Philip of Acarnia gave me. More and more, he used opium for everything. I didn't want opium, so I put up with a lot of aches and pains.

Four thousand sets of boots, going up the gravel to the fort.

Arrows began to fall on us. They'd been lofted high to get over our shields.

The men behind me raised their shields.

I began to go forward faster. It is the natural reaction to incoming arrows.

I was almost to the base of the main breach. We'd pounded three of them at last light, and the batteries had opened up again at first light, pounding the mud-brick wall to dirt and wrecking the attempts at repair. Baskets of gravel had cleared the workers off the walls.

We were quite good at sieges, by the Jaxartes.

Even as I reached the ditch at the base of the devastated mud-brick wall, I saw that the pioneers had filled it in with fascine bundles, and crossbow bolts were going over my head into the archers on the walls shooting down at me. It didn't make me feel *safe*, but it is reassuring to a soldier to know that the other parts of the machine are functioning to support him.

The poor bastard in the breach had been unlucky. A five-talent machine had hit his feet square on and effectively pulped them, and he lay in an immense pool of his own blood and screamed. His screams were horrible, because his fate represented exactly the sort of thing we all feared.

I should have looked back to call the troops forward, and I should have kept an eye on the archers shooting down from the embrasures, but I let my focus fall on the poor bastard screaming his guts out. I ran to him and killed him – spiked him in the head. He went out like a lamp being blown out.

May someone do as much for me.

Now I was halfway up the breach. Amyntas son of Gordidas, one of my former grooms, and Marsyas were right behind me, and Laertes and Polystratus were a pace behind, their shields *full* of arrows, and behind them were a dozen more officers and gentlemen.

The enemy tribesmen were lining the breach.

There was no one behind my officers.

The taxeis had stopped dead, about fifty paces out from the wall.

There comes a point in a charge when you can't really go back. I was just beyond the spear range of the men in the breach. To turn and run back to the taxeis under the wall would be to turn my back on healthy enemies and run the gauntlet of their archery – again – this time with my back to them.

No thanks, I thought.

So I turned and charged the enemy. Or rather, fifteen or twenty of us charged a thousand or so of them.

I had assumed that when the taxeis saw us committed to the fight, they would come forward.

I was wrong.

It should have been easy. The enemy Sogdians were dismounted nomad cavalry, and they had neither shields nor armour nor real spears. They threw javelins with deadly force and excellent aim – but we were fully armoured men with heavy aspides. Their archery was deadly – but we'd survived that.

And they'd been chewed over pretty hard by our artillery.

It should have been easy, but the odds of fifteen fully armoured men against a thousand unarmoured archers were just too long, and we had no impact when we struck them. The breach we went up was only about ten men wide, and so, for a while, our little group held its own. A hundred heartbeats, perhaps.

The spear is a deadly weapon, when the wielder is armoured and shielded and his opponents are not. I must have wounded ten men in those hundred heartbeats.

But the Sogdians did something I had never seen before. They began to use their bows at point-blank range – releasing arrows from so close that there was no possibility of a miss. As they began to get around the ends of our little line, archers began to shoot into our unprotected thighs and backs, and in moments, half of my friends were down.

Marsyas gave a choked scream and dropped by my side.

Laertes fell atop him.

My spear hadn't broken. I had a short spear that day – pikes are useless in a storming action, and I had one of my fine Athenian spears, all blue and gilt work, with a long, heavy head and a vicious butt-spike. The haft was octagonal, which allowed me to know where the edges of the spearhead were without looking, and I'd been practising with the thing for a year.

The proper Homeric thing to do was to die standing over my friends, but I elected to go in among the archers and live a little longer.

I leaped forward from where I had straddled Marsyas. The Sogdians' use of archery to finish us off had caused them to draw back instead of pressing the last little knot of us, and that left me space that shock troops wouldn't have given me. I let my shield fall from my arm – it was full of arrows, and one of them was in my lower bicep by a finger's width.

Then I put my left hand near the head of my spear as if I were boar-hunting, and stepped into their ranks. I didn't stop moving, and

Ares lent me his strength, and for as long as it takes a man to drink his canteen dry, I rampaged through their ranks, too close to be shot, too fast to be tracked, and I thrust with the spear two-handed, and *cut* with the spearhead as if it were the point of a sword. I felt pain – I was taking blows, and my forearms burned, but to stop was to surrender to death.

Marsyas rose from the pile of our dead, his sword in his hand. I saw him – a flash, but a complete impression, because his armour was beautifully worked, and because his battle cry was 'Helen', of all things.

And then Hephaestion came up behind Marsyas, and behind him were the hypaspitoi. They ploughed over the Sogdians in the breach and I was swept along with them into a fort that had, by the time I was in control of myself, already fallen.

The hypaspitoi and the Bactrians under Cyrus, who had come up the gully unopposed and stormed the south wall, now butchered the garrison. No one tried to surrender, and the fighting went on and on – new pockets of resistance were found in alleys, on rooftops, and as the men began to break formation to loot and rape, they found men cowering in basements or tight-lipped in courtyards, and killed them.

Polyperchon's men came late into the town. They had baulked, left me to die and then been threatened with decimation – death for one man in every ten – by Alexander in person, lying on a litter. I missed it, but he went mad, so I was told by Cleitus, spitting, calling them the sons of whores. Alexander, who never swore. Well, almost never.

When they came into the town, they went on an orgy of destruction and killing. The hypaspitoi had rounded up fifty or so women and some children – to be sold as slaves. Don't imagine they were rescued for any altruistic purpose. Polyperchon's men found them by the breach and killed them all.

And then they started killing Cyrus's men.

At first, the Bactrians ran, or called for help, or pleaded that they were allies – friends.

Then they started fighting back.

I was sitting on a chair in the former agora – a looted chair. I had a nasty gash on my thigh and something was wrong in my lower back, and there was blood trickling from somewhere and running down my arse and my leg – all I wanted to do was sleep, or at least rest. And Polystratus, bless him, had found me some pomegranate juice – in the midst of a massacre, that's a miracle. He'd been knocked out – clean unconscious – by a blow to the head, but taken no other wound.

I saw the fighting start across the square.

I cursed.

Got to my feet. And, I'm not ashamed to say, I finished my juice before I went to save Polyperchon's men.

I was so angry that I didn't bother to think. I walked up to the fighting, and I killed one of the Macedonians with a thrust to the face.

He was a phylarch, and he'd probably fought at Chaeronea. I didn't particularly care. I put him down, and I stood over him and let my rage have voice.

'You stupid fucks are killing our Bactrians!' I roared.

They flinched.

I smacked one man who had his sword raised – I swung the spear so hard he moved a foot or two and fell in a heap, out cold.

'Anyone else?' I roared.

My friends – my own companions – began to close around me.

Alexander was there. He'd been carried into the fort on a litter, and had Hephaestion with him.

There wasn't much I could say, standing there with the blood of a Macedonian officer on my spear.

Alexander was white with pain, but he nodded to me. 'Your precious pezhetaeroi,' he said. 'The sooner have I replaced them ...'

I had never heard him say it. Just at that moment, I was angry enough to agree, but even an hour later, I was calm, and I began to think of what it meant that Alexander no longer trusted his troops. I wondered if he even knew what was wrong.

They wanted to go home. And they *hated* our Persian and Bactrian 'allies'.

And when Cyrus embraced me, he said, 'I tell my men! That you are not like the others.'

In other words, our Bactrians and Persians didn't love us, either.

Two days later, Alexander was off his litter and leading another assault. I was the one on the litter – it turned out that I had an arrow in my back. It had penetrated my thorax and the wool chiton under it, and gone in the distance of a man's finger to the first joint, right over the fat that surrounds the kidney.

Most of the men who'd taken arrow wounds were raving. The Sogdians poisoned their arrows, and while only a few men died, the rest were in pain, groaning, screaming, with fevers and sweats.

I was, it turned out, suddenly very unpopular indeed with the army. My killing of a Macedonian made me one of 'them'. One of the men who was against the old ways. No one seemed to care that the useless fucks had left me to die in the breach. Men I'd led at Gaugamela turned away when my litter passed them.

That's how bad the army was getting.

Alexander was wounded again at the sixth fort. He took a rock – thrown from high on the wall – to the head, and went down.

Our Bactrians and our Persians stormed the fort with the hypaspitoi. Hephaestion stood over Alexander with his shield, and Black Cleitus got him clear of the fighting.

The seventh fort surrendered, with a garrison of six thousand men. But that day, a hundred men came in from the steppe and reported that Pharnuches had been ambushed by the Sakje, or the Massagetae, or possibly Spitamenes himself. He'd lost his entire command. Fewer than three hundred men had survived.

Alexander ordered the prisoners from the last fort to be executed. He had the most recent Sogdian recruits and the men of Polyperchon's taxeis do it as a test, or a punishment. The Sogdians were killing their own brothers. The Macedonians were performing an ugly task, and they knew why.

Eumenes convinced him *not* to execute the survivors or Pharnuches's column. But they were sworn to secrecy. Eumenes had joined the inner circle, and the conspiracy to keep Alexander sane.

But pain made the king savage, and the atmosphere of the camp reflected it.

After a week of recuperating, we raced west to rescue Marakanda, because its loss would sever our supply chain. Spitamenes melted away, and we relieved the city.

Craterus went off with a column to pursue Spitamenes – lost him at the edge of the steppe and managed to get into a fight with a party of Sauromatae and Sakje who had disciplined Greek cavalry with them. He lost, and retreated, abandoning his wounded – our third defeat in a month. We'd lost thousands of mercenaries in the forts, in the storming actions, to Spitamenes' raids and now to the Sauromatae on the steppe.

Alexander's wounds were so bad that he couldn't see from time to time, and bone splinters were continually appearing from the leg wound and his collarbone. He was in so much pain that he stayed in his tent, and the Persians he'd surrounded himself with used the time to wall the rest of us off from the king.

Worst of all, Spitamenes was gathering men on the steppe.

Using Marakanda as a headquarters, the king devised a new strategy from his bed. He had the infantry move along the rivers, fortifying. We began to plant garrisons in every valley and on every hilltop, and using the wonderful horses we were taking as tribute from every chieftain we conquered, we mounted as many men as we could and divided the mounted army into five mobile columns. The infantry garrisoned the new forts we built over the winter and the cavalry swept between the forts.

Hephaestion had a column. Alexander had one for himself. Craterus had one. Coenus shared one with Artabazus. And I had one.

Spitamenes beat Coenus and took one of our border posts. I had a brush with your pater across the Jaxartes. I'm not ashamed to say I did everything wrong. My column was almost all Sogdians – recent converts – and I *thought* I was shadowing Spitamenes, but he'd slipped between our columns and raided south.

Instead, I caught a tiger. We fought in a dust storm – I've never seen the like – and it was virtually impossible to see across the battlefield. My men held the battlefield – but only because your pater wanted to slip away, and he did.

Your Spartan friend Philokles brought me in as a prisoner. Do you know this story? I said some unfortunate things to your father. I met your mother – not as a prisoner, but as a mother. I saw you at her breast.

You know, lad, when I sit here – beside his tomb – in the fullness of my power, King of Aegypt, Pharaoh of the Two Crowns – I can see them around the fire, at the edge of the great steppe. Your pater and his men. Philokles, who made me feel a complete fool – he still does – and your pater, who reminded me that he had been thrown away by Alexander and owed Macedon nothing. Your mother, who'd been our prisoner.

And yet I was happy to be with them. They were great men, and they were philoi. In my thoughts, I have often compared Kineas and the king. Your pater loved war – he loved the planning, the scouting, the organisation, the movement, the action. But he never loved the killing, nor did he ever tell me stories of his prowess. And when, on the banks of the river, he and Diodorus offered to let me join them – I should have been outraged. But I was tempted, because the king was losing his mind from hubris and from pain.

And because he loved war a different way, and he didn't want the company of his peers. He wanted only to be the absolute master of all men.

Your pater released me, and Philokles rode me clear of the Sakje and down to the edge of the Jaxartes.

'Last chance,' he said. He smiled. 'I know you won't change sides. But I'd bet a cup of good wine you could just ride away.'

I smiled, because he had the right of it. I would never have betrayed the king, but I was tempted to use the moment and vanish. Harpalus did, later.

Philokles clasped hands with me. 'Remember what Srayanka said,' he added. 'Tell Alexander not to cross the river. Spitamenes' time is almost done. The Massagetae are tired of him.'

That was precious information.

I rejoined my command south of the Jaxartes and we swept east along the river, staying well away from the Massagetae. When we returned to the army, I gave the king a severely edited brief – I knew how to edit a scouting report.

Alexander could not sort out the Massagetae from Spitamenes. That is, he understood that they weren't the same, that Spitamenes used Massagetae goodwill and manpower but didn't actually control them. But Alexander wasn't interested in listening to me. I'd been defeated, and I joined the ranks of the disgraced commanders.

He concentrated his columns around Marakanda and pushed north and east, and finally, east of Cyropolis, he faced the Massagetae confederation and all of Spitamenes' Persians across the Jaxartes.

We neither won nor lost.

I fought all day – two charges in the morning and two in the afternoon at the head of my Hetaeroi. Alexander was wounded in the fighting by the river when the Sauromatae almost collapsed our right flank, and the Macedonian infantry – the phalanx – had to cover our withdrawal across the river. I think it was the worst day that the Hetaeroi ever had. We lost men – we lost horses.

But the Massagetae could make no headway against the phalanx, and Spitamenes' men took a beating from our left-flank cavalry. I almost reached him myself. By the time we withdrew, the Massagetae may have felt victorious, but the Persian rebels had ceased to be an effective field force.

I've heard a hundred men who say we lost at Jaxartes river. But by Ares – we went across the river into the arrow storm, and we crushed Spitamenes. He mounted one more raid – *one*, and then he was through. Nor did the Massagetae want any more of fighting us.

Best of all, the situation forced our Macedonians to fight. They didn't fight well, but as Alexander put them in a position where the choices were to fight or to die, they chose to fight. After Jaxartes, the pezhetaeroi began to regain discipline. We didn't lose. Had we lost, we'd have been exterminated.

Alexander, however, was deeply affected by the battle. It was the closest he'd ever come to a loss, and he had never before failed to take the enemy camp, seize the enemy's baggage, provide his army with the benefits of victory.

Combined with four wounds in as many months, his lack of victory made him all too human. The god was hidden.

The man was angry.

As I have mentioned, the greatest internal problem facing our army – since we marched into Hyrkania – had been the division between 'old' Macedonian officers and 'new' Persian officers. This is a gross oversimplification. First, the rift was built on the factions left over from Parmenio's time. Alexander had begun to employ non-Macedonian officers from the first – Erigyus of Mytilene is a fine example. Philip did it as well. Philip was never afraid to employ Athenians, Spartans, Ionians – he'd hire whomever he could get, the best men, the most expensive.

Alexander merely continued that policy in Asia. He drafted Lydian cavalry after the Granicus, and as soon as we had Persian defectors, they were given rank and employment. Why not? I still cannot fully understand the anger of the 'old' faction.

But after Parmenio's death, the question was complicated by Alexander's attempts to be all things to all men – to be a Persian king for the Persians while remaining a Macedonian to us and being a Greek for the Greeks. He thought he was both clever and successful. He was not. And the worst of it was that none of us could tell him that he had failed – he never believed us. His hubris blinded him to the simple ignorant anger of his Macedonian phalangites, who wanted no part of putting Asians in the ranks of the phalanx.

The sad truth was that we knew – we, the officers – that there was nothing remarkable about Pella, or Amphilopolis – or Athens or Sparta. We could take young Bactrians or Persians or Lydians or Sogdians and make them passable pikemen. The phalanx – ours, not the Greek kind – won battles by walking forward relentlessly with courage, good training and really, really long pikes. Our veterans imagined themselves irreplaceable, but they were not.

We knew it, but again, the problem was far more complex than it appeared. Because the phalanx couldn't be replaced. They were the heart of the army, and if they mutinied – well, they could turn on us. Alexander had taken them on a five-year rampage across Asia, and he'd taught them that *anything* can be taken at the point of the spear. Including the King of Macedon.

We're still paying for that lesson. Eh?

At the same time, the king was losing touch with his staff. Even at Marakanda, even on campaign, he had a growing personal staff of subservient Asians. He liked it that way. Let's not mince words. He didn't want to be surrounded by the teasing and mockery of peers. He didn't want sharp-tongued friends reminding him of the consequences of his actions.

He was not Kineas.

That summer, the conflict boiled over and people died.

So did friendships.

Alexander gave a dinner to celebrate the appointment of Black Cleitus as the satrap of Bactria. Cleitus deserved the post – ten years of absolute loyalty – and we were getting Nearchus back, so Alexander could spare Cleitus.

And Cleitus had developed an unfortunate habit on campaign – the habit of needling Alexander about his own failings. Cleitus didn't have the brilliant mind that Alexander had, but he was thoughtful, penetrating – and as the man who had most often saved the king's life, he was free to speak his mind.

Increasingly, he did. And thus it came as no surprise to me that Alexander was sending him away.

I was lying on my couch, far from the inner circle. No amount of hard fighting at Jaxartes could restore my reputation. I had lost a fight, even though I had had only Sogdian tribesmen in my command and had taken very few casualties. And as I say, the king was isolating himself from anyone who might have spoken out, and that included me.

Which, I must confess, was fine. I was sick of him.

That night, I had just decided to be unfaithful to my Thaïs. It was a funny sort of decision – we'd never pledged to each other and thus, I felt, my honour was fully engaged. She was free to take lovers – she was, after all, a courtesan, a matter of which she never ceased to remind me when she was angry. I hadn't seen her in a year.

I'm making excuses. I had purchased a Circassian – fine-looking – as a slave. I hadn't allowed myself to think what I was doing, but the longer I owned her – well, make your own conclusions. I lay on my couch in the dust, angry with myself and drunk and ready to behave badly. I was anxious to leave the dinner, go back to my tent and see how far her willingness would extend. I assumed that it would extend quite far.

I drank more. We are never worse than when we are about to behave badly. And conscience – I have to laugh. I could have fucked a slave a day, and no man in that army would have thought the worse of me.

Alexander was busy rehashing every battle he'd fought. He was talking about the enemy commanders he'd killed or maimed in single combat.

I'd heard it all before, and I tuned him out, until he mentioned Memnon.

I was daydreaming of my soon-to-be concubine – a mixture of salacious thoughts and anger at my own weakness – when I realised that the king had just claimed that he had killed Memnon at Halicarnassus.

I shook my head.

Black Cleitus laughed. He was lying on the king's right, as was proper since it was his day. He snorted, as he used to do when they were boys and he thought that Alexander was getting above himself.

'Memnon died of the flux at Mytilene,' Cleitus said.

Alexander stopped. Who knew what went on in that head? But he shrugged. 'Who are you to argue with me?' he asked. He was very drunk. 'I am the very god of war, and you are merely one of my warriors.'

Cleitus barked his snorting laugh again. 'You're a drunk fuck, and saying you are the god of war is blasphemy. Don't be an arse!'

Alexander got to his feet, and then tripped over something on the floor and almost fell. The unaccustomed clumsiness made him angrier. 'Zeus is my father! I have waded in blood and made war across the earth, and I don't have to listen to you – what have you ever done for me?'

Cleitus had thus far played carefully, but this stung him, and he leaped from his couch. 'Saved your useless life, ingrate!' he roared.

Never tell the truth to the powerful.

Lysimachus rolled off his couch. Hephaestion got a hand on the king, and Lysimachus and Perdiccas both got between the king and Cleitus.

Alexander, in the hands of Lysimachus, leaned forward, his face red, and yelled, 'Your sword couldn't have kept a child alive! Name me a victory *you* have won? Any of you? Of the lot of you, I'm the only one who can fight and win.'

I'd got hold of Cleitus by then. I could see what was coming, and I was damned if I was going to allow Cleitus to lose his position in the army. But I couldn't get anyone to help me and I couldn't shut him up – a problem I'd had since childhood, to be frank.

'You know who you remind me of?' Cleitus shouted. 'Philip. Your fucking drunk *father*. It is a shameful thing, for you – the King of fucking Macedon – to humiliate your own men – who have followed you across the world – in the midst of these enemies and foreign traitors!' Cleitus spat. 'You insult your best men – who have been unfortunate – while jackals laugh at them, who have never faced an enemy sword!'

Alexander turned to Perdiccas. 'I have never before heard cowardice described as misfortune,' he said, intending to be heard. 'Although now that I hear it so described, I suppose it is the bitterest misfortune a man can endure!'

696

Cleitus got a hand free from me. I was trying to get anyone to help, but the men closest to the king on couches were sycophants, flatterers, vultures – not men who would help me, even if they had the courage to try.

'Was I a coward at the Granicus? If my sword hadn't been by you, you would have been dead there and twenty other places.' Cleitus slammed his elbow into my stomach to get me off him, but I was ready – I rolled with the blow and got an arm around his neck.

'It is by our blood, our wounds, that you have risen so high!' Cleitus called. 'You think that *you* did this, Alexander? You think that *you* won those victories? Your hubris disgusts every *man* here. Your father built this army – your father Philip. You pretend that a god is your father! It's a lie! You are a man!'

'That's how you talk about me behind my back, isn't it!' Alexander said, quite clearly. And he wasn't looking at Cleitus. He was looking at me. Perdiccas later told me that Alexander looked at him, too.

I believe it. I think, by then, the king wanted us all gone. All the boys of his childhood. All the ones who knew that he was a man, and not a god.

Alexander turned back to Cleitus, suddenly icy and calm. 'I know the things you say behind my back,' he said. He turned slowly, and pointed with his free hand – Lysimachus still had his left – at Cleitus. 'You and your friends cause all the bad blood between my Macedonians and my Persians. Don't imagine you are going to get away with it!'

Cleitus stood straight. Something in Alexander's tone sobered him for a moment. 'Get away with it?' he asked. 'We're dying for you every day, Alexander. And the ones who live get to bow down like sodomites and show their arses like these Persian fucks! While you wander around in a white dress and a diadem like a play-actor!'

Alexander turned to Eumenes, who had joined the men trying to restrain him. 'Don't you feel that the Macedonians are like beasts? Any Greek is like a god by comparison.'

Cleitus punched me in the eye. It hurt, and he was about to launch himself at the king, so I swung hard and hit him in the head.

Alexander picked up an apple – it was the first thing under his hand – and threw it at Cleitus, hitting him in the face.

I think Cleitus confused the two blows. Either way, he went off his head, drink and pain combining to make him bellow like a bull. But by then Marsyas had his other arm, together with Philip the Red.

We began to drag him, step by step, from the tent.

Perdiccas got the king in a choke hold, and Leonatus – the king's friend – took the king's sword from its scabbard and hurled it across the tent as Alexander reached for it. He went for the knife he always wore around his neck, but Lysimachus beat him to it – the king was so enraged he was ready to knife the men who had hold of him. As he wrestled with three men, his inhuman strength bearing *all three* of them down, he shouted, 'It is a plot! To me! They are trying to murder me! Sound the alarm!'

His hyperetes refused. He had his trumpet, and he shook his head, eyes narrowed – like a proper Macedonian, he could make his own decisions about the king's state. He wasn't a slave. And when one of the Persian vultures grabbed for the trumpet to blow it – to sound the alarm, and summon the hypaspitoi – the king's hyperetes bashed the Persian with the trumpet and put him down.

I had Cleitus clear of the tent by then, and I wrestled him out into the cooler night air, and Marsyas, whose wounds were suddenly bleeding again – Cleitus was struggling as hard as the king – kicked Cleitus in the balls.

Cleitus bellowed again, and flattened Marsyas with one blow, breaking his nose. And I missed my hold, and Cleitus stumbled back into the tent, where the king was shouting 'Turn out the guard!' at the top of his lungs and Perdiccas was trying to get a hand over his mouth.

I was right behind Cleitus. He got all the way into the command tent, and drew himself up. 'Alas!' he roared. 'What evil government is come to Hellas?'

The hypaspitoi surged in through the doors, and it was over – I could tell just looking at the men coming in, in full armour, that they had been warned. Their faces were set, and they didn't move to surround the king – rather, they moved to prevent any further violence. Alexander sagged against his captors.

Cleitus held his arms wide. 'When the public sets up a war trophy, do the men who sweated get the credit? Oh, no – some strategos takes all the prestige!' He was quoting from Euripides' *Andromache*. 'Who, waving his spear, one among thousands, did one man's work, but receives a world of praise. Such self-important "fathers of their country" think they are better than other men. They are worth nothing!'

Alexander ripped his arms free from Perdiccas and Leonatus. And in one step, he had the spear – a short longche – from the hypaspist closest to him, and he plunged it to the socket through Cleitus, who was, of course, wearing no armour.

I saw the spear-point come through his back.

His mouth opened.

I'm told his eyes never left the king's face.

And he died.

Coenus, Perdiccas and I were exiled a few weeks later to chase Spitamenes. That's not how it was put to us, but that was the truth of it. Leonatus had already been sent away.

The king mourned for three days, until the weasel Anaxarchus told him that as he was a god, he was above the law. He justified the king's actions, and the king accepted his word and moved on.

So much for his closest friend, the man who had stood by him since infancy.

After Cleitus died, we – the former inner circle – knew that no man was safe. Philotas, to some extent, had it coming – Parmenio had always been the king's rival. But Cleitus was merely blunt – his loyalty had never been questioned, and without him, the king would have died. Several times.

I wanted no more of it. When I was sent to find and defeat Spitamenes, I went happily.

And we caught him. He had three thousand Dahae cavalry and several hundred of his Persian adherents, but the forts kept us informed by beacon, and too many villagers had had enough – or perhaps they were more scared of us than they were of Spitamenes. We cornered him in a deep valley, and while Perdiccas took his taxeis up the hillside to block their retreat, Coenus and I charged home. We broke the Dahae easily enough – they didn't want our kind of fight – and most of the Persians surrendered. They had had enough.

In a matter of weeks, we had Spitamenes' head. And that was the end of his revolt. Overnight, a man who had held us longer than Memnon *or* Darius was gone, killed by his own wife, and we were, at last, masters of Sogdiana.

I was between Coenus and Perdiccas, riding slowly, because our column was tired and because we were done and our men weren't in the mood to be hurried.

I took a breath, enjoying the mountain air for the first time in two years. 'I think ...' I said, and Perdiccas grinned.

'Do you?' he asked. 'I thought I smelled something.'

I punched him. 'I think we have to make him go home now,' I said.

Perdiccas nodded, the happy look wiped from his face. 'Do you think – if we get him home ...'

Coenus laughed. It was a desperate laugh.

I turned. 'We can get him home,' I said. 'If we work at it.'

Coenus wiped his eyes for a moment. 'We're not going home,' he said. 'We're invading India. In the spring.'

I was still in charge of the army's food and supplies, and I hadn't heard a word of it. But then, I'd been out of favour half a year.

In fact, it was another year before we marched on India. The king was careful about the reconquest of Sogdiana, and he developed a lust of heroic proportions (the only kind of lust he ever had, really) for the daughter of one of the Sogdian chieftains – Roxanne – or so he claimed. She probably saved a lot of lives with her superb face and lush, velvety skin.

We received drafts from home, and Alexander mustered our veterans – as many as he could. And he began to bring foreign officers closer in – he tried to appoint Cyrus to command half of the Hetaeroi in place of Cleitus, and Hephaestion talked him out of it.

I was scarcely paying attention. With the Prodromoi and all the intelligence I could muster, I was trying to figure out how to feed the army when it marched east, to India. The king arrested Callisthenes on a trumped-up charge, and I can't pretend I'd ever loved him, although he was better than the lickspittle Anaxarchus. Alexander tried – repeatedly – to induce us to perform the proskynesis. Leonatus mocked any man who did, and Polyperchon was arrested in Alexander's presence for direct refusal. And again, Hephaestion went to the king and begged him to relent.

A group of pages plotted to kill the king. But, in the best tradition of Philip's court, they fell out among themselves – sex and dominance were involved. Alexander had them executed, and used the incident to justify moving against the Macedonian faction, which had been 'proved' disloyal, and after the fact he implicated Callisthenes in the plot and executed him.

He had become quite dangerous to be around.

I avoided him. I spent the year riding as far east as Taxila, the ruler of which was already an ally. I was laying in stores for thirty thousand men. I had given up on getting the king home. I was willing to get him into a war.

THIRTY-SIX

~~~

When we sat on the stone bench in the Gardens of Midas, Aristotle taught us about the shape of the world, and the shape of the universe. He taught us ethics and morals and ideals of rulership, and I dare say he was wrong about a great many things. After all, he was chiefly responsible for Alexander.

I like to think that he did better with me. For one thing, he felt free to correct me more often.

But I am dithering.

One of the things that Aristotle had quite horribly wrong was the geography of the East. And it is odd, when you are a grown man, the commander of armies, the lord of millions, how mistakes learned in your youth continue to shape your thinking, despite some intellectual awareness that all is not quite right. I knew a man once – a Persian slave who was freed in Athens. He had adopted Greek ways – he abjured the worship of Ahuru Mazda, and worshipped Zeus and Apollo. But he always turned to the sun to pray in the morning, regardless of circumstance.

Or put another way, all of us make the peasant signs for luck, for aversion of evil, even long after we accept that they are nothing but superstition.

And who does not remember their first lover with a sudden bolt of lust?

Hah! How would you know? But you will.

The point is, Alexander's confusion about the shape of the world had profound consequences. And he continued to make strategic decisions based on those confusions, despite a constant stream of scouting reports and intelligence reports provided by trustworthy agents and edited by his staff. He believed that if we crossed the Jaxartes and travelled north, we would come to the Euxine. I knew better – but then I had met Kineas and Philokles, and they had *come* from the Euxine.

Likewise, Alexander believed, when we were relaxing at Persepolis, that Cyrus's former province of India marked the edge of the world – that beyond the land of elephants and spices lay the ocean, and beyond that the rim of the world.

By the time we crossed the Kush, I knew better, and Craterus knew better, and Ariston certainly knew better. But Alexander either didn't read our reports, or didn't understand them – little possibility of that – or didn't care.

He planned an invasion based on any number of false assumptions. He assumed that India was roughly the size of Bactria, and that it had a finite end – at the ocean.

As was often the case, his views communicated themselves to the army. And he reputedly said – I was not there – that India was the last, because it had been part of Cyrus's empire, and Alexander felt that if he reconquered all of the mighty Cyrus's possessions, he would be accepted by the Persians as a legitimate ruler.

And he was right.

We had most of the great nobles of the empire serving in the army by the time we crossed the passes. Alexander reorganised the army *again* at Alexandria-the-Farthest, our base in the endless mountains of Bactria at the head of the Khyber. This time, he put a squadron of Persian noble cavalry with every squadron of Hetaeroi. I got one of these pairs, with Cyrus and his retinue now promoted to command the other – we had been the experiment from the first, which, to be honest, I'd always suspected. I liked Persians – I was used as a test case for everything from acceptable rations (Greeks and Persians won't always feel the same way about food) to matters of sex and cleanliness.

The Persian cavalry was excellent. Thaïs told me in a letter that Alexander had also recruited thirty thousand Persian and Mede youths as infantry, and they were receiving training. He used the old Kardakes system, and it ran well enough.

Before we departed Alexandria, we received drafts from home – recruits from Macedon and Greek mercenaries, as well as some Lydians and Phrygians. The Macedonians looked outlandish to all of us, in their clean white wool chitons, bare necks (we all wore the local scarves) and wide-eyed innocence – and these were men who had survived to march out to us from Macedon, so they were hardly *new*. By the time we headed south, we had almost sixty thousand men for the invasion of India – but fewer than fifteen thousand of them were Macedonians. We were, to all intents and purposes, a Persian army.

And Alexander was a Persian king, with a court, a harem he never visited, and priests, augurs and other useless mouths I had to feed. He wanted an audience for the conquest of one more province.

But from the height of the main pass into Taxila, any doubts the king may have had about the extent of India were dispelled. Aristotle had insisted that we would see the mighty outer ocean from the height of the Kush. Alexander kept asking men about the ocean – we knew that Scylax, the Greek explorer, had been to India by sea in the time of Marathon, and I had his book, which wasn't especially useful, but it did name port cities in India.

We looked out from the height of the Khyber Pass and saw – India. Hill country, and folds of hills running away to the south, into a lower range of mountains at the edge of vision far away beyond the vale of the Indus.

Cavalry scouts who had been to Taxila and beyond reported that from the height of the Orminus range – the very limit of the geography of our Persian officers – you could see green fields stretching away south for five hundred stades, at least.

We were invading a country the size of Greece, at the very least, and perhaps the size of Europe. Or Asia.

I gathered the reports, and no one could tell me how big India was. I had one report from a merchant who said that to travel from one side of the country to another took more than a year. If this was true, then India was the size of Asia, and we were doomed to an eternal war.

I remember that I stopped my horse – a handsome Sakje mare that Kineas had given me and I still rode by preference – at the height of the pass. The column had been slowing and stopping all day as men paused to take in the view. I was with Perdiccas's taxeis.

A familiar voice growled by my left foot.

'Where's the fewkin' ocean, then?' Amyntas son of Philip, phylarch of the third company of Craterus's taxeis, was standing looking under his hand at the rolling brown hills of Tiausa.

I looked down. 'A little farther,' I said, the eternal staff officer.

Amyntas spat. Looked up. 'How's the daughter, then?' he said.

'Olympias will be ordained a full priestess at the Great Feast of Artemis,' I said, and he grinned.

'Good for her.' He smiled wickedly. 'And that nice priest boy?'

'A stade away. A fine soldier.'

'He is, at that,' said the old bastard. 'I see him all the time. And you, old man?'

'Amyntas son of Philip, you dare call me old? Weren't you at Marathon? Still alive?' I took his hand. 'And you are older, I think.'

He waved at the hills in the far distance. Men filed past us. And suddenly, he turned and said, 'He's fuckin' insane, ain't he? I mean,

703

he'll just march east until we all die – and then he'll replace us with local sods, right? Am I right?'

Men around us were murmuring.

'How's Dion?' I asked. Then I winced. I'd forgotten.

'Dead at Arabela. Bloody flux,' he said. 'Told you that last year, when you held the sacrifice.'

'And the young man? Charmides?' I asked.

'Dead – can't exactly remember where. Hey, Red, where'd Charmides go to earth?' he called out to a phylarch who was resting both hands on his spear and staring out over the earth.

'After Marakanda?' The man shrugged. There was a pause, and then he said, 'I think. Aphrodite's tits, Amyntas – he died – at ...?'

Amyntas shrugged. 'Boys like him come and go so fast, we don't bother to learn their names any more. The shit they send us from Pella – Zeus Soter, sir, are they out of men in Macedon?' He looked at a dozen new recruits filling the two nearest files. They weren't big men.

'Antipater's keeping the best for hisself,' another man suggested. 'Sending us thieves and urchins.'

'I'm no thief!' a young man protested with some spirit, and Amyntas stepped right up to him. His hand moved as if for a blow, but paused with perfect efficiency to stroke the boy's cheek as gently as a mother.

'No,' he said, laughing. 'If you were a thief, you'd have a useful skill. As it is, you're not worth a fuck. And that's the *literal* truth.'

The boy was shaking.

'Go easy, soldier. You need him to press his shield into your back when we fight in India.' I smiled at the new boy.

Amyntas spat. 'Then I'm fuckin' dead already, sir.' But he laughed. 'I'm the right phylarch, now.' The senior file leader. The man responsible for the dressing of the battalion, the order of march – a very important man indeed.

'Congratulations,' I said.

He smiled. 'All the people who could do the job better are dead. That don't say much for me.'

The column had started to move out. Sweating bearers – servants of the common soldiers – were carrying enormous bundles on their backs and heads and heavy forked sticks on their shoulders like yokes. They marched with their masters, in files in between the soldiers' files.

The bearers picked up their packs, the soldiers took one last gulp of water or wine, and the column began to move.

'Of the ten men in my file, when we left Macedon, I'm the only one still alive,' Amyntas said.

Those words stuck with me, all the way down the pass.

*

The next night, Alexander summoned a council. It was remarkably like the old days – consciously so – and no sooner was I handed a cup of wine than I saw that he was elated, his eyes glittering, his face almost unlined, the energy glowing in his skin.

He embraced me as soon as I had a cup of wine. 'I have missed you, Ptolemy!' he said.

An odd remark, if you consider that I briefed him twice a week on matters related to food and logistics – and more often still about geography and intelligence. But it is true, we had had little enough to say to each other as men since before Marakanda.

'I'm right here,' I said, or something equally inane – but Alexander, on his way to his next embrace, stopped, and looked back. Perhaps I'd put more emotion into my statement than I meant.

'You sound bitter, Ptolemy.' Alexander's eyes met mine, and they were brimful of power. Not madness. Just will.

I shook my head.

Alexander greeted Perdiccas, Lysimachus, Coenus. But he made a point of coming back and standing by me.

'Listen, then!' he said, and the babble of gossip stopped.

It was years since I'd seen him look so well rested – and so happy.

'India,' he said. 'Our last campaign together,' he added, with a smile in my direction. 'I suppose there will be some hill tribes to subdue. But this is Cyrus's last conquest – and I know you all want me to go home.'

It took my breath away – that he said it right out, without whining, or crying, or killing someone.

And yet, the cynic in my soul whispered that a wine-bibber is always telling his wife he'll quit, too.

But it made me happy. Of course, the wine-bibber's wife is happy, too. For a little while.

He looked around, and my feelings were exposed on every face – even men like Craterus. Relief. Quiet joy, or merely exhaustion.

He nodded, as if he'd been talking to someone else. 'But I have one favour to ask,' he said. Nodded again. 'I want you all to be at your very *best*. You think you are tired and far from home?' He looked around. 'We are living in myth. We are the cutting edge of an epic. We are the heroes of the *Iliad*. When we march home to Babylon and Pella, we will be leaving behind *this* – the existence that is greater than the merely mortal. If this is my last great campaign – make it your best. Eh?'

I don't think his words reached Craterus. But Perdiccas met my eye. We were both smiling.

Alexander never gave speeches. Or when he did, they sounded a little forced.

Coenus was smiling, and Lysimachus, and Seleucus, now commanding the hypaspitoi.

'I'm going to send Perdiccas and Hephaestion down the Indus, to pick off the cities on the river. Craterus, you and I and Seleucus will go north on the Choaspes. The rendezvous is Gandaris. The Raja of Taxila is our ally – Ptolemy is in contact with him already, and we have depots marked on your itineraries. The order of march is here. Any questions?'

People asked questions – Seleucus especially. He always did.

When they ran out of questions, Alexander looked around. He had set himself a Herculean task, and that put him on the plane of the gods. He was happy. He was also not wearing the diadem, not wearing a white robe. He was in a plain chitoniskos, dressed like any Macedonian aristocrat after a day of war, or hunting. First among equals.

'Anything more?' he asked. He looked around.

He was *beaming*.

'Let's go and conquer India, then,' he said.

While Hephaestion took the main army straight downriver – straight being a remarkable thing to say of the upper Indus – and Alexander went off into the trackless wooded mountains of the Chaispes, I had a different role – as the linchpin between the two columns. I had my squadrons and Philip the Red with me, and together we kept the two columns in contact. I had the Paoenians and most of the Prodromoi and Ariston to command them, and all the Agrianians, who we'd mounted on mules, and Strako's Angeloi, who'd been expanded with locals into a small squadron. It was one of my favourite commands – the perfect instrument for the job. We could cover hundreds of stades of ground – at one point I had men along both banks of the Indus all the way down to the plains below Taxila – or combine to fight. And the preponderance of scouts allowed me to gather information for the future while supporting the king and Hephaestion. And my central location allowed me to control supplies to both columns. I was in constant contact with Eumenes. Information flowed, logistics were put in place.

We were a superb instrument of war. Even if that meant we ate men's souls.

From a purely military standpoint, the oddest thing about the Taxila campaign was that the Raja had already made submission, and his city provided us with supplies and convoys of grain, which came from *in front*. The usual problem of supply is bringing it up from the rear, and supplying our army over the Hindu Kush would have been brutal. But from the front – I never experienced anything like it – all I had to do was move my cavalry and cover the convoys.

Alexander plunged into the mountains with a fervor that verged on the reckless, and got an arrow in his arm leading the first assault on a hill town a week later. I arrived a few days after, with a convoy of wine and olive oil all the way from Syria – a convoy that *had* come over the Hindu Kush. Greek and Macedonian soldiers need wine and olive oil. Without them, they will function, but they won't like it. With them, they may go without food, but they will fight.

At any rate, he was lying on a kline, reading one of my reports and eating grapes. He looked up and made a face.

'Ptolemy!' he said.

I had to grin. It was good to be liked and valued. Again.

'I brought you wine,' I said. 'Good wine. There's some Lesbian stuff and some Chian.' I handed him a small amphora. 'And this. Antipater sent it.'

Alexander raised an eyebrow.

'What happened?' I asked, pointing at the heavy bandage on his sword arm.

'Hephaestion will scold me,' he said. He rolled his eyes. 'I led an assault and I got shot.' He shrugged. 'It was fun. And it is just a scratch.' He sat up on his bed. 'I don't mean to make a scene, Ptolemy, but take that amphora out and smash it on a rock.'

I made a face. 'I'll take it and drink it,' I said.

He turned. 'Do not,' he said. 'It's sure to be poisoned, and you are one of my few remaining friends.'

I was? Who knew? I was tempted to say as much, but instead, I shook my head. 'Antipater?' I asked.

'I'm sure of it,' he said. He shrugged, winced when he moved his right shoulder. Lay back. 'Thaïs says so,' he went on.

That was the first I had heard that Thaïs was continuing to provide the king with information. We exchanged our own letters.

I had freed the Circassian. Cleitus's death had that good effect – I never bedded her. Funny – when I told Thaïs the story, she shook her head, touched my face and said I was a fool.

Am I a fool? I am what I am. And I suppose that Alexander would say the same.

I stayed with him for two days, while his siege engines pounded a high stone keep to flinders and Seleucus stormed it. Then we moved on, and Alexander's shoulder was better, and at the next big stone keep – they seemed to grow on the mountains like mushrooms – Alexander insisted on leading the assault. Again.

'I'll go with you,' I said.

Alexander nodded. 'Of course you will,' he said.

They should have surrendered. Mind you, no bandit chief on the wheel of the earth could have imagined that the Great King, King of Kings, would drag eighty war engines through the Hindu Kush and over the Khyber Pass simply to break the tyranny of the chiefs in the Swat hills.

'This region has raided Taxila and the plains for generations,' Alexander said as the men behind us fidgeted in the pre-dawn mist. 'I intend to crush the warlords and break the war bands down into manageable sizes.'

I made a face. I assumed he couldn't see me in the dark.

But we *had* grown up together, and he shook his head. 'You're thinking that it is a lot of trouble,' he said. I saw his teeth gleam. 'But it is worth doing well. War is a craft like any other – but you know that – you put the food in my army's gullet.'

'I try,' I said. It was nice to have him talking. 'What about the chiefs and their retinues?'

'Shed no tears for them. Ask any peasant in the valley what it's like to live under – literally under – these bandits.' He sounded passionate. Interesting.

'These people don't even know who we are,' I pointed out.

'They will before morning,' the king said.

We crept up the hill in the last darkness. We put ten ladders up against the wall, and then, far too late to save themselves, the defenders threw lit torches into the ditch and began to loose arrows at us.

Alexander was wearing greaves, but one of the arrows caught him in the ankle and he almost fell off the ladder. I pinned him against it. Then, because going down was out of the question, we went up.

He was the first on the wall, and he moved like the athlete he was, and his sword rose and fell and stabbed the way a skilled seamstress's needle moves, with perfect economy. I was only heartbeats behind him, and still he had killed or mortally wounded three men before I had my feet over the parapet.

There was a rush along the top of the wall, and it came at my side. I turned, put my shield into my attackers and my aspis all but filled the catwalk. They pushed me back, and I cut under the shield – and then back over. My opponents were being pushed forward by their mates. I scored across one man's thigh under my shield and raked another's nose – no kills, but they flinched, and I backed up a full step and then *pushed*, caught one man off balance and he fell off the wall.

I couldn't risk a glance, but I did wonder where in Hades the king was.

Behind me, I could hear him. He bellowed, 'Spear! Throw it!'

I had my right thumb in the hollow of my blade – a nasty technique I'd been taught by a hoplomachos, a Keltoi trick, and one I used when I had to fight at night. With your thumb pressed into the blade, your blade becomes the perfect companion to a circular shield. Your hand and elbow allow the blade to travel around the edge – parrying and striking in the same action.

I cut low – cut all the way around my shield – and a man groaned and fell to his knees. I kicked him and the rest pushed me back.

Something hit the crest of my helmet.

I stepped back, and a spear came over my shoulder and punched into the throat-bole of the man in front of me. And then, fast as lightning, a thrown spear hit the man to my right.

I stepped forward into the space left by the sudden corpses, and cut overhand – feint, backhand.

Another man fell.

Alexander stepped up so close that his knee was against my hip as I crouched, and he shot his spear out overhand and caught another man in the thigh, and he went down, and the knot of men behind him broke and ran for the tower.

Without speaking, we chased them – two men against a dozen.

Some fool opened the iron-bound door of the keep to let them in, and we were on them, hacking, cutting, side by side – they slammed the door, but Alexander put his spearhead into the door jamb with godlike precision, and the spear-point stuck in the wood of the jamb as he intended, and the door smashed against it and bounced from the fine steel.

The courtyard was filling with blood-mad hypaspitoi, and Seleucus led them against the door. The men inside struggled to hold it.

They failed.

We killed everyone in the tower.

Then we walked down the hill, back to camp. Alexander was de-lighted. He kept slapping my back and telling me he had missed me.

I kept wanting to tell him to stop playing war. I was tired, and I had a long scratch down the inside of my leg that had almost touched my testicles, and I was not in a particularly good mood. Slaughtering men raising their hands to surrender – it always sticks in my craw, like the last bite of a meal that's too big.

At the base of the hill, the sycophant Anaxarchus the priest stood with Anximander, the seer – brothers in crime, if you ask me.

Anaxarchus saw the blood flowing from the royal ankle. 'Ah, ichor from the wound of an immortal god!' he said. Always the man to go for the grossest flattery.

Alexander glanced at me. He flashed me a grin, and turned on Anaxarchus. 'Blood,' he said in weary disgust. 'Just blood. Don't blaspheme.'

All things to all people. Even me.

I loved him.

I went back to Hephaestion, coaxed a convoy over the brown ridges from Taxila, read reports on Porus, whose trans-Hydaspian kingdom was our immediate target south of the mountains, and was back with the king in time to see him open the siege of Nyasa. The town didn't resist more than a day, and surrendered on terms. It was *not* a bandit hold, but a small town full of people who looked nothing like the other inhabitants – they had strange customs, but beautiful women; they hung their dead in cedar coffins, from trees, but they were the first people in Asia to make decent wine. The vines grew on the mountains behind Nyasa, and we celebrated the Feast of Dionysus there, and we were all royally drunk, and Alexander didn't kill anyone.

I took another convoy north a week later, and Alexander was at the Rock of Aornus. The place was so high that the top was lost in clouds when I arrived – legend had it that Herakles and Dionysus had both failed to take the place.

Alexander refused to leave it alone. It was parasanges off our route, and we didn't need it, as we had Nyasa, but the mere mention of Herakles and he was off, armed with a fresh pothos, to do his best to emulate or exceed the hero.

We set the siege engines, which loosed their first rocks. They went up and up, and at perihedron, they were still *below* the level of the walls.

A week later, and Hephaestion was at the rendezvous. He willingly took my advice and started to build a set of bridges over the Indus while the main army built a fortified camp and supply magazine – more to make work than because we needed such a thing.

Back at Aornus, I was stunned by the scale of the king's ambition – I, who had known every one of his ambitions. He was building a trestle – a web of wood – that rose from the *next mountain*. It was *immense*.

It was almost complete. The troops were working like daimons.

Morale was incredibly high. Word was out – as the king intended – that this was the last campaign, and that the king had asked that every man do his best. It was a heady combination.

I went back south to meet another convoy from Taxila, then ordered

Ariston to scout south of Taxila, and then I went back to the king.

Eight days after opening his siege, the engines mounted on the trestle of wood began to loose stones into the town. The effect was devastating, and the dry-stone wall that crowned the fortress collapsed in eight or ten hits.

We stormed the place in the morning, right over the new breaches. The defenders weren't ready. Incredible, really.

We rolled south, linked up with Hephaestion and marched to Taxila.

THIRTY-SEVEN

S outh of Taxila, the hills rise once more in a shield, and then fall away into the endless plain of the Indus. We already had scouts in the plains, and we picked them up as we advanced, and used them as guides. And the Raja of Taxila, towering in the howdah of his elephant, was there in person to direct us. It was for his alliance that we were marching to fight Porus.

We marched from Taxila to the banks of the Hydaspes in two days – because we heard at Taxila that Porus was forging alliances in the plains and had eighty thousand men and two hundred elephants.

The army was just growing accustomed to elephants. We had forty of them, and we drilled alongside them, and our horses were often picketed near them – horses can be spooked by elephants; both their noises and their smell can affront even a battle-hardened mount. But we had no notion what squadrons of elephants could be like. Forty seemed like an army.

We had no notion what rain was like, either, until the monsoons broke. The king intended to fight in the monsoon, presumably because the Indians *didn't* and it would add to the sense of adventure. In fact, it reduced their archery to manageable proportions, which was good, as they had expert archers with great bows of bamboo that shot shafts heavy enough to penetrate a bronze thorax.

So we marched in rain so thick that at times it was difficult to breathe, and over roads that either became swamps or torrents. Despite that, we made eight to ten parasanges a day.

The Indians of the plains used chariots, too, which added to the Homeric element for all of us – enormous battle cars, with four or six horses yoked in a line, and four archers per swordsman and a pair of drivers. I encountered one in person on our third day after Taxila, when the Paeonians and a handful of our allied Indian cavalry ran into one of Porus's patrols across the river. The enemy commander was in a chariot as big, it seemed, as an elephant. His cavalry outnumbered mine by two to one or more.

I sent scouts out into the fields on either side, and they reported that the ground was solid enough. So I closed up my column, prepped my officers and rode straight at my opponent.

He began to deploy his cavalry.

A little more than a stade from the head of his column, and the rain stopped. I pumped my fist in the air – my only order of the hour – and my column unravelled in heartbeats. My units never attempted to form a line. Instead, as soon as any unit came up, they charged. The Indians were hit with a rolling series of squadron charges – every impact had its effect, and by the time Cyrus's second half-squadron of Persians rolled forward, the Indians were shattered.

We lost three troopers wounded and two dead, and we took fifty prisoners. Best of all, the action was over in the time it takes to sing a hymn. It was a small action – no empires fell – but I feel it shows where we were as a force – what we were capable of. Persians, Thracians, Greeks and Macedonians in one force, well trained, well disciplined, and I rather like to think well led. The Indians were good, but not like us at all. They couldn't fight from a column on a road.

That night, I was huddling by a spitting fire in the rain, happy as only a victorious commander with low casualties can be, and Bubores came to me with a wreath of some local plant – from the king, for my victory. He gave me a hug, and stayed to drink my wine.

I remember because he asked me to tell him how the fight had gone, and I just shrugged. 'Bubores, do you think this army has ever been a better weapon than it is right now?'

The Nubian looked into the fire – the coals, anyway – for a long time. 'No,' he said. 'The drill—'

'The high morale,' I said.

'The teamwork,' Polystratus said at my shoulder. 'It's never been better.'

I nodded. 'When it is like this,' I said quietly, 'I almost enjoy it. Hades, brothers – I *do* enjoy it. But those poor Indians never knew what hit them.'

Bubores nodded. 'But it is only because he says he'll go home, after.'

We all nodded, and the wine went around.

Anyway, I got a crown of laurel – or whatever India had that looked like laurel – because I captured their strategos's chariot. I sent it to Alexander, who received it with delight.

But Porus had beaten us to the river, despite our best efforts. And five days after we left Taxila, we were staring across the river at an army with almost a hundred thousand men and two hundred elephants. Porus was no fool. He covered the fords, and all the fords for parasanges up and down the river.

The rain fell.

The army moved up, and built a camp. I doubt that anyone, from footslogger to the King of Macedon, was *comfortable*, but one of the advantages of years of campaigning in every climate in the world is that your men learn to construct shelters, and this time, since it was clear we might be here for months, we floated logs down the river and built huts.

In fact, the king kept the troops moving, marching up and down the river, building small forts and feinting at various crossings.

Sometimes his brilliance lay in being a thorough master of his craft. For three weeks, every time a detachment marched out of camp, Porus sent twice the number of his Indian cavalry to shadow it along the far side of the river. Our men were still eager, but the wine and olive oil were mostly gone, and we were stymied in an endless quagmire of mud by a foe who outnumbered us.

I kept my lights together as a division. I enjoyed commanding them, and I expected the king to break them up into task forces every day, but he did not, and so I kept them busy, scouting the riverbanks.

Ariston found Adama Island, four parasanges north of the army, outside of Porus's patrol area. We poured men and supplies north once we'd found it, and all the engineers – twice they tried to bridge it, first with piling driven into the swollen banks, and the second time with a bridge of boats assembled on one bank and swayed across, as we'd done against the Thracians at the Danube.

The river was falling – the rains tapering off – but they couldn't get a bridge across.

Another week passed. Every day, the king was more difficult to live with – nervous, anxious, quick to anger. He expected Porus to find the potential crossing site any day, and build a fortification to cover it.

I had volunteered to take command at the island and get the advance guard across, and I was on my way to take my leave – already up to my ankles in mud, standing in *warm* rain – when Hephaestion came out of the king's tent, his face red and angry even in the watery light.

'Good morning,' I said.

He grunted. 'Going to see him? Good luck to you, Ptolemy. I'm ready to go home to Macedon and leave him.'

I gave him half a grin and went into the tent.

Alexander was staring at a sketch of the river. He looked at me. 'What?' he shot at me.

'I'm on my way upriver to try and get the bridge across.' I saluted. 'If it can be done, I'll do it.'

'If it can't be done, we're finished,' he said with uncharacteristic candour.

'So?' I asked.

He pursed his lips.

'Answer me this, Lord King – what difference does it make? Why are we fighting Porus?'

Alexander wrinkled his nose and made a face as if I'd asked a childish question. 'He lies across our path and you ask this?'

I shook my head. 'We're *invading his country*.' I laughed. 'We could just march away and *not* invade his country.'

'Perhaps I should send someone else to the island,' he said, only half joking.

We set the next night for our attempt to force the river. Alexander's plan was subtle, but simple. He was going to march the elites upriver – the Hetaeroi with their Persian counterparts, the hypaspitoi, three cavalry commands under Hephaestion, Perdiccas and Demetrios, as well as two big phalanx divisions with all the veteran Macedonians, and my command. We would cross, and try to turn Porus's position. At first light, on a day that promised to be fair, Craterus was to lead the main army across the river.

I had gathered every boat for ten parasanges, and floated them to our bank, as we had at the Danube. I had sixty Agrianians across already, in four forward pickets with fires.

Alexander arrived before full darkness, with the hypaspitoi. Diades floated the pontoon bridge, Helios got it staked in hard to the far bank and we had some long moments in the torchlit, soaking darkness until it swayed out into the current and stayed put. And then it broke loose.

It was just too short, and came all the way around, breaking ropes, to land against our bank. Luckily, we had dozens of Greek sailors, and they fended the boats off and then pulled them back upstream. Ropes were shifted for another try, and four more boats were lashed on to the end of the pontoon platform, and we had lost an hour.

Diades begged the king's forgiveness. Alexander sat bareheaded in the torchlight, surrounded by his officers, and watched, his eyes never leaving the ropes, the sailors and the boats.

Again they swayed the bridge out into the current. Again we saw Helios and his men drive in palings on the far side.

This time, they got their grapples into the far bank properly, and the bridge steadied in the current. The current took the bridge and slammed it downstream, but the hawsers held.

We waited.

They held.

I caught Cyrus's eye. 'Let's go,' I said, and led my household companions across the bucking bridge. But Alexander was ahead of me, with Seleucus and Lysimachus.

He cantered across the bridge. I rode more slowly.

The engineers began to hold men back, only allowing men to cross in tens, and meanwhile the infantry was embarking in the rafts and boats I had collected for a week.

The boards on the bridge were slick, the oils in the new wood combining with the water to make them treacherous. To make matters worse, the rain turned into a lightning storm, and bolts from heaven began to lash the column.

A bolt struck a file of phalangites, killing three men outright.

In midstream, with the river rushing under my horse's feet like a live thing, the sky criss-crossed with purple lightning, as if Zeus had set up a trestle to lay siege to the sky, the banks on either shore lost in the darkness and the torrential fall of rain that was, itself, the negation of all sound, I felt as if I were no longer of this world, but had followed the king into the nether regions.

Indeed, when my charger got his forefeet on the far bank, with a loud whinny to announce himself to the waiting horses, or perhaps a prayer to Poseidon for his deliverance, the king spoke out of the flashing darkness.

'Welcome to Tartarus,' he said bitterly.

'What's wrong?' I asked.

'Follow me,' he yelled. We could barely make ourselves heard.

It was a short ride.

The rising river had cut a new channel.

We were not on the far shore.

We were on a new island, and on the far bank, an enemy signal fire burned despite the torrential rain.

Sometimes, he was a god.

He turned to me and his face, streaming with water, was almost alight with his determination.

'It can't be very old,' he shouted. 'I'm going to try it. It can't be deep.'

Before I could say anything, he made Bucephalus – perhaps, by then, the oldest horse in the army – jump into the water.

716

It was deep. But the horse swam well, and the water had almost no current to it – the channel was fresh, and had not yet cut deep. I saw no point in watching further, and urged my mount into the water – my Nisean, one of the army's tallest horses. His feet touched the mud underneath – my feet got wet, but they were wet already. We were across in a hundred heartbeats, and we scrambled up the new far bank side by side, rode to the enemy watch fire, scattered it and killed the sentries.

My Paeonians were beginning to ford the river behind me. The Prodromoi were hard on their heels, and behind them came the Hetaeroi and their Persian equivalents.

There was an element of humour, sitting there with the king, watching them come. We were the first two across, and had the enemy been alert, Alexander's conquest of the world could have ended in ignominious capture on the banks of the Hydaspes river.

But the rain was letting off, and the show of heaven's wrath. Already, it was possible to hear the creak of oars. Already, men were singing the paean from the boats. The Paeonians and Prodromoi crossed and I sent them off into the darkness. The rest of the Agrianians crossed, and I followed them into the last of the rain. Behind us, the barges of the hypaspitoi and the pezhetaeroi were nudging the shore.

We were across. We had fourteen thousand men, to fight a hundred thousand men and two hundred elephants.

As the rain settled, Alexander took on a glow; never had I seen him so sure of himself. Suddenly he was everywhere – with Seleucus, getting the hypaspitoi moving off the riverbank, and forward with me, asking me for a report. My pathfinder Agrianians, who had been across for days, came in as soon as I lit the patterned signal fires in the locations I had briefed them on – men came from as far as four parasanges, men who had laid the trees at the edge of Porus's camp, reporting on his troop movements. Now they told us that Porus's son, Porus the younger, with two hundred chariots and two thousand cavalry, was coming at us out of the rain.

We manoeuvred in silence in the growing grey light. There was almost no cover, but we moved the Paeonians as far forward on the left as could be managed, and Hephaestion took the royal Hetaeroi forward on the far right, with Demetrius's men forming the centre well back. There weren't enough infantry across yet to make a difference.

The king himself insisted on leading the centre, and then we could see the Indians coming. They'd formed well – they probably formed right outside their camp, fearful of our speed, which shows how competent they really were. Young Porus was in a chariot, and he drove it across the front of his force, haranguing them. Then he charged our centre, and we charged his flanks. He was young and foolish, and he died. We killed or captured his entire force in about as long as it takes to tell the story, because they hadn't expected us to outflank the ends of their line. Thorough, but not good enough. They had not faced Spitamenes, or Memnon.

We had.

When I rode up to the king, he was weeping, standing beside Bucephalus, who was putting his muzzle into the king's hand. The old horse had four huge arrows, almost the size of javelins, in his body, and another in his neck. Even as I watched, he subsided to his knees with a sigh.

A white charger was brought up, and the king paused and kissed Bucephalus on the head. 'Good horse,' he said.

Better than Cleitus got.

Then he remounted, and we were off, southward.

We pursued the broken Indians as hard as we could, until we had three of the fords that the Indians had been holding for three weeks in our hands. The water was high, but Meleager and two other taxeis got across, the men soaked, their pikes unaffected.

The phalanx was starting to form.

Ahead, Ariston was watching Porus, and sending a stream of messages to the king. Porus had begun to form his battle line to our front, and he'd left adequate forces to keep Craterus bottled up across the river.

Alexander rode forward to see for himself, and I followed him. The sun was just emerging from the clouds – the first sun we'd seen in days.

I thought of Issus.

Scouts led us to a stand of acacia, where the king sat on his new charger with Ariston, Perdiccas, Coenus, Hephaestion and me, and watched Porus form his army, a seemingly endless crenellation of bow and long-sword-armed infantry as the wall, interspersed with elephants as the teeth.

Alexander sniffed. 'There goes another one,' he said. He meant messengers, but none of us got that. Yet. Porus was sending quite a few, and Alexander was watching them, but we hadn't noticed.

At the flanks, Porus's cavalry shifted. They didn't seem to form well – especially on their right, our left, they kept moving – forward, back – it drew the eye.

Alexander watched under his hand. 'You have to assume that his son was his most trusted commander,' he said. 'And hence, that he commanded the right-flank cavalry.'

He looked around, and his eyes glittered.

'Watch the cavalry on the right. They are under an inexperienced commander, and one that Porus does not really trust.' He smiled, watching intently.

I'll be honest. I didn't see anything like that. I saw a well-formed army, waiting to repel an invader. And I saw us about to fight a truly unnecessary battle.

I looked at the king. 'How do you know the king mistrusts him?' I asked.

Alexander laughed aloud. 'Look! Watch!' He looked at the battlefield. 'And another one.'

Seleucus solved the riddle. 'Messengers!' he said.

'Well reasoned!' the king said. 'Since I arrived in this patch of woods – no great time – Porus has sent five messengers to his right flank. Now, why does the right flank keep shifting?'

We were all silent.

Alexander slapped Seleucus on the back. 'Some day, you will be a great general, lad. Listen, friends.' He laughed – the sheer joy of his face made him seem like one of the deathless gods.

'Porus is planning to pull all his cavalry off his right and use them all on the left, under a commander he trusts,' he said.

Lysimachus grunted. I made a similar sound. He was the greatest military genius I've ever known or heard of, but it was an absurd conclusion to draw from the evidence.

'Coenus – take your hipparchy and Demetrios, and all of you ride wide round our left. If Porus's left-flank cavalry stand fast – charge them. If they cross his rear, follow them, ignoring the line of archers and elephants, and charge the *rear* of their cavalry.' He nodded. 'That's what will happen. The right will ride around his rear to the left.'

Seleucus grinned. 'Care to wager?' he asked.

'My career against yours?' the king said, and Seleucus turned grey.

But Alexander laughed. 'Your turn will come, young man.'

It was the first time he'd ever used that phrase in my hearing. *Young man.*

He turned to me. 'Left of my line. Form your Hetaeroi, and put the Paeonians and Prodromoi behind you.'

I nodded. He was going to charge from the right in a cavalry column. As it turned out, we formed six squadrons wide and three deep – a formation not entirely unlike a wedge, except that it was more flexible.

As we came through the trees and formed, we were the only troops Porus could see. By the time the king's squadron was forming, Porus was sending messengers to the flanks – right and left.

I had Cyrus with me, chewing on onion sausage, and Polystratus and Theodore and Laertes.

Even as we watched, squadrons from Porus's right-flank cavalry began to wheel about and vanish behind his line of elephants and infantry.

I shook my head in disbelief. 'I've known him all my life,' I said aloud. 'He still—'

Polystratus started to laugh, and then his face closed. 'Company coming,' he said, and then Alexander was there on his magnificent new white horse, almost as tall as my Triton. He had a dozen Persians around him, and no other Macedonians, and he wore the diadem on the crown of his helmet, but otherwise, he seemed himself.

He beckoned, and as I started forward, he turned his horse – merely by moving his hips, because he was part of any horse he rode – and I followed him.

When we were all together, Alexander pointed at the gathering mass of Indian cavalry.

'As I may have mentioned,' he said with insufferable smugness, 'Porus is now moving all his cavalry to face me. The power of reputation and a really fancy helmet. Listen, my friends,' he said, leaning forward, and his face was as open as I had ever seen it. 'This is the last army between us and the ocean. The gods have graciously given me this one last great day – against great warriors and giant beasts, the like of which no Hellene has ever faced.'

He looked at us all. 'I didn't mean to make a speech,' he said with a sudden flash of his rare humour. 'I just wanted to say – if this is the last one, let's make it magnificent.'

I know I grinned back at him. It's facile to say we wanted the battle. I, for one, knew perfectly well that we were fighting an army that was merely defending its homeland. We didn't even need to fight – the gods knew, we weren't going to conquer all of India with sixty thousand men.

But he was infectious, like one of Apollo's arrows, and I was infected. I *wanted* to be my best.

He rode that white charger to the middle of the line. Our infantry was just coming through the scrub – the Agrianians first, in skirmish order, and behind them the hypaspitoi in a long file on the right, closest to us, with the phalanx in the centre, and the left – empty. Coenus was out of sight beyond the line of poplars that seemed to demarcate the far left of our battle line.

The Indians thought we'd wait for our infantry.

I grabbed Laertes. 'Ride to Briso with the archers. Tell him to pull all the lights back behind the phalanx and wait for orders. The Agrianians too.'

Laertes gave a nod and rode off into the grain fields. The soil underfoot was sandy, and despite days of rain, it was easy riding. And for the first time in my long military career, I was going to fight a battle with no dust.

Alexander raised his spear.

The Indians were not ready.

We were.

The king lowered his spear, and we rolled forward.

I remember a moment in that charge unlike any other charge I've ever been in, when I could see all the way across the front rank – remember, there was no dust. I could see Alexander, a little in advance of the line, his shoulders square, his posture relaxed, his spear-tip rising and falling a fraction with the canter of his great horse, and I could see Hephaestion just behind him, Lysimachus, far off on a magnificent bay – and our front rank, just at the edge of the gallop, was well closed up and the dress across the front was superb. The sun shone on our helmets and turned everyone's armour to gold.

And I thought, *This is all I want.* And then I realised that I was seeing it as he saw it. Because I wanted something else entirely. I wanted home and a family, and he wanted – this. An eternity of this.

But in that moment, in the heart of the charge, I felt it, as one man may see, for a moment, why another man worships another woman or a god.

I had a long lance, for a change. I'd practised with it in Sogdiana, and now I held it two-handed, the way the Sauromatae use it, and we were moments from impact with a badly formed Indian squadron that compounded its doom by trying to cover more ground to our flank. They were only formed four deep, and their whole squadron vanished in a spray of blood, like an insect swatted by the hand of a god.

To resist a cavalry charge, enemy cavalry must be well formed, and, preferably, moving. Horses may well not charge a line of men – who can look like a wall or a fence, because horses are *not* smart – but a line of horses is merely a challenge to the manhood of a stallion. And a loosely formed line of horses is an invitation to a war horse. Like the king, our mounts lived for these moments.

We swept through their front-rank squadrons without losing our formation and crashed into their second line, which was better formed and moving forward, and I snapped my kontos gaffing a man who seemed to be wearing armour of solid gold, and used the butt-spike to smash another helmet, and then we were through them – I could see Cyrus's squadron to my right, and Polystratus was at my heels, and I risked a glance back – full ranks at my back – and I put my head down, thumped Triton with my heels and we were pushing forward.

Alexander's timing was, as usual, perfect.

We crashed into their third line of cavalry, and they held us – they were the right-flank cavalry, sent to finish us off, of course, and their ranks were no firmer than ours. And we were hopelessly intermixed with the enemy. The enemy cavalry began to press us back, and I could see the king killing his way forward, but he was virtually alone.

I was damned if I was going to let him go down alone.

I had my long kopis in my hand, and no idea when I'd drawn it, but it was a better sword than anything the Indians had – their steel was poor. And my horse was the largest horse in the melee.

So I pressed forward.

Behind me, Polystratus shouted 'The king!' and my Hetaeroi took up the cry, and then Cyrus's men began to shout it, in Persian – 'The king!'

We held them. Or perhaps they held us.

I had a rumble of thunder between my legs, the most powerful war horse I'd ever ridden, and this was his first real taste of the hipposthismos – the horse push. Suddenly, like a river freezing in deep winter, the melee began to gel, the friction of horse against horse slowing movement.

But like a strong swimmer against an adverse current, Triton pushed forward. And no horse could stop him. He bit, he strained, he kicked, and I was another horse length closer to the king.

And another.

I fought, but I fought to keep Triton alive, not to put men down. Alexander was truly alone. I have often wondered whether, having seen it was his last battle, he sought to die there. I only know he'd never outridden the line by so far. Perhaps his new horse was faster than he imagined ...

And then I was at his back. And Polystratus was at mine – Lysimachus came up, and Hephaestion, just as his white horse reared and fell and I caught him, so that he got his feet clear of the wreck of his mount, and in heartbeats he was mounted again, as Hephaestion killed a man and dumped his body from his saddle. The Indian mounts were smaller and bonier than ours, but good horses, as we had reason to know. Alexander was on one.

The enemy threw in their last line of cavalry, and the whole melee shifted again, and I was facing a sea of foes.

Elbow to elbow with an Indian – we both cut, and his sword bent, but my beautiful Athenian kopis snapped at the hilt. He leaned back to cut at me, and I got my bridle hand under his elbow and then punched my right fist and the stub of my blade at his face until the blood gouted and he was dead. He fell into the sea of horses and was swallowed up.

And then, with a roar like a river in flood, Coenus fell on their rear.

Obedient to the king's orders, he had ridden all the way around our left, and around the rear of the enemy, and now he fell on the cavalry melee with the finality of a lion bringing down an antelope.

The Indian cavalry broke in every direction. And the battle was won.

Unfortunately, no one had told King Porus.

As Porus's cavalry streamed from the field with the Hetaeroi and the Persians in pursuit, the phalanx, formed at last – we'd been stades ahead of them on to the field, and our charge had been swift – elected to advance. I assume that Perdiccas thought to take advantage of the chaos of our cavalry victory to press Porus right off the field.

Alexander had given the pikemen a brief pre-battle speech, or so Perdiccas told me later – on how invincible the pike was.

When you are a god, men believe everything you say.

The wall of pikes and shields pressed forward down the field.

Porus – a giant of a man, seven feet tall, on an elephant that towered almost a full head above all the other monsters on the field – didn't even glance at the wreck of his cavalry. He raised his goad, and his bull elephant trumpeted – a sound that reached above the neigh and screams of horses and men – and his crenellated line began to move slowly down the field towards our advancing phalanx. I could see him, about two stades away, and he looked huge at that distance.

Let no man doubt the courage of the Macedonian phalanx. Faced with a line of monsters, they walked steadily forward. For the first time in years, they sang the paean – we'd never had a field to sing on, in Sogdiana.

I was rallying my squadrons. I was never the strategos that Alexander was, but I had enough sense to see that our infantry might need help, and that help would have to come from the cavalry. But it was a mess – the Indian cavalry had mostly cut and run, but we were dreadfully intermixed, my front squadron had threaded through Coenus's front squadron, and all the trumpets were sounding the rally. With the cries of the elephants and the tortured sounds of wounded animals, it took the will of the gods to get a man back to his place in the ranks.

I watched the two mighty lines close on each other. I waited for one or the other to flinch.

No one flinched.

When they met – when they met, it turned out that Alexander was wrong about the efficacy of the pike.

A lot of our men died, in the front rank. Veterans – men who had crossed the Granicus, men who had stood their ground at Chaeronea, stormed Thebes, crossed the Danube ...

The men who made us what we were.

They died because elephants cared nothing for age, skill, armour, shields or the length of the spear. They snapped the spears, and their great feet crushed men, and their trunks grabbed men from their ground and lifted them high in the air, and their tusks, often sawn short and replaced with swords, swept along like the scythes on Darius's chariots.

The taxeis were not in the same state of high training they had once been. The ranks were full of recruits and foreigners. When the phylarchs ordered whole files to double to the rear to make lanes, some taxeis, like that of Perdiccas, executed this flawlessly, and the monsters walked on, doing no harm. But in other taxeis, the attempt to manoeuvre in the face of the beasts led to chaos.

And collapse.

Meleager's taxeis broke first. It didn't run – because the better men weren't capable of running. But the lesser men hesitated, the files fell apart and then suddenly the pikes were falling to the ground and men were falling back, or running, leaving their phylarchs and their half-file leaders to fight alone.

Attalus's mob broke next. They unravelled faster, and by the time they started to go, I was in motion. I looked back for the king, and I couldn't see him, so I acted on my own.

I led the Prodromoi forward into the flank of the Indian line. It wasn't really a *line* so much as a thin horde. They were having trouble with their bows, which probably saved a lot of Macedonian lives, but they didn't have any trouble with their long swords, and they were using them to batter through the front of the spear wall, where the elephants caused any hesitation.

Right on the end of their line, closest to me, was a hard knot of elephants – five of the brutes.

We charged them.

Our horses baulked.

A mahout swung his animal to face us, the men on the animal's back showering us with darts and arrows. Above us in the swirl of a cavalry fight, they had a superb advantage. It is very hard to throw a javelin *up*. Especially when trying to control a panicked horse.

Indian cavalry had taken refuge with their elephants, and their horses weren't panicked by the monsters – a matter of habituation.

An old Thracian, Sitalkes – I'd sat around a hundred fires with him – downed a mahout with his javelin. Most of the Paeonians saw it, and the cry went up to kill the drivers – because no sooner did the mahout fall from between the giant beast's ears than the animal came to a dead stop.

But it was easier said than done, and most cavalrymen had only two or three javelins, and most had spent them in the cavalry fight. Before long, we were riding in among the animals, but doing them no harm – washing about their feet as the ocean washes against the pilings of a pier.

I rode clear of the fight.

There was the king, rallying his household Hetaeroi.

I rode up and saluted. He bellowed at his trumpeter, Agon – the same man who refused to summon the guard the night that Cleitus died, a fine man and a hero many times over – bellowed for Agon to sound the rally again.

He looked back at me.

'We're not having any effect,' I shouted. 'We need javelins. *You* need javelins. And the beasts panic our horses.'

Alexander watched the melee behind me for the space of twenty heartbeats.

'Not true,' he said. 'Your men have pulled five elephants out of the line. That's something.'

'What do we do?' I asked.

Alexander backed his beautiful white horse – his fourth mount of the day – and fought the stallion's desire to fidget. 'I'm thinking,' he said.

From any other man, that would have promoted panic.

I turned my horse, intending to go back into the melee. Not because I wanted to. Fighting elephants is pure terror – fighting them on horseback is fighting the monster, fighting your own fear and the fears of a dumb animal who controls your fate.

Alexander grabbed my shoulder. 'Stay,' he said. 'I need you.'

So I waited.

I had never had leisure, in the middle of a fight, to watch him. I had seen him at the height of battles – but never at the height of a battle in the balance.

He rode back and forth in front of the Hetaeroi. He was learning his mount – he walked, he trotted, he sat back, he rolled his hips. Meanwhile, his men were collecting javelins from the ground, and from corpses, and the last slackers were rejoining.

To our front, the elephants were surrounded by the Paeonians and the Prodromoi. Men were trying to cut the elephants with their swords, and failing. They were brave.

They were dying.

Beyond them, the elephants were pressing forward. Closest to me, Seleucus and the hypaspists were retiring slowly, in perfect order. A dead elephant testified to their prowess, and the Indians let them go.

They were retreating because the phalanx was *gone.* The five taxeis were huddled in the scrubby trees.

Porus and his elephants rumbled to a stop. His Indian infantry didn't leave the shelter of the great beasts. They reformed their line and began to loft arrows at the hypaspitoi, the last infantry on the field.

Alexander grabbed my bridle.

'Go to the centre and rally the phalanx,' he said. 'Get them back on to the field. They will not want to come. Make them move.' His eyes glinted like polished silver, and he was smiling inside his helmet. 'Look at the five monsters you charged.'

One elephant had simply wandered away, its mahout dead. The other four had stopped. They were confused by all the horses, by the pain of a thousand minor cuts, and now they were baulking at their mahouts' commands, turning and moving away, into the flank of the Indians. Killing their own men.

'Get the centre back,' he said. 'I'll defeat the elephants.'

He sounded very, very happy.

I rode to Seleucus, first. He was on foot – his horse had dumped him as soon as the elephants closed, a young horse and not fully broken.

He looked stricken. 'We ... we've lost?'

I managed a smile. 'Look at the king,' I said. 'Does he look beaten?'

Seleucus nodded. And grunted.

'I'm going to try to get the pezhetaeroi back on the field,' I said. 'Retreat slowly, and when the centre comes back, go forward.'

Alectus laughed. 'Forward, is it?' He pointed at a pair of elephants, tusks dripping. They had a hypaspist – both had their trunks around him – and they were both pulling. Pulling him apart. Like cats playing with a mouse.

'Forward when I come,' I said.

I spurred Triton, who was delighted to ride *away* from the beasts.

Back among the scrub, there was a sight I had never had to see. The pezhetaeroi were angry, terrified and humiliated. Men were sitting on the ground, weeping, or staring dumbly. A few phylarchs were trying to form the men, but most were standing, watching disaster without any idea how to fix it. Rout was something that happened to other armies, not ours.

And a lot of our phylarchs were dead.

Meleager was at the rear of the mess, out on the open ground north of the woods, hitting men with the flat of his sword, herding them back into the woods.

I rode to him. 'Alexander says get them back into the field,' I said.

Meleager looked at me. 'Fuck you,' he said. 'They're not going, and neither am I. Why don't you go and face the elephants, and see how you like it?'

'I already have,' I said. 'I can't pretend I like it. But I'll do it. And so will you.'

Meleager spat. 'Fuck off,' he shouted.

I left him to his despair and rode to Attalus.

Attalus had the nucleus of his taxeis formed *behind* the woods, and more men were joining the ranks, and the surviving phylarchs were appointing new file leaders. The awful truth of a rout like that is that the best men *die*. They're the ones who stand. The lesser men run, and survive.

'Alexander orders you back on to the field,' I shouted.

As soon as men heard me shout, they started walking to the rear.

'Are you insane?' Attalus screamed at me. 'It's all I can do to hold them here!'

I rode on.

Just beyond the wreck of the phalanx, behind the centre of the woods – open oak woods, here – stood an island of order. Briso, with the Psiloi – the archers, the Agrianians. Right where I had left them.

'Trouble?' Briso asked.

Three hundred archers and six hundred Agrianians. And sixty of Diades' own specialists, the bowmen carrying gastraphetes and oxybeles, the two-man crossbow, under Helios.

I motioned to Attalus – the Agrianian Attalus, not the Macedonian one. I slid from my horse's back, and my muscles screamed in protest. There's nothing worse – to me, because I am just a mortal man – than leaving combat, and then having to return to it. I had been in a mortal fight, survived, triumphed, faced the monsters and survived again. And now I had to steel myself to go back. *Again.* I had to lead other men.

I took several breaths while I dismounted. Then, to goad myself, I took my helmet off – my beautiful Athenian helmet – and threw it away. I needed a clear head and good vision.

Ochrid had followed me all morning, and now he appeared at my side and I took my two best javelins from him. Their blue and gold magnificence steadied me. It sounds childish, but their octagonal ash shafts were friendly to my hands.

I nodded to my officers.

'We're losing,' I said.

They all looked as if I'd punched them.

'Don't fool yourselves,' I said. 'If we don't do it, the army is done. So we're going to go right up the field into the teeth of the fucking monsters and we're going to kill them – close up. With everything we've got. If we can get in close, maybe the gastraphetes can shoot the monsters. Helios, that's your job – to get the machines as close as can be managed. Attalus, cover the archers and press forward – right into them. We'll go in among their legs and try for the crews. The mahouts – the drivers – are vulnerable. Get them. But mostly, don't let the beasts into the archers.'

I looked at them. They were scared. That was fair enough – no one had ever faced anything like this before. And I was about to lead a thousand men to do what twelve thousand had failed to do.

'We can do this,' I said. 'The one thing I've learned today is that the beasts are slow, and tire easily. If we have to retreat – then we'll run.' I moved my eyes from face to face. 'And go back. Until the king has his counter-punch ready.'

Briso nodded, and Attalus took a deep breath, and Helios looked thoughtful.

'We're all he has left,' I said.

That stiffened their spines.

Attalus formed the Agrianians in a long skirmish line behind the woods, and the Toxitoi formed behind them – one long, long rank, three hundred men long, with a horse length between men, so that our whole front covered six stades – almost the frontage of the phalanx. The crossbowmen stood in knots, or as individuals, where Diades assigned them, well behind the skirmish line.

We moved through the woods – and the wreck of the phalanx – to the sound of the hunting horns.

My last act before we went forward was to send Ochrid to the baggage with orders to fetch more bolts, arrows and javelins. Then I remounted, so that I could see to give orders, and followed.

The phalangites in the woods were angry, and they jeered at the Agrianians and the Toxitoi, taunting them that they were going to their deaths.

At the forward edge of the woods, the better men crouched and watched the enemy. Most of these men still had their sarissas, and so had never entered the trees.

And there was Amyntas, son of Philip. He had a nasty face wound – the skin on his scalp was ripped and his helmet was gone. But he had his aspis and he had his spear.

I raised my javelins to him.

'Dress the line,' Attalus roared. The hunting horns gave their low, mournful call.

The Agrianian line trotted out of the edge of the woods. The Toxitoi emerged behind them.

Amyntas trotted to my foot. 'You are going forward?' he croaked.

'Yes,' I said. 'If you can form any kind of a line, follow us.'

He nodded. He never really looked at me. His eyes were on the enemy.

'Alexander says we are not beaten yet!' I turned to the men hesitating at the edge of the woods. 'Follow us. Form the phalanx. Let the Psiloi hurt the elephants. Come and protect us from the Indians. Come and be men!'

Men looked at me, and looked at Amyntas.

And stood where they were.

My curse on all of you, I thought.

And I went forward with a thousand men, to face the elephants.

It is very lonely, as a Psiloi.

There's no comfort from your file mate, because he's a horse length behind you. No comfort from your rank partners, your zuegotes, the men you are yoked to in the battle line. They're too far away to touch, to look in the eye, to wink at or to moan at.

I had never realised how very brave the Psiloi were, until that day, against the elephants.

The Agrianians went forward fast, at a trot. The Indians made the same mistake we'd made. They thought that the battle was over. And they were probably contemptuous of the thin screen trotting down the field towards them.

I was huffing by the time we came within a long javelin throw of their line. The Agrianians, obedient to the shouts of Attalus, began to gather in loose clumps facing the pairs of elephants. They ignored the Indian foot soldiers and ran straight to the elephants.

The Indians began to loose arrows, but their aim was poor. Skirmishers are a difficult target for massed archery – especially skirmishers making a concerted dash forward.

The men they hit died, however. Their arrows were enormous.

Archers on the backs of the elephants shot, too.

The Agrianians went forward into the arrow storm, heads up, legs pumping them forward. Right into the monsters.

Off to my right, the hypaspitoi watched us come up, pass their front and move on. They cheered us, but they didn't follow.

Farther to the right, I could see the king – far, far off, gleaming on his white horse. He had formed the Hetaeroi into four wedges, and that's all I had time to see.

'The king is coming!' I called.

And then the Agrianians went in among the elephants, and the madness began.

The Indian infantry stopped being stunned by our reckless approach – really, a charge – and started forward, eager to crush our Psiloi.

I put my bare head down and rode for the hypaspitoi. But Seleucus waved me off, and I saw him march off his half-files to the left, doubling his front, and then the whole of the hypaspitoi started forward at the Indian infantry. They, naturally enough, flinched, and responded to the charge of the hypaspitoi.

Triton had decided that he could survive facing elephants. He shied, but he went where I pointed him, and now I pointed him at the largest struggle – fifty of my Psiloi and twenty archers against five or six elephants right in the centre of the field.

There were Paeonians there, too, because the Prodromoi and the Paeonians had filtered all the way along the Indian line by this time – the battle was breaking down into a desperate, every-man-for-himself engagement of a kind I had never seen. The Indians were surrounded, but so far their monsters were untouchable.

Even as I watched, an Agrianian punched his heavy javelin into the side of one of the towering beasts, and then threw himself at the shaft, stabbing deeper and deeper. The great animal bellowed, and its trunk licked out and caught him and ripped him free, throwing him over its head – but another man had a shaft in, and a bold pair of Toxitoi stood almost at its feet and shot – shot quickly and accurately, despite the bestial death that towered over them, and they cleared the crew off the beast's back, and an engineer leaned in, almost touching the animal, and his bolt vanished into the behemoth's guts and the animal screamed in agony.

The archers shot into its face, and their shafts bounced off its thick skull, and then a lucky shaft, Athena-guided, or moved by Apollo's hand, went into an eye, and the creature stumbled, bowed its mighty head and slumped to its knees.

The other animals nudged it – it was somehow more horrible than anything to see their concern for their fellow monster.

And then they shuffled their great, flat feet and moved back, away from the pinpricks of the Psiloi.

I rode back down the field to the pezhetaeroi. 'Come on, you bastards!' I shouted.

And they came.

Meleager had a handful, when he first started back up the field. Antigenes and Gorgias had even fewer.

But Philip son of Amyntas, senior phylarch, had a lot of good men – men of all six taxeis. He ignored the officers. His full-throated roar was as loud as an elephant's scream of pain, and carried across the field.

'Get in the ranks! Get in the ranks! Pick up any spear you see and get in the fucking ranks! Are you cowards? Are the fucking barbarians better men? Are the *archers* better men? *Get up!*' he screamed. Spittle shot from his mouth as I rode up to him, and he ignored me. 'Get in the ranks! Fill in! Now. *The king needs us!*'

And they came.

They came in tens, and then they came in hundreds, and then it was like an avalanche of pikemen. They came with swords, with daggers, with broken spears, with stolen javelins, with bare hands.

I had never seen anything like it.

Gorgias and Meleager ran to the front to take command, but I cantered past them to Amyntas son of Philip.

'Into the Indians!' I shouted. 'Stop their gods-forsaken archers from coming to grips with the Psiloi!'

He put a hand to his ear – an ear covered by the flaps of his helmet.

'Forward!' I shouted.

He grinned. It was a hard grin – an evil grin. 'Here we come,' he growled.

I galloped back to the elephant fight. Dozens – in some cases hundreds – of Indian archers were clearing our Psiloi off the beasts, pushing our men back, and back.

Until the hypaspitoi and the phalanx struck them, and crushed them. In three hundred paces, the battle was transformed and the Indian archers broke, running for the safety of their elephant line, which had retreated several hundred paces, the great beasts lumbering away and putting heart into our phalangites.

The Psiloi ran down the gaps between the taxeis, and reformed in the rear, drinking from canteens, and slumping to the ground in blank-eyed exhaustion. They had faced the monsters for about as long as a man and a woman make love. No longer. And they were spent.

Nonetheless, Ochrid arrived with a train of slaves bearing arrows, javelins, bolts and darts.

Briso was missing. Attalus was badly cut by a sword, and Helios was commanding all the Psiloi. I waved a javelin at him in thanks. 'I think you're finished,' I said.

His look of relief said everything.

I turned Triton and rode for the front.

There was almost no fighting. The Indian infantry was lightly armoured and when they ran, our men couldn't keep up, even if they broke ranks. All along the front, our men reclaimed fallen spears, some picking up shields. To be honest, men were *still* coming up from the woods, convinced by the victory that it was safe to emerge from their cowardice.

They were wrong.

Porus wasn't beaten. Porus was regrouping.

The king had begun to throw his wedges into Porus's flanks, but Porus, with real brilliance, countered them with elephants, sending companies of elephants into the point of the wedges, shredding their formation.

He had saved a squadron of giant chariots, and now he released them against the king's flank, but that, at least, we were prepared for, and Alexander sent his tame Saka, Massagetae who had taken service and Sogdian nomads, to shoot the chariot horses. They destroyed the whole force – a thousand chariots – before the infantry had time to panic.

But, Porus rallied the bulk of his elephants, and placed himself in the centre. Any infantry that could be rallied – and they were brave men, those sword-armed archers – came forward on the flanks of a veritable phalanx of elephants, with the giant of giants leading the way.

It was a slow attack – scarcely a charge, but a shuffling, lumbering advance, slower than the march of a closed-up phalanx.

But our men were not going to stand it. They began to shuffle back.

And then the king was there.

He appeared out of the woods, and he rode unerringly to Amyntas's side even as I reached him.

'The infantry!' he said. He smiled. 'Just hold their infantry. Oblique right and left from the centre – avoid the elephants.' Men heard him. The words 'Avoid the elephants' were wildly popular.

And his presence was like a bolt of energy.

The retreat stopped.

I remember the king looking at Meleager, who was not in the front rank, not in his proper station, and clearly not in command. His glance only lasted a heartbeat. He didn't show anger, or pity.

Just a complete lack of understanding, like a man facing the sudden appearance of an alien god.

Then he turned his horse.

I didn't wait for him. I knew what he needed. I just waved.

And rode for Helios.

*

'One more time!' I called.

Even the Agrianians – the bravest of the brave – shuffled their feet.

There are times when you yell at troops, and times when you coax them.

And sometimes, when brave men have already done all that you can ask – all you can do is lead them.

I rode to the front of them, and I raised my javelins, as yet unthrown, over my head.

'I'm going,' I said. 'Do as you wish.'

And I pointed Triton's head at the elephants and walked forward.

I didn't look back. I had time to think of the hill fort, and the taxeis that left me to die. The Agrianians were men I'd served with for years – but they weren't *mine*. I was best with troops who knew me. I didn't have the magic Alexander had. I was the plain farm boy, and it took men time to love me.

So I let Triton walk forward, and the elephants were close – fifty of them, formed in a mass.

The phalanx had broken in two, and each half marched obliquely to its flank – or flowed that way like a mob. Discipline was breaking down. It was already the longest battle any of us had ever seen, and darkness was not so very far away, and the main lines were on their third effort.

There would be no fourth effort.

This, then, was it.

Alexander appeared at my bridle hand. He was smiling, and the sun gilded his helmet. He pulled it off his head, and waved it. 'Nicely done, Ptolemy,' he said, his eyes on the men behind me, who were following, formed in a compact mass roughly the width of the elephants to our front. The Toxitoi and the engineers and the Agrianians were all intermixed.

To my left, Amyntas was leaning forward towards the enemy as he walked behind his pike-head like a man leaning into a wind. To my right, Seleucus was almost perfectly aligned with us.

I could see men I knew, and men I had never seen before – Macedonians and Ionians and Greeks and Persians and Bactrians and Sogdians, Lydians, Agrianians. I think that I saw men who had been dead a long time – men who fell at the Danube, men who fell at Tyre, men who fell in pointless fights in Sogdiana.

I certainly saw Black Cleitus.

And next to me, Alexander made his horse rear. He laughed, and the sound of his laughter was like a battle cry, and the sarissas came down, points glittering in the last of the sun.

Alexander turned to me and laughed again. 'Watch this,' he said, as he used to when we were ten and he wanted to impress me.

He put his heels to his new horse, and he was off like a boy in a race – alone. We were close to the elephants, then. He rode at them all alone. I was too stunned to follow, for a moment ...

He put his spear under the crook of his arm, and he put that horse right through the formation of enemy elephants – in a magnificent feat of horsemanship, passing between two huge beasts who appeared from three horse lengths away to be touching. But his reckless charge was not purposeless.

Oh, no.

He left his spear an arm's length deep in the chest of the nearest elephant, and the great thing coughed blood and reared, dropping his crew to the ground and then trampling them to death.

The whole of Porus's line shuddered, and the king rode out again, having passed behind the elephants, and he burst out of their left flank, still all alone, and rode along the front of the hypaspitoi.

That's when the cheers started.

He killed an *elephant*. In *single combat*.

It was like the sound a summer thunderstorm makes as it rushes across a flat plain, driven by a high wind that you have yet to feel. It started well off to the right, among the royal Hetaeroi, who now launched themselves at the rallied Indian infantry.

ALEXANDER!

The hypaspitoi had the god of war himself riding in front of them, and their shouts rose like a paean.

ALEXANDER!

The pezhetaeroi picked it up, and the Agrianians, the Toxitoi. It spread and spread, and he rode to the centre, spinning a new spear in his hand, horse perfectly under control, head bare, and those horns of blond hair protruding from his brows.

ALEXANDER!

The sunset made his pale hair flare with fire, and the blood on his arms and hands glow an inhuman red.

ALEXANDER!

I happened to be in the centre of the line, and he rode to me – a little ahead of me. He paused and looked back at me, and his eyes glowed.

'This is it!' he shouted to me.

At the time, I think he meant that this was the end of the battle. In retrospect, I wonder if this was what his whole life had waited for. This was it – the moment, perhaps, of apotheosis. Certainly, and I was there, the gods and the ghosts were there – the fabric of the world was rent and torn like an old temple screen when a crowd rushes the image of the god, and everything was possible at once, as Heraklitus once said.

'*CHARGE!*' he shouted.

And we all went forward together.

The rest is hardly worth telling. I wounded Porus, and captured him – with fifty men to help me. Porus's army broke, and ours hunted them, killing any man they caught – men who have been as terrified as ours show no mercy.

The carnage of that day was enough, by itself, to change the balance of the world.

If apotheosis came at Hydaspes, the end was near.

After the turn of the year, after Porus swore fealty (which he kept) and after the gods stopped walking the earth and went back to Olympus – after it was all over, and the slaves buried our dead – Alexander went back on his promise and marched east. We marched after the summer feasts, and we marched into more rain – rain and rain, day after day.

Victory gave us wings, for a few days. Alexander gave the troops wine, oil and cash, the takings of Porus's camp, more women, more slaves.

Cities surrendered, and cities were sacked. We marched farther east. And three weeks later, on the banks of the Beas, the army stopped.

Amyntas son of Philip caught the king's foot as he rode across the front of the army. The army was formed to march, but the pikes were grounded, all along the line, and the cavalry were not mounted, even though the men stood by their horses.

Amyntas pulled at the king's foot.

The king looked down at him. 'Speak,' he commanded.

Amyntas didn't grovel. He met the king's rage with a level glance. It is hard to stare *up* into a man's eyes and keep steady. But Amyntas had faced fire and stone, ice and heat, scythed chariots, insects and elephants, and the king did not terrify him.

'Take us home, lord,' Amyntas begged. But in that voice you could hear not terror, but steel.

Alexander tried to buy them. He ordered the army to disperse and plunder – two days of licence to rape, murder and destroy, rob, loot and seize, burn if they wanted.

They did.

And he assembled the camp followers – wives, slaves, sex toys, matrons, mothers – and promised them increased rations and better pay – manumission – anything they wanted, to convince their warriors to go east.

That night, we lay on our klines and listened to the endless rain fall outside. It was so wet that the falling rain gradually soaked the hemp fibre of the great tent, and there was a sort of mist of moisture even inside.

Hephaestion drank deep, and I heard him laugh. 'They're like dogs, lord. They'll come to heel.'

Meleager laughed, and the Persians all nodded. Even Cyrus. Craterus smiled a thin smile.

Perdiccas looked at me.

I shrugged.

But Alexander caught my shrug. 'Oh dear. Ptolemy thinks otherwise.'

He was close to the edge. I could tell. Hydaspes had taken him too high – I truly feared what was to come. I should have been careful.

I didn't feel careful.

'They will not change their minds. They are finished.' I looked around. 'They were finished years ago, but they comtinued. For you. Their god. Their living, breathing god.' I shrugged, and my rage brewed up like the flames in a hearth when the door is opened and the wind sweeps in. 'They are *men*, not dogs. They have given you *everything* and you give them a district to rape.' I shook my head. 'They are finished. They mean what they say.'

Alexander shook his head. 'So eloquent. But you cannot imagine that I would turn back for *them*.'

And then Coenus shocked me. He stood up, as I was standing. 'Then turn back for me,' he said. 'I am finished. I need rest, even if you do not.'

Alexander's eyes might have burned a man, they were so hot.

But Perdiccas stood up. 'I stand with Coenus and Ptolemy,' he said. 'I will fight for you until I die, but I want to stop marching east.'

Lysimachus stood.

Craterus looked from man to man. He was looking for the main chance. Looking for his moment.

Seleucus stood.

Nearchus stood.

The king rose, and hurled his golden cup across the tent, so that it struck the statue of Herakles and seemed to explode.

'You cannot!' he cried. 'We are on the verge of immortality! After this, there will be nothing worthy, nothing great – merely the maintenance of an empire and bureaucracy, where I was a *god*.'

It was a plea.

'You seek to limit me. But what limit should a man of the noblest nature put on his labours? I, for one, do not think there should be *any limit*, so long as every labour leads to noble accomplishments!' He looked around. 'We here are like the undying. I am going from triumph to worthy triumph!'

He was standing by his couch, in a swirl of muddy water and matted wet grass where the rising rains had flooded our camp. I mention this because Coenus looked at the floor.

'Is this Olympus, then?' he said with a snort.

'If you just want to know when our wars will end,' Alexander said, 'we are not far from the Ganges. After the Ganges is the Eastern Sea. And the Eastern Sea will link to the Hyrkanian Sea, for Aristotle says the great sea girdles the earth.'

Of course, I knew from Kineas – who had sailed the Hyrkanian Sea – that it did not join with any other body of water. And I ran the scouts. I knew that no peasant we had met could tell me how far it was to the Ganges.

'It is more than a thousand parasanges to the Ganges,' I said into the silence.

'*You don't know that!*' he shouted at me.

Craterus lay on his couch, and stared into the cup of wine in his hand as if it might tell him what to say.

Hephaestion sat up on his couch. But he didn't stand. Nor did he speak.

Alexander looked at me, and the last time I'd seen that look was the night he killed Cleitus.

But I was tired, and I met his murderous glare with indifference. Only when you have killed as many men as I have, lad, and seen as many worthless victories, can you be truly indifferent. And nothing is more effective against hubris than indifference.

'You traitors! Worthless weaklings!' Spittle flew from his mouth.

It's odd, but I thought of the pezhetaeroi huddled in the woods behind our lines, indifferent to my pleas that they go forward to win the battle. Indifferent.

Yes. They weren't cowards.

They just didn't have any more to give.

'If we turn back now,' he said, once more in control, 'the warlike tribes of the East – every spearman in that thousand-parasange plain – will rise against us, and all our conquests will be pointless, or we shall have to undertake them again, and our sons will face these men.'

I might have said, *So you agree that it is a thousand parasanges to the Ganges?* Or I might have said, *You used this argument about defeating Bessus, and then Spitamenes.* Any of us might have refuted him.

But we had heard it all before, and like the drunkard's proverbial wife, we shook our heads, tired of his lies.

He stormed from the tent.

Alexander spent two days alone, except for his slaves. He wouldn't see Hephaestion, or Craterus, much less us, the *mutineers*.

Then he sent an ultimatum to the army via Agon, his *hyperetes*. March, or be left behind. Alexander threatened to go forward with only his Persian levies and his subject Indian troops.

Amyntas son of Philip came to my pavilion. My floor was a hand's breadth deep in water. He sat on an iron stool that rusted as fast as Ochrid's slaves could polish it, and he shook his head.

'I want to tell him,' Amyntas began.

I raised my hand. 'I won't conspire,' I said. 'Tell him yourself, or don't.'

Amyntas shrugged and got to his feet in the water. 'He's fucking insane,' he said.

He stood there, waiting for my reaction.

'By Zeus the saviour of the world, Lord Ptolemy, he *promised*!' Amyntas cried suddenly, in almost the same tone in which Alexander had pleaded that we would end as bureaucrats.

I remember that I nodded.

Amyntas left my tent and went to the king.

A day later, Alexander emerged, summoned the command council and announced that we were turning the army and marching for home.

THIRTY-EIGHT

e never forgave any of us. Not the pezhetaeroi, and not the commanders.

What followed was horrible, and it made Sogdiana pale. Even now, I take no pleasure in the telling.

He tried to kill the army. He didn't retreat along our lines of supply, but went down the Indus river to the sea.

Again, I return to the simile of the woman married to a drunkard. At first, we listened to the complex excuses he offered as to why we had to march down the Indus to the delta, and we affected to believe them. It scarcely mattered to us – we were going home. And I don't think there were five hundred men in the whole army who didn't feel the same.

But it turned out that marching down the Indus meant fighting our way through a vast, hostile plain. He wasn't done – he was still on a binge.

And, in my opinion, he had determined to die, or achieve an even greater level of heroism, if that was possible, than he had achieved against the elephants.

He began well. He held an assembly and announced we would march back. Men applauded – men cheered him as they had cheered him when he charged the elephants. He ordered us to build twelve giant altars to the gods, and we sacrificed like the gods themselves, and we had games that went on twelve days. I did not win in a single event. My hands hurt so much when I awoke most mornings that I couldn't hold a sword to spar. Men I'd never heard of won most of the events – recruits, just two years out from Pella, or Athens, or Amphilopolis, or Plataea.

One of Cyrus's men won the archery.

Polystratus won the horse race, and received a golden crown, which he still wears at feasts.

His friend Laertes won the mounted javelin competition.

Then he made Porus, our erstwhile enemy, the satrap of India, and put the army to work as labourers, repairing dams and dykes and towns along the Indus. This was mostly make-work, as Nearchus and Helios and all the engineers spent the summer building triaconters – thirty-oared ships – to sail down the Indus, which we were told was navigable all the way to the great sea.

I remember that it was about this time that we met Kalanos and his disciple Apollonaris – that wasn't his name, then. They were members of a sect that went naked but for their beards – serious ascetics, men dedicated to meditation and prayer and fasting. Hephaestion had the notion that they would make the king feel better, and brought their leader, Dandamis, to the king.

He was a great mind, and he and the king debated for hours – through interpreters—the nature of men's souls, the size of the world, the purpose of creation. As Hephaestion had guessed, Dandamis filled a need in the king.

But the next morning, he was gone.

The king rode in person to fetch him from his camp. I wasn't there, but I heard the story from Nearchus, and also from my son, who was there. The king found Dandamis sitting naked by a cold firepit. He sat on his horse for a while, looking down at the dirty, naked man, and then said, 'Brother, come and follow me across the world, and we will learn together.'

Dandamis didn't speak for a while, and the king repeated himself with great patience, according to my son.

But after the sun had moved in the heavens, the king's horse began to fret, and the king sat up. 'Come, philosopher,' he said. 'Follow the son of Zeus.'

And Dandamis laughed. 'If you are the son of the greatest god, so am I!' he said, and Barsulas says there was real mockery in his voice.

'Are you a fool?' Alexander asked. 'You are naked, and I can clothe you – you have no fire, and I can feed you.'

Dandamis then looked at Alexander with pity. 'You have nothing I want,' he said. 'Once, you might have made a passable philosopher, but now you value no opinion save your own. You wander because you cannot bear to be still – you conquer because you cannot bear to rule. Please go.'

Well, well.

But Kalanos and his disciple came with us – the young Chela, who became Apollonaris the Philosopher, here at court.

I hadn't received a letter from Thaïs in a year, and I had no command and no real role. Craterus now worked the logistika directly. The king scarcely spoke to any of us, and never to me, and although I attended him daily, he never even turned his head towards me.

Of course, it might have been worse.

Coenus died of poisoning. Coenus, who had been with us his whole life. He died vomiting black bile. I held his head.

After that, Laertes and Ochrid found me a slave boy to taste all my food. About a week later, he died, vomiting black bile.

We found another.

Macedon, eh?

We had two thousand ships, crewed by our Aegyptians, our Carians, our Greeks – anyone who had ever even *heard* of a ship. Nearchus had the command, and we started downriver in autumn. Craterus had a third of the army, on the right bank of the river, and Hephaestion had almost half the army on the left bank, including all of our elephants. Alexander was very keen to get the elephants home – two hundred of them. Coenus had openly speculated that we weren't going home via Sogdiana specifically because the king feared losing animals in the high passes. He may have been right.

We sailed along the banks of the Indus for a week. It *was* idyllic. Indians gathered on the banks and waved, or sang. Some knelt and prayed to Alexander as he passed, as a living god.

But where the Hydaspes and the Akesinos joined, there was a set of rapids, a narrow gorge and a whirlpool.

That is where I began to suspect that Alexander meant to kill us all. He ordered us to pass the rapids by rowing. In three days, we would have been able to unload, carry our ships across the portage and reload. We were the finest, most organised army on the face of earth, and we knew how to do such things.

He ordered us to row, and men died.

Ships were spun around, and collided with the rocks and capsized. Ships ran afoul of each other and capsized. Ships were simply sucked into the whirlpool.

We lost *only* seven ships, as Alexander mentioned with a laugh and a toss of his head that night, at dinner. He had the look of a smart boy who had pulled off a difficult prank.

Fifteen hundred men drowned.

South of the rapids, the river became broad and flat. We heard that the Malloi, a barbarian people, intended to resist. Alexander brightened up.

I was sitting on my bed, drinking too much, to be honest, when

Theodore, Polystratus's friend, came and banged my tent pole with his spear. 'Message for Lord Ptolemy!' he called.

I got up, threw a chlamys over my shoulders and went out into the brilliant sun. Even in evening, India is pounded by the sun.

Ochrid was just giving him a cup of wine.

Theodore drew himself up to attention when I came out. 'I have a message from the king,' he said.

I took it.

It was a wax tablet, and on it, in the king's own writing, it said – 'Ptolemy – too long have I missed your face over the rim of my wine bowl. Join me tonight, and stop sulking in your tent.'

Apis! He thought *I was sulking*?

I reported in a clean chiton, and the king beamed at me. 'Did I offend you?' he asked me, clasping both my hands.

What, exactly, do you say?

'I've been unwell,' I said, with utter cowardice. But Perdiccas laughed, and Hephaestion gave me a look – of thanks?

'Are you fit for a command?' he asked.

It turned out that I was to have half the Hetaeroi – Black Cleitus's former command. A dream command – with Cyrus and Polystratus as squadron commanders, and some attached Indian cavalry.

We were to be the army rearguard.

With his usual brilliance, Alexander had worked out a plan of march that would allow us to travel at intervals – spread over a thousand stades – to minimise supply difficulties, and yet allow us to recombine in any direction. Alexander was using his Aegema to flush opposition, and Hephaestion and I were the anvils against which he would crush any who opposed us.

If you leave aside the morality of it, it was a well-thought-out plan, and just executing such a complex operation was heady stuff. And damn it, it was a pleasure to be in command again.

We swept south, into the Malloi.

They didn't deserve what happened, but then, no one did.

We found their army just south and east of the river, and it broke before Alexander was on the field. I wasn't there – I've heard of this from others. Hephaestion says that he watched it – a whole army shredding and fleeing rather than face Alexander. And why did they try to stand in the first place?

Men are fools.

Idealism was no doubt involved.

We got orders by messenger to close up to the main body, and we pressed on into the darkness, so that night we caught up with

Hephaestion's forces at a sort of muddy ditch that the Prodromoi claimed was a river. I watered my latest war horse in it – my horses were dying like flies on a cold day, and I was out of Niseans and Saka horses, riding only the local bony Indian nags. But I had one fine horse left – a beautiful Arab mare, the only mare I've ever ridden in combat. She was a genius among horses – like my Poseidon – and I called her Amphitrite. My adoptive son loved her, and blessed her every morning.

At any rate, I ignored my grooms and took Amphitrite down to the 'river' to water her. If we hadn't been in a near desert, I wouldn't have let her drink, and even as it was, I dismounted in the lukewarm water that smelled of human excrement and only let her drink in little nips.

At dawn, Alexander took the Aegema, every man carrying his helmet full of that awful water, and headed east after the fleeing enemy.

Why?

No idea.

We followed an hour later.

We literally ran them down. As we had learned, way back in the pages. We didn't moralise. We simply drank our foul water and kept going, killing every Mallian who slowed, or stumbled, or gave up. The path of their retreat was lined with corpses, and eventually there weren't enough vultures to eat the dead.

And still our pursuit continued.

Perdiccas had a dozen units under his command, and Alexander sent him to ring a major town. Then Alexander stormed another Mallian city – in an hour. I hadn't even caught up yet. They were utterly broken as a people, and *still we hunted them and killed them.*

Alexander rallied what troops he had under his hand – his Aegema, and the light troops under Perdiccas. Remember, I was supposed to be the rearguard – behind Hephaestion. Hephaestion was by this time behind me, and the only time I saw Alexander that day, he cursed his best friend for tardiness because the crushing of the poor Mallians was his newest pothos.

We marched back towards the river, almost due south. My scouts were in touch with Perdiccas, but I had already lost the king ahead of me. Peithon, newly promoted to command, was sent farther south, on a sweep through the jungle to destroy any Mallians hiding there, and he exterminated them.

This was our fourth day of pursuit. We were all fighting a little and killing fleeing, desperate, tired men a great deal. It was wearing, hot, sweaty and horrible.

On the fifth day, I had lost Hephaestion behind me and I had lost the king altogether, although I had Peithon just south of me and we turned west together to get to the river faster. Our cavalry needed water – abundant water – and we needed some forage. I came across Peithon, who was standing by his foundered horse, a lovely Nisean who was dying in the brilliant sunlight, the blood at her nostrils startling in its intensity.

Peithon was younger than me, and he all but hid his head. 'I didn't want to kill her,' he said, deeply affected. 'I . . . Ptolemy, when will this stop?'

I had no comfort to offer. So I put a hand on his shoulder, found him another horse and rode on.

Hephaestion caught us at midday.

'Where's Alexander?' he asked me as he rode up. Even *his* horse was exhausted, and he had access to the king's horses. His pikemen looked exhausted. We were all done in – a five-day pursuit? Ares' torment.

I pointed west. 'My scouts say there's a fight going on right now just across the river,' I said. it was true. The report was fifteen minutes old. Strakos was sitting on another blown horse at the brow of a low hill to my left.

'Ares wept,' Hephaestion said.

We didn't pause to reorder. I rode for the river, now just five stades away, and the closer I got, the more surely I knew that there was a battle.

Just at the edge of the river was a low ridge – really, just a mound. I rode to the top, and across the river I could see an army – fifty thousand men, at least.

I turned to Polystratus. 'Sound the rally,' I ordered. 'Form wedge.'

Then I did what Alexander would have done.

I sat on my horse and watched the battle.

I couldn't find Alexander. All his white horses were dead, and he was mounted on a bay, and that made him harder to find. But mostly, he was hard to find because he was herding fifty thousand men with about two thousand cavalry. He was fighting a battle of infinite pinpricks, the way a small, agile man fights an enormous giant in a sword fight. He had only cavalry, and the Mallians – if, indeed, these were Mallians – had five hundred elephants, but they couldn't be everywhere and wherever they were *not*, Alexander was.

He had all the Hippo-toxitoi, the horse archers from Bactria and the Saka, and they were literally riding rings around the Indians.

I sent Theodore to find the king and tell him where I was, that I had four squadrons formed and ready to charge. Then I sent Laertes for Hephaestion, and told him that the king needed the pezhetaeroi. Immediately.

Then I led the formed wedges across the river in a column, a formation that was purely expedient and worked beautifully. The Indians had no idea of our force until I displayed a line of wedges – every wedge with a thousand elite cavalrymen.

Their front shuddered.

While my line of wedges was forming, the king appeared, as if by the will of the gods. He dismounted, snapped his fingers at Leannatos, one of my Hetaeroi, and took his horse.

He grinned at me. 'I can always count on you, my friend,' he said warmly.

Drunkard. Wife.

He pointed at the Mallians. 'We are outnumbered ten to one. They have more elephants on this field than we have horses.' An exaggeration, but not much of one. 'And they are on the defensive! I beat them across the river, and now – thanks to you – we have them.' He looked into the dust at the rear of my column. Cyrus's Persians were just forming on our side of the river.

Pikes glinted in the sun.

'Hephaestion is right behind me,' I said.

Alexander laughed.

'We will exterminate them!' he said.

The Mallians were not waiting to be exterminated. As soon as they saw the pikes, their army broke, and our seven thousand cavalry were not enough to destroy them. Their elephants simply rode away, and their cavalry all escaped, and the infantry glutted the roads so that we had to cut a path – a literal statement, and a disgusting task.

Alexander didn't hesitate. He took the cream of the Aegema and ploughed through them, racing for the gates of their city. He was just too late, but he stormed the outer wall with two hundred men.

I was three stades behind him, wondering what the *fuck* he thought he was doing, and then I put it together. He was reliving the pursuit of Darius.

I began to cut my way forward with vigour. He was going to die.

On and on. *He was going to die.*

I went over the wall, where a trio of wounded Hetaeroi told me he had gone over an hour before. The city was too damned big. And it was paralysed with fear, and yet full of fight – desperate men. Rats. Rats who outnumbered us by many hundreds to one. Remember that our army had been pursuing the Mallians for five days. Horses were foundering. Men were simply coming to a stop.

I had Polystratus and Leonnatus, who, by a quirk of fate, was astride the king's winded horse. Which was such a fine animal that it just kept going. We all dismounted at the outer wall, and after that, we were running through narrow streets, trying to reach the king through a mob of armed and unarmed Mallians who wanted only to flee.

On and on.

I stopped killing the enemy, and just ran past them.

We came to the base of the citadel wall, and a group of hypaspitoi told us that he had gone off to the left, and we ran – ran – around the wall, gathering any Macedonian or Greek or Persian we found. There were shouts and screams ahead of us to the left.

It was like a nightmare, when you wander lost through a burning city and cannot find the king.

I have such nightmares.

And then we found five men, and I knew them, and they were trying to climb the stones of the wall using plants that grew there. A broken ladder lay at their feet.

'He went over the wall!' screamed one. 'He's going to die in there!'

I had perhaps sixty men at my back.

The citadel wall was six men tall and crenellated.

Abreas, the man screaming, kept pointing at the top of the wall.

Astibus lay dead, his body broken, where the ladder had collapsed.

Bubores ...

I took a deep breath and looked around. There were no more ladders.

'Climb it,' I said. 'Use your daggers as pegs.'

Had the top of the wall been defended, it would have been foolish suicide. But there wasn't an enemy to be seen.

Men threw their daggers on the ground and Abreas was off, climbing the wall, and Leonnatus went behind him, handing him new daggers, and they went faster than I thought possible. Men brought billets of sharp wood, bronze rods, anything they could pillage ...

Laertes came with a silk rope – some sort of decorative rope, but we got it up to Leonnatus.

'The king lives!' Abreas roared from the top of the wall, and he jumped down inside to aid the king.

Leonnatus paused to tie the silk rope to a stanchion, and then he, too, jumped down inside.

I took the rope in my hand and turned to Laertes. 'No one climbs until I'm at the top,' I said.

I went up the rope. Try it, lad – try climbing a narrow silk cord, in armour, in the heat of the sun, after five days without sleep.

I made it.

I looked down.

Alexander stood with Peukestas on one side and Abreas on the other, and Leonnatus was just rising, having taken an arrow in the thigh. Blood was *spurting* out of the king's right side, under his arm.

Even as I watched, Abreas took an arrow in the throat.

They were facing a hundred men. Or more.

They were surrounded by corpses, and it was clear that the Mallians wouldn't face them. They were, most of them, without bows, and they threw rocks, refuse – anything.

They had half a dozen archers with the great Indian longbows, and they were the most dangerous men.

I ran along the wall.

An archer saw me, and loosed. For a heartbeat, that arrow and I were all there was in the world, and then it hissed past me, and I reached the point I had selected on the wall and jumped.

Thirty feet.

I landed behind the archers, and I killed one before I knew I'd turned my ankle. Then I killed another.

Then I realised that I was between the enemy and their own gate.

I did the bravest thing of my life. The best thought-out. The most amazing.

I turned, and ran to the gate. Away from the king. Away from the fight. With my back to the remaining archers.

I lifted the bar, and a hundred Macedonians burst into the courtyard like an avenging flood. I turned and ran back towards the king, cursing my ankle, with the daimon of combat filling me, and there was Peukestas standing over the king with the king's shield from Troy on his arm, and the king lay at his feet, and Leonnatus was on his knees, swinging a kopis as the Mallians tried desperately to kill all three.

I ran along the colonnade, and Hermes gave me wings.

I saw the spear meant for the king.

I threw myself between the spearman and his victim without thought, as if my whole life had been lived for this moment, to save the king from a death that he richly deserved.

The spear hit my aspis and skidded away.

The king's eyes met mine, and he smiled.

And the king was saved.

He almost died.

We killed every man, woman and child in the town.

THIRTY-NINE

—◊◊◊—

We didn't march south again until spring. The king teetered on the edge of death for two months, and blood from his lungs flowed over his breast whenever he took a deep breath. The army became increasingly nervous, like a young horse facing an elephant. They realised that, without him, we probably wouldn't make it home. It's odd, but I had come to the same conclusion. We were sailing a sea of enemies. We had slaughtered so many people that we were universally feared and hated – there was no hope, now, of making an ally. And here, in the midst of the chaos he had created, if the god of war left us, we would all drown.

Or that's how it looked, on the banks of the Indus.

He recovered around midwinter – emerged from his tent, spoke to the troops. Was cheered like a god. He ordered the surviving Mallians to build us more ships. He enslaved virtually the entire surviving population and put them to work, and in the spring, we sailed south, leaving a desert of destroyed farms, burned cities and corpses. I have heard angry young people tell me that war never changes anything.

Tell that to the Mallians.

I look at the pages of the Journal, and I see that we fought our way down the Indus. It's a blur to me. We did not truly rest among the Mallians – no more than an exhausted man rests when he has three hours of sleep – and the spring campaign was more rapid marches and more killing. By late spring, no one in the Valley of the Indus would stand against us. Whole populations moved east, emptying towns before us.

There was one exception.

South of the land of the Osetae, we were marching – I was marching, anyway. The king had left Nearchus to command the river fleet, and the whole of the Aegema was travelling on the banks of the river, broad spring meadows carpeted in flowers. It was beautiful, unless you looked too closely and realised that these were supposed to be farm fields.

It was mid-morning, as I remember. I was riding with the king, and the Prodromoi came up to inform us that there were Indians – unarmed – in the fields ahead.

The Indians had an entire class of philosophers – fascinating men, like priests, except that they were born to their caste, and never left it – called Brahmins. Waiting in the fields were hundreds of Brahmins, dressed in the sombre colours of a funeral.

Alexander cantered over to them, with his bodyguards, fifty Hetaeroi of the household, and some hypaspists. I rode alongside him on my mare. We were a brilliant riot of colour – horses, gold and silver buckles, brilliant bronze breastplates, helmets, silk and wool and linen, strips and furs.

One man stood forth – a tall man with a long beard. As we approached, he and his companions began to stomp their feet on the ground.

Alexander laughed. He turned to one of our many interpreters – a Mallian slave. 'Why are they stomping their feet? Is it some form of applause?'

The king's interpreter rode forward, dismounted and touched his head to the ground respectfully. They spoke in the local language.

Then the Brahmin stepped forward. His Greek was not wonderful, but it was clear.

'We own the ground under our feet,' he said. 'And you, conqueror, own no more than we.'

As a veteran of the Sogdian War, I knew we never owned any more than the ground under our feet. So I laughed.

The Brahmin glared.

Alexander nodded. 'So very true,' he said, with no interest at all. He turned to me. 'Perhaps you should befriend him, Ptolemy, since his humour seems to suit you.'

We rode on.

By midsummer, we had taken Patala, the greatest city at the mouth of the Indus, and a few weeks later, I stood looking out at the Great Ocean.

It stretched, a dirty grey-white sheet of sun-sparkled seawater, to the horizon – stinking in the heat, rippled like a new-washed chiton of linen, and it was obvious to a child that this was an enormous body of water and that it did not flow into the sea near Libya or any other sea. It had tides – great tides.

I was with a cavalry patrol when I first saw it.

I remember reining Amphitrite in and sitting on her back, looking out at its white-hot immensity, and thinking that we were doomed.

But we were not doomed. We were merely very far from home. After a pause to gather supplies, Alexander reorganised the survivors, picked march routes himself without consulting any of the rest of us and marched us west towards Persia.

Morale was high, because any man who could see the sun could see that *at last* we'd turned west, into the setting sun, and we were marching home, or at least towards Macedon, as was evident to the meanest understanding.

Of course, they hadn't heard of the Gedrosian Desert.

I had. I had patrols out all the time. And it was clear to me that we were about to undertake one of the labours of Herakles.

Let me be clear. We could have taken the route Craterus took, across the mountains. We knew how to do mountains, and most mountains have water.

We could have ferried the army home by sea, sending three lifts.

I was with the king, and Leonnatus, who was his new favourite (fair enough – he had saved the king's life), lying on a couch with Perdiccas. Strako – now an officer of the Prodromoi – was going through the options.

And that useless fuck, the seer, stood and poured a libation. 'Cyrus lost his entire army crossing the Gedrosian Desert,' he said, the pompous fuck. 'No army has ever crossed it, O King.'

'My army will cross it,' Alexander shot back. He looked around, and Leonnatus, who was another driven man, grinned.

'Or die trying,' Hephaestion said wearily.

'Oh, as for that ...' the king said. He grinned. 'They made me turn back. They can't complain about my route home.'

I felt as if I'd been punched in the stomach.

More men died in the desert than died at Hydaspes.

I ran the logistika for as long as we had any meaningful amount of supplies. I didn't do it for the king. I did it for the army.

To be fair, he was, as usual, of two minds. He didn't care if they died, but he wanted to get them across triumphantly. But I think he wanted enough of them to die to make it look Herculean.

He *did* order supplies to be gathered. He sent out members of Thaïs's Angeloi on racing camels, headed north-west and due west, to the satraps, ordering them to prepare magazines for our march. I helped with this, and while I thought that the king was setting an impossible pace for his army, assuming that they could cross a hundred stades of desert

750

a day, I nonetheless had to be satisfied with the other preparations. The satrap of Gedrosia was ordered to have fifty thousand mythemnoi of water at every depot – not enough for surfeit, but a realistic amount. The grain, the meat on the hoof, the remounts – I planned them all. Spare saddles, cloth for chitons, baskets to replace baskets, pack animals to replace dead pack animals.

I had three days, and I doubt I slept. When I closed my eyes, the Greek letters danced in front of my eyes, and when I awoke, it was with the thought that I hadn't counted on the weight of water jars in my calculations for cartage.

Alexander had an air about him – of amusement, perhaps – that I found frightening. As if he knew that the result was a foregone conclusion, but insisted on playing his part with a light heart.

Nonetheless, he signed and sealed my orders for Apollophanes, satrap of Gedrosia, and for the satraps of Carmania and Archosia. We pillaged Patala for carts and draught animals, and when we formed to march west for good, we had forty-two thousand men and twenty-two thousand women and children, as well as a little over two hundred thousand animals. And that did *not* include Craterus with the elephants, who took another route, nor Nearchus with the fleet, which now ventured out of the river and on to the open sea.

Alexander imagined that the fleet would be in touch with us as we marched, but most of the coastline of Gedrosia is a single massive cliff, fifty men high, and barbed like a phalanx with spears.

For two days, we were still in the plain of the Indus.

On the third day, we began to climb, and the climate grew drier, although the air was humid. We reached a set of low hills, and when we climbed them, we found ourselves on a narrow plateau between the mountains – the endless, tall, barbed mountains of Archosia – with the cliff and the sea to our left.

An army of seventy thousand men and women and children, on a single march route, with a single track just wide enough for two wagons to travel abreast – in places, it narrowed to a single cart track.

So, a little mathematics. How long is an army of seventy thousand, if there is only room for four men to march abreast?

About a hundred stades. A *hundred* stades. And that's without intervals between units and divisions, without stragglers, without a single broken cartwheel or dying horse blocking the path.

And never mind the corpses.

An army strung out over a hundred stades, which only marches fifty stades a day, has to travel in multiple divisions, and they must all form at the same hour and march at the same time, or they cause each other brutal traffic delays in the boiling sun.

All of which we did.

We had excellent march discipline, or we'd all have died. But after the first two weeks, we were losing a hundred men a day, and the officers knew we couldn't turn back. And the rocky ground had no habitation to strip, no peasants whose water and food we could forage. Even in Bactria, there had been wells and streams. Gedrosia had nothing.

Alexander seemed delighted. Because it was *so hard*.

After the fourth week, the king had to move up and down the column constantly to keep people moving. We were all doing it, but he was the most active. I met him, repeatedly, and he'd always halt, accept my salute and smile.

'Not as bad as it might be,' he'd say, while a twenty-three-year-old Persian concubine died of heat exhaustion at the feet of his riding horse.

On and on.

In the fifth week, we were losing five hundred people a day, most of them at first light when they simply refused to march. The phylarchs had orders not to waste energy on the dying, but simply to keep the men moving. We were just a day or two from the first great depot, and Alexander felt our losses so far were *acceptable*. I could have spent my time in rage, but I was as hot and tired as the others, and my little Arabian mare was finally showing signs of wear, and I wanted her to live, so I gave her all my water that evening.

I barely slept. Once you have no water, everything goes wrong in your body.

The next day, Laertes forced me to drink a cup of his own water. Bless him. And we started again.

Alexander came up, saluted and informed me that he was riding ahead with the Hetaeroi of the royal household to the depot.

'I'll be back in three hours,' he said. He looked around. 'When I tell them it's only six stades away, the men will perk up.'

I wasn't sure that was true at all, but I let him go with a wave and started to rove the column. I saw Bubores threaten to kill a man who wanted to sit down, and I saw Amyntas carry a child.

The king didn't return until sunset.

We made about twenty-two stades, by my reckoning. A poor march. And we didn't get to the depot.

I was standing with Hephaestion, where we'd gathered two hundred Hetaeroi to guard the two dozen water wagons that still held water. In the animal park, we had another twelve hundred empty carts – most drawn by oxen – and the draught animals were increasingly difficult.

Oxen are too big to control, when they lose their heads, and my experience as a logistics officer told me that the oxen had been taken a few marches too far.

'We're not going to make it,' Hephaestion said.

I was stunned by this pronouncement. 'It can't be more than a day's march to the supplies,' I said.

Hephaestion shook his head. 'I have a bad feeling about this,' he responded.

Perdiccas was watching a crowd of soldiers form near the baggage animals. 'They may just decide to kill the animals in the lines,' he said. 'Blood is as good as water, if you can keep it down.' He shrugged. 'I learned that in Bactria.'

Philip the Red was dressing his troop of Hetaeroi, making a good show to overawe the pezhetaeroi and their women – women who were often as dangerous as the men – when the king rode up. He didn't dash up to us – he rode slowly, and there were fewer than a dozen knights behind him.

We saluted.

He shook his head. 'There's no depot at Gelas,' he said. 'Not an amphora of wine, not a mythemna of water, nor of grain, not one bullock.'

We looked at him in silence.

He sat up straighter. 'It is a betrayal. Someone wants this army dead.' He shrugged.

We were silent. I couldn't think what to say. Apollophanes was never much of a leader, but I didn't see him as a traitor.

It didn't matter, though. If there was no depot ...

I rode over to the king's side. 'We must order the draught oxen slaughtered,' I said. 'They will provide food and drink – buy us some time.'

Alexander looked at me, and in the last light of the sun, his eyes burned like fire. 'If only they hadn't forced me to stop,' he said. 'We would all be comfortable in some marching camp on the Ganges.'

Oh, how I hated him, in that moment.

Perdiccas and I ordered the excess baggage animals slaughtered. The pezhetaeroi and their women killed them, drained their blood, and in the morning we marched, leaving a field of animal corpses, as if they had fought us, like the Mallians. And the men and women marched with brown blood flaking from their hands and mouths, because there was not one drop of water with which to wash.

Alexander took his bodyguard and rode for the coast, to find the fleet.

He came back four days later, and we were still moving. We had used up all the rest of the water, and he led us to the coast – three days out of our way – where he'd found a spring.

We marched along the coast for six days, and we filled the remaining sixty wagons with water in skins and jars and anything that would hold it, and men marched with their helmets in their arms, full of water, children tried to walk holding a poor cup of water.

There weren't many children left.

I do not remember when it happened. I merely remember that one night Bubores came into my camp – I should explain. I was sitting on my saddlecloth, with my military cloak wrapped around me. Laertes and I were repairing our tack, to make our horses' lives as easy as we could. We had no tents, no baggage of any kind – everything I owned was on my body or on Amphitrite's rump. I'd killed my last riding horse the night before, for food, and from him I'd fed forty Hetaeroi and all the surviving Angeloi.

At any rate, Bubores came, and sat on his haunches in that African way in the dying light of the sun. He had a young boy with him, a wizened, dark-skinned boy of four or five.

Laertes held out a cup. 'Share, friend,' he said. He'd found us some water, and we didn't ask him where. Ochrid had done the same, the day before.

Bubores took the cup and gave it to the boy. 'You remember,' he said, and his deep voice was strong and even, 'when the hypaspitoi were new, and we marched on to your farm – and you had slaves and bronze kettles for every man?' He grinned. 'I wanted to thank you. Ever since then. I had never owned a slave before, nor had any man treated me that way.'

I laughed. 'Bubores – you are a soldier of the Aegema, an officer, and you stand by the king. You can tell me this any time. Why now?'

Bubores rattled the necklace of bones he wore around his neck. 'I will die soon. Perhaps tonight or tomorrow.' He shrugged. 'I am paying my debts. I owed you my thanks – never managed to tell you.'

I laughed. 'Don't be an irrational arse. You won't die here.'

His bright eyes met mine, and his look was calm – and like the look new lovers give each other. Trust. Belief. 'I will die soon,' he said. 'And so will most of us. Here? In the desert? Back at Babylon? What does it matter? The king will kill us all.' He smiled, but it was a bitter smile. 'It is a hard thing, to reach this point on this long road, and know that I am not the hero. I am the villain. I have killed a thousand men, taken a thousand women, enslaved ten thousand.' He raised his hands. 'What does that make me?'

I had never heard him speak this way.

Laertes shook his head and Polystratus, behind me, grunted. 'Got that right,' he said quietly.

'This boy is my son,' Bubores said. 'The mother is dead now. The boy is a good boy, and all I have left – what treasure is worth a fuck, out here? Listen, Ptolemy. You are a great man – an aristocrat, a friend of the king. When there is no more food, you will have food. When there is no more water, you will have water for a few more days. I beg you, as an old comrade, to take my son when I am dead.'

Polystratus turned. 'Just say yes, and don't protest. Bubores, we'll protect your son. You have my word.'

Bubores shook my hand, and Laertes' and Polystratus's. And then he and the boy went back into the silent darkness.

Two days later, while I walked next to Amphitrite, I saw him. He was walking at my mare's tail.

I looked at him, and he met my eyes.

'Pater dead,' he said.

I gave him water and we walked on.

When we had been fifty days in Gedrosia, give or take a few days, I was with the king. The light was gone from his face. We were burned red brown, and we hadn't had *any* water in four days. We were losing a thousand men and women a day. There were fewer than two hundred horses left.

We were marching only at night, which made it easier – if stumbling blindly across an endless waste of grit and rock, with no sandals and bleeding feet, bleeding gums, parched throat and no sweat – can be called *easier* – but the sun was rising and we were still going. Alexander was sure we were close to the capital of Gedrosia, called Poura.

We came over a rise, and entered a long valley – a barren, rocky valley that had ancient trees – myrrh trees, the largest any of us had ever seen, with myrrh gum so abundant that we crushed it under our feet as we marched, so that the whole valley smelled as if the gods had come to us. It was absurd, and beautiful, and the smell rose to the heavens, and we had very few dead that day. And I have hated the smell of myrrh ever since.

The next day, we were losing men so fast that I couldn't stop to prod one without another falling over near by, and men had begun to die – literally, to *die* – on their feet.

I left Amphitrite and Bubores' son with Polystratus and headed for the king at the very front.

He was walking quickly, using a spear as a staff. Perdiccas and a handful of his bodyguard were with him, and the rest of the army trailed away behind him like an army of spectres, spread, I expect, as far as three hundred stades – at the rate we were moving, there were still living men two weeks' march behind us.

Again, we marched – or shuffled – all night, and kept going into the dawn.

I had intended to say something to the king. But now that I was following this slim figure into the dawn – with the print of blood from his reopened wounds clear on his chiton – I realised that there was nothing to say. The time to speak, or to act, was so long past ...

Agrianians came out of the morning murk. There were half a dozen, without an officer, and they clustered around the king as I came up.

They had a Thracian helmet full of water.

It fixed our attention the way a beautiful woman can fix the attention of a hundred men in the agora. I noticed that it was not just water, but *cool* water, which formed condensation on the bronze of the helmet.

The Agrianians knelt, and their leader gave the helmet to Alexander, handing it over with head bowed.

Alexander looked into the bowl of the helmet for a moment. Then he looked around. By then, in the first light of day, there must have been a thousand men, perhaps three or four women, and Bubores' son.

He smiled.

'Did you bring enough for everyone?' he asked.

The Agrianians shook their heads.

Alexander poured the water out on to the sand. 'I will drink when everyone has drunk. Now lead us to the spring.'

Sometimes, he was easy to love.

On the fifty-ninth day since we had left Patala, we marched into Poura.

We did not march. We shuffled.

Men died from drinking too much water, or too much wine.

When we mustered, six days later, we had eleven thousand infantry, seven thousand cavalry and fewer than six hundred women. Eleven children. Thirty-one horses.

One was Amphitrite.

One of the children was Bubores' son.

And there was a letter from Thaïs waiting for me. It was lovely – I still have it. It was like water in the desert. And I know what the phrase means.

As soon as we reached civilisation, the killing began again. It was Philotas and Callisthenes and Cleitus the Black, but at a new level of horror, and there were no attacks of remorse in the aftermath. Just a feast of crows.

Cleander died. Sitalkes was killed. A row of Persian satraps, whose principal guilt lay in assuming that their barbarian conqueror would never return. Apollophanes was arrested and dismissed and then executed for failure to supply us. He hadn't even tried. He never offered an excuse, even under torture.

Astaspes was killed, and a host of men more junior found themselves arrested and murdered. Alexander informed us – and the army – that there had been a conspiracy against him – against all of us – and that the disaster in the Gedrosian was the result of their attempt to murder the army.

Not the result of one man's hubris.

We marched into Persepolis. More satraps were executed.

What did I do? Heroically, I kept my head down, went to the king's tent as seldom as possible and commanded my Hetaeroi.

I have not gone into detail about the king's adoption of Asian ways – beyond asserting that, as always, he tried to please everyone and ended pleasing no one. But after the massacre of the satraps – with Cleitus dead, Nearchus terrified, Perdiccas and I in virtual in-army exile – after that, the king did whatever he liked. And what he liked was to become the King of Kings. He adopted the court costume. He hid himself in the midst of a vast horde of perfumed functionaries who had never held a piece of wood, much less a pike.

At Susa, he held a review of his new army. He had raised a new army – I think I mentioned it – thirty thousand pikemen, all Persians and Medes, trained to a degree of perfection in drill that was both beautiful and a little scary to watch. He reviewed them at Susa, and called them 'Successors'.

The name meant just what it seemed to mean.

His Macedonians had served their turn, and he was through with them – those he hadn't killed in the desert, that is. And when the phalanx – that is, the old, at least partially Macedonian phalanx – grumbled, he referred to the Successors by another name. Because the assembly of the pezhetaeroi was often called the 'Tagma'. And Alexander called his Persian phalanx the 'Antitagma'.

Another name that meant just what it seemed to mean.

It took months for the king to lay his plans, but when he acted, he did so with the thorough planning that characterised him on the battlefield.

He held the mass wedding – everyone knows the story – and thousands of his men took Persian wives. It was a magnificent ceremony.

It was also one of the truly good, well-thought-out, well-devised acts of his reign.

I was no longer needed for military planning, but at Susa, one afternoon, the king met Thaïs, recently come up from Babylon – or rather, he heard her unmistakable fingers on a kithara and invited her to help him plan the weddings. And she brought me.

Once again, the king looked at me over a military desk and smiled. 'Too long since I have seen you,' he said, and embraced me.

Again.

It required the kind of planning that a fortress requires, or a campaign. Ten thousand men, ten thousand brides. Gifts, priests of every religion required, dowries, food.

Twenty thousand people drink forty thousand amphorae of wine. Eat five thousand sheep and five thousand goats. Require twenty thousand slaves to wait on them, and the slaves have to be fed, too.

Ten thousand brides require ten thousand bridal dresses. Even if you want them to sew their own, the cloth has to come from somewhere. So does the jewellery.

Inside? What building can house this? Outside, what place is beautiful enough?

And so on.

The weddings were in the Persian manner, the men sitting in chairs, the women coming to stand by them. So we needed ten thousand chairs.

It might have been chaos, but the king put ten thousand talents of silver at our disposal, and we did the thing well. The king offered me a Persian bride, and I grinned.

'I want to marry Thaïs,' I said.

He nodded. 'I intend to marry Barsines,' he said.

'Barsines?' I remember smiling. 'Not Banugul? I thought you preferred her.'

He looked very human, then. Looked out over the mountains, towards Hyrkania. 'Perhaps it is the very fact that she prefers to rule her little kingdom among the wolves,' he said. 'I generally prefer what I cannot have.'

I was still stunned by the self-knowledge evident in that statement when I reported it to Thaïs that night, as we lay, she half atop me, her head on my shoulder. She still smelled like herself, she still looked like herself ...

'He knows what he is,' she said. 'He merely ignores it, most of the time.'

I shook my head in the darkness lit by a single lamp. Her skin glowed.

As usual, I wanted her.

'Will you marry me?' I asked, when we had made love.

She shrugged. 'I don't charge you, either way,' she mocked me.

'If I don't marry you, the king means to give me a Persian girl of fourteen years,' I shot back.

'I could use someone to help around the tent,' she said, running her hand across my penis. 'To watch Eurydike. Perhaps teach her Persian, since it will be *such* an *important* language when she is grown.' She was matching actions to the rhythm of her words.

We giggled.

We made love again, which, after all my body had suffered over the last years, was a sort of Aphrodite-sent miracle in itself. And I asked her again.

'Will you marry me?'

The lamp was out, and the tent was dark.

'I really have to ask Bella,' she said. 'And what of all my other clients?'

'Thaïs!' I said.

She laughed and laughed.

And when I was slipping off into a sated sleep, she whispered, 'Of course.'

The weddings were superb. The food was good, and the priests – all six hundred of them – were on time. Our adoptive children were officiants – both of them. Barsulas had sailed with Nearchus and had swum with whales in the eastern Ocean, and Olympias was a full priestess of Artemis and had come all the way from Ephesus with ten other priests of the goddess.

People today speak of the weddings as if they all passed off in one meadow, or one great temple, but in fact the weddings took over every part of Susa, and our part was at the Temple of Astarte, to which I gave two talents in gold for offerings and a great gold amphora that I'd taken in India and my son had got home by ship – because, if you are wondering, not a single coin of plunder made it across the Gedrosian Desert. And I sat in my Persian chair, in Persian dress – oh, a nice long coat, baggy trousers, the whole costume – because the king's actual intention was to begin the acculturation of his Macedonian staff to the world of ruling the Persian Empire.

I sat in my chair, and Thaïs came, veiled in silk gauze, and after the Priestess of Aphrodite had said all the words, I rose, threw back her veil and kissed her lips, and her blue eyes stayed on mine for a long time.

I think that would be a good place to end. Thaïs and I, on thrones, and Polystratus and his Persian bride Artacama, Laertes and Theodore with their brides, Barsulas with his bride, a magnificent girl and a rich heiress named Artonis, and all of our friends who we could gather – all the survivors of my group of pages. Philip the Red was there, and he wed another beauty, Amastrine, who seemed shocked to be offered a cup of wine by a man not her husband. You see – we carried through the weddings in the Persian manner, because the king had commanded it, and he was paying.

But the feasts that followed were pure Greek. I'd say Macedonian, except that among the thousand men and women dining on the portico of the Temple of Astarte at Susa, no boy was raped and no man's gullet slit – so it can't have been a Macedonian feast.

Thaïs played the kithara, and everyone was silent – the highest compliment that a crowd can pay a musician. We had performers – jugglers, and an old rhapsode, and then we danced – women with women and men with men, and Cyrus, my friend from Sogdiana, danced the Plataean Pyricche with Strakos and Amyntas and Polystratus and me. We were pretty drunk, but we did it well. And when the aulos pipes stopped and we were merely human again, we saw that the king had joined us.

Thaïs led the women out – Persian as well as Macedonian, more than twenty women with whom, we saw immediately, she had practised in secret – and they danced one of the dances of Artemis that all Greek women know. Olympias danced next to Thaïs, and the Persian women danced – and Cyrus smiled. We all smiled. Wine flowed, and people were happy.

It would be a good place to end this story.

But I will not end here.

A few weeks after the wedding, the king paid off the army's debts. The men saw it as a favourable sign.

They were wrong.

He had himself declared a god. He assumed he had bought the army's acceptance.

He was wrong.

He began to move the army – Aegema, Tagma and Antitagma all together – back to Babylon, and he paraded them at Opis.

It was a clear, dry day. The army bore no resemblance to the ragged horde that had stumbled out of the Gedrosian Desert. We had the new phalanx, magnificent in bronze armour, crisp, white chitons and the new helmets with Persian-style tiaras atop them. The old Macedonian infantry – fewer than ten thousand men, even with a recent infusion of recruits from home and a thousand Greek mercenaries – stood looking second-best. The hypaspitoi had absorbed more men out of the pezhetaeroi – yet they, too, had received drafts of the very best of the new Persians. They gleamed with gold. And they stood separate, more like a tyrant's bodyguard than the elite of the army. Seleucus commanded them, but he had multiple lieutenants who were clearly there to watch him – new men, fresh out of Greece, and one from Lydia.

The Hetaeroi were more Persian than Greek. We had new horses and new armour and thousands of new men.

Alexander came out and sat on a throne, surrounded by advisers and functionaries, under an awning. Then he stood, and in a loud, clear voice, informed them of his plans.

'It is my wish that the men who conquered the world,' he said with an easy smile, 'should have the retirement they deserve – that men who should long ago have gone home to Pella to plant their farms should go, richly rewarded, and live lives of ease and splendour.'

If he imagined that they would be pleased, he was wrong.

The ranks began to move – the Tagma writhed as if it had to face elephants. The pikes wavered.

The very air became still.

Alexander still had that smile fixed on his face.

Amyntas son of Philip stepped forward – he was the right file leader of the rightmost taxeis – the senior phalangites of the army. Every man knew him – every man knew he had declined to become the king's shield-bearer, or the senior phylarch of the hypaspitoi. He stepped forward at parade-ground pace, until he was three paces in front of the taxeis.

'Do you think you can just send us away?' he roared. 'We shat blood for you!'

Alexander watched him, the way a man looks at a snake that has suddenly appeared near his foot.

The phalanx began to shout abuse – at the king.

Alexander's face grew red.

Amyntas raised his arm and pointed his spear at the Antitagma. 'You plan to conquer the rest of the world with your *war dancers?*' he shouted.

The Tagma took up the cry – War Dancers! War Dancers!

Men began to laugh.

Now spears in the Antitagma began to shake – with rage.

Alexander's face was as red as the sun had turned it in the Gedrosian Desert. He raised his hand to speak.

But the Tagma was not cowed.

'With your pretty boys and your father Amon!' called another front-ranker, and men laughed.

761

They all laughed.

Every Macedonian in the army began to laugh at the king.

'God Alexander!' men laughed. 'Father Amon! War dancers!'

Alexander walked rapidly up to Amyntas. He motioned to the hypaspitoi, and his personal guard detached themselves and ran to him. Not Bubores or Alectus, or Astibus – all dead. Men we didn't know.

Amyntas saluted. He said something. I was too far away to hear it.

Alexander's face became ugly – white and red, his mouth thin and set.

A hypaspist drove his spear into Amyntas, under the arm with which he was saluting the king.

He killed about fifty of them – veterans, every one. Later, in a fit of remorse, he held funerals, and a dinner to celebrate the friendship of Macedon and Persia.

And then he ordered all the veterans home. Oh, they were well paid. But he sent them under Craterus, with orders to displace – and murder – old Antipater.

And then Hephaestion died.

Alexander was almost human for a month after Hephaestion died. He died of a hard life under brutal conditions – of a love of excess and hard drinking. I suppose it is possible that he was poisoned. I don't think so.

But his death revealed something to the king. Alexander looked around him like a man awakened from a dream – I think because Hephaestion, for all his failings, had helped to protect the king from the hardest truths, and without him, Alexander was like a man wearing armour without padding.

But Hephaestion had also been our last conduit to the king – our last way of protesting, of demanding that he remain a Macedonian. And after a funeral that alternated between high drama and darkest comedy, heavy drinking and flights of royal fancy that made me want to vomit – he was lost.

By the time we moved to Babylon, I had had enough. I sent Thaïs away, with the children, and all my men but Polystratus. They were discharged veterans now, anyway.

I sent them west, to Aegypt. Thaïs had her orders, and Laertes had his.

FORTY

After Hephaestion's death, all I could think of was Philip – Philip, the King of Macedon. The only excuse for his murder was hubris and tyranny. He had made himself a god, and begun to act like a selfish tyrant.

And Amyntas son of Philip – a ranker, a phalangite, a man who loved his king and marched to his wars, and died, spitted on a spear on the tyrant's orders.

Oh, yes.

Bubores, dead in the desert. Astibus, at the foot of a wall that didn't need to be stormed. Charmides, who shat himself to death in Bactria. Dion, who died at Guagamela.

And another million men and women.

It was me.

After Hephaestion died, I was invited to the banquets again. It was odd – it was as if the gods gave him to me. At the funeral banquet, he put a hand on my shoulder and called me his 'last friend'.

Once I would have wept at those words.

I had no more tears to shed.

I sent Thaïs away, but I kept her things. I was a student of Aristotle, and a good one – I have a curious mind, and I like to read.

It is not difficult, if your target drinks unwatered wine. And Alexander drank more and more – more every night, and longer, while he planned his next extravagant conquest.

I am not ashamed to say that I tried twice. Twice, I went to his parties, lay on a couch near him, and I could not do it. I conjured the death of Cleitus – the death of Philotas, the death of Amyntas. The murder of Coenus. His attempt on my life. The march through the Gedrosian. The massacre of the Mallians.

It is hard to kill even the shell of something you love.

But some weeks after the funeral for Hephaestion, Cassander came.

He was a nervous youth who was too used to having his own way too close to his school days. He came from Macedon – from Antipater – to negotiate. The old man knew Alexander wanted him dead, and with the same callous indifference to other men's lives that he always showed, he stayed home and sent his young son.

Cassander is and was no man's friend. He was a boy on a dangerous mission. He was a fool then and he's not much better now.

But ...

He came into the dining hall with a clatter, because he'd tripped over his own feet at the entrance, and the men near the door laughed at him. I was lying three couches from the king – Bagoas was sharing his couch, painted like a woman.

Cyrus – now a squadron commander in his own right – approached the king, and threw himself on his face – full proskynesis in order to approach and receive the kiss of a king's friend.

Cassander laughed. It was a nervous, reedy laugh, but I suppose he meant it – he had never seen such a thing in all his life.

Alexander rose to a sitting position on his couch, and then kissed Cyrus and exchanged a comment or two, all the while beckoning to Cassander to approach. When the young man came, Alexander smiled at him – smiled and held his glance, still beckoning, until Cassander came close enough to kiss.

Alexander grabbed his ears and smashed his head into the marble floor – not once, but five or six times, until the blood poured from the boy's scalp, and he shrieked and soiled himself.

Alexander rose to his feet and kicked him in the crotch, and then turned and ordered the body removed. His expression was one of mild distaste.

That night, I opened the gold container I had found among Thaïs's belongings, and poured the powder of strychnos nuts carefully into the king's wine after his taster sniffed it and set it at the king's side on a low table by his couch.

He developed a high fever, went to the bathhouse and sweated it off.

I was haunted by the notion that he was, in fact, greater than human.

But I knew better. And I believed then, and still believe, that all that was greatest in Alexander – the part that was greater than merely human – left him after Hydaspes. Perhaps it was his apotheosis. And afterwards, only the bestial shell – less than human – was left.

Listen to me – the philosopher.

You can purchase anything in Babylon.

I purchased fresh nuts and ground them myself, as Alexander and I had learned to do at Aristotle's hands. As I had seen Thaïs do, before Memnon died.

Instead of dry powder, I had a damp mush.

I dried it in the sun, and put it in his wine. He was drinking deep, unwatered wine straight from the amphora, and it was the work of a moment to brush the foul stuff into his cup.

Why wasn't I caught?

Because the gods willed it so.

And because, by that summer in Babylon, *no one wanted him to live.*

I thought of my conversation with Cleitus, the day Philip was murdered.

Of what could justify regicide.

Boy, if I ever act the tyrant that he was, you have my permission to kill me.

He lay near death for two days. The soldiers – the same Macedonians he had already disbanded and ordered home – crowded around the palace doors, openly praying for his survival.

Because that is how men are.

The old circle gathered by his bedside, and it was telling – I think we all thought it – that there were no Persians at all to attend his last days. He lay, barely able to move or speak.

When he asked for wine, I gave it to him.

With more poison.

Craterus was beside himself – he, alone of us, wanted to conquer more worlds, march farther. He was unchanged. His feelings for the king were unchanged. But he had missed the Gedrosian Desert.

He leaned over the king and asked, 'Lord – who should inherit your kingdom? To whom should it go?'

There was silence for so long that we all, I think, assumed the king was too far gone to speak.

But he did not speak. He giggled.

His head rose a fraction, and his eyes met mine squarely. As if he knew ... everything.

'To the strongest,' he said.

HISTORICAL NOTE

Writing a novel – several novels, now – about the wars of the Diadochi, or Successors, is a difficult game for an amateur historian to play. There are many, many players, and many sides, and frankly, none of them are 'good.' From the first, I had to make certain decisions, and most of them had to do with limiting the cast of characters to a size that the reader could assimilate without insulting anyone's intelligence. Antigonus One-Eye and his older son Demetrios deserve novels of their own – as do Cassander, Eumenes, Ptolemy, Seleucus, Olympia and the rest. Every one of them could be portrayed as the hero and the others as villains.

If you feel that you need a scorecard, consider visiting my website at www.hippeis.com where you can at least review the biographies of some of the main players. Wikipedia also has full biographies on most of the players in the period.

From a standpoint of purely military history, I've made some decisions that knowledgeable readers may find odd. For example, I no longer believe in the linothorax or linen breastplate, and I've written it out of the novels. Nor do I believe that the Macedonian pike system – the sarissa armed phalanx – was really any better than the old Greek hoplite system. In fact, I suspect it was worse, as the experience of early modern warfare suggests that the longer your pikes are, the less you trust your troops. Macedonian farm boys were not hoplites – they lacked the whole societal and cultural support system that created the hoplite. They were decisive in their day but as to whether they were 'better' than the earlier system ... well, as with much of military change, it was a cultural change, not really a technological one. Or so it seems to me.

Elephants were not tanks, nor were they a magical victory tool. They could be very effective, or utterly ineffective. I've tried to show both situations.

The same can be said of horse-archery. On open ground, with end-less remounts and a limitless arrow supply, a horse-archer army must have been a nightmare. But a few hundred horse-archers on the vast expanse of an Alexandrian battlefield might only have been a nuisance.

Ultimately though, I don't believe in 'military' history. War is about economics, religion, art, society – war is inseparable from culture. You could not, in this period, train an Egyptian peasant to be a horse-archer without changing his way of life and his economy, his social status, perhaps his religion. Questions about military technology – 'Why didn't Alexander create an army of [insert technological wonder here]?' – ignore the constraints imposed by the realities of the day – the culture of Macedon, which carried, it seems to me, the seeds of its own destruction from the first.

And then there is the problem of sources. In as much as we know *anything* about the world of the Diadochi, we owe that knowledge to a few authors, none of whom are actually contemporary. I used Diodorus Siculus throughout the writing of the *Tyrant* books – in most cases I prefer him to Arrian or Polybius, and in many cases he's the sole source.

In this book I deal with the life of Alexander in detail. I owe a deep debt to Peter Greene, whose biography of Alexander I followed in many respects. However, I also used sources as widely separated as Arrian (whose hero worship makes him suspect) and the Alexander Romance (mostly fabrication, but with hidden gems), tempered by Plutarch despite his moralizing ways. I suspect that Alexander was the Adolf Hitler of his era, not the golden hero. I suspect that he was both a gifted general *and* the beneficiary of some unbelievable strokes of luck.

For anyone who wants to get a quick lesson in the difficulties of the sources for the period, I recommend visiting the website www.livius.org. The articles on the sources will, I hope, go a long way to demonstrating how little we know about Alexander and his successors.

Of course, as I'm a novelist and only an historian on weekends, sometimes the loopholes in the evidence – or even the vast gaps – are the very space in which my characters operate. Sometimes, a lack of knowledge is what creates the appeal. Either way, I hope that I have created a believable version of the world of Alexander. I hope that you enjoy this book, and its companions, the Tyrant series.

And as usual, I'm always happy to hear your comments – and even your criticisms – at the Online Agora on www.hippeis.com. See you there, I hope!

Christian Cameron
Toronto, 2011

ACKNOWLEDGEMENTS

I've been accused – by friends – of only writing to recruit new people for re-enacting. This is not true. I write because I love it, and because it is the best job in the world – what other job allows me to travel to Greece to do research? Or travel to Finland to become a better long sword fighter – as research?

Besides, I have to write books to earn the money to be able to *afford* re-enacting.

That said, though, I am always recruiting. Right now, in 2011, we've just completed the first recreation of the Battle of Marathon. We had about 100 participants. When we do it again in 2014, I'd like to see five hundred. In 2020, when we go to Thermopylae and Plataea ... a thousand? Two thousand?

That could be you.

Okay, let me try to convince you, in a roundabout way.

I approach every historical era with a basket full of questions – How did they eat? What did they wear? How does that weapon work? Books are only so useful. That is to say, books and learning are the ultimate resource, and professional historians rank among my favourite people – but there is no substitute for *doing it*. The world's Classical re-enactors have been an enormous resource to me while writing, both with details of costume and armour and food, and as a fountain of inspiration. In that regard I'd like to thank Craig Sitch and Cheryl Fuhlbohm of Manning Imperial, who make some of the finest recreations of material culture from Classical antiquity in the world (www.manningimperial.com), as well as Joe Piela of Lonely Mountain Forge for helping recreate equipment on tight schedules. I'd also like to thank Paul McDonnell-Staff, Paul Bardunias, and Giannis Kadoglou for their depth of knowledge and constant willingness to answer questions – as well as the members of various ancient Greek re-enactment societies all over the world, from Spain to Australia. Thanks to the UK Hoplite Association for supporting my book talks in Britain. Thanks most of all to the members of my own group, Hoplologia and the Taxeis Plataea, for being the guinea-pigs on a great deal of material culture and martial-arts experimentation, and to Guy Windsor (who wrote *The Swordsman's Companion* and *The Duelist's Companion*, and is an actual master swordsman himself) for advice on martial arts.

Speaking of re-enactors, my friend Steven Sandford draws the maps for these books, and he deserves a special word of thanks, as does my friend Dmitry Bondarenko, who draws the figures and borders on the maps. My friend Rebecca Jordan works tirelessly at the website and the various web spin-offs like the Agora, and deserves a great deal more praise than she receives.

Speaking of friends, I owe a debt or gratitude to Christine Szego, who provides daily criticisms and support from her store, Bakka Phoenix, in Toronto. Thanks Christine!

My interpretation of Alexander and his world – which is also Kineas's world, and Philokles's world, and Thais's world, and Ptolemy's world – began with my desire to write a book that would allow me to discuss the serious issues of war and politics that are around all of us today. I was returning to school and returning to my first love – Classical history. I am also an unashamed fan of Patrick O'Brian, and I wanted to write a series with depth and length that would allow me to explore the whole period, with the relationships that define men, and women, in war and peace – not just one snippet. The combination – Classical history, the philosophy of war, and the ethics of the world of arête – gave rise to the volume you hold in your hand.

Along the way, I met Professor Wallace and Professor Young, both very learned men with long association to the University of Toronto. Professor Wallace answered any question that I asked him, providing me with sources and sources and sources, introducing me to the labyrinthine wonders of Diodorus Siculus, and finally, to T. Cuyler Young. Cuyler was kind enough to start my education on the Persian Empire of Alexander's day, and to discuss the possibility that Alexander was not infallible, or even close to it. I wish to give my profoundest thanks and gratitude to these two men for their help in re-creating the world of fourth century BC Greece, and the theory of Alexander's campaigns that underpins this series of novels. Any brilliant scholarship is theirs, and any errors of scholarship are certainly mine. I will never forget the pleasure of sitting in Professor Wallace's office, nor in Cuyler's living room, eating chocolate cake and debating the myth of Alexander's invincibility. Both men have passed on now, since this book was written, but none of the Tyrant books would have been the same without them. They were great men, and great academics – the kind of scholars who keep civilization alive.

I'd also like to thank the staff of the University of Toronto's Classics department for their support, and for reviving my dormant interest in Classical Greek, as well as the staffs of the University of Toronto Library and the Toronto Metro Reference Library for their dedication and interest. Libraries matter!

I couldn't have approached so many Greek texts without the Perseus Project. This online resource, sponsored by Tufts University, gives on-line access to almost all classical texts in Greek and in English. Without it I would still be working on the second line of *Medea*, never mind the *Iliad* or the *Hymn to Demeter*.

I owe a debt of thanks to my excellent editor, Bill Massey at Orion, for giving these books constant attention and a great deal of much needed flattery, for his good humour in the face of authorial dicta, and for his support at every stage. I'd also like to thank Shelley Power, my agent, for her unflagging efforts on my behalf, and for many excellent dinners, the most recent of which, at the world's only Ancient Greek restaurant, Archeon Gefsis in Athens, resulted in some hasty culinary re-writing. Thanks Shelley!

Finally, I would like to thank the muses of the Luna Café, who serve both coffee and good humour, and without whom there would certainly not have been a book. And all my thanks – a lifetime of them – for my wife Sarah.

If you have any questions, wish to see more or participate (ah, we're back to that ... want to be a hoplite? A Persian Immortal?) please come and visit www.hippeis.com. Go to the 'Agora' (that's Greek for forum, folks,) sign in and post to the welcome board. And let me recruit you for re-enacting. We call it living history. It makes history come to life.

And history matters.

Christian Cameron
Toronto, 2011

ABOUT THE AUTHOR

Christian Cameron is a writer and military historian. He is a veteran of the United States Navy, where he served as both an aviator and an intelligence officer. He lives in Toronto where he is currently writing his next novel while working on a Masters in Classics.